THE LAST CONTENDER
SONG OF THE LOST
BOOK ONE

LIV SAVELL

STERLING D'ESTE

L & S
FABLES

Copyright © 2022 by L&S Fables

All rights reserved.

The characters and events portrayed in this book are fictitious. Any similarity to real persons, living or dead, is coincidental and not intended by the author.

No part of this book may be reproduced in any form or by any electronic or mechanical means, including information storage and retrieval systems, without written permission from the author, except for the use of brief quotations in a book review.

ISBN-13: 9798352535776

Cover art by: Merilliza Chan

Cover design by: Nerdy Book Mama

Library of Congress Control Number: 2022919426

Printed in the United States of America

DEAR READER

In this book, the use of they or them with a singular subject is used for characters who prefer gender-neutral pronouns or when a character's gender is not immediately apparent.

To each other

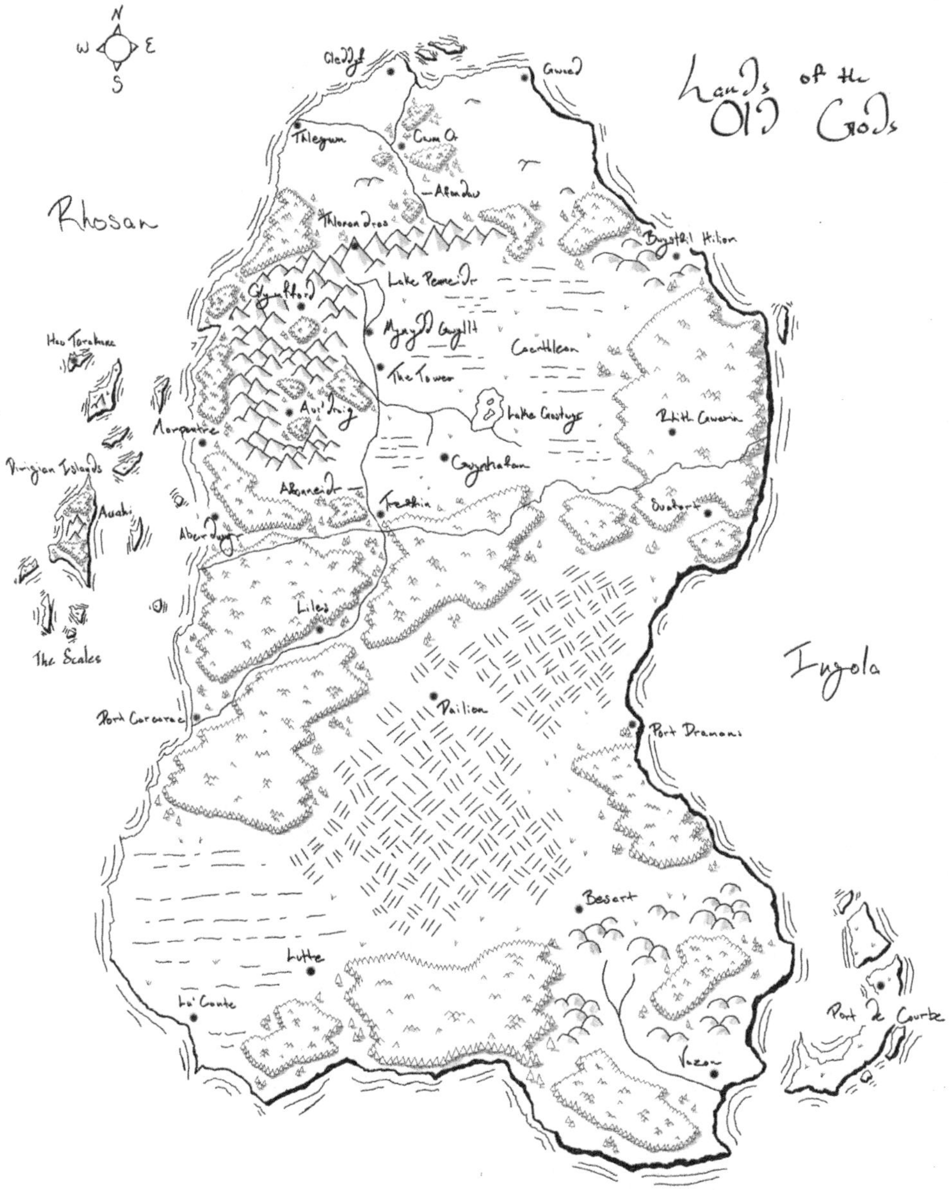

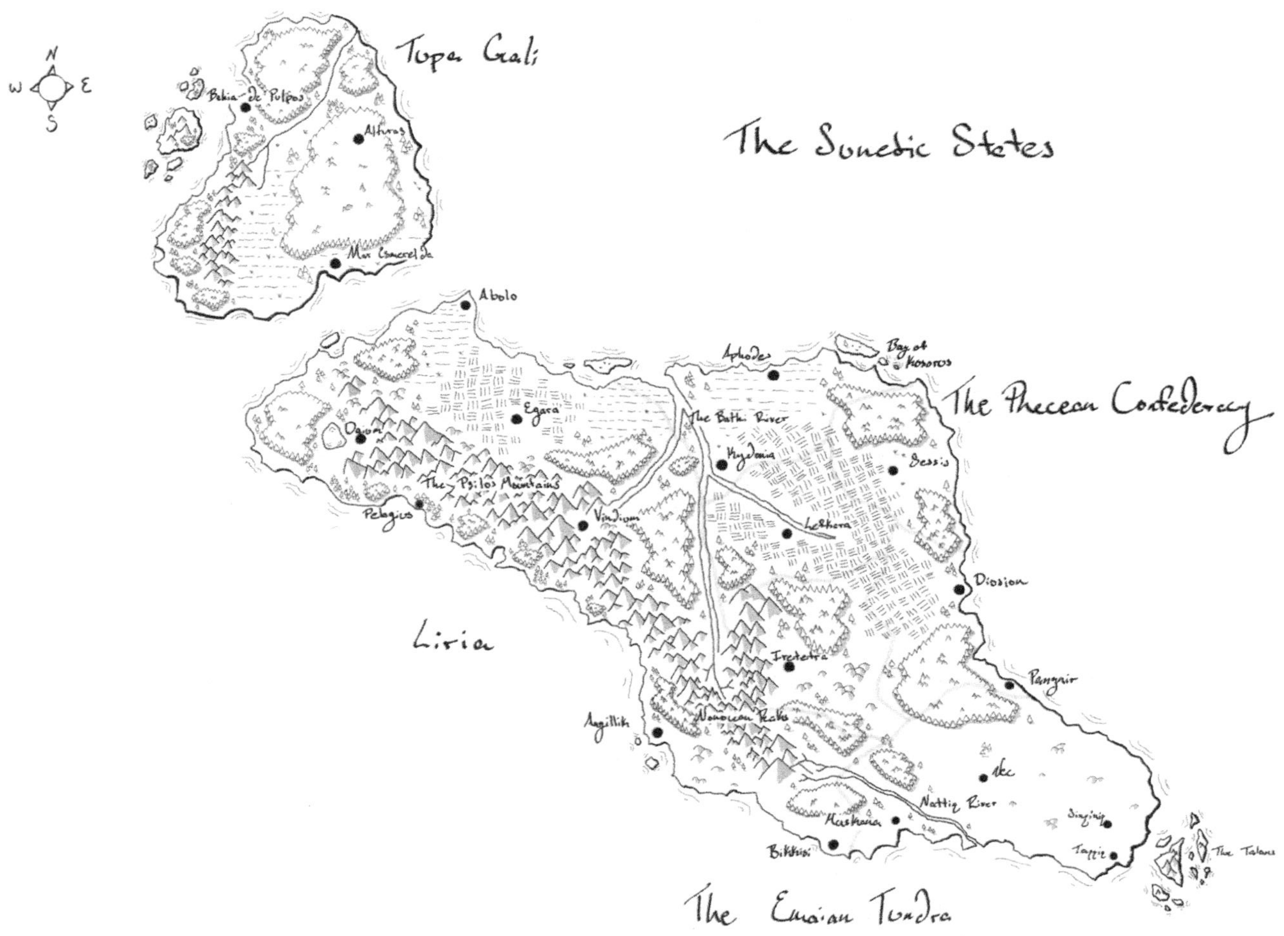

CHAPTER 1: RHOSAN

FIRST MOON, 1794, BRYNTREF

Eleven Years before the Proclamation

A fire nibbled in the hearth. It was a messy eater, snapping and crumbling as it burnt through rich, winter-dry pine. Its sounds mingled with Wynn's wood knife moving rhythmically over the toy he was carving— a bear still mostly lacking in distinguishing features. It felt good in his palm, a sturdy chunk of apple wood that smelled reminiscent of the fruit the tree had once borne. His eyes slipped closed, and he blinked too long. The night was calling to him of dreams and peaceful slumber…

Until the happy patter of soft, bare baby feet came rush-stumbling by. Owynn tumbled into his mother's knees where she sat mending one of his shirts, his hands clutched around something Wynn could not quite see. "Look!" Owynn burbled, holding up long, spiraling wood shavings to his head to mimic his mother's curls. "I look like you now!"

Nia's gaze, soft with affection, shifted to the wood shavings, and she nodded. "You do. Just like mama." She reached out to brush a long finger across his plump cheek, pink with excitement, and then glanced to the window.

Dark had long since come, and the evening was shifting into night.

Owynn needed to be abed. Nia didn't have to speak for Wynn to understand the meaning of the look she cast his way, and he set aside his carving knife.

"Come here, son," he said, opening his arms. "Let's sing together before bed."

The boy came in a giggling rush, still clutching the wood shavings, and barreled into Wynn, who swept him up into his arms as easily as if he was one of the planks of wood lying in the workshop below. He giggled when Wynn tickled him and breathlessly tucked his soft head against Wynn's neck. He smelled slightly sweet, a sticky child scent.

"Do you remember the words?"

Obstinately, the little boy shook his head. "It's too early for singing."

"All the birds have gone to bed," Nia chimed, her tone helpful.

"See? Even the birds have finished their evening songs. You don't want to be late, do you? Do you remember how it starts?

The boy shook his head again, but it was out of a desire to stay up later, not ignorance. They sang the song often enough. Wynn tickled the boy's head with his beard to get him to look up and then mouthed the first few words. Owynn joined in, and they sang together as they got ready to sleep.

"THERE ARE nine Gods to guide our lives
    To help and test and teach us
    They watch from sky and earth and water,
    They listen, kind or capricious.

ENYO GROWS rich fields and forests
    Esha cradles mothers and babes
    Tha'et gives us sunlight for planting
    Iluka sings the waves.

THE HUNTER, Maoz, guides arrows true,

Kirit favors the brave,
Va'al sends tricks to confound the clever,
Ruyaa knows what we crave,

When we die, Aryus will hold us,
  Take us to a land of peace,
  Never there will illness reach us,
  All our cares will cease.

There are nine gods to—"

A scream pierced the night, and Wynn turned away from the blanket he was tucking around his son. Only a few sporadic lights were visible through the window of the small, one-room apartment above his carpentry shop. In his trundle bed, Owynn pulled the covers over his head.

"Nia? Did you hear that?"

Wynn's wife pressed her lips into a line, taking light steps to the window. She stood off to one side to keep anyone in the garden from seeing her. The hairs on Wynn's neck stood up, and he compulsively clenched his fists. Nia inhaled sharply and pulled the curtains across the window, obscuring whatever she saw from view.

"Wynn," she hissed, her tone even as her eyes darted to Owynn's huddled form. Whatever it was, she didn't want to frighten their son. The carpenter hurried to Nia's side and peeled back the curtain.

His woodcarver's shop was inside the small village of Bryntref proper, surrounded by the shops of other craftspeople. He could smell the smoke of burning wood, see the lick of fire north of them—his neighbors' houses going up in flames.

"Raids?" Nia kept her voice low, and he felt her slip her fingers into the crook of his elbow, holding him tight. It wasn't impossible. They were on the Southern edge of the Kirit Territories, but not below the mountains which officially ended the Kirit worshippers' domain. It was early for a raid, only the first moon, but then when did Victors care about such things?

As he scanned the dark and counted the winking lights of torches between his neighbor's houses, Wynn could not delude himself. There was nothing this could be but a raid. The Victors had come to Defeat them, and there was no question in his mind of what the outcome might be. His home would fall, as all small villages did beneath the might of Kirit's people.

A preternatural calm fell over him, a stillness or understanding that ran as deep as his bones. His fingers, calloused by the use of tools, trailed along the persimmon-soft surface of the windowsill. He had lived here as a young child before his father's success as a carpenter and growing family had precipitated a move into a bigger residence outside of town. When Wynn's father had retired and left him the shop, he'd never been more proud.

And yet, all children of the north knew that even such seasoned wood would burn if the Victors came.

Belatedly, he answered his wife. "Yes."

She inhaled sharply but didn't sound afraid as she replied, "What do we do?" Everyone knew what a raid meant. Victors were searching for people to Defeat as their religion demanded. Once one was Defeated, there was no escape. Some Defeated worked as field hands or miners; others took care of the laborious tasks within a Victor's home.

Some were even made to fight other Defeated like kept dogs.

When Victors came to a village, they came to win. To claim everything worth taking and burn the rest. Nothing could be done except fight or flee. If Bryntref were larger or boasted a fighting force, they could deter the Victors, but as it was, they were still recovering from the fever that had decimated their population two years prior. He knew they didn't stand a chance against a greater, more violent force.

When your home catches fire, you save what can't be lost.

Wynn turned to Nia, searching her face and finding fear there. He must look much the same. "Our son will not grow up as a slave."

"Wynn—"

"Take all the food you can carry. You know how to find water and make it safe to drink. Run until you can no longer see the fires, and then ward every place you stop. The Old Ways will keep you both safe and warm. Try not to hunt until you reach the mountains— it'd just slow you down."

"Papa?"

Wynn smoothed a lick in his son's thick, red hair and began to collect warm clothes for the toddler, sliding a little carved wolf out of his way. "Come on now, into your leggings and boots."

Nia remained by the window a moment longer, looking beyond the curtain. Whatever she saw there seemed to fortify her will as she turned away, her back as straight as a birch. "Wynn, come with us. They aren't on us yet. We could escape together."

He acted as though he had not heard her, keeping his expression soft as he helped his son dress. "I'll be right behind you," he lied. "I just have to make sure you two get away first. The food, Nia. Enough to see all three of us to the mountains."

When he looked up, Nia hadn't started to pack the food. She stood, her normally soft gaze wide with fear. "Wynn-" she was going to fight with him about it; he knew she would. And they didn't have time for that.

If his son and his wife stood a chance of escape, it was now. *Right now.*

He grabbed Nia by the arm, too harshly, he knew, but he couldn't help it. She had to *go*. "Every moment you waste, you risk losing Owynn to them. Do you want our son to grow up Defeated?"

Nia recoiled at his words, her expression pained. "And you want him to grow up without a father?"

"Better free and fatherless than a Defeated. Besides, you've always said I was too lucky for my own good." He relaxed his grip and pulled her into his arms, kissing her soundly. "I don't see why that has to stop now."

She struggled only for a moment before she stiffened and melted into him. Nia wrapped her arms around his neck, trembling. The moment broke as the sound of shouting reached them. Nia pulled away from their embrace, and then it was just Wynn and his son.

His little boy stood knock-kneed, eyes darting between Wynn and

Nia as she hurried around the cottage, collecting the supplies they would need to make it in the dead of winter. He knelt, running a knuckle across a sweet cheek. Would this be the last time he ever saw his little boy?

"I love you, Owynn," he said, and his voice cracked, raw around the edges. "The day you were born was the best day of my life."

"Papa, what is a raid? Why are we up?" The smooth, round planes of his son's brow were furrowed, uncertain.

"You're going to have to be very brave. Take care of your mother and do everything she tells you." He pressed his hands to Owynn's cheeks, squeezed his shoulders, and pulled him close. Tiny, new-formed hands clutched him.

"Papa, what's wrong?"

Wynn released him and began to roll up the blanket on Owynn's bed. "Quickly now, fetch me the pack Mama made for you to carry to market." When his son handed it to him, Wynn placed the blanket inside along with a water skin, rope, needles and thread, and the wolf carving, then helped Owynn settle it onto his shoulders.

"Too heavy?"

The boy shook his head, eyes glassy and afraid.

"Nia? Are you ready?"

Instead of answering, she reappeared at the stairs, a heavy bag slung over her shoulder, thick layers of clothes disguising her form. She pulled their son into her arms, smoothing his brow with kisses. When she looked up, she met Wynn's gaze.

Fear was apparent there, but also determination. That gave him a sliver of hope. If she could be brave and remember the runes for protection, fire, and speed, then they could make it.

All he had to do was buy them the precious time to flee undetected.

He took her shoulder, leading her down the stairs and toward the back of the cottage. If she could slip into the darkness, into the thick of the forest, they might avoid the Victors.

As Wynn opened the back door, Nia paused. She looked into his face, moonlight painting her normally warm features into something silver and foreign. "I love you, Wynn."

He touched her face and kissed her again. "Due south. No Victor will follow you into the lands of the Valley Gods. Be swift. May the Gods guide your path. Take care of our son. And, Nia, I love you."

Her hand found his, giving it one last squeeze before she disappeared into the darkness. He shut the door behind her and turned to find his spear, his lungs thick with the smell of his neighbors' homes burning.

Fear lent Wynn speed. He took the stairs two at a time and fell to his knees at his cot, thrusting his arm beneath it to grab his weapon. His fingers closed on air. It was gone, and smoke grew in bulging pustules to fill the room. He coughed and searched again, shaking now that his family had left. It was as if all his strength had fled with them.

Below, fists hammered at his door. There were tools on the first floor. Chisels and mallets that might serve as weapons. He wanted nothing more than to run, to follow his family into the welcoming darkness of the forest beyond the village. Only, if he went now, the Victors would know they'd let a family get away. They'd send the dogs.

Wynn scrambled back down the stairs and into the dark shop, picking up a heavy chisel. His door creaked and groaned.

Gods, let his father forgive him for spilling blood with these tools. Let them have gotten away too. Let Nia and Owynn stay free.

The door shuttered again, the hearty, well-cared-for wood finally beginning to splinter. Wynn still remembered crafting it with his father, his first real project. Gods, what was he doing? He was no fighter, he—

The door fell in, and Wynn leaped forward, his shaking hands raised to fight off those who would tear everything from him.

CHAPTER 2: LIRIA

SECOND MOON, 1779, EGARA

Twenty-six Years before the Proclamation

The sun overhead was hot, sweat beading along Lucilius's brow. He impatiently wiped it away, pausing as a carriage trundled past. A man dressed in the army's gold uniform stood impassive at the corner. Young men and boys eyed him enviously, and women smiled as they walked past. He was a recruitment man, a soldier who told the glories of being within the Imperial Legion. He caught Lucilius looking and nodded.

"Have you served your proud nation?" he asked, putting Lucilius on the spot. The tactic was used to embarrass and enlighten those who had not yet heeded the call to protect Liria.

Lucilius saluted the man. "Yes, Legionnaire. I serve under General Caius."

The soldier only nodded, stoic and proud, the women around him glancing Lucilius's way appreciatively. He smiled, but their charms held no allure for him. After all, his own Camilla was far fairer.

With the street clear, he darted out, jumping over a fallen poster of the Imperator's profile, and jogging along the walkway. Camilla and her family would be leaving for services soon, and if he wanted to catch a few moments with her, he'd have to be waiting. Already he was pushing it, the sun almost to its zenith.

When he saw her, he stumbled.

She trailed her parents ahead of him, her dark tresses pinned up and falling in thick curls down her back. Her head was slightly tilted, her hands clasped in front of her soft yellow gown, and the gentle color set off her warm skin.

Luce had a moment of doubt. Could this woman truly be as interested in him as he was in her? He wasn't sure if it could be possible. She was too beautiful, too smart, too *good*. And yet, even while he watched, she searched the open street to her right as though looking for someone. Her head swiveled one way, then the other, and when she finally turned enough to see him, her eyes lit up, and a coy smile softened her proud features.

How could any man doubt such a smile?

He hurried forward as she touched her father's arm to let him know she would be walking to the service with another. She slowed until he reached her, then threaded one arm through his with a squeeze that said she'd missed him. "Luce! I thought you wouldn't make it in time."

He flushed. Timeliness was something a soldier was supposed to have mastered, especially one who had been with the Legion for more than ten years. He had taken an exceedingly long time applying the dark paint about his eyes, making sure the lines were smudged and his gaze heavy. Camilla Pontius boasted some of the best, oldest bloodlines, but Lucilius Horatius Nonus was merely a soldier's name. He knew she was too good for him, but his heart didn't care. He so wanted to impress her and her parents, but by being particular, he'd nearly been late— a fate worse than poorly shined boots.

"A Legionnaire asked me if I had served my nation yet. I had to set him straight." He covered Camilla's hand with his, marveling at how smooth her skin was. His was blistered and rough, marred with scars. A soldier's hand.

"Mmmm... and was he duly impressed by your position with General Caius?" A half-smile hovered about her lips, and her eyes turned coyly up to his. Was she teasing him? It was hard to tell with

Camilla, but he felt an answering smile touch his cheeks all the same. Just up ahead, the great church bells chimed the quarter hour. Did they really have so little time this morning? It seemed to be flying by.

"He nodded," Lucilius replied, brows arching to prove how very impressed the Legionnaire had been. A *full* head nod. "I saluted. It was all *very* impressive."

She laughed, just like he'd hoped she would, and the sound mingled with that of church bells ringing over the square and the crunch of recruitment pamphlets dusting the pavement and the swell of voices as the city's denizens made their way home from the morning's sermon. Camilla smiled into it and pressed against his arm. "With that endorsement, I'm surprised you didn't have ladies falling over you all the way here!"

His neck warmed, and Lucilius tightened his grip ever so slightly on Camilla's hand. "Why do you think I was nearly late?" He didn't want her to think his gaze or affection would ever wander, even if those other ladies *had* noticed him, but it was fun to tease. "I had to evade them. Climbed two roofs and a garden trellis before I escaped. A poor boy like me, I wouldn't know what to do with so much attention." It was a bit laughable to call Lucilius a boy. He was nearly ten years older than Camilla, yet she could leave him tongue-tied with butterflies in his belly. His twenty-eight years seemed nothing in comparison to her beauty and quick wit.

"You don't seem to mind *my* attention…." Camilla's gaze was as sly as it was sweet—she'd seen right through his attempt at levity. "After all, you did climb *two* roofs *and* a garden trellis to get here."

There was nothing he could say to that. She was right, after all. He'd run over hot coals and broken glass to have these few minutes walking with Camilla. Swallowing back any retort he might have tried to make, Lucilius only brought her hand up from his arm to kiss her fingertips. She knew she was more than some fawning city girl, impressed with his envious role within the general's command. He had only worked up the nerve to openly court her three moons ago, but he couldn't imagine a day without seeing her.

Even if it was all impossible. She was a true noble, and his family barely ranked above merchants. Someday she'd go off and marry as befitting her blood, and he'd have a good, honorable, but decidedly poorer life as a soldier.

But not today. Not now. Today he had Camilla on his arm and her fingers pressed to his lips. That was good enough for him. A moment in the sun. A memory to hold onto for the rest of time.

⇑   ⇑   ⇑

Sixth Moon, 1779, Egara

The first rains of autumn were always a relief. Cold winds broke the sweltering summer heat, and the roadways' dust washed away. Everything would look new and clean.

Despite this, Lucilius felt ill. No matter his protestations, Camilla had continued to allow him to court her, and while he knew it was an exercise in futility, he was incapable of staying away. So he came to church sermons, announcements from the Imperator, dinners, galas and any functions where they would both be in attendance and properly supervised. He walked by her family's grand townhouse and stared up at her window, hoping for a glimpse of her. He smiled and nodded in understanding as her father explained that while it was an honor for Camilla to be admired by one of the soldiers of the Lirian Legion, ultimately, she would marry elsewhere.

But Camilla was growing tired of public meetings and hand holding. Only three days before, she had been so bold as to pull him into an alleyway on the way to church and kiss him. His head had swam, and his heart had stopped, and, damn him, Lucilius had pulled her closer and kissed her back! She tasted of honey and cardamom.

This was beyond stupid! They had no future, and he couldn't let Camilla sully her good name. So, that was why he had agreed to meet her today, in secret, in the cafe. He *would* tell her today. Break things off.

Which was why he felt so sick.

He couldn't stand the idea of making her cry, the thought of not seeing her every day. It made his guts boil, and his heart weep. He had spoken with his commander about these terrible symptoms, and the older man had laughed, pity coloring his gaze as he looked at Lucilius. "That's love, you fool," he said, clasping him on the shoulder. "It's called being heart sick."

He *was* sick. He was going to throw up any minute; he was sure of it.

Swallowing down bile, he eagerly waited for Camilla to enter the cafe. She would be windswept with rain in her hair, excited by the escape, and bold as always. He'd just have to break it off, right then and there. Tell her that she was behaving foolishly and he *wouldn't* let her put her future in jeopardy over him. That he loved her too much to allow it. He would put his foot down. Draw the line.

Camilla breezed into the cafe like a summer rain—all soft grace and unstoppable. He watched, stomach clenching as her dark eyes swept the room in a divisive arc until they came to rest on him. At no moment did she seem uncertain or unnerved. She knew precisely what she wanted.

And he was going to have to tell her no.

She wasted no time coming to his table, shaking back the cloak she'd held tight about her shoulders, hiding the proud lines of her face. He thought that if she had kept it on, he would have still known her—by the force of her stride if nothing else.

"Luce," she said when she reached him, breathless and eager, "I wasn't sure you would come, but I am *so* glad that you did."

"Camilla..." he croaked, suddenly hoarse with emotion. Hastily Lucilius swallowed, trying to clear his throat, to find his voice. He had to tell her *now*. Before she sat and ordered one of her overly complicated drinks and smiled at him. Before she pushed past his reason and logic and confounded him into doing whatever she wanted.

It was how Camilla had claimed his heart. A warrior. She simply took it without asking.

"Camilla." He started again, readying the speech he had memorized on the way. "Yes—I came but *only* to tell you that we cannot let this —*us*—continue."

"What?" Camilla was—of all things—smiling. She pulled at the fingers of her right glove, revealing, in millimeters, the smooth skin of her wrist, her palm. "Don't be ridiculous, Luce. You love me."

As though it could be as simple as that.

Her right glove slipped free, unveiling the length of her slender fingers even as she moved to work on the other. A waiter came by, and when Camilla ordered something with four different sets of instructions, he hardly noticed. He was too busy watching her hands, trying to find a way to make her understand.

"Smile, love," Camilla commanded, turning back to him. "We've never had this much time to ourselves. Isn't it exciting?"

"Camilla—" Lucilius knew he sounded like a bleating sheep at this point, mesmerized by her flesh and her smile and her immovable will. "Your family—"

"Yes, they will cling to rather tiresome notions, but I believe they will see that I am right in time, and—well, Luce, don't look so glum—they aren't here now." She reached out to place her bared hands on his arm where it lay across the table, her smooth, honey skin making stripes of his more sun-hardened brown. "Haven't you *missed* me?"

Damn him. He was too weak. He couldn't stand and leave! Tell her it was over. That she would come to regret seeing him. Lucilius didn't bother to argue about his station, how small his house was compared to hers, or that most of the bluebloods smirked at him and his kind when they attended formal events. Camilla wouldn't hear it, and she wouldn't care.

And he *had* missed her.

He missed her every second that they were apart. So despite knowing that this could not end well, that no one would allow this to pass, Lucilius only covered her hand with his, his grip nearing desperate.

"Of course I missed you. I love you." Her wide smirk only made him love her more. She had known well before he did that Lucilius Horatius Nonus would love her. After all, she was Camilla.

⇑   ⇑   ⇑

Third Moon, 1780, Egara

The dancers looked like jewels bouncing upon a dowager's ample bosom, glittering as they did on the mirrored floors and walls of the Pontius mansion ballroom. Camilla was among them, swaying in the arms of some suitor her parents were pushing on her. Though she smiled graciously enough, her eyes found Lucilius at every turn, where he stood in a knot of other officers, nodding for all that his mind considered only Camilla.

She was wearing red— no muted pink or sable crimson but the brightest cardinal-breast red Lucilius had ever seen pressed on fabric. No color had ever suited her better. She was vibrant, a sun among dim stars.

He could find her no matter how far apart they stood. It was nearing midnight, and guests began to trickle off into the night. Soon he would slip away to find her without the ever-present press of eyes. For now, he could only observe as she bowed to another heir, thin and smooth-skinned and of her class. Could only watch as the other man touched her arm, her waist, his eyes blurring with tiredness and alcohol.

He would leave tomorrow. Would she still be waiting when he returned?

The Imperator had ordained more raids on the Emaian savages, and while Lucilius found little sport in hunting down the inferior heathens, it was his duty to obey. After all, they brought back slaves from such raids, and within the safety and order of Liria, they educated, fed, and trained the savages. It was a fair trade. The Lirians tamed and helped the savages; in exchange, they labored for housing, food, and guidance. It was a comfortable system, and, over generations, it had helped grow Liria into a mighty Empire.

And yet, Lucilius didn't want to go. Never had he found following orders so distasteful before. He hated to see these bluebloods pawing at his Camilla. It made his head swim, his blood boil, and his heart weep.

He'd be gone a moon or *more*. Would she be engaged when he got back?

Lucilius swallowed down the rest of the contents of his cup and turned away from the dance floor, unable to watch any longer. One of the other soldiers slapped Luce heartily on the shoulder, startling him from his thoughts. "Why so glum?" Amus was an old friend and drunk, his rambunctious nature only fed by the strong liquor. "We're off to spill a little 'maian blood tomorrow! Do you think it's as colorless as their faces? Perhaps the stuff won't even show against snow. C'mon Luce! Since when have you gotten down in your cups?"

Across the floor, Camilla slipped out of her suitor's hands and off towards the wall, angling to ease out of the room. She might have been subtle if not for the red of her dress, pulling gazes in as she passed.

"I'm not down in my cups," Luce complained, straining against the urge to let his eyes follow Camilla as she slipped out of sight. They'd been playing at these foolish games for moons now, and he knew where to meet her. *Later*. For now, he had to be seen and remembered. "Come on! Another round!"

"Now that's more like it!" Amus swung an arm across Luce's shoulders and shook him good-naturedly. Luce tried to shrug him off, but the other man's grip only tightened. He turned his head towards Luce's ear and lowered his voice. "All you need is a drink and a bit of fighting, eh? By the time we get back, you won't even remember being heart sick." Amus was wheeling away to refill his cup before Luce could respond, jostling with other soldiers and smiling at women.

For an hour, Luce remained with his companions, his brothers in arms. They drank and he pretended to drink and they all laughed and joked and danced around playfully. Finally, they started to teeter off, ready to sleep before shipping out the next morning. Luce managed to slip away in the shuffle for their coats and blades and arguing over whose carriage they would take or if they should just walk. Amus wouldn't remember or care who Lucilius got a ride with as long as he showed up at the barracks bleary-eyed and ready for marching orders tomorrow.

Lucilius snuck through the back halls of the Pontius mansion, sticking to the servants' and slaves' corridors until he finally came out in a secluded garden. This space was purely Camilla's. She tended to these plants, and the garden was overlooked by her rooms. The public never visited these sequestered, private places. Except Luce.

And while his morals objected to meeting her, alone, unchaperoned, he had been able to ignore those protestations in lieu of secret embraces and sweet words. This could be the last time he held her in his arms. When he returned from the raids, she could be engaged.

When he arrived she was already in the garden, her back turned to him and her hair loose. She stood quietly, her face turning to inspect the blossom of a moonflower whose petals had been closed in the day's heat. Gone was the elaborate red confection of the evening; she wore only a simple blue dress, her shoulders draped with a cashmere shawl.

He had never seen anything so beautiful, so simple and good. He sighed, and she must have heard him, though she didn't turn around. "I was starting to think you might not come." Was her voice a little vulnerable? "That you might leave without coming to see me."

"I would never leave without saying goodbye," his voice rumbled, and he stepped closer. Lucilius held out his hand. "Would you?" While the question sounded simple, he knew she understood the complexity beneath it.

Would she marry another while he was gone? Would she 'leave' without saying goodbye to him? Was this the goodbye for both of them? She to her proper life, and he to his role as a soldier?

Finally, she turned, but in the dark, he could not quite make out her eyes. Her face was unreadable. "No." The word seemed to catch in her throat as though it was heavier than it ought to have been.

He tugged her into his grip, wrapping his arm about her waist, his free hand tracing the proud lines of her face. In the moonlight, she looked impossibly beautiful. Lucilius smiled. "We're alike then." He kissed Camilla, trying to memorize the feel of her lips, the smell of her in this garden, in his arms. How strong and warm she was pressed to him.

When they broke apart, Lucilius wasn't ashamed that he was panting. Every emotion and thought he had was welling up and colliding within him until he was nothing more than a raw, aching heart. "I love you, Camilla. I'll *always* love you."

She leaned into him, the thin layers of her dress and shawl a paltry separation. "Luce. I wish you did not have to go." There was something a little wild in her eyes, in the way her lips parted. He realized with a jolt of surprise that she was breathing hard as well, her pupils so large, they made her already dark eyes seem black. "I want—" she breathed, but for once, she didn't seem to be able to find the words. She kissed him again, urgent and eager.

His pulse jumped and doubled, and Lucilius held Camilla tighter. When she looked at him like that he couldn't think! Perhaps he should've stopped drinking earlier in the evening.

"You want?" he asked, uncertain. His hands wandered down her body, and despite himself, Lucilius couldn't help but notice the narrowness of her waist, the slope of her hips. Never had they stood so entangled for so long. Never had he seen her in such... thin clothing. He could feel the heat of her body radiating through the linen of her dress.

"I want *you*, Lucilius. Now. Before you go off to fight, before it's too late." Her words were coming in a mad rush, her pulse throbbing in her neck, visible even in the dim light.

His heart stopped. "*Now?*" he repeated lamely. He wanted her too, but, "but we're not married! We're not even engaged!" And how he had longed to ask her, but her father had denied his request. Friendly, but denial all the same.

'Soldiers are the backbone of our nation,' he said, all smiles and expensive wine. 'But my daughter isn't a backbone. She's the heart or the head. You understand, don't you, Lucilius Nonus?'

And he had. Because Camilla was an Empress or a Queen, not some lowly soldier's wife.

She squeezed her eyes shut as if to block out the words. "Why does that *matter*? I love you. You've just said you love me. Why do you care so much about all of their rules?"

She took a shaky breath, and her bottom lip quivered with it, still damp from his kisses. She suddenly felt fragile in his arms, something he had never thought of her as before. She was unstoppable, and small against his chest.

"It's *because* I love you," he explained, cupping her cheek. "I want to show you to the world and be with you in the light of day. In public. You don't deserve having to sneak and act as if this is shameful. *I'm* shameful. For someone like you, Camilla—"

The tension went out of her shoulders, and she turned her face away. "It doesn't feel shameful to me."

That shut him up. Her face closed off; her shoulders slumped in disappointment. He couldn't stand it. He could never disappoint her.

"Camilla," he whispered, carefully turning her face back to his. Lips swept gently against hers, then trailed along her jaw, past her ear. The smell of the floral oils she used in her hair was overwhelming. He could feel her hands balled into fists at his back, clinging to his coat and pulling him closer. How someone so delicate could haul him about was baffling. He couldn't stand to see her cry. He wouldn't allow it.

Lucilius lifted his hand to weave through her hair, cradling her skull, pressing kisses to her flesh as she urged him on. Anything to make her happy again.

Camilla sighed into his mouth and let the shawl fall from her shoulders, baring dusky skin to the glow of the waning moon and cool night air. Her throat convulsed as she swallowed, her eyes doe-soft. Small hands tugged at his jacket, his shirt, the ties of his trousers. She put his hands to her skirts. "Love me, Luce. I will never take another."

A thousand reasons clamored in his head as to why he should deny her, turn away and keep her safe for the future she deserved. Part of him leaped with joy at her words.

And he was leaving in the morning and would be gone for moons, and when he came back, maybe her parents would realize he could honor her as she deserved. Maybe this wasn't the end, but the beginning. Hope blossomed in his chest as Luce bent to kiss Camilla again.

⇑ ⇑ ⇑

Sixth Moon, 1780, Emai-Lirian Border

Winter dawns in the Emaian wasteland were bleak. The light was weak, barely breaking through the sky, and took forever to properly transform into daybreak. Lucilius waited alongside his comrades, steam rising from their collective breaths, mimicking smoke from a fire.

But there was no fire. No heat, no warmth, no shelter in these terrible lands. How the natives survived was beyond him. They were lucky when the Lirians came and took them to the civilized north. Not that they showed gratitude—always fighting and wailing like cats, garbling in their simplistic language.

They were like children. Incapable of understanding what was best.

Lucilius hated going on raids. He hated the tundra, hated the cold and the bland rations. He hated being away from Camilla.

And it was all so he could collect these graceless heathens and deliver them to Liria? He was a trained soldier, not a shepherd looking after errant sheep! Still, those who did well in the raids were often rewarded. If he was promoted and able to afford a larger home, then Camilla's family might be willing to let him marry her.

The snow behind him crunched, and Lucilius turned to see who had approached. His General, Caius. Respectfully he bowed.

"Corporal Nonus, see that your cohort is prepared to move at daybreak. You are being sent to raid a small Emaian stronghold. Capture as many as possible."

The general's face was inscrutable, but the underlying meaning of his words was clear: Luce was to lead a raid, and its success or failure would reflect on the rest of his career. Doing well meant stepping up. That was the way of things in the Legion. Only results mattered, and nothing was more reviled than failure.

General Caius had already turned to survey their encampment as though compliance was so expected that he did not even bother to see it carried out any longer. It was nothing to him whether or not Luce answered. "An encouraging prospect, isn't it? An orderly camp."

"Indeed, sir," Lucilius agreed, following his gaze. Neat rows, straight lines, everything in its place, and every man in his place too. Ordered. Clean. *Perfect.*

For a long moment, they stood in silence, surveying the collection of tents before the sun finally decided to rise. With a nod to the General, Lucilius turned to gather his men. If he was leading a raid, then this was his chance. Ten years within the Legion and a handful of promotions. This was just the next step to glory and proclaiming his love for Camilla to all the world.

⇑　　⇑　　⇑

Hefting his ax, Lucilius blocked a poorly aimed spear thrust to his shield arm, knocking it aside and bashing the man in the stomach with the butt of his ax. The man wheezed and collapsed, Lucilius turning away to face the next heathen.

It was a tidy raid. The Emai hadn't been ready for them. They never were. Of course, the Emai couldn't think ahead or plan such things. That was too complex for the simple ice people.

Already Lucilius saw lines of the captured men and women being led away with shackles about their necks, heads bowed subserviently. So easy to get into line. A few young men had tried to fight, but they were falling into order as well. They would likely come away with twenty new slaves. A good number for such a small village, and Lucilius had been careful to direct his men. Only the strong and healthy should be taken. He'd not be blamed if some died on the voyage back to Liria or were too weak for good labor.

A bellow broke through his thoughts, and Lucilius looked around. A massive woman, if she could be called that, guarded one of their stinking tents. She was more bear than person, with white hair hanging down her face and her gray eyes wide. She picked up a bucket and chucked it at one of his men's heads. It collided, and the warrior fell. Another man stepped in, but she kicked up the coals of her fire, and he retreated, afraid to be burned.

Ridiculous. These heathens were no better than animals.

She blocked the entrance to her little tent, and Lucilius suspected she was protecting something within to drive her to such insanity. Readjusting the grip on his ax, he strode forward. He'd end this now and reduce the number of injuries this beast would inflict.

"Woman!" he shouted in their basic language, crude and lacking nuance. "Stop your attack. Look around—" Her eyes darted to all the warriors, but he could see her comprehension was low. Too stupid to understand. Lucilius sighed and gestured with his ax to the line of Emai being led away. Quiet. Peaceful. "Look—They know we've come to help. Your life will be better in Liria. You won't freeze, and you'll be fed and clothed—" He eyed the scraps of animal hide covering her now. Crude and ineffective. "You'll even be able to read and speak a real language."

Her eyes narrowed, and her chin came up, mulish. Too stupid to understand but too stubborn to stop. "You have your slaves. Go," she spat out, reaching from beneath her rags to pull out a long knife.

Lucilius sighed again. He just wanted to wrap up the raid, claim the promotion he was likely earning and return to his beloved Camilla! It had been three moons since he held her last, and this idiotic trollop was all that stood in the way of the raiding season ending.

He was seriously considering just letting the woman go. If she wanted to starve on this frozen block of ice, so be it, but then, a small cry pierced the air. He understood now. There was a child within the tent. Perhaps more.

Children made poor slaves. They often died on the journey up to Liria. They were too weak and malnourished to be useful for the first few years and couldn't withstand the harsher punishments that Emai slaves needed to learn properly. They took longer to train than the adults.

He didn't want her mewling babes.

Lucilius stepped forward, hand out to calm the wild beast. "Your child—" With a move too fast to track, the blade in the woman's hand swept through the air.

There was a blinding pain in Lucilius's left wrist, and when he looked down, it was to see his hand was gone. It lay on the snow beneath him, and blood bloomed all around it. His men lunged forward, and between three of them, they subdued the woman, thrashing and screaming as if *she* were the one who had lost something precious.

Lucilius couldn't even think as he slumped down to his knees, cradling his stump with his good hand.

CHAPTER 3: RHOSAN

THIRD MOON, 1794, CWM OR

Eleven Years before the Proclamation

They didn't keep him in chains. No great walls surrounded the Victor's estate, and only a few guards patrolled the grounds. They did not need more. Outside, Victor Gruffyd's land rolled nothing but endless, unforgiving snow-drenched terrain, and his kennel boasted huge, thick-coated wolfhounds who could track down a man before he'd gone a mile.

The Defeated had been quick to tell Wynn this as he lay in his bunk among them. He thought they meant the words out of kindness, their way of giving him advice: *be quiet, lie low, stay safe.* He wished they had just kept it to themselves. Hope here was a fragile thing.

He lay in the cot, his head at the top and his heels balanced on the bottom edge, a thin, rough blanket thrown over thin, rough clothes. He was surrounded by the sleeping sounds of nineteen other men, all grunting and snoring and sniffling. Morning light oozed beneath the barracks door, but no one had yet stirred.

Wynn closed his eyes and deepened his breathing, trying to pretend that it was Nia and Owynn he was listening to as they slept late one rest day morning.

The illusion was broken by the sound of shuffling feet. The door to the male Defeateds' quarters creaked as it opened, and Wynn kept his eyes shut even as he heard an exasperated sigh.

"Up!" A familiar voice called. It seemed that word was all they needed to hear because the slumbering, snoring, farting men started to shift. Some groaned, and a particularly deep sleeper continued his loud snores in the corner, but most rose. Wynn peeled one eye open to see the Defeated filtering out of their quarters. Off to eat breakfast and to endure another day of labor, all to line the pockets of Victor Gruffyd.

Standing beside the door was Linn. She was an older Defeated woman—housekeeper, cook, and leader of the female Defeated. She watched with a steady gaze, and when she caught Wynn looking her way, she cocked an eyebrow. He was still abed. "If you don't get up, Wynn, you'll miss breakfast."

Hunger gnawed at the lining of his belly. Wynn had lost everything. His profession, his home, his wife, his child. How odd was it that even after all the pain and anger had torn through him, he still needed to perform such mundane tasks as eating? Life just struggled on, like new shoots pushing up from the burnt carcasses of dead trees.

He stood. "What's for breakfast?"

Linn's nostrils flared, and she gave Wynn another appraising look before she shook her head. Breakfast, for the last *three* moons, had been rye porridge and eggs. Everyday. Why he bothered to ask if it was anything different was beyond Wynn. Maybe it was just something to say. Habitual.

Nia used to make sweetened porridge with berries and apple slices. Or fry stale pieces of bread soaked in egg. In the summer, they'd just have fresh fruit and a cup of goat's milk.

He doubted the Defeated would ever have the pleasure of fresh fruit. That luxury would surely be reserved for the mighty Victors.

"You're working with Jeston in the back field today. The fence has been damaged, and the goats keep getting out." Linn made a beckoning gesture, and Wynn hurried his step. He wondered if Linn was Battle Defeated, like he was, or born into it. It was impossible to tell, really. Both the Defeated and their Victors were of the same general ethnicity, the only difference being that the Victors followed a God that claimed the strong had dominion over the weak, that the Victors should take and rule over what they had stolen.

The pain hit him then, a deep-chest ache as though he'd been struck with a boulder on his breastbone. Gods, he missed Nia. He wished they had killed him that night as the village burned around him.

It was like that sometimes, the hurt. Though more often, these days, Wynn felt little at all. He turned to the well for a drink and to wash his face, then stumbled into the long, rough hall where the Defeated ate their meals. His porridge was as tasteless and lukewarm as always, but at least the eggs were fresh. When he finished, he left to begin his day. If nothing else, the mind-numbing sequence of chores would dull his pain.

Jeston brushed by him, their face in the air as they whistled a jovial tune. They always seemed lively, no matter the situation or the chore forced upon them. Jeston had told him once that they followed the Death God, Aryus, above all others and didn't need to worry about this life when something better was waiting for them in the next. They also refused any implication on gender, much like the God they served, though the Victors forced them into the clothing and barracks of a male Defeated.

As dark as he felt just then, Wynn would have rather accompanied anyone else out to the fence. Even silent Keeley or the ever-cantankerous Lugh. He turned abruptly from Jeston and strode toward the broken fence, stopping only to pick up a tool or two.

When he returned, it was to find Jeston smiling as they piled rocks to one side of the dilapidated stone wall. They looked up as Wynn approached and nodded. "Do you want to hear a riddle?" Jeston was full of riddles, another trait they shared with their God. He wondered if the God of Death would want their followers to be happy in captivity.

It seemed wrong to Wynn that Jeston should just accept their role in all this. Just smile and whistle and work without pay or respect or even human kindness. Wynn's Pa had always said that the Gods helped those that helped themselves. To merely accept this captivity, to do nothing to free himself, would be like giving himself freely to the Victors.

"Go on then." They were going to tell Wynn regardless, so they might as well get it over with. He picked up one of the stones from Jeston's pile and tested its weight in one hand before laying it on the wall to find a place it might fit.

Without the proper mud to cement the stone, the wall would fall again, but that was the way of things on Victor Gruffyd's compound. Everything was repaired halfway, craftsmanship tossed aside for quantity. Wynn hated it all.

"What has one eye but cannot see?" Jeston asked, setting their stone down.

Wynn looked at the lumpy piece of rock in his hand. "I don't know. A potato." He placed another rock on the wall, trying to fit them together so they would hold each other in place. Owynn would probably do better with his stacking blocks.

Jeston laughed. "A potato? That's a good guess. But potatoes have many eyes. It was a needle."

Wynn's mind flashed to the night of the raid, to packing sewing supplies and putting his son's arms through the straps of the bag. He closed his eyes for a long moment, letting his lungs fill with cold air. He needed to calm his breathing, to move his thoughts to anything else. He couldn't have another fit. Not while someone was watching.

"Got another one?" he asked, sweat beading his forehead.

"Of course. Riddles were Aryus's favorite thing." Jeston took up another stone, seemingly oblivious to the hammering of Wynn's heart. "What must be broken before it can be used?"

The answer flew out of his mouth before Wynn thought it through. "A man."

Jeston stopped with their stone hovering next to Wynn's, their eyes widening at the dark answer. But it was true, wasn't it? These Defeated, battle or otherwise, they were all broken. Broken to the will of Victor Gruffyd. Wynn didn't want to be like that. He wanted to be free. Free and whole.

Jeston blinked and set their stone down, wedging it in so that the wall would be as sturdy as something so shoddily made could ever be.

"An egg," they answered, their voice softer now, as if afraid to be overheard. They should be. To talk of freedom within the compound was to ask for a beating.

But Wynn didn't care. He had to get out. He was suffocating here.

He could just leave. Just walk out of the compound. There weren't that many guards on the fringes of the property where the animal pens were kept. And since he and Jeston had been sent off to do a job that would ostensibly take half the day, it would be hours before anyone thought to come looking.

"You weren't born to this place either," Wynn said, his voice low. "Come with me. We can leave now. I know enough of the Old Way to keep us alive."

"The Old Ways are forbidden," Jeston replied, which was neither agreement to escape nor a dismissal of the idea.

"Not outside of this Godsforsaken place they're not."

Jeston straightened up. Wynn figured they were perhaps thirty summers old. Older than he was, but not by that much. When had they been Defeated? Ten years ago? More? They glanced across the ruined wall and into the forest. The trees were heavy with snow, limbs drooping like a farmer after bringing the fall harvest. They shook their head. "Wynn, I don't have anywhere else to go. My village is gone, my family too. This is my home now. It could be yours too. I'd like to be your friend." They reached for Wynn then, trying to take him by the shoulder in what the carpenter assumed was supposed to be a comforting gesture, but he pulled away, angry.

He didn't want this to be his home! He didn't want to be friends with people who kept themselves wrapped in invisible chains. "You're as much your own captor as they are. Stay here then, but I'm going. Tell them I overpowered you or knocked you out or something."

Jeston widened their eyes and turned away. Was that hurt in their expression? Wynn didn't care. He was leaving. Now. He dropped the rock he'd been holding and strode off, keeping his shoulders square, and his eyes focused ahead. Purposeful. As though he had every right to be stepping off of Gruffyd's property. And he did, didn't he? He was a free man. A free man who'd been forced from his home.

No one called out to stop him. No horns blared. No hounds bayed.

Jeston did not say a word. There was no sound at all but the squeak of powder snow beneath the thin leather boots he'd been given to wear, and he was grateful now that he'd done as Linn said and oiled them. His feet were still dry.

Wynn walked for hours. The air, still mostly untouched by spring, warmed as the sun reached its zenith, then began to cool again as she slipped lower down the horizon. Perhaps Jeston had found a way to keep from alerting the Victors. Maybe he would truly get away.

His steps lightened. The forests surrounding the city of Cwm Or were stunning— thick, heavy-limbed oaks stood beneath towering pines and warmly dressed spruces. At one point, he traveled through a stand of straight-backed birches that reminded him sharply of Nia. She had wanted Owynn's crib carved from the soft, pale wood, and he'd made her a bangle from some of the same lumber, the contrast stark against her dark skin.

She'd been wearing it when they fled. Did she think of him when she saw it now? Did she think him a coward or dead? He hoped they had made it away, crossing to the other side of the mountains. They could find shelter with one of the Valley Gods' temples, or perhaps Nia would find her mother's people in Esha's territory. They would be safe. Owynn would grow up strong and tall off the fruits of a softer place; one day, if Wynn was very lucky, he would find them again.

It was dark, the trees no longer beautiful statues but menacing sentries guarding the path forward. Wynn knew he should stop, should ward a sheltering fir or hollow and sleep till light returned, but he wanted to get farther away, to put more distance between himself and the Victors. He stumbled, tripping over tree roots and covering his face with his hands to avoid hitting branches. Somewhere, not terribly far off, it seemed, a wolf howled, followed by barks and yips.

Wynn went suddenly, numbingly cold—colder even than the chill of the late-winter night could have made him.

Those weren't wolves.

They were dogs. The deep-voiced, bear-sized wolfhounds that Victor Gruffyd bred to guard his lands and hunt down escaped Defeated.

Wynn surged forward, his heart thudding in his chest like a prey animal running before a predator. Tree branches scratched at his arms and sides, tearing into his clothes and leaving long scratches on his skin. His chest heaved for air, straining against the biting cold. He tripped, falling flat against the snow, the damp soaking his skin, and then he was off, hands held out before him like a blind man to keep from running into any trees.

He could hear the heavy footfalls of dogs getting closer, the excited bursts of sound when they caught his scent anew. Thank the Gods Nia could not see him now, could not watch as he was hunted down with no more dignity than a wild boar. Thank the Gods they had not been taken.

A large, furred shape loomed suddenly to Wynn's left, and he skidded to change directions, gasping for air, for anything that might help him survive this night. The dog kept pace with him easily, one eye glinting off whatever moon or starlight could filter through the trees. A dog was on his other side, tongue lolling even as it yipped to the others. Both animals surged past him into the night, and, for a second, he allowed himself to hope. Perhaps they weren't hunting him after all, but some—

The dogs wheeled around and Wynn skidded to a halt, backpedaling to avoid two sets of snapping teeth, their pale canines seeming to glow in the dim light. He turned, so numb with fear that he could not feel his hands or feet. Wolfhounds closed in from every direction, six hulking beasts each standing taller than his hip, and as long as a bear. A few of them growled even as they tightened the circle around him.

There was nowhere to escape except through Gruffyd's hounds, but, futile as that would be, Wynn had to try, had to give everything to this escape attempt. There might not come another. He rushed forward, headed for a gap between two of the dogs, but one of them moved as well, darting in low and eerily silent, its ears forward and mouth open. Wynn put an arm up to protect himself and the dog clamped down, his teeth sliding through skin and fat and flesh like knives through stewed meat. The dog's eyes were wild, showing white. Blood dripped on snow and smoke fur.

Wynn's world was a wash of pain and fury. He beat at the dog's head, almost oblivious to the arrival of men and horses. When they dismounted and called off the hound, he flew at them instead, scratching and pounding them with rocks and ragged fingernails.

"Knock him out!"

"Get the ropes!"

No. *Never*. Never again would they own him. Wynn would fight until they killed him. Better to die free than live in a cage of their making. He ran at their knives and clawed at their eyes. He knew only red, raw rage until something blunt connected with the back of his skull, and darkness fell.

CHAPTER 4: THE EMAI

FOURTH MOON, 1787, VILLAGE OF NEC

Eighteen Years before the Proclamation

The illu where Iniabi lived had one room. It was large, but not the largest in the village, with walls of overlapping skins sewn to great, curving spars of whale bone with the waxy thread they spun from goat and elk intestines. There were scents of damp fur and fish from the specimens hanging above her head, drying alongside root vegetables and the hardy shrubs that sprouted when the snow was thinnest. Mostly, though, it smelled of oil and smoke and dung.

Everything her mother owned was piled against the walls: a blackened clay stove; animal skins and baskets; two rough beds; a table lined with jars, mortar, and pestle; and Iniabi. She stood still, her bony spine pressed into the curve of a whalebone spar, the illu walls enfolding her shoulders, and wished that there were two rooms so that she might stand within her home and not be in sight of her mother.

The mending was finished. She had hauled the elk rugs outside to beat them free of dust and debris. Their two pots were clean, and so were their mugs and plates. The goats were milked. Their dung had been mixed with fibrous shrubs and left to dry so they could later burn it. There was no other task that needed doing, to Iniabi's eyes, so she could only make herself still and quiet where her mother might not notice her idle hands.

So far, she had not. Iniabi's mother knelt in illu's center with her back to Iniabi, but her thick-knuckled hand was reflected in the black eyes of the fish she held before she plunged a bone needle through the plump skin of its lower lip. She picked up the next and repeated the motion, then again, until she had a long string of them bound together by their gap-mouthed grins. They would hang like that for moons, all glass-eyed, laughing at the illu above them until their skins wrinkled and their eyes turned goat-milk white.

"Iniabi." The sound of her name made her jump. She was frozen as a snow hare, heart pumping furiously below thin skin.

"Yes, Aada?"

"Take two jars to Sani's illu and return once she fills them with whale oil."

Iniabi relaxed at the command, but there was still something of the prey animal to her pulse as she lifted the jars and scurried, light-footed, from the illu. It was noon, sun reflecting against new snow.

There was a time in her life when Iniabi thought that all the world must be white. The snow around her village never melted, and the ice never thawed. The Emai were pale people that wore pale furs. The wise women pressed gypsum into their skin to bleach away the hints of peach and pink. They told stories in it, too, on tent walls. What color there was did not seem to exist for its own sake but to serve the vast white. The orange of flame and the red of spilled animal blood only reminded those who saw them of the unending, colorless press.

Now though, she knew that all the world was not so.

When Iniabi was six or seven years old, strong enough to follow her mother and carry buckets, they traveled to the sea to collect urchins from freezing tide pools along the water's edge. It was an expanse that it might have swallowed everything Iniabi had ever known, perhaps all of Emai if it so chose, and the slavers as well.

The whole world was not white but black. An ocean of ink surrounding their little white home.

Iniabi shook her head as she walked, trying to banish thoughts of a dark sea. She was already in the village proper. The gray-white of fur tents surrounded her, a slight break from the pure white snow. Emaian women sat before them, pounding vegetables or feeding babes. Their men walked by, over-large and hauling impossible loads.

Not far from her, a group of warm-skinned children in dark furs played in the village's streets. Not Emaian, but slavers' children, the product of banished northerners from Liria or Phecea. People said that they had been filling Emaian towns for years, that there were places so thick with them that the pale Emai were drowning in a dark sea of foreign people. Some Emaians even spoke of a time before the banished had come, though that made little sense to Iniabi. Hadn't they always been here?

The other children looked up as she approached, and Iniabi instinctively held the empty jars closer to her chest. They'd been playing a game; their faces were ruddy with exertion, and one of them held a skin ball. She kept walking towards them but stopped a few feet away and scuffed the toe of her boot. Her mother would be angry if she delayed.

"Can I play?" Iniabi asked in her native tongue, and her voice sounded small even to her. The other kids didn't move. They were all warm-skinned foreigners; no Emaian children played among them.

"Isn't that the witch's daughter?"

"Oooh, what if she puts a curse on us?" They erupted into giggles, and overhead, the clouds shifted away from the sun. The world around her was suddenly too-bright, glaring.

"I will not!"

"Want to know what we do to witches back in my country?" The boy who swaggered towards her had high cheekbones and a long nose too big for his face. His hands were fists, and he wore Emaian furs. They all did.

"You make them into slaves," Iniabi said, her lip curling. He couldn't scare her with something she already knew. "Or you would if you weren't exiled."

"No," he laughed and raised a hand to throw something she hadn't seen. "We stone them."

The rock hit her below the cheekbone, and the pain was like blood on snow, hot and shocking. When she lifted a hand to touch the place, her fingers came away red, and all the whites around her were sharp again. The rock had fallen a few feet away, and when she picked it up, the rough edges bit into her palm as though it were trying to mold her skin to its form.

A woman's voice called from a nearby doorway, harsh in reprimand. The other children scattered, calling to each other. "You're cursed for sure, now!"

Iniabi clutched the rock all the way to Sani's illu, dreaming she dared to throw it at each of their faces.

⇑ ⇑ ⇑

Sani wasn't at her home when Iniabi arrived, but her daughter was. Mika was a couple years older than Iniabi— eleven or twelve— and they had sat together before at prayers.

The older girl was stitching elk skins outside their illu, but she stood when Iniabi arrived. "Aada told me you'd be by, daughter of Manaba." The other Emai always said her mother's name that way, with a little bit of awe.

"I'm to ask Sani to fill these with whale oil." She shuffled her grip on the jars, shoving the rock into her coat so Mika wouldn't see it. The older girl nodded and held open the flap hanging over the door to their illu. It was similar to Iniabi's, only without the table for making tinctures and with the addition of a man's boots and spears. It smelled of whale oil, but so did most of the village.

"What happened to your face?"

Iniabi's hand half-raised to her cheek then halted and lowered back to her side. Should she lie? Brush it off? She hesitated for too long, then held out the rock. "Banished kids."

Mika turned and spat, the spray of spittle landing between them where it bubbled: white against the dirt floor. "You should have thrown it back."

Iniabi didn't respond, but Mika didn't seem to think she needed to. The older girl turned towards several carefully corked earthenware jugs and began to fill the jars with golden oil. "I'm surprised they bother you, your mother being the healer. And you look more like them than any of us."

"I do not!" Iniabi's skin and hair were the same ash-white as Mika's. They might have been sisters, but Mika was already as tall as her mother, and Iniabi never seemed to grow.

Mika straightened carefully under the weight of now-full jars. "Your eyes are just as black as theirs are. As black as the sea," she said, and her Emaian winter-sky gaze felt like an accusation.

Iniabi had never seen her eyes. She had no way of telling whether Mika was speaking the truth or not unless she asked Aada. Iniabi shifted her weight from foot to foot. Aada didn't like any mention of the banished.

Mika handed Iniabi the filled jars, and her too-narrow shoulders bent under the weight. She shifted her hands to better grip the bottom of the jars and set her spine. "Are you sure you don't want to make two trips?" Mika sounded doubtful, as though she didn't expect Iniabi to make it all the way home with her load.

"No." They weren't all that heavy, and Aada was waiting. Iniabi slipped out the door before she could wonder anymore about slaver eyes.

CHAPTER 5: THE EMAI

THIRD MOON, 1789, VILLAGE OF NEC

Sixteen Years before the Proclamation

On the first day of the third moon, the chief of Nec died, and Manaba, daughter of Ooyu, stood before the people to guide them through their grief.

It was a gray morning. Great swaths of cloud blotted out the sky in a mirror image of the snow below so that the village balanced precariously on the edge of two opposing forces. Iniabi sat in that liminal space, her legs crossed and her arm brushing Mika's. The older girl's face was solemn, and she didn't seem to mind the contact.

Around them, the Emai huddled in twos and threes, their lumpen-fur forms hunched against cold and grief. In their center, the chief's wife wailed her sorrow into the snow-sky, her children tucked against her. A few softer voices joined in from the people, but no one cried. The Emai could not shed tears.

Manaba let them grieve for a time, as was fitting, before she stepped forward to place her hands on the shoulders of the chief's wife and her eldest son, a grown man. "My people," she called, and her voice reverberated off snow and fur and illu, the wails of the people becoming a song to buoy her words. "The Great Sea has heard your grief, and with the gentleness of the slow-tide, she has sent me a vision."

Manaba lifted gypsum-caked hands to the sky above them, her gypsum-painted face framed by the curve of rock walls pointing up towards the sky like fingers in a cupped hand that held the village in its palm. Her eyes rolled backward, spheres of veined white, and she took a breath that filled her belly with air. "I see Chief Nakos standing on the shore, and in his hands are the spear and net, for he was both a great warrior and provider for his tribe. Behind him lies the snow—his family and his people—but he will not turn. Nakos is a brave man and knows what he must do. His spear falls outward, a challenge. His net inwards, a promise. His spirit will yet protect the People. Nakos steps forward, arms raised, and the waves rise to meet him."

Iniabi stood, her knees wobbling. She had to hold the whalebone bowl, and her fingers could not shake. She approached Manaba as one of the village elders led an elk forward from the other side. It was a beautiful creature with fanning antlers and a thick snow coat softer than any Iniabi had ever seen. Its eyes were deep and solemn, and Iniabi had the bizarre desire to rush forward and place her arms around the elk's strong neck.

She held still, though, for Manaba, her Aada.

"Let us give salt back to the Great Sea in Nakos's name so that she may protect him on his journey through her depths and continue to provide for the people."

Iniabi positioned herself just below the elk's crowned head, her black eyes on his. Her knuckles were bloodless against the bone bowl. All around her, the people opened their mouths, their voices tumbling over one another in a keening song, growing and crashing like wave rhythm until the rock walls caught the sound and multiplied it a thousand times. Manaba joined in, her high call floating over all. She reached forward, a knife suddenly in her hand, and drew a deep, straight cut across the animal's throat.

The elk made no noise but turned its round eyes on Iniabi. Blood fountained from its neck, splashing into the bowl, up her arms, across the elk's chest. It no longer looked soft but wet and red. Slowly, as though being lulled to sleep, the animal's legs began to buckle, bending at the knees first in its front legs and then in the back. Iniabi sank with it, her arms trembling beneath the weight of bone and blood.

Manaba bent at the waist, her lined face coming close to Iniabi's before she dipped a finger into sacrificial red and smeared it down her own face in a long, straight line that began at the center of her forehead and stopped where her neck ended in furs. It bled into the gypsum to either side, a branching river. "Rejoice, Emai, for the Great Sea has heard your song! Nakos will return to us through the leadership of his son. May the Great Sea provide!"

Dozens of voices, echoing and bodiless, repeated her words from the depths of their furs. "May the Great Sea provide."

The elk was dragged away, its blood taken from Iniabi's hands so that all the Emai might partake, and in the sudden bustle of work, Iniabi felt Aada's hand on her shoulder. "Well done, daughter."

⇑ ⇑ ⇑

It was after dark when they returned to their illu. Iniabi's mouth still tasted of boiled elk blood mixed with root liquor, bitter-burning down her throat. Aada's eyes were too bright, but her steps did not falter. She swept into the skin room and stoked the fire, humming. Iniabi found a wall in which to hide her shoulders.

Manaba did not stoke the fires.

"Come here, child." The medicine woman laid something in the fire that Iniabi could not see, then turned, her white braids swinging in tandem with beaded necklaces. Iniabi stepped forward until she could see the uneven stitches in her Aada's elk-skin tunic. It was stained, in places, by the spray of sacrificial blood.

"You did well today," Manaba said for the second time, and Iniabi's chest swelled. She had done well. Aada was *proud*. "You will make a fine medicine woman."

"Yes, Aada." It was the correct answer, even if Iniabi could not see herself howling for the dead, her face bisected by a red river.

"Good girl." Manaba turned to the fire, her hands hidden by the curve of her back. "What does the medicine woman do?"

"Heals the sick, keeps our histories, comforts the tribe… receives visions?"

"Mmmm, and where do the visions come from?"

"The Great Sea."

Manaba turned and in her hands was a knife, the blade so hot that it glowed orange-white, the color of the sun dipping below the horizon. "Yes, The Great Sea gives visions, but only if you ask for them with blood and poison." She reached forward and gripped Iniabi's jaw, forcing her fingers into the joint, so the girl's mouth opened. Manaba snarled. "This is a *privilege*, girl. Don't you dare fight me."

Iniabi squeezed her eyes shut, damp breaths panting past Manaba's gnarled fingers. There was a moment of still, and then the blade lay against her tongue, and the flesh leaped away from the heat like hair curling in flames. The smell of cooking meat filled her nose, and for the second time that day, Iniabi's mouth tasted of salt and steel. Manaba shook her.

"Quit whining. Would you rather be a slave?" The medicine woman's fingers tightened, five thick nails, and Iniabi opened her eyes to see the black bottle of poison tipping into her wound. It was cold and salty-sweet.

Manaba let go, and Iniabi fell, inching backward toward the ground away from gypsum skin and knife and bottle. Even sound seemed too slow, the crackling of the fire drawn out like whistles. The dark, though, came fast.

Before she hit the floor, Iniabi *dreamed*.

She stood on a mound of bones, and around her throat was a collar of iron, the links that should have held her captive broken. In her right hand was a sword, in her left a net. Behind her stood an army of snow; before her lay fields of blood.

Men ran towards her, their hands dripping with chains; only the Iniabi in the vision did not fear them. She stepped forward and slid her blade through an eye with the ease that Manaba hooked fish mouths. She sliced open a belly and lobbed off a limb. The bones made new mounds for her to step on, and for every foot of ground she took, the white behind her came forward, swallowing up the field of blood and the corpses upon it.

The battle continued, and gradually, Iniabi became aware of forms standing alongside her. Their faces were blurred, but they wore Emaian furs and shouted Emaian war cries. With them, the battle raged faster. There were fewer of the enemy for Iniabi to fight, but occasionally one of the others would fall, adding their bodies to the bone piles. The enemy was never-ending, but Iniabi was not fighting to destroy all that stood before her. She needed to reach something precious.

Iniabi knew she had come to the end of her fight when she saw her. A woman stood amid the blood, though it did not touch her sandaled feet or linen robes. She had dusky, nut-brown skin and a mass of hair curling in tight ringlets. Her body was soft, her face angled, and her eyes warm. She was beautiful in a way that Iniabi had not realized people could be.

Around them, the Emai still clashed with slavers in flashes of white and red, but they all kept clear of the woman. She stepped towards Iniabi, her un-calloused hand outstretched. When she was near enough, Iniabi dropped her sword and laid the net in that gentle palm. It began to snow, and everywhere the flakes touched blood, it billowed up in smoke and wafted away.

When Iniabi woke, her skin was fish-scale clammy, and her thighs were sticky with red.

CHAPTER 6: LIRIA

SIXTH MOON, 1780, VINDIUM

Twenty-five Years before the Proclamation

Winter in Vindium was beautiful. Crystalline frost layered the windows, citizens prepared for the deliverance festival, and the smells of roasting nuts wafted through the streets. It was bright and happy and horrible to watch from the medical ward of a Legion hospital.

The field surgeons had sewn up Luce's wrist and saved his life. He hadn't bled to death and hadn't gotten the rot that some soldiers did. His injury, weeks later, was much improved. He was weak, tired, and his arm ached. At night he woke to cramps in his hand, only to remember it was gone. How strange to feel pain in something that didn't exist anymore.

And what did it matter? Hand, no hand… real or unreal pain. His future was over.

In a moment of weakness, he wrote to Camilla and told her that he was coming back and would be in the hospital, but not why. Since then, Lucilius had realized his folly. Camilla could never marry him. He was a cripple. While he had still received his promotion and retained his place in the Legion, he was no longer whole.

She deserved a life without catering to a man who dripped food into his lap and couldn't dress or tie his own boots. He had stopped answering her letters and refused to tell her which hospital or ward he was within. It would be easier for them if they never saw each other again. She would marry a good, noble man and have a family and a life that was proper and beautiful.

He—

Sighing, Lucilius looked at his stump. He knew many soldiers who had injuries. He didn't think less of them. But most had earned their marks in battle, not from a demented heathen wielding a knife. How could he walk around honorably when he had been so shamed?

He couldn't. And without honor, he couldn't have Camilla.

He resigned himself to life without her for her sake, so it was a shock to find her standing in his doorway. She should not have known where he was, should not have come to see him even if she had... And yet there she was, in a soft, winter gown, her hair braided smoothly back. Neither of them spoke for a long moment, then she stepped forward, and he realized with another jolt that she was *angry*, her face taut and her dark eyes flashing.

"Was it all a lie, then?" He flinched at the sound of her voice. "Is that why you have stopped answering my letters?"

Although he was a warrior and she was the woman he loved, Lucilius felt a ripple of fear coursing through him. Why couldn't she have just let it go?

"It wasn't a lie," he muttered, glancing down at his good hand. The wrist was wrapped in bandages and hidden under the blankets. She couldn't see his injury. Would it be easier to just show her? But what if she looked at him in shame and disgust? Could he take it?

No. He wasn't strong enough to bear that.

"Then *why*, Lucilius?" Her shoulders were tense about her neck, and she shook slightly when she spoke. He had never seen her so upset, so hurt. And he had done it. "Why won't you speak to me?"

Lucilius painted the ceiling with his gaze. He couldn't look at her, not when she seemed so hurt. He had cut things off to avoid harming her more.

"Camilla—" he started, his voice strained. He knew her stubbornness. She'd want to stay with him despite the injury if she wasn't repulsed by it. And he would never, *never* let her. Not when the likelihood of him receiving battle promotions was slim to none. Not when he'd be a Legion grunt for the rest of his life. "I can't. Not anymore."

"Luce, what kind of explanation is that? What could have possibly made you turn your back on me?" She took another step forward, then hesitated, resting a hand on her stomach. He hadn't realized it yet, but she seemed reduced, as though she had been ill in his absence. "If you refuse to marry me, then I am ruined."

"Don't be dramatic, Camilla. You've never been the type," Luce murmured, closing his eyes tight to avoid seeing her drawn face. She must have lost sleep, wondering what had happened to crush their happy, beautiful love. "It will hurt for a time—to be apart. But you'll heal. You'll learn to love again. You'll be happy." He tried to tell himself it was true for him, too, but Lucilius knew they were lies.

"No, I have not ever been the type." Camilla's voice had gone cold. He couldn't help it; he opened his eyes again. She glared at him as fiercely as any commander he'd ever served under. Like a coward, he looked away. "But perhaps, it is true what they say about how your emotions change while you are pregnant."

"It's not the time to start, Camilla. I can't explain, but you have to believe me, this is for the best. I'm not what you want. I'm not what you need. I'm not— " She glared and stood spear-straight as her words sunk in. His breath hitched, and Lucilius blinked stupidly at the woman he loved. He didn't think she was making it up— Camilla had never been a liar or a story weaver. And he didn't think she'd say such things to get him to return to their courtship. Which meant it was the truth. She would have his child, and here he was a useless, invalid! "It's early enough; surely you could marry another and convince him?" he said, eyes drifting down to her belly, unassuming and ordinary. Lucilius held his breath as he pulled his stump out from under the blankets, placing it gingerly on his lap so she would see and understand he wasn't a whole man anymore.

"Marrying me is that repugnant to you then?" she scoffed, her cheeks flushing. "You did not seem to think so before. I have risked everything for a way to marry you, to love you for the rest of my life, and you will still insist on turning me aside, on abandoning your child to be raised by another at best. If no one will have a ruined wife, what then? I suppose your child and I will live in a poorhouse? On the streets?"

"Camilla!" Lucilius protested, horrified at her blatant words. "I'm trying to offer you an alternative. A happy, beautiful life. One you deserve, and I cannot provide!" He held up his stump in explanation. Didn't she understand what this injury would do to his military career? "You're a Pontius. I'm a Nonus." Her family was old and established. He was barely noble. "Our child would be a Nonus if we wed..."

"Our child will be a Nonus or have no name at all. There is no place for an unwed woman and bastard child among the ranks of the Lirian nobility." She swallowed hard and straightened her shoulders. "I am sorry you were injured, but the talk about you has been that of a promising young leader. You did well on the raids. You will have a career with or without that hand. I will only have a place in this world if you give it to me." The tendons along her jaw stood out for a moment, and she took a deep breath. "I thought you would have been joyous to marry me, to be a father, but I will not beg."

His gut twisted, and he reached out to take her hand, only to remember that his left one was gone. The bandaged appendage hung in the air between them before Lucilius lowered it to his lap once more.

"I *am* happy. Unbelievably happy, but, Camilla, I never wanted to saddle you with a cripple. A *poor* cripple...." Despite himself, Lucilius felt his voice break. Hastily, he looked away. Shameful tears were welling up in his eyes. He didn't want her to see him so weak.

She softened, her eyes gentling. "Luce, I want *you*. Rich or poor. Two hands or one." Camilla came to stand in reach of his bed. "You will recover from this. You will learn to adapt."

With a shuddering breath, he was careful to keep his face turned away from Camilla, but Luce finally offered his good hand, palm up, to her. To take. To hold.

He would adapt.

Tenth Moon, 1781, Liria

"Camilla!?" Lucilius's voice echoed through the house's foyer, bouncing off walls and distorting as it traveled. He closed the front door behind himself and let the maid take his stiff-collared jacket. Normally he wouldn't wear such a formal uniform, but the commander had called a special meeting, and Lucilius had thought it wise to dress strictly. He was glad to have the highly decorated uniform to keep him sitting upright during the meeting, as it had been full of surprises.

"Camilla!?" he called again, taking the stairs two at a time as he climbed to find his wife. If she wasn't answering, it was likely she was in the babe's nursery, playing with Ignatious or perhaps holding him in her arms as he slept.

Only, Ignatious was sleeping soundly in his cradle, an older nurse watching over him as she sewed. Camilla was not in their rooms, or the kitchens, or organizing their expenses. She was not meeting with the staff or writing letters.

Luce was beginning to worry, unease worming through his veins until he thought to check the garden. She was laboring there, sweat beading her brow and her delicate fingers brushed with soil, bracing up thin, scraggly vines. They seemed hardly worth the effort to him, but when she heard his entrance, she turned and beamed.

"Look, Luce! My mother has sent me clippings from their garden! I will have moon flowers again." He was almost breathless watching her. She was still as beautiful to him as she had been the first night he met her among the vines. "They don't look like much now, but in a few moons, this trellis will be heavy with blooms. Our courtyard will be the envy of all our friends."

He highly doubted it. Most of their friends were military men like himself. While some of Camilla's social circle had remained, most distanced themselves. With the sudden wedding followed by an 'early' baby and a poor match with a one-handed soldier, many nobles looked down on them. Still, they were left with a good group—a good group who did *not* visit their humble abode on the *west* side of Egara.

But he'd never argue with Camilla. Never again. She saved their budding romance by taking fate into her hands, she concocted their marriage when he could only see boundaries, she birthed their perfect son, and she insisted Lucilius work harder than all the other officers in the Legion. She was right, of course.

"Certainly," he agreed, offering her a hand and then pulling her close to steal a kiss. "I met with the General today. He's giving me a promotion." He squeezed her tight. Another promotion, so soon, was surely a good sign. All those extra days writing reports, attending drills, and inspecting his cohort had paid off. The General liked what a 'tight group' Lucilius was running. 'Efficient,' he had called it.

"That's wonderful!" She hugged him back, though she was careful to keep her dirty hands from his dress shirt. "And so soon! I knew your hard work would pay off." She was happy, he realized, her cheeks warm and her eyes creased from her smile. Though he may never understand why she had chosen this life with him, it suited her. "I'm so proud of you, Luce. Just today, the Speakers talked about how important your work for the Emai is to the Almighty."

"It includes more responsibility but also more pay. We might afford to move to the southern quarter in a few years." It was a more desirable, affluent area. Maybe then, some of her friends would come to visit.

He brushed his thumb along her cheekbone and kissed Camilla. His life was turning out better than he had ever dreamed, even before his injury.

Camilla was a little pink and breathless when she pulled back, her eyes dancing. "Let me see if I can't get the cook to make something special tonight. To celebrate." She kissed his cheek. "Ignatious will be happy too!"

Lucilius sighed as she left. How had he gotten so lucky?

CHAPTER 7: RHOSAN

THIRD MOON, 1794, CWM OR

Eleven Years before the Proclamation

Wynn gasped awake to cold. It was just past dark, the sun and all her warmth slow and lazy with sleep. It would be a while longer still before they arrived. His hands were manacled, each iron loop ending in a chain binding him to a post. He half-hung between them, the length of the chains and the height of the poles keeping him from kneeling in the snow. Only his bare feet reached the ground, and he could not make himself look at them. His few glances so far had only revealed strange, red, and swollen masses that he could not quite feel any longer. His hands were hardly better off, and he shook in his blood-smeared clothing, sinking with drowsiness but unable to sleep. Every time he got close, he sagged in his bonds, and the pain of hanging from his shoulders pulled him to consciousness again.

It was impossible to tell how long he had been bound here. Wynn remembered waking up dazed, his hands and feet trussed and his head slapping rhythmically against the side of a thick-coated horse, its hide filling his nose with scents of sweat and manure. He'd waned in and out of consciousness, coming back to life briefly to struggle as he was forced into the bonds that held him now. After that, the freeze and the dark had rendered time meaningless. He existed only in a state of exhausted pain, unable to sink into sleep or oblivion, his head ringing with waves of agony and his bruised body struggling against the onslaught of cold.

Sometime later, Defeated began to arrive. He knew he made a pitiful sight, his left arm raw and pulpy from dog bites and his extremities frostbite-red. Wynn didn't look up to see them, but from the murmured whispers, it was both men and women, and there were enough of them to make up most of Gruffyd's holdings. No one moved to speak to him or untie his bonds. No one stepped forward to help him at all.

Victor Gruffyd's big bay horse snorted as it wound through the Defeated, and despite himself, Wynn flinched. He had no idea what torture was coming next, what horrible abuse. Surely he was to serve as an example to the rest.

Victor Gruffyd grunted as he dismounted, and Wynn blinked in confusion as the large man came forward. Gruffyd had beady eyes and cheeks crisscrossed with too-large capillaries. He should have looked jolly, but he didn't. Rough hands brought a key to one of Wynn's manacles, and he couldn't help but moan in pain as his malformed wrist was twisted to afford Gruffyd a clear view.

As his second hand was released, Wynn fell onto his knees, his feet no longer able to hold him up. He sank down, shivering, huddling small for warmth. For the second time in as many days, he was glad his wife was nowhere near him, that she could not see this.

"Well, Wynn? Why aren't you running? Now is your chance. You're *free*." Wynn tried to at least stand, to have some ounce of pride, but he couldn't manage it. His body resisted the simplest of commands. He couldn't raise his head, his neck made of willow branches. "Come on! Run! Go! You think you're better off? Take the opportunity granted to you, boy."

Slowly, painstakingly, Wynn maneuvered one foot beneath him and braced against his knee. He rocked his weight slowly onto it, pushing up to stand, but fell again with a strangled cry. Tears coursed down his cheeks at the pain of trying to put weight on the damaged foot, like millions of needles puncturing sensitive skin and swollen muscle. He made no further move to rise.

"Why aren't you going, Wynn? Isn't this what you wanted? To be free?" Gruffyd's voice was chiding. When Wynn didn't answer, Gruffyd knelt, yanking Wynn's head up by the roots of his hair. It should have hurt, but he couldn't feel anything. Not anymore. Gruffyd's face was blurry before his eyes. "Tell me what you want, boy."

Wynn closed his eyes, the tears he had already shed freezing on his cheeks. His voice came out in a ragged whisper. "Warm," he begged. "I want to be warm."

"Warm? But where would you be warm? You don't have a home. There aren't any villages around here for miles. Well… except Cwm Or. Which you ran away from, so clearly you don't want to be there." He released his grip on Wynn's hair, and his head lolled on his neck uselessly. Like a newborn babe, vulnerable and weak. "I thought you wanted to be free?"

Gruffyd's mock-confused tone barely registered in Wynn's mind. He was so tired. Everything hurt. His body, his heart. His skull pounded like war drums. "You took it," he sobbed. "Home. Wife. Son. You brought me here to be used until I die."

Wynn opened his eyes again in time to see Gruffyd smile. "That's right. *I* took it. I Defeated you in battle. If you had won, you'd still have a home. But you lost. I am your better. The sooner you accept that the sooner you can be warm again, Wynn." Gruffyd stood, leaving nothing for Wynn to look at but his muddy boots.

Instead, the Defeated man looked to his swollen toes, even now losing color, paling into the same dead white as the snow. It was like his flesh was dead before he had even left it. He trembled, his shoulders sagging as the fight left him. "You are my better, Victor Gruffyd."

⇑　⇑　⇑

The blisters were the worst part of frostbite. They'd erupted on his fingers, toes, face, and even on the soles of his feet. White, fluid-filled pustules that burst only to spill foul-smelling pus. They made every step an unbearable reminder of Wynn's humiliation.

He sat in a chair in the barracks, empty now with the day. Most of Gruffyd's Defeated were in the fields, preparing the earth for planting after this last frost finally broke. The Defeated mender, Iorath, ground bark and herbs into a thick, pale-green paste that smelled refreshingly of the forest outside. He was a young man—light-haired and taken only just a few weeks after Wynn.

"How'd they find out you were a healer?" Wynn asked after a time, raising himself slightly from the miasma of grief and depression that had clung to him since his escape attempt.

"I told them." The healer, finally satisfied with the consistency of his poultice, began to remove strips of cloth from Wynn's aching feet,

"Isn't that just asking to be taken?"

He took a breath. "They already had my sister and me. This way, I was able to get us out of the mines, and I can practice my craft. Not on the Victors, of course, but on my people."

Wynn grunted and sank back into darkness, only half aware as the mender began to remove the bandages on his hands as well.

"You know," Iorath said after a time, "these are healing well. There is fresh, healthy skin beneath the sores. You won't lose any toes."

Small mercies.

Footsteps announced the newcomer before their knock did, and Wynn didn't bother to look up until someone spoke his name. "Wynn?"

Linn stood in the doorway, her normally dark complexion somewhat pale. She could see the state his feet were in, still exposed to the room. He supposed he'd flinch too if he were her. "Yes?"

Linn blinked and tilted her head in a beckoning manner. "Victor Gruffyd wants you now."

"He shouldn't be walking," Iorath explained, starting to smear his poultice across Wynn's disfigured toes.

"He'll have to," Linn replied.

"Then at least wait until he's been bandaged up. Here, take some of this. It needs to be applied to his hands and face as well."

The older woman hesitated a moment, but she took the bowl of green Iorath held out. She settled onto her haunches beside Wynn and dipped her fingers into the stuff. When she touched him, she was gentle.

With the two of them working on him, it did not take long before he was once more bound in clean strips of linen. Linn had to recruit the aid of another Defeated man, as Wynn's bandaged feet would no longer fit in his boots, but with the clumsy, borrowed pair on, they managed to get him out the door. Leaning heavily on Iorath, they soon had Wynn to the road before the great house where Gruffyd waited impatiently beside a small cart drawn by a mule. A young Defeated girl checked the mule's harness, but she leaped aside when Gruffyd rode by. He kicked his horse over to Wynn and gazed down at him, an unfortunate glint in his eye.

"Get in the cart," he ordered.

It took Iorath and Linn's assistance, but Wynn settled in the cart. He couldn't help but worry about where this mysterious trip would end. Iorath had a point about making himself useful to the Victors. The mine was a back-breaking, unrelenting place. Most who worked there didn't last very long, and the conditions made Gruffyd's Defeated quarters look like a temple. Was Gruffyd so fed up with Wynn that he was ready to sell him? Should Wynn make his case as a craftsman?

Even after the humiliation of proclaiming Gruffyd his superior, the idea left a bad taste in Wynn's mouth.

The mule brayed as Gruffyd urged his mount into a trot, and the wagon lurched forward. Wynn grabbed the sides of the cart, his bandaged hands providing him with poor purchase.

They ambled through the town of Cwm Or, down the rutted, muddy streets, and past the square where farmers and smiths pawned their goods. Mostly the people who walked by looked normal, like the villagers of Wynn's home. But what had he expected? Defeated milling around, heads hanging, and hands dirty? Victors residing over it all like foreign Kings? No.

Victors were rich, powerful warriors who amassed their status and wealth by conducting raids and claiming Defeated. You had to have plenty of land to work and money to feed your captives. Most of Kirit's followers couldn't afford such a life.

The cart turned abruptly, leaving the main road to bump across a pitted path, the rough ride tearing at Wynn's blisters beneath the cloth on his hands. The land around Cwm Or was flat, the forest looming in the distance without touching the town. As the mule kept pace with Gruffyd's horse, they made their way westward, leaving the civilization of Cwm Or and slipping into the scruffy, uninspiring wilderness.

They rode that way, with Wynn's aches and pains doubling and Gruffyd silently urging them on, for an hour or more. Wynn wished he could at least fall asleep, but his heart was beating too quickly to allow it. Any moment, he would see the pitted, ill-formed hills of the mines. Any minute, Gruffyd would hand him over to a short lifetime of darkness for nothing more than a fistful of silver.

Wynn should have stayed out in the cold to die.

He jerked in surprise as the cart came to a halt. The structure in front of him wasn't a mine, that was to be sure. He frowned, watching as Gruffyd dismounted and a man hurried out from the roughly constructed building.

"I'm sorry, Victor," he mumbled and nodded respectfully. Gruffyd's fine furs would make it clear to anyone that he was a Victor and not some ordinary man. "The matches are already set today. We don't have room for another bout."

Gruffyd looped the reins of his horse around one of the cross ties and waved the man off. "We're not here to enter, only to spectate. What fights do you have for today?"

The man nodded again, not quite a bow but certainly pathetic—like groveling. "Two girls. Been causing their Victor some trouble so… And then there is the usual lot."

"No animals?"

"None, Victor. We haven't caught any bears lately."

Gruffyd turned to look at Wynn, lips curving into a mournful frown. "Pity. Oh well, I'm sure the betting will still be worth the trouble. Do you have some men that can assist in getting my Defeated into the stands?"

A strange look crossed the man's face as though he were unused to the idea of helping Defeated, but he didn't challenge Gruffyd. He turned and stuck his head into the building and called, reappearing briefly with two bulky, scarred Defeated. They helped Wynn out of the cart and around the building with no particular gentleness or rough treatment, following behind Gruffyd as though they merely led his horse rather than a human.

Behind the building, the forest opened up to feature a rough, muddy pit surrounded on all sides by stone walls. It stood in the center of a natural depression so that the land around it looked down into the pit—empty now but for a couple of rusted cages, their doors swinging open like hungry maws.

Gruffyd led the way to a set of stands where he climbed to a seat. Wynn was unceremoniously deposited in the space where the Victors rested their feet, but at the moment, all he could feel was how grateful he was to be off his sores.

"You ever been to a pit fight, Wynn?" Gruffyd's voice was casual, relaxed even. He shifted and placed his mud-covered boots on the seat beside Wynn. If the Victor moved his foot so much as an inch, he'd get dirt all over Wynn's breeches.

Of all the humiliations of being Defeated, dirt was certainly not the worst of them.

"No, Victor Gruffyd." Wynn kept his tone level, breathing against the anger in his chest. He packed it down, hammering and hardening that kernel of heat until none of it showed through his skin. Down below, activity had begun to stir in the mud— two people being dragged before the small audience.

"That's a pity. If you had, maybe you'd have known enough to not be Defeated. Your people are too soft. That's why they are never Victors." Gruffyd leaned forward, his gaze not on Wynn but on the two girls below. They must be the Defeated the man at the entrance had spoken of. They'd displeased their Victor, so he'd brought them here as some sort of punishment.

As Wynn looked around the 'pit,' he noted the poor state of the place. The stands where the audience sat were made of cobbled-together wood, half rotten with wet. The arena, where the two girls stood in little more than rags, was the type of mud created by snow thawing and refreezing over and over again until the earth was nothing more than clumps of clay, manure, and slush. Even with the cold air nipping at his nose, he could smell the stench of blood and something rotting.

Weren't the pit fighters supposed to be revered? Didn't Kirit prize the strongest, cruelest of his warriors? This seemed more despicable than glorious.

A man's voice rose from the edge of the pit. He spoke to the girls but pitched his voice to carry into the stands. "For the trouble you two have brought your Victor, only one of you will return with him tonight. The other will stay in the lesser pits to take on Cwm Or's most dangerous competitors!"

The two girls looked at each other, but Wynn couldn't hear what was said. Had they been friends? Lovers? What had they done to so anger their Victor?

Gruffyd grunted and leaned forward even more as if he wanted a better view.

"Now, fight!"

At first, neither of the girls moved, and the people around them—Victors and townspeople—crowed their disappointment. They were here for blood, and they were not used to waiting for it. One of the girls looked around at the assembled people and spat on the ground, but the other took no such stance. She straightened her shoulders, and then she lunged.

Wynn looked down, suddenly horrified. He had no desire to watch these girls destroy themselves. They couldn't be older than sixteen.

Perhaps it was worse that he didn't watch because the groans and cheers of the crowd let his imagination run wild. People, ordinary townspeople and roughened warriors, screamed advice and insults, the few who had been seated before coming to their feet to stand. The crowd turned into a living thing, writhing and thrashing against each other obscenely. Wynn felt the press of strange bodies against him, their unwashed smell mixing with the arena to make his stomach churn.

It was over quickly, whatever it was the two girls did. Gruffyd bumped Wynn with his dirty boot, indicating that he ought to stand up. The man beside Gruffyd passed over a handful of coppers. It looked as if it was all he owned, his arms as thin as reeds and his cheeks hollow. What did Gruffyd need with coppers?

"Not as impressive as the real pits," Gruffyd announced as he started down the stands. "But then that's why they're called lesser, eh?" Gruffyd stopped by the arena's edge and turned to study the mess. Wynn couldn't help it; he looked.

One girl stood, long scratches down her face, lip bloodied, and hands hanging limply by her side. At her feet, the other girl lay, a stray shaft of wood sticking out of her eye. The girl who had spat in distaste. A Victor stood nearby, collecting a tidy sum from the man who seemed to be in charge of the festering place. Had he sanctioned the rudimentary weapon being tossed into the pit, or had the girl just found it in the mud?

"Want to know how I knew to bet on her and not the stronger one?" Gruffyd asked, a smirk tainting his lips.

Wynn reeled from the senseless violence of it, the desperation it would take one human to kill another so coldly. Would he have done it to avoid fighting in pitched battles or against wild animals? "No, Victor Gruffyd."

Gruffyd's smirk disappeared faster than a cloud's shadow. The scowl made him look ten years older. "I knew because she had something left to lose. She thought she was too good for this place, so she lost. You keep acting like you're too good for your place in *my* world, and we'll see where you end up, boy."

CHAPTER 8: RHOSAN

NINTH MOON, 1794, FOREST WEST OF THE AFONDAU

Eleven Years before the Proclamation

The ride to the southeast corner of Kirit Territory was a long one. The autumn winds were bitter and salty with ocean storms, and the roads were churned to mush, so it took three days longer than it should have. It was a hard journey for a healthy man, and Wynn found himself grateful that the frostbite sores on his hands and feet had finally healed with new pink skin.

There was some debate among the Victors as to whether or not this would affect the Dragon Hunt, but there did not seem to be a consensus on yes or no, and all agreed the damp would only slow the Hunters down since the Dragons could fly if the frigid weather didn't keep them grounded.

Either way, the hunting party arrived on the edge of the last known Dragon Territory. The scent hounds caught a trail, and Victors and Defeated geared up to follow the dogs. Wynn kept a careful distance from the hounds, resisting the urge to rub the bite scar on his arm. He wasn't sure exactly why he had been brought along for this hunt. Maybe it was a test, and Gruffyd was simply using it to determine whether or not his lesson had sunk in. Maybe Gruffyd just didn't want to leave Wynn behind while he and his dogs hunted someone else.

Victors Eurig and Gruffyd were the first to draw bent arrows, so their Defeated were allowed the *honor* of leading the hunt and the ten-minute head start. Victor Eurig presented his prize stud, Dyfan, who, Wynn had overheard Victor Eurig telling Gruffyd, started in the fighting pits at sixteen and quickly became one of the best fighters in his weight group—notoriously vicious in the pit. The Victors placed bets. Dyfan was favored to kill the dragon.

Victor Eurig's red beard hid a smile as he approached Victor Gruffyd, who looked crestfallen to have Wynn teamed with Dyfan. "Freshly Defeated, isn't he?" Victor Eurig asked, looking over Wynn with an appraising eye.

Next to Dyfan, Wynn felt rather small. He had never considered himself a short or skinny man. Lean, perhaps, but not weak. Carpentry took a certain amount of muscle; however it was not difficult to tell what the Victors had been looking for when they bred Dyfan. He was massive, a beast of a man. All thick limbs and shoulders twice the breadth of Wynn. Dyfan had a younger face, but next to him, Wynn felt like a gangly adolescent.

"What's he called?" Victor Eurig asked, and Victor Gruffyd grunted in displeasure. "Wynn."

"Well, it's not your fault!" He clapped the other Victor on the shoulder, and they turned away to place private bets. "It's not like you got to name him."

Wynn turned away from them, his teeth grinding together. His name was a proud one among his people—taken from the name of an ocean Goddess descended from Illuka and Tha'et. His wife loved it. His son carried it even now. The people below the mountains would respect it when his family arrived safely. They were not as barbarous as these Victors.

His skin was hot with anger. It was a wonder he did not glow, did not melt the snow beneath him. He could reach for a weapon—a spear, if possible. He would put it through Gruffyd's belly so that he took a long, agonizing time to die. They would kill him, but so be it.

The dogs hadn't done the job before, but maybe he could get a Victor to end this for him.

There was little point to his life any longer.

Gruffyd returned from gambling with Eurig and pulled Wynn aside.

"You have the privilege of aiding Dyfan in this hunt, Defeated. See that you honor yourself and your betters." Gruffyd's voice was stern. As though there was any honor in this ceaseless, pointless bloodshed. A hand shoved his shoulder again, and Wynn shook it off, taking a couple steps forward. Someone pressed a spear into his arms. He looked down at it a long moment, imagining turning, plunging it into the bodies of his "betters."

He couldn't do it, couldn't give up his life so easily. He was too much of a coward with the threat of the lesser pits hanging above his head.

Wynn clutched the weapon until his knuckles matched the snow beneath his feet, then stepped forward in the direction the Victors had set him on.

⇑ ⇑ ⇑

"Cold?"

After a half hour of silence, the sudden noise startled Wynn awake. He had not been thinking, only walking, devoid of feeling.

Dyfan spent the trek prowling ahead of Wynn—he had not noticed the other man slow to walk beside him. Wynn was surprised at his distraction; it was not as though Dyfan was easy to miss. His bulk was impressive at best and intimidating at worst. Even with layers of hides and wool to keep him warm, it was easy to make out the shape of his build and the ease of his movements. Dyfan had been well-trained and well-fed his entire life.

He was a weapon as much as the spear he held.

Dyfan's hands were bare, like Wynn's, and were covered in scars and marks, his skin chapped red from the long journey in the cold. The sides of his head were shaved and tattooed in blue woad, intricate designs branding his status as a fighter and a Defeated. The hair atop his head was short and blond.

Why would this prized dog care if he was cold or not? Shouldn't he have been more concerned with licking the boots of his Victors? Wynn scowled, ready to be angry at everything, though his conscience smote him for it. Did he really mean to shove aside a hint of kindness in this cursed place?

"No," he sighed finally. "I mean, at least not any colder than usual."

After all, the lands north of the Brig'ian mountains were never exactly warm. Nothing like the fertile plains farther south.

Dyfan seemed to think about that for a minute and finally nodded. "Dragons don't feel cold," he murmured, his voice rough from lack of speaking. He continued to walk, looking for tracks in the mud and tilting his head as he listened to the baying of the hounds.

"Lucky them," Wynn muttered under his breath, dragging his own feet in the snow.

He did not want to hunt these people. It was too like the raid of his village— the Victors' revered sport and conquest as though they were made somehow stronger by the taking.

But so long as he wanted to keep his life, Wynn's options were limited. One man could not take down a hunting party. Should he try to aid the dragons? Or take his chances in the wilderness once more? Would he even be able to get away from Dyfan?

So consumed was he that Wynn did not at first notice the smell of a campfire in the air, the column of smoke rising above the trees. He would have kept walking into that camp had Dyfan's thick arm not swung out to block his way.

With his hand still pressed to Wynn's chest, Dyfan jerked his chin towards the brush to their right and began to move through it, slowly and with little noise. The howls in the distance faded to pained cries. Three dogs came galloping past them, darting back to the other hunters and relative safety. Another limped along seconds later, bleeding from a gash on its leg. Still, they could hear the rest of the pack barking and fighting. Wynn tightened his grip on the spear. He knew the feel of teeth on skin.

A roar split the forest, deeper and more frightening than any sound an ordinary beast could make. Dyfan's hand dropped from Wynn's chest as he gestured for them to crouch and move towards the commotion.

Wynn's heart beat painfully in his chest at the raw scream, and he went still in the underbrush. He could see nothing but fire, the twisted faces of his friends and neighbors as they fell, and feel nothing but the desperation that kept him fighting well past his limit if only his wife and son could get away.

They had been Defeated, he knew now. The men he had killed.

Another scream rent the air, and Wynn couldn't tell who it came from. Was he back in the village? Was it happening all over again?

He took deep, shaking breaths, trying to get a hold of himself, but he could only tremble. *It's alright. This is not the village. It's over.*

His body couldn't listen.

Pale blue eyes came into Wynn's field of vision, and then he wasn't looking at the brush or a village or even the muddy, snow-slick earth. Dyfan's eyes were widely spaced and unblinking as he met Wynn's gaze. He took Wynn's empty hand and pulled it up to his throat, pressing cold fingers to his pulse.

"Breathe," he instructed, his gravel voice vibrating through Wynn's hand as he spoke.

Wynn's fingers twitched against Dyfan's throat, his gaze filling with blue. When the other man's chest lifted, he inhaled. When it dropped, he exhaled. The sounds of fighting were fainter now. Perhaps they always had been, and Wynn's mind had merely magnified them.

He became aware of the skin beneath his hand, scarred and cool, of the bulk of Dyfan, of the smell of salt and fir. He pulled away. "Let's get this over with."

Together, they slid closer to the clearing, where a strange pair stood with their backs pressed against a boulder. Their cooking fire was scattered, and a ring of the Victors' dogs pinned them in. A few were dead already, though the man and woman seemed to lack weapons.

The woman was normal enough, if tall for a human female, with raven-dark hair and a swollen belly. It was the male that drew Wynn's attention. Huge and muscled, he was a match for Dyfan in reach and weight, but the spiraling horns atop his head and great black wings made him seem even larger. His skin was pale in the way of the mountain people, his eyes a piercing blue, though it was hard to focus on anything but the enormity of his wings. The dragon half-breed was one of the God Children, descendants of a time when the Gods still walked Illygad and took mortals as lovers. There were several races scattered through Rhosan and Ingola, though they were rare.

It was just the two travelers against a company of Victors and their Defeated. Wynn's heart sank. He didn't want to attack them.

Dyfan watched the scene unfold for a heartbeat and then stepped forward into the clearing. The dogs, recognizing him, started to yip and grow even more excited. The blood would spill soon.

A splitting whistle left Dyfan's lips, and the dogs backed off, though they still circled the pair. The woman's chest rose and fell rapidly, but the male just looked through them, his eyes like ice.

"You understand?" Dyfan asked, and the male hesitated before he nodded. He knew what this was. A hunt. "Fists or spear?" Dyfan asked, hefting his weapon casually. The woman shivered, and the male turned toward her slightly. They couldn't hear the words, but it looked like a goodbye.

The male stepped forward, his great black wings spreading to keep the pregnant woman from their view. As if that would protect her from harm.

"Spear."

Wynn swallowed, his mouth suddenly dry. He could not kill this man in cold blood. Not for merely trying to protect the woman carrying his child. It was wrong. Inhuman.

And yet, the dragon advanced. Wynn could make out his eye color and the rough patches of scales on his hands and jaw. He shivered, white-knuckled hands gripping his spear tighter. If they must fight, then let the dragon attack first.

In the end, Wynn got his wish.

The winged creature launched at them faster than Wynn had ever seen a human move. He seemed to hope to defeat them, to buy himself and the woman enough space to escape.

Dyfan leaped back, leveling his spear at the dragon's chest. The male swatted it away, but Dyfan only brought it back. He retreated two steps and advanced one, methodical and unflinching in his attack. This fight was more a contest of wills than skill, the two men equally matched. They seemed to have forgotten Wynn and the dogs.

Dyfan managed to slam the butt of his spear into the dragon's belly, but he recovered quickly, throwing a punch that forced a grunt from Dyfan. The two men flew apart, panting, but just as it seemed they would launch at each other again, Dyfan pulled back his spear and threw it with deadly accuracy. The dragon had enough time to turn to the side, but the shaft still entered his belly.

The woman screamed, tears streaking down her face, and Dyfan came forward as the dragon slumped to his knees, clutching the weapon still lodged in his gut. His breaths were labored, his eyes glazing over with pain. Dyfan waited, blood trickling from the corner of his mouth.

The dragon was taking too long to die. His breaths came shallowly, his side leaking blood, and still, he hung on to life, his eyes fixed on the woman. Her face was thick with tears, her body convulsing with them. One hand supported her bulging belly.

The dogs howled around them, pining for blood, for meat.

Wynn swallowed. He took a few steps forward, lifted his spear, and put it to the halfbreed's temple. "Rest well and do not suffer." He plunged the point through the dying man's head.

Behind them, the sounds of the party reaching the thicket of woods was audible. Branches cracked, boots thudded. They moved slowly but relentlessly like blood over snow.

Wynn ignored Dyfan and caught the eyes of the woman. "Go, and quickly. There are temples in the south that will help you. Just get free of this place. Too much blood has spilled already."

The woman stood, confused and startled, watching her lover's body, but something must have snapped within her as she turned to look at Wynn. Her head dipped in a silent nod before she hurried away from the sounds of hunters and certain Defeat.

Dyfan watched her go steadily, his mouth opening to speak, to say something. Only the Victors were there, crashing through the brush and cawing as they saw the fallen dragon.

"Who did it? Who killed him?" Victor Eurig examined the two spears, his eyes flashing. Dyfan held Wynn's gaze for a moment longer and then nodded towards him.

"Ha! Good hunt!" Victor Gruffyd clamped his hand on Wynn's shoulder, proud to have a winner, a good hunter. "As the one who made the kill, we have the first choice at the spoils."

As the Victors clustered around the male's body, Dyfan slowly walked over to the boulder the dragon and his woman had been backed against. It seemed as if he was just wandering, but his tracks mixed with theirs, obscuring the woman's passage. Blue eyes met Wynn's from across the clearing, impossible to read as he kicked at the muddy snow.

Wynn did not nod or smile or gesture. Nothing to give Dyfan away. He just met the other man's gaze while the Victors slapped his back and knew that somehow, despite having been bred to his role, the other Defeated was no more a trained dog than he was.

CHAPTER 9: PHECEA

ELEVENTH MOON, 1792, DIOSION

Thirteen Years before the Proclamation

The ballroom might have been a zoo for all the feathers that adorned its inhabitants. Feathers of vibrant green lined bronze walls. Great vaulting ones of indigo crowned lady's heads. Gentlemen wore pins of tiny red and gold ones upon their vests. When they danced, the whole world came awash with color.

Biton loved it.

At eight years old, this was only the second time he had been permitted to attend a council gathering, and the first was two years prior, when the meetings had taken place in the nearby province of Aetirieum. Practically ages ago. Now, with the rhythm of the drum and dulcimer in the air and the thud of dancers' steps beneath their feet, his parents seemed set on standing quietly to listen while their Councilor, the great Arsenio Othonos, spoke of trade.

"The Imperator demanded a reappraisal of trade agreements between Liria and the Confederacy, though they are not due to expire for another three years," he said, and Biton cast a furtive eye toward his father, trying to gauge how closely he listened.

Cyril Mavros was the picture of rapt attention, the skin between his brows puckering with worry or thought. They often drew together: so much so that Biton could see just how they would fold even when his father's face was still. "Surely, the council won't agree," he was saying. "It would set a precedent. Liria would no longer consider themselves bound by our agreements if they could change them as they pleased."

Biton glanced over his shoulder at the ballroom floor, littered with feathers of a thousand different colors. He was small enough to dodge between the twirling dancers and so might collect feathers until he outshined all of them. Maybe even his cousin, Acantha, who he had heard someone call the fairest creature of the hour.

He would be so bright that his father would see him and say, "My, Biton, what a princely figure you make. Perhaps you are old enough for your own horse."

Or perhaps not, but it was certainly worth the try.

Another figure moved towards their little party, and Biton used his presence to disguise a retreat of a few more steps. The newcomer was not someone Biton recognized, but he had no trouble joining the conversation. "The latest intelligence from Liria suggests that these new terms would be considerably less favorable if the Imperator gets his way...."

Biton's father turned to address this new concern, and the chance for escape was wide open. He didn't hesitate to take it but swept away to dart through the teetering pairs of dancers. He found a brilliant maroon feather the length of his arm. A turquoise followed, and soon he added a handful of tiny violet feathers to his collection. Biton had just stooped to swipe a brilliant emerald one when something quick and light brushed his ear. "Tag, you're it!"

"What—" Biton started, careening back upright. What kind of rule was that? You couldn't be it if you weren't even playing! Near him, a few noble children scattered, giggling as they tried not to get caught. Biton grinned. His bundle of feathers became a sword, and off he went to battle the fleeing Emai.

Children wove in and out of the adults, ignoring shouts to slow down or grunts of pain as they stepped on toes. Quickly the chase led out of the formal ballroom, past the feasting tables, and into the gardens. Without furniture and adults in their way, the play sped up.

Bushes and shrubs became hiding places and fountains a means to escape 'it.'

Inevitably someone new got tagged and the game would begin once more. A gaggle of Leos children darted past the steps to the patio when a small figure slipped onto the path. They ignored her and kept going, and she watched dispassionately. Much smaller than the rest of the children and clearly not part of the game, the little girl's dress was tidy and clean. Her hair was hilariously large compared to her frame making her head look strangely gigantic. Two girls slowed as they ran past her, seeming to recognize her enough to nod cordially before returning to their sprint. Sighing, the smallest girl sat on the patio steps, chin in her hands as she watched the tag game moving onto the back lawn and towards the pond.

Biton slowed. She seemed... sad. He would be sad watching as everyone else played. Perhaps they should tell her to play too, and then she wouldn't have to sit alone on the steps.

He hesitated a moment, and in that second, a younger kid slammed into him, half knocking him down. The boy giggled. "Got you!"

Biton looked at the others and then back to the girl and stomped determinedly over, his breath still puffing from running so hard. Somewhere along the way, he had torn the knee of his silk trousers, and his sharp face was smeared with dirt. "I'm *it*, so, you've gotta run, or I'll get you!"

The girl looked up, startled, and the jerky movement made her plume of curly hair float around her head. "You're *it*?" The voice that came out of her was high-pitched, squeaky, and nervous. It was too dark to tell her eye or skin color, but it was easy to see how she considered Biton and his status as 'it.' Clearly, she had wanted to play with the others, but now she hesitated.

"You're a lot bigger than I am," she observed, standing slowly but not running. "If I'm it, I'll never catch anyone and ruin the game. Won't I?"

"I don't see how being little would make you slower than me." Though come to think of it, perhaps he was faster now than he used to be. Maybe she would have to get older to be quick... He shrugged.

"If you *are* slow then, you'll still be able to fit places I can't, and that probably makes it fair."

That seemed to make sense to the girl, and she nodded sagely, much as their parents would during debates. Then, she took off, running as fast as her little legs could carry her. Which, she had been right, was not all that fast.

What did it matter? She was in the game now!

CHAPTER 10: THE EMAI

ELEVENTH MOON, 1794, VILLAGE OF NEC

Eleven Years before the Proclamation

*I*niabi stepped from the warmth of her illu into the sort of powder snow that held no shape but clung to everything it touched, like road dust or fish scales. All the world had been coated in it during the night, but it wouldn't last long. It was the eleventh moon—spring well on its way. Soon, the Emai would leave their villages to raid the sea for its fruits: fish and kelp, clams and mussels, the urchins with which they made poison.

Iniabi would go with them, as she was sixteen and knew the secrets of the seer's draft.

Behind her came the sounds of goats stirring in their skin and whalebone enclosure. Manaba would not be long behind them, so Iniabi hurried about her morning chores, breaking the ice on the goats' water into so many bobbing knife-shard pieces and packing the kettle with the brightest new snow.

There was a root that the banished bought from Phecean traders and then sold to the Emai. They called it kava and claimed it had first come from the warm isle of Tupa Gali far to the north. It had a spicy, bitter scent when steeped in hot water, and on mornings such as these, when Manaba pulled herself with agonizing slowness from poison dreams, it would cure her headache and dull her temper.

Iniabi perched at the center of their illu and built a dung fire within the circle of stones. The kettle hung above it on a little iron hook made for that purpose. Balanced on her toes, Iniabi folded in upon herself in the heat of the new flame and ground a palm-full of roasted kava root in their mortar and pestle—the mortar and pestle for food. Her mother's medicine-making toolset sat upon the table where she worked: the only real wood they owned.

The kava smelled as rich as bare earth or fatty fish dripping above a roaring blaze. She raised the bowl to her nose and breathed deeply, letting it tickle through her airways. Perhaps, she could taste it today if there was time before her mother woke. The ground powder went into a mug with boiling water, and Iniabi glanced around. All was still quiet. She raised the fragrant pestle to place ground kava on her tongue.

"Iniabi." She jumped, and the mortar clattered to the stone fire pit in a clamor of clacking rock. Manaba's voice held all the warning of a thunderclap. "Don't make so much noise. And bring me my kava."

Her mother hadn't seen. Relief flooded Iniabi, but her heart rate was still the pace of hare feet, and her slender hands shook as she pressed the hot cup into Manaba's grip. "Here, Aada."

"Good," the medicine woman croaked. "Go into town and fetch me a bundle each of kelp and adawora. We'll continue your instruction on medicine in the afternoon if you aren't late."

"Yes, Aada," Iniabi said and slipped out into the snow.

⇑ ⇑ ⇑

The village of Nec was already busy, despite the early hour. Emaian men sat outside their illus, mending nets or binding new spears while their husbands and wives bustled about other chores. No dark-skinned children played in the spaces between homes. Mika's Aada claimed that their parents had come in search of rumored riches and left again when there was none to be found. All except a few. One had married an Emaian woman and moved into her illu, much to the chagrin of the village. And another had made an illu of her own. She was clever both at catching fish and convincing Banished traders to part with their kava and wheat, so there were fewer grumbles about her staying when the other Banished returned to the port cities on the edge of Emaian lands. Manaba didn't seem to care what the Banished did. She hated all of them.

Iniabi found the adawora first, stopping at the illu of Meriwa and Tonraq, who were great tundra-walkers. They had the best luck finding shrubs amid the snow. They lived the farthest out from the village, except for Manaba, and on the other side of the enormous, cupped ice hands that sheltered Nec from the worst of winter's storms. Manaba called them Ice Hearted when she met them, for Tonraq and Meriwa were fearsome warriors. They were the first defense raiders met, and they held their place as village protectors with a straight-backed calm that Iniabi idolized. When she offered payment, Meriwa shook her head.

"No, bright one."

Her husband clasped Iniabi's hands in his strong, scarred fingers. "Just ask Manaba to keep us in her dreams."

It was always so.

Piav was sitting outside the illu he shared with Mika and her Aada, and he smiled at Iniabi as she approached. He was a gentle-looking man, with eyes so big and round that they might have belonged to an elk if they were not as pale as his snowy hair. His big hands worked with the delicacy of spider legs over a web as he wove a new net. He knew the work so well that he did not look at his hands but at Iniabi so they might talk. "Have you come to see Mika?"

Iniabi drew herself up. "I came for kelp, if you've a bunch to spare for Manaba."

"Of course," he said, though he too refused payment.

"Piav, why do the Emai not take fair payment from Manaba?"

"It is the way of things. Did Manaba not tell you? One day we will say, 'Keep us in your dreams, Iniabi, Daughter of Manaba.' Then we will give you kelp and whale oil and skins and shrubs and ask nothing but that you heal us and deliver our babies and protect us all from slavers and ice storms."

"I suppose it is payment, then."

Piav laughed and ruffled Iniabi's blizzard hair as though she were still much younger than sixteen. She shrugged him off, trying to put it back in order. "Mika is inside, mending. Why don't you go speak to her while I finish this net? Then I will send you back to Manaba with the kelp she needs."

Anxiety pierced Iniabi's belly like a sharp knife on a ceremonial elk's throat. If talking to Mika made her late, Manaba would be angry, and no amount of kava would calm her. Still, it would take time for Piav to finish his net. She would have to stay until he was finished mending, right? She might as well spend time with Mika while she was here. Iniabi smiled. All she needed was to talk for a short while. Manaba didn't need to know.

"Hello," Iniabi said, stepping out of the cold and into the cluttered warmth of Mika's home. The older girl sat on the floor before the fire, her long legs crossed in their hide leggings beneath a shirt she was mending. Her silver hair had fallen forward as she worked to cling to her forehead and cheekbones, and when she looked up, Iniabi froze like the top of the goats' water in the mornings. She had to shatter the ice to keep moving. "Piav said you'd be in. I'm just waiting for kelp to take to Manaba."

"Iniabi!" Mika's smile was sun on the rock spars that rose up around the village, all warmth and shine. "Why haven't you come to talk or visit the traders with me? They came just a few days ago."

"Manaba has been teaching me to make tinctures." Iniabi folded herself into an imitation of Mika's posture, their knees just touching. She felt too hot, as though she had stayed too long in the cold and could no longer bear the easy warmth of an illu.

Mika's sharp eyes missed nothing. She dropped her mending and gripped Iniabi's elbow, holding her arm so the purpling bruise on her wrist was visible. "Again, Iniabi?"

"I—" She flushed, warmth flooding her neck. "It's just because of the poison."

"You can't keep telling people you're clumsy. What Emai wants a clumsy wife?"

Mika always seemed to be talking of marriage lately. Perhaps because her mother spoke of it as much as Manaba spoke of wounds. Whatever the reason, Iniabi grasped at the chance to change the topic.

"Perhaps some wouldn't mind, especially if they knew I wasn't actually clumsy." She darted a glance at Mika. "Do you want a wife or a husband?"

Mika seemed to have given this significant consideration. She cocked her head to the side and lay her cheek in a palm. "Wives are lovely and warm and clever, but a man's strength might be more useful."

"I'll be strong as any man," Iniabi said, puffing her chest out in imitation of Piav. It made Mika laugh, as she'd meant it to.

"You're sixteen and still small as a newborn kid." Mika pushed Iniabi, playing, but Iniabi flushed all the same.

"That doesn't mean I'll always be."

Mika had already turned back to her favorite subject. "Maybe I'll have one of each like Yura. I'll have children at the same time as my wife, and we won't tell anyone whose child is whose so that we *both* get presents on their birthdays."

Iniabi snorted. "I know which of their children are Yura's and which of them are Tapeesa's. And so does Manaba."

"So? No one else can keep it straight."

Piav came in then, kelp cradled in one arm, but his face was no longer cheerful. "Get back home, Iniabi. You have to warn Manaba.

Iniabi stilled. She wanted to stay longer; Iniabi wanted to sit with her knee touching Mika's and listen to her friend speak of marriages and whatever else she wished. It was strange for Piav to usher her away. "What's wrong?"

He made to hand the kelp to Iniabi and then froze at the sound of screams. Booted feet crunched through the snow between the illus, and Iniabi shrunk closer to Mika in sudden fear. It sounded as though hundreds of people were descending on their little home.

"Girls." Piav opened his arms as if to shepherd them. "You must find—"

A black-tipped arrow punched through his throat with a spray of glistening blood, the splatter falling over the rug, the hearth, the shirt draped across Mika's lap. Iniabi raised a hand to her face, and the tips came away damp and crimson.

The arrow point filled Iniabi's vision, a perfect triangle of cast steel. It had exploded just above Piav's voice box so that when he gasped, it bobbed in a macabre dance. Around her, the air was rent with screams that might have been Mika's or hers or some other villager's, though she could not tell. Iniabi couldn't think of anything except that the scene before her wasn't real. It was like a poison dream, full of death and terror but divorced from reality. She, Mika, and Piav were all still safe. They *had* to be.

And then, Piav fell forward. The arrow hit the ground before the rest of him and slid part way out the back of his neck, gore clinging to its shaft like ice on twigs. It had bright, blue fletching—a color Iniabi had never come across in such vibrancy. Like someone had distilled the sky into a living being only for it to be killed and made into weapons of war.

In the kind man's absence, there stood a stranger.

He was dressed in plate and mail, and from his waist hung a steel helm beside an empty scabbard. He had eyes almost as slanted as a cat's, and his warm, brown skin was scar-crossed, even over his skull, where his hair was shaved to the scalp. In his right hand, he held a sword.

Beside her, Mika gripped Iniabi's arm, her perfect, even fingernails digging into Iniabi's skin. The older girl was screaming, and it seemed like she had been screaming for a long time, but Iniabi had only just become aware of it.

"Silence," the man barked, followed by a smattering of words in a language Iniabi did not know. Where was the bow? This man carried a sword. Where was the bow that had killed Piav?

Iniabi shook Mika's arm to quiet her, the other girl's skin strangely cold beneath her fingers. "Mika! They will kill us too!"

Iniabi knew who these raiders were and, from the stories of her people, what would come next. They would kill and rape and steal, put the young and strong in chains to be taken as slaves, and slaughter the rest. To survive, they would need to keep their heads down, to let themselves be taken, and pray for escape.

Mika's screams cut off, her eyes wide and red. She had bitten her bottom lip bloody, and the thin mixture of crimson and spit flecked her chin.

"Out." The man moved out of the way, pointing to the door with his bare blade. Iniabi stood, dragging Mika up with her. Her mending fell to the ground to mingle with blood and tainted kelp.

"Ataat," Mika croaked, her voice like the wet crack of ice on water. She reached for Piav's body, but Iniabi hauled her past him, slipping outside the illu without looking at the slaver. He was so much bigger than them, terrifying with his sword and armor. He smelled strongly of sweat, blood, and animal fur.

Then they were past him and standing huddled together in the snow. The air was rent with screams and smoke. Tonraq's body lay sprawled in the snow, a gaping sword wound bleeding sluggishly from his chest and his red-coated mouth open in death. Nearby, Yura's illu burned, filling Iniabi's nose with the scents of cooking fish and whale oil. Behind her, the soldier shoved them forward.

"Move," he said and sent them careening towards the village center. They passed more bodies along the way: Adara lay bleeding over her dead wife, slain even though her face bore the same dark tint of the invaders. The chief's sons had fallen together, two dead from blue-fletched arrows and the third still struggling to breathe past the arrow in his chest. His ax still lay nearby, the handle bathing white snow in crimson. Meriwa lay on her belly over a barrel, her leggings torn open and a slaver panting above her, his breath coming in shuddering gasps of pleasure. Even as Iniabi watched, Meriwa lifted a shard of pottery from the snow, but instead of turning it on her attacker, she slid it across her own throat, soaking the whalebone beneath her in black.

Iniabi forced Mika's face away, making soft, cooing noises like those mothers made to their newborns. "Keep your eyes on the snow, Mika," she sang, her voice ragged and broken around the edges. "Don't remember the village like this. We will survive."

The soldier shoved them to their knees in the village center in a circle of other huddled fur-laden forms. Manaba was not there, but Mika's Aada was, and the two girls pressed against her like seal puppies, hiding their faces to keep from seeing more of the destruction. Iniabi did not know how much time passed before she was hauled upright and shackled to Mika, but she would never forget the image of her home burning beneath the curving rock they thought would protect them.

CHAPTER 11: THE EMAI

ELEVENTH MOON, 1794, NORTH OF NEC

Eleven Years before the Proclamation

They walked in chains, the shackles frigid even at the turn of the season. All that was left of Iniabi's village was strung out in a line across the snow, boots crunching as they struggled northwards. There were just eighty of them left. Mika marched before Iniabi and behind her Aada, Sani. Tapeesa marched before her. Every few hours, Tapeesa wailed, and her husband, Kallik, answered her grief from farther ahead. Their children and wife were dead.

Iniabi's eyes remained on Mika's back. Someone— Sani, probably — had sewn a design there, tiny white beads in the shape of a short-tailed weasel. Its eyes and nose were black as the sea in winter, its long body seeming to shimmer as they walked. Iniabi tried to count the number of beads in the design, but before she got far, the jingle of tack from one of the Lirians' huge mounts sent a jolt of fear through her. Iniabi did not fear the horses—they were smaller than elk—but the men who rode them terrified her. She shrunk against Mika, careful not to trip the older girl, and for a second, Mika leaned back into the touch. It was an instant of comfort, too small to leave her anything but hollow and desperate, but better than trudging in these chains alone.

The Lirians didn't see; these men who had destroyed all Iniabi knew were not omnipotent. On the third day, one had frozen in the night, too stupid or drunk or lazy to take off the metal armor that had killed him. They stank of piss, smoke, and sweat, and they did not know to rub their faces with fat to keep their skin from cracking in the cold and wind. They had destroyed the village.

Corpses did not last long on the Tundra. The ravens would find the village first, descending on the dead they had left behind to pick at frozen flesh. The wolves would come after— savage, round-shouldered beasts who would fight and tear at the remains. By the time the foxes and the wolverines came, there would be nothing recognizable but bones. Snow and ice would fall, thaw slightly, fall again. In a year, not even the illus would be left standing.

Iniabi shuddered. Manaba was dead. Manaba, daughter of Ooyu, was dead, and Iniabi did not feel the well of grief rising within her breast. Her Aada was dead, and she felt nothing at all.

That night when they stopped, the men dropped their bags beside Sani and turned to set up the camp. Iniabi watched them shake out their strange, small tents, hammering iron stakes into the snow to keep the fabric from being torn from them in the night. Everything they did was in fear of the Tundra, of the people, of the cold. They did not see how they might survive from the Tundra as the Emai did. They were like children in this way, afraid of everything.

In front of Iniabi, Mika watched their captors. The Emai were huddled in their chains, the day's long summer light fading rapidly back to black so that long shadows spilled over the snow like blood. The Lirians built a fire at the center of their camp and sat clustered around it, eating stewed hare and talking loudly in their brash language. Iniabi huddled against Mika's back, a few mouthfuls of dried meat clutched in one ungloved hand, hoping her body heat would warm it enough to chew. They shared a blanket with Sani, Tapeesa, and two other Emai.

The dried meat was hard between Iniabi's teeth—half-frozen and so salt-packed that it stung her tongue. It wasn't anything she recognized— not fish or goat or elk. It took too long to soften and swallow. Tapeesa did not even try to eat it, her round cheeks still beneath pale, wide-set eyes. The set of her jaw was so stubborn that Iniabi doubted even iron could pry it open.

Beside her, Mika shifted, letting a sudden draft of cold air in beneath the blanket. Sani hissed, but she dared not make any louder noise. They had all learned quickly not to draw attention from their captors. The cold after dark on the Emaian Tundra was a living, biting thing, but neither this nor her Aada's displeasure seemed to bother Mika. The other girl's eyes were fixed on the nearby packs, full of the food and supplies meant to keep eighty slaves and fifty soldiers alive through this journey. Dread pooled in Iniabi's belly like poison.

"No, Mika." They were the first words Iniabi had spoken in days, and they came out cracked and quiet. The other girl rounded on her, gray eyes flashing like wind—cold and angry.

"Hush! You'll get some too." The skin around Mika's lips had cracked, wind rash spreading across it like scales. The slavers knew nothing of how to protect them from the cold.

Behind them, Tapeesa stirred, listless and half-aware, then settled back into her stupor. Sani glared at them both. Iniabi had overheard them whispering several nights before. "No matter what, you survive," Sani had said. Iniabi already knew how to survive, but it was not something Mika had practiced before. She didn't know how to stand still and hide her shoulders between whalebone spars.

The older girl slipped forward, planting one gloved hand in the snow so that she could reach out with the other. Mika pulled wonders from the sack—rounds of flat bread and bags of dried fruit that she passed to Iniabi, her mother, and lastly, up and down the line of Emai. Iniabi placed something orange on her tongue. It was dry, soft, and wrinkly, but when she bit into it, a bright, cheerful flavor burst to life in her mouth like the first rays of a summer sun on shoots of green. It was sweet enough to make her jaw ache, this food from the north, and she shoved a second into her mouth before passing the bag along.

"See?" Mika whispered, but her voice was pride-filled.

"Yes." Iniabi nodded wearily, her belly full—*really* full— for the first time since they had been taken from their village weeks before. "You were right."

Mika's sweet lips twisted into a smirk, and she held Iniabi's gaze for a breath longer before she tucked into her own feast of stolen food. Iniabi sighed and leaned against her, sleep a dear friend on the horizon. It was so much easier to drift off when you weren't hungry. Somewhere far away, a snowy owl hooted as if in agreement.

At the front of the line, a slaver stopped on his way to the tent and shouted, tearing an empty bag from pale hands. Iniabi came wide awake at once, hunching her shoulders and pressing herself closer to the earth. Beside her, Mika stiffened.

Iniabi did not look up. She kept her black eyes—slaver's eyes—on the ground beneath her feet. They sat crouched on a rock, wet from the snow that had melted between them. It stained her soft leather boots dark.

The owl hooted again as the slavers came closer. It did not take long to measure the distance between their supplies and the slaves most likely to have stolen from them. Their metal-shod feet came to a stop before Mika. Iniabi's fingers were fisted in the other girl's jacket, though she did not remember reaching out. What should she do? If she looked up, would they take her instead? Would she be able to stop this from happening?

Instead, one of the soldiers hauled Sani up by her hair, and relief, sick and yellow flooded Iniabi's chest. It wasn't Mika.

The older girl gasped as her mother was yanked to her feet and moved as if to stand. Iniabi pulled her back down hard, fear lending her strength. "Survive, remember? You have to survive."

The soldier turned to one of the others—the scarred man who had killed Piav, and he stammered in the language of the Tundra. "To steal from Liria is to ask for pain." The soldier that held Sani began to tear at her furs.

Mika lurched against Iniabi again, desperate to get free. "No! No! Aada!"

The scarred soldier took a whip from his hip and let it uncoil, the weighted ends pooling in the snow. The other shoved Sani to the ground. Her milk-pale back was bare to the snow, smooth and perfect but for the line of her spine and the blue creases left after carrying a child. Sani closed her eyes, breathing low, and Iniabi released her friend, too frightened to keep struggling. She sank back down, flattening herself like a scared dog. "Mika," she whispered. "Mika..."

She didn't listen, darting forward until her chains went taut and yanked her back by the manacle around her neck. Mika cried out as she fell, just as the whip the slaver held lashed across Sani's back. The older woman screeched, and bright red stripes appeared across her skin. Mika struggled back to her feet, but Lirians came, slapping Mika hard across the face. Twice more, she tried to rise, to aid her mother, and twice more, they threw her down.

Sani wept, and Mika howled, and Iniabi could do nothing but press herself to the ground and hope that Sani would not be too hurt and Mika would not catch the slavers' attention, and they might all live another day. If they were dead, they could do nothing. Not escape, not fight back.

"Stop! Stop! Please stop!" Mika begged, crawling to the feet of the slavers. It looked as if one might kick her, but Mika held on tight. "It wasn't her. She didn't do it. She didn't steal." The fall of the whip ceased, and Sani's ragged breathing filled the clearing.

"What did you say?" the Lirian asked in his heavily accented voice.

"She didn't steal your food." Mika's cheeks were red with fear or anger. Iniabi didn't know which.

"Who did, then?"

Mika hesitated, and the man whipping Sani raised his arm as if to let the lash fall again. "Someone will pay, slut. It can be her or whoever *did* steal, but be certain someone *will* pay."

Iniabi winced at the venom in his voice. It was the same tone that Manaba used when she gripped Iniabi's mouth and forced open her lips. *Would you rather be a slave, girl?* When Iniabi looked up, it was to see Mika staring at her mother, weeping and beaten. Then the older girl turned and pointed to Iniabi. "She did it. She stole from you. She's half-slaver. She thought she was owed some food."

A great chasm opened within Iniabi's chest as though she were a hollow thing made of ice that might shatter during times of thaw. She could see nothing but Mika's gray-white snow eyes and feel nothing but the warmth of having the other girl near. A soldier tugged her to her feet, a sharp pain in her arm and a rattling of chains. They tore off the fur she wore over her thick coat, then the parka.

Sani pulled her clothes back on, but tears in the fur showed the moon-white of skin. Tapeesa wailed. Mika wouldn't meet Iniabi's eyes, but Iniabi couldn't look anywhere else. Mika's silver hair fell in a curtain across her cheek, the strands kissing the curve of her cheekbone, the ends sticking on her rash-red lips. Kallik answered Tapeesa's cry, and Sani voiced her sorrow with him. One of the soldiers kicked her back.

They pulled Iniabi's kiati—her long-sleeved tunic with its narrowing, knee-length hem— over her head and shoved it at her chest as though the worst part of this was not the mutilation of her form but its nakedness. These men who had raped the women of her village saw something harder to stomach in her chest than the gouges they scored in her back.

They shoved her to her knees, the cold pressing in like a hungry animal, eager to tear at her flesh. Iniabi thought it hurt, that chill, and then the first lash cut across her back. She screamed until she choked, the lines like fire in her skin. She bit her tongue, vomited the contents of her stomach, and screamed until she was hoarse. Still, the blows kept coming. "To steal from Liria is to ask for pain," the man chanted. "To steal from Liria is to ask for pain."

It was only when she fell silent and lay prone in the snow did they cease. The soldiers let the other Emai take her back and then went to their tents, leaving more white snow splattered red.

ᛏ ᛏ ᛏ

The next morning, Mika shook Iniabi awake. She was clothed again, her kiati sticking to the bloody mess of her back. The other Emai were standing, the soldiers collecting their things to leave. The packs full of food had been moved, but the blood and vomit from Iniabi's whipping lay frozen over the snow.

"I am sorry, Daughter of Manaba." Sani did not say the name with awe anymore. Perhaps the reverence for a medicine woman ended with her death, or else Sani had seen the still-healing bruises on

Iniabi's arms and ribs the night before. "You *must* stand. They will offer you no mercy."

This, Iniabi knew. The soldiers were not people like the Emai were. They did not see her and know her pain. In this, they were like crows—cunning and swift and lacking any semblance of empathy. Iniabi spat into the snow. Her mouth tasted of blood.

The soldiers might be like crows, but Mika was a girl. And it was Mika who had done this.

Iniabi forced herself to her feet, groaning as the scabs on her back caught on fabric and tore. Warm blood trickled across her skin like water for cleansing. This time, it was Iniabi that would not meet Mika's eyes. She shook, a sick chill, like weakness forcing her body to tremble. Behind her, a boy not much older than her put his hand on the top of her head. "Strength, little sister." The Emai who heard him repeated the word.

"Strength," Mika whispered, and Iniabi hated her for it, hated her for the pain, hated her for the kindness afterward. Her world was heat and fire.

The first step was agony. Iniabi screamed, and someone else along the line called out in answer as if trying to hide her from the notice of soldiers. From then on, she stayed silent, but the pain did not cease. Time had no meaning. There was nothing but the fire and the snow. A world of white bordered on all sides by black.

She slept again and was roused to walk. Mika tried to speak to her, but the words were like snowflakes on a hot tongue. They did not stick. The second day passed as the first had. When they stopped, Iniabi slept and did not eat.

On the third day, Mika shook Iniabi awake. She walked until the snow rose up to meet her. When the slavers came to open her chains, Iniabi told them that there was poison in the sea. It lived inside the veins of the Emai, and with every Emaian they took into their lands, they heaped more poison down their own throats.

The soldiers left her to die in the snow.

While she lay there, Iniabi dreamed as vividly as she had the first night her mother touched poison to her bloody tongue. She dreamed again of the white tide, of the bodies fighting with her, only this time, instead of warcries, they shouted, "Dasan! Dasan!" as though they fought beside the great warrior who had flown an eagle into the sun. The sun descended among them and burned wicked stripes across Iniabi's back. With the pain came darkness once more.

When Iniabi woke next, it was not to the shake of a human hand but to the light-sharp hop of bird talons. She peeled her eyes open, fighting the frost that had formed in her eyelashes. It was day—still or again, she did not know, but she thought it unlikely that she would have lived through a night alone in the cold.

A second raven landed in the snow, cocking its head to the side to examine her with a sly, shining black-bead eye. Its feathers were as black as her eyes, with a fat-slick sheen. It hopped closer, and its partner pecked her hard in the cheek. Corpses did not last long on the Tundra.

Iniabi flung out an arm, scattering them both, and forced herself to sit up. The birds took flight, screaming raucous insults in their wakes. How dare she not be dead? Had she a sling and the strength, Iniabi might have shot them from the sky, but she had neither, and besides, Manaba did not allow the pointless harming of animals. She would get little to eat from a raven.

All around her, the snow was trampled, darkened in places from piss or horse dung. Iniabi could see where her people had lain for the night and where they had shuffled in their long, eel-chain farther to the north-west. Iniabi did not know where she was or how to get to other Emaian towns, but she knew that the slavers lived in fear of the Tundra and would not stay in its power long. She rose, the movement full of pain, that steadfast companion, but so long as she had lungs that could breathe in cold air, she would not be food for ravens.

After a time, Iniabi came across a water skin, carelessly dropped into the ice. She poured the contents into her mouth, packed it with snow, and tucked it against her body to melt. There was nothing on the skin to speak of where it had come from, but no slaver would leave such a thing for an Emaian, much less one half-dead from whipping. To steal from Liria is to ask for pain.

Iniabi did not stop at nightfall. To slow down would be to freeze, to ask for death. She was a daughter of this endless white. She would not let it bury her like a stranger, lost and unmarked. The village that raised Iniabi was gone with its medicine woman, but she was trained in the arts of blood and poison and history. She would not let it be forgotten. Iniabi began a litany of the dead and sang it under her breath as she walked.

"Manaba, Piav, Yura, Tonraq, Meriwa…" After a while, she came upon a length of wolverine fur, half buried in the snow. Iniabi pulled it over her head and kept going. "Xanthe, Adara…"

Dawn was slow to come, inching over the world like thaw in spring. The horizon melted around the sun, absorbing her colors and spreading them farther up the sky. Even the snow glowed pink at the birth of day. When the world had brightened into visibility, it was no longer a flat plane of white. Black buildings rose from it in the shape of urchin spines, and Iniabi had never been more grateful for the poison people within them. She turned towards the settlement to the sound of raven curses.

CHAPTER 12: LIRIA

SIXTH MOON, 1788, EGARA

Seventeen Years before the Proclamation

Murmuring voices merged into a dull hum until Luce couldn't make out any individual conversations. He resisted the urge to drum his fingers against the polished stone tabletop and instead watched the doors leading to the Imperial chambers for the first sign that the Imperator was on his way. No one knew precisely why this meeting had been called, but Luce would be a fool to think it was to congratulate the soldiers. Raids had been down in the past year, coming back with fewer Emaians. Without inventory, the Lirians had to increase the prices of bred slaves; in return, the Phecean Confederacy bought less. The economy was struggling. Liria had always kept the captured Emai, breaking and training them, while they exported the slaves from their breeding programs to neighboring countries.

There were rumors that the gold and iron mines in the Psilos range were starting to run dry.

He glanced to his left, seeing no one with a lower rank than captain. To his right, predominantly naval officers, the lowest rank was a vice admiral. Luce straightened up more, smoothing his hand over the front of his uniform. Camilla had made sure it was pressed that morning. He looked precisely as he should.

A steward stepped forward from the doors and announced the Imperator. Everyone in the room stood, brought their fisted hands to their chests, and bowed. The doors slammed open, and Luce kept himself from blinking.

No one spoke for a long time, waiting obediently for the Imperator to allow them to stop bowing, and the Imperator, in turn, said nothing at all. Luce used this tactic sometimes with trainees who had disappointed him. Let them sweat and worry about what he would say or what punishment they had earned.

"Rise."

Though granted permission to straighten, they still stood in formal lines, backs stiff, gazes fixed ahead. As Luce stared blankly at the man across from him, he could hear the Imperator's boot heels clicking against the floor, striding behind his line of military personnel and across the head of the table. Instead of taking a seat, the Imperator prowled down the far line of waiting soldiers, finally coming into Luce's view.

He'd been in a few meetings with the Imperator during his years of service, but only rarely, and never had he seen the Imperator so stern. His handsome, olive face was set in a scowl as he scanned each man, going so far as to stop beside one general and glare at the medals pinned to his chest as if they somehow offended him. Luce could see a bead of sweat running down the general's forehead as he stood at perfect attention, waiting for whatever pronouncement the Imperator would make. Instead, the Imperator resumed his inspection.

When he had circled the table and come once more to the head, he sat but did not grant them permission to sit or even to go at ease. Luce suspected the men around him were holding their breaths, as he was, because he could hear the Imperator's loud exhales.

"Do you know what I see when I look at this group of the most highly decorated military leaders in all of Liria?" Luce's heart stopped in anticipation for the hammer to fall. "Failure!" The Imperator slammed his fists on the stone tabletop, and the captain across from

Luce flicked his gaze towards the Imperator and back away. "Absolute failure!"

Luce could see the Imperator through his periphery as Liria's leader smacked the table again. His face was a red blur.

"How could the finest military in Illygad fail to bring in a bunch of heathens from the bottom of the world?!?! How could the finest military fail *me*, their sworn leader?! How could they fail Liria?! Due to your failures, your families will go hungry! Liria will fall into disrepair and ruin! Is that what you want?!" The chair the Imperator had been sitting in clattered to the floor as he bolted to his feet. "I can only assume this failure is due to the lazy nature of men. Your soldiers are complacent and fat. This isn't their fault, but *yours*, gentlemen! A soldier is only as good as his leader, and you are all the leaders of *my* military. Therefore, you have *failed*. You have failed me, you have failed Liria, and you have failed yourselves. Thanks to these failures, we are using up all of our breeding stock. Without new inventory, Liria's largest export is becoming sparse."

Shame coated Luce's throat as he waited for the Imperator to dismiss them. He had worked hard through the years to gain his rank, and he relentlessly drilled the men under his command. How had he failed them? Where had he gone astray? It wasn't as if they were lacking in discipline or training. The Emaians hadn't changed their ways in hundreds of years, so why were they becoming so scarce now?

Would the Imperator simply remove their ranks and promote better, more worthy candidates, or was this failure enough to warrant more extreme consequences? Shame warred with fear for the prominent place in Luce's gut. Camilla told him just that morning that she believed she was pregnant, which would make their third child. Ignatious was eight, and Sabina only three. What would they do if he was demoted to foot soldier again? The pay wouldn't allow them to keep their home in the prosperous southern quarter, not to mention the strain of an additional mouth to feed. That wouldn't matter if the Imperator felt their failings were severe enough to arrest them. With Luce locked away, Camilla would be forced to take the children back to her parents and *beg* for shelter.

He couldn't do that to her. That wasn't the life he promised her.

Despite the shaking in his knees, Luce pivoted to face the Imperator, clasped his fist to his chest, and bowed again. The other captains, generals, and admirals turned and mimicked Luce's respectful prostration. The Imperator growled but waited.

"Imperator! I am your loyal servant. Tell me what I can do to rectify this terrible failing, and I will do it," Luce said to his highly polished boots. He would go. Even if it was the wrong season. Even if they froze.

The silence stretched to the point that Luce thought his heart might explode, and then the Imperator of Liria spoke.

"Bring me back more Emaians. Do your duty. Do not fail me again."

⇑ ⇑ ⇑

Eighth Moon, 1788, Tundra

The wailing around him was the sweetest song Luce had heard in moons—perhaps years. A ship full of Emaian slaves was noisy, and the clamoring, screaming, and shouting filled him with grim euphoria. This haul—eight hundred fresh Emaians— would prove his men were good soldiers and he an adept leader. Pushing further into the treacherous lands of the Emai produced several villages of underfed, uneducated barbarians. Clearly, the area had been missed over the years, likely due to its isolated location. Most Emaian holdings didn't have more than two hundred adults, but these had yielded incredible numbers. Childlike in their inability to fight or comprehend what was happening.

Even now, the adults moaned as openly as the sniveling children. Shameful. They couldn't even properly cry—like cows or pigs.

The wind whipped at Lucilius's face, and he welcomed the salt air, tilting his chin back as the waves crashed against the ship's hull. He used to take pride in bringing the heathens back to Liria, knowing they would live better lives. Now, he didn't care about the Emai or the improvement in hygiene, education, and medical care they would receive in Liria. He didn't even feel relief that the Imperator would know that Luce was the right commander. He only felt satisfaction in completing his mission and returning to Camilla.

Let other Legionnaires preen and primp over their prowess in battle, or let the priests bring the heathens into the fold. Lucilius would always serve Liria, but his family's happiness and safety would forever take precedence in his heart and mind.

"Sir?"

Lucilius turned to face one of his corporals and nodded. "Yes?"

"Five more have died in the holdings."

"What from?"

"I'm not sure, sir; it stinks down there. Perhaps rot from injuries?"

"Yes, those beasts don't bathe. Very well, corporal. Toss the bodies overboard."

The corporal nodded, clasping his fist to his chest. "And those around the bodies? They're weeping and clinging to them."

"If they want to go with the dead, they can." Luce turned back to watch the waves passing by.

"Sir?"

"Toss them overboard too if they make your job difficult, corporal. You don't deserve the bother."

"Ah... yes, sir."

CHAPTER 13: RHOSAN

FIFTH MOON, 1795, CWM OR

Ten Years before the Proclamation

Perhaps the Victors called their arenas 'fighting pits' in reference to something their God, Kirit, said because they were not, in truth, *pits*. The ground in northern Rhosan was too hard to dig out. At some point, someone must have tried because the pits were three feet below the surface level of the earth, but no more. When the digging wasn't fruitful, they built upwards. Stones stacked upon stones to create walls, cells, and rooms, all circular, windowless and solid. The fighting pits could withstand any blizzard, any fire. They had, over the years. Maybe that was why people respected them enough to call them pits.

The Pits was more than just the name of the arena, but also that of the compound. An outer wall three times Dyfan's height surrounded the enormous round building where the fights took place as well as stables, barracks for visiting fighters, and smaller living quarters for the Defeated who maintained the compound attached to the kitchen where they made meals on training days.

Dyfan spent much of his time here. His Victors, Victor Eurig and his wife Blodwyn, ensured he had plenty of training sessions. He had been competing since his sixteenth summer and most times won. He was a good combatant, and he made his Victors proud. He even had won Contender matches three years running. The better he was, the more often they sent him to the pits to train with the best at swords, axes, or spears. And if he wasn't training, he was fighting.

It felt good to win, to know his meals would have extra portions to keep him strong, that his bed would be warm with blankets and sometimes companions. It meant his life was better. He liked it when his life was better. Easier.

The clash of shields echoed, a familiar and comforting sound, as Dyfan stood outside the fighting arena. There would be matches all day. Because he was a better fighter, he'd have to wait until late afternoon. Victors wanted to watch good matches, and Victors didn't arrive until after the noontime meal, so the interesting matches were held later. He wasn't the only one watching either—several other arena Defeated were passing the time the same way, standing nearby rather than sitting in the stands.

The morning bouts were usually new or young Defeated from the breeding stock. Now, two boys, likely no more than sixteen, crashed, pummeling one another with fists and shields. They were enthusiastic and energetic but used very little technique besides brute force.

Dyfan turned away, uninterested in those who didn't have respect for the artform of pit fighting. His gaze fell on a figure that sparked something in his memory: red hair shorn close to his skull, fair skin, a distinctly unhappy look about the mouth.

It was the Defeated from the dragon hunt. The man was strange, a new Defeated, captured in battle rather than bred to purpose. Dyfan was surprised he had made it ten lunar cycles. His experience with Battle Defeated was mostly poor. They chafed against tradition and often caused trouble for themselves. Victors only had so much patience, and Battle Defeated tended to test it. Most were killed by their Victors or deliberately entered into fights and bets they had no chance of surviving.

It seemed the redheaded man had more sense than impulse, though Dyfan remembered his crazed look from the hunt. He had seen plenty of fighters in the pits bore the same look— old Defeated who had fought for so long they could not remember which battle they were in, which contest was real and which was only a memory.

Dyfan knew one day he'd relive every fight and carry fear around — as much a shackle as the tattoos on his skull—and so he liked to help those who struggled now, hoping some young Defeated would help him when he was old.

If he lived that long.

The yelps behind him indicated the match was over and another would be starting soon. He suspected the redhead would be up quickly since he was not a highly ranked fighter. Dyfan had never seen him in the pits.

Dyfan approached him. "You fighting today?" Dyfan asked by way of greeting, pausing out of arm's reach of the man. Sometimes, the ones who couldn't remember what was real and what was the past spooked easily and lashed out. Best not to scare them if you could avoid it. Dyfan crossed his arms over his chest and himself leaned against the cool stone wall, becoming just another boulder in the cells.

The look the man gave him was wary, distrustful—a raw look, like that of a cornered dog. He considered the question over-long, giving it much more time than it deserved. "Yes," he said, examining Dyfan as if scanning for danger. Recognition stole across his features only slowly. Dawn on a cloudy day. His eyes narrowed, then widened.

He did not look as though he were reliving a battle.

"Dyfan." The redheaded man spoke his name slowly. "From the hunt."

It didn't seem like a question, so Dyfan only nodded. "They were calling you Wynn." Others would have smiled or laughed at the name, considered it soft or overly feminine, but Dyfan didn't see the point. It wasn't as if Wynn had picked out the name himself. His mother had. Dyfan's mother hadn't picked out his name. Victor Eurig had. "The fear can help you, sometimes. If you let it." He shrugged, uncomfortable giving advice. "Makes you faster."

"They'll not be able to catch me, then." Wynn attempted a smile. As readily as that, he admitted his fear. Laughed at it even. Most Defeated did not dare. Wynn was looking at him again, the same searching expression, though perhaps a little less uncertain. "Is that what makes you so deadly?"

Dyfan didn't know how to respond to that. He wasn't particularly deadly; he just wasn't lazy or sloppy. He worked hard every day, and pain didn't leave its mark on him like it did on others. He refused pain entry into his mind, so even when his leg was sliced by a blade or his lips were crushed and bruised by fists, he kept fighting. It wasn't that he was brave; it was that he was strong.

That was too much to say, too much to think, so he only shrugged, turning from the redheaded Wynn. From time to time, Dyfan thought about the female, pregnant and sobbing, that the redheaded Defeated had let escape—had *encouraged* to escape.

He wondered if she had gone south, to those soft peoples who knew nothing but warmth and happiness, separated from the Kirit clans so long ago. He wondered why he hadn't tried to stop her. His Victor certainly would have wanted a dragon spawn to keep for himself, to raise up as a mighty Defeated fighter. But Dyfan had looked at her trembling lips and the dead dragon at his feet and felt no urge to stop her. He didn't need another warrior to compete with, after all.

A tightness entered his chest, and Dyfan rubbed at the muscles, wondering why he was feeling tension *now*. He wasn't afraid of these fights, and while Wynn would likely lose, that didn't matter to Dyfan. Perhaps the memory of the hunt was making him uneasy.

The Defeated straightened up and leveled Wynn with another appraising look. "I'm not deadly." He stated, tone blunt. "Just better than most."

"Me neither— well, not deadly, that is. I wouldn't say that I was better than most." Wynn's hands drew Dyfan's gaze, where he held a short length of the spiny, thorned brambles that grew thickly against the outside walls of the pit. They were just about the only thing that thrived in that hard, cold soil. Even as Dyfan watched, Wynn pressed one of the thorns into the pad of his forefinger until a ruby drop welled there, deep and glistening. Wynn looked up at him, warm eyes resolute. "I will survive this, though. This place will not destroy me."

He raised his bleeding finger to his forearm and drew a rune in quick, sure strokes.

The design was foreign to Dyfan's eyes. He couldn't read or write, and he certainly couldn't do magic. No Defeated could. He reached out, covering the lines of blood with his hand before he could think better of it. When Wynn jerked back, Dyfan shook his head. If the Victors or the training masters saw him doing magic…

"They'll behead you," he murmured, keeping his voice low and his shoulders relaxed. He didn't want anyone looking their way.

Wynn's jaw was tight enough that Dyfan could see the thick lump of muscle at its corner. He pulled away again, this time with enough force to break Dyfan's grip. His arm showed only a bloody blur, and he spoke through clenched teeth. "Do you know how dangerous that was? If I had not already released the power, changing its direction could have hurt or killed one of us!"

Dyfan glanced down at his palm, smeared with Wynn's blood. He closed his fingers over the red stuff, hiding it from sight. He hadn't known rune magic could be so potent. He didn't know anything about it, aside from the fact that it was the fastest, surest way to get a Victor to kill you. Two summers ago, a rune user, a Battle Defeated like Wynn, was flogged and had his nails torn out before the Victors beheaded him.

It wasn't worth it. Any Defeated knew that.

He looked up again to see Wynn was still staring at him. "It doesn't matter. Don't do it again."

Wynn looked away. "It's a gift from the Gods to their people. No human should be able to control another's use of the Old Ways. It'd be like… like stopping them from worshiping the Gods."

That was too complicated a topic for Dyfan. He didn't know of the Old Gods except for Kirit, who ruled the far north. He made the Victors, the most powerful fighters, and he decreed the Defeated were the lesser subjects in his land. The weak served the powerful, and if they were too weak to be used, they were put down. The better they fought, the more they honored Kirit and gained status.

Unless you were born to be Defeated, like Dyfan.

That was just the way, and he didn't know what the Gods had to do with Victors chopping off your head if you did magic. It didn't matter.

"Just. Don't." He tried to meet Wynn's gaze, to impress on him without words how important it was that he not do magic *ever* again.

Wynn rubbed at the drying blood on his arm and dropped the brambles into the dirt beneath their feet. It seemed that he had meant what he'd said earlier: he would try to survive. "Alright. At least, not where anyone can see."

CHAPTER 14: RHOSAN

Twelfth Moon, 1795, Cwm Or

Ten Years before the Proclamation

"Don't worry about it, Nimue. Victor Ifanna is sending Wynn to take over. Even *he* can handle collecting eggs." The two women smirked, and Linn bumped Nimue with her hip. Playful. "Ah! There he is now. Defeated Wynn, do you know how to collect eggs?"

Despite his escape attempt and entrance into the pits, the other Defeated in Gruffyd's compound found him harmless. Less than harmless, really, which suited Wynn fine. The women appeared comfortable around him, and the men seemed unconcerned by him even though he was a Battle Defeated. It was lonely not belonging to any group, but he knew that was better than being hated.

"I'm sure I can manage," Wynn said dryly, rolling his eyes, though she didn't seem to notice.

Nimue nervously brushed her hands over the plain brown of her woolen tunic and handed Wynn the basket she had been using to collect the eggs. "Should I go now or wait for them to call for me?" she asked Linn, ignoring Wynn as she returned to their conversation. Wynn still remembered her coming to escort him to Gruffyd's cart before he saw the lesser pits, her dark hands making quick work of ointment and bandages.

"Don't worry, girl. He's not so bad, from what I hear. Not rough. Go on now, else you'll over think it." Nimue looked at Wynn, but Linn clucked her tongue again, and that sent the younger woman off.

"Young people, always worrying about things they can't control—even the bred Defeated, though you Battle ones are worse." Linn eyed his grip on the basket and tilted her chin. "You going to start winning some fights, or do you enjoy walking around with your eyes blackened and your lips split?"

"What, you don't think this look suits me?" It was a poor attempt at a joke; nothing was appealing about the damage done to his face in the last round of fights. His left eye was so swollen he could hardly see out of it, and he woke to find his lashes glued together where it leaked in the night.

He wasn't about to say otherwise, though. It wouldn't help him to start complaining about his losses. The truth was that you couldn't turn a carpenter into a prize fighter by throwing him into the ring. It was one thing to lash out in fear and desperation and quite another to walk calmly into an arena against a trained fighter.

"What's the girl so upset about?" he asked, more to change the topic than anything else.

"Things she can't control. Victor Gruffyd paid Victor Eurig for some breeding rights to his big stud. You've seen him. Wins a lot. He's sired a couple of Victor Gruffyd's Defeated, and they turn out real big and strong. They're too young now to know if they'll be as good as he is in the pits, but his prices keep going up, so I reckon Victor Gruffyd is trying to get a few more on the cheap. Nimue hasn't been with a Pit Fighter before. Bit jumpy is all."

Wynn's eyes turned away from the older woman to the direction in which Nimue had gone. She was going to be used like chattel, but he could not imagine how she could go into it so calmly.

He swallowed hard.

Perhaps it was just a way of life here. Breeding when the Victors demanded it kept the Defeated from worse punishments, but if it was his wife in Nimue's place, he would have gone mad trying to stop it. And likely lost his life as well.

"Who's the stud?" He didn't envy that position either.

"Dyfan. He started in the pits five years ago, and each season he's taken most titles and ranked well. Been a Contender three times over." Her light blue eyes shifted from Wynn's face to the front yards of the compound where a few riders trotted in.

"What does that mean? He's been a Contender?"

"You really aren't a Kirit follower, are you?"

"My people prayed to all the Old Gods."

"Mhm. Well," Linn said. She seemed particularly unimpressed with him now. "The best fighters in each weight class fight at the end of the season. Winning makes you a Contender."

"Well, I suppose I won't have to worry about that." And hopefully, being a poor fighter would keep him out of breeding too.

"I wouldn't be so sure. The lesser pits have their own versions of Contender matches. You wouldn't want to end up there." Linn's blue eyes narrowed when Wynn met her gaze, and he thought he understood what she meant. His situation could get *much* worse. "It's better to be like Dyfan."

As if summoned by his name, Dyfan dismounted and trudged their way. He stopped three lengths away and looked between Wynn and Linn. "Getting eggs?" he asked, voice as rough as ever.

Wynn looked up at him, swinging the basket and raising his eyebrows. "What, you didn't get enough breakfast?"

It had been seven moons since Wynn had seen Dyfan in the pits, and in the intervening time, he had forgotten just how physically imposing Dyfan was. At least if he kept losing, Wynn would never have to fight him. Though the lesser pits were certainly no better.

The look Dyfan leveled on Wynn was unwavering and cold. Empty really. He didn't smile at the joke though Linn's lips twitched. "What's her name?"

"Nimue," Linn said.

He only nodded. "Good luck with the eggs."

"Thanks," Wynn said, his voice small and lacking humor. He shouldn't have needled the man. Not when he already seemed so unhappy. Wynn just hadn't known what to say and had fallen back on half-hearted jibes. He stood silent, watching Dyfan walk away, and then turned to fill his basket.

The rest of the day passed uneventfully for Wynn—just another barrage of simple and often inefficient tasks meant to keep him fit enough to fight and tired enough not to cause trouble. He supposed they did their job, though no amount of labor was going to make him a decent fighter. There was nothing to fight *for* in this Gods-forsaken place.

When the horns finally blew for the evening meal, Wynn was damp with sweat despite the winter chill, and his clothes and skin were smeared with dirt. He brushed at it with his fingernails, wrinkling his nose at the beginnings of scruff on his cheeks. He'd never been keen on growing a beard.

The Defeated dining building was plain in the extreme—just four walls raised around tables and a room that kept more smoke in than cold out. Still, his stomach complained at the smell of food, and he slipped inside, trying to banish memories of better meals with friends and family. He had gone down that road before and did not mean to tread there again if he could help it.

His face set, Wynn took the simple mash offered him and found a place to sit away from the others. The room was filled with murmuring voices. Defeated weren't prone to shouting over one another or even chatting loudly, but they would converse quietly. Even with that dull hum of voices mixed together, the room dipped in volume as another entered.

Dyfan didn't seem to notice. He stood in line, collected up a bowl of the same slop as the rest of them despite his reputation, and turned to look for a place to sit. No one looked up, made eye contact, or called out. Some even ducked their heads. The response startled Wynn because of how well Linn spoke of Dyfan—most of the Defeated looked like they disliked or feared him. Wynn suspected

Dyfan was less than twenty years old, despite his intimidating physique, four or so years younger than him.

Wynn didn't look away, didn't hunch his shoulders. He kept his eyes on Dyfan when he scanned the room and gestured vaguely to a nearby seat. He wasn't sure why he did it—what was the point in forming an acquaintance with someone who one day might fight you? Though Dyfan was champion weight and Wynn only a mid. Perhaps Wynn simply saw another outcast.

Or maybe he remembered the feel of rough fingers teaching him to breathe when fear rose up to steal the knowledge from him.

Dyfan neither seemed surprised by the invitation nor relieved, but he did come to sit across from Wynn. Their eyes met for a moment, and then the pit fighter took up his spoon and started eating. He made his way through the contents of the bowl, as uninspiring as it was, with the same stoic manner he approached most things.

Half his bowl was empty before he looked up. "You don't win much." They never fought together, obviously, and they hadn't spoken since their interaction at the pits, but Dyfan must have been paying attention. "I used to lose too. Sometimes still do. Miss it, sometimes. Losing."

Wynn's head tilted to one side as he considered the other warrior. It didn't make sense that any Defeated that had known the pain and punishments of losing would miss them, but something recalled his mind to their interaction earlier.

'What's her name?' Dyfan had asked, and his eyes had been empty.

Wynn swallowed.

"What do you mean? Don't tell me you want to look as pretty as I do." He palpated the swollen flesh around his eye with the tips of his fingers

"Losing enough makes you invisible. Sure it hurts, but being invisible isn't so bad." Dyfan stabbed a potato with an ungodly clang. His spoon was the wrong tool for the job, but with enough force, he speared it. Defeated looked over their shoulders at Wynn and Dyfan's table.

Wynn wasn't quite sure what to make of that. On one hand, Dyfan was right. Wynn's lack of ability in the arena left him beneath the notice of Victors and Defeated. But then, it didn't last forever. Linn had a point—if you didn't honor your Victor, they would find another use for you. It was even stranger that *Dyfan* was the one telling him this. He was one of the pit's best.

Dyfan didn't seem to notice the silence stretching between them as he inspected the harpooned vegetable. "Good dinner."

"It's really not." Wynn lifted his spoon and let some soup slop back into the bowl. Behind Dyfan, he could see the other Defeated sitting at their bowls, shoveling spoonfuls of soup into their mouths between quiet words and smiles. Few men were as bruised as Wynn or as dreaded as Dyfan. "Perhaps the best place to be is somewhere in the middle. Good enough to escape regular beatings or the lesser pits and bad enough to escape fame."

⇑ ⇑ ⇑

Second Moon, 1796, Cwm Or

Nine Years before the Proclamation

THE DEFEATED in Cym Or were rarely bound. The estates and fighting pits were walled and guarded, they were kept too tired to steal, and the great expanse of cold, punishing wilderness outside the settlement was an excellent deterrent from escape. Most often, they were sequestered to meager quarters and held there by threats of severe reprimand rather than physical restraint.

And yet, the possibility of ropes or shackles was never too far off. They could be brought out to address disobedience, to tame violence. They might be used to separate mothers from their children. Or to punish fighters who would not win.

Wynn entered the pits, tied at the wrist and hobbled at the ankle, flanked by two men of Cym Or. They stopped as a party before the training master, interrupting his work.

"Excuse us, training master," one of the men began, "But Victor Gruffyd has sent this one to be trained by you." The Victor hadn't bothered to come himself. Wynn rarely saw him outside of the compound except to see the fights.

"If he does not shape up, he is to be sold." The second had a long scar and a bored look across his face as though he had lost any patience he'd ever had with this life. They both worked for Gruffyd—paid men who lived in the town, not Defeated.

Scar Face shoved Wynn forward, and from his position on his knees, he watched coin exchange hands. He supposed he ought to feel honored that Gruffyd was still willing to spend anything on him. Wynn turned his face to the side and spat.

The training master didn't seem impressed. "Gruffyd's mad if he thinks this one will ever become a Contender. Well, mad or broke. I don't suppose he has the funds for another." He shrugged. "Cut him free. I want to see what he can do."

Wynn only barely kept himself from sighing as they released him from the bite of the rope, but he could not resist the urge to rub at the chafed skin.

"Well, what are you waiting for?" The training master's voice was as rough as a dog's bark. "Run! Five laps around the edge of the field!"

Wynn leaped to his feet and sprinted.

Most of the Defeated were already in their training routines. Some were lifting heavy buckets of ice; others did lunges or squats. More jogged around the edge of the arena, slower than Wynn but obediently plodding away. It was a cold day, but sun streamed through the open top of the arena, and sweat beaded Wynn's brow. A few pairs of eyes followed him as he ran, but most had the empty stares of those uninterested in the world beyond. It was enough simply to work out and let their minds wander.

"Alright enough!" The training master shouted for Wynn to stop running. "You're not the slowest slug on the riverbank. Lift those stones."

There was a collection of stones piled in the center of the arena. Presumably, they had measured their weight and knew their values. Dyfan, already sweating through his coarse tunic, hefted a large rock and carried it to the opposite side of the arena to form a second pile.

Wynn watched Dyfan for a moment, noting his posture and the

place he was dropping off the rocks, then went to do the same. It had been two moons since they had sat with each other over dinner and talked of the visibility of slaves, and he couldn't seem to catch the other man's gaze.

If anything, Wynn's presence in the training grounds today proved that invisibility was not something that could last forever—sooner or later, the Victors saw you and demanded more.

He picked up a stone, smaller than Dyfan's but large enough to strain his legs and shoulders. It seemed to take a lifetime to start a new pile next to Dyfan's, but as soon as he had done it, he went for another. There was something almost... *nice* about the mindlessness of it. It was a simple directive. It took no thought—comforting in its monotony. Perhaps that was why some of the fighters enjoyed training. That and the fact that it likely kept them alive.

The training master forgot about Wynn for a while, letting him go back and forth between the piles of rocks. At one point, Dyfan and Wynn passed each other, going opposite directions, and Dyfan murmured, "Nice rock." Which, at this point, was starting to seem like Dyfan's standard greeting—short observations made in a rough voice. On the tenth circuit, the training master remembered Wynn or had seen enough and called him to cease.

"Alright. You're not completely useless. Let's see you against Ifor."

The man was no Dyfan. Ifor was much closer to Wynn in size and stature but tougher looking. He made eye contact as Wynn approached, but he didn't growl or flex to intimidate Wynn, as some fighters were prone to do.

"First man on the ground loses," he instructed, pointing towards a cleared patch of earth.

Wynn rolled his neck, keeping his eyes on his opponent. Neither of them moved. The sounds of thuds and grunts from the rest of the field faded into oblivion. Ifor seemed content to stand and watch— he hadn't even bothered to stretch or take up some ready position but just stood there, waiting. Well, if they had to fight and this Defeated would not get the cursed thing over with, then Wynn supposed he'd have to start it. He took a deep breath and launched at Ifor.

Only, when his fist ought to have connected, the man was no

longer there. Some instinct of self-preservation sent Wynn skittering to one side, just in time to miss getting struck by Ifor's counter, a rough fist whistling inches from his ear. He backed up, putting some distance between them again.

This time, Wynn approached more cautiously. His breath was coming faster, his heart speeding from anxiety and adrenaline as though his body dreaded the pain of fighting. He realized that he *wanted* to win, not to please his Victor, but for the sake of winning.

Wynn side-stepped nearer, keeping his eyes on Ifor, his fisted hands up to his chest, all the while the other fighter made no move. When he was almost within arm's reach, Wynn paused, then jumped forward, swinging. Ifor turned, dodging the punch, and caught Wynn's arm in both hands. Then, Wynn was on his back, gasping up at a gray sky for air.

"Terrible instincts. We'll sharpen those up. Not too weak, though." With his pronouncement handed down, the training master hollered for a few other Defeated to show Wynn the routines.

There was no noontime meal in the pits unless their Victors paid extra, so when supper came around, most of the fighters were ravenous, hurrying and elbowing each other to get a better spot in line for the food being dished up.

Despite not making any aggressive moves, Dyfan ended up near the front of the line. Wynn was at the back, but as Dyfan walked by with his plate of food and a hunk of bread, he caught Wynn's eye. "I eat near the doors." They still stood open from when Wynn stepped through them, a little bit of sky visible above the compound's main gates in the distance. They'd be able to see more, if they could sit closer, but the Defeated didn't leave the arena floor during training, and the expanse of space left for villagers to stand and watch the fights lay between the arena and the outside doors.

It took Wynn a long moment to realize that Dyfan was inviting him to eat there too. The shorter fighter stared up at him a little stupidly, dazed from exhaustion. He did not remember ever being so tired. "I'll eat with you."

Out of the corner of his eye, Wynn could see the man in front of him shift uneasily at their conversation, though he did not turn.

Perhaps they thought it odd that one of the Contenders they so feared was befriending the new, weak Battle Defeated. If this could even be considered befriending. He had spoken to the big warrior only a handful of times since being captured almost two years ago—there were a few in Victor Gruffyd's complement of Defeated that he knew much better. But there was an understanding between them, something born when they had silently agreed to free the dragon's pregnant mate from the Victors.

When he had filled a bowl with the typical, un-imaginative fare, Wynn turned towards the doors and settled himself near Dyfan. He gestured towards the bare earth. "Is this what you do every day?"

Though the question wasn't complicated, Dyfan took his time thinking about it. Chewing on his hunk of bread, he eventually shrugged. "Sometimes. Being strong is good. Having stamina is good. Sometimes the best fighter doesn't win, just the fittest. It's good that the training master will make you strong. Maybe you won't fall so soon then."

Dyfan looked at Wynn for a moment longer and then returned his attention to his plate of food. While the flavors weren't interesting, the portions were larger than in Victor Gruffyd's settlement. Bigger fighters probably made for more entertaining fights.

"You know, I was beginning to think that black and blue were my colors… What will happen if I'm sold? If I don't win some fights, I mean. Is one Victor really any worse than another?" Unless, he supposed, he was sold to a Victor whose interests lay in the lesser pits.

"Depends." Dyfan set down his bread and settled his palms on his knees. He was sitting cross-legged on the ground, as they all were. No one was going to waste expensive chairs on Defeated. A few sat on the rocks they had used that morning to lift and carry, but most just lounged on the packed mud. "Are you useful in other ways? If you have good skills, sometimes a new Victor will buy you for that. But if you embarrass Victor Gruffyd, he won't keep you. Probably try to sell you to the mines or lesser pits. If it got out that you're just stubborn, you might get a new Victor who enjoys breaking stubborn Defeated.…"

Wynn's jaw tightened, and he pressed his teeth together until they ached. Either of those fates would mean his death sooner rather than later, and he didn't want to die. Despite it all.

"I was a carpenter before." Wynn kept his eyes on the purpling sky. It didn't sound like that way was open for him here, though. He would have to learn to fight, or else his life would take a frightening turn for the worse. "Do you think that training master has experience turning carpenters into pit fighters?"

Dyfan

Before. Before he was Defeated. Before he had a Victor and lived in Cwm Or. The idea of *Before* was a strange one. Dyfan didn't have a Before. Just an Always.

"No." His reply was quiet, gaze drifting over Wynn's hardened features. That looked like pain. Was it from the day or from 'Before'? "But Cadel was a fisherman, and he's not too bad. So maybe you can be like him."

Dyfan picked up his plate, scraping the last few bites of supper into his mouth and stuffing the bread on top of it. His cheeks bulged as he chewed the mouthful, but it gave him a reason not to speak anymore.

Some part of him wanted to ask about 'Before,' but he shut down the idea. There wasn't *Before* anymore, just *Now*. And *now*, Wynn was a terrible fighter, Dyfan would never have a Before, and it didn't matter anyway.

"Yeah, maybe so." Wynn examined Dyfan's face for a moment and turned back to the vista in front of them. They both ate in silence, neither willing to break it. When the horn sounded, Wynn stood and offered Dyfan a hand. Training was done for the day and would start again early the next morning.

Dyfan looked at the hand and put his plate in it, standing up on his own. He took the plate back and nodded his farewell to Wynn. It was unsettling to share the meal with him. Most of the time, people left Dyfan alone. The other pit fighters were polite but not openly friendly. In general, that was the way of things in the pits. After all, they *were* competitors.

When Dyfan was at Victor Eurig's compound, he spent time with the other Defeated who lived there, and, of course, Victor Eurig often watched Dyfan train. But mostly, Dyfan was a solitary man. He entered the pits abnormally young, and training took up most of his time. It wasn't as if he was lonely. He liked being on his own, for the most part.

He turned away from Wynn without a farewell and headed towards the cell he slept in when he stayed at the fighting pits. He'd not talk to Wynn tomorrow. That would be easier. Better.

CHAPTER 15: PHECEA

SIXTH MOON, 1794, DIOSION

Eleven Years before the Proclamation

For his tenth birthday, Biton was given a man.

Of course, his mother insisted that the Emai were not people the same way she was or that he would be. They lived in rough tents in a frozen wasteland and should be allowed to stay in Phecea to serve and learn from a more educated civilization.

He was to be kind but not overly familiar. There needed to be space between man and Emai, just as between a ruler and their people. It was a rite of passage for noble-born children, a way of learning to govern.

In the end, his parents found the right Emai two weeks before Biton's birthday, so when they met, Biton felt he was not entirely prepared. He was nervous—his belly tingling into jellied thighs and his palms slick against the silk of his trousers. He was a little indignant—the confidence surely would have come by the time he was ten.

It was a mild day for the sixth moon, and his mother insisted upon formality. He stood beside her in the family courtyard, surrounded by extended cousins and family friends. His father entered from the opposite side, followed by the palest, plainest person Biton had ever seen.

The Emaian had short, white hair and an effeminate face with a soft mouth and rounded cheeks. His skin was almost as pale as the unadorned shift he wore. Biton bit his lip, and his mother laid a hand on his shoulder, squeezing a silent reprimand. He tried to stand a little taller.

"Son," his father said, standing before him. "I have with me your first charge, should you accept it."

Biton's mouth went dry. "Yes, father."

Cyril Mavros placed a heavy key around Biton's neck. "Treat those who serve you well, and they will serve all the better."

"Yes, father."

The crowd murmured in agreement, and with a gesture from Biton's father, the Emaian went to stand behind Biton. The boy let out a sigh of relief. That part, at least, was over.

His parents linked hands and then turned to the gathered onlookers—friends, family, and nobility invited to celebrate this step in Biton's life. "My son has accepted the first burden of adulthood!" Cyril said, taking up a glass filled with a clear, bubbling drink. His mother beamed, her gaze proud as it lingered on Biton. The group raised their glasses and turned to look at him. "To Biton Mavros!" they cried and then drank.

As was Phecean tradition, Biton and his new Emaian stood and greeted the party-goers, thanking them for coming. Many looked the Emaian over and complemented Biton on having a nice, clean specimen. Others focused on Biton, commenting that he was growing up so fast, so well. Surely he would follow in his father's footsteps and join the treasury?

Biton scrunched his nose but only when he thought no one was looking. Everything about the treasury seemed *boring*.

All through the party, the Emaian stayed by Biton's side, a silent and solid presence. Despite this celebration being for Biton, it was primarily attended by adults. Biton's younger sisters had long since vanished upstairs to their rooms.

As the afternoon turned to evening, Biton's mother, Iris, came to his side.

"My son. So handsome." She smoothed his black silk hair and

leaned in to kiss his forehead. She left red smears of her face paint behind. A reminder of a kiss. "It is getting late. Go on up to bed." Her gaze flickered to the Emaian at his side, and she nodded, dismissive.

Biton blanched slightly, his nerves returning. What did the Emaian think of all this? Of him? Did he have a name?

Trying to stand straight and look as though he were already ten years old, Biton nodded to his mother, wiped off the smudge of lip rouge, and trudged up towards his room. He wanted to turn around and look at the Emaian, but his father never looked at his slaves, so he kept his face forward, his back crawling with the imagined press of the slave's gaze.

He left his door open when he arrived in his room, passing the guard posted there without paying much attention. It was Davos this time, and he never laughed.

Once inside, though, Biton was uncertain. Should he give an order? Should he dismiss the Emaian? All he wanted to do was ask questions.

Davos shut the door behind them, so it was just the Emaian and Biton alone in his room. They stood facing each other for a breath before the Emaian glided toward Biton's bed. Carefully, he pulled back linen sheets and coverlets, smoothing the pillow. Another slave had already laid out his sleeping garments, so the Emaian only had to pick them up. Linen from the Tupa Galan jungles. The Emaian fingered the soft fabric and then turned to Biton.

Biton flushed. "I can dress myself." The words came out over-loud and too highly pitched, though he had meant to sound self-assured.

"You can…"

He trailed off, pulling his brows together. He didn't want anything to eat so soon after the party, and there was nothing in his room that needed picking up. What did he want then?

"You can tell me a story." He pulled off his stiff dress tunic and pulled on his bedclothes, taking them from the Emaian's hand. "And your name. I want to know what that is too."

The Emaian looked at him for a second. "Keme." A simple name. The way the Emaian said it drew out the eh sounds. Keem-eh. And his voice. The slave had a strangely deep voice for such a bland person. Or—Bland-looking *slave*.

Keme took the chair by Biton's bed, folding his hands carefully. "What kind of story would you like to hear? A happy story? A sad story?"

Biton considered this. His mother liked sad stories. Sometimes she even cried over them, but then she went and still read more. "How about a story about bravery?" Biton screwed up his face when he realized he'd phrased it as a question. "I mean, yes, I would like a story about bravery, Keme."

If Keme noticed his slip up, he was good enough not to react. Instead, the Emai resettled in the chair and crossed his legs. "A story about bravery. Very good, Master Biton." Keme took a deep breath, closing those empty eyes as if to better remember how the story started.

"A long time ago, before countries, kingdoms, or tribes, there was only night and day and people who lived by the sun's rule. Day was a celebration. The sun rose, the plants grew, and all was well. But night —" Keme shook his head. "Night was frightening. Creatures prowled the land and hunted the people. The darkness ate up all in its path, and the people lived in fear of the things that moved within it. They prayed for a way to scare away the darkness until one woman decided to change it all. You see, she didn't want people to suffer anymore, to fear night and the dangers it brought. So she climbed the highest of the Nonoccan Peaks and convinced a hawk to carry her to the sun. She asked the sun to stay, to keep the people forever in light."

Keme's eyes opened again, but his stare still seemed distant as if seeing that woman on the hawk's back.

"The sun denied her. Though the people did not like the darkness, it was necessary. It let people and animals rest, brought the oceans closer, and kept the mountain's snow from melting. Darkness, night—they are important. But this woman would not let her people down. So she begged the sun to give her a piece of its light. Just the smallest bit, to give her people hope in the night."

The Emai gestured towards the hearth, crackling with a merry fire.

"She brought back the sun's flame and tamed its ravenous hunger.

None were afraid of the dark with her light to guide them. The people named her Dasan for this brave deed."

"Dasan," Biton murmured, tasting the word. "Was she the only one called Dasan, or were there others?"

"There were others, though no one has been so named in generations."

"Do you know where I can find a hawk to carry me? I think I would like to meet the sun."

Perhaps he could ask her what he should be. Surely the sun would know of a better job than Treasurer for the Othonos family. Or maybe she would give him a present as good as fire, and people everywhere would come to see him and bring him gifts like puppies and silks and jewels and swords and horses. He blinked a few times, sinking further into his soft mattress. It had been, after all, a very busy day.

"All the hawks strong enough to fly up to the sun left generations ago. They didn't like to be kept in cages, so they flew to the islands of the far south. You would have to travel great distances to find one." Keme's voice was hollow. "Maybe one day."

Biton shrugged, pillowing his cheek on one hand, his eyes sliding closed. "I'll probably be big enough next year." He might have said more, but he had already fallen into the warm embrace of sleep.

CHAPTER 16: THE EMAI

EIGHTH MOON, 1794, ANGILLIK/IFRATEM

Eleven Years before the Proclamation

On her seventeenth birthday, Iniabi woke in a cave. It was a small space, narrower at the front than the back, so when she came or went, she had to squeeze through the opening. A bigger person wouldn't be able to follow. In the back was her nest of treasures—enough stolen furs to keep her warm through the cold late-winter nights, a sling made of scrap leather and cords she'd found near the docks, and a dwindling cache of food and clean water.

She pulled herself from the furs, grimacing at the cold, and checked to ensure that no creatures had slipped inside during the night to use her shelter. So far, the horse blanket she had nailed up over the inside of the entrance was doing a decent job of keeping out the larger pests. Iniabi stood, pulled back her hair, and tugged on her boots.

She would need to sell poison soon. Her stores were low though she took none for herself. What poison dreams she had experienced showed a future that confounded and frightened her. Even if she wanted to delve back into them, she understood the poison. You could not take it more than once a season if you wanted to live without it.

Outside the narrow crack of Iniabi's cave, the cliffs dropped to pockmarked stone. At high tide, there was nothing but sea below her, but while it was low, the sea's grasping fingers revealed tidepools brimming with the urchins from which the Emai made poison. Iniabi picked her way down to them, murmuring as she climbed. "Manaba, Piav, Yura, Tonraq, Meriwa, Xanthe, Adara, Mika, Sani, Toklo, Tampeesa..."

For weeks after she had made it to the port of Angillik (Ifratem if you asked a Lirian), Iniabi had searched for the other Emai from her village. She hid among crowds or between buildings and watched the selling of slaves in the town's little slave market. She watched as silver-haired people were led into boats in chains. Eventually, she gave up hope. While she lay feverish in the streets of Angillik and burned or shook with chills, her people had slipped from her grasp and into the land of thieves. They would not return.

The tide pools were almost sea-black, lighter than the deep water past the rock's edge but darker than the rock they lay in. The first one Iniabi came across was half-empty—she had already taken much from it—so she moved on to the next. Manaba's voice rang through her mind as she went. "Take too much, and the urchins will not come back."

The next pool housed a tiny world. Barnacles clung to the sides, interspersed with mussels and deep purple sea urchins. Two fire-red anemones waved delicate tendrils at the bottom, and as her shadow fell over the edge, tiny crabs skittered away. Iniabi slipped her hand into the frigid water, past rough-barked barnacles to dig up the mussels that clamped shut their shells at her touch. She made quick work of them, prying them open to divulge the salty, chewy middle, and after a handful, her growling belly subsided. It was harder work to get the urchins from their rock perches as stings were dangerous, but it did not take Iniabi long to fill her net. She left the fresh urchins in her cave to dry and carried up what she had already made to the town above.

Angillik no longer looked like an Emaian village, though Iniabi knew tales of its past from the old Emaian fishers who still sold their catches in its streets. It had not truly been Emaian for more years than anyone still living could remember. No illus graced the narrow streets, and there was no common center for people to gather. Instead, it was a dirty, ramshackle place of close stone buildings and refuse-laden alleys. There were enough white-haired, black-eyed brats that Iniabi went easily unnoticed, and she liked it that way just fine. So long as she could pass as a child, she could stay free of the stares of Lirian men.

Iniabi went to the brothel first, slipping around back with a stone weighing down her sling just in case any patrons wanted their pleasure or their poison for free. Inside, she relaxed. This early in the day, Angillik's brothel was a sleepy place, quiet and so warm that it felt over-hot after the chill of the tidepools. Several of the ladies sat in the kitchen, drinking kava or spreading roe on bread, their faces streaked with the remains of their previous night's work—kohl and rouge melting from eyes and lips like ice.

"Oh, look," one of them said, leaning back from the table. Her skin was as dark as her hair, a rich brown like earth buried under snow. She did not look like a slaver or the Emai. Many people in Angillik did not, and it had shocked Iniabi at first that there were people besides hers and those who hunted them. "Someone fetch the matron. Her little poison girl is here to peddle dreams."

"I don't suppose you have one that will convince my favorite client to marry me?" The woman who stood up was of Lirian ancestry, but Iniabi had heard the others call her a bastard, someone born outside of a partnership. She was only a year older than the "little poison girl," though she didn't know it.

"Don't work that way," Iniabi answered in Lirian. Her grasp of the language was terrible, heavily accented by her childhood in Nec. It made the women laugh, and a few spoke too quickly for Iniabi to understand. They thought her slow for being unable to speak their language, but she wondered if any of them would have survived as well in an Emaian village as she did in their town.

The door to the kitchens banged open hard enough to rattle the dishes on their wall-bound shelves. The painted ladies ceased their noise.

"Hello, Iniabi." The matron was a tall woman in her forties with hair just as white and eyes just as black as Iniabi's. She had a long, severe nose and the corners of her fish-like mouth perpetually frowned. She wore a full-skirted Lirian dress as though it would make her look like one of them. "Your last batch made one of our clients ill."

Iniabi shrugged. The men from Liria wanted poison to carry them away, so the matron would not stop selling it. "It *is* poison. It isn't easy on the body."

Besides, it was not meant for men.

Her answer sparked anger in the matron's eyes, and she slapped Iniabi hard across the cheek. It stung, but the girl had known worse pain than the soft hands of this woman could inflict. "It is poison, *matron*," she hissed, and Iniabi had to bite down on her own fury. This matron was just as much of a half-breed as she was.

Iniabi took a breath. "Yes, matron."

"Give the poison here and take your coin. I'll not pay full price for rancid things." The matron dropped a few coins on the table, and Iniabi scooped them up, leaving behind a string of carefully sealed mussel shells, each filled with a few drops of poison.

It would not do to fight now. The matron would only have her girls hold Iniabi down and beat her. No. But the next time she brought the brothel poison, half of their precious shells would be empty. The thought made Iniabi grin as she slipped back out into the cold. No slaver-friend would get the better of her.

⇑ ⇑ ⇑

Tenth Moon, 1794, Angillik/Ifratem

WINTER HUNG over them late that year. The sky poured snow into the sea and froze the cliff face, so it became more precarious to reach Iniabi's cave. She spent the nights struggling to stay warm and the mornings selling poison, as though the colder it got, the more the people of Angillik wanted to escape.

Manaba would have hated them for it, but Iniabi woke every day, slipped bloody fingers into the tide pools, and made them dreams to pour into their veins. Let them take the poison. Let it creep into their minds and their hearts and rot them from the inside. Addiction to urchin spine was a subtle way to kill yourself, and they wouldn't know that they'd die without the poison until she stopped making it and killed them all.

For all her anger, Manaba had revered life. She taught Iniabi of the cycle of the Emai, of the tundra. She killed nothing unnecessarily and took no more than what she needed. But somehow, while Iniabi pulled urchins from tide pools and sang her list of names, she did not think that Manaba would have minded all the slaver deaths this poison would cause.

That morning, Iniabi started her rounds with the tavern. She sold poison to the man who worked the bar and the one who owned the inn. The auctioneer paid double and would charge twice that to the men and women who came to buy slaves. At the brothel, the matron was waiting on Iniabi, impatient in a room empty of painted ladies. When she saw that the matron was alone, Iniabi slowed, and her pulse quickened. Her sling was in her hand, as always on these rounds.

"Hello, matron," she said politely, standing in the doorway rather than coming inside. The kitchen around the stern woman gave nothing away. No one seemed to be hiding behind barrels of salt fish and grain. The big, round table was still littered with the remains of breakfast.

The Emaian woman met Iniabi's gaze coolly. "The esteemed Captain, Leo Demetrias, died in his bed last night, coughing black slime. He has not taken the spine in three days. There must have been a mistake, you see, because last time you delivered, half of the shells were empty, and I ran out of poison to sell."

Anxiety gnawed at Iniabi's middle like starving rats after old scrap. It had been stupid to test the matron like she'd done, but some brazen spike of anger boiled her blood at the idea of backing down and apologizing. Instead, she kept her eyes on the matron's and shrugged purposely. "You get what you pay for, matron."

The woman snarled. "You don't deny it, then? It was going without the spine that killed him?"

Iniabi took a step back. Suddenly, the kitchen smelled like desperation, and there was something in the matron's eyes that reminded her of how Mika looked when she begged the slavers to beat her friend instead of her mother. The girl's thoughts surged like a quick tide. "The poison takes everyone differently," she lied in her mother tongue, "and some take it worse than others. There are reasons why the medicine women use it so rarely."

"Reasons you seem to know a lot about. I think we'll need the recipe. Just in case." The Emaian matron refused to answer her in their language and picked up a large, metal tankard. This she rapped sharply against the counter, and a sound like a whip crack sliced through the air. Iniabi flinched instinctively, bracing for the fall of the lash. Instead, two long shadows darkened the light coming in through the doorway around her.

Iniabi darted forward, her sling already in motion. The stone couched within its pouch took flight, striking the first of two large men in the center of his throat. He went down in a splay of limbs, fouling the approach of his partner. The sound he made was like nothing Iniabi had heard before— a thick, broken wheezing. She clutched her poison as the matron reached for it and dashed through the door behind her.

There was no one in the brothel's gaudy seating room. Once-rich cloth in reds and purples lay stained over thread-bare chairs and sofas. Lanterns swung unlit overhead, and tankards sat empty on worn tables. It was not hard to imagine why this place was more sought after at night when the day could not illuminate its flaws. Iniabi ran through the room on light feet, flinging open the front door just as the kitchen door crashed behind her. She didn't waste the time it would take to look.

Like the brothel, the streets of Angillik didn't take kindly to daylight. Piss and shit dribbled down the gutters; scraps of food, rucksacks, and splintered wood littered the cobblestone paths. When Iniabi sprinted down the first alley, she had to dodge a wiry-haired dog gorging itself on something red and bloody, leaping over crates left by the businesses to either side. Behind her, the heavy whomp of booted feet followed steadily after.

If Iniabi could only get to her little cave, she would be safe. These men could not fit through the entrance— she doubted they could even make it down the cliff face. Though, if she led them there, they could wait above the cliff until she was driven out by hunger or thirst and she'd be all the more easily taken. She would need to lose them first.

Iniabi took the next left at random, the walls of the buildings on either side pressing in so close that she could touch them if she stretched out her hand. A crash echoed behind her, and Iniabi hazarded a look at the storm of curses. There were three behind her now—one man with skin the color of elk eyes and two Lirians. The man whose throat she had crushed was not one of them. She turned back and skidded to a halt.

A third wall rose before her, blackened from smoke and damp, cutting off her escape. The footsteps slowed. One of her pursuers laughed.

Iniabi shoved her string of poison into her belt and took a running leap onto the wall. For moons now, every morning and every evening before high tide, she had climbed the cliffs to her little cave. They were slick with ice, what little hand and footholds made small and treacherous. In comparison, this hastily put up brick with its regular finger-thick crevasses was easy.

She was halfway up when they began to throw rocks. The first hit her in the shoulder, a glancing blow. The next hit her back. She kept climbing; these strikes weren't as painful as a slaver's whip. Then, a rock caught her in the back of the head, slamming her forehead into the stone wall. Her vision blurred, darkening around the edges. Another rock hit her right hand, and then she was hanging, the only thing keeping her from capture a single crack between two bricks hardly as deep as the first joint of her pointer finger. Iniabi swayed, gasping. Another rock caught her in the calf.

And then she kicked at the wall and hauled herself over the edge.

She lay there panting for a long moment, her limbs trembling and her chest tight with fear. They knew what building she was on. They could climb up to the roof from the inside, get ladders, or just surround her and wait until she was too cold and tired to do anything.

"Get up, Iniabi," she told herself, her voice a harsh whisper. "Move, you stupid girl. Would you rather be a slave?"

If Manaba saw her now, she would call Iniabi weak. Stupid. She deserved everything she got. Iniabi always deserved everything she got.

"Yeah, maybe. But I'm alive, and you're dead. Dead and left to scavengers in the snow."

Iniabi pushed herself to her feet. Shouts rose up from below, but she paid them no attention. On the other side of the building was another roof, lower than the one Iniabi stood on and about a cart's width away. She stepped back from the edge.

It was too far. She wouldn't make it—not without injuring herself. She'd have to find some other—

The sharp clack of wood against stone rang out behind her, and Iniabi turned to see a ladder leaning against the side of the building.

Would you rather be a slave?

She ran, and when her feet reached the end of her roof, she threw herself at the next one. There was a long moment where she hung weightless in the air, then she was falling, arms flailing, her sling slapping her thighs from its place tied to her belt. She hit the next roof hard, stumbling forward into a loose-limbed tumble, and fell right off the opposite side.

There was a shock of pain, bright and hot against her back, and all the air left Iniabi's lungs. Her body shuddered for it, gasping, choking. The air wouldn't come! She couldn't fill her lungs, and—

Iniabi managed one breath, then another. She rolled shakily off the crate that had broken her fall, now cracked open beneath her, and heaved on her hands and knees.

"That was quite the fall."

Iniabi scrambled up, heart pounding. The voice came from a woman—tall and dark. Her black hair was braided into a thousand tiny strands and pulled high on her head in a horse tail. A couple loose braids swung before ears heavy with gold hoops. She had a high forehead, prominent cheekbones, and one of her eyes was hollow—a scarred lid sewn shut over an empty cavity. Beside her stood two men, one shorter than Iniabi and the other broader than the men from the brothel combined. He had yellow hair, and his skin was pale—more pink than snow like hers.

The woman regarded her curiously. "What's chasing you, girl?"

"I— They—" Iniabi panted, sliding back. Her mind was a panicked thing, a rabbit on the run from a wolf.

"Slowly. Take a breath. That's it."

"My mother worked at the brothel," she lied, gasping for air around the words. "Men lent her money for poison, but now she's dead, and they say they'll get what they're owed from me."

The woman exchanged a look with the short man. "Do you speak Emaian, girl?"

The man grumbled something pretty in a language that Iniabi didn't know. He looked unhappy with the way things were going.

"Please! Just don't tell them where I am!"

The woman put a hand on her hip, braids swaying around her face. "Do we look like people who turn girls over to low-lifes? Answer the question."

Iniabi wasn't sure what sort of people they looked like at all. They didn't wear anything that looked Emaian or Lirian. All three were in tall boots and loose trousers. The short man and the woman wore coats that looked like whale or seal skin, and the woman had tied a bright red sash about her waist. All three carried swords and knives.

"I— Yes. Emaian is my language." Iniabi pressed herself into the curve of the wall. She could hear shouting again. Would they assume she had come this way?

"Excellent! How would you like to leave this place for good?"

In that moment, Iniabi had never heard a better proposal. Leave Angillik with its slavers and brothels and poison-lovers? "Yes! I mean, yes, please. Can we go now?"

The woman laughed and untied the sash at her waist, draping it over Iniabi's white hair. "Come on. Our ship leaves tonight."

CHAPTER 17: THE WESTERN SEA

TENTH MOON, 1794, THE FLYING NIGHT

Eleven Years before the Proclamation

The ship was the strangest place Iniabi had ever been. It was as big as a village, but one structure made of enough wood to keep a southern Emaian settlement warm through winter. Three great sails rose above the deck, their trunks thicker and taller than any tree in the Tundra. Hulking people shoved past her on small stairwells, going about business she did not understand. So far, the only sailors who spoke Lirian were the ones she'd met in Angillik and the captain, though Iniabi only had the misfortune of crossing paths with that formidable woman infrequently during her first two moons. No one spoke Emaian.

Iniabi lay in an oblong strip of thick cloth hung between two hooks in the place where the sailors slept. They all swung from similar contraptions, swaying through the night in a way that had made her feel ill the first time. What was wrong with the ground? They certainly had enough cloth for pallets.

A boy stepped into the room, tall, lanky, and round-cheeked. He had dark hair and warm, brown skin just a little lighter than elk hide. He approached as Iniabi carefully maneuvered one leg out of the swinging bed, her toes reaching for the safety of the wood below. He laughed, but she didn't think he did it out of cruelty. He had a soft face. Softer than any of the others on board.

Iniabi straightened the long, narrowing length of her kiati and pointed to the thing she'd been sleeping on. Yesterday, this boy had led her around the ship, pointing out various objects and naming them in the pretty, flowing language the pirates all spoke in between chores. When she showed interest now, he brightened.

"Hammock," he said.

Alright, then. They slept in death traps called *hammocks*. She pointed at him.

"Iago."

She pointed to herself. "Iniabi."

This seemed to make him happy, and he launched into a string of words she did not know. Thankfully, he didn't seem to expect her to. Nearby, a sleepy sailor grumbled from her hammock, and Iago hushed, steering Iniabi between the stirring forms of people preparing to rise.

The day passed like the previous one—in a flurry of chores. She and a handful of other young crew mates scoured the deck with sand and brittle stones. Then she sluiced it off with salt water and went to move crates and coils of rope and wash dishes for the cook, who also seemed to go by the name of Cook. She wasn't entirely sure. He told her a little about the ship in Lirian.

It was called the *Flying Night*, and it was the fastest ship in the Western Sea. Cook could not tell her why they wanted her on board. There were no other Emaians.

That evening, after finishing in the kitchen, Iniabi dragged sore, tired feet down into the belly of the ship, where her *hammock* awaited her. Her hands were blistered, her back aching. Iniabi had never minded hard work, but now all she wanted was to sleep for the next two days.

Halfway down a narrow stair, a man blocked her way. His expression was tight with annoyance, and he pointed back up with a string of the sailors' language in gruff tones. She picked out the word *deck*, the topmost level of the ship, and their words for *night* and *girl*.

Wearily, Iniabi turned and climbed back up. It did not seem like he would let her sleep otherwise.

She followed the gruff man to a spot near the rail and waited. He spoke longer in their language, pointing first to the deck and then to the open sea, its roiling surface black as poison in the night. She thought he said *ships* a few times and was confused. There was only *one*, as far as she could tell. Did he mean for her to sleep out here all night? Even a hammock would be better than the hard deck and seaspray.

"Hammock?" Iniabi asked, cocking her head to the side in hopes the man would understand the question. He laughed in her face and pointed sternly to the deck again before bowing and walking away.

What had she done to deserve to sleep on the deck? Was this a punishment? Or a trick, like the ones the Banished children would play on her back home? She lifted her hand to the small scar under her eye and sighed.

Whatever the reason, she was too tired to protest. They would have her cleaning and running errands all day again tomorrow, and it would be even more miserable if she were awake all night. Iniabi put her back to the frigid sea and lay down, resting her head on an arm. Even in the cold and damp, she dropped off quickly.

⇑ ⇑ ⇑

Rough hands shook Iniabi awake, her head thudding into the ship's deck. It was still dark, probably only a few hours after she'd been told to sleep there. The back of her kiati was soaked through, and she shivered despite the mildness of the spring night. There was a pair of boots in front of her nose—the person who had woken her. The leather was connected to Taaliah, the woman who had offered her an escape from Angillik. The presence of someone who spoke enough Lirian to understand her brought a sudden, pronounced wave of relief.

"What is it?" Iniabi asked, yawning.

"What?!" It was strange to hear such venom from the typically even-tempered woman. "You're sleeping on watch duty, that's what!"

Iniabi didn't know the meaning of the words *watch* or *duty*, but she could tell she had done something wrong. "What is *watch duty*? The man who brought me here only pointed to the deck."

"Fucking... Look. You were supposed to look out for other ships or problems. Because you were sleeping, you put us all in danger! It's good it was me who found you because—"

"What's going on here?" The captain strode past Taaliah, who paled at the sight of the stocky, warm-skinned woman. Iniabi pushed herself onto her feet, trying not to draw attention.

"I was just explaining watch duty to Iniabi, Captain," Taaliah said. She took a half step away from Iniabi as if she didn't want to be associated with her anymore. Iniabi shot her a grateful look anyway for not telling the captain she'd been asleep.

The captain's gaze felt heavy on her shoulders, like Manaba's when she was angry. "Explaining watch duty to someone already on watch? Really? It looked as if you were waking up a stupid girl who was shirking her duty."

Iniabi wasn't sure of the Lirian word *shirk*, but the captain's tone made it clear. She was in trouble. "Captain, Nico just brought her up here and pointed to the deck. He knows she doesn't speak Phecean, but he still—"

"I don't give a shit about Nico or what the girl can and cannot understand. She put the entire ship at risk. I'm of half a mind to let you take her punishment, Taaliah, since you're the one who brought this leech on board."

Taaliah, shut her mouth. It seemed her loyalty to Iniabi only went so far. Like Mika.

"I'm sorry! I understand now, Captain. I—"

"Shut up." Iniabi clamped her jaws closed so fast they made her teeth clack. If this were Manaba, she would look for a way to fix it, but she didn't understand the captain well enough to know what to do. When Iniabi didn't speak, the captain turned. "Come with me. Taaliah, you take over watch."

The captain led Iniabi the length of the ship, passing sailors, their faces turned out to sea. Iniabi should have watched them for what to do, but in her exhaustion, the idea had not occurred to her.

If only she'd stayed awake a little longer, she might have avoided all of this.

Beside the ladders leading to the quarterdeck was a room Iniabi had never visited. The captain hauled the door open, and they stepped into a chamber as opulent as it was cluttered and unorganized. Iniabi pressed her back to the door as though it was a whalebone spar.

Striding to a large wooden desk, the captain settled into a chair and steepled her fingers. "Taaliah has these dreams of trading with the Emai, which is why she brought you here. She thinks we'll get better prices for whale oil from them, but I don't think you're worth the effort. You can't tie a decent knot. You don't seem to have any useful skills besides grunt work, which I have plenty of hands for, and now you put my ship and my crew at risk."

I can hide, Iniabi thought. *I can survive in the Tundra. I know how to catch a hare, birth a baby, or heal a wound.*

I can make poison.

"I can get something else you can sell. Something worth even more than whale oil."

The captain's frown lessened. "What is worth more than whale oil?"

"Dreams. The slavers covet Tuqunnaqtuq, our vision bringer."

"What?" The captain leaned back in her seat, a smirk twitching at the corners of her lips. "Some sacred item? A special statue or icon? You'll have to be better than that. I'm not some uneducated Lirian swine."

No. The captain was not Lirian, but Iniabi didn't know from what land she hailed. "I don't know enough words in this language to explain. In Ifratem, I sold it to the brothels, the pubs, and the inns. The auctioneers bought it before they sold their flesh wares. You take it in a cut or drink it straight, and it takes your mind from this world. They called me a peddler of dreams."

"So it's a medicine of some sort?" The captain leaned forward, her attention focused keenly on Iniabi.

"A medicine that men long for. That they want and want and want and can't ever get enough of. It makes you escape."

The older woman licked her lips, the scar bisecting her lower one glistening. "And you have this medicine *now*? If this is some trick where we have to go find it, just for you to jump ship to avoid your punishment...."

Iniabi had never been more grateful that she'd escaped with the brothel's poison. "There is some in my hammock. Enough for several gold pieces."

"Bring it here, Iniabi."

CHAPTER 18: THE WESTERN SEA

FIRST MOON, 1795, THE FLYING NIGHT

Ten Years before the Proclamation

*L*ife aboard the ship was no harder than living with Manaba; in some ways it was easier. The captain was happy now that she had poison, and the expectations of the rest of the crew stayed largely the same each day. Iniabi did not have to worry about sudden bursts of anger or poison dreams.

Most of these expectations consisted of chores, but Iniabi was no stranger to work. She scoured the deck or went to see if Cook needed pans scraped out or the bosun needed help stitching sails. She learned to coil rope, tie knots properly, and scurry up the rigging. Now, when she looked at her hands, she found them hardened, lumps of rough skin growing on her palms and fingers to protect her.

No one else on the ship spoke Emaian—Iniabi was the only white-haired, alabaster-skinned person among them. They spoke a beautiful, lilting language called Phecean because that was where the captain was from. The rest of the crew were from more places than she knew existed—Tupa Gala, Araria, Ingola, Phecea. Only one or two were Lirian, and these were Banished like those in the village of Nec.

When Iniabi put together enough words in Phecean to form her question, she went to the other girl on board close to her age. It was a clear day, with nothing obstructing the pale sky overhead, and the deck was still damp from its recent cleansing. People of every description went about their duties, including the girl Iniabi sought. She was warm-skinned with lips a little darker around the edges so that they drew Iniabi's gaze. She had long, dark hair she kept braided and wide brown eyes. "Why do we scrub the deck with sand and salt water?"

The girl didn't look up as Iniabi spoke, instead continuing her task. "To keep mold and fungus from growing, and so the planks will swell up to keep out water." Her accent differed from the others, with discordant notes and slippery S's.

"Where are we sailing to?"

"We're running the shipping lane from Ifratem to Pelagius." Again the girl stayed focused on her task, her answers leaving Iniabi feeling a little irritated and confused. It was odd to speak with someone who wouldn't look at you, but then she had interrupted the other girl, and she wanted to know the answers. It had been a long two moons since she'd been able to speak much with anyone.

"Where's that?"

The girl heaved a great sigh and finally straightened up. She was taller than Iniabi, but then most people were. "Don't you know anything? It's in Liria."

"We're going to Liria?" Alarm blossomed in Iniabi's chest. This ship wasn't carrying any slaves. She'd checked. So why were they going to the land of the slavers? She was the only Emaian—or half-Emaian—on board. Had she failed to please the captain? Would she be sold rather than her poison?

The girl scoffed and propped her hands on her hips. "No. We're not going *to* Liria. We're searching for Lirian merchant ships. Ships full of goods bound for Ifratem." She paused, looking at Iniabi with a haughty, expectant expression. When it was obvious Iniabi didn't fully understand, the taller girl rolled her eyes. "So we can take those goods. So we can sell them ourselves. We're pirates. That's what pirates do."

Slowly, Iniabi's lips cracked open in a smile, the movement painful, like the muscles hadn't seen much use. They were going to steal from the Lirians and then sell their goods back to them! "When will we find their ships?" She thought that even the difficulty of speaking in a strange language couldn't keep the excitement out of her voice.

"We'll find them when we find them, fish brain. What do they call you?"

"Iniabi." Just Iniabi. She'd not wear Manaba's name here. "What about you?"

"Jaya." The girl glanced over her shoulder. The captain was at the helm, but she wasn't looking their way just yet. "You're an escaped slave, right?"

Iniabi considered the other girl's dark eyes for a moment. "Yes. I escaped from Vindium and made my way back to the Emai. When I reached my village, nothing was left, so I went to Angillik looking for work." She had no idea where Vindium was, but the Lirians in Angillik spoke of it longingly enough that it must be in Liria.

"Angillik?" Jaya's thick brows pinched together in confusion. Iniabi was sure Phecean was not her native language, and it certainly wasn't Iniabi's. She hesitated for a moment, trying to put together an explanation that made sense.

"Ifratem is what Lirians call Angillik. It was Angillik before."

"Before..." Jaya nodded, her expression softening somewhat. "Well, that's a long way to travel all alone." Iniabi wondered if the other girl suspected she wasn't telling the full truth and resisted the urge to squirm. Instead, she made herself shrug.

"What about you? Where are you from?" The girl didn't look like anyone Iniabi had met before—full-lipped and dark-eyed. She was beautiful in a hard, dangerous sort of way.

"You ask a lot of questions, you know." Jaya glanced at the captain again and knelt, eyes on the rope. "You better get back to work, fish brain."

"Alright. Bye, Jaya." Iniabi slipped below decks to see if the Quartermaster wanted a hand in the supply room.

⇑　　⇑　　⇑

Not long after her conversation with Jaya, Iniabi woke to the pounding of the ship's drums. They felt like thunder, traveling through the planks and down the ropes of her hammock, where she swung gently above stores of grain. She pushed herself up, uncertain. The distant sounds of shouting filtered down from the deck, and the whole world shook as one of the great ballistae fired.

Iniabi half-fell from her hammock in her rush for her boots and ran pell-mell up the steep steps onto the deck. Everything was a blur of chaos. Sailors shouted for the sails, for the ballista, for archers and spear throwers. Seaspray showered them as the *Flying Night* turned, and the great drums beneath the deck thundered their fury into the wind. Just beyond the railing, Iniabi could see another ship circling closer in the gray light before dawn, the two great vessels like wolves sizing each other up before a fight.

"Fish brain!" The shout startled Iniabi back to herself, and she looked down the ladder to see Jaya trying to climb up. Hurriedly, Iniabi moved out of the way, and Jaya got onto the deck, pulling two wicked, curving blades out of the sash at her waist. "Now get back down to the Quartermaster! You'll need a weapon tonight."

Weapons. Yes. She needed to be able to fight.

Iniabi slipped back into the bowels of the ship, pressing herself to the side whenever pirates came barrelling past, weapons in hand. The Quartermaster was in the armory—a room that had once been the brig when this was a Phecean military vessel and not a pirate ship. He shifted through barrels of quarrels when Iniabi came in, filling a pouch at his waist, his crossbow thrown over his back.

"Quartermaster Vlassis?" Iniabi asked, and the man looked up. He hadn't changed since she first met him in Angillik—short, dark-haired, and disapproving. He didn't grace her with a reply, just fixed her with a black-eyed glare. "I need weapons."

"What can you use?" She showed him her sling, and he raised a brow. "Well, mam always said the best weapon is the one you know, but if you make it through this with nothing but a fancy rock thrower, you'll be the luckiest girl alive."

She swallowed. "I'll take a knife too."

Vlassis laughed, throwing his head back so that she could see the lump bobbing under his chin. "Well then, here's a knife, and—" He went rummaging around in one of the crates behind him— "some lead shot too. Board that merchant vessel and come back alive, and I'll teach you how to use every weapon in the arsenal."

Iniabi reached out to take the man's vast hand. She shook it once like she'd seen people do in Angillik. "Deal."

Back above deck, the sky was lightening. The chaos had diminished, the crew standing at the portside rail watching as the ship slid up next to an enormous, lumbering galleon. Fires sparked across her deck while desperate sailors fought to put them out before the pirates reached them.

Iniabi tucked her new dagger into her right boot and fitted a lumpen hunk of lead into her sling. As soon as the merchant ship was within reach, pirates swarmed her, swinging onto the other deck or stomping across hastily laid planks. When Iniabi reached one of these, she looked down through the space between the ships and swallowed at the roiling foam beneath them, black and tumultuous. The fall wouldn't kill her, but the cold and the deep would.

"Move it!" Behind her, more pirates waited their turn, grinning and cold. The two youths that scrubbed the deck with her every morning were there, each holding knives. Iniabi turned and stepped onto the plank, crossing it without looking down again.

Being on the deck of the Lirian merchant ship was like walking through a poison dream. There was noise everywhere, shouts and thuds and grunts of pain and effort. Lirians in plain tunics and breeches struggled against pirates in a dizzying mismatch of colors. Bodies struggled against bodies, thrusting out with blades meant to disgorge organs. There was more piss than she expected.

Iniabi's fingers white-knuckled around her sling as bigger and stronger bodies shoved into her, cursing. Someone ran by, blades in each hand, both dripping blood. They didn't seem to notice who they cut. Iniabi backed up until she felt the railings press into her spine. Her breath was coming in pants, and all the world smelled of iron. She swung her sling around herself—a looping path about either side, just as Piav had done. Another pirate fought nearby, their face sweat-streaked as they attempted to disarm a larger opponent. Behind them, a Lirian reared back, and before they could strike, before Iniabi really knew it herself, she let loose the lead shot that took the Lirian in the skull. He crumpled.

This— she could do this. She just had to avoid being a coward and then get back across the plank, and then Vlassis would teach her to fight. She placed another rough chunk of lead into the sling and imagined each Lirian with the faces of those who held her down in the snow and lashed her until the white was misted red. Never again. She would never be helpless again.

A few feet away, a Lirian sliced through the throat of one of the pirates, and Iniabi threw a stone that broke his sword arm. Someone else finished him off. She landed a shot on a man's mouth in a shower of blood and ducked out of the way when struggling bodies slammed into the ship's rail. A Lirian turned away from his kill to find her and smiled, his yellow teeth catching the morning light so that he looked like he'd swallowed the sun. Iniabi released, but the ball missed him, screaming over the writhing heads to disappear somewhere out to sea. She dropped her sling and pulled out her knife, her palm slick on the simple eel-skin hilt.

"Come here, slave bitch," he said. He caught her by the face with one hand and the wrist with the other, then threw her bodily onto the deck. There was the sharp crack of her skull against wood, the world blurring around her. An enormous boot filled her vision, and then there was nothing.

⇑ ⇑ ⇑

Iniabi woke on Cook's table, her face awash with pain. She struggled to sit up, her limbs aching. Cook, the enormous pink-skinned, yellow-haired man she'd met with Vlassis and Bosun Taaliah in Angillik, looked up from where he was cleaning his hands on a cloth. He had a strange, soft-vowelled accent from somewhere far north of Liria and Phecea. "I set your nose as best I could, but it'll never be quite as straight as it was."

The girl started to raise her hand to her face and stopped herself. Best not to mess with it, probably. "Did we win?"

Cook guffawed. "Didn't take you long to turn pirate, did it? Aye, the hull's full of cargo."

"I took out three of them."

"Really? I heard it was four. Now get your sorry ass off my table. I did what the captain asked and kept you in one piece. I guess she means to make a fortune off you after all."

Iniabi blinked at him, still dazed from the battle and unconsciousness. "The captain wanted you to heal me?"

"That's what I said, isn't it? Don't get to thinking you're special, girl. The captain's just got a nose for gold. Now go wash up! You smell like blood, and I need help peeling potatoes for all these sailors. We're eating Lirian food tonight!"

CHAPTER 19: LIRIA

FIRST MOON, 1795, LIRIA

Ten Years before the Proclamation

The white stone walls of the western barn made Luce's eyes water from the glare of morning light. He was grateful when the director of the breeding facility led him and Commander Vitus into the building. The halls smelled of soap, and there were bundles of dried herbs every four windows.

"We're honored by the accommodations the Imperator granted us. We strive for excellence in our breeding stock, of course, and it is nice to be recognized for our efforts," the director said as he showed them down tiled halls and into the main barn. The high ceilings gave the place a sense of grandeur. Luce turned down one of the aisles, inspecting the cleanliness here. The tiles were so polished he could see a warped version of himself reflected back.

"It's impeccable," Commander Vitus said, his tone dry. Luce suspected he knew why the tall Lirian was irritated. The breeding facilities for the slaves were likely cleaner and more handsomely appointed than his home. Vitus was a young man, working his way up the ranks as Luce had.

"Yes! Well, we've noticed a correlation between successful pregnancies or coverings and the well-being of our stock. They're fed only the finest grains and vegetables, and each slave gets six hours of sunlight and exercise time, weather permitting. Healthy slaves make healthy profits." The director chuckled as he paused by a stall where several men and women of Emaian descent sat, practicing mending and weaving.

"They work?" Commander Vitus sounded surprised, his eyes wide beneath the traditional black eye paint all Lirian soldiers wore.

"Of course! It's not like being part of the breeding program takes up all their time. In between fertile cycles, the females make cloth, dye, or other textiles. The males are on loan from certain farms. They're selected for temperament and conformation, and we rotate them every few weeks, so we have a nice spread of options. Don't want underbred slaves after all."

"The slaves on loan are bred as well, though? The ones you're using in your program to sire the next generation? Not captured ones." They had the comfortable, docile look that Luce never saw in captured Emaians.

"Of course! Captured slaves rarely make good breeders. Too stressed. We've a nice stock here, so we haven't bred a captured one in…oh…four generations?" The director gestured for Luce and Commander Vitus to follow him down the rows of stalls to the far side of the barn. "Though, if we keep having to ship out more and more of our breeding stock to meet the trade demands, I suppose we'll have to resort to introducing captured slaves into our program."

"We're not there yet," Luce said as the director bowed him and Vitus into an office. "We've increased raids on the tundra. More stock will show up."

Commander Vitus nodded as well, his expression bland. He had an excellent poker face since he knew as well as Luce that supplies were dwindling on the raiding front. But that wasn't for civilians to know. Luce was here to comfort the most profitable breeding program's director and keep the lines of production flowing.

"I don't see how that will help, no offense intended, Vice General Nonus. It's not as if we can sell those savages to Tupa Gali or Araria. Only bred slaves are suitable, and they are Liria's main exported good." He rubbed at his temples. The poor man must have headaches, trying to keep up with demand. He did a commendable job of it too, and Luce was under strict orders to keep the director happy.

"We're creating a gentling program for those newly captured. It trains them in manners and household skills. We think in a few years, it'll make captured Emaians suitable for the open market. Perhaps not for Pheceans—" Luce laughed with the others. Soft-handed Pheceans couldn't handle captured Emaians. "But certainly appropriate for most buyers."

The director smiled, relief relaxing his features, and Luce returned the expression. "That's excellent news! Here gentlemen, let me make you some mint tea, and then we'll go over the expected output for next quarter."

CHAPTER 20: PHECEA

ELEVENTH MOON, 1794, KYDONIA

Eleven Years before the Proclamation

*B*iton's tutors called Kydonia the Jewel of Bathi, as though the river bisecting the continent was as dainty as a necklace from which a jewel might hang. Still, as absurd as the metaphor was, Biton could not deny that there was something jewel-like about the city from which the Leos family ruled their province. Like many cities in Leonis, the buildings were painted to ward off mildew, prevalent in the humid climate. Each stood out in bright colors, glittering in the light of metal whale-oil lamps that burned nightly in the city's wealthier areas. Great copper-coated bridges spanned waterways almost as populated as the well-cobbled roads, and the streets were hung with glass garlands in sapphire, emerald, and gold.

Few places better showed the true wealth of the Phecean Confederacy, a wealth that had always lain in the work of its craftspeople.

Hopefully, his father would allow Biton to explore. He was ten now and had Keme. Surely, he would be allowed to see more of the city? It was all he could do not to press his nose to the windows of their coach, trying to soak up as much of it as possible.

People in colorful clothes stopped to watch them as they passed, some even waving before going about their tasks. Biton smiled at all of them until—too soon— the coach rolled into the grounds of the Leos Estate, and the great copper and oak gates swung shut behind them.

Biton would have minded more if the estate was not one of the grandest places he had ever seen. He would never say it was better than the Othonos Estate in Diosion, his home city, but it was perhaps just as good. He turned full circle to see it all, taking in walls and towers of rich, red stone and doors and windows accented in hammered bronze. When he bumped into his mother, Iris Mavros looked down with one eyebrow raised, her expression weary from travel. He *knew* that she would get on to him for his overzealousness.

"Well?" she said, her voice more amused than stern. "Off you go then. Explore. But Biton, stay within the Estate walls, and if I hear that you have disturbed the residents, animals, or slaves of this estate, you will be kept in our rooms the remainder of this visit."

"Yes, mama!" Biton called his response over his shoulder, already dashing away.

Danae

Most Council children weren't allowed to attend the annual Council meeting until they were at least nine—usually ten— but Danae wasn't *most* children. She was the sole daughter of Arsenio and Andromyda Othonos, who sat on the Council as one of the five ruling families of the Phecean Confederacy. As their only child, Danae would one day inherit the council seats and their responsibilities. So, despite being eight years old, she was brought along. This year it was hosted in the Leos family territory, and Danae was determined to prove herself as valuable and mature as the other children.

Twisting the hem of her vest, Danae lingered by her father's side well after the other children had been dismissed from the breakfast. Talks wouldn't start until luncheon since some families had yet to arrive. The Othonos, of course, came two days early, as it was her father's habit to enjoy the city before getting to business.

Quiet as a shadow and lingering nearly as close as one, Danae was still there when her father stopped mid-ramble on the taxation concerns recently brought up by the glassblower's guild. He bumped into Danae and looked down in surprise, his brow raising and a smile touching his lips.

"Danae, my darling. You don't have to stay for all this. I know it's boring." He brought his hand down to run over her fluffy hair, teasing his fingers through it to make her curls stand even more on end. Andromyda fussed that he ruined her hair, but Arsenio always insisted he loved her too much to let her have perfectly controlled locks. Danae liked the affection and didn't mind having a halo of sandy brown curls. Today though, she did wish he hadn't ruined it so early on.

"I don't mind, father," she whispered, uncomfortable with the number of adult eyes on her.

"Shoo. Go play." He patted her back as he pressed her away from his side, and Danae couldn't bring herself to beg or cling to his leg as she might have done in the past.

Dismissed and alone, Danae wandered the halls of the Leos estates. She could hear the echoes of children playing, but she had no idea where they could be. Instead of hunting them down, Danae occupied herself by studying the art placed at intervals down the hallways.

While the Othonos family boasted a fine collection of sculptures, paintings, glass pieces, and topiary, the Leos also displayed indoor fountains and windchimes hanging in windows. It was a feast for the senses, and Danae quickly became absorbed with discovering each one.

It was a surprise when the call went out for luncheon. The adults would dine in the meeting hall, eating and discussing politics and the state of Phecea, but the children were being served a picnic that afternoon. Spring was mild in the Kydonian valley, and once summer set in, no one wanted to be out in the frequent rain. These were some of the last good days of sunshine.

Danae found her way down to the lower halls and the glass doors leading to the patio and back lawn. Trees bloomed fragrant flowers, though some fell in a gust of wind. A slave fetched her cloak and then helped her into it.

Children gathered on the blankets, chattering and sitting in little clusters of threes and fours. Most knew each other well already. Some were siblings or cousins. Othonos was a proud family, but its branches were slim.

Danae swallowed and trotted down the patio steps, standing on the edge of one of the blankets. Those gathered there didn't notice when she approached or say anything as she silently sat down on the corner.

"*Of course*, I know how to eat Ingolan food! Only a *baby* wouldn't know how." A large boy boasted, lifting the food in question with a strange tool. It looked like he had harpooned the dripping dumpling, and yet he managed not to ruin his fine red cloak.

Danae glanced down. The meal before them didn't have grains or flatbread to pick the food up with. She didn't even see deep-set spoons for ladling sauces. Would she embarrass herself in front of the older children by proving she didn't know how to eat in the international style? Dread filled her belly, and Danae reached for a cup of tea. At least she could drink that safely without making a fool of herself.

The tea was a frothy green color and tasted like grass, but she made an effort not to grimace or pull a face. Everyone else was drinking it as if it were some great delicacy! Well, almost everyone.

One of the others stared at Danae. They were perhaps two years her senior but had delicate features and wore brightly colored silks that made it difficult to tell whether they were a boy or girl. "You actually *like* this?" they asked, "But it's—it's *green*. The dumplings are *much* better." They picked one up with their fingers and stuffed it in their mouth.

The boy who had been so proud of his ability to eat them correctly sneered. "You're not doing it right."

"I'm eating them how I eat. You can copy the Ingolans if you want, but *I'm* a Phecean, and I don't see why I shouldn't do as I like."

Danae watched the exchange with a mixture of discomfort and amazement. The silk-clad child was happy to stand out, be noticed, and be 'wrong.' They were so *confident*, and she drank gross tea so she wouldn't look ignorant. Everyone else was using the little pitchfork.

Four dumplings in, the silken child didn't show signs of embarrassment. The grouchy boy turned away, muttering about low-born people, and Danae quickly popped a dumpling in her mouth. No one was looking.

A startlingly sweet and spicy filling burst over her tongue despite the bland look of the things. With another careful scan of the group, she picked up one more before anyone could see her faux pas. When she reached for her third, Danae's hand collided with another, and she yanked it back. Her eyes stuck on slender, bejeweled fingers and followed the progress up their arm to find the pretty rebel.

"Apologies," she murmured politely, sticking her hand behind her back to hide that she had been eating with it in the first place.

They just grinned, showing two rows of small, white teeth, perfect but for a chip missing from one of the large ones in front. Another of the dumplings was in their fingers. "My name's Biton. What's yours?"

She watched Biton for a moment longer, trying to place the name, but without a family tied to it, Biton was not enough information.

"Danae. Danae Othonos."

"You're just as Phecean as me!" Biton said, mumbling around a mouthful. "Which is the best thing you can be, of course."

A few other children glanced up at this, and one small boy dropped his fork and grabbed a dumpling, shoving it in his mouth almost defiantly. He choked and Biton laughed, though he—it must be he with a name like Biton— thumped the smaller boy on the back good-naturedly.

"I found a secret ruin today." Biton's face had gone suddenly solemn. "It must be thousands of years old—maybe even *haunted*. Wanna see?"

"Haunted?" She wasn't sure if she believed in ghosts or spirits, but the risk that they were real made her hesitate. The others seemed amazed by this news, not afraid. "Wh-where?"

"I can't tell you. It's an arduous journey—probably like an *hour* away! And only I know the secret path."

"Ummmm." She postponed answering by chewing. If she said no, she'd be left out *again*. If she said yes, she might have to go into a haunted ruin. And that didn't sound like any fun! "I... guess?"

Biton nodded sagely as though this were a mission of the greatest importance. "Everyone brave enough to go has to eat two— no *three* more dumplings! Because you never know how long a quest will take. And take a sip of the magical green potion prepared for us. It'll keep you from being lulled asleep by spirits."

Biton screwed up his face and forced himself to take a big gulp of the tea, eyes watering as he swallowed it. Some others did, too, though few looked as unhappy about it as he did.

"I'll be your fearless leader, Dasan, after the girl who rode a hawk to the sun, and you can pick names if you want."

Immediately, squabbling broke out. The boy who had known how to use the Tupa Galan utensils wanted to have the same name as another boy— Avel, like the Phecean soldier who had sailed north across the sea and put to sleep the great sea monster he found there. "Look," Biton said, too eager to leave to wait for them to resolve it, "You can be Av, and you El so that you're both named after him. Let's go! We have a long journey ahead of us."

Danae debated which name to use, but all her favorite historical and fantasy figures were quickly claimed. Still, Biton's excitement was contagious, and he was grinning down at her, eager.

"I'll just be Danae," she finally announced, slipping her hand into his and letting him haul her to her feet.

Biton

"Danae and Dasan, off to the Hidden City. That has a nice ring, don't you think?" Biton grinned and waved at the others. "Come on, this way!"

He led them around the estate garden, careful to jump only on every other paving stone since the middle ones were *always* trapped, to a place where there was a little space between two hedges.

"From here on, we have to be *really* quiet," he whispered, pressing a finger to his lips. "The approach to the ancient city is guarded by Lirian cultists!" Biton's eyes went wide, and he made a show of peering through the bushes where several men in Leonis livery trained in fenced areas, some sparring and others practicing archery.

Biton wiggled through the hedges and ran to hide behind a small building between two of the largest fields, waving energetically at the little troop. When they came, breathless and pink-faced, he led them off again, dashing to the safety of the estate walls, where they tiptoed along until they reached the shade behind the stables.

"Alright, we're almost there," Biton whispered, breathless. "Are you ready for the last part of our quest?"

The group circled around Biton, nodding, except for Danae Othonos, who was a beat behind everyone else. Somewhere along the line, she had picked up several twigs and leaves in her hair, and the knees of her leggings were grass-stained.

"What if we're caught by the Lirians?" Av and El asked.

"What if we need to go potty?!" said a smaller boy with dark eyes and freckled skin. The others snickered, but all fell quiet, watching Biton weave his spell.

"If you're got by the Lirians, you *must* swear on your life that you'll never tell them what our mission was—even if you get tortured, or they take away all your nice clothes or make you eat rotten food."

Av nodded, but El's eyes went even wider. "But I don't want to wear bad clothes and eat bad food."

Biton placed his hand on the taller boy's shoulder. "It's for your country, El."

After a few moments in the shade, they were off again, careening around the garden's edge until the old gardener's shed was in sight.

"There it is," Biton whispered, huddled with the others beneath the hedges. "How should we get past the monsters guarding it?"

"Run at them!" Av said, his voice rising. El shushed him.

"Let's be sneaky!" the littlest boy said

"What do you think, Danae?" Biton turned towards her, taking in her slightly disgruntled appearance. He didn't want her to feel left out or like she wasn't important to the game.

Her eyes grew wide with terror as everyone turned to look at her, ready for her suggestion. "Um—Couldn't we—just..." she trailed off, looking towards the invisible monsters guarding the shed. As if she could really see them there. "Maybe they want to make friends?"

El sneered. "You can't make friends with monsters! Everyone knows that."

Biton looked solemnly at the circle of children. "You saw how many Lirians were here! What if they attacked? We *need* the monsters on our side. Do you see them sleeping there? One's a two-headed chimera, and the other is a flaming hawk on fire from her trip to the sun. They would protect us from the Lirians if only someone was brave enough to befriend them." Biton turned his gaze to Danae. "Will you do it, Danae? For the sake of the Phecean Confederacy and all your friends and family?"

Danae looked past him at the shed and squared her shoulders, hands coming to smooth the front of her vest, even going so far as to try and flatten her puffy hair. "Very well," she said, voice quivering. "For Phecea."

She stepped carefully into the open, Biton crossing his fingers as she snuck toward the door. When he saw the gardener coming up behind her, his heart sank. Mother had told him not to get in the way.

Danae's gaze was locked on the door, and she didn't see the gardener until it was too late. She shrieked, and the others took off, not wanting to get caught being somewhere they oughtn't.

"What are you doing here?" the gardener asked, tone severe. Despite her attempts at bravery, Danae dissolved into tears and ran. "Wait!"

Biton ran after her, pumping his legs to keep close enough that he didn't lose her in the maze of hedges. By all order, she was fast, but he was determined to catch up. "Danae, wait! It's alright! We escaped!" It took a while, but she slowed eventually, and then he came forward and wrapped his skinny arms around her little shoulders. "Don't cry, Danae."

She tensed at his touch but turned into the embrace, hiding her face against his silk shirt. "I ruined the game!" Her voice was breathy as she panted from the run, and when she pulled back to look up at Biton, her eyes were swollen and red. Tears streaked through the grime on her face.

"You did exactly right," Biton said, assuming his story voice again. "That was the Lirian Imperator! We weren't ready to battle him yet, but because you were smart enough to run away, we can live to fight another day!"

"Really?"

"Really! And your idea to befriend the monsters was very brave."

"You think so?" Danae stepped back, hastily wiping at her tears. Already she had left smudges on his silk shirt. Not that he cared. "Won't the others think I'm a baby for crying and running? I'm only eight.... " Danae dropped her voice. "Maybe I *am* a baby...."

"Nah, you're brave! And who cares what the others say? You're Danae Othonos and you escaped the Imperator at eight years old!"

Biton wasn't sure why he wanted her to be happy again so badly—maybe it was because she was the youngest and the quietest of the group or because she reminded him of his little sisters. She had stopped crying, though, and that was good. "Want to go get some sweets from the kitchen?"

A watery smile crossed her face, and Danae nodded enthusiastically. "Are we allowed?" Her eyes had an almost adventurous glint, and she took his hand with an encouraging squeeze. They could have another adventure.

"Probably not," Biton said. "The Lirians want to guard everything nice and keep it only for themselves, but Danae and Dasan can get through together!"

Off they went again, racing across the grounds.

CHAPTER 21: RHOSAN

FIFTH MOON, 1797, CWM OR

Eight Years before the Proclamation

*B*lood spattered the packed-earth floors of the arena, droplets of the stuff turning the red-brown dirt darker. Still, it wasn't as much as it might have been, not enough to have come from a corpse or serious injury. It wasn't even enough blood to warrant notice, but Dyfan was within arm's reach of one spatter, and it kept catching his eye.

Wynn spat mouthfuls of the stuff. It was his first fight since Victor Gruffyd had coughed up enough coin to enter the man in proper training—three days a week, three weeks of the moon cycle, for more than a year. It seemed Victor Gruffyd was determined to make a real fighter out of Wynn; likewise, Wynn was determined to try.

The training was paying off. The fight had lasted three minutes, and Wynn hadn't fallen. Sure, his brow was split and his mouth bloody, but his opponent was marked too. They exchanged blows, grappled with each other, and neither was tossed from the ring. Neither had fallen or been severely injured.

It was a fair match, and something tight within Dyfan's belly loosened an inch. There was no pleasure in watching a lesser man be beaten by a better fighter. Dyfan leaned forward against the bars of his cell, the window a view into the arena.

Three moons back, Victor Eurig paid for Dyfan to have one of the windowed cells leaning over the pits. The view, he had murmured to Dyfan in secret, would also give Dyfan an additional advantage; he could watch his opponents to learn their strengths and weaknesses. He usually enjoyed the view, though it grew tiresome at times to always be watching the matches.

Now, his gaze steadily followed as Cadel charged forward, head down. He rammed into Wynn's belly and wrapped his arms about the shorter man's torso. Wynn struck Cadel's back, delivering a volley of blows that thumped loudly over their panting breaths. Cadel ignored the hits and jammed his fist against Wynn's side, digging his shoulder in as he continued plowing forward. He would simply knock Wynn from the ring.

Dyfan had seen Cadel use the move before, distracting another fighter with attacks to their side while he tried to shove him out of the ring. They were of the same weight, and while Cadel had more experience, Wynn was younger and in better shape.

With blood and sweat streaking their bare upper bodies, Wynn finally wrenched himself free, stepping aside to let Cadel plummet. Slick, Cadel couldn't stop himself from hitting the earth and scrambled to regain his feet.

Wynn darted forward, and as Cadel rolled to his back, Wynn was there. He brought up a fist. Without the hesitation he sometimes showed in training, he slammed it into Cadel's jaw. Cadel's eyes fluttered and rolled back into his head.

The few onlookers hooted, and the training master announced that Wynn was the winner. Not a Victor. Defeated were never proclaimed Victors, but they could win in the pits. They could earn certain titles, the most respected of which was Contender.

Victor Gruffyd's face was visible in the mass of onlookers, red with triumph and pleasure as people handed over pieces of gold. No one outside the arena knew how hard Wynn trained. The odds were stacked against him, and he had made Victor Gruffyd a nice fistful of gold.

Dyfan watched a moment longer, then turned away. He was glad it had been a good fight. He didn't know if he considered Wynn a familiar or not. Sometimes they would sit next to the gate and eat their meals. Sometimes they would talk, though not much and never of their lives or Wynn's life before. Anytime they got close to something too important, too big, Dyfan would stop speaking. He didn't like how it made his mind whirl or his stomach clench. It was useless to bring up things that made him feel so... uncomfortable.

Wynn was one of the few Defeated who didn't seem afraid of him. At least not openly so. And that was nice. Sometimes. Being too companionable with other Defeated in the pits was never a good idea. For now, it seemed unlikely that Wynn would ever have to fight Dyfan, but one day they might. And it was harder to fight someone you shared bread with and knew had a 'Before.'

Settling on the cot in the corner of his cell, Dyfan closed his eyes. Maybe he could nap some before his own matches that afternoon.

Wynn

Victor Gruffyd didn't show up again until hours after the fight though he had been right there when it was over. It was afternoon, the sun just passed its zenith, and though it wasn't summer yet, Wynn was hot. He leaned against the rough wall outside the pits watching as Gruffyd stumbled up the path from the compound's gates, his footsteps sloppy and uncertain. He slung an arm about Wynn's neck as if they were old friends and pulled him in close, wafts of alcohol-soured breath barraging Wynn's face.

"I won back all that I spent on you and more!" he said in a whisper that was too loud to really deserve the name. "Such a good boy!" He jostled Wynn in a semblance of a hug and leaned against him, heavy. "What do you want as your reward, eh? Extra rations for the week? You have 'em!"

Dyfan strode by, led by Victor Eurig and a man who wore the white furs of a healer. Dyfan's fight had included weapons, not just fists, and he had a series of long but shallow cuts along his arms and torso.

Victor Gruffyd spotted them and hauled Wynn around as he turned to speak. Or rather, holler. "Eurig! Good matches today, eh? Good matches—" He stumbled forward, and if Wynn hadn't been there supporting his weight, he likely would have fallen. Victor Eurig and Dyfan stopped, the healer pausing as well.

"Yes. Good matches. I'm happy your… *fighter* turned out so well today." Victor Eurig's tone was subtle but implied clearly he didn't think Wynn was any prize.

"Ha! Didn't I tell you? That girl of mine dropped his second babe few moons back," Victor Gruffyd gestured vaguely towards Dyfan. "A girl. Such a pity. Just a little girl."

"Well, these things are never sure, and they have female pits too. She could be a Contender in her—"

"Pah! No one bets as much on the girls." Dyfan's gaze was ice, fixed on Wynn's bruised face with nothing close to emotion showing. Victor Eurig kept silent, waiting for Victor Gruffyd to say whatever he was getting at, but the drunk man seemed to think better of it. "Maybe I should just breed you, eh, Wynn? You'd give me good boys. Make me a lot of money."

"He's only won one fight, Gruffyd. You might be seeing a little more than there really is."

"Ha! Did you see him? Hitting that man while he was down? No mercy. He's a good one. I know it."

"It was mercy." Wynn looked up at the voice—rough and gravely and so rarely heard. Dyfan even seemed a bit surprised that he had spoken.

"What?" Victor Gruffyd asked, his tone bordering on belligerent.

"To end the fight swiftly. It's mercy," Dyfan said.

"You tryin' to insult me?" Gruffyd's ruddy face darkened to purple. "Eurig, your stud is trying to tell me I have a soft fighter."

Victor Eurig glanced at Dyfan. He didn't look afraid or apologetic. "I'm sorry, Gruffyd. You know how these prized studs can be. Dangerous and willful. I'll have him whipped for the offense, I assure you."

That seemed to settle Gruffyd's feathers. Victor Eurig, Dyfan, and the healing man continued on their way.

"Mercy. Pah. That boy don't know nothing about mercy. Oh well. I hear he's insane. A lot of those arena-bred ones are. But you!!" He shook Wynn's shoulder. "You're a gem! I knew it when we took you from that little spit of civilization. You just fought and refused to give up despite being so terrible. I knew you'd be a winner."

Wynn's eyes were still on Dyfan's back as they walked away, his mind turning over the other Defeated's words.

Had he meant to be merciful when he struck Cadel? Wynn wanted to think so, wanted to believe that he had walked into that arena and saw another man, not just a body he had been told to break, an animal. In truth, he could only remember wanting it all to end. Was that mercy? Or cowardice?

Gruffyd took another step and nearly fell when his knee buckled, forcing Wynn to turn and catch him. For all that he was clumsy as a boy after his first ale, the Victor was still the most dangerous force in Wynn's life. There would always be the threat of the mines.

"Should I get a buggy, Victor?" Wynn pitched his voice to sound soothing, even as his face twisted with disgust at the man's fetid breath. In a cart, he would be less likely to vomit over Wynn's toes.

"Home?! What?" he laughed loudly. "To Ifanna? I know—I know! I'll give you my tunic and my—my hat, and you'll go instead!"

Wynn laughed as though that was an excellent joke, grimacing at the stares of bystanders. "If you'd rather take a room, I can bring word back to the estate that you had important business to attend to in the city."

Gods and God-children, how was he supposed to deal with this idiocy? Gruffyd needed nothing more than a quick plunge into icy water, but it was out of the question when he could as easily order Wynn's death as not.

"No, no, I don't want to lose the money you just won me," his words were starting to slur significantly, and his head bobbed. "Walk me home. To my compound."

It initially seemed impossible that Victor Gruffyd would make it all the way there, but with fresh air, movement, and a few gulps of water, he seemed to perk up. Soon he was walking mostly under his own power, and while he wasn't chipper, he wasn't completely falling down. They padded between the squat buildings of Cym Or, away from the Pits and all their violence.

"I was right about you, you know. Wynn. You're a winner. You know how much I spent on those stud fees for Dyfan? Too much! You could sire winners. Boys. Boys make good money—Sell for more too, you know."

Wynn couldn't make himself answer. He had a boy if he was still alive. And he'd had him with a woman he loved. He was no animal to be bred against someone he did not care for. And, yet, if he was told to do it, what then? Refusing would mean physical beatings, denial of food, or a sentence of slow execution in the mines. Could he give up his life to say no? It was not as though his life was worth very much these days.

Wynn glanced at Gruffyd, at his cheery step and ruddy cheeks. The Victor had been speaking as though they were friends…

"I wanted a boy, once, but was never able. For the longest time, we thought it was my wife's issue, that she could not bear children, but—" He let his head hang. Wynn could not make himself apologize, but he could find sorrow to color his voice. There was plenty of it to go around. "She found another man and became pregnant with him. The village medicine woman said I will never be a sire. All I can do now is become a better fighter."

He held his breath, hoping he would not be killed for the lie. It was a gamble, of course, but perhaps it would save him from being used more than he had to.

Victor Gruffyd was quiet as they walked, presumably thinking about it before he finally chuffed Wynn on the shoulder. "I guess we don't have to tell people interested in your stud fee, eh?!"

It wasn't even time for the evening meal, but by the looks of it, Victor Gruffyd was ready for bed. He sent Wynn off with more congratulations and affectionate hugging and then teetered into the main house.

That left Wynn to find his supper in the Defeated meal hall. News had spread of his win, and other Defeated smiled or nodded in his direction. Linn even patted his cheek before sending him to collect more firewood.

It was a strange feeling to be so accepted among the Defeated for his win, as though they approved of him doing what the Victors said he ought. Perhaps they did believe their place in the world was as it should be—enough of them had been born to the life. But no creature that had been free would be able to live quietly in a cage. He would never feel completely comfortable among them.

When their quiet voices grew unbearable, Wynn left the crowded room, found his way to the edge of the Defeated quarter, and pressed his forehead to the fence. If only he had been born a dragon half-breed and so might escape into the skies.

CHAPTER 22: RHOSAN

TWELFTH MOON, 1797, CWM OR

Eight Years before the Proclamation

Snow softened Cwm Or. It hid the filth and rounded the sharp edges of stone buildings and wood houses with steep-pitched roofs. Even straggly fir trees lost their shape beneath clinging winter coats, and the hardened people of this far Northern land were bundled beneath feathery furs and thick skins.

It was a deceptive softness, Wynn thought. This was still a place ruled by Kirit's most devoted followers, and the presence of the God of War was clear in the tight faces of Defeated in the streets, following their Victors on errands. Much of the city was normal—plain even. There were blacksmiths and tanners, bakers and butchers— and yet, even these did not go unmarked by the God they served. Many bore scars, and none seemed to be without a weapon close at hand.

Wynn wondered what Dyfan would have thought if it had been him displaced into Wynn's life and not the other way around. Would he find the people of Bryntref village weak, or would he love them as Wynn had? For all his strength and ferocity, there was a softer side to Dyfan. Perhaps he would have melded much better into a quiet village life than Wynn had the roar and violence of Cwm Or.

The sleigh slid to a halt, and Wynn was pulled roughly from his musings. He sat beside Jeston on the driver's seat of a gilded sled, Victor Gruffyd's wife, Ifanna, sitting in state in the higher seat behind them. Jeston had tugged her matched pair of thick-coated gray mares to a halt before the second-largest building in Cwm Or.

Smaller only than the fighting pits, the temple stood in symmetrical brilliance, each turret widening to a heavy bulb and tapering to nothing at its peak. Pointed arches topped wide, double doors, and the brickwork was laid in a pattern of light and dark stones that were almost dizzying to look at. It was not a beautiful structure, but it was undoubtedly impressive.

Ifanna jumped down from the sleigh and slung her heavy braid over her shoulder with a derisive look. "Haven't you ever seen a Kirit Temple before? Don't just stand there and gawk! Get the barrels!"

Wynn did as he was bid, balancing one barrel against his shoulder and the other under his opposite arm. Whatever they held sloshed as he moved, their contents adding a wet slap to each step. If nothing else, training with the other fighting Defeated made him stronger. He followed Ifanna into the temple obediently, trying to resist the urge to wrinkle his nose at the great wafts of her floral perfume floating back towards him.

Inside, the temple was much like the exterior—grand and intimidating. Rich tapestries lined the stone walls, displaying likenesses of the God of War. In one, he stood upon a body, holding a flaming ax aloft. In another, he was battling a foe. Still more showed Kirit wreathed in fire or with molten rock pouring from his lips. Wynn shuddered as he passed them. Nothing good came of worshiping one God more than all the others. Each of their roles was important, and where one held undue sway, the world swung out of balance.

Ifanna didn't look back as she led the way farther into the temple, confident in knowing her obedient dog would heel. The Victors' assurance in their own superiority was so complete that none thought twice about it. She paused at one of the many altars and pricked a finger against the naked blade balanced there. Her blood dripped down the length of iron, joining the thousands of other red stains. It didn't seem the Defeated were expected to pay tribute to Kirit, as he and Jeston trailing after their mistress didn't stop and do the same.

Perhaps their servitude was tribute enough, or the Victors thought Defeated blood too poor a tribute for their God.

In the dim light afforded by oil lamps, a luxury Wynn hadn't seen in Cwm Or as even the Victors used simple candles, Ifanna's brown braid looked black, and her red-stained lips curled into a simpering smile.

She held up one hand, and they stopped. She bowed respectfully to a man in deep red robes, his bald head shining in the lamp light. "High priest Govannon."

"Victor Ifanna," he said.

"I've brought our offering for this quarter."

The priest turned to look at Wynn and Jeston and nodded approvingly.

Wynn went cold, his mind replaying the images from the tapestries lining the walls of the halls behind them. Was he going to be given as a sacrifice after the training Gruffyd was putting him through? Even now, even after he had lost everything, Wynn did not want to die.

He set down the barrels at the priest's feet when Ifanna glared at him, his forehand damp with sweat and his body shaking. If he ran now, the priests would get him, and these were no soft-bodied robe-wearers but men and women who believed themselves Kirit's finest warriors.

Ifanna recovered enough to give the high priest another half-smile half-snarl and made an elegant gesture toward Jeston, standing at Wynn's side. They set their barrel down and tried to step back, but Ifanna was too fast. She grabbed them by their arm and held them in place.

"This Defeated is a worshiper of Aryus. I thought Kirit would enjoy an Offering slated for another."

The priest bowed graciously to Ifanna as Wynn drowned in fear and shame. Of course, it wouldn't be him, not when Gruffyd still hoped to profit off him in the ring. Of course, it was calm, gentle Jeston who bore their life in unflagging equanimity in honor of their God.

Wynn should have never cast them aside.

Govannon stepped forward to examine Jeston. "Would you like to make the Offering, or shall I in your name?"

"You're the expert."

The high priest offered his hand to Ifanna. She kissed the back of it ardently before he turned to Jeston. They were tranquil as Govannon led them to the apex of the dais raised behind Wynn, the slightest tinges of a smile hovering about their lips. They were made to kneel.

"Highest Warrior, Lord of War and Strife, I make this Offering to you in the name of the Victor, Ifanna, who has become strong in might and influence among our people. May she and her husband, Gruffyd, exult as the blood they have given feeds your unimaginable power."

Govannon raised the knife, but before he could slide it across Jeston's neck, they gave him a dazzling, beatific smile and sang so that all in the temple could hear them:

"We all serve Aryus in the end!"

The knife fell, and Jeston died grinning.

The temple was silent too long, the drops of Jeston's blood ringing in the quiet, their gentle, wet splashes filling grooves set into the dais to carry the blood. Wynn watched it, stunned into non-action as it flowed away.

"Worry not, loyal Victors!" Wynn flinched at Govannon's breathless volume as he recovered from the shock of being so thwarted by a mere Defeated. "The Offering's soul is of no concern so long as his blood—"

"Their—" The word was small, just a step towards defiance, but Wynn's voice grew as he continued. "It is *their* blood you have spilled in the name of upsetting the balance!"

Govannon snarled and raised his voice even louder. "—so long as *his* blood feeds the Greatest God! Will there be another to follow him?"

"Them!" Wynn no longer could make himself quiet and small for these monsters. "You killed *THEM*!"

"Do you offer to join *him*?" Govannon held up the bloody dagger, but much to Wynn's surprise, Ifanna stepped beside him, her body partially shielding him.

"Forgive our Defeated, High Priest Govannon." Her voice was a purr. "I would offer him, but he is already in service to Kirit, whether or not he knows it. You see, he is training to become a Contender, should he prove himself worthy. A mighty fighter, as Kirit declared we all should be."

Govannon's gaze flickered over Ifanna's shoulder to Wynn. His jaw stood out in stark relief, but after a few breaths, he nodded curtly. "Get this Defeated out of our temple. Do not bring him back here, Victor Ifanna, unless it is as a tribute."

Ifanna bowed deeper than before and slipped her hand about his elbow. Even through the furs, Wynn could feel her nails, clawlike, digging into his arm. "Move," she hissed.

The eyes of the priests were on them, their bodies tense as if they were ready to attack any moment. Wynn, coward as he was, took a step.

He did not want to die.

Wynn did nothing, staying quiet as she led him out at a furious pace and ordered him into the driver's seat. He could not push the horses fast enough to please her until the temple disappeared behind them. Then, he let up to give the poor mares a chance to breathe.

Ifanna leaned forward, her movement catching his attention. She watched him with the keen focus of a hunter. "Are you simple-minded? Or simply wishing to waste my husband's coin on your training?"

The same madness that came over him in the temple rose up within Wynn like a tide of fire. "I am neither, Victor."

Ifanna's eyes widened in what Wynn suspected was shock. She'd probably never been spoken to like that by a Defeated. Perhaps by anyone. Her lips twitched. "Then what are you, *Defeated*?"

A coward.

"A man that was free too long to bow to this madness."

Whatever Ifanna had been expecting, it clearly hadn't been that. She closed her jaws so quickly her teeth clacked and settled back in her fur-covered seat.

"Carry on," she commanded. As if that were it. As if Wynn hadn't seen Jeston sacrificed like they weren't a living, breathing, thinking person. As if he hadn't just insulted her High Priest and her religion all in one.

With trembling fingers, Wynn tightened his grip on the reins and urged the mares back into a trot. It was all Wynn could do to avoid looking at Jeston's empty seat.

CHAPTER 23: THE WESTERN SEA

SEVENTH MOON, 1795, THE FLYING NIGHT

Ten Years before the Proclamation

"Again."

Iniabi pushed herself off the smooth wood of the quarterdeck and went after her staff. When she straightened, she was careful not to look toward Jaya and Cai on the other side of the deck. Hopefully, they were more interested in sparring with each other than noticing how bad she was.

Quartermaster Vlassis stood next to Iniabi's sparring partner, Iago, the old sailor's tattooed arms crossed in front of his chest. "Hurry up, girl! When we made that bargain about teaching you to fight, I didn't think I'd be spending this much time waiting for you to scrape yourself off the deck! On your feet! Attack!"

Iago raised his staff in a diagonal guard across his body, but the Tupa Galan boy looked thoroughly dubious at the idea of fighting Iniabi again. He was an easy two heads taller than she was, still long and lanky at eighteen. His jawline was well-structured beneath big seal-pup eyes with lashes longer than a girl's. He wore his brown hair in a messy knot on the back of his head so that strands fell down around his face, and he was by far the softest pirate Iniabi had met. She liked him, but she was starting to wonder if this exercise was to teach her to fight or if Vlassis hoped that kicking her ass would toughen up Iago.

Either way, Iniabi raised her weapon. *She* wasn't going to give up. No matter how many times Iago knocked her down. Their weapons met with a sharp wooden clack. Iniabi ducked beneath a swing, air whistling over the top of her head as Iago's staff ruffled her hair. Iago easily parried her response and caught her sharply on the ankle for good measure. Iniabi went down in a tangle of limbs. At least the Quartermaster had wandered off to comment on Jaya and Cai.

"Iago, what am I doing wrong?"

Iago glanced over his shoulder to ensure Vlassis couldn't hear them and gestured to Iniabi's entire body. "You're always in the wrong place at the wrong time. Instead of attacking and then darting off or continuing to attack, you just stand there. Like a rock. You don't move enough—" He cut himself off as Vlassis shouted at Jaya and Cai.

Jaya scowled beneath the newly shaved side of her head. She looked wholly untouchable. Iniabi turned back to Iago and took a deep breath, holding out a hand so that he could help her up. "So I just need to move more?"

"I mean..." Iago huffed as he helped Iniabi to her feet, dropping her hand quickly, as if it burned him to touch, and shrugged. "You also need better aim, to strike harder, and to be less predictable... But other than those things, yeah, move more."

"You're really great at this whole teaching thing," Iniabi rolled her eyes and lifted her staff in front of her chest. "Let's go again."

Iago hefted his staff one-handed and, without blinking or changing his expression at all, swung at her. Iniabi jumped back just in time, feeling the push of air as Iago's staff missed her head. Had it made contact, she would be on her ass *again*. While she regained her balance, Iago reversed his grip and struck at her knees to knock her off her feet once more.

Iniabi tumbled away, and quite suddenly, she got it. The trick wasn't to be able to block or parry each one of Iago's blows—she was too much smaller and weaker than him to manage that. Instead, she just needed to be where he wasn't striking, and she *was* more nimble. She could climb the rigging faster than anyone but the twins, Nil and

Neus, and they were the youngest people on the ship. Iniabi dodged a swipe at her shoulder, darted in, and jabbed the butt of her staff into Iago's belly. It wasn't enough to knock him down, but when he put her on the deck a few minutes later, Vlassis walked over and said, "Better, Iniabi."

And that was enough to put her in high spirits all day, even through helping Taaliah with the sails and Cook with the dishes. When she, Cai, Iago, and Jaya took over the night watch, she still felt like it was an excellent day. They walked in pairs—Iniabi and Cai, Jaya and Iago— taking turns watching from the foc'sle or moving around the deck.

"I heard we'll be putting into a new port soon," Iniabi said as she and Cai passed through the main deck. It was always a little eerily quiet after dark, all of the shouts and bustle of the day gone to sleep. There was nothing but the creak of ropes and timbers, the odd squeak of a lantern swinging on its hook. It was enough to drive anyone to fill the silence.

"We're *always* putting into port," Cai muttered, scratching at a patch of hair she supposed was meant to be a beard. It was pretty barren, but Iniabi found the thick hair on northern men's faces strange anyway. The Emai didn't grow so much facial hair.

"Yes, but it isn't Ifratem or Bikkisi this time." The Lirian name for Angillik still felt strange in Iniabi's mouth, but the rest of the crew didn't know it as Angillik. "We're going to stop in Emaian lands— a town called Muscana."

"Emaians have *towns?*"

Iniabi shoved him. "Where did you think they lived, numbskull? In ice castles below the ground?" Teasing aside, it had shocked Iniabi to learn how little most people knew of the Emai, though she supposed it shouldn't have. The Emai knew little of other lands and went out of their way to avoid outsiders. Years of being taken as slaves would do that to a people.

"My mama always said your type popped up from little warrens in the ground like rabbits."

"That's cause your mama is a northern-born, pirate-loving whore who packed you onto a ship as soon as you were tall enough to walk."

Iniabi scowled at him. "Which just shows how little she knows about the Emai."

Cai stiffened. "Who told you that about my mama?"

Jaya had, but there was no way Iniabi was going to rat her out. Cai looked mad, like she had said something that upset him. Well, fine then. He'd said something that pissed her off too. "Anyone can tell just by looking at you!"

"Better a whore's son than a slaver's daughter, I'd say."

Iniabi swung at him, fury bubbling up when he dodged the blow. "Fuck you, and that nasty, scraggly thing on your chin you keep pretending is a beard!"

"You're one to talk! You call those tits?"

Iniabi flung herself at him like one of the ship's cats that lived belowdecks, all bristles and claws. She scratched his face and pulled his hair, and he landed two hard punches in her gut that left her gasping for breath.

An iron grip pulled her back. Iniabi struggled, teeth bared, trying to return to her foe, and a voice boomed over her head. "Enough!"

Iniabi shrank down like a struck dog, looking up into the scarred face of the ship's bosun. Taaliah was probably the most formidable pirate on board, except perhaps, the captain. Her full lips were pressed into a thin line in anger, and she gestured one-handed at Iago to douse them both in a bucket of seawater. Iniabi gasped at the shock of cold but was secretly glad that Cai seemed even more uncomfortable.

"*I'll* handle this." The captain's voice shocked them all into momentary stillness– she and Cai in their sopping clothes, Iago with his bucket in the air, and the bosun with her arms crossed over her chest. The captain wanted to address the simple matter of a spat between younger crewmates? It was unheard of.

Beside Iniabi, Cai began to shiver.

Taaliah turned to the captain. "Surely, this is too menial a problem to trouble yourself with, Captain? I wouldn't dare intrude on your time."

"Then stop wasting it now. Cai, Iniabi, come with me."

CHAPTER 24: THE WESTERN SEA

SEVENTH MOON, 1795, THE FLYING NIGHT

Ten Years before the Proclamation

Iniabi followed Cai into the captain's quarters, too nervous to take in the richness or the clutter. She was out of options. Iniabi had given Captain Ira the poison when it seemed her only other choice was to die at sea. What could she say now if the captain decided she no longer wanted Iniabi aboard? She had nothing else to give, and she had to give something. The world required.

Iniabi wiped sweating palms on her trousers and tried to appear calm as the captain sat behind her desk to stare at them both.

"Cai, you've been on my ship the longest. What is the punishment for fighting?"

"Scrubbing the decks, cleaning the bilge, or breaming what crusties we can reach, Captain." He spoke clearly, but Iniabi thought she could detect the tremor in his voice. He ought to know the punishment, given how many brawls he'd gotten himself into since Iniabi came aboard.

It had been stupid of her to let him pull her into one.

Captain Ira nodded slowly, her gaze drifting between Iniabi and Cai. When she stared at Iniabi, the Emaian girl felt her skin go tight. Would the punishments be worse for her? Cai was a northerner like the captain. There was no telling what might be in store for a half-Emaian bastard girl.

"What is your favorite chore, Cai?"

The question seemed to throw him off, and he fidgeted suddenly, shifting his weight. He mumbled his answer uncertainly. "Kitchen duty."

"I see. Very well. Cai, since you insist on getting into squabbles like a child, I will presume you are too young to be left unattended. For the next three moons, you will have kitchen duty whenever you are not performing your other tasks. Any time that might have been categorized as free shall now belong to the kitchen. Do you understand?"

"Yes, captain." Iniabi couldn't see his face, but he sounded resigned.

"Iniabi, you will scrub the deck for the next week." Captain Ira straightened as if she were about to dismiss them, scratching idly at the back of one hand. The movement caught Iniabi's attention as she mumbled her understanding and turned to go. Cai shot her a dirty look, but what did she care? It was his own stinking fault, getting into so many fights. "Iniabi, stay here."

Iniabi froze, all the relief from the captain's easy dismissal dissolving like sea fog in the summer. Cai's dirty look only darkened, but she would have given a ship's worth of gold to leave with him. She turned slowly, her shoulders tense around her ears. "Yes, captain?"

The taller woman stood up from her place behind the desk and walked around the front of it, scratching at her hand once more. "I need you to get more of the Emaian medicine you had when you first came aboard."

Iniabi went cold. There had been almost six dozen doses of poison when she was taken aboard— enough for the brothel in Angillik to go for a few weeks without needing more. She'd never heard of anyone taking so much—not even the slavers were so interested in killing themselves for a few dreams.

She hadn't told the captain it could kill.

"You... you took them all, Captain?"

"What? No. But I'll be running low soon enough. Where do we need to go so you can get more?" Captain Ira's eyes weren't red-rimmed as some would be, and though she had the intensity of a fox listening for snow-buried mice, she wasn't rambling or rail thin. Iniabi relaxed. The captain wasn't going to die from taking too much poison yet, but she obviously didn't understand the limits.

What would the crew do if they knew she had given their captain poison? There was just as much danger in her running out as in her taking too much. Poison had the captain now, and Iniabi would have to keep it from killing her if she wanted to live much longer.

"If you take too much of it too quickly, the medicine will not work effectively. You could stop seeing dreams and start seeing nightmares, or the dream world could follow you into your waking hours."

The older woman narrowed her eyes. "Why didn't you tell me this before? How much is too much?"

"I believed you meant only to sell it, Captain. How often are you taking it?"

She broke her stare, looking away. "Half of it is gone. I started with very little, but lately... Lately, the dreams have been compelling."

If the captain truly had half the doses, she could make it last another couple of moons at least. Maybe even a little more. "Would you like me to help you? To make sure the dreams stay as sharp and lovely as possible?"

"How?" The captain glanced up and then away again, like a child almost. Uncertain.

"Just by making sure you get the exact dose you need. It is medicine, after all, something that should be handled with care. You could have it three times a week, easily."

The captain stood still for a long moment and then let out a big breath. She turned to a box on her desk, just a simple thing with waves carved into the sides. She ran her fingers over the lid and then across the lock, keeping it shut. Her touch was slow, almost delicate, like a mother touching a babe's cheek. Her addiction to the stuff was further along than Iniabi had ever seen. Most killed themselves quickly by indulging too much and then doing without. What would taking a small amount over a long time even do to a person?

After a final stroke, the captain reached into her blouse and pulled out a chain. It held a key. She pulled the chain over her neck but stood holding it in her palm, not letting it go. "How did you learn to make this medicine, anyway?"

Iniabi hesitated. Would the captain trust her more or less to know the truth? "My mother, Manaba, was an Emaian medicine woman. I trained with her in the arts of healing and dreams."

"Before you were made into a slave?"

"Yes, Captain. I was taken at fifteen," she lied, "and will reach my eighteenth year in a couple moons. I was taken after I learned much of my Aada's ways."

Captain Ira closed her fingers around the chain and its key, hand partially raised to Iniabi but still lingering just out of reach. "Aada?"

"Our word for mother." Iniabi resisted the urge to snatch the key out of the other woman's grasp.

"Ah. Very well." Captain Ira reached out, and Iniabi suppressed a sigh of relief as the key fell into her palm.

"We will need to attain more from Emaian tribes, Captain. I can make it given rich tidepools and an open space where I might build a hot fire, but it would be dangerous aboard the ship. Best to get it in trade. The Emaians will want weapons, grain, or kava in exchange."

Instead of looking at her, the captain watched Iniabi's hand, where she still held the key. Iniabi tucked it into one of her pockets, out of sight. That seemed to break the spell. Captain Ira blinked and smiled at Iniabi.

"Then send Taaliah to me. I want us in Muscana in record time."

CHAPTER 25: LIRIA

TENTH MOON, 1795, EGARA

Ten Years before the Proclamation

Spring breezes drifted through the city's southwestern quarter and through the Nonus house windows. They carried white-pink petals and the scents of ranunculus flowers. It gave Luce's home an almost romantic air, and he instructed the servants, with Camilla's permission, not to sweep them up. Though his home would seem less organized, he thought the signs of spring were worth it. After all, an early spring would mean easier sailing conditions for his men and safer passage to the Emaian territories.

Though it seemed that while Luce thought of tactics and raids and safe waters, Camilla thought of more political maneuvers. "It's time to select a bride for your son," she announced as she delivered his afternoon tea. Mint.

"Really? Tulio isn't even three yet; I think that's a touch young to be thinking about marriage, don't you?" Luce lifted his cup to inhale the fragrant steam, enjoying the exasperated look Camilla gave him. Tulio had been their surprise baby, arriving so stealthily that Camilla had been nearly halfway through with the pregnancy before she knew she was even with child. After all, she was getting older, and it seemed unlikely they would have more children.

And Luce had been happy with that. Ignatious, Sabina, and his second daughter, Cassia, were more than enough to make him proud. But, if he was candid, he had dearly wanted another son, one he could have a larger part in raising. Luce had been a lowly soldier and gone frequently when Ignatious was young. With Tulio, Luce managed to stay in Liria the entirety of his infanthood, and it seemed likely that would be the same for his toddler and child years.

"Not *that* son, my love. Ignatious is fifteen now." She made a gesture that Luce knew meant he ought to keep drinking, so he obeyed. Fifteen? How could his firstborn already be fifteen? Time couldn't have passed so quickly.

"That seems young to me."

"It's on the young side of marriage arrangements, but not unheard of," Camilla propped herself on Luce's desk, long-lashed gaze steady on his face. He knew that look too. She had a plan.

"Alright, then why push to find him a bride so early?"

Camilla smiled, and Luce felt a swelling of pride. She approved of his asking. "Because we want to be the first to follow the Imperator's trend."

"Trend? Do you mean the alliance with Tupa Gali?" Just that winter, the Imperator had taken a Tupa Galan Princess as his bride. As it had seemed he would never marry again after the death of his first wife, the nation was overjoyed at the promise of a strong succession—people still spoke about the bride's riches, the gold-spun gown, and the jewels in her hair. Besides, by tying Liria to Tupa Gali, trade from the fertile jungle lands would be secure. It had been a brilliant move for the increased strength of Liria.

"Of course, I do. If we have Ignatious marry a Tupa Galan girl, like the Imperator did, we will be acknowledging his alliance and create one of our own."

Luce frowned. "The Tupa Gali don't have a class system the way we do. They're not very cultured or civilized." Even *if* the Tupa Galans possessed inordinate wealth. He had always imagined his son marrying into noble bloodlines like he had.

Camilla shook her head, eyes narrowing. "Culture and class we can help her acquire. Besides, while they are not as proud a country, it was good enough for the Imperator, and they do have very wealthy merchants and tradespeople. I'm certain we can find someone suitable."

He knew he ought to concede to Camilla's practicality, as she understood the workings of society better than he did, but still, Luce hesitated. He had married the love of his life, the most beautiful, tenacious, and well-bred girl in all of Liria. Was it really fair to ask Ignatious not only to marry a complete stranger but one without Lirian blood?

Their children would be half Tupa Galan…

Camilla's hand came to rest on his shoulder, drawing him from his musings. "Beauty resides in all of Illygad, my love, not just Liria. I am certain Ignatious can be happy with an untraditional bride, and it will surely raise the notoriety of this family."

She was right. He smiled and put his tea down to cover her hand with his.

CHAPTER 26: PHECEA

SECOND MOON, 1797, DIOSION

Seven Years before the Proclamation

The formal tunic Andromyda presented to Danae was the most glamorous thing she had ever worn. It was also the most hazardous. The tunic's hem fell nearly to her ankles, and the leggings were woven of a slick linen material that made her legs slip past each other too fast. The length of her tunic made her worry every step that she would trip or rip the hem, but it was traditional court garb, and her mother expected her to wear it.

She didn't look glorious. Her mother assured her that her odd-angled limbs and overly large hair would smooth out into sinewy grace like her father, but for the time being, Danae was all elbows and frizz. The peach color of the court tunic *was* flattering to her caramel skin and the little yellow gems sewn into the neckline and cuffs whispered as she walked.

She was in her first formal outfit because she was finally old enough for etiquette classes. A mistress of fashion and rules would teach her and all other council members' children in Diosion how to behave like a proper Phecean. They would be exposed to the arts and encouraged to dabble wherever their passions lay. They would be taught to walk, dance, eat, and above all else, to be perfect.

Danae knew she needed as much help as she could get. She had been a short child, but some time between her ninth and tenth birthday she grew a good six inches. Now, she felt like a giant on stilts, prone to knocking things over.

As the coach pulled up to the hall used for court celebrations and gatherings, Danae swallowed her fear. The etiquette mistress would instruct here between council events. Other children of nobility were already present. Some new, like her, others older kids who had been attending classes for years.

Everyone wore bright colors: silks, gems, hats, and feathers. It was all very ostentatious. Danae wondered if her bejeweled tunic was enough. A slave helped her out of the coach, and Danae picked up her tunic gingerly, walking carefully to avoid ruin.

The inside of the hall was surprisingly plain. The walls were pale blue and without decoration. She supposed it was kept blank between events like a canvas waiting for an artist to apply detail. It was spacious, easily accommodating the ten children milling about.

Hanging back by a wall, Danae scanned for anyone she knew, but none were immediate friends. Her palms were sweating, and Danae looked down, wondering if she should wipe them on her tunic or find a handkerchief. There were tables laden with snacks and drinks across the way, and it seemed likely there would be something to dry her perspiring palms. She had just about made up her mind to try anyway when someone caught her eye.

The boy was the prettiest thing she'd seen in years. He wore red silk trousers and a black silk vest, the lapel studded with garnets, and even in a sea of color and glamor, he was the height of beauty.

Danae stared openly as he strode past, noticing the ease of it despite the confining formal tunic he wore. She knew she was gaping when the boy turned to face her.

"You!" she cried, then hastened to lower her voice. Shouting was rude. Even excited shouting. Of course, she knew Biton Marvos. His father was the province treasurer, and he handled things for her parents as well. They'd been friendly in the past, and it was a relief to think she might have a familiar companion here.

Biton smiled warmly, his almond eyes crinkling despite the

volume of her cry. He bowed with a grace that she envied and straightened with a greeting. "Danae Othonos, a pleasure, as always."

He might have said more, she thought, but then a sharp female voice cut through the noise. "Is everyone present? Good. Let us begin. Today we will focus on greetings, your first display of etiquette."

The woman's voice droned on, slightly grating in a way that made it difficult to pay attention to. Still, Danae was doing her best—she did so *want* to be elegant—until she caught sight of Biton.

He stood slightly behind the teacher so that any time she began a demonstration, he could perform it in an exaggerated fashion, his expression held purposefully sorrowful and his arms thrown out dramatically. He flopped forward in a jester's bow, and several students erupted in giggles.

Danae didn't know how to react. It was funny, but surely the severe Mistress of Etiquette would not appreciate his levity? Occasionally, the woman looked Biton's way but never caught him being a tease. When she was done explaining, she paired them off.

Her partner was not Biton, unfortunately, but a beautiful girl with shiny, straight black hair and long-lashed eyes. Danae suspected they were the same age, but Danae was half a head taller. How could she have gone from runt to giant in only two summers?!

Danae mimicked the bows and curtsies, but each time she found Mistress Afin, who had finally introduced herself, gazing at her, it was disapproving.

"Don't stiffen your neck like that. Be elegant. Smooth. Like water flowing over stones." She bowed, neck curving along with her spine. Danae tried again, and the Mistress only nodded, lips tight.

Biton looked like a boneless cat. If a boneless cat could exude grace. He caught her looking and winked. Danae felt her face turning ruddy, and she turned back to her partner, who, while not Biton, was at least closer to water over stones than she was.

"Othonos! Lower those shoulders!" Mistress Afin called from the other side of the room. *She must have eyes in the back of her head*, Danae thought, *to have caught me while her back was turned.*

For all she tried, the next few lessons were no better. Danae was simply too long. She had more height than she knew what to do with, and it made her clumsy. She could never seem to remember to keep her shoulders down and her neck relaxed *and* slide the correct foot out all at the same time. And no matter how many times she told herself to "be like water," she didn't once begin to feel any smoother.

Biton, of course, seemed to have no issue at all, even though he played around rather than listening while the instructor explained the finer points of etiquette. By the end of the third day, she half-wanted to shake him when he came to speak to her after another frustrating lesson. It wasn't fair that he could be so careless and still do well.

"Danae, do you want to stay late with me today?" As always, he looked dashing, today in deep blue and gray silks that made his dark eyes seem stormy. His friendly face was just as open as ever.

"Stay late? I can't wait to escape," she said, watching as their fellows flooded past, waving and calling goodbye to Biton. Not to her. He was very popular. Probably because of how dashing and funny he was. She'd run her hands through her hair so much it looked like a bird had built a nest on her head. Sighing because it was a bit rude to make that remark, Danae turned towards Biton. "Apologies. Why are you staying late?"

"Well, I thought you might like to practice with me, though if you'd rather not, I understand." He phrased the offer almost as though she would be doing a favor for him, but it was a thin veil.

Danae stared up at Biton for a long moment. She was taller than most girls, even the older ones, but he had a few inches on her.

Danae only wanted to jump in her coach, ride home, and rest her aching back, but Biton was offering her an audience-free opportunity to improve. Danae waved her driver off. His expression didn't change as he looped back around to wait, and Danae turned to Biton.

"Alright. Let the torture begin."

⇑ ⇑ ⇑

Third Moon, 1797, Diosion

The Othonos colors were white and gold. While the family wasn't prone to slathering their sigil everywhere, as some nobility did, their estate subtly nodded to their prestigious bloodline. The pavers making up the drive to the front of the estate were cream, despite how difficult it was to keep them that way, and the gate was painted gold. The flowers along the stucco manor's sides were a gay yellow, and the trees lining the drive bloomed white.

The knocker on the door was gold. Real gold. Of course, the Othonos were wealthy, a product of their long standing as one of Phecea's ruling families. A slave showed Biton into a waiting room, leaving him a tray of cold drinks and pastries seasoned with cardamom and anise. He didn't have to wait long before a scurrying of feet announced Danae. She held out her long court tunic precariously, her movements unnatural and stiff, but she grinned brightly upon seeing him.

"Biton!" she cried and hurried over, nearly tripping on the knotted rug in the center of the mosaic floor. Danae caught herself on Biton's arm and, flushing, straightened. "Oh! Apologies. I'm *so* glad you're here. Mother and father are at a gallery opening this afternoon and should be gone for hours."

"That should give us plenty of time!" He smiled back at her and gave her arm a little pat as though she were one of his overzealous younger sisters, eager to play. "Are you ready to get started?"

Biton loved dancing, the music and grace of it, and part of him wanted Danae to like it as well. Perhaps because she was his friend, he supposed. Or just to save her from the discomfort of Mistress Afin's stinging remarks.

Instead of answering, Danae flared out her skirts and bowed to Biton as one noble would another. Only her elbows stuck out, and the movement was less a sweeping of her dress tunic and more a yank—not at all the fluid grace she was supposed to portray.

Biton stood, dusting crumbs from his doublet. He bowed to Danae in turn, keeping his face warm. He wasn't quite sure where to start—Biton was no dance instructor, just someone who loved to dance.

"Let's try that again," he said gently. "I'll bow to you and you to me, only this time, instead of trying to do it right, do it in the most comfortable way."

Her frown was slight as Danae bowed, ignoring her tunic altogether in favor of the simple bow one gave friends or family. Right arm wrapped about her waist, left tucked behind her back. The movement was more refined, something she likely did every day to her mother and father. It wasn't that she was utterly lacking finesse or coordination, but rather seemed to get in her own way, over-thinking or exaggerating the movements.

"Better?" she asked, tone nervous, perhaps anticipating a harsh rebuff.

"Much better."

Biton repeated the same simple bow, his mind whirling. He needed to get Danae out of her head, to get her feeling the steps rather than trying to remember how to execute them perfectly. What better way to do that than to simply move?

Biton held out his hand to her, smiling brightly. "My lady, may I have this dance?"

When she put her hand in his, he started singing in his squeaky tenor. It wasn't a piece they knew the steps to but a new song popular in the courts at the time. Three of Biton's sisters were taking turns learning it on the harp.

"Just dance however you like."

Danae was stiff in his grip, looking down at his feet as he stepped up, side, back, up, side, back. "I don't dance if I don't have to. My papa says I'm nearly as bad as he is." Danae stepped forward when she should have stepped back, and their heads thumped together. "I'm sorry! Are you alright? Maybe I'm hopeless."

"I don't think so," Biton said, laughing. "But let's not worry about doing it the right way now." He dropped her hands and stepped away, singing the same lovely, lilting melody as before. He took a step forward, then back, then spun in a circle and leaped into the air, giggling as he came down unsteadily on both feet. "Are you going to let me dance by myself the whole afternoon?"

"You're so much better than I am; it's more fun to watch *you* dance." Still, she started to sway to the tune he was humming. As he spun again, Danae gave a small twirl in place.

"That's beside the point," Biton panted, flopping a strand of dark hair back and out of his face. "The music is pretty, and no one can see you. There is no being good or being bad."

He took a deep breath and began to sing again, stomping his foot on the strong beats of every measure. "*One* two three, *la* ti-da three, *one* two-and three-and, *one*...."

He stopped and cocked his head, catching his breath. Danae still didn't seem comfortable enough to just dance with him. Still, he felt that if she could only move, could only feel the rhythm of it, then dancing would be so much easier for her.

"I know!" He twirled in place, unable to be still with such a great idea in his head. "Let's make it a game! I'll sing, and the only rules are that you have to stomp when I say 'one,' and you can't stop moving until I stop singing. What do you think?"

Danae

It sounded crazy, but Danae couldn't possibly be worse than she already was. "Alright. What do I get if I win?"

Biton cocked his head a moment, then sang his answer in the same tune. "*I'll* ask-dad if *you* can-come with *next* time-we go *out!*"

Taking a steadying breath, Danae picked up her tunic so the long hem wouldn't be underfoot and braced herself for the start. She could do this. Stomp on one; don't stop moving. She'd probably just walk and stomp every three, but that was better than bashing her head against Biton's.

"Yes!" Biton embellished his own heavy-light-light step with a sashay and then another twirl, then gulped in air and began another verse, his voice cracking on the higher notes. "*Don't* forget-to *move* your-arms too!"

Her arms *too*? That seemed impossible, but Danae walk-stomped around and added erratic arm flaps. She suspected she looked like a demented stork, strutting around the banks of the Bathi River, but she maintained the beat he sang.

It grew easier, and Danae played with making her arms float rather than flap. She felt pretty silly, but Biton didn't laugh or comment. He just kept singing and dancing along, and Danae felt her chest loosen. This wasn't so terrible. But then, was it really dancing?

After long minutes of singing and dancing, Biton tripped, stumbled over a footstool, and fell lightly to his knees. With a deep sigh, he flopped onto his back and lay there with his eyes closed above a wide grin, his chest rising and falling with thick gasps of air. "Whew. You win. Let's take a break."

"Very well." Danae settled on the stool he had tripped over and stared down at his flushed face. "Why are you the way you are? How can you be so nice, so confident? I'm a lot younger than you... Wouldn't you have more fun with the nobility in your age group?"

"Well, I can't be anyone else." Biton cracked one eye open and peered up at her as though he was thinking hard. He had a funny way of chewing on the inside of his cheek whenever he was pensive so that his lips twisted to one side and his normally fine features smooshed out of symmetry. He shrugged as if there really wasn't all that much to it. "I'm nice cause I like it when people are nice to me. And you're not that young. You're older than all of my sisters." He pushed himself up and stretched, his breathing almost normal and his warm cheeks fading to their usual cream. "Did you have fun dancing, though?"

"That wasn't dancing! That was stomping every three steps." But she had found it *almost* fun. Her palms weren't sweating, and she hadn't ripped out her seams, and that was as close to fun as she had ever been while dancing. The realization sunk in, and Danae's smile fell. *Had* she been dancing? Had it been *fun*? "I mean... I guess... I guess I was having *some* fun...."

"It was *too* dancing! All dancing is, is moving in rhythm with music. You've just got to feel it." He pulled himself to his feet and found the tray of pastries again so he could shove several of them into his mouth. "I'm glad you had fun, though. That's what I was hoping. I love dancing more than just about anything—except riding."

Danae took up a pastry of her own, carefully taking a bite, not allowing a single crumb to drop. He was so free of inhibitions. She wished she could be like him, but then he wasn't the sole heir of a ruling family. Or maybe he had just been made that way.

"Maybe next time, we can add some actual steps, but we'll keep it fun. I promise." Biton wiped his face carelessly, knocking crumbs to the floor. "What do you say?"

Before today, Danae would have said it wasn't possible for dancing to be fun, but Biton had proved a creative teacher. If anyone could make the torture of veering around and stepping on toes fun, it was him.

"Alright. But don't be surprised when I ruin your pretty shoes."

CHAPTER 27: PHECEA

EIGHTH MOON, 1797, DIOSION

Seven Years before the Proclamation

"*B*iton, don't sing any louder than Callista or Adohnis."
The music instructor had a glare that could curdle milk, a way of narrowing one eye, drawing his brows together, and staring directly at you until you fixed whatever it was that he disapproved of. Biton shifted and lowered his dynamic to blend more, and Adohnis shot him a superior look beneath his mop of caramel curls. His birthday was two days after Biton's, and he was always trying to prove he was better.

They all stood around a harp in the music room at Biton's home, with Danae playing the accompaniment. Master Karan never seemed to have any reason to give *her* the look. Danae's curly head was cocked slightly to the side, her mouth open as her fingers traced lovely, arching arpeggios in simple time. One of Biton's sisters had left a half-eaten sweet beneath her chair, but thankfully, Danae hadn't noticed it.

Biton took a deep breath, and Callista started her solo. She had a pretty voice, high and trilling, to go with her diminutive stature and delicate nose. Biton's mind began to wander. Had it been an hour of practice yet? Adohnis would leave with his sister, Callista, and then finally, Biton could take Danae to go see his horse.

Behind Master Karan, a side door opened just a crack so that Biton could see two of his sister's heads, stacked one above each other like the Lirian dolls his father had bought them last spring. It was Dido and Andara, the littlest, and they both had their hands over their mouths to stifle giggles. Biton glared at them, trying to get them to close the door and stop disrupting practice, but that made them smile all the wider. Dido even waved at him.

"Stop!" The music faltered around them, even Danae twanging a wrong note in alarm. Master Karan leveled his look on Biton again, his eye bulging behind its squint. "Biton! That was your entrance!"

"But—" Biton withered as Dido and Dara had already disappeared. "Sorry, Master Karan."

The instructor harrumphed and raised his hands once more. "From the beginning, please, Danae."

Behind him came a squeal and a torrent of giggles as one of the girls thundered past to the accompaniment of the opening theme, and then—thank the stars— the great clock in the hall sang out the hour. Biton sighed his relief, but Master Karan missed it beneath the noise.

"Alright," he said. "That's it for today. A beautiful job, Danae, truly beautiful. Nice work, Callista, Adohnis. Biton, I cannot stress enough the importance of practice!"

"Yes, Master Karan," Biton intoned, but already, he was full of excitement. He could show Danae around now! And they could play all night since she was sleeping over!

Callista and Adohnis folded up the music and ate the little hors d'oeuvres his mother had laid out. Danae didn't move from her place behind the beginners' harp, fingers stroking the strings to produce muted notes. For once, she wasn't worrying, perhaps focusing on the music or how the instrument tucked against her shoulder.

A small plate in hand, Adohnis approached Biton with an affable smile. "Are you going to Ion's tomorrow?" The other boy kept his voice low, likely to ensure Danae wouldn't overhear. Despite her place in a highly esteemed family, she still had not fallen into the social structures that made up the Phecean youth.

"No. I have plans with Danae." He had never much cared for the structures of social hierarchy. Besides, Danae was of a higher rank than all of them.

"Oh." Adohnis shrugged, uninterested in anything other than what he wanted to do. "Ion says the artist, Talia Perridi, will be there talking about technique." Biton yawned.

As Master Karan billowed out of the room in a swishing of silk robes, his sisters piled in—the twins, Dido and Andara, both five and more creatures than humans, and the next youngest, Voleta. Skipping over, Voleta tugged on Biton's favorite red tunic. "Bitttttttt-toooooonnn."

"What is it Leta?" Her dark hair was coming out of its braid in messy wisps that he tucked behind her ears. "I don't think you're supposed to be in here."

"You said we'd play Pirates when you were done. I heard the master. You're done!" It was amazing that she had made it waiting through the entire music lesson.

"What's the pirate game?" Callista asked. She was the youngest of their music group—even younger than Danae. She had the lightest hair of anyone Biton knew, other than the Emai, and they didn't have any color hair at all. Just white or sometimes silver.

Biton sighed. So much for showing Danae his horse. "Give me a minute, and I'll tell you." He trotted over to Danae and squatted down beside her chair. "We're gonna play pirates. Do you wanna come?"

She brushed her thumb over one chord, tilting her head as it resonated through the room. "You have a lot of demands on your time, don't you?"

He had been to her home; it was quiet and ordered. By contrast, the Mavros estate was a constant whirlwind of color and noise. With five daughters and one son, Cyril and Iris Mavros kept busy. Tutors came and went, lessons took place in every room, and of course, they also attended events and meetings.

"Nah, not really. I have plenty of time to play." Biton smiled at her with all his teeth. "Do you want to be the captain? Or what about the first mate or the lookout?"

He glanced over his shoulder at his sisters. Dido and Dara were busy peppering Callista with questions, but Leta scooted closer. She looked shyly over Biton's head where he crouched beside Danae. "How long did you have to practice to get so good at the harp? I've been taking lessons for a year, but I'm still not as good as you."

"I— umm. I only started a few years ago, but... I just like the harp, is all." Danae smiled tentatively at Leta, who was much younger than her, yet Danae treated her shyly. "It's the only thing I'm good at."

"I'm going to be good at it too, one day," Leta said, and then Dido, the little animal, charged in, bowling Biton over.

"Biton! Tell Dara I get to be the lookout this time! She got to do it last time, and I'm so good at it! Listen! Land ahooooooy!" She devolved into a fit of gasping laughter. "Laaaaand ahooooooy!"

Biton shoved her off onto the carpet, and she kept rolling until she hit a music stand and sent it toppling over, giggling all the while. He pressed his hands to his face. "That's not the only thing you're good at, Danae. You—"

"Biton, Dido's lying! She was the lookout last time too. She just wants to do it again." Dara wrapped her arms around Biton's neck, draping over him from behind. "It's *my* turn, really! I promise it is!"

Callista joined in laughing, and Adohnis couldn't hide his smirk despite his efforts to seem old and mature. Danae winced at all the noise but startled everyone by standing. "Alright. Alright. We'll draw straws for the lookout since it is clearly a coveted position. Here, Biton." Danae offered him her hand, helping him to his feet. "You're the captain."

⇑   ⇑   ⇑

Danae watched from her perch on Biton's bed as he dug for something he wanted to show her. The dyed silk comforter felt like water beneath her fingers as she nervously ran them over the surface. The game of pirates ended with Adohnis and Callista tossed overboard and Danae promoted to the second mate before Biton's sisters started a mutiny and elected to have Biton and Danae abandoned on a remote, unnamed island.

On the island—one of the Mavros's horse stalls—Biton convinced Danae to try and build a raft so they could make it to land and reap their revenge. It was an elaborate story and consumed her thoughts so wholly that Danae hadn't realized it was nearing nightfall until his mother came to fetch them for dinner. Callista even smiled goodbye to Danae before they left.

So Danae was their only guest for supper, a loud meal with many complaints and compliments tossed around. His sisters rarely wiped their hands on the napkins provided, and his parents hardly reminded the girls of manners. Biton was immaculate, and Danae stole glances across the table at him whenever she had the chance because he seemed so grown up. She felt like one of his little sisters, not a lady of a higher rank.

When it came time to retire to Biton's bedroom, Danae's supper turned to a lump in her tummy. She hadn't ever been on a sleepover before. Her mother didn't have a satisfying answer either, just, "mind your manners and thank his parents" when Danae asked her about the rules. Which didn't tell Danae how to act now that the actual sleepover part was here.

"Um... So," she started, trying to find a topic for conversation. What did one discuss before bed? "Do you like... being an older brother?"

"It's a lot of work. Oh! Here it is!" Biton said, pulling a beautifully painted box from one of the drawers. He brought it over to the bed and motioned her to come closer, his warm, dark eyes as liquid as hot chocolate or kava. "Do you wish you had siblings? You could have a couple of mine."

Without thinking much, Danae shook her head. She liked playing with Biton's sisters, but she couldn't keep up with that much energy or demands for fun. How he came up with the games and stories he told, she had no idea. "I think they'd be bored with me."

Biton shrugged from his place on the bed, his shoulders scrunching up the blue silk beneath him. He pulled a small, toothless key from a chain beneath his tunic and inserted it into a hole in the box she hadn't yet seen between the tails of two lush, red foxes. It clicked open. Inside, two figures in beautiful ballroom attire in blue and green began to twirl to the sound of a waltz, reflected in a pane of glass glued to the inside of the box's lid. The music came from a turning metal cylinder with spokes at random intervals.

"Aren't they beautiful?" Biton asked, "I want to dance in a ball full of people all bedecked in silk and feathers."

"Which one are you?" Danae supposed either figure could be Biton, as they were both dressed in his house colors, but the one on the left looked more joyful, arms thrown up, black hair flying out behind them as they twirled. The one on the right, for some unknown reason, had been painted with an expression akin to a grimace. Despite herself, Danae smiled. "That one is me, see? He's scowling."

"Then the other one is me, of course. Though why would anyone scowl while dancing? It's the best thing there is after riding and swimming. Right up there with playing pirates."

"He's scowling cause she's so much better, and no matter how much he practices, she'll always be. And that makes him happy and grumpy at the same time. It's alright. He's happy she's so good at stuff. Because they're friends." Danae glanced at Biton, feeling her face flush. She wasn't any good at storytelling.

"Hmm... Maybe they're friends, but he's a Councilor like your parents, and she's a pirate captain that keeps raiding the coast, and all they want to do is be friends and dance, but in the morning, he'll have to send the fleet to stop her." Biton scooted closer as he warmed to his tale. "The Great Pirate Queen is in love with him, but she doesn't think he could ever love her back because he already has a husband, so they meet as friends. Besides, her crew would lose respect if they found out she wanted to spare this noble, and they all need the money to feed their families."

He'd completely missed what Danae meant, about how having a friend that was good at everything could be hard. Not that she'd say anything. Letting the pillows behind her back embrace her, Danae tried to decide the next part of the tale. "So... So, to spend time with her friend and make the money her crew needs, she...uhh... kidnaps the Councilor and wears a mask, so he won't know it's her?"

"Yes! She whisks him away to her pirate ship and demands a ransom. At first, she thinks she'll tell him there, where no one can barge in or change his mind, but everything keeps going wrong.

There's a storm and a fight, and she has to save the Councilor from enemy pirates before he ever finds out that she took him in the first place. So she gets caught between the Councilor and her pirates again because he thinks she saved him, and they still want to get the ransom."

"That's terrible. How come they don't get a happy ending? Do you mean because they are so different, they can't be friends?" Danae's stomach suddenly had a very odd feeling. Maybe Biton was only her friend because she was a Councilmember's daughter.

"Maybe they *do* get a happy ending. Maybe the pirate tells the truth, and the Councilman forgives her for it. He offers her crew honest jobs in return for getting him home safely despite attacks from other pirates, and the Pirate Queen becomes the Councilman's head guard, and they're friends always." He yawned widely, already half-asleep. "Different people can be friends. Keme told me."

"Oh." Danae nodded as she thought about that. She liked the story more if they could be friends despite their differences. "Alright. But then..."

⇑ ⇑ ⇑

His father's voice droned from the dining room. It was his habit to read the weekly print aloud to Biton's mother and any other children who had managed to arrive at breakfast on time—usually only Biton. Today though, he had woken to find Danae already gone. She must have dressed and headed to breakfast since her things were still in his room.

When Biton entered the dining room with bows for his parents and Danae, he found her beside his father, a place of honor at the table. She had eaten there last night too, but she looked more relaxed now, her hands wrapped around a steaming cup of kava.

"—the increased raids on our border have been met without response from our neighbor, Liria. While the raids have been numerous, the raiders appear to be typical bandits. However, the survivors of these attacks have stated that the raiders exclusively spoke Lirian and were too well trained to be simple brigands."

Danae offered him a shy smile while he settled at the table. They had stayed up late into the night, telling stories and playing with the impressive collection of toys Biton had in various trunks. As the evening progressed, Danae seemed happier, even going so far as to wallop Biton with a pillow when he told a story of a chicken who learned to poop on cue. Of course, she had apologized profusely until he returned the blow, starting a pillow fight that left his bedroom covered in down.

"The Council is understandably loath to confront Liria about this issue, given that they deny any involvement with the raids; however, these attacks could end up placing strain on citizens all over the Phecean Confederacy. Most of the nation's agriculture comes from Zodrafi Province, where the attacks have been centered: agriculture that feeds our craftsmen and sustains trade with other nations." Biton took another bite of warm eggs cushioned with soft, white cheese and wrapped in flatbread, then dragged the bowl of honeyed yogurt closer. Uncharacteristically, Cyril Mavros stopped halfway through the article and set the print down on the table between himself and his wife.

"Well, that sums it up rather neatly." His voice was dry, his eyes tired.

"Why would Liria want to raid us, father?" Biton asked.

Cyril didn't treat the question any less seriously because it came from a child. Biton loved that about his father. The older Mavros always answered him as if he was an equal. "Liria is largely a mountainous region. It is rich with ore, and the valleys make suitable grazing land for livestock, but they do not have the space for agriculture that we do. Better fed people mean better labor and ultimately, more money."

"So they're raiding us over money?" Biton chewed the inside of his cheek. It wasn't grand or heroic, but the people fighting the raiders would be. "Why don't we send soldiers to protect the land?"

"We are, but we must do so carefully. We do not want to provoke a war with Liria: it would be far worse for our farms than a few border raids."

Trying not to provoke a war didn't sound all that heroic either.

Biton's mother laid her hand on her husband's arm. "Surely, we can speak more of this later, Cyril. We have a guest. Danae, how have you enjoyed your stay?"

The girl nodded, swallowing hastily to answer his mother. "It was very nice. I've never stayed in anyone's home besides my own before. I thought I would be afraid away from my parents, but Biton is good company. Thank you for having me over. Next time—I mean, if there is a next time, not that there will be—"

Mother and Father exchanged a look, but Biton was already speaking. "What? You didn't tell me it was your first sleepover! That's like—a *momentous* occasion. You've got to come back, right, Papa? Please? Danae tells great stories."

"Of course!" Cyril said. "Danae, you are welcome over anytime. Be sure to tell your parents that you had fun, and we hope you'll come to visit again."

"I will. I'm certain Biton will be invited over too, but I don't have as many dress up outfits or sisters to play with, so maybe… it wouldn't be as fun." Danae glanced at Biton, brows furrowed over golden brown eyes.

"I'm sure that's not true. Isn't that right, Biton?" She looked at him, her chin dipping in the slightest of nods. "You would have fun even, especially without your sisters underfoot."

"Of course, we would! You don't need sisters or clothes to have fun. You can do that anywhere! You just need to tell a story."

"But, the dressing up was fun too," Danae murmured.

"Then you'll just have to come over again!"

CHAPTER 28: RHOSAN

EIGHTH MOON, 1798: CWM OR

Seven Years before the Proclamation

The gates of Victor Kerwyn's compound were nicer than Gruffyd's. They were wrought iron, twisted into spiraling spikes that made a deadly, if graceful, arch. Wynn took them in carefully, trying to think of anything but why they were here. Behind him, Gruffyd sat up and straightened his tunic as the horses slowed and their wagon rolled to a stop. On the other side, a few Defeated leaped into action and pulled open the gates. There was no squeak or grumble from the well-oiled iron, so the buzzing of bees and the stamping of horses were the only noises that interrupted the lazy summer day.

Kerwyn waited for Gruffyd just inside his walls, glimpses of a vast, well-tended land sprawling behind him. How many Defeated must Victor Kerwyn have to be able to plant and farm so much? Wynn gritted his teeth, frustrated by the pointless excess. Why should one man stand on the backs of others just to own more than he could ever use?

Gruffyd left the wagon with a hand on Wynn's shoulder as he made the small jump down from his lofty perch. Wynn stayed respectfully behind, his stomach roiling.

Kerwyn's back was straight despite the lines on his face and silver-white hair. Wynn tried not to stare. He'd never seen someone this aged in Cwm Or. Defeated simply didn't make it that long, and Victors likewise tended to die off in battles or raids. Regular townspeople reached more than sixty summers.

What did the people of Cwm Or do with their elderly? Their God certainly didn't seem to preach caring for the weak, so it seemed unlikely that families would give their seniors easier tasks. His stomach clenched. Did they... kill them?

"Victor Gruffyd." Kerwyn spoke clearly and smiled wide, showing that he had most of his teeth.

"Victor Kerwyn."

The two men clasped forearms, and then Kerwyn turned to look at Wynn. "So this is the pit fighter you wanted me to see. Training him up for the Contender Matches?"

"Yep. Eating up my coin, but when he works out, he'll pay it back tenfold."

Victor Kerwyn nodded slowly, his gaze lingering on Wynn's chest and shoulders before working its way down his body. Finally, he smiled again and looked into Wynn's eyes. It was strange for a Victor to meet his gaze, but Wynn didn't look away. His pa had taught him to look other men in the eye, to treat everyone he met like they were equals. "And a good investment for me to get a few of his offspring for cheap before he does. Like I did with young Dyfan. You know I have his eldest son? Big fucker, bout..." Victor Kerwyn scratched at his lined cheeks, and Wynn saw he was missing two fingers. "Eight summers now."

Eight summers? From talking to him during training, Wynn had gathered that Dyfan was younger than him by a few years. How old had he been when they first made him breed? Sixteen? Fifteen? How many children did Dyfan have? Wynn knew of two children by Nimue, a son and a daughter, and Kerwyn's boy. How many others were there?

"That old!? How much did you get him for?" Gruffyd asked.

Kerwyn smiled, his weathered face creasing into a sly mask. "Cheaper than what I'm getting this boy for now."

Gruffyd grunted in what Wynn assumed was jealousy and clasped Wynn on the shoulder. "Well, this'll be just as good an investment as Eurig's stud!"

Kerwyn made a noncommittal sound and gestured for Wynn and Gruffyd to come farther into his compound. The place was tidy, and everywhere Wynn looked he saw signs of additional improvements: covered pathways from the main house to the slave quarters and kitchens, even the woodshed. Sloped wooden troughs to carry water to fields of barley and rye. It was the sort of place any farmer in Rhosan might be proud of or would have been if it wasn't tended by a small army of Defeated.

Shortly before they reached the main house, a couple of Kerwyn's Defeated came to escort Wynn from the Victors and towards their quarters. He wasn't particularly surprised. It had been much the same when he had seen Dyfan visit Gruffyd's estate for this purpose back when Wynn was newly Defeated. He found himself hoping the girl had someone like Linn to ease her mind before meeting him. If she were calm, it might be easier to get her to agree to his plan.

They took him past the main Defeated barracks and into a building filled with smaller individual rooms, most of which would be used for nursing mothers or kept open for breeding. Some Victors also kept private rooms for their Contenders, the fighters who reached the top of their weight class.

Wynn's mouth was dry, his chest a hollow chasm heavy with sloshing dread. He did not want to breed, forced into rutting with a stranger so that the Victors might fill their games. He was a thinking man, a skilled carpenter, and a father.

He was not an animal.

They reached the door before he was ready, one of the Defeated behind him, a young woman, stepping forward to knock on the thin wood. "Liliwen, are you ready?"

A high voice replied, "Yes."

Then the door opened and the Defeated propelled Wynn through. With a soft shucking sound, the door closed behind him, and there was nothing between Wynn and a complete stranger but a bed. He inhaled sharply, trying to collect his thoughts, but then coughed. The room smelled heavily of garlic and cloves, a strange combination.

The girl, because really she was just a girl, perhaps seventeen or so, smiled apologetically. "The herbs. You get used to them after a while. Victor Kerwyn says they ward off pests. I don't complain cause I don't get mite bites."

Wynn fumbled for an answer, thrown off by the suddenness of this meeting and the strange topic. "No mite bites is good. Perhaps someone should tell Victor Gruffyd."

"Oh! Do you have fleas? Victor Kerwyn said you should wash before…." She glanced toward a basin set in one corner with a pitcher beside it. The girl, Liliwen presumably, was as tall as Wynn and broad-shouldered, with generous hips. It was easy to guess why she'd been chosen. Kerwyn wanted another Contender, after all. With her height and his 'natural ability,' as Gruffyd called it, Kerwyn seemed to be hedging his bets. The thought made a muscle in Wynn's jaw twitch.

"No, I don't have fleas." Wynn looked at the door and tried to turn the knob. It was locked. From there, he walked to the wash basin and scrubbed his hands.

"They said they would come back after lunch. Is that enough time, do you think?"

"Plenty." Wynn pulled a sharp nail hidden in his pocket and washed that too for good measure. "They didn't leave anyone to stay and listen? You know, to make sure we do as we're told?"

Liliwen's eyes were wide as she watched him. They were dark brown like tilled earth. Like Nia's had been. "I don't know. I've not been around when breedings happen before. I mean… Wouldn't they know cause you'd be all tired and such?"

She had a point, he supposed. It was a detail to keep in mind. Wynn looked at her again. "I'm sure this is not going how you expected it to. I promise not to harm you. Just let me take care of one thing, and I'll explain."

"Alright," she said, though her tone was skeptical.

Wynn pressed the sharp end of the nail into the pad of his forefinger until blood welled there, hot and thick and threatening to spill down his wrist. In his mind, he pictured seclusion, silence, and protection, summoning these to him with the power of his offering. It was important to focus—if you got distracted the magic would have nowhere to go, and it was not a safe thing to keep inside you.

Liliwen gasped and stepped forward, hand outstretched as if to help him. "Ouch! Don't do that; you'll—"

"Hush now." He spoke softly, gently—like he might be speaking to Owynn before the boy fell asleep. Odd, that. It had been a long time since thoughts of his family had arisen. He banished that guilt and pushed all his energy into the spell, drawing runes on the stone around the door. When he finished, he sighed in relief. Holding the magic within him was like wrapping his hands around potential. It felt good to let it go. "There. Now we can talk without being overheard."

"What?" Liliwen looked at his runes as if he had made a mess she'd have to clean up. Well, that was probably true. "What is that?" Wynn realized that the girl probably was born Defeated, perhaps hadn't ever heard of the Old Ways.

He took a seat on the floor and stretched his neck. "If it's alright with you, I'd rather not go on with this whole breeding business. I told Gruffyd that I was infertile, and he brought me here to collect the gold anyway. He certainly won't be surprised if nothing comes of it. I mean no offense. I married once for love before I was Defeated, and I have no wish to have sex now at the whim of tyrants."

Liliwen just stared at him, her lips slightly parted. After a few seconds, her brows creased, and she glanced at the runes he'd made around the door. "And…You painted on the walls with your blood to prove to Victor Gruffyd that you're…mad?"

He laughed. "Have you ever heard of the Old Ways?"

"You mean like traditions? Like we always boil the well water before drinking cause its tradition?"

"They are traditions, in a way. And it certainly makes a good story. You might as well lie down so that the bed will look rumpled when they come to let us out."

"But," even as she protested, the girl sat on the bed, "won't they hear you talking like this, like you said?"

"Not with the runes there. You know there are other Gods, right? Besides Kirit?"

"You mean…" She cast a furtive glance toward the door as if she wasn't certain Wynn's runes would actually work. He was sure. He felt the magic even now. "Like Esha or Aryus?"

"Yes, like both of them. There are many Gods because the original Gods had children who became Gods in turn, though they tend to favor the south with its warmth and cities and mages. The first was Enyo, Goddess of Nature, in all its strength and beauty. Her followers call her Un Cyntaf. First One. Though, she is not the greatest of the Gods any more than Kirit is. They all contribute to the balance of the world." Wynn's voice caught in his throat, tears pricking at his eyes as he remembered the song he and Owynn sang together that last night before everything was taken from him. "Though she is not the greatest of the Gods, Enyo did give us one of their greatest gifts— that of magic, or the Old Ways."

"Enyo?" Liliwen's voice was thoughtful as she pulled one of the flat pillows over to her lap, hugging it. "But I thought she was the one who fought Kirit and made the mountains. She denied the southerners Kirit so they would never know glory."

"There are people south of the mountains that serve Kirit, though not as the only God."

"But Kirit is our Overseer. Why wouldn't they want him guiding them?"

"Because there is more to life than war. Don't you want to eat healthy crops, or fall in love, or—"

"—or have babies?" Liliwen gave Wynn an assessing look.

He raised an eyebrow. "That too. The other Gods govern those things. They have for a thousand years—from the days when they first came to Illygad and walked the land, through the Great War and their banishment, and they still do now, though from afar."

"I know," Liliwen smiled at him suddenly, straightening up. "Esha is fertility. She helps the female Defeated by giving us strong babies. When Mona had Afan, she got a room to herself and extra rations. Even now, she gets the kitchen work cause she has to keep an eye on Afan."

Did Esha lend her blessings to these women? Wynn wasn't sure. She was the Goddess of Love and Fertility, the being who closed marriage vows and listened to prayers for safe pregnancies. Wasn't what the Victors forced upon them a corruption of that?

Then again, if the prayers came from these women, the Defeated and not the Victors... Wasn't that a prayer worth listening to? Wynn had listened to the priests all his life, but he had no answers.

Instead of continuing in that vein, he went on. "There is also Tha'et who governs the sun, the moon, and the seasons. Iluka rules over the sea. Maoz is the hunter, protector of beasts and those who hunt them respectfully. Va'al is a trickster who knows truth from falsehood—"

"You're going to talk of Old Gods all morning, aren't you?" Liliwen gave Wynn the look of long suffering that only a woman could give an irritating man.

"Is there something you'd prefer to talk about?"

"Well... You're certain you won't bed me?" She smiled again, her irritated frown disappearing faster than a hummingbird after nectar.

"That I am."

"And they can't hear us cause of your blood scribblings?"

"That about sums it up."

Liliwen cast the door one more glance, then curled onto her side, propping her head up on her palm. "Then... have you met the Contender, Dyfan?" Her voice was hopeful, her eyes bright, and Wynn was taken abruptly back to growing up with gossiping teenage sisters.

He sighed again, for good measure, and then indulged her. After all, she was playing along with his plan.

CHAPTER 29: RHOSAN

EIGHTH MOON, 1798, CYM OR

Seven Years before the Proclamation

On the day Dyfan lost, Wynn was at the fighting pits.

It was not the first time—everyone lost— but it had been so long since it had last happened. Years, probably, if the whispers of the other Defeated were to be believed. Perhaps even before Wynn was captured and brought to this cursed place. He watched the fight, or most of it, though from a poor vantage point.

Two sets of stone seats like stairs overlooked the fights where the Victors could sit and watch the matches beneath canvas tarps. Villagers stood and jeered between them, some hanging over the arena wall, others pointing to the lists and talking excitedly to their neighbors. Cells ringed the opposite side where wealthy Victors kept their fighters, two stories of blocky rooms set in a semicircle. The other Defeated, Wynn included, crowded into the spaces between, squatting in the dirt or leaning on stone walls to watch.

Wynn preferred to sit against walls where there were fewer shoulders to bump into and fewer unwashed bodies to assault his senses. He closed his eyes and pressed the back of his head into the rock, trying to empty his mind of thoughts. That was until he heard the crier announce Dyfan's fight that day.

His eyes flickered open, and he twitched upright, shouldering forward past the other fighters until he could stand at the pit's edge. Wynn had bested all of these men in the last year, so they gave way to him. Still, Dyfan and his opponent had already exchanged a flurry of blows before he could see what was going on.

Standing in the middle of the ring, Dyfan and his opponent, Ein, grappled with one another. One spear lay on the ground off to the side, the shaft broken. The other was the focus of their wrestling, each trying to wrench it away from the other. It was unclear whether the weapon was poorly constructed or was snapped by a kick.

Dyfan and Ein kept a grip on the spear shaft and exchanged pummeling blows with their free hands. Muffled grunts punctuated the impacts, each Defeated taking a beating on the ribs and back. The match hadn't been going long, yet they were both covered in sweat. Neither gained the weapon. Victors screamed at the fighters, Victor Eurig bellowing to forget the spear and finish the bout. It was a wonder that Dyfan could hear him over the din, but he broke away from Ein. He jumped back, and though Ein's recovery was swift, the larger Defeated managed to escape with a thin slice across his belly. He rolled and came up, holding the broken shaft of the spear previously abandoned on the ground.

It was no more than a couple hand lengths long, ridiculously short compared to the weapon in Ein's grip, but Dyfan hefted it steadily as Ein charged. With a glancing swipe, Dyfan used his truncated weapon to deflect Ein's, shoving the tip to the side. He grabbed the shaft with his free hand, but Ein yanked it back, forcing Dyfan to stumble forward to his knees.

Dyfan ducked as Ein kicked out, the heel of his foot coming to graze against the top of Dyfan's head rather than hitting his jaw. The blow would have knocked Dyfan out had it made contact, and he was clearly disoriented, shaking his head as he scrambled back to his feet. Wynn's jaw tightened, his arms tightening across his chest. He wanted to stop the fight.

With a strangled roar, Dyfan launched himself forward, ignoring another swipe from Ein's spear. Then Dyfan was atop Ein, beating him with the butt of the broken spear.

"He always goes insane like that when he's losing," a Defeated said. Dyfan was usually a collected fighter. Fierce, to be certain, but effective and methodical. Now he was desperate.

Ein threw him to his back, turning the tide, then tossed aside his spear and grappled Dyfan. He pinned one of Dyfan's hands beneath his knee, crushing his fingers. Dyfan shouted and thrashed, nearly unseating him.

"He better do something quick, or Dyfan will get out of it, and then it'll be over."

"Wouldn't want it to be me."

"Good hold, though."

Blood spread from the cuts on Dyfan's belly and chest, and his ruddy skin paled as he fought. Ein brought back his fist and slammed it into Dyfan's jaw. Dyfan fell back, eyes wide but open. Feebly he stirred, still trying to fight. Ein raised his fist again and brought it down on Dyfan's temple.

Wynn closed his eyes, wincing at the blow. That sort of thing could kill a man or else leave him damaged.

Ein struggled to his feet. He had managed to avoid cuts from the spears, but he was bruised and bloody. It had been a quick fight. No more than ten minutes, but brutal.

The other Defeated parted as the match ended, returning to their conversations. Victor Eurig glowered as he came down from the stands, a healer in white furs trailing behind. They bent over Dyfan. Was he dead?

For a long time, he didn't move, but finally, the healer nodded to Victor Eurig, and they loaded Dyfan's limp body onto a stretcher. Wynn could just hear Eurig. "—shouldn't have broken so easily. Who is in charge of the weapons? That fight should have lasted at least twenty minutes, and instead, they spent half the time fighting over a spear. When will he be ready to go again? I need to recoup my losses."

"Not for some days, Victor Eurig. As I've told you before, if Dyfan takes too many more strikes to the head, I suspect his mind will fade as the older fighters' do. Some become too aggressive to be useful. Let him rest. He will make you more earnings when he is well."

"He better. Today was disgraceful. Rolling around like children!"

As they carried Dyfan past, his hand dangled from the stretcher. It looked as if Ein had broken several of Dyfan's fingers when he pinned Dyfan's hand with his knee.

On impulse, Wynn followed them. He fought earlier than Dyfan and had won his match that day. Victor Gruffyd would be drinking himself into a stupor to celebrate the win and would not think to send for him until much later. Dyfan's party paid no notice of him. What was one more Defeated in the pits?

They steered out of the cavernous main room and into a cell furnished with a straw-lined cot that served the Defeated as both bench and bed. Wynn settled himself on his ankle bones to one side of the door, listening to the murmur of voices as the healers continued to speak with Victor Eurig. After a minute, the master trainer hurried past Wynn and into the cell. He looked worried.

"Is he awake yet?" Wynn recognized the voice of the trainer.

"No," Eurig said.

"Ein has been dropping weight to qualify for the lighter classes, but he's still in Dyfan's category. With this win, he's ahead for the Contender matches."

"Victor Henwas is making him lose weight deliberately?" Wynn didn't know that voice, so it must belong to the healer.

"Well, if he loses ten more pounds, he'll not have to fight Dyfan for the title," the trainer said.

There was a scoffing sound, most likely the healer.

"I don't care about Ein or Victor Henwas and his plans. What about Dyfan? What does this loss do to his chances of qualifying for the Contender matches?"

Anger heated Wynn's skin, hot and sudden. Eurig cared less for Dyfan than he did his horses. He was only interested in how much he could win.

"This loss isn't good, but I'm less worried about this event and more concerned about how long he'll be out of commission. Next week's bouts are important pre-qualifying rounds. The season has barely begun, and he's already lost one match and will miss another."

"How many must he win to qualify?"

"Ten, and of course, he'll have to beat Ein later unless Ein drops the weight by next moon."

"If he makes it to next week's match—"

"Victor Eurig, I am telling you, no. You've hired me to keep Dyfan in the best fighting shape for as long as possible. If you keep him going now, you'll lose him sooner." It surprised Wynn that the healer was willing to stand up to a Victor like that, but then he supposed their reputation would be on the line. If Dyfan couldn't fight a few years from now, people would blame the healer.

There was a long silence, and finally, Eurig sighed. "Fine. No matches next week. Come, training master. I want you to explain precisely how you will get Dyfan into the Contender matches this season."

The Victor and his party swept out without a glance towards Wynn, and then, there was nothing but the clinking of instruments against stone and the brush of the healer's robes.

The healer stayed with Dyfan for an hour before they were satisfied enough with their work to leave, and for a time afterward, Wynn still did not move. Now, in the relative quiet, he could not remember why he had come.

He stood and stepped through the door of the cell. Dyfan lay motionless, his chest bare but for a swath of bandages, and the fingers of one hand splinted straight. Wynn strode forward until he stood above him and was surprised to find the big man's good eye open. "I thought you'd be out for hours after that knock to the skull."

Dyfan stared at Wynn for a long moment before blinking and looking away. The other eye was swollen shut. Despite Wynn's advantageous position hovering above Dyfan, the pit fighter made no move to get up or to even the odds. Most fighters didn't like being vulnerable and did everything in their power to remain on even ground. Dyfan even went so far as to roll over onto his side, grunting with pain and exposing his back.

Wynn snorted and sat down in the space that Dyfan had vacated, though there was hardly room for him with the other man's bulk. "Hello to you too." When that didn't produce any answer, Wynn took a deep breath. "Did they rattle your brains one too many times? Or do you still have a few left?"

Dyfan's shoulders hunched defensively, and he curled tighter on his side. While he had never been a particularly talkative man, he seemed rendered mute. Wynn was ready to get up, to give up on the other fighter saying anything. Why had he even come here? What had been the point in trying to speak to Dyfan after his defeat? There wasn't anything to say, really. Nothing that the both of them didn't already know.

Wynn turned slightly, freezing at the visible shake of Dyfan's shoulders, at the wet breaks in his breathing.

For a long, stiff moment, Wynn did nothing. He did not speak or stretch out a hand or get up to leave the other man in peace. Instead, when he finally did move, he just let himself down onto his side on the sliver of available stone, his back pressed into the Dyfan's spine and the corner of the slab digging into his ribs.

Dyfan shook for a long time, and still, neither man spoke. Voices rose and fell in the rooms beyond. Feet tramped past. The flicker of lanterns grew and faded. It was impossible to tell how much time passed in quiet and body heat, but evening was deepening.

Eventually, Dyfan stilled. His breaths evened, and the tense muscles softened. It was quieter then, the last matches of the day complete, but Wynn waited long minutes before he rose, leaving soundlessly on poorly-shod feet.

⇑ ⇑ ⇑

The last fight of the evening was a bloody one. The two Defeated started the match with staves but resorted to grappling when the flimsy wooden shafts shattered. They clawed at each other's faces, teeth barred like dogs.

It was artless, savage. And the Victors ate it up.

Dyfan stood in his cell overlooking the pit and turned his gaze away from the melee. The ranks of Defeated watching had grown—many arrived to sleep in the rough communal barracks outside the main building so that they could fight in morning bouts without traveling from outside the city. No Victor wanted their Defeated to fight tired. It lowered their chance of a win and moving up in the ranks to compete in the Contender bouts.

One of the Defeated below stood out, not because of his size or stature, but because he alone watched the stands rather than the bout, reddish hair taking on the hues of lantern flames. His thoughtful face was creased, his arms crossed. When the Victors erupted at some escalation in the ring, the Defeated spat on the ground and raised his eyes to Dyfan's cell.

Wynn.

Irritation saturated Dyfan. Wynn should watch the matches. One day he'd fight these men, and if he knew their old injuries or their style, he would have a better chance of winning against them. Instead, he scorned the Victors and the sport. Dyfan jutted his chin towards the fight, a silent reminder that Wynn should be spectating.

The fighters were tired, sweat-slick and grappling ineffectively against one another. There was no clear winner, which irked the Victors. Someone would have to end it decisively. One man wrapped his hands about the back of the other man's neck. He tried to slip free, but instead, his opponent forced his head into their knee. It wasn't a particularly impressive blow, but as disoriented as they both were, he collapsed in the dirt.

The fallen fighter shook his head, trying to clear it as he pushed himself to his knees. If he stayed down, the bout would be over, but his Victor might claim he had not tried his hardest. If he managed to stand again, he'd be hurt worse. Dyfan could see his opponent huffing for breath and bringing back his foot. He'd kick out if the felled man tried to stand.

The crowd screamed. Some for him to stand, others for his opponent to finish the bout. Dyfan blinked as the fallen Defeated surged to his feet, only to be met with a kick to the stomach. He flopped back on his back, clutching his belly and struggling to breathe.

Dyfan slipped out of his cell and made his way down to the gathered Defeated. He found Wynn watching as the two Defeated were carted off the arena floor and brushed his hand against Wynn's shoulder. Angry eyes flickered to Dyfan, and the larger man nodded.

It hadn't been a good match.

"Come." He nodded towards the private cells. *His* cell.

Wynn met his gaze, then turned back to watch the injured fighters until they disappeared outside the building. Likely, a healer was waiting in the barracks. Neither he nor Dyfan moved, and the space around them filled with the sound of voices. The Victors argued over the match, and nearby, a female Defeated swore vehemently.

Wynn looked up at him again, warm eyes blank of any emotion. He nodded once, a sharp, bird-like movement, and let Dyfan lead the way. A few of the other Defeated watched them go, but no one asked questions. Dyfan was too well-known among them.

They were silent as they moved through the press of bodies and into the empty halls. Even as they entered Dyfan's cell, indistinguishable from any other. Turning towards the cot he slept on, Dyfan sat with a grunt. He watched as Wynn looked out the barred window, across his view into the arena, and back.

"You're angry," Dyfan said, tilting his head slightly to take in the tight way Wynn held his shoulders and jaw. "Don't be *angry*. Be smart. What did you learn about Elis and Jac?"

"I learned the Victors like bloody fights, and one of the easiest ways to get them is to make sure that one or both of the weapons in the ring will break after a few hits." Wynn's voice was lower than usual. Darker. "They don't want us fighting fair."

Wynn reached up to wrap his hands around the bars of Dyfan's window, gripping them until his knuckles paled to a chalky white. He looked like a caged animal, for all that the door was open behind him. The bars only kept battle-fevered Defeated from joining the fights out of turn.

"I learned that those farm Defeated don't have stamina. They fight fast and hard and hope it's over at the start. If I hold out longer, evade, and take a few hits, they will fade, and then I can make my strike. End the bout in one or two select attacks. They are higher ranked than you are, Wynn. You'll have to fight them someday." Didn't he see? This had been his opportunity to get an edge on his competitors. He had wasted it being angry that it was unfair. "Come here."

Wynn didn't move at first, and the muscles all along his back tensed. For a long moment, it seemed as though he might lash out. At Dyfan, at the Victors, at anything at all, if only it would alleviate his anger. He had never looked so much like he *wanted* to fight.

And then it was over. Wynn took a deep, steadying breath and uncoiled his fingers from their vice-like hold around the bars. He took the two steps necessary to cross the room and sat beside Dyfan on his rough bed. "Alright. I'm listening."

"Tomorrow, you're in the border matches. They don't hold them often because Defeated usually don't bleed. You and another Defeated will enter the circle drawn in colored sand and crouch opposite each other. When they bang the drum, you'll try to knock your opponent from the ring. No blades, no fists, just brute strength and cunning."

Dyfan actually preferred this type of contest. While perhaps less refined in specific skills, there was something about pitting your strength against another just to see who would come out on top. But Wynn hadn't trained in this style, as it was frowned upon.

"Though it seems your only choice is to run at each other, this is not true." Dyfan pushed off his cot to crouch in front of Wynn. He placed his hand on the ground before him, fingers splayed out. "Knock me down."

Wynn looked at him doubtfully. "Wouldn't my opponent be easier to knock down while moving towards me?" He didn't look like he really wanted to try to push Dyfan over. They were in totally different weight classes, and Dyfan's low position wouldn't give him much leverage. It wasn't surprising when Wynn didn't put much effort into his attempt to shove Dyfan; he didn't think it would succeed. He was right. Wynn braced his shoulder against Dyfan and pushed with hardly any give.

Dyfan let Wynn press against him for a few more moments to see if he might gain some tipping force and shove Dyfan to the ground. Wynn's hair brushed against Dyfan's cheek as the smaller man wrapped his arms about Dyfan's shoulders and pressed harder. He smelled like soap and something earthy. Dyfan ducked his head and shoved Wynn back onto the cot.

"You both start in a crouch." He nodded for Wynn to come at him, and Wynn complied with a look that told Dyfan he thought this was pointless. This time, with Dyfan's weight back, he shifted to the side as Wynn rammed into him, and Wynn went sprawling past him.

Swiftly, Dyfan pivoted and grabbed Wynn by the back of the skull, pulling his head up and gaining control. "Why did you fall?" he asked, hoping Wynn had caught that shift in his weight, how Dyfan had been ready to slip off rather than let the brunt of Wynn's attack plow into him.

"Because you turned," Wynn growled. "What is it you're trying to tell me? To use my opponent's weight against him?"

"No." Dyfan waited until Wynn straightened up again, then resumed his crouch. He looked down at his hand on the ground before him. His fingers were splayed out, knuckles white from the weight bearing down on them. Leaning forward. Ready to charge. Dyfan shifted back, and his knuckles returned to their usual color. Full of blood because he wasn't putting pressure on them. He moved forward slightly, white knuckles. Back, flushed. "Do you see? If you know what your opponent will do, you can plan a counter that will win. It's not as glorious to use your wits, but winning is winning after all."

"There is no glory in the pits."

"Is there glory in dying when you could have survived?" Dyfan asked.

Wynn sighed and looked down, coming to terms with an internal struggle that Dyfan did not understand. To him, this was simple. If you won, you didn't end up in the mines. For Wynn, though, everything seemed to be more complicated, to have more nuances than black and white. Dyfan didn't envy him.

Wynn sighed and looked up, resigned. "Can we go again?"

CHAPTER 30: THE WESTERN SEA

TWELFTH MOON, 1796, MUSCANA

Nine Years before the Proclamation

Muscana wasn't Nec, not exactly. It wasn't a small Emaian village in the Tundra, set in a cupped bowl of rock, erupting from the snow like so many eager talons. It did not have faces Iniabi recognized— no Manaba, Piav, or Tampeesa. No Mika. Instead, Muscana was a small Emaian village on the sea.

Illus, like those that Iniabi had grown up in, rose like gray buds from the snow, set in rings around a central meeting place invisible from the rowboat. The medicine woman's house would be on the other side, set off from the rest of Muscana. On the seaside, a few rickety piers jutted out over the water, held in place by sheer stubbornness of will. It was there they angled the rowboat, Jaya and Iniabi heaving the oars in unison. Taaliah sat behind them with the captain in the prow. They were silent, though if it was out of anticipation or deference to the captain, Iniabi did not know. She could only pull on the wooden handle of the oar, lean into the pain of sore muscles, and wonder about what lay before them.

More than two years had passed since Iniabi stepped foot among her people. More than two years had passed since Nec had been razed by slavers, its citizens taken like chattel to be sold for hard labor or household slaves or whatever else the Lirians and Pheceans wanted. Should this feel like a homecoming? Should she be weighed down by guilt? The other villagers of Nec were dead or slaves, and Iniabi, daughter of their medicine woman, was free.

She shook her head, the spray-dampened tendrils of her white hair sticking to her face where they fell out of their tie. She would not regret surviving. No one should ask that of her. Still, as they tied up the rowboat and stepped onto Muscana's rickety pier, unease stirred in Iniabi's belly like rats in the bilge. The Tundra might not see it that way.

The captain surveyed them for a moment, and Iniabi met her gaze, standing a little straighter. Aside from the wicked scar curving through her bottom lip, the captain did not look like a pirate officer. She was a stout, heavy-limbed Phecean woman in her late forties, her salt-and-pepper coils tied back away from her face. She wore tall boots, breeches, and a coat that looked like it might have been a military jacket at one point, but there were no insignias left on it anymore. She turned back to the village. "Let's see if you two are as useful as Vlassis swears you'll be."

Of course, Vlassis and the others did not know that they came to fill the captain's carved wooden chest with poison so that she could keep her dreams and her life as well. They knew only that they had an Emaian translator and that whale oil and seal skin were worth more than gold in the north.

Iniabi looked to Jaya, but her eyes were on the captain's back, calm and focused. She wore her curved sword on her hip and stood straight as a pine. Iniabi took a deep breath and followed them to the edge of the village, where a small party waited.

Four warriors wielding whalebone spears and flint knives stood to either side of an older man and woman. Each one wore the stony expression of the Ice Hearted, their gloved hands tight about their weapons. They did not look directly at the approaching pirates, but Iniabi had the feeling that they were being sized up. The older pair— not husband and wife as some might assume, but chief and medicine woman— were clothed in much the same way as the people of Nec— elk skin and wolverine pelts and tiny, beaded designs. The woman's neck was as heavy with necklaces as Manaba's, though more wrinkled with age. The captain stopped before them, and the chief raised his hands.

"All those who wish to speak must do so peacefully."

None of the pirates reacted except the captain, who looked back. Iniabi wet her lips. "He's asking us to lay down our weapons so we can talk."

Jaya's nostrils flared, and Iniabi saw the hand flex as she tightened her grip on her sword. It seemed the captain shared Jaya's misgivings because she frowned and made no move to comply. "How do we know they won't attack us the moment we do?"

"When you lay down your weapons, you become guests. It would be wrong to attack guests. The Emai believe their ancestors would refuse to protect them if they did." She was careful to separate herself from the Emai where the captain could hear. They were them, and she was one of the crew. The survivor. Not the medicine woman's daughter.

But she had been one of them once, and part of her ached for the smell of snow, sea, and smoking fish. These were her people, not the pirates, yet there was no real guarantee they would take her back. She was a traitor now, an Emaian following northerners. Standing with them across from the people of her birth.

She missed home.

Time stretched between the pirates and the Emaians, and the captain hissed through her teeth and tossed down her blade. Jaya followed suit obediently, Iniabi only a second behind the older girl.

Taaliah was the last to put down her sword, but the moment she did, the Ice Hearted relaxed and stepped back so that they could approach the chief and the medicine woman. The captain put a hand on Iniabi's shoulder and drew her to the front of their party.

Up close, the Emaians smelled like salt and whale oil. Iniabi swallowed, fighting the urge to close her eyes, to breathe in. Could these people be hers? Could she go home? "I am Iniabi," she said finally, "and I will translate your words for Captain Ira Minelli."

If the Emaians were startled to see one of their own translating for a pirate Captain, they didn't show it. Their pale eyes were level as

Captain Ira stepped forward. "We are here to make fair trades. We have a ship full of supplies and gold, whichever you will take in exchange for goods we can sell in port: furs, oil, and *medicine*."

Iniabi looked to the captain and then repeated this, adding to the end, "We can bring you weapons, things that will protect you when the slavers come." It was a strange sort of power, languages. The captain could not understand her, and the Emai could not understand the pirates. Iniabi could decide much of how this would go. The thought made her stand straighter.

"What would these sea-walkers know of poison?" The medicine woman's voice was gravelly as if she rarely spoke anymore and wasn't used to doing so now. Her eyes were grayer than the other Emaian's, painted milky white with age and rheumatism. They swiveled from Captain Ira to Iniabi, and the weight of their gaze felt real as if a snow-damp blanket had been laid across Iniabi's back.

"There are those who sell it in the taverns and brothels of Bikkisi and Angillik. It takes the slavers from this world, and so they pour it down their throats like water, and when it kills them, it does not dissuade the others. They will pay anything for it." Iniabi carefully left out any mention of selling it or the captain using it—she did not think it would aid them.

The medicine woman stared at Iniabi for a breath longer and then tilted her chin toward their chief. The two exchanged a silent conversation with just the meeting of eyes, and then the man nodded as if in agreement. "The Poison is a secret of the Emai. To sell this secret will cost much. Two barrels of millet or barley for every shellful."

Iniabi gritted her teeth. A shell was perhaps six doses, and grains were tricky to come by these days. At that price, Iniabi couldn't have sold it in Angillik, and they would need to restock too soon.

"At such a price, it will not sell even in the cities," she said, keeping her eyes on the woman rather than the captain, "and we will have no use for it. No more than a barrel, or we won't trade."

The old woman snarled, showing several missing teeth. Contempt made her wrinkled face look all the more haggard. "Where is your loyalty, daughter of the tundra?"

"Iniabi!" the captain hissed.

"If you would be reasonable, elder, this could help you. You could have grain and protection for the spare whale oil you distill and the poison you can make plenty more of." Iniabi took a deep breath and switched to Phecean. "The medicine woman is considering a price, Captain."

"Then why does she look so sour? Don't ruin this deal for me."

The medicine woman spoke before Iniabi could reply. "Do not speak to me, girl, of reasonable. There is nothing reasonable about life anymore. Not when we sell our sacred ways to survive. Tell me, Iniabi, are you proud of what you have become?" The old woman's gaze moved over her, taking in her sailing clothes and sun-kissed skin. She was Emaian, and always would be, but the more she stayed at sea, the more she saw her slaver blood.

"I survived," she said, letting disdain color her voice. She would not let this old woman cow her. "I might have been a slave. The children of Muscana still might unless you do what you can to prevent it."

The chief stiffened, but then he laid a hand on the medicine woman's shoulder, and after a moment, she turned away, visibly shamed. "We have been hurt badly, Iniabi. Our pride is the only thing we have left, and selling sacred poison to these...*merchants*... It hurts that pride. But pride won't feed us, so we will accept her terms."

Iniabi nodded stiffly, suddenly wracked with guilt. These people were Emaian, blood of her blood. She could not join them now. This wasn't how the Emai acted, and Manaba would have punished her for it. She all but felt her mother's hand close over her jaw. *You're dead. You're dead you're dead you're dead.*

He turned then and nodded to Captain Ira. "We trade," he said in poor Phecean. When Iniabi gave him the captain's terms, he accepted though the medicine woman would not meet his eyes, and all the time they waited for the exchange of goods, the captain kept her hand on Iniabi's shoulder. The girl tried to smile at Jaya, to celebrate, but the Ararian pirate huffed and turned away. Only the captain was left smiling.

CHAPTER 31: LIRIA

TENTH MOON, 1797, EGARA

Eight Years before the Proclamation

"Congratulations, Vice General Nonus." Commander Vitus raised his glass as Luce walked by. He smiled at the Commander but didn't stop to talk. After the wedding, he would have time to socialize and receive well wishes and toasts, but now he had to be by his son's side and prepare him for the biggest day of his life. The temple's courtyard, well shaded by cypress and full of the bubbling of water, was empty of all guests. They would remain in the atrium, enjoying food and drink before the ceremony started. No, the courtyard was reserved for family and the place where the bride and groom would meet before they walked to the dais hand in hand and tied their lives together.

Luce thought about sitting on one of the benches along the circular walls of the courtyard but then decided not to. No matter how sore his knees were these days, Camilla would not be pleased if he creased the pants of his dress uniform. Instead, he occupied himself with studying the fountain in the middle. It depicted the First Imperator holding an ax in one hand and a cup in the other. At his feet, water burbled, washing his toes before splashing into the pool below. It was obviously of Lirian make, with strong, clean lines and proper subject matter. Not like those Phecean constructs, all weak angles and soft edges.

"Father?"

Luce turned to see his son, dressed in the formal uniform of a soldier. Pride swelled in his breast, and the older man beckoned to Ignatious. The boy's face was strained, the tendons in his neck standing out as he approached, saluting to Lucillius's rank.

"None of that," Luce said, and Ignatious smiled hesitantly. "*Well, here we are.*"

"Yes. I haven't seen her yet." Despite his controlled expression, Luce could see the nervous twitch of his son's hand.

"Don't worry, Ignatious. Your mother and I have worked long and hard to find the right girl. You know we started searching two years ago when you were only fifteen. We had our pick of girls, but we didn't rush. She is educated, wealthy, and beautiful."

"I know, but... She's Tupa Galan."

"Yes, she is. And with her comes trade alliances not only for our family but also for our nation. Next to the Princess, Valeria has the greatest ties to their largest shipping companies. We must tie their wealth to ours." Luce clasped his hand on Ignatious's shoulder. "Let me give you one last piece of advice, my son, before you marry and become a man."

Tonight, after the wedding, he and Valeria would move into a much smaller home in a less prominent quarter of the city, and in the morning, Ignatious would begin his basic training to follow in his father's footsteps. Today, though, he was still Luce's first son.

"This will not be a typical or traditional marriage, but neither was your mother's and mine. She is so much better than I am, but she saw that I would work hard to provide her with the life she deserved. So too will this girl. She is not Lirian, but you are giving her the chance to better her life. Treat her with kindness and honesty, as your mother has treated me, and I am certain she will not let you down. Though she is Tupa Galan, she *wants* to be Lirian, and that is admirable."

Ignatious rubbed the back of his neck with one hand, then threw his arms around Luce, like he had when he was small. Luce didn't hesitate to hug his son back. When they broke apart, Luce had to wipe at a few tears threatening to escape the corners of his eyes. "Alright, straighten your uniform before your mother and Valeria arrive; we don't want to look unseemly."

Ignatious smiled and complied.

CHAPTER 31: THE WESTERN SEA

SEVENTH MOON, 1798, THE FLYING NIGHT

Seven Years before the Proclamation

Iniabi stood on the deck of the ship, *Flying Night*, her home for the last four years, and pointed the butt of her staff at Jaya. "Are you ready to hit the deck, bilge rat?"

The other girl had grown another couple inches over the last year and acquired a half dozen more tattoos so that her arms dripped with the ferocious beasts of the northern Ararian jungle. The sides of her head were shaved, the center bound in a braid that fell to her waist, and she wore gold hoops in her ears and brow. Even Jaya had not changed as much as Iniabi, though, with her corded arms flushed pink from good health and sunshine. She would never be tall or curvaceous, but she had hardened into a whipcord tautness with sharp features below dark eyes. She wore her hair braided back in the female pirates' style and carried a sword on one hip.

Nearby, Iago knocked Cai down for the third time that morning, and the twins' sparring match dissolved into disorganized grappling, Nil grabbing a double handful of his brother's hair while Neus struggled to hold him down. Vlassis watched Iniabi and Jaya, though, and Iniabi wasn't about to fall.

"Only if it is with you beneath me, sea urchin, and my staff buried in your gut." Jaya's retort was a good one, her tone more intimidating than Iniabi's. She was better at insults. Jaya spun her staff in her grip, and it blurred in the air before she brought it to a halt, pointing at Iniabi's core.

Vlassis gestured, and the sparring match started. Jaya attacked at once, not allowing Iniabi to do so. Her staff flew through the air, and Iniabi bent backward to avoid it, whipping her staff down and to the side. Jaya's vicious swipe exposed her legs, and Iniabi whacked her in the meat of her thigh.

The taller girl winced when Iniabi's strike made contact, and Jaya took one step back, putting more weight onto her good leg and allowing Iniabi to straighten up. Both girls resettled their grips on their weapons, and Jaya's brow arched up her forehead, a cocky invitation for Iniabi to attack.

So she did, bringing her staff around in a crescent moon, aiming for Jaya's good leg. Jaya blocked the attack, sweeping the butt of her staff up and stopping Iniabi's strike. In the same fluid motion, Jaya spun on her good leg and whipped her staff around, aiming for Iniabi's unprotected shoulder. The Emaian ducked just in time, feeling the woosh of Jaya's staff overhead. Sometimes her short height was an advantage; opponents misgauged how low they should aim.

Jaya hissed between her teeth and kept coming, but Iniabi was faster, dancing away from most strikes, blocking a few, and landing a series of small but painful hits on Jaya. If Jaya got one blow in with her strength and power, it would likely end the fight, but that was only if she could make contact.

Both girls panted, sweat beading on Iniabi's brow and the back of her neck. She could feel it creeping between her breasts and over her belly. Jaya's tunic was drenched.

"Stop," Vlassis said, and Jaya froze. Iniabi stilled, but an odd mix of annoyance and anger shuffled through her. She hadn't wanted to stop.

"Jaya, you have lost this match."

"What?" Jaya sounded breathless. "She's barely made contact!"

"She's peppered you with jabs. If it were real steel in her hands, you would have half a dozen small, bleeding wounds, and she would have none. By now, you'd be drained not only of stamina and wind but also your blood. Iniabi would only have to stay out of range long enough for you to succumb to your wounds."

Iniabi wanted to grin—she had won, hadn't she?— only it didn't quite feel like as much of a win as knocking Jaya down would have. These days she was great at moving, and not getting hit, but would that really be enough? She wanted more physical power. Instead, she only nodded. "Should we go again?"

Jaya frowned at Vlassis, who turned away to watch Nil and Neus squabble. She rubbed at her thigh and shook her head. "I have chores to do and my pride to nurse. Who would have thought you'd ever really beat me?"

Iniabi felt her face warm. "Yeah, well. That's what you get for teaching me all your tricks, pirate girl." What did she have to do to get Jaya to look at her like that all the time? Win a dozen battles? Give her all Iniabi's cut of the goods?

Jaya laughed, the sound deep and musical. "That'll teach me to give out charity." She slung her sweaty arm over Iniabi's shoulder and jostled her, going so far as to ruffle the Emaian's hair. Iniabi snaked an arm around the other girl's waist, squeezing them together for a heartbeat, then Jaya walked away, leaving Iniabi half-drunk off the salt and sun smell of her.

Vlassis snorted. "Iniabi, since you're so eager to continue, why don't you give Cai a break from Iago?" The Tupa Galan boy stood over his opponent again, looking sheepish. Time might be helping Iago to fill out and grow into his height, but it wasn't exactly turning him into a hardened killer, even if he was the best fighter in their little group. With a final glance in the direction Jaya had gone, Iniabi squared off against Cai for another round.

Cai spat on the deck between them. "If I beat you, are you going to complain to your mama?"

Iniabi rolled her eyes. "Yeah, sure. Her spirit will come to haunt your sorry ass to give you an excuse for losing all the time."

Cai launched himself at Iniabi without warning. She'd seen him use this tactic before and brought her staff up in time to protect her collarbone from his blow. The wood clacked, and Iniabi tightened her jaw. Had the strike made contact, it might have broken her bone. She angled her staff to the left, and he stumbled as his staff slipped. Amateur. He should have better footing, but he was sloppy, relying on brute strength and tricks.

She popped him on the backs of his legs as he stumbled past. He yelped and turned, bringing his weapon up. "Not that mama!" He hissed, inching to the left. Iniabi followed his progress, keeping herself in a strong guard position. "The one whose boots you're always licking. Captain's pet. I bet you just go in there every night and sit on her lap when you're not kneeling between her legs."

Iniabi knocked his staff aside with one heavy blow and then thrust the butt of her weapon into the center of his belly before he got a chance to recover. Cai made a satisfying gasp and curled around himself. "You better not let anyone hear you talking about the captain like that. You'd get a lot worse if it was Taaliah or Vlassis."

Cai backed up, the coward, but managed to lift his head and give her a venomous look. "Why would they care? Everyone knows you're the captain's little whore."

Iniabi knew that she could not have possibly kept the frequent trips to the captain's quarters secret, and yet she was still surprised that Cai believed the captain wanted her for sex. She supposed he wasn't creative enough to figure out the real reason. Maybe it was better that way. "You've got it all wrong, Cai, but then you were never much of a pirate. The crew doesn't give a damn about anything except for the gold we make, and that's thanks to the captain."

He glared at her a moment longer and lifted his staff as if he were going to attack again, but Vlassis called out just then, proclaiming weapons training over. Cai gave Iniabi another dirty look and turned away, but not before she noticed the twins and Iago watching them. Had they overheard Cai's insults? Was he right? Did everyone know about Iniabi's trips to the captain? Did they all think she was the captain's pet?

Iniabi sighed and ran her hands over the smooth surface of her staff. What did it matter? It wasn't as if she could stop supplying Captain Ira with her poison. The woman would die of withdrawal, but not before she had Iniabi drowned.

⇑ ⇑ ⇑

That evening, while Jaya was stuck below decks with the Navigator learning to read star charts, and Cai was working with the ship's carpenter on a new sail, Iniabi begged food from Cook. She carried two bowls and a couple of wrinkly apples up to the deck, where Iago sat with his legs dangling off the ship and his arms crossed over the bottom railing.

"Here," she said, handing one of each to him. "We both know you're starving."

He looked up and smiled, his lank hair falling over his forehead. "Thanks."

Iniabi sat down next to her friend, putting a spoonful of Cook's hot seafood stew in her mouth. This time it was crab, fish, barley, and okra, simmered in something spicy from their last prize and full of flavor. "Lost souls, Cook's outdone himself again."

From their place against the railing, the sea spread black and fathomless for untold miles, no land marring the horizon. They could have been alone in all the world beneath a red evening sky. "Nice job knocking Cai on his ass today," Iniabi said, shooting a grin at the tall Tupa Galan boy. "He's been insufferable since he managed to grow that beard."

"You have to admit, though, it does look pretty good."

Iniabi recoiled and shoved Iago in the shoulder. "No way! Cai? Look good? You've gone crazy."

"How do you think I'd look with a beard? More fearsome? More handsome?" He turned his head, showing off his naked jawline.

"You'd look like a skinny walrus," she laughed. "But all your enemies would probably flee in terror. Maybe it wouldn't be so bad of an idea. We could send you over each time we got ready to board and then just take the goods after all the Lirians had thrown themselves in the sea!"

Iago gave Iniabi a harsh look, but as he took another bite of the stew, she could see the smallest smile creeping onto his lips. He was the least easily offended of the pirates; perhaps that was why they were friends. "What would you know of what makes a man handsome anyway? You only have eyes for ladies with swords. I've seen that drawing you keep under your pillow."

"What—?" Iniabi was thoroughly bewildered. "I don't have any drawings! Anything paper on the ship gets wet or eaten by rats."

He smirked and continued eating his stew as if Iniabi was lying about drawings of beautiful women with big *swords*. Where would she even get such a thing? She rolled her eyes. "Oh yeah, so who do you keep pictures of, then? Boys with beards?"

"Why would I need drawings of that when I have such a perfect specimen in front of me?" he said. Iago paused long enough to look down at Iniabi, his gaze lingering on her chin as if she had a beard, and then he took another bite. She couldn't help it; she rubbed at her jaw.

Iago laughed and shook his head. She shoved him again. "Fish brain."

"I'm like you. I like ladies with swords."

She eyed him curiously as Iago slurped more of the stew. "Any sword-wielding women in particular?"

Iago hesitated in his last bite, looking down into the spoon as if it would have the answers he sought. Finally, he sighed and finished the stew, setting aside the empty bowl to look at her fully. "I already said I'm like you. I like someone who can't like me back."

Something in Iniabi's chest plummeted, and she felt her heartbeat speed up. "How do you know I like someone who can't like me back?" She was careful not to allude to the person she did like, in case he was wrong. Did he know something about Jaya that she didn't?

"Because I know that person. They…well, *she*… I don't think you understand where she comes from. She…she *can't* like you, Iniabi." Even though there was urgency in his tone, Iago was careful to keep his voice low, and Iniabi was grateful for that. She absolutely did not want this conversation to be overheard.

"What does it matter where she comes from? We all come from different places here. We've all started over on the ship for some reason or another."

"They… The Ararians teach really different things to their kids. Really strict things. She doesn't live there anymore, but I think she still believes those teachings. Besides, Iniabi, haven't you noticed she doesn't flirt with *anyone*? Ever?"

"If she believes those strict teachings, how come she's a pirate?" Iniabi was so confused. "And what teachings do you mean anyway? That she can't like people?"

"Never mind, Iniabi."

"No, you can't say things like that and then refuse to explain them." She shook his arm. "Tell me."

"She can like *men*, Iniabi. I don't know if she does, but she can't like women. It's not... Her people say it's wrong."

Iniabi blinked at him and then put her chin on her arms folded over the railing, her bowl of stew forgotten beside her. "That's— that's the strangest thing I've ever heard." It made her feel hollow. She wasn't even sure she believed it—after all, it was normal for some people to not like the same gender, but for a whole country to say it was wrong? She shook her head.

"I know. I'm sorry, Iniabi. If it makes it any better, I understand. It's disappointing to like someone who can't feel that way about you. I just wanted to warn you... you know... so you wouldn't get hurt."

"I guess no one warned you, then?" Iniabi still wasn't sure how she felt. Iago could be wrong, couldn't he? Maybe he'd gotten Jaya's beliefs mixed up. She patted his knee.

"No, no one warned me. I had to discover it all on my own."

They sat like that until the red sky darkened to purple, and the sea took on the appearance of jagged glass.

She needed to prepare the captain's dose of poison soon. Iniabi glanced up at the crescent moon, wishing she had a giant hawk to take her there. She was trapped here aboard this ship, in this situation with the captain, constantly balancing on a knife's edge between death and discovery. With a grunt, she pushed herself to her feet, collecting her bowl. She would be sore from her fights with Jaya and Cai today, her muscles already protesting their abuse.

"Where are you going?"

"To my bunk. I don't have watch tonight." She never had watch on the nights the captain needed poison.

"Oh. To your bunk...." Iago plucked up his empty bowl and stood.

"You know, Iniabi, you don't have to lie to me or Jaya. Not anymore. We know what's going on."

Iniabi froze. Did they think what Cai thought? That she went to the captain to provide sexual favors? Would that be better or worse than the truth? She certainly didn't want Jaya to think that, and Iago had been talking about how he knew who she wanted... "What do you mean?"

He shrugged. "I mean, we're not stupid. All those times we go to Emaian villages to buy that medicine, but never sell it... The captain keeps looking sicker. She's the one taking it, isn't she? And you're helping her?"

Her heart was thumping hard in her chest. Had they put together that the so-called 'medicine' hurt the captain? That Iniabi was poisoning her slowly in the hopes of keeping her alive as long as possible?

The crew couldn't know.

"I'm doing what I can for her."

Iago nodded as if this was what he expected her to say. As he turned to go, Iniabi resisted the urge to call out. If he knew the truth, he wouldn't be able to help her and probably just hate her instead. She needed to handle this on her own.

CHAPTER 31: LIRIA

FIFTH MOON, 1798, DAIUM

Six Years before the Proclamation

Streamers and flags of red and gold fluttered in the streets of Daium as legions of soldiers marched by, boots so well shined that they reflected the sun overhead. Their sword hilts and belt buckles glittered as they passed beneath cream buildings. Half Liria's population seemed to have come to watch. The force was breathtaking in its formal glory, and Luce smiled down at Tulio as he gasped and clung to his father's arm. The six-year-old pointed as the next row of soldiers rounded the corner. "There he is! Look! There's Ignatious! Papa! Look!"

"I see him, Tulio."

"Wave, papa! Wave!"

"He's busy, Tulio. He can't wave back,"

"Isn't he happy to see us?" Tulio sounded put out.

Luce crouched to better see into his second son's blue-green eyes. Not brown or black like most Lirians, but as vibrant as the sea. "Of course, he's happy to see us, but it is his duty to Liria to stay in formation. When the Foundation Day celebrations are over, he will join us at the lake, *then* he'll greet you."

Tulio's lower lip trembled, threatening a pout. Luce couldn't see how the boy could really recall what it was like to live in the same home, as it had been well over a year since Ignatious had married, but Tulio still complained of not having a brother to play with anymore. "But—"

"Here now, son. Be brave like Ignatious. I know it's disappointing not to see him right away, but I promise he will be very glad to be with us once he has done his duty." Luce brushed his thumb along Tulio's cheek, whisking away any tears that might have escaped. Though it was the highest honor to serve Liria as a soldier, Luce suspected his youngest child would not be suited to the life of discipline. Perhaps he'd be more prone to politics or trade— useful but less structured.

Tulio's frustration seemed to linger, so Luce hauled the boy up to ride on his hip. There was no point in watching the rest of the Foundation Day parade if Tulio was crying. "Let's find a good spot by the lake now, so we have the best view when Ignatious is free."

"How will he know where to find us?"

Luce scanned the crowd and gestured for a young Corporal to approach. He saluted. "Sir?"

"Find my son, Ignatious Nonus, when the parade has finished. Tell him his father and brother wait by the lake."

The Corporal nodded and saluted again. "Yes, sir."

Perhaps it was an abuse of power to make some unsuspecting Corporal run his errands, but the older Luce got, the more comfortable he was with utilizing all the benefits of his status. After all, he was second in command of the entire Lirian Army. Surely that could come with a few comforts.

Weaving through the cobbled streets of Daium, Luce let his footfalls head downhill. The city was constructed at the edge of Liria's largest natural lake, on a bluff overlooking the glittering splendor. All one had to do to find water was to move downhill. Easy enough, even with a cranky six-year-old on one hip.

"Do you remember what you learned from your tutors about Foundation Day?" Luce adjusted his grip on Tulio's side as they started half-jogging down a steep street.

"Uhuh, the Lorotos—"

"Loratos," Luce corrected. Tulio flushed.

"The Loratos broke Liria away from the other city-states of Phecea, making it its own great country. Today is the day the Pheceans signed the accord admitting separation." Luce was glad to hear the tutors he paid so much were doing a good job.

"Very good, Tulio. And why did the Loratos want to make Liria into its own country?" Luce paused by a large flower bed, catching his breath. He wasn't an old man, per se, but toting his son around like a sack of flour was certainly more exercise than he got most days. He needed to resume training, even if he wasn't in active combat anymore. After all, soldiers looked up to their leaders.

"Was it because Pheceans only care about music and food and art and dancing, and they don't care about the Almighty or serving their country?" Luce was doubly impressed. Those were big concepts for a little boy.

"Yes! Excellent Tulio." The boy turned pink, but this time Luce thought it was with pride. He squirmed then to be put down, and Luce happily complied. "The Pheceans only cared about bettering *themselves*, not their families or nation. They are selfish and lazy. The Almighty gave the Loratos the strength to break free from the sickness of Phecea, and in return for saving us, the Loratos inherited the divine right to rule. One day, The Almighty will reward our faith—maybe even in your lifetime."

Tulio started walking again, and Luce followed suit. "Is that why we fight the Pheceans now?"

"We don't fight them."

"But I thought you said the border—"

"Those are little skirmishes because the Pheceans keep coming onto our land." Or rather, land that had rightfully belonged to Liria ages ago.

"Oh, so they're stealing?"

"Something like that. Here, look down there. What do you see?" Luce said, pointing to the shimmering lake below.

Tulio squinted and then smiled. "Baby battleships!"

"Yes, they were made for the Foundation Day celebrations. Are you excited to see the reenactments?"

"Yes!" Tulio's voice was high-pitched with glee, and he started to run down the hill. Almighty, he was fast. Luce sighed and picked up a jog. At least his son wasn't crying anymore.

For a time, Tulio was happy to throw rocks into the lake and chase the gulls, the banks slowly filling with parade-goers. Ignatious was among them, following the Corporal Luce had assigned the task. Tulio ran for his brother, clinging to his legs as Ignatious took huge steps, and the two cackled with mirth. Between sessions of wrestling, Ignatious smiled shyly at Luce. "Has mother told you the news?"

"Hmm?"

"About Valeria?" Luce hadn't heard anything about Ignatious's wife, but then he'd been buried in mountains of paperwork for the Imperator the last few weeks.

"No, is everything well?"

"More than well! She's pregnant." Ignatious beamed, and Luce felt his heart swell.

"That is fantastic news, son!"

"What is?" Tulio asked.

"Your brother is going to be a father," Luce said, and Tulio frowned.

"Don't you have to make babies with girls?"

"Generally speaking, yes." Luce tried to hide his smile as Tulio's expression turned to one of horror.

"Yuck!"

Ignatious laughed, and Tulio ran off, collecting more rocks to throw into the lake. Luce turned to his eldest son and clasped his shoulder. "I'm glad to hear you suffered through the process of making a child. Your devotion to your country is estimable."

Ignatious managed a shy smile. "I heard Phecea is threatening to cut off trade with us."

"They are," Luce agreed. Ignatious looked worried, so he hurried to reassure his son. He probably feared rationing or scarcity if Phecea cut off trade. That was no environment for his wife and coming child. Luce would have felt the same way. "They've threatened us in the past and never have the nerve to go through with it. Besides, we have a strong trade agreement with Tupa Gali. If the Pheceans cut us off from their commerce, what does that mean? No more poetry. How ever will we survive?"

The words had their intended effect because Ignatious's frown smoothed away, replaced with a sarcastic pout. "What will I do without my hand creams and scalp massages?"

They both laughed, and the tense moment passed. It wasn't as if Liria needed Phecea anyway. Liria was strong. Phecea was weak.

CHAPTER 34: PHECEA

SEVENTH MOON, 1799, DIOSION

Six Years before the Proclamation

Though he had been Danae's friend for years, Biton still received a generous welcome when he went to the Othonos estate. The servants showed him to the formal sitting room, gave him a drink in a gold-enameled glass, and fed him luxurious little treats. More often than not, Danae arrived to play, but sometimes one or both of her parents came to greet him.

Today, it was Councilor Arsenio Othonos, Danae's father. He was a tall man with the same creamy brown skin and soft, curling hair as his daughter. Though Councilor Arsenio exuded an authoritative air, his daughter still presented a shy awkwardness in social situations.

Councilor Arsenio bowed politely to Biton as he entered the sitting room, taking a cup of kava. "Biton, I'm glad to see you today. I heard you were starting your apprenticeship soon." Danae had bemoaned this fact for weeks, afraid to go back to etiquette classes without Biton as a shield and a guide. He had mixed feelings about it too. It would be exciting to start learning more about the inner workings of the Phecean Confederacy, but it would mean spending time away from his friends and family.

"Yes, sir," Biton said, rising to dip into a low, formal bow. Councilor Arsenio was one of the ten most powerful people in their nation, and he should always be shown respect. "It will be an honor to start serving the Confederacy."

"Indeed. Perhaps you'd enjoy working within my office, should you have the time? Danae says you've a keen mind, and she'd be happiest if you didn't travel too far."

Biton's eyes widened, and he couldn't think what to say. It was a tremendous offer, something that could change his career and increase his rank. He took a deep breath, as his father had taught him, so that he might respond in a collected manner. "Yes, sir. Thank you. I will endeavor to serve you and our nation to the best of my abilities."

The sitting room flew open, and Danae bowed as one would to a family member. "Papa! I thought you had already left."

Her father stood, gripping Biton on the shoulder with something akin to affection. Without even having to stoop, he turned to Danae and kissed the top of her head. She might be as tall as her father by the time she finished growing. "I was just leaving when I heard Biton arrive. He and I enjoy our little visits, so I said hello. But now, I must go."

She watched him leave before hurrying over to Biton. They were past bowing, so she kissed his cheek in greeting. "Hello, I'm sorry I kept you waiting."

"Danae." Biton was all but shaking with excitement. "Your father just offered me the chance to work in his office as an apprentice."

He still could hardly believe it. It was too good an opportunity. Like getting to study with the best artist in one's craft.

"Of course he did! You're clever and well-liked!" She didn't seem all that surprised, so it must have been something she had mentioned before. "I'll miss you, but at least you will stay in the city proper now." Pulling away from their embrace, she smoothed the front of her tunic. "Now, do you want to hear the piece I've been working on?"

"Yes, of course!" Biton said, still a little dazed. "Should we go up to your music room then?"

Biton had always wanted to be Danae's friend, but he was beginning to understand why it was so important to his parents. They had ensured he saw as much of her as possible over the last couple of years. It suited Biton perfectly well, but now it looked like it would solidify his future too.

"Yes, of course, if you're done with your tea?" Danae's manners were impeccable. Even as excited as she was to show off the piece she had been working on, she remembered to be polite. Still, he could see her brimming with energy and ready to pull him up the stairs.

Biton put down his tea with a smile. "A cup of tea wouldn't keep me from your performance."

Danae

Settled before her harp, Danae brought the instrument back to brace against her shoulder—a friend, familiar and warm. The well-polished wood glowed, and as Danae bowed her head to concentrate, rays of sunlight warmed her cheeks. Music had become her salvation these last few years, her harp especially. It offered her a place of repute with other musicians and gave her something to demonstrate at parties. She could sit and play for hours, being part of the room without the awkward discomfort of not knowing what to say.

Danae had only owned this harp for a year; since she became too long for the children's one she started on. Each instrument had a personality: Her children's harp had been a little slow to respond, lazy but amenable. This harp was sensitive to her touch, fickle, and demanding in its frequent tunings. It took moons of working with the more refined instrument before her melodies sounded as they had before, but Danae learned a valuable lesson.

Anything worth having took effort to keep.

Now, she enjoyed how precisely she must play for her harp to agree and make music. Lovingly, she ran her fingers over the chords, eliciting a beautiful hum before setting her hands on either side, quieting it once more. "Are you ready?"

"Yes," he said as he settled on a cushion, his fine blue silks set off by the room's cream walls. "Whenever you're ready."

"Alright. It's better if you close your eyes."

She laid her hands against the strings and turned her mind inward to that picture of motifs and melodies, chords and dynamic contrasts: her map of the journey ahead. She took a deep breath and plucked the first notes.

The piece started softly, a triple-meter lullaby in longing lines that reached ever towards a cadence they could not obtain before a more agitated, arpeggiated accompaniment pushed up from underneath, creeping out of the shadows of the melody and into a raucous crescendo. The music grew wild here: storms of wind-tossed runs all in that same lilting, three-step beat. Strong-weak-weak. Strong-weak-weak. Like a trembling heart.

Dimly, Danae was aware of Biton standing, his eyes still closed in the center of the room. He began to move, to dance in that typhoon of melody and rhythm, swaying like a windswept tree or a hawk looking down above the chaos.

Then, there was a moment of quiet, a pin-drop of silence where everything kept still, before the return of the original melody, changed and darkened by the passage of the tempest, but still whole, still in that opening key, the home they had been searching for since the first steps away. And finally, with tender trills, she found the cadence, the rest at the end.

"You can open your eyes," she murmured to Biton, who obediently had kept them shut even during his dance. He knew she didn't like to be watched while she played. "Well?"

"That was beautiful, Lady Artist. An experience from the first note to the last. You tell such amazing stories with that instrument." Biton stepped forward and kissed her cheek. "Really, Danae. That was amazing."

The heat of her skin felt like the sun's warm glow. "Thank you, Biton. Come on, I have a new shipment of dyed silks from Tupa Gali; let's see which ones you should keep and which ones I'll make into outfits."

Biton

Biton picked up a ream of silk in the purest, most vibrant gold and wrapped a yard around himself, luxuriating in the feel of the fabric. It was less like touching something tangible than slipping one's hand in a stream of warm, sparkling water.

"Danae, you *have* to take this one! It will set off the tones of your skin and eyes perfectly. You'll look like a fallen star." He shrugged it off his shoulders and draped it about Danae's, where she stood before a mirror in her room. The space around her was an explosion of color. Fabrics of every imaginable shade spilled onto the floors and furniture so that it seemed less like reality and more like a dream world where everything was made of bright sweets. "What do you think?"

She moved to look at the effect in the standing mirror, shifting left and then right so the silk could catch the sunlight. "Don't you think it's too... bold? Here." She turned, draping a yard of midnight black across Biton's chest. It made his black hair and slate eyes all the darker, his almond skin richer. "Oh, and I have the gems that go with that."

Danae turned, discarding the golden silk as she hurried to her jewelry box, or as Biton affectionately referred to it, her treasure chest. As the sole heir to the Othonos family, Danae often received gifts that were not entirely suitable for a girl of thirteen— diamonds and rubies, silks and velvets, imported laces from Zolela.

"I don't think gold is too bold a color choice for you," Biton said absently, turning back to the mirror. "In fact, I think that it was made for you."

He pulled the midnight fabric tight down the front of his chest like the two panels of a gentleman's doublet and puffed himself up, pretending to be as strong or filled out as one of the heroes in the stories Melba was always sighing over. He didn't much like the effect it had on him. It just wasn't... right.

Keme would understand.

"Danae, what are you looking for?" She was still digging around in her box of treasures, so Biton turned back to the mirror and arranged the silk in a sash slung across his chest, shoving down the collar of his tunic so that his warm-skinned clavicles would show above the pretend neckline. It had a much more pronounced effect on the length of his neck. Danae was right: this color was nice with his eyes. It even made his lashes seem longer.

"Do you remember when Master Barak came over for supper a few moons ago with his husband and their daughter, and papa talked with them about changing the shipping route to avoid Tupa Galan waters even though it'd increase the voyage by three weeks?" Danae had been stuck home, smiling at the important merchants to keep them feeling respected and happy. An additional three weeks at sea was no small matter, and it was a dangerous route. The waters farther to the north were choppy, prone to storms. Still, Danae's father had said it was better to lose their goods to the sea than the "pirates" that seemed to infest Lirian waters.

"I remember," Biton said, only half paying attention. He draped another swath of black silk across his lap.

Danae straightened up, holding out a necklace of onyx. It had one teardrop stone that would lay flat against one's chest, then smaller round ones that made up the chain. "Here." His friend came up behind him, setting the necklace, not around his throat, but as a circlet around his skull, the teardrop stone dipping onto his forehead.

Long fingers worked through Biton's inky hair, braiding it away and wrapping it artfully around the necklace until the stones were woven into his locks, black stars on a black sky. "Well, he gave this to me. Mother got emeralds." Onyx, while a striking stone, was not all that expensive.

"I—it's beautiful." Biton looked into his reflection, and for a moment, he saw himself. It wasn't a new sensation, not really. Biton made a habit of being as much himself as he could be. He spoke and acted in the most authentic way. He told stories that made his chest swell because he loved them, and he danced how his soul wanted him to dance.

It was just that the mirror had never shown him before a picture of him how he really, truly ought to look.

"Thank you, Danae." Biton felt a little dizzy. He needed to talk to Keme.

"Of course, you're much more glamorous anyway, and I think

black makes me look sallow." She brushed her hands over his shoulders before turning back to the bed strewn with silks. "Now, do you want to keep the red too?"

CHAPTER 35: PHECEA

NINTH MOON, 1799, DIOSION

Six Years before the Proclamation

The early spring breeze smelled of spices and salt, and the bay echoed through the marketplace. Danae waited in the rear of a pack of girls from etiquette class. Mistress Afin had let them out earlier than usual, and Danae was slowly being accepted into their social circles. She wasn't foolish enough to think this reflected her popularity but rather the leftover shadow of Biton and her family name. Still, it was better to careen from stall to stall with noble girls than to go home alone. Danae's parents were in Sessis for the week, so until Biton finished his work for the day, the Othonos estate would be empty aside from servants and slaves.

"Danae, what do you think about this perfume? The man says it's all the way from Ingola. I've never owned anything from Ingola before…." Yolanta held out the bottle for Danae to sniff.

To Danae, the scent was too floral, but she could tell from the way Yolanta's eyes gleamed that she wanted Danae to like it. "If it really is from Ingola, it's like having a piece of another country," Danae said diplomatically, neither offering her opinion on the sickly sweet scent nor blatantly lying.

Yolanta sniffed the bottle again, humming as she debated whether she wanted it or not. Having shopped with the other girls before, Danae knew it could take Yolanta a while to make up her mind, so she wandered away from the group.

Rows of chimes swayed in the breeze, singing out in bright voices. Bolts of fabric dazzled her eyes, and spices warred with perfumes. The marketplace could be an overwhelming adventure, but Danae found it inviting. People shouted and laughed, and children played in front of street musicians and performers. Occasionally a soldier in a Phecean uniform strolled past. The military presence in Diosion grew every year, it seemed.

As a little girl, the soldiers frightened her. They were loud with their shined boots and sharp angles. They dressed like no one else she knew and smiled far less. In parades, they walked all the same, and the music played on drums and brass trumpets hurt her ears. They seemed so out of place in Phecea, a country that loved the arts and the passions. Dancers, philosophers, great thinkers, and creators. That was what Phecea meant to Danae, and the soldiers clashed with that idea.

Danae could still hear Yolanta, so she felt no need to hurry shopping for something less stuffy and more unique. She and Biton often tried to outdo one another, producing the most bizarre or beautiful items from around the world. Since he would come over that evening, Danae wanted something impressive. A stall with bright flags of Illygad caught her eye, and Danae crossed the street to see what they might have when a familiar figure caught her eye: Keme, stepping aside to let Pheceans have the right of way.

Danae knew Keme was Biton's personal slave and often went out for him on errands, but she had never seen the man outside of the Mavros estate. His white skin and ashen hair stood out against the predominantly dark-haired and dark-skinned Pheceans, and the strange context startled her.

Beside him stood a servant girl in sackcloth trousers, her shirt half-untucked. Her short, black hair was shoved into a simple cap. She might have been anyone. A runner for the Mavros estate, perhaps, or someone who worked for one of the stall keepers, only she wasn't carrying any packages. Why would Biton send Keme out with a lowborn girl?

Danae put down the basket and waved to the shopkeeper. She'd be back; she just had to get a closer look first.

The girl wasn't acting like a servant. She walked with a straight spine and her shoulders back and had all the lithe grace of a professional dancer. She kept stopping, touching Keme's arm to direct him to some stall or another, and smelling the perfume or touching the fabrics there. She even bought a few things while Danae watched: wax for removing hair, a lovely silk tunic, and a delicate crystal bottle of perfume. All of the coin came from her own pockets: gold and silver. What servant girl would have such money?

And then, Danae watched the girl turn and flash a wide grin at Keme, her face in full view for the first time.

Without thinking, Danae spun on her heel, walking away from Keme and Biton. Because the girl with the slave wasn't some servant with mysterious handfuls of gold but Biton. Why he was dressed as a servant or sneaking around when he told her he would be busy at his apprenticeship all day, she couldn't fathom.

But the idea of being caught following him and Keme around, watching him behaving so oddly, or worse, catching him in a lie, felt decidedly uncomfortable. Danae slipped back amongst the other girls just in time for Yolanta to buy the Ingolan perfume and tucked her hands tightly against her belly.

"Where were you?" Yolanta asked as they left the stall and meandered back towards their carriages.

"I thought I saw someone I knew," Danae said, wondering if Biton had wandered up this line of stalls yet. She didn't want him to know she had seen him out with Keme.

"Who was it?"

"It was the wrong person."

⇑   ⇑   ⇑

Biton sat at the long, stone table in the Othonos dining room, its white marble surface littered with gold-inlaid plates brimming with delicacies. It was situated so that floor-to-ceiling windows ringed three of its four sides, and most of these were open, their sheer curtains blowing gently with an evening breeze coming off the bay.

It was unusually quiet. Biton was used to eating in state at Danae's home, especially when her parents were there, but things were typically lighter when it was just the two of them. He couldn't guess what bothered Danae so much that she wouldn't speak, but he supposed he would just have to cheer her up.

"One of Father's mares just gave birth to a foal! You should see her, Danae. She's so ungainly. Like a puppy on stilts. She has the softest nose in all the world and black legs like she's wearing leggings!"

"Oh? What are you going to call her?" The question wasn't a poor one, but the lack of enthusiasm on Danae's part was odd.

"I think I'll call her Dasan, after the story of the warrior and the eagle that took her to the sun. Unless you can think of a better name?"

Shaking her head, Danae returned her gaze to her still-full plate. She hadn't eaten much despite the lack of conversation.

"Or maybe I should save that name for you if you get another horse. You could be Danae and Dasan, remember?"

"No, you can use it."

Well, that didn't work. Biton chewed on the inside of his cheek. "I've been learning so much at work! They have me study records to see what has worked in past years."

"In the past?" Danae asked golden brown eyes fixed on her plate rather than his face.

"Yes! But they're all talking about what's going on now. Evidently, Liria has refused to acknowledge threats to stop trading, even though they depend on us for grain and crafted goods. The raids haven't died down, and some people are even speculating that the Imperator married that Tupa Galan wife of his to gain access to their corn fields. It might mean war if Liria keeps cutting diplomatic ties and the raids keep increasing."

"War would be bad. I know mother and father don't want that." She pushed a bit of food around, her demeanor fretful before she seemed to remember something. "I saw soldiers in the market today."

Danae hadn't mentioned that she went into the market today,

though normally, if she did go shopping, she would show him her prizes. Biton fidgeted in his seat. He hadn't told her *he* would be at the market either.

"Did you find anything interesting?"

Her soft lips parted several times as if she would speak, but in the end, Danae only shook her head. "No, Yolanta bought this perfume from Ingola, and that took so long we had to leave after."

"Yolanta always takes forever. Was the perfume any good at least?"

"It wasn't to my taste," Danae said in her diplomat's voice.

"So it was absolutely terrible?"

A small smile tried to escape the confines of Danae's lips, making the corners of her mouth twitch slightly. "I didn't say that."

Biton could have cheered. It was a start. "That's what it sounded like to me."

⇑   ⇑   ⇑

Eleventh Moon, 1799, Iretetra

Despite the unseasonably cold weather blowing up from the south, the noble children bundled up, tacked up, and took their horses out. The fields around the Adamos estates were well maintained with little stone walls and groomed hedges that the more adventurous riders could jump should they please. And for those, like Danae, who preferred to trot or canter leisurely, the gently sloping hills were just the thing. Callista and Yolanta trotted alongside Danae, their geldings nearly as docile as her mare, watching as the boys raced one another over the hill and across a stream.

Biton was amongst the racers, with Adohnis and Ion hot on his heels. Much like everything Biton did, he rode enthusiastically and as if he were born to it. "I don't know why they bother to race him anymore," Erose said as she cantered over and pulled her gelding down to trot alongside the other girls. Danae noticed how closely Erose watched the race. "He *always* wins."

She meant Biton and it was true. He was a fantastic rider: totally fearless. Already, she could see Adohnis lagging behind, slowing his mount to a more reasonable pace to ford the creek. Sensible but certainly not the tactic of someone who would win against Biton.

"Well, he's so nice about winning; it doesn't really feel like losing," Callista said.

"Hmm, well, if we want to make it back before the others eat all the food, we'd better hurry."

Even with their hurrying, the racers made it back to the stables well ahead of the slower group, so Danae watched from her position on Lois as they jostled one another, wrapping arms about each other's necks and cajoling. Biton was in the thick of it, his coat mud splattered, but his cheeks high with color.

Biton hooked an arm over Adohnis's shoulders and pulled him over so that he could ruffle the other boy's thick head of curls. Ion and Adohnis had inches on him, and Danae was at his height, if not a little taller, but that didn't stop Biton from playing rough with the others. "Oh, come on, Adohnis. You'd have probably beat me if I wasn't on Crane. He's the fastest horse in Father's stable, or he will be until his filly grows up. You should see her!"

Adohnis shoved Biton's arm off, laughing. "Maybe you ought to lend us your stable master. The man just keeps breeding faster horses for you. My papa said yours used to race just like you do."

Ion snorted. "Adohnis, you weren't even that close. *I* was second! It's not all about how great your horse is."

"Yeah, you could probably show me a few tricks." Biton's face split into a wide, happy smile. "Hey Danae, what do you think? Is it the horse or the rider?"

Relaxing her grip on Lois's reins, Danae straightened up in the saddle as the others looked her way. "Ah, well... A good rider will only get so far on a three-legged horse, and the fastest stallion in the stable will run in the wrong direction if his rider doesn't know how to direct him."

Erose pulled her gelding to a stop on the opposite side of Biton. "Biton, will you help me down?" Her smile was too broad to be demure, but the effect was pleasant, her bright, Tupa Galan features lighting up and her copper skin glowing despite the harsh spring day.

Biton met her happy gaze with one of his own and reached up to lay a hand on her waist. Erose swung her far leg over the front of her horse's saddle in a way Danae disapproved of. What riding instructor had taught her that? She placed her hands on Biton's shoulders so that as he helped her down, he could not help but look up at her breasts.

"There you are," he said once she was safely on the ground. "Did you have a nice ride? Your gelding is a beautiful animal."

Erose tossed her thick hair, wild from the ride but in a way that just looked voluminous and free. Danae's hair, also teased by the wind, looked like a bush. "Oh, you know... a nice little trot. Nothing as exciting as the race."

Danae gathered both reins in her left hand along with a handful of mane, grasped the pommel of her saddle with her right hand, and swung her right leg over the back of the saddle. Landing on her feet *properly*, she pulled Lois's reins over her mare's head to hold them loosely with both hands. As any decent rider would.

Erose still stood with her gelding waiting, blinking up at Biton.

His face lit up. "Oh? Do you race then?"

"I don't know. I've never tried. Maybe you could show me?"

Danae turned away, heading back into the stable. Biton's popularity usually didn't bother her, but there were days when the flock of admirers became a *bit* too much. Always chatting and laughing and coming up with new things to do.

The warmth of the stable seeped into Danae as she led Lois to the stall the Adamos family made available for her mare, sliding the stall door shut behind herself before removing the bridle. Lois turned towards the few pieces of hay left in the corner as if she were starved.

Danae smiled, brushing her hand along the smooth flank of her mare before starting to untack. Most of the other nobles would likely head to lunch and let the stablehands tend to the horses, but Danae thought a few minutes alone with her mare would be welcome.

The quiet didn't last.

Biton and the others led their horses in after only a few moments, and while Ion and the other two girls quickly passed their horses off to slaves, Adohnis and Biton stayed behind to untack their own mounts.

"Don't take too long!" Erose called over her shoulder, and then the stable was quiet once more, but for the rustle and scrape of leather and stable doors.

Brushing the curry comb over Lois's withers, Danae fell into the comforting habit of grooming, the only thing occupying her mind the movement of her hand and the weight of Lois beside her. Peaceful, meditative. Danae bent to pick up her hard brush, flicking it across Lois's sides, which were hardly sweaty.

Adohnis finished first, sliding out of his horse's stall with an armful of tack he dropped into the hands of the nearest slave. He stuck his head over the stall next to him. "Hey, I'm starving. I'm going to go catch up with the others. Don't take too long, eh? We might just eat all of the good stuff."

Biton's voice came back muffled. "Yeah, alright! I just want to look over Crane. That was a hard run."

For a few minutes, there was just the sound of horses munching on hay and the shifting of great bodies. Danae nearly forgot about her rumbling stomach as she rubbed down Lois. And then, Crane's stall door opened. Danae peaked over the edge of Lois's door as Biton stepped out, his saddle in his hands. One of the slaves stepped closer to take it, but he shook his head and placed three fingers to his lips. "Thank you, friend, but I can set these in the tack room."

The Emaian woman looked as though she had been struck: wary and surprised, but it quickly melted into gratitude. She returned the gesture, hand to her mouth, and bowed low.

Then, Biton was gone, sweeping first into the tack room and out into the sun.

The interaction struck Danae, though she wasn't entirely sure why. Biton was kind to everyone, and she had seen him interact politely with Keme, but the slaves in the Adamos stables were strangers to him. To everyone. And yet he went out of his way to behave almost deferentially.

She had never seen someone act that way before.

As Biton left the stable, the slaves watched him go and gathered together, murmuring in their blunted language.

She waited a long time to leave the stable, not wanting Biton to know she had seen his strange treatment of the Emai slaves. What would the others think if they saw him being so... peculiar?

Hours later, Danae lay beneath sheer purple valances in the four-poster bed given her by the Adamos family. She watched Yuka, her personal Emai slave, move around the room on silent feet. She banked the fire in the hearth and pulled the curtains over the windows to block the full moon. As she turned back to the small vanity, pouring a glass of water, Danae tried the gesture she had seen Biton demonstrate in the stable earlier.

"Thank you, Yuka," she murmured, pressing her three fingers to her lips.

The woman's eyes widened, her gaze dropped to the floor, and she bowed low. "Yes, of course, mistress," she said, and her voice was soft, careful. "Is there anything else I can do for you this evening?"

Her reaction made Danae feel odd. Yuka wasn't happy or thankful as the Emai in the stables had been. If anything, she seemed put off. And why wouldn't she be? Danae was acting as if she were Emai too. The falseness made her belly writhe, and Danae shook her head. "No. Goodnight, Yuka."

When Yuka bowed and closed the bedroom door, Danae sighed. She had known Yuka her entire life and Yuka's mother as well. And her grandmother. All of the Emai in the Othonos estate had been with her family for generations. When an Emai in the Othonos estate expressed an interest in having children, Danae's mother contacted other council members to see if there were any suitable matches. If agreeable, they purchased the new spouse and added to their staff, taking on the responsibility of another Emai so that children could be raised by both parents.

Yuka was probably offended that Danae had treated her as she would a captured Emai from the south. Like an uneducated tribesperson. She pressed her fingers to her burning cheeks, wishing the flush would fade. Yuka had been born in Phecea, in the Othonos estate! She was cultured and educated. It had been wrong of Danae to treat her otherwise.

CHAPTER 36: THE WESTERN SEA

SEVENTH MOON, 1799, THE FLYING NIGHT

Six Years before the Proclamation

*I*niabi woke to someone shaking her shoulder and groaned, pressing her face into the canvas of her hammock. It was cold, and she was not yet ready to leave the warmth of her blankets for the day. "What time is it?"

"Early," Jaya whispered, her voice tense.

She opened her eyes then, taking in the sight of Jaya standing over her. She had thrown a hardened leather breastplate over her usual tunic. There was a crossbow strapped to her back, and extra knives jammed into her belt. No war drums vibrated the ship, though, and Iniabi could not hear the sounds of pirates preparing to attack.

Iniabi sat up in her hammock. "What's wrong?"

"Captain thinks it's another Lirian raid." That would be the fourth one in six moons. "A warship was spotted a few leagues from here. We're trying to outpace them and lose them in the fog, but...." Jaya shook her head. The *Flying Night* wasn't much of a match for the new Lirian warships. Fastest on the sea, armed to the sails with soldiers, and as hungry as a bear after hibernation, the Lirians were formidable.

Iniabi flung off the blankets covering her and pushed herself to her feet, feeling around the decking below for her boots and her sword. "I'll need to get down to the armory. Meet me on deck?"

Jaya only grunted before she dashed off, her boots thudding against the ladder as she climbed above.

Fully armed and dressed, Iniabi reached the deck in the near-dark of predawn. The *Flying Night's* lanterns were doused, her three massive masts supporting full sail. They were running just as fast as the ship could go under a good wind in clear seas. Iniabi hoped it would be enough.

She found Jaya and the others clustered around Taaliah on the quarterdeck, their expressions solemn and their hands on their weapons. Iniabi joined them, hurrying across the deck in a clink of weaponry. Taaliah nodded to her. "Good, you're here. I need you four to prep the deck, just in case. Get spikes to throw, tar to pour—any nasty trap you can think of to help even the odds. I don't care what the others say— We're not outpacing that piece of Lirian junk, and we've only got a few hours before the sun burns up the fog and all our cover is gone. Best get to it and be ready to fight when the time comes."

Iniabi nodded. "I can talk to Cook. If he has oil to spare, we could use it to light their ship on fire."

"Good thinking. The rest of you find other methods. I want this ship to feel like a fortress in an hour."

As she worked, Iniabi kept an eye on the lightening sky, on the tendrils of grasping fog that clung to the masts and the great sheets stretched between them. The crew was unnaturally silent, going about their duties with drawn faces and too-watchful eyes. They all knew what was coming, and Iniabi didn't think that many of them expected to survive it. Perhaps it was determination or stubbornness or a belief that the future she'd seen in poison dreams as a child, but Iniabi was sure she would still be here come the next morning.

When she and Cook finished making bombs with oil and alcohol, Iniabi went to find Iago, where he hauled great sacks of spikes into the rigging to be dumped on their enemies if they were boarded. Iniabi took a rope and lent her weight to his.

"It's odd having to wait for a battle, isn't it? Usually, we decide when we fight." Iniabi heaved, watching the sack lift away from the deck. Hopefully, they wouldn't need all this.

Iago's angular face was pale in the morning light as if he rarely saw the sun. He glanced at Iniabi and shook his head. "Normally, when we raid other ships, we're not fighting soldiers. People don't die, not really. We scare 'em a bit, and they give us their goods. What do we fight for now? Our lives."

Iniabi shook her head. "All fighting is for our lives. Or at least all fighting where our opponents want us dead. Whether the opponents are soldiers or merchantmen, anyone could get a lucky shot."

Iago swallowed, his throat bobbing, but nodded though he didn't look any less pale. Cai's sharp whistle cut through the air, and Iago waved vaguely to Iniabi before walking off to help the other boy with his preparations. Iniabi watched him go, uncertain of what she had said to make him leave.

"You're not very good at comforting people, are you, Iniabi?" Jaya had snuck up on her in the fog and stood coiling a rope at the rail, ensuring it would be out of the way and not a tripping hazard.

"I thought it would be comforting not to think of this battle as something different, but rather as something we're already good at." Iniabi went to lend Jaya a hand. "I thought I was projecting confidence in us."

"You do seem confident," Jaya agreed, glancing up through thick lashes as she knelt to straighten the pile of rope. "But if you're confident, he's alone in his fear. It would be inspiring, I guess, if you were the captain, but you're just a skinny Emaian girl. If you're not afraid, and he is, then maybe that makes him a coward."

"Iago's not a coward. He can best any of us in a fight." Still, she said it uncertainly. "What would you have said to make him feel better?"

Jaya straightened up, her long black hair already braided and pinned to the back of her skull. She looked sleek as a seal and ready for battle. She didn't look afraid, as Iago had. "I probably would have told him he's a good fighter, and I'd have his back. Then maybe he wouldn't feel alone. Maybe I'd say my gut is roiling, and I might puke my brains out any minute, if it were true."

"It's not true, though, is it? You're like me. Fighting only excites you."

The older girl studied Iniabi for a long moment. "I'm not afraid. But then, I'm not afraid of dying either. I know what awaits me in the end. Iago… He doesn't have that, so I suppose that's scary."

Movement on the prow caught Jaya's attention, and Iniabi turned to see what it was. The fog parted in a gust of wind, briefly revealing the outline of a massive warship. It flew the Lirian flag, garish and bold, with an ax and a cup crossed in its center. In another instant, the fog shifted and hid them from sight.

Away from other Emaians, where there was no medicine woman to sing her spirit to the shore, Iniabi was not sure where she would go when she died. Most likely, her spirit would wander the Tundra for an eternity, tormenting the lost and wailing her regret to the sky. She wouldn't die tonight, though. Iniabi had seen her future in the grip of poison dreams, and she had never known the urchin to lie to an Emaian woman.

Perhaps that fate awaited her anyway—punishment for the poison she'd delivered.

The Lirians struck before the fog burned away, their sleek warship sliding out of the mist like an enormous wraith, wreathed in cloud tendrils and full of swords. Men in red and navy uniforms swarmed onto the *Flying Night*, their hands full of steel and their bodies armored in thin strips of metal. They crashed into them the way the sea crashed into the shore—relentless, unstopping.

The deck was a chaos of stomping feet, writhing bodies, and whistling blades. Iniabi moved through it, mostly dodging but weakening the enemy where she could. She cut an ankle tendon here, added a stab wound there—little blows that made their recipients easier to take down. Someone had scattered spikes across the ship, and the pirates, more used to maneuvering on uncertain ground, were doing a better job of avoiding them than the soldiers, but still, the *Flying Night's* sailors fell in droves.

They would be taken. Anyone could see it. The *Flying Night* was going to fall to these soldiers.

"Help! Iniabi!"

Iniabi spun, dread filling up her chest cavity so that there was no room left to breathe. Iago stood in a knot of bigger, better-armed men, swinging his sword in a wild attempt to keep them off him. Iniabi leaped forward, ducking in behind one of his captors to slip her knife between his ribs, then behind another to slice open the backs of his knees. The third managed to get a grip on Iniabi's arm and threw her bodily against the side of the crates stacked on the deck.

She lay there for a time, relearning how to breathe, her vision dancing over a foggy sky. When she pushed herself up again, it was only to watch as a Lirian sword slid through Iago's throat. She screamed his name over the tumult, trying to push herself to her feet. She swayed alarmingly. Where had her sword gone?

"Iago!" Shouting only drew the attention of others to her, and Iniabi backed up, heart pounding as a big Lirian soldier turned her way. She needed a blade—anything to protect herself, but even as she cast about for something, the soldier made his move, lunging forward in a soft rustle of well-oiled armor as he swung at her throat with an ax. Iniabi jumped backward, tripping over herself in her haste to avoid him, to survive. She barely caught herself and retreated again, throwing anything she could reach in his way—barrels, rope, some of Iago's spikes. He dodged them all nimbly.

Behind the soldier, free of any bout of his own, Cai stalked the deck, his stride purposeful and his blade stained red. There was a bloody slash across his temple, but otherwise, he looked none the worse for wear.

"Cai!" Iniabi screamed for him, praying that he would reach the soldier in time, that he would be able to save her from the onslaught. She was almost to the railings, almost out of space to run, and the soldier knew it. He grinned under his helm and slowed slightly, taking his time pursuing her. "*Cai!*"

The boy turned and took in the scene—Iniabi pressed nearly to the railing, an enemy soldier bearing down on her and no sword in sight, no way to fight back. Slowly, wretchedly, Cai smiled. And then he turned his back on Iniabi.

Iniabi's chest opened like a chasm, real fear, hot and corrosive, flooding in to fill the space. Cai was gone, had chosen not to help her. The Lirian only kept coming. There was the glint of morning sun on his ax, the light of triumph in his eyes. Had he helped kill Iago? Had he wielded the blade?

Death awaited Iniabi on the edge of that ax, but she had seen the dreams. She would not die today. She took two quick breaths and then flung herself over the ship's railing, dropping into the icy sea below.

Iniabi made an arrow of herself, pointing her toes to the waves so when they reached up to swallow her, it was with a gentle caress rather than the slap of taut water against skin. The cold took her breath away, but even if the sea were to kill her, it would be a better death than that from a Lirian's hand.

The sea tore at Iniabi, dragging at her boots, her hair, her clothes. It grasped her limbs with icy tongues and sang of the peace and silence of its hungry abyss. She didn't listen. There was a life out there for her, a place for her to take even if she had to carve it from the body of the earth, even if she had to snatch it from the hands of others. She would live. She would survive.

She would *thrive*.

Iniabi fought back to the surface, clawing out of the sea's grasp with aching shoulders. Let them ache. She wouldn't let it stop her. Not now. Not when Cai would be up on deck laughing at her demise. Fuck him. Fuck them all.

The sides of the *Flying Night* were slime-ridden and fraught with sharp-edged barnacles, but slowly, she pulled herself up using fallen netting, spitting salt water and strands of matted, soaked hair, her fingers numb with cold and a thousand small, bleeding cuts from rope and the ship's hard parasites. By the time she reached the top, she could hardly breathe, her shoulders spasming beneath the effort of hauling her weight back onto the deck. Panting, Iniabi drug herself to the nearest Lirian corpse, drew the knife from his belt, and staggered back to her feet.

Only, all around her, the chaos had died down. Fire erupted on the deck of the Lirian warship. Someone had used the oil, and the flames licked hungrily over salt-swollen planks to leap towards the sails. The fight was over. The Lirians surged back towards their ship, desperate to put out the flames before she sunk, and they died in greater numbers in their haste to clamber back aboard their warship. They were running away, and Iniabi had survived. She had survived, damn them all!

The knife flew from her grasp, her jaw tight with anger, and buried itself in the back of a fleeing soldier.

⇑   ⇑   ⇑

In the aftermath of the battle, Iniabi walked through a sea of corpses. Nil moved with her, his shoulders slumped with exhaustion and grief. There was a red gash across his forehead, hastily tied with a strip of cloth, and he walked with a limp, as though one of his knees pained him. Each time they came across a body in a Lirian uniform, they stripped it of its weapons and valuables before tossing the corpse over the railing and into the sea. There must have been a line of sharks stretched out behind them for a league by the time they were done, ripping through gaudy uniforms and into flesh. Iniabi wondered what came after them, like how the foxes came after the wolves on the Tundra.

Iniabi did not see Jaya's body among the fallen pirates, but neither did she see the other girl among the living. Vlassis was dead, as was Neus, Nil's twin, but Taaliah still relayed the captain's orders at the helm. When the last Lirian body fell to the sea, Iniabi approached her and asked the one question on her mind: "Jaya?"

The walnut-skinned woman just shook her head. She didn't know, hadn't seen her either. Iniabi asked the captain, the navigator, and each sailor she came across on the deck. She was growing panicked, her breath coming in frantic gasps. She could not lose both Iago and Jaya on the same day.

"Iniabi!" The girl looked up to see Nil shuffling towards her on the deck. Someone had bandaged his head properly, though Iniabi couldn't imagine how. Had that much time passed? He looked as if he'd lost his whole world. "She's with Cook!"

Iniabi raced below decks just as Jaya stumbled from the galley. Her shirt bulged over the bulky forms of bandages, but she was awake. She was alive. Iniabi could have crowed, but instead, she slipped a shoulder under one of the older girl's arms and helped her navigate the steps.

"We survived," Iniabi told her. "We got away. In spite of fucking Cai. Jaya, he left me to die."

The older girl frowned, squinting down at Iniabi for a breath before she shook her head. "It was a *battle*, Iniabi; it's not as if we can always save each other."

"He wasn't fighting anyone! He saw me being attacked, saw that I had lost my sword, and— Jaya, he *grinned*."

"He was probably grimacing in fear," Jaya grunted, leaning heavily against Iniabi. Whatever her injuries were, they seemed severe. "I don't like Cai either, but he wouldn't just let one of us die. He's part of the crew."

"Maybe not most of us. But he would me." Iniabi sighed, shifting so she could better help Jaya up another few steps.

"Iniabi, you're being paranoid. We'll ask Iago, and he'll tell you the same as I am. In the heat of battle, things happen. Even if Cai did look at you—"

"Jaya, Iago is dead." The words caught in her throat like fishbones threatening to tear her apart from within.

The older girl stopped then, her grip around Iniabi's waist growing uncomfortably tight. "He is?" Her voice was distant, her gaze fixed on a pool of blood a few feet away.

"I saw— I couldn't save—" Inabi's chest felt too tight to pull in air, and in the aftermath of the battle, her limbs began to quake. "I didn't even find time to tell him I would have his back."

Jaya blinked, finally looking away from the puddle of blood and straight into Iniabi's eyes. The pirate's were red-rimmed as if she had been crying. From fear? From pain? Iniabi didn't know. "You were his friend, and he knew that even if you didn't tell him today. It doesn't matter, Iniabi. In his heart, he knew you were friends." She slowly draped her good arm around the Emaian's shoulder, pulling her close.

Despite her trembling, Iniabi could feel Jaya shudder as well. She put her head in the curve of Jaya's shoulder, and together they stood on the deck as evening broke the sky.

CHAPTER 37: RHOSAN

SEVENTH MOON, 1799, RHOSAN

Six Years before the Proclamation

*E*in rolled his neck and shoulders as he walked from the list of tomorrow's matches. He was prone to this behavior whenever he felt his opponent was weaker than him. Confident of a win, he'd strut about like a wood pigeon trying to impress a mate, and it was even more noticeable since he'd lost enough weight to drop below Champion Class. The other Defeated crowded into the standing room area near the doors, peering over each other's heads to see who the Victors slotted them against.

The list held little interest for Dyfan. While he cared about knowing his opponents, he'd find out when Victor Eurig came to discuss tactics with him that evening. Besides, it was not as if he could read the thing. Most Defeated didn't know how to read or write. But as he polished off the last of his canteen, watching Ein strut about, Dyfan caught a piece of conversation that interested him.

"Wynn has been getting bigger and winning more. I suppose they thought he was ready for Ein."

"Laughable. He's getting better, but it's a fixed match, I guarantee it. They're not even in the same weights. Besides, didn't you see Victor

Gruffyd losing in the dog races? He needs coin fast, and Victor Henwas wants another win for Ein."

"If Wynn loses, Victor Gruffyd will lose the opportunity for Wynn to qualify," the more reasonable voice argued.

"Heh! Coin now is better than the promise of coin tomorrow. Just wait and see. I'll even bet Victor Gruffyd wins a tidy sum when Wynn loses to Ein."

Dyfan didn't bother to see who was speaking, instead tossing the empty canteen to the basket where some arena Defeated would collect them up and refill them. He didn't need to read to know the news was true, others whispering and glancing in the direction Wynn had gone. He likely hadn't seen the list yet, instead choosing to exercise or find a moment of peace.

Uncomfortable emotions mixed within Dyfan's belly and he stood frozen for a long, painful minute. Should he give Wynn hints on how to beat Ein, as he had been doing for moons now? Give him lessons on polearms, Ein's favorite weapon?

What would the use be? Wynn was improving as a fighter, but Ein had been in the pits for most of his life. While he wasn't as heavy as Dyfan anymore, he was nearly as tall, and Ein was certainly swift, ruthless, and well-trained. He was too much of a match for Wynn. No hints, no last-minute training would change that.

Perhaps he could convince Wynn to pretend to be ill, so he would forfeit the match? It was dishonorable, but there was no honor in fighting in a bout you had no business being in. Why did it matter? Wynn was a grown man, who wasn't Defeated all his life. He could make his own choices and win or lose on his own merits.

Dyfan watched as Ein punched another Defeated in the arm. They were laughing. Sure of his win and his qualification for the Heavyweight Class Contender matches.

Without knowing it, Dyfan turned to search the barracks of the arena. Victor Gruffyd still did not pay for Wynn to have a cell when he stayed here despite his numerous successes. If Wynn were resting, he would be there.

Constructed of scraggly pieces of wood and mud, the barracks were hotter than the stone cells within the arena proper. It smelled of sweat and dried blood, and Dyfan opened his mouth to breathe rather than inhale through his nose. At first, it seemed as if no one was inside, and Dyfan wondered where else Wynn could be, but a muffled grunt made Dyfan sweep the inside of the barracks again.

Wynn squatted next to a cot. Dyfan recognized the look. His fits of anger and melancholy had become more frequent over the moons, and he was becoming detached and paranoid. Usually, Dyfan ignored these shifts, continuing to eat and discussing training with his ally. Wynn might sweat, stop speaking, or scan, wide-eyed for invisible threats, but then, Dyfan just kept behaving as he always did, and Wynn often shook it off, returning to himself. Of course, there were times that nothing would help, and Wynn would be lost to his fears until they released him. It frustrated Dyfan to be useless, but he had known enough fighters to understand it couldn't be helped.

"Wynn," Dyfan murmured as he came to stand out of reach of the other man. They may be allies, but in these moments, Wynn was dangerous. Sweat beaded his brow, and his hands trembled. He kept his eyes tightly closed except for once to glance at Dyfan.

It felt like this would be a long bout, and Dyfan breathed heavily through his mouth before settling on a rickety cot. It groaned under him. He could wait.

Wynn

Wynn's chest was under an anvil. The pressure was immense—rib-cracking, lung-crushing weight. He felt that if he could just fill up with air, if he could just get one decent breath, he would be able to pull himself up. His throat was a straw, too thin and ragged to aid him. Even the air was too thick. Smoke-thick. Like on the day he was taken.

He crouched on rough, wooden floors, and his nose was full of the smell of blood. Footsteps were coming nearer, and his wife and son had just slipped from the door, just disappeared into the snow and dark. Gods, let them make it away before the Victors noticed. He would fight to keep them away from the cottage long enough. They wouldn't know it was empty until his family was far away.

He was losing feeling in his hands, his feet. How could it be that cold with the village in flames around them? There ought to have been enough fuel to warm the Brig'ian mountains for a moment.

Wynn curled his fingers, but they were slow to react. Where was his spear? He had to fight off the Victors, had to make time. He scrambled backward, thrust his hands under his cot, and froze. It wasn't there. He had no weapon, and they were coming with their fire and hounds.

"Where is it?" he hissed, catching sight of Dyfan seated nearby. "They're coming."

But Dyfan hadn't been there. He hadn't been with the Victors who tore through the village. He was too valuable…

Wynn fisted sweating hands in the quilt of the cot Dyfan sat on and pressed his head to its edge. He could feel his body tremble, the heavy, earth-quake shake of his broken mind. The voices of other Defeated were just audible, though none bothered him with Dyfan on watch.

In the privacy of the cloth pressed to his face, Wynn squeezed his eyes shut until tears leaked from them, forced free like the liquid pressed from fruit. It had gotten so hard to cry, like the years since his capture dried him out. Perhaps one day, there'd be nothing left but sand.

Gradually, Wynn found he could breathe again. His lungs filled out in shaking gasps. The trembling in his shoulders eased. He still could not feel his hands or feet. He reached out and gripped Dyfan's leg, just below where it bent at the knee, and hoped he understood. Wynn was so Gods-damned grateful for that boulder of a man. He always would be.

Dyfan's hand came within view, hesitating slightly before covering Wynn's with a squeeze. They sat for a time, quiet and breathing, acknowledging their circumstances without speaking. Then Dyfan's voice rumbled from above Wynn's head. "It doesn't like to let go, does it?"

"No. It doesn't." Wynn recovered a moment longer before pushing himself up to sit beside Dyfan on the cot, his hands still unsteady before him. He pressed them to his thighs to keep them from shaking. "Do fighters ever recover from this?"

The appraising look Dyfan gave him was answer enough. No. They didn't. They were put down like rabid dogs. "Sometimes, Victors will have a fighter trained for other work." The corner of his mouth twitched upwards, gaze flickering to Wynn's too-long hair. "You look like a field worker."

Wynn shoved him. Dyfan didn't budge. "Yeah, well, you look like a rock. A big chunk of stone."

"The strongest, best stone?"

Wynn just snorted, but he was beginning to smile. He could feel the tension in his temples ease. He stood and nodded at the door of the barracks. "Kirit's left nut, I hate this place. Let's go."

Wynn stepped into the wan light of a northern Rhosan morning and walked with Dyfan to the arena. Defeated gathered around the fighting lists when he made his way among them, shouldering past a couple in his weight class so that he could read the lists, Dyfan close behind. Not much of it was worth paying any attention to, but he was a little surprised by the name next to his. Ein. Did that mean he was moving up?

"Do you have any tips for Ein?" Wynn asked, turning to look at his ally.

Dyfan's gaze was already on Wynn, steady as he considered the question. "No. You'll be fine."

The rest of the day passed without incident, though it was a difficult one. Wynn's hands still shook hours after the morning's attack, and he dropped most of the stones he bent to carry. In sparring, his head spun, and he ended with a whole host of new bruises.

At dinner, Dyfan seemed affected by whatever miasma hung over Wynn's shoulders. He was unusually distant, eating his food mechanically, his eyes locked on the gates. "You alright?" Wynn asked after a while, but all he received was a grunt in answer.

Dyfan

The sun had fallen below the edge of the compound walls, and rowdy voices floated on the summer air, the Defeated full enough to start joking and debating. Soon escorts would arrive to take some Defeated back to their compounds. Everyone else would go to bed. It was time.

"Hold my bowl." Dyfan handed the wooden vessel to Wynn.

"Alright… Why? Where are you going?"

Dyfan made no effort to reply. Turning towards a big group of other fighters, he crouched to palm a stone. It would do well enough. Ein was in the group, finishing his meal and laughing at something Cadel said.

One of the older fighters noticed Dyfan's approach and motioned for the others to quiet down. "Dyfan. Do you need something?"

"Yes." He had noticed the shaking in Wynn's grip, the clumsy responses to basic sparring routines. The other man was in no condition to fight, let alone Ein, who was well beyond Wynn's training.

"What do you need?" Everyone had turned to look at him now, Ein's smirk grating against Dyfan's stone resolve. Heating him. Making him angry.

Dyfan could still feel Wynn's hand on his leg. His touch had been cold despite the moderate weather, his body chilled from the terrors gripping him. Dyfan resettled his hold on the rock in his hand.

"Ein," he said. As Ein looked up with a hubristic grin, Dyfan let the rock fall. The tricky fighter didn't even have a moment to change his expression. Dyfan's fist rose and fell, bashing the other man's face and head with the stone. Blood spattered against his skin and stained his knuckles. The impacts bruised his fingers, but he hardly felt the pain until trainers hauled him off the bleeding, unconscious man.

"What happened?!"

"—insult him?"

"—insane, you know how they—"

"STOP!"

Dyfan made no effort to fight the trainer's grip, dropping the gore-slick stone before they made him. With his arms pinned behind his back, he walked calmly towards his cell. Only once did he look over his shoulder to where Wynn still sat, clutching their empty bowls. Their gazes met as the trainers propelled him out of sight.

CHAPTER 38: RHOSAN

SEVENTH MOON, 1799, RHOSAN

Six Years before the Proclamation

The next morning, Wynn woke to the sound of angry voices. The barracks were nearly empty, the other fighters having left to catch the first few matches of the day or to find the source of the altercation. In that relative stillness, Wynn closed his eyes. Dyfan would be punished today, most likely after the matches.

He pushed himself up and out into the sun, threading his way towards the entrance to the pits. Dyfan's cell was in there—likely barred. A cage, like one for a dangerous animal.

The crowd thickened the closer he moved to that great stone building. It was a strange mix, both Defeated and Victors mingling. Individual Victors might speak to or walk amongst their Defeated, but they held largely separate, except to give or receive instruction.

The source of the argument that had woken him lay at the crowd's center. Victor Henwas, Ein's owner, was purple with rage and drink, his fists balled at his sides. He stood so close to Eurig that his spittle flecked the other man's face as he spoke. "You had him do it on purpose! That creature of yours! You had him slaughter Ein!"

Eurig showed no fear, but neither did he rise to Henwas's accusations. "Come now; you know how these Defeated are! Crazy as fighting dogs."

"You did it so your scum wouldn't lose! He would have made me a fortune."

"There'll always be more Defeated, eh? What's one between friends?" Eurig unbelted a pouch from his waist and pressed it into Henwas's hands. "You could buy another Ein. Besides, don't you have a bitch pregnant with one of Dyfan's spawn? He'll make a fine fighter."

With the immediate threat of violence lifted, the crowd began to thin, and Wynn angled back towards the pits, shouldering past other Defeated and avoiding the Victors altogether. Inside, it was as empty as he'd ever seen it, and his bare feet slapped unmusically against the stone, the sound echoing throughout the building.

He knew the path to Dyfan's cell without thinking, despite having been there only twice, and when he reached it, he stopped at the bars newly covering the entrance to peer inside.

Dyfan sat on his cot, head lulling back against the stone wall, feet braced against the edge. With his legs up and his wrist dangling from one knee, he was the picture of a dozy fighter. His eyes were even shut as if, despite the clamor, he was sleeping. He only opened them as Wynn knocked his knuckle against one bar.

Ocean eyes swept over Wynn and then beyond before Dyfan closed them again. "Morning," he drawled. Utterly unphased.

Wynn shifted and raised his hands to grip the bars. "Well, you don't look crazy to me. That's what they're saying, you know. That you're losing your mind."

The larger fighter didn't even bother to make his usual grunt of a reply. He just opened his eyes to stare at Wynn, unimpressed.

"So why'd you do it?"

Dyfan sat for so long without speaking that it seemed like he wasn't going to say anything at all. Wynn glanced back down the hall. The building was starting to fill up with fighters and spectators. "You weren't going to fight Ein," Dyfan said.

"Why? You said I'd be fine. You know I've been getting stronger."

"Victor Henwas fixes fights. It was rigged."

"Since when has that mattered? What happened to being smart, not angry?" Wynn felt his face heat. "You're going to be whipped for this. You know that, right? They are going to beat you."

Dyfan only shrugged in response, irritatingly unconcerned. He let his feet drop down to the earth, and the cot groaned as he stood and pointlessly straightened the threadbare blankets.

Wynn banged his fist against the bar and turned his back on the cell. "You dumbass. I don't need you to get hurt for me. I could have handled it."

What even was this? What had he done to earn that kind of loyalty from Dyfan? It hadn't been long since the other fighter had squatted in that cell and told him how important it was to stay cool-minded. And now he was maiming Defeated so that Wynn wouldn't have to fight in a fixed bout?

He rubbed his face with his hands and sank slowly to the floor, the bars to Dyfan's cell biting into his back. Shuffling footsteps indicated that Dyfan was attempting to sweep. As if it mattered. He worked for a while in silence before finally asking, "Who are you fighting now?"

"No one's updated the lists, but I'm sure the Victors have figured it out between themselves." Wynn stiffened at the sound of footsteps, preparing to leap up to his feet, but whoever it was, they reached their destination before he saw them.

The sounds behind him stopped, and there was sudden warmth as Dyfan reached through the bars to grip Wynn's shoulder. His touch was firm, lingering as his thumb brushed the back of Wynn's neck. As Wynn stilled, Dyfan's fingers moved to smooth away the long locks of hair on his collar.

"What would they do if the Victors knew you were protecting me?"

Dyfan's gentle touch tightened. "I... I had to, Wynn."

"I—you—" Wynn's voice was quiet even in the echoing hall, but he cut off when the sounds of footsteps returned, quicker this time. He stood up too fast and overbalanced, placing a hand on the wall to steady himself. There was hardly enough time to glance at Dyfan before a voice cut between them.

"What are you doing up here? Defeated should be in a cell or watching the matches." It was a villager in a smith's apron, likely here to fix something.

Wynn just shrugged and walked away, his feet making lonely slaps against the stone.

⇑   ⇑   ⇑

They held the whipping at sunset. The sky was a bloody smear of red on sickly yellow, the rust-red stones of the arena painted in it like doused sacrifices in a hedonistic ritual. Dyfan alone stood in the center of the dirt pit, the stands around him packed to the point of discomfort— every pit fighter in the city and nearby settlements was there to watch.

Wynn stood among them, oblivious to everything but the ocean eyes of the man who waited in the center of that pit. He could not look away. He could hardly breathe. It should never have been Dyfan chained to that post, his muscular back bare, his head held up defiantly. Dyfan had been whipped before, his skin already scarred, and Wynn deserved every lash Dyfan was about to receive. If it weren't for him, Dyfan would be safe.

Well, whole. Not safe. No Defeated was ever truly safe.

The murmured voices of fighters around him hushed as Victor Eurig and the training master entered the arena. The training master looked grim, like a father unhappy with disciplining a wayward child, but Victor Eurig just looked mad. He'd lost money because of Dyfan's stunt, paying off Ein's Victor. He stopped six paces from Dyfan and gestured for the training master to pass over the padded whip. He probably paid extra to ensure Dyfan got the softest punishment possible. Not out of affection, but because Dyfan's place in the Contender Matches was already tenuous. If Eurig wanted even the slimmest chance of Dyfan qualifying, he needed to keep the fighter in the best shape possible.

For the first time, Wynn was grateful Dyfan was such a prized possession. If he was anything less to Eurig then this could have been so much worse. That whip could have had multiple prongs or knots at the end. It could have been tipped with metal barbs. Instead of being carted away to shudder through fever and crippling muscle damage, Dyfan would walk out of this ring and fight again.

Godsdamn him for doing this to himself. Dyfan should have just let Wynn lose the match, should have just let things be. There was no point in defying the Victors for this of all things, not when they would hurt him for it. Wynn forced himself to take a deep breath. He would watch this. He owed Dyfan that much.

The training master stepped forward, and the already quiet crowd held its breath. "Defeated Dyfan attacked another fighter outside of a sanctioned bout. He cost a Victor a fighter; he interfered with the natural order of the pits. For trying to take fate into his own hands, Defeated Dyfan will receive twenty lashes. Kirit teaches us that the Victors act as his right hand, and the Defeated are their lessers. For a Defeated to go against the rules set by the Victors and Kirit, he goes against his God."

Wynn gritted his teeth. The Gods had never set some mortals above others. These people had twisted everything he believed in to suit their violent ways.

The training master stepped back to allow Eurig a view of Dyfan's back and the space to use the whip. Eurig pulled his arm back, the whip dropping behind him with all the sinewy, slimy grace of a worm. It hung there, limp and waiting, a dark thing about to strike.

And then, it fell.

The Victor grunted as he first swung the whip, putting in the effort to ensure this punishment would last. It thwacked against Dyfan's back, and though the large man didn't yell, he did jerk involuntarily.

Wynn shuddered, fighting the need to close his eyes. He would do this for Dyfan, but as the whip continued to fly and blood sprayed around the form of that gentle rock of a man, Wynn's will crumbled. He closed his eyes and let his chin fall to his chest, shaking with the senseless violence of it all.

CHAPTER 39: LIRIA

NINTH MOON, 1799, EGARA

Six Years before the Proclamation

"Balbina Nonus," Camilla crooned as she laid the baby girl in Luce's handless arm. He placed his remaining hand on the babe's belly, tucking her firmly against his body. He would never drop her. Despite her first miscarriage, it seemed Valeria had given Ignatious a beautiful, healthy daughter. True, her skin was already darker than a true-blooded Lirian's would be, and what little hair she had on the crown of her head was thick and curling, but she was a Nonus, and she was perfect.

"Shall I take our granddaughter for a little stroll around the courtyard?" he asked Balbina, who only yawned.

"That's a good idea. Take Ignatious with you so I can help Valeria. With a newborn in the house, she needs all the help she can get. Especially with no mother here to assist her." Camilla was already rolling up her sleeves, and Luce knew she would clean the house, wash their clothes, and help Valeria bathe. Valeria might be Tupa Galan, but Camilla treated her as one of her children.

Her generosity seemed to know no bounds.

Luce stood, careful not to jostle the sleeping baby, and left the sitting room. Ignatious was in the kitchen, half-asleep over a cup of mint tea. Maybe it would be better if Luce didn't rouse him. Balbina made a happy sleeping sound, and Ignatious's eyes flew open. He jumped to his feet and looked around in confusion. Spotting Luce and Balbina, the tension lessened in Ignatious's body, and he sighed, scrubbing his hands over his face. "Father."

"Here, come into the sunlight with us. We're taking a turn around the courtyard, and the fresh air will do you good."

Ignatious followed Luce into the modest courtyard of the house he and Valeria lived in. The Emaian slave Ignatious had bought with his first commission entered the kitchen as they left, and distrust filled Luce. He fought the urge to tighten his hold on Balbina. The Emaian was freshly captured, not bred. Ignatious would never be able to afford a bred slave. Especially not with prices creeping higher and higher. Luce turned away from the unpleasant sight and back to his son. "How do you like fatherhood so far?"

"It's exhausting. She wakes in the middle of the night, and I worry something is wrong. All she does is cry and sleep."

"Babies are like that, in the very beginning."

"I don't remember Tulio or Cassia being that way."

"You slept in your own room Ingatious. How would you know what your mother and I went through?" Besides, by the time Cassia and Tulio were born, Luce was making enough money to have nannies for the babes.

Luce caught movement out of the corner of his eye, and the Emaian slave walked past with a bucket full of soapy water. Probably for scrubbing something. "You're right," Ignatious conceded and sat on the nearby bench. He stared at the lone cypress tree in the courtyard, its vibrant greens stark contrast against the tan stone of the house. Luce knew his son wasn't actually admiring the scrubby little tree but worrying.

Fatherhood was all about worrying for one's children. His heart tightened. "I will pay for you and Valeria to have a nanny."

"I can provide for my family, father." Offense made his fine features all the sharper, and Luce felt pride and annoyance fight each other in his breast. It was only fitting that Ignatious would want to fend for himself, but Luce was *his* father, Balbina's grandfather, and he wanted nothing but the best for the little family. They were an extension of himself. His blood.

"And *I* can afford a nanny for my granddaughter. I do not want that Emaian touching her. Not once. If you and Valeria require additional help, then so be it."

"Father—"

"Enough, Ignatious. It is a gift I offer. What do you say to a gift?"

Ignatious seemed to struggle with himself, and then his shoulders slumped. "Thank you, Father."

CHAPTER 40: PHECEA

TWELFTH MOON, 1799, DIOSION

Six Years before the Proclamation

The Mavros house was hectic the last afternoon of the twelfth moon, with people coming to leave little gifts or admire the artwork Biton and his sisters had made. Administrator Iris welcomed Danae with a hug before heading to a celebration for the end of the year, where the renowned singer, Pavlina, would be showcasing her latest piece.

"Biton is somewhere up there." Administrator Iris gestured to the stairs and then floated out the door. Danae supposed Biton got his grace from his mother because it seemed to her that the woman glided everywhere.

Danae barely reached the stairs when Biton's sisters, Dido and Dara, stopped her. "Danae! Look at my painting; can you tell what it is?"

Dido held up a small framed piece, and no matter how Danae squinted, she wasn't quite sure what the seven-year-old had created. Perhaps it was supposed to be a pond with flowers or the sky with oddly colored trees? "I think the purpose of art is not to portray a specific scene, but instead to invoke emotion. Your painting certainly inspires energy and joy."

Dara giggled until tears leaked from the corners of her eyes. "It's a bowl of yogurt with berries! I told you she wouldn't be able to tell."

Dido raised her little rounded nose into the air. "Berries give *me* energy and joy."

"As long as you feel something, then it is good art."

The twins skipped off to pester someone else, and Danae climbed the stairs, listening to the chords of a harp and the humming of voices warming up. Later, while she and Biton were at the Leos' end-of-year celebration, his sisters would likely have small celebrations with their friends.

Danae hurried to Biton's room and found his door ajar. Inside, Biton was at his vanity, preparing for the party. Keme stood behind him, braiding Biton's thick, black hair around the onyx circlet Danae had given him. His shoulders were draped in black silk, his warm collarbones on display, unlike the traditional paneled tunics that men usually wore. Black onyx drops hung from his ears, and his face was painted in bold strokes, dark around his eyes and red on his lips. Keme said something, and Biton smiled, radiant as the sun on a spring day. Keme didn't avert his eyes or say something demure like a slave ought but laughed, full-throated and happy. They seemed as close as brothers.

Danae yanked her head from Biton's door. She didn't know why he was dressed up so lavishly or why he and Keme were so close, but she recognized a private moment when she saw one. She should have knocked, not just entered.

Danae crept back down the hall and stepped into the first open doorway she found. It was the music room, and Voleta stopped singing. "Danae!" Alarm shocked Danae's heart, but she moved forward to embrace Voleta. She didn't want Biton to hear Voleta calling her name.

"What are you singing?" Danae asked, her voice soft in the hopes of inspiring Voleta to whisper too.

Despite her best efforts, Danae could not focus on Voleta's explanation. Instead, her mind kept returning to Keme's hand on Biton's shoulder or the way Biton smiled. So familiar. So warm.

Biton

Biton looked into the mirror of his vanity, Keme standing quietly behind him, his white hair hanging down over startlingly pale eyes as he worked on some intricacy of the braids around Biton's circlet. The picture he saw was not of the administrator-in-training or the dutiful son but of himself—bold and striking. The adventurer. The storyteller.

He looked remarkably different. And remarkably different from anyone else.

The circlet, with its dangling stone, and the drops of onyx at his ears all moved in ways he was unfamiliar with. They touched his skin, ice-brushes, and he was uncomfortably aware of his neck and clavicles.

"Will people act... differently now?" he asked. He was who he was, no matter who reacted, and yet, it was new to be so obviously outside of the societal norm. Males in Phecea traditionally wore much less revealing clothing, but Pheceans weren't Lirians, hung up on rules and roles for each gender.

"If they do, will you change? Will you wipe off your paint and clothe yourself in the ways they expect?"

Biton met his own gaze in the mirror: black eyes and black-eyed reflection, and saw again the glimpse he had first found in Danae's room, wrapped in a yard of newly arrived cloth.

He could be himself, or he could try to please all those around him, torn in as many directions as there were faces. Never would they all be sated.

"No," he said, raising his eyes to meet Keme's. "No, I won't."

Keme smiled and smoothed down the braid. "I would expect nothing less."

⇑ ⇑ ⇑

Dido and Dara claimed that Danae was in the music room and insisted on escorting Biton.

"Biton! Can't we come with you? You look like a pirate king!"

"Yeah, like you've won all the treasure!"

"I want to wear jewels and paints and sweep beautiful people off their feet!"

Biton smiled, taking them each by the hand so they'd stop tugging on his clothes. "You will! You just have to wait a really short—minuscule really—eight years."

"Eight years?" Dido made it sound like a century.

"Yep! It'll be over before you know it."

They passed through the double doors of the music room, and Biton found Danae seated at the harp in a pretty blue formal tunic with silver necklaces and a silver cinch about her waist. She was playing for Leta, who stood up to interrupt her even as Biton watched.

"Wait, can I see you play that passage again? How do you reach all the notes in that chord?"

"Don't pester her while she's playing, Leta." Biton smiled at Danae across the room, though his stomach was tight with nerves, and he could feel the texture of the paint on his eyelids. "Are you ready to go to the party?"

Danae set the harp back on its feet and ran her hands over the curve of her knees before nodding. Her gaze lingered on the circlet of onyx on his brow. "Am I underdressed?"

Biton flushed but kept his hands away from his clothes. "No. I think you look lovely."

"Danae looks like a cloud or fluffy hydrangea blossom," Leta said, her keen eyes moving over his friend's untamable hair and blue silk. While she hadn't meant it as an insult, Danae flushed, obviously uncomfortable.

"And what does Biton look like?" Danae asked.

His sister turned to study him and then shrugged. "Sparkly. Like he always does."

Biton sighed out his relief. "Thanks, Leta. I think Danae and I should head to our carriage. The Leos's townhouse is on the other side of Diosion, and we don't want to be late." Danae moved to stand with him, but Dido and Dara whined.

"When will you be back?"

"Why can't we go?"

"How many treats will you bring us?"

"Probably a hundred," Biton assured them as he took Danae by the hand, leading her away from his over-eager sisters. By the time they climbed into the Mavros carriage, he had warded off dozens of questions from the twins. The quiet of the cabin as they pulled away from his home was a welcome reprieve.

Danae watched the streets passing by, filled with finely dressed people calling out greetings. The cream stucco buildings of Diosion shone with blown glass balls sparkling in the light of lanterns, and festivity gathered in the air like excitement. Those not invited to noble houses celebrated in the markets, eating sticky, honey-soaked phyllo and drinking wine.

"Are you excited for the party? I can't wait. The Leos always find the best entertainers. And last time, they had sweet spoons at every single table. Mine was kumquat. I love kumquats. Maybe they'll have them again." Biton grinned over the seat between them, trying to catch her attention. Danae had gotten so quiet.

"Oh." She blinked and looked his way as if he were pulling her from consuming thoughts. "I didn't know you loved kumquats."

"What's on your mind, Danae?"

"I just thought I knew everything about you, is all," she said.

"Don't you?"

"It doesn't seem like it since you like kumquats, and I didn't know that. And I didn't know the Leos party would be so formal," Danae gestured to his clothes, cheeks flushing. "I just… didn't know."

Biton's shoulders slumped, and he thought back to his conversation with Keme at the vanity. "You're upset because of my clothes? You gave me the silks and the circlet."

"No, I'm sorry, Biton. I'm just… Nervous. I've never been invited to these types of parties before."

Biton reached out and took her hand. "I understand. New things are scary, but you really do look nice. All our friends will be there, and we'll have a good time."

New parties and new looks. They would be nervous together tonight.

Danae nodded slowly, squeezing his hand. "I'm sorry, Biton. I've been a bad friend. I'll try to do better."

"You could never be a bad friend."

Danae

For the rest of the carriage ride, Danae tried to convince herself she *was* a good friend. She hadn't deliberately spied on Biton, and it wasn't as if she caught him doing something shameful or deeply private. There was no reason to feel such guilt over the moment exchanged between Biton and his slave. He was only getting ready for a party.

The more she thought about it, the easier she felt. Biton didn't believe she was a bad friend, and that was the most important thing. Next time, she would just knock before entering his room. Having found a solution to her guilt, Danae started to feel excitement as the carriage pulled along the cobblestones leading up to the Leos's townhouse.

The Leos family must have commissioned the building, as the green roof tiles and cream stucco matched their house colors. The entrance was carved iron shaped into the family crest and framed by decorative bushels of wheat and vines of grapes. The servants that helped them from the carriage wore a cream and green livery and, Danae was startled to realize, white masks.

All the servants were masked, as were the Emaian slaves and entertainers. It made the guests stand out, with their bold faces on display. Danae thought it was a clever choice, turning the nobility into artwork. And, of course, Biton was the height of artistry. His bold outfit had their peers flocking around him.

"Where did you get that tunic?"

"Of course, he designed it!"

"Adohnis, you should wear your hair like that."

Biton made room as Erose and Ion crowded closer, and Danae looked around the great hall, noticing artists setting up paint and canvas or great mounds of clay. One already was starting to wet his hands and spin his wheel, the first step in discovering what sculpture the earth wanted to reveal. Art as entertainment: a very Phecean concept.

Emai slaves, recognizable only due to their colorless hands, offered trays of delicate sweets and savories, and servants carried bottles of juice, liquor, and wine along with cups.

"Biton," Erose said, "you have to make me a tunic *just* like yours, only in purple." Her house color. When Danae glanced back, Erose had woven her hand into the crook of Biton's arm.

Music echoed from a distant ballroom, and Danae followed the group as they started to make their way towards the sound, stopping every so often to admire an artist's first strokes of brush on canvas or the way one used a sharp knife to cut into wood. She supposed the artists would be there all night, creating on display. The thought made Danae wince. She would hate to compose music in front of a crowd, the experience too personal to put on a stage.

By the time they reached the ballroom, many people were already dancing. Not the free-flowing dances that Biton would erupt into when the spirit moved him, but structured group compositions. Danae let the group of her peers move towards the edge of the dance floor without her, instead standing near two old administrators drinking and talking.

Erose wore a gown rather than a formal tunic, and it reminded Danae of a flower opening as she flared her skirts and bowed her head to Biton. He bowed as well, his hand offered palm-up for her to take. The older children paired off, joining the dance. Danae took the pomegranate juice provided by a passing, masked servant and watched the whirl of spinning bodies.

"General Corinna Strataki says the few scouting reports she has gathered indicate an alarming amount of Lirian troops milling around mountain passes and the Bathi River," one of the old administrators said.

"Of course, if mentioned to the Imperator, they are just undergoing training exercises."

"*Of course.* I find it's really only effective to train troops near the border."

"*Precisely,*" the man chuckled, though the sound held no humor in Danae's ears.

The two men moved away from the wall, joining the dance together despite their advanced years. Even old men could move more gracefully than Danae. A slave came by with a tray of green things. She took one, a little apprehensive, and sniffed.

"What is it?"

"It is kelp, mistress." The voice of the woman was muffled from her mask.

"Kelp? You mean seaweed?"

Tentatively, Danae brought it to her lips and then took a small bite. It was squishy and salty and tasted of the sea. While it was not something Danae would have chosen, she didn't find it entirely unenjoyable. She nodded, and the Emai slave left, offering her tray to the next person.

Danae was wondering if there would be a proper supper or just little treats when a loud chime rang through the building. The musicians stopped, and people started to flock out of the ballroom. Looking around for Biton or the others, Danae let the tide of party goers take her.

Biton

The entertainment for the night was a play that won raving reviews in the halls of Kydonia, Leonis Province's capital city. It was an excellent choice. A means to share the Leos's pride in their home province with the people of Diosion. Biton found a place to sit next to Erose and then saved the seat on his other side for Danae, where she might sit between him and Adohnis.

When she found them, he smiled. "Danae! You're just in time. Did you have any interesting experiences while we were dancing?"

"I didn't dance, which was good enough for me," she said, settling beside Biton with a grateful sigh. "Did you have fun?"

"Yes!" Biton smiled, though he didn't want her to think he liked any of their other friends' company more than hers. "Leos have some really great musicians, but it's not my favorite music to dance to."

Erose leaned across him, laying a hand on Biton's knee. "Hush. It's starting!"

The play opened on a white background. There were snow-dusted rocks littering the stage beneath a sheer gray canopy for the sky, and in the center stood a single, ill-made tent. Musicians seated to the side started a hollow, airy tune, and for a moment, all was still. Then a solemn-faced narrator with fish-like frowning lips began to speak in a resonant baritone.

"The Emai lead rough lives amid the snow and the ice of the southern tundra, barely surviving as the seasons pass. They cram themselves into dirty, crowded tents for warmth and live off what meat they can glean from fish and elk. Their medicine women drink the blood of these offerings, claiming that it gives them the power to see into the future so they might rule their ice-caked kingdoms."

Behind him, Phecean actors slipped out of the tent to struggle through the fake ice on the stage. Their skin was coated in white chalk, and they wore white wigs over their hair. Still, it was not difficult to see that they were not Emai themselves. It was the eyes. Even at a distance, theirs were visibly dark.

Biton shifted uncomfortably in his seat and glanced to either side of himself. Danae and Erose watched the scene, but Biton knew Keme would not enjoy such a presentation. His stories of the Emai and their whalebone villages were much different and more likely. How could there be so many Emai if they couldn't thrive in their homeland? Besides, weren't his tutors always telling him to consider the source of information? Keme had known the Emai first hand. He had been born in those lands.

"The savage fears being taken from his cold hut because he does not understand what enlightenment can be found through the development of the six humors: philosophy, politics, art, science, music, and craftsmanship. If there is one occurrence the savage should fear, however, it is his enslavement by Lirian masters."

On the stage, the 'Emaians' were attacked by a phalanx of Lirian troops, their grotesque masks rendered large so that they could be seen from the stage. The actors played out a slaughter in red ribbons and falling spears. Biton closed his eyes. Was this really just the Lirians? Or did Phecean troops attack Emaian villages in the same way?

When he opened his eyes again, the Emai were in manacles, chained together like prisoners. Like slaves. The play went on to showcase the story of a single Emaian "rescued" by Pheceans, who taught him to read, write, and better himself through service and clean habits. It ended with him happily serving his Phecean family, but Biton could think of nothing but that moment when the soldiers raided the village and took the people there like chattel. It was the stuff of nightmares, being torn away from one's home in screams and blood and dying bodies.

As people started to stand and leave the stage area, Danae turned to Biton with a frown. "Wouldn't it be better to explain to the Emai why learning and creating is the way to a full life? I know they don't speak a real language, but certainly, there would be a Phecean scholar who could communicate our good intentions?"

But that wasn't right at all. Why did either Phecea or Liria have to steal people from their homes? Weren't there enough citizens already to do the work?

Erose shook out her mane of thick black hair. "Biton, the dancing is starting again."

He let her lead him away though his heart was no longer in the music.

CHAPTER 41: RHOSAN

EIGHTH MOON, 1799, CYM OR

Six Years before the Proclamation

The smell of roasting hares, hogs, elk, and fish crowded the air, and Dyfan's stomach twisted. Defeated weren't fed rich foods. The trainers found that fighters who subsisted on vegetables and grains had better stamina and strength, whereas those fed heavy meats and milk were sluggish and prone to long-lasting injuries. It had been the way of things since the time of Kirit, so Dyfan had never eaten animal flesh.

Watching the Victors slicing into their feast, Dyfan was glad he hadn't. It seemed barbaric in a way that he, a pit fighter, could not name. He turned away, his gaze passing over the rest of the space. Wooden tables draped with colorful runners in knotted yellows and greens stood arranged in a cobblestone courtyard. Braziers provided light in the darkening evening, though it was hot enough during the eighth moon that they didn't need them for warmth. Defeated servants carried cups of cider and plates of food while the Victors devoured their first course.

Victor Gruffyd arranged this gathering at his compound, inviting most of the local Victors and their pit fighters. Of course, the Defeated weren't guests, but art or entertainment, scattered around the open front yard of Victor Gruffyd's holdings so their Victors could boast and demand various physical feats from them. Thankfully, it seemed enough for Victor Eurig that Dyfan stood bare-chested, a short sarong tied about his hips so that most of his body was on display. The tapestry of scars and tattoos over Dyfan's chest, back, and legs were testament enough to his various accomplishments as a fighter.

Victor Gruffyd had already made Wynn do several rounds of squats and heavy lifting. He was dressed as Dyfan was, as most of the Defeated were, and Dyfan could see sweat beading his back as Wynn dropped into a push-up position.

"Look how much stronger he is now! He'll be joining the middleweights soon enough!" Victor Gruffyd placed an earthen jug of mulled wine between Wynn's shoulder blades. It wasn't unreasonably heavy but certainly cumbersome.

Victor Eurig wasn't having him parade about to keep the still-healing lash marks from reopening. Even with a padded flail, Dyfan had a few abrasions and many bruises. It was worth it. Every lash. He would do it again to keep Wynn from fighting Ein. The match had been fixed, Dyfan was sure of it, and Wynn hadn't been himself. No one should have to fight like that.

Victor Gruffyd led the other Victors back to the tables for the second course. Dyfan fell in to stand behind Victor Eurig as he sat, observing as the Victors laughed and toasted one another. The wine vats were draining alarmingly fast.

Wynn stood nearby, brow sweaty and reddish-brown hair clinging to his face. Despite the dangers of fighting with hair that length, Dyfan often caught himself looking at it. The way it lay against Wynn's neck or across his eyes distracted Dyfan, drawing too much attention to the angle of his cheekbones and curve of his mouth.

"Hot?" Dyfan whispered as Wynn looked his way, trusting the jovial conversation at the Victor's tables to keep attention off of them.

"Beats being cold. How's your back?" The expression on his face could have easily been guilt or concern, and Wynn craned his neck to see the damage.

That was enough to catch Eurig's eye. The Victor leaned over to whisper to Gruffyd, and Wynn was called forward again. This time, rather than feats of strength, they made him run to gauge his speed.

It wasn't until later that he managed to get back to Dyfan. One of the other Victors was taking a turn showing off his fighters, and a good thing too. Wynn dripped sweat, his breaths just now evening out. "Alright," he said as he came closer, "I'm hot now."

"It's good for you to practice instead of just lazing about here. Fat fighters lose." And since no one was looking their way, Dyfan let himself cast an appraising look over Wynn's chest and stomach. It was a good joke because Wynn certainly wasn't fat. If anything, the man was prone to being too skinny.

"I'll show you fat, you boulder. You make two of me!" It was an exaggeration, but Wynn was smiling. He didn't have enough reasons to smile.

Blodwyn and Ifanna, Eurig and Gruffyd's wives, walked arm-in-arm, turning around the yard to view the fighters up close. They'd drunk as much as the men, it seemed to Dyfan, but both women were clear-eyed as they approached. Beside him, Wynn stiffened.

Ifanna's gaze lingered on Wynn's chest and thighs, and Dyfan fought the urge to step in front of him. The two women walked around the corner and out of sight before Dyfan stopped watching her back. A strange and uncomfortable sensation was coiling in his gut.

"You should tell Victor Gruffyd you'd win more if you trained all moon." Of course, Wynn couldn't *tell* his Victor anything, but... it was true. If he was at the pits and working more, he'd only improve. Dyfan forced himself not to stare at Wynn, and turned back to surveying the courtyard.

"I think I know how to frame it," Wynn said. Dyfan could see the other fighter looking up at him out of the corner of his eye, but he didn't turn to meet his gaze.

Before them, the Victors had finally lost interest in sparring and turned into the table, laughing in the good-natured way of happy drunks and boasting about their abilities.

"I've brought in a hundred Defeated!"

"I can double that!"

When he looked again, Wynn had turned away, his eyes fixed on the dirt between his feet. The talk of bringing in Defeated from raids seemed to upset him. Perhaps he thought of his Defeat. Dyfan had never asked Wynn about it. Never would. That piece of his life was over, and Dyfan didn't want to bring more distress to the other man.

Wynn's fist clenched at his side, and concern trickled through Dyfan's veins. If Wynn had a bout of fear here, Victor Gruffyd would be shamed. A shamed Victor was a dangerous thing. Dyfan stepped forward, bending to murmur into Victor Eurig's ear. The man was heavily into his drink but still less ridiculous than the other Victors.

He stood, feet still steady.

"You know what would be a real test?" he said. Victor Eurig didn't bother to raise his voice. "Our fighters have trained and worked to become the best. But is it a fluke, or is it in their blood?" Dyfan stepped back to stand beside Wynn, closer than before. Heat radiated off Wynn, his scent bathing Dyfan. "I know plenty of you have bred your fighters. Let's see if their offspring are as impressive!"

They gestured for messengers to go fetch various children from compounds. Dyfan reckoned it would take hours for all of them to arrive and hoped that by the time the children did, the Victors would be so drunk they would lose interest in testing them all together. In the meantime, they would debate which child would do the best and keep off the topic of battle Defeated. And since Wynn didn't have any offspring that Dyfan knew of, it seemed likely he'd not submit to fear.

Immediately, debates broke out over who had the purest, strongest bloodlines, and Dyfan found himself stealing glances at Wynn again. The sweat was drying on his skin now. The evening was becoming milder.

Wynn

It was not long before Ifanna summoned someone to escort those on display to the Defeated quarters. The Victors seated around the table seemed to be making every effort to drink themselves unconscious, and Wynn supposed they didn't like being that vulnerable in the presence of their human fighting dogs. He didn't blame them.

Wynn wasn't so sure that he would have the ability to refrain from taking that kind of opportunity. Especially if it meant freedom.

The Defeated moved away in a group. It was a clear night—that time when the stars were brightest, well after the moon had passed her zenith. Wynn followed the others for a time, walking beside Dyfan in quiet companionship. When they reached the group of poorly-lit buildings where he slept each night, he nodded to his ally and walked away.

Wynn's room had only belonged to him a few short moons. It was just wide enough for a cot and a chair, but it had a door—a privacy few Defeated knew— and it was all his. It had been a reward for his improving status as a fighter and the only one he was grateful to have.

The chair held Wynn's few clothes, and he lifted his trousers to replace the garb Gruffyd displayed him in. They were worn but not overly rough and molded to his body. He settled in the cot, as he always did, and shut his eyes. Sleep, however, would not come.

He lay there and imagined he felt Dyfan's hand on his shoulder, fingers stroking his neck, curling into his hair. Sometimes he thought he must have dreamed that moment in the corridor outside of Dyfan's cell. Sometimes he wished he had. The alternative was so much more complicated.

He shifted and tried instead to remember the exact shape of his wife's face, the tilt of her chin, the curve of her lips. It had been so long since he had attempted to visualize her, and now he found that he could not. It had been five years. The same length of time that he had been married to her. Surely that was not enough time to forget her face? Would he still recognize her? Wynn thought so. If she was alive. The idea didn't bring him any comfort.

There was a sound in the corridor—bare feet and the swish of trousers. Whoever it was stopped at Wynn's door, and the longer they stood there, the more certain Wynn became. Dyfan stood on the other side.

Should he call out, invite him in? Wynn couldn't quite make himself do it, but neither could he tell Dyfan to leave. He lay there, hardly breathing, just waiting for the big fighter to decide what to do.

It seemed to take hours.

Finally, there was a brush of knuckles against Wynn's thin door, a knock so quiet it was barely audible.

Wynn shut his eyes and drew in a breath. If he made no noise, then Dyfan would leave. Everything would stay as it had been. Changeless, unceasing. Year after year of fights and Victors until he lost himself entirely, either to a broken mind or an early death.

He felt himself rise, almost without conscious decision. Wynn took the step to the door and opened it.

Dyfan's eyes blazed with unknown heat. He scanned the interior of Wynn's room, always a fighter, always assessing for some potential advantage. When his focus returned to Wynn, it was a nearly physical thing, the weight of his gaze heavier than stone.

Slowly, painstakingly so, Dyfan entered Wynn's room, coming to stand half a hand width away. The door swung shut as Dyfan reached for Wynn's shoulder, tracing the curve of muscle there and then down the length until he gripped Wynn's elbow. This close, Dyfan towered over Wynn, his sheer bulk overwhelming.

"Tell me to leave, and I will." Dyfan's voice, usually gruff with disuse or battle, was silken. Unspeakably tender.

Wynn opened his lips to respond, only to close them again. His stomach was a battlefield between desire and hesitation. His heart was beating their war cries. He shut his eyes against the dark and breathed in, a long, low rising of his chest. "No." It came out in a whisper. "Don't go."

Having said the words, Wynn was at a loss for what to do with himself. With Nia— but no. He didn't want to think about how it had been with the wife he'd loved in a different life. This thing, this growing bud between him and Dyfan, was something else entirely. A kinship, a warmth of soul, and longing for each other born out of kindness shared in the bleak landscape they were forced to exist in. Dyfan was not the lover he had sought but the one he needed, this steady, tender man.

Wynn let his forehead fall to Dyfan's shoulder, feeling the even fullness of his breaths, the scent of him, sharp and hot and earthen. He put his palm flat on the rough top of Dyfan's forearm, leaning into the brush of hair as he slid his hand up his bicep. He felt real, the nearness of him filling Wynn's senses like a river, swollen with spring. Dyfan's hands on him through the bars of his cell must have been real too. "What is this?"

Dyfan leaned against Wynn's touch, his chin tilting down, so his ocean eyes followed every move Wynn made. He stood in silence for a long time, his free hand resting firmly against Wynn's hip, pulling him closer. Finally, he answered, his voice softer than Wynn had heard it before. "Something ours."

In Cwm Or, the Defeated did not own anything. Their food, their clothes, their bodies— all were the property of the Victors. And yet, some soul-deep part of Wynn knew that Dyfan was right. He had seen it on the other man's face as Wynn dragged himself from the depths of his terrors, had felt it lying with his back pressed against Dyfan's while he cried.

This was something that no Victor could take away.

His hand tightened around Dyfan's bicep, his face turning up to look into blue eyes made storms in the dim light above a jaw like mountain crags. The desire in his core surged, a wildfire, and Wynn kissed him hard, his teeth grazing Dyfan's lower lip in his haste.

Dyfan stiffened at that first brush of teeth but then melted, softening into Wynn's grip despite his superior height and strength. As they kissed, time stretched between them, morphing until Wynn wasn't sure if a minute or an hour or an entire day had passed. The longer their lips explored each other's contours, the closer Dyfan pulled him until there was no space between them. Not even a breath —they shared that too.

Finally, Dyfan pulled away, his normally stoic expression transformed into something nervous but eager, and Wynn remembered Dyfan was younger than him. He was not a beast but a young man, expectant and shy. A smile curved the corners of his mouth, and he tentatively brought a calloused hand up to cup Wynn's face, brushing his thumb along the curve of his cheekbone.

Wynn closed his eyes, pressing his skin to Dyfan's palm, reveling in the impossibility of him. How could someone like this have survived this place so long? How had he not been crushed or changed?

Dyfan was so much stronger than any of them knew, someone true to himself in the face of any storm.

He pressed his lips into Dyfan's hand and slowly lifted the simple shirt that had replaced his early feast garb until he could tug it over Dyfan's head, exposing the planes of his body, a heart-twisting mix of hard and soft. Wynn placed a hand on Dyfan's chest and slid it flat against his neck and into his hair.

When they came together again, nothing lay between them—their heat rebounding across the silken press of their chests, and warmth blossomed loving and deep within Wynn, an earnestness that caught in his throat and made tears prickle behind his eyes. He had not been touched in so very long.

Dyfan's clothes fell away like charcoal, crumbling to the floor at Wynn's touch. He lost his trousers shortly after, only half aware of the motion, drowning as he was in the tastes and smells of male skin. They tumbled together into the bed, Dyfan's body pressed as close as a hot summer's night, coiling around his chest and between his thighs. He was over-full with need—taut with it, like his body would overturn at the slightest provocation, spilling him out onto the floor.

Strong hands moved across Wynn's shoulders and down his back, trailing fire lines, drawing Wynn closer. He could see the contours of his room over the other fighter's shoulder, the corners made strange by sheltering shadow. He groaned, and the space seemed to reverberate as muscles, knotted with years of work, ached at the massage. The sound only seemed to encourage Dyfan, and he repeated the long stroke, pressing the meat of his thumb into the groove of Wynn's shoulder blade.

Wynn hissed, turning his face towards Dyfan, biting at his throat. They were together, unclothed and alone. This was theirs, and Wynn wanted more of it. He let his hands explore the hidden spaces of Dyfan's body, arching as the big man's questing fingers found him. They lay like that, panting, the sounds of the night thick around them, and yet unaware of anything but their closeness, brown eyes into gray eyes into black. When they crested together, all lay silent again, safe in the curl of each other's arms.

CHAPTER 42: THE WESTERN SEA

TWELFTH MOON, 1799, THE FLYING NIGHT

Six Years before the Proclamation

"Heave! Heave!" Rain sheeted across the deck, heavier than wet sail cloth and falling in an unending barrage. Iniabi's hair plastered to her skull, her clothes slick against her skin. Water streamed down her face, was pulled into her mouth with each panting breath, and blurred her vision until she could see nothing but the rope in her hands and Cai's back in front of her. Farther up the line, Jaya called out the count, and every time her battle-horn voice called, "Heave!" Iniabi flung her weight back, pulling on the thick mainsail rope. The friction was so great it had eaten through the palms of her gloves, and the rough fibers tore into her hands.

Far overhead, the mainsail inched closer to the yard, the immense canvas cloth folding in upon itself. It had only a few more feet to go—another half-dozen heaves, and then Iniabi would be able to rest, to give her aching palms some respite. Perhaps there would even be time for Cook to bandage her up before the next storm duty she'd be needed for. Maybe. Ever since her promotion to bosun, Jaya had become a pain in the ass. Iniabi wished Vlassis had never died and the captain hadn't made Taaliah Quartermaster.

"HEAVE!"

Iniabi's skin tore, and somewhere up above, a rope snapped like the crack of a whip, and still, even after all these years, Iniabi flinched hard. Above them, the mainsail sagged open to one side, and the storm winds grabbed it, straining against the ropes. The coil threatened to leap out of Iniabi's hands, but the long line of sailors kept it from moving.

"Iniabi! Cai!" Jaya's voice echoed above the storm, and Iniabi looked around to see her pointing to the rigging. "Get up there and get that cursed sail furled!" Iniabi blanched at climbing the rigging in a winter storm of this magnitude, but she knew what would happen if someone didn't. The storm would tear the mainsail to shreds, and then there would be no chance of making it to port alive, not with all the Lirian ships in these waters—they'd be a lame elk in a sea of wolves.

There was nothing for it. Iniabi tore strips of cloth from her shirt and wound them around her palms. The damp fabric stung, but it was better than testing her raw skin against the rigging. She stepped out of the line of heaving bodies and wrapped her hands in the net of ropes that would allow her access to the mainmast.

She felt a slap on her arm, a dull thing since her body was mostly numb with cold. "Stop, fish brain!" Cai shouted over the roar of the sea and the crash of the thunderheads. "We need the ropes to secure us!"

"Leave it! There's no time! That sail will be shredded in minutes!" Iniabi shrugged him off and pulled herself up from the deck, climbing hand-over-foot. "Come on, Cai! Get up here! We've been climbing these ropes for years; don't tell me you're scared of a little rain!"

She glanced back over her shoulder to see Cai scowling up at her. When she continued to climb, he spat and started after her. He was a prideful prick, and Iniabi had known that if she was brave enough to take the sail in this gale, he would too, simply to prove no slaver girl was better than him. Well *fine*, if it got the blasted sail furled and the *Flying Night* safely back to port.

Iniabi reached the yardarm first, sliding out across it with careful steps. This high, the sailors below looked small and far away. Everything was slick with rain, and the usually stable ship rocked and groaned with every wave. Iniabi slipped, losing her footing on the precarious surface, and had to reach out and grab the nearest line to right herself. By the time she was vertical again, her heart was throbbing like a caught rat's, and her hands shook against the rope.

"Are you just going to sit there and diddle yourself or get the fucking job done!?"Cai shouted behind her.

Iniabi shook her head, grimacing at the pain in her hands and the body-numbing freeze, but she kept going, sliding out along the other side until she could reach the sail. Behind her, Cai did the same, and slowly, they began to pull in the sail despite the wind's cold grasp. Iniabi's fingers closed over the first gasket, the pieces of rope used to tie a sail to the yardarm, and the ship gave a powerful lurch, the mast swinging wildly through the air.

Her stomach rose into her throat, and though she never got seasick, Iniabi thought she might puke. It would splatter the people below her, and the absurd hilarity of the thought brought her back to the moment. She could do this. She had done it a thousand times, though admittedly not in a storm like this one. The swirling mass of clouds above them crackled with electricity, and she could hear Cai cursing a steady stream of insults as he hurried to fasten the sail.

The ship bucked again, and Cai let out a short, sharp scream, letting go of his hold on the sail. Suddenly, Iniabi was holding the weight of it alone, pounds and pounds of fabric held closed by nothing more than the short gasket rope she'd been attempting to tie around the yardarm. "Cai, you baby! Grab the fucking sail!" The wind tore at Iniabi's hands, at her face, at the cloth beneath her. The rope began to slip through her numbed fingers. "Cai!"

Iniabi turned to look at him, to get the idiot coward to do the job, but there was no one on the yardarm behind her. "Cai!?" The cry was torn from Iniabi's lips, tossed back at her face by a sharp wind. There was no use. Cai was gone, and alone, Iniabi could not hold the sail.

Desperately, Iniabi hauled on the gasket. She had to get it up above the yardarm, just long enough to tie it off, to protect the sail, but it slipped through her fingers. The sail billowed beneath her and tore through the center, the wind making ribbons of frayed edges.

⇑ ⇑ ⇑

"You stupid fucking slut!" The crash of a glass bottle against the cabin wall echoed like the storm's lightning, and Iniabi flinched. She didn't speak—she wasn't foolish enough to interrupt the captain in a rage.

Captain Ira's quarters were the nicest part of the ship if in a gaudy way, all colorful fabrics and thick couches. There was a wide, rumpled bed half-hidden behind a folding screen and a mahogany desk littered with maps and letters Iniabi could not read. The captain herself stood leaning against this, her hands pressed to the wood and her face nearly as dark with rage. She had lost so much weight that her skin seemed to hang loose from her frame, and there were poison-dark circles around her eyes.

"Do you know how much you've cost me, Iniabi? And you, Jaya?! Is your command of mere sailors so tenuous that they won't follow simple orders?! Are they so ill-trained that they would even think of climbing without a rope?! The entire sail will have to be replaced! That's coming out of your earnings, Iniabi. Jaya, you are obviously not ready to be bosun."

Jaya was going to hate her. Iniabi would have given up enough earnings to re-sail the entire ship rather than Jaya lose her new position because of her. Even if Jaya was annoying in charge. More frightening, though, was the change in the captain. Four years of weekly poison consumption had turned her into a wraith of her former self, skin striped with scratch marks and her movements tense and clumsy.

"Bread and water rations for both of you. If we somehow make it to port without a mainsail, Jaya will recruit and train someone to replace Cai." She stumbled forward, knocking another glass off her desk, the sound of it shattering like the crack of thunder.

Jaya nodded, her first sign of life. "Yes, Captain."

"As you two have endangered the entire crew of the *Flying Night*—" She slammed her fist on the table, hair falling greasy and unwashed across her face. She seemed to lose focus, her eyes catching on the box of poison and then flicking back up to Iniabi. "You— You— Because, because you've endangered the crew, you'll... take their night watches on top of your usual duties." She straightened up, her gaze wavering. "Both of you get out of my sight."

Jaya bowed and turned on her heel. Iniabi fled, slipping through the cracked door so close after Jaya that she stepped on the other girl's heel. "Shit, sorry," Iniabi muttered, then, when the other girl didn't turn, ran to catch up. "Wait! Jaya, I am sorry. I don't want to get in the way of you becoming bosun. We can find some way to fix this."

Jaya strode purposefully across the deck, still scattered with debris from the storm, and down the ladder into the belly of the ship. She didn't pause to acknowledge Iniabi or anyone else.

Iniabi sucked in a breath. Jaya could stand on her pride if she wanted to, but she wasn't about to let a wound fester. It was the fastest way to lose a limb, Cook said, and with Cai and Iago gone, Iniabi was coming closer and closer to losing everyone on this ship that she cared about. She flung herself down the ladder.

"Look, I know you're angry, and rightfully so, but Jaya, it's just us left. Let's not let one mistake mess that up."

"Mess it up?" Entering the barracks, Jaya spun to face Iniabi with surprising speed, and before the Emaian could react, the other girl was shoving her away. "Apparently, my one mistake was trusting you to do as you were told! My mistake was relying on *you*, Iniabi!"

Iniabi shoved her hands away. "I did exactly what you told me! The only thing I didn't do was take a security line. How was I supposed to know Cai would fall? Look, can we just put this behind us?"

"How were you to know?!" Jaya's dark cheeks turned crimson. "That's the entire fucking point of the security line! And the captain? *What the* fuck *have you done to her, Iniabi?*"

"You know what, fine! If you want someone to blame so badly, go on and blame me! Good luck getting your promotion back, and have fun having no one else on this ice-damned ship!" Iniabi spun on her heel and stalked off, shaking, Jaya's words echoing in her mind. *What have you done to her, Iniabi?*

CHAPTER 43: THE WESTERN SEA

FIRST MOON, 1800, THE FLYING NIGHT

Five Years before the Proclamation

"Iniabi, I've been thinking...." Captain Ira's voice was slurred, her gaze not on Iniabi, who stood at the desk, counting out shells of poison, but on something across the cabin. Something unreal, of the dream world.

"Oh?" Iniabi murmured, double-checking her math instead of paying attention.

"Maybe I should take more medicine. Just a drop."

Iniabi suppressed a sigh and started piling poison shells back into the box with a lock. This was not the first time the captain had made this suggestion. But it was clear just how much of an effect the *medicine* already had on her body. Even as Iniabi turned to look at her, the captain began to rock herself, childlike under the drug's hold. "Remember what I said about needing the right amount for dreams? You don't want to lose them, do you?"

The older woman stopped rocking, looking up at Iniabi with startlingly intense precision. "How do you know what dose is right for me? I'm a warrior. I need more."

Iniabi knew what would come next if she didn't placate the captain. Her moods were volatile as the sea and less productive. Twice this moon, Captain Ira had screamed at her, calling her names and dissolving into begging fits. The crew overheard and asked Iniabi questions she couldn't answer. So far, they believed it was the captain's 'sickness,' but that wouldn't last forever.

She could just give in, but she worried about how much worse the captain would get on a higher dosage. Would she lose her mind entirely? Slide into dreams one night and just... not wake up again? Not to mention, it would mean running out of their supply that much sooner. If anything, Iniabi should be decreasing the doses by a drop or two, but she didn't think she'd be able to get away with it.

"You might be right. Pheceans are different than Emaians, after all...." They were weak-minded fools that dosed themselves with the poison they were meant to sell— "but our supplies are getting low. You don't want to run out, do you? We should keep the dose the same until we restock."

"What do you mean we're getting low?!" The captain hauled herself to her feet, stumbling over to look into the box Iniabi filled with shells. "How could we be getting low?! You're supposed to keep an eye on this! How much time do we have?"

The desperation in Ira's voice made her shrill, and Iniabi winced. It would be audible outside. "A moon cycle, Captain. Plenty of time to get to the Emaian coast. It's just been slow going since the storm damaged the mainsail."

Iniabi locked the lid of the box where she kept the captain's poison, taking a half-involuntary step back when the woman lunged towards her as if to swipe the keys out of her hand. Iniabi clutched them to her chest, heart pounding like she was a little girl again, under Manaba's control.

"Don't speak to me like I'm a half-wit, you bitch!" Ira spat as she spoke, her words forceful but ill-formed. It was incredible she was on her feet right now, given the dose she had just taken. She shambled forward and swung her fist at Iniabi, the blow painful but not powerful. Iniabi stepped back again, waiting for Ira's dreams to take her away. Then she could leave and tell Leon to plot a course for the nearest Emaian holding.

The captain glared at her, but as the ship heaved and swayed, the fire in her gaze dimmed. She muttered and made her way back to her desk, leaning heavily before she half-fell, half-sat into her chair.

By the time Iniabi opened the door to the captain's quarters, the woman was unconscious, face down on a stack of charts. Iniabi shut the door and smoothed shaking hands across her shirt. Even if she did get another allotment of poison in time, how much longer could she do this?

She climbed the ladder to the quarterdeck, looking for Leon. Jaya stood next to the wheel, but Iniabi didn't bother to try and talk to her. She was still mad about her demotion. Instead, she approached the pink man next to Jaya, clearing her throat when he didn't look up from his maps.

"Let me guess, the captain wants us to drop all our plans and head to the nearest Emaian settlement, post haste? Regardless of our torn sail? No tent-dweller will have one." The navigator had a strange accent and an even stranger manner of speech. The crew said he was from Ingola. Wherever that was.

Iniabi hesitated, her belly going cold. "That's what she wanted me to pass on." How much did he know?

He looked up then, his sandy brown eyes skeptical. "And if I told you to remind the captain of the Lirian merchant ships we were chasing down? Would you do it?"

"Careful, Leon," Jaya's sharp voice cut between them, startling Iniabi. "If you seem against Iniabi, you might have a little accident."

"I'm not some pubescent deckhand. I doubt she'd get the drop on me that easily." He smirked, but it didn't seem to hold any humor. They were talking about Cai. They thought she'd killed him deliberately? The idea left Iniabi cold, hollow. Guilt welled up in tar-like bubbles between the planks of her ribs.

"The Captain knows what she wants," she said too sharply. "If you don't like it, perhaps *you* should be the one to remind her."

For a moment, there weren't any sounds but the snapping of sails and the rhythm of the waves lapping the ship's hull. Jaya and Leon looked at each other, something dark flickering between them.

Leon pulled out a different stack of maps, clearly preparing to plot a new course. As ordered. Iniabi wavered, wondering if she should watch him, but thought better of it. She turned and strode away, but not before she could hear the snide tone of Jaya's voice. Leon laughed coldly at whatever Jaya had said, and it was all Iniabi could do not to look over her shoulder at the pair as she climbed down the ladder and onto the main deck.

Thunder grumbled overhead, and Iniabi turned her face to gray storm clouds, feeling the first drops of cold rain plop against her cheeks.

ᛏ ᛏ ᛏ

In the dim of early morning, the mess was all but deserted. A handful of night-watch sailors sat together, talking softly, the morning watch already taking over their positions on deck. It smelled of the stale stew, watered whiskey, and bread served for dinner the night before. The sailors quieted for a moment when Iniabi entered, her feet dragging with exhaustion after another long night on the deck. It seemed the captain's punishment that she and Jaya take night shifts had no foreseeable end, and Jaya's contempt only made the long shifts harder. Iniabi missed Iago more than ever. She missed having a friend.

Breakfast, as always, was a serving of ship's biscuit, cheese, and salted fish. Iniabi took hers unenthusiastically, sitting alone in the middle of the room. None of it looked particularly fresh, and they weren't likely to get anything else from the other ships in the area. Perhaps the next Emaian settlement they stopped at would have caribou, seaweed, and summer berries.

That was if Iniabi lived that long. She brushed a hand against her shoulder where the captain had most recently lashed out. She needed a way out. And soon.

The sailors nearest Iniabi seemed to have forgotten she was there, voices rising again to fill the room. She placed another bite of shriveled bread into her mouth, chasing it down with big gulps of weak, lukewarm beer. The conversation was certainly more interesting than her meal.

"Did you hear her screaming again last night?"

"More like crying," a gruff voice said. Iniabi thought it belonged to Bastien, but she didn't dare shift around to look and see who it was.

"There are some illnesses that cause madness." That could only be Leon.

Bastien scoffed. "Don't be an idiot. She's not sick."

"What are you talking about? She's wasting away—"

"Haven't you ever seen someone taken with dream potions?"

The silence made Iniabi's ears ring. If the crew figured out the captain was a poison addict, they'd figure out who was giving her the drug. It wouldn't be a hard guess, as she was the only Emaian, likely the only person who knew how to curate the doses. All the feeling drained from Iniabi's face and fingers. Great sea, they were going to kill her.

"Then she *is* insane. If she wasn't before the tinctures, then she is now. That shit warps everything." Leon said.

"You're one to talk," someone else hissed, their voice much lower than the rest. "You drink yourself sick anytime we're in port."

"I might indulge," he said, "but the next morning, I'm myself again. You can see what the dream potions are doing to the captain. She's losing her mind. Do you want to follow a crazy woman?"

No one spoke again. Iniabi held herself stiff as a barnacle, her heart pumping a too rapid, uneven stutter.

"Think about it," Leon said after the heavy pause, and the scraping of benches indicated a few had stood up to leave. Iniabi didn't dare move. She didn't breathe again until they were all gone.

The simple fact of her situation was that the captain would not improve. Stopping the poison would only kill her, and continuing to give it to her in slow, small doses would only stave off her inevitable ruin by a few moons—a year at the most. She was sailing a leaking ship and running out of buckets to bail with.

If those sailors rallied behind Leon and mutinied, Iniabi would be out of time that much faster. She had seen the poison dreams. She knew that she would live through this, that there was some greater destiny for her, didn't she? Or was that her own insanity, brought on by a little girl trying to live up to her mother's impossible demands?

Whatever it was, Iniabi would not die on this spirit-forsaken ship.

She stood, leaving the rest of her breakfast lying untouched on the table, and climbed the decks to the captain's quarters to speak with her privately. The gaudy cabin was dark and musty with last night's excess, and Iniabi squinted against the dim light. Someone sat in the captain's chair, but it wasn't Ira. "Who—" Iniabi started when Cai's bloody face caught the light coming in through the door. She gave a throttled scream, falling back, but when she looked up again, he was gone.

Iniabi cursed, scrambling out of the cabin and into the light. It was just exhaustion that made her see him. She'd been attending to her regular duties, dealing with the captain, and keeping night watches for weeks. This was nothing. And it certainly didn't have anything to do with what she planned to tell the captain. It was their fault for being traitors.

Iniabi made her way to the deck above the captain's cabin, where the helm stood with a full view of the ship before it. The captain stood behind the helm, though it was locked in place, set as they were on their current course.

"Captain," the nerves roiling in Iniabi's gut made it difficult to catch her breath, and the word came out airless. "I've overheard something you'll want to know."

WHAT THE CAPTAIN did with that information would taint her dreams forever. The images were seared onto the backs of her eyelids like the spidering of lightning strikes after staring at a flash across the sky, but blinking did nothing to make them go away. In some part of her mind, Captain Ira would always be standing triumphantly on the deck, cheerfully chanting to herself as she slowly cooked Leon's eyes with red-hot pokers. It smelled like meat—mild and porky— and his screams rang out over the water in a discordant, throat-tearing counterpoint to the captain. "Eyes for Ira, you fucking dogs! Ira gets your eyes!"

Iniabi was not the only one relieved when the spikes finally found Leon's brain.

CHAPTER 44: LIRIA

FIRST MOON, 1800, EGARA

Five Years before the Proclamation

"Calm down, Camilla. Ignatious is well trained, and he's only fighting Pheceans. You know Lirian steel wins out over the gilded excuses Pheceans use." Though Luce tried his best to use a calm, confident tone, his mind raced at the thought of his son out on some battlefield. The Pheceans were more organized, better fed and better educated than the Emaians. While the barbarians were wild and unpredictable, they didn't command any military force. Most of their weapons were made of bone, not steel.

But it wouldn't help Camilla, who paced before Luce's desk, twisting her hands, to admit this. She needed his strength and his confidence that all would be well with their son. It *had* to be.

"Calm down?! He's going to war! *War*, Luce. Even you haven't done that, and you are *far* more experienced. What will his family do if he should *fall*?" Her voice faltered on the word, and Camilla clutched at her chest as if her heart were about to burst.

"Then we will care for Valeria and Balbina," Luce said. Already he had started setting aside funds. For his family, for his son's. Provisions too. Anything that could be preserved had been. Paper, ink, food. Luce had a nice stockpile in his home, hidden from even Camilla, for he knew why the Imperator allowed this war with Phecea. The mines had run dry decades ago, and the influx of trade with the Tupa Galans was not enough to keep Liria afloat. They needed Phecean goods, Phecean land. So Liria would take what was rightfully theirs, and he would be prepared for the slaughter.

He did not doubt his country, but Luce was a man with one hand, and he knew even the most decrepit and low-born creatures could cause chaos. He would not be caught unawares. He would not let his family suffer. Never again.

CHAPTER 45: PHECEA

FIRST MOON, 1800, DIOSION

Five Years before the Proclamation

Three moons ago, if anyone had asked Danae what the worst form of torture was, she would have said sitting through Mistress Afin's discussion on the greeting protocols of foreign dignitaries, eating the raw fish favored by coastal farmers, or possibly dancing in public. Now, she thought it was watching Erose Cirillo conduct her little court at her new year tea party. Apparently, it was an annual event, but Danae hadn't been old enough to invite until now.

Danae regretted being invited because the moment she climbed out of her carriage, she was greeted by girls up to four years older than her. And while Danae was taller than most, she was acutely aware of how young she was. The older girls, mostly of good families but not council members, wore dresses with tight bodices that draped over their curves. Not the comfortable standard tunic that most wore in Phecea. And despite the ocean wind, they did not wear shawls.

Gathered in the back garden, cheeks flushed from the wind, older boys and girls sat around on cushions. The low tea tables were heavy with steaming pots, bowls of dates, and olives soaked in brine. It was a beautiful summer day, and wisteria-draped trellises spilled scent over the guests. They spoke loudly over one another and laughed too much, and in the center, sat Biton. He wore one of his newest fashions, a simple gray silk tunic with a steep neckline cinched at his waist with a jaunty sash in brilliant red. Rubies dripped from his ears and throat, and his hair was tied loosely back. Biton's face was only lightly painted: red lips and silver liner around his eyes.

He looked like the center of a great mural, bright and lively, with everything else revolving around him. Erose showed Danae her seat, a place of honor at her right side, yet somehow isolated as everyone else down the table faced Biton and away from her.

"I think it is a *good* thing that we have finally begun fighting back. Phecea cannot stand for the raids on our soil. It's been years, and the people of Zodrafi have had too many hard winters." Biton raised a spoonful of tart, preserved cherries to his mouth. They were the same color as his lips.

"I don't know," Adohnis said. "My father thinks that war is never the answer. He says that we have only invited more strife."

Biton cocked an eyebrow. "What would he have us do then? Diplomacy has failed in the past. No amount of talks, threats, or sanctions made a difference to the Lirians."

"How hard did we really try, though? From the beginning, we layered the Imperator with accusations. Surely there could be a way to find peace without hurting his pride?"

"This isn't a matter of personal pride, but of the fate of two peoples. Liria has no respect for softer measures." Biton leaned back, placing another cherry on his tongue. "Danae, what do you think? You are perhaps the most eloquent diplomat among us."

Erose made a rude disbelieving noise, not quite loud enough for the others to hear, but she did not stop Danae from speaking.

Danae had heard recreations of debates made in council chambers on the topic of Phecea declaring war on Liria—after all, her mother and father held some of the most esteemed seats on the council. Her father said war was coming no matter how sensibly Phecea handled the issue of Lirian aggression.

"It is difficult to see the best path forward when fear and hunger cloud our judgment. Perhaps in years to come, we will be seen as wise for acting proactively, or perhaps we will be considered fools for starting a war we could have avoided. The past is easy to judge while the future invites only speculation."

Erose snorted. "That didn't answer the question at all!"

"Maybe, that is because there isn't an answer. At least not yet." Biton smiled at Danae across the table. "Perhaps we should speak of topics that are more forthright?"

Before Danae spoke, Erose murmured in agreement as if he had said something particularly sage. Danae picked up her cup of tea, swallowing it too quickly. Her tongue burned, her throat constricted, and Danae coughed and sputtered.

No one noticed much.

Erose, playing hostess, stood from her cushion in a swishing of skirts. She flounced about the table, refilling cups and freshening treats. As she reached Biton, Erose placed her empty hand on his shoulder, as if her balance was suddenly terrible and she needed him to brace her up. Danae bit back a sigh, though she nearly spat out her second sip of tea as the older girl bent such that her low neckline was astoundingly close to Biton's face.

His almond-shaped eyes darted over Erose's offering and then up to her face as if he hadn't just stared down her chest. Danae glanced at the others at the table. No one seemed to mind or care. In fact, Adohnis was smirking.

Danae brushed invisible crumbs off her sage-green tunic, noticing how the cloth did not rise or fall. Flat.

Sighing, she set down her cup.

"Why don't we play a game?" Ion was the only one who looked as tired of the affair as Danae felt, and his eyes followed Adohnis's gaze with a troubled expression. "Biton, you've always had an ear for entertainment. Do you know any good ones?"

Erose straightened, and Biton dropped his chin into his hand. "Hmmm... maybe we could take turns humming to see if anyone can guess the song, or we could go around the table, and each make up part of a story. Does anyone else have any ideas?"

"I'm too chilled to sit still for so long. Let's play fish in a barrel," Erose said. Callista nodded as if this were a splendid idea, but it struck

Danae as odd. She and Biton played fish in a barrel with his sisters, who were still quite young, but the game seemed juvenile for this crowd. Erose's eyes flickered over her party guests and landed on Biton. "I know, Biton, *you'll* hide first."

At least Ion looked as confused as Danae felt.

Biton just shrugged. "I warn you, though, I'm *excellent* at this game. My sisters keep me in practice. Now! Everyone, face the wall and keep your eyes closed!"

Somewhere down the line, Erose began to count, and when the time was up, Biton was gone.

"Remind me," some girl Danae didn't know spoke, scanning the area as if Biton would hide nearby, "When we find him, we shout, right?"

"No! You hide *with* him. And each time a person finds the hider, Biton in this case, they join in hiding too."

"But there are so many of us! How will we all fit?"

Erose laughed, the sound grating against Danae's nerves as she walked away. "You *don't*, silly! You just try to hide nearby if you have to. That's when it gets funny."

Uninterested in the amusing aspects of fish in a barrel, Danae circled the little garden, peering at benches and rose bushes and tinkling fountains. There weren't any good hiding places here unless Biton was willing to scale one of the well-groomed trees. Just in case, Danae glanced up, careful to keep her demeanor casual to not alert the other seekers. No flash of silk.

No. He wasn't in a tree.

And since Erose, unwisely, hadn't proclaimed the rules, that would mean the house was not off limits. A townhouse, even for a smaller family like the Cirillo's, would offer many hiding places.

As Erose continued to explain the concepts of a children's game, Danae slipped inside. She discounted the floor-to-ceiling curtains, as it was the first place someone like Dido would hide. A closet might do, but it seemed rude to hide in one of Erose's linen cupboards. Not to mention, with so many seekers, it would get crowded and give away his spot. The other hiders would loiter around the closet until everyone else realized that they were "hiding in plain sight," a tactic his little sisters didn't understand very well.

Under a bed would be good, but it would be awfully bold to enter a Cirill bedroom uninvited. Biton was bold, but he wasn't oblivious to social rules.

Even if he *did* stare at Erose's chest.

Sighing, Danae turned towards the kitchens. Servants stairwells and the hidden passageways between rooms to hide their slaves seemed the safest choice. Technically open to all in the house, but often overlooked.

She paused by a discreet door, the paneling blending in like part of the wall. The other seekers were starting to filter into the house now, clearly having come to the same conclusion she had, that the garden had no hiding places. The hidden door opened as an Emai slave came through, a bundle of firewood under his arm. As the door started to whisk shut, Danae eased into the darkened hall. Her eyes adjusted slowly to the dim lighting, and she took a few steps forward, careful to keep her tread light. If Biton heard her coming, he'd hold his breath.

She let one hand run along the wall, feeling for crevices that might indicate a closet or another door. The space hummed with noble voices on the other side of the wall, but the hallway was eerie. No shifts of movement. No pants or nervous breaths.

She took the time to check the entire space, but he was not there. Danae slipped down the stairs and waited on the kitchen's threshold to watch the cook and servants move around. A few noticed her and bowed but continued at their work. After all, this was their domain.

Another Emai slave entered from the opposite wall, the door beyond revealing steps down. A cellar. Perfect.

Danae skirted around the edge of the kitchen, careful to keep out of the way. No one tried to stop her—why would they? She was an Othonos— and she reached the door to the cellar without trouble.

The stairs leading down turned into darkness, and Danae hesitated. It was just a cellar, but the cold air wafting from the space felt creepy.

Silly, she chided herself. It's just a cellar. Straightening her shoulders, Danae trotted down the steps, determined to be confident, where in reality, she was a little afraid. She wasn't a baby, scared of the dark!

The bottom revealed a room much like any cellar she had been in, which were just the Mavros and Othonos ones. Shelves of root vegetables and hanging herbs, barrels of dried grains. Perhaps less well lit than her family's and more drafty, but a cellar.

She walked along the lines of shelves until she came to the back row, where wines and casks of other liquors sat. And at the end of the row, a barrel was moved forward. Perhaps just sat there by a lazy servant and never put into the proper little row, or perhaps Biton had moved it to create a space to hide behind.

Danae tiptoed to the last barrel and peered behind it. Sure enough, Biton grinned up at her like a fool.

"Danae! That didn't take you long at all. Of course, I shouldn't be surprised. You're the cleverest out of all of us." He scooted over so that she could crouch beside him. "Were the others behind you? Or did you leave them all chasing their tails in the garden?"

"Someone must have realized there weren't any good hiding places," Danae said as she climbed over the barrel, glad she wore a tunic and trousers. It would be difficult to maneuver in a skirt. "Because they were headed inside when I found the servant's door."

Settling beside Biton, Danae listened to the noises overhead. Just the murmured voices of the servants and cooks. Either no one had come into the back of the townhouse yet, or they were sneaking as she had.

"Good! I didn't think it would take them long to figure that out. Erose is pretty smart too." He peaked over the barrel and then gave Danae another of his wide smiles. "Fish in a barrel is no fun if you're hiding alone for a long time."

"No. You wouldn't want to be here by yourself the whole time. Especially not when you have *so* many friends here." Danae tried for her usual tone, but even to her ears, the words sounded clipped. She kept thinking about how all the boys and girls were fawning over Biton. How much they complimented him and asked for his opinions. As if he were a councilor!

"What does that mean?" Biton asked, taking the flesh of his cheek in between his molars. "You have friends here too! There's Callista and Adohnis and Ion and Yolanta and Erose—"

"Erose is *not* my friend. She's *your* friend."

"Why can't we *all* be friends? Why does it have to be my friends and your friends like it's two different groups?"

"Well, she doesn't try to show *me* her new neckline as she does you. And even if she did, I wouldn't look!"

"Don't act so superior! How do you know you wouldn't if someone handsome, beautiful, or dashing leaned over you like that?! Just give it a couple years."

Danae clamped her lips together to keep back the words that wanted to flow forth. No one would look at or lean over her that way. She was taller than most of the boys and thinner than a winter poplar. Erose's attitude said it all. Danae was just the boring daughter of Councilor Arsenio and Councilor Andromyda. Invited because of her status.

Biton flushed as red as his ruby earrings and opened his mouth to say more when Ion's head appeared over the top of the barrel. "Whatever it is, I don't want to know about it. But I found you because neither of you knows how to *whisper*."

Biton's mouth clamped shut again, and he looked away, sliding behind the next barrel over so that Ion could squeeze in between him and Danae.

"Well, this is cheerful."

⇑   ⇑   ⇑

Summer came fast. It was only the third moon, yet flowers poked through the soil. Trees donned themselves in vibrancy, and the Bathi River swelled until she burst from her banks and sent mountain water running down to the sea. It was Biton's favorite time of year. Parties were held outside or in open rooms, and even the administrators in the city offices began to relax their rules on opening windows.

This summer, however, was fundamentally lacking. His work was becoming more interesting, he still had parties to attend, and he and Keme had been slipping out to see more of the city away from the sheltered world of Phecea's aristocrats. It was, however, incomplete without Danae.

It had been two moons since their argument in the Cirillo cellar, and they had not made up. Danae still attended the events she was invited to, but she spoke very little, and the last time he had seen her, she had left early, slipping out to her carriage before they even served the meal. Today, they were supposed to have gone riding at Callista and Adohnis's home, but Danae hadn't come.

Something was wrong, and whatever it was had to be deeper than Danae being angry about his—admittedly untasteful— behavior at Erose's tea party moons ago. Didn't it? Danae wouldn't still be mad about that.

Biton stepped out of his carriage, the window still smudged where he had sat with his face pressed against the glass to enjoy the season. The path up to the manor was as lovely as ever: white marble stepping stones lined with basket-of-gold flowers up to the gilded gate. Biton put his hand on the gold knocker and tapped it into the oak of the main double doors, feeling like a guest at Danae's home for the first time since he came over to teach her initial dance lesson.

It was answered by an Emaian slave who did not raise her eyes from Biton's shined black boots. "Apologies, sir, but the Councilors are currently busy. Please send a note to their secretary, Spyro Mundas, to make an appointment."

"Actually, I came to see Danae."

Her eyes flicked up briefly then. "Ah, but the young mistress is ill. Would you like me to take a note?"

Biton chewed the inside of his cheek. "No, I think I'll chance it. It is imperative that I speak to her. Please, friend. I will take any blame."

The slave must have recognized Biton from all the time he spent at the Othonos home because she stepped aside to let him enter.

The beautiful manor was quieter than usual. The servants watched their steps and no strains of lilting harp music coiled through the halls. Danae's parents must have had business away from home. Biton almost wanted to hold his breath as he climbed the great staircase to the third floor, where Danae's room was tucked into a west-facing corner. He only hesitated slightly when he rapped on her door. "Danae? Are you awake?"

There was a long pause before her voice finally floated to him. It sounded muffled. "Go away, Biton. I'm not well."

"Then I suppose I'll just have to shout to you through the door." Biton leaned against the wood hard enough so that she would hear the audible thump. "I'm not going until you talk to me."

Another long pause and then a sigh so loud he could hear it from outside. When Danae pulled her door open, it looked like she really *was* ill. Her hair, often a halo around her head, was completely untamed, frizzled and ill-formed. Brown-gold eyes were red-rimmed and puffy, the tip of her nose pink.

"I don't want to go horseback riding today, Biton," Danae's voice was even more choked, and she sniffed heartily while she pulled her shawl tighter across her body. Beyond her bed was a nest of covers and pillows, uncharacteristically untidy.

"You've been *crying*," Biton said, an observation rather than a question. He tucked her shawl around her and pulled the slender girl into a hug. "I've missed you."

Initially, she was stiff, but little tremors rippled through Danae until she broke into sobbing gasps, wrapping her arms about Biton as if he were her anchor in an angry sea.

"There, there." Biton patted Danae's back, trying to hide his awkwardness. When he or one of his sisters cried, Mama would pat their backs and hold them close, and Papa would fake cry until he had them laughing. Biton didn't think that would work with Danae.

"Biton! I can't go to those parties anymore." She stepped aside so he could enter her room, which for once in her life looked like Biton's: clothes were piled about, and the dresser and standing chest were open and empty.

"Why not?" Biton rubbed her shoulder. "Do you want to sit down?"

Maybe that would help. People sat down when they weren't feeling well, right? And they drank tea. Where was Yuka? Danae definitely needed some tea.

She shuffled over to her unmade bed and sat down, the feather-filled blankets puffing up around her. He would never say it aloud, but

Danae looked like a baby bird, with her feathers poofed and her long limbs folded tight against her torso like wings. She looked miserable. "I'm the ugliest one there, and everyone knows it. They only invite me because I'm an Othonos."

"That's not true at all! You're beautiful! I'd invite you to anything because you're my friend and Callista, Yolanta, Adohnis, and Ion all like it when you're around. They asked after you." Biton looked around and found a tea service set carefully atop her otherwise cluttered desk. The tea inside was over-steeped, but it was still warm, and there was sugar to sweeten it. He poured Danae a cup and stirred a few spoonfuls in. "Here. Drink a few sips of tea."

Taking the cup, Danae shook her head in denial. "I'm not. You just get more glamorous, and I only get- get taller!" She hiccuped as she spoke, and her hair jiggled as she did so. "Everyone thinks you're *so* beautiful and suave and fashionable, and I just... Don't belong."

"Danae, you're the best of all of us! Saying you don't belong is like saying Pavlina doesn't belong with singers or that my papa doesn't belong at the treasurer's office." He sat down beside her and draped an arm over her shoulders. "If you want to be glamorous as well as beautiful, I could help?"

She hiccuped again, watery eyes lifting to Biton's face. "What do you mean? You can't make me prettier or more feminine. I'm just a stick with big hair and knobby elbows. Not like you."

Biton blinked at her. She was lovely, and he had to *work* to appear more graceful while his growing body betrayed him with hair and odor. "Danae, I make myself prettier and more feminine all the time. I don't just wake up this way," he indicated his deep blue blouse and lapis necklace.

This news seemed to genuinely shock Danae, and she stopped weeping altogether. "But... But you've always looked so...good."

"Not always. The first time I dressed this boldly, I was so nervous. It was for the end-of-year celebrations at the Leos estate. Do you remember?" It was only a few moons ago.

"You've always looked glamorous, Biton." Danae wiped at the drying tears on her face. "You're just more so now. And I'm...not." She gestured to her rumpled clothes and swollen eyes. It wasn't a fair comparison, she was two years younger; still trying to figure out how to dress and move. Most of the other noble girls were older and more experienced in fashion and makeup.

"You just need more practice." Biton stooped to rummage through the piles, tossing tunics and leggings aside until he found one of a gemstone-red that he liked. He lifted and shook it to remove some of the wrinkles. It wasn't perfect, but it would do for now. He tossed it over his arm and continued his search.

"It's pointless," Danae huffed, flopping back on her bed. At least she wasn't weeping anymore, though she was undoubtedly wallowing. "I only fit in little girls' clothes. I only *own* little girls' clothes."

"That's not true; this red is dashing." He picked up a pair of satiny black pants: straight-legged and slim around the ankles. "Here. Put these on."

Danae caught the outfit, and Biton searched for her treasure chest, which happened to be buried under a mountain of plain leather slippers. He sighed. They were going to have to order a few new things.

With a huff, Danae complied, mumbling nonsensical things about her appearance and how pointless it was to try and make it better. However, when she caught sight of herself in the mirror, her complaining stopped. Biton cleared the bench before her vanity of discarded shawls and patted it. "Sit."

Mute, Danae sat, though when she caught sight of her hair and blotchy face, she winced. "Biton, it's not going to work."

Biton ignored her and held up a black scarf patterned with silver. Yes, that would work. He set it on her vanity with the box of jewels and produced a string of opals to go about her neck. "I think this is a particularly nice color on you. And the opals match the embroidery perfectly."

"But, Biton, my hair...."

There was no denying that her hair needed care. It was a different texture than his and her mother's, and her father didn't keep his very long. Biton didn't think that Danae would want to cut hers short, but neither did he know what it needed. He chewed the inside of his cheek. "We'll braid it today, and you should ask your father when he comes home."

He lifted the comb from her vanity and began to separate her hair into sections. He wasn't as good at this as Keme, but he did know how to braid.

The room was quiet as he worked, Danae watching Biton through the mirror, eyes considering before she finally spoke. "Thank you, Biton."

"Of course!" Biton smiled at her in the mirror and tied the end of her long rope of hair off with a black ribbon. He found a simple silver circlet in her treasure box to lay on her brow and then asked her to stand up so that he could tie the scarf about her waist. "Alright, look in the mirror now."

Danae hesitated before turning to look. She swallowed hard, staring for a long time at the impressive figure she struck. Admittedly, she was still lean and tall—there was no getting around that—but her hair was tamed by the braids, and the red tunic lit her skin. She was young but she looked less childlike with the scarf about her waist and the jewels at her throat.

She reached out to the mirror, touching her reflection tentatively, a small smile curving her lips. He hadn't realized how much Danae's appearance had been weighing on her, and he could see how the parties and the older girls might have made things worse. "Do you like it?" he asked.

"I think so," she whispered, almost shy now.

Biton smiled and kissed her on the top of her head as he might one of his sisters. "Do you have any face paints?"

CHAPTER 46: PHECEA

FIFTH MOON, 1800, DIOSION

Five Years before the Proclamation

"Do I look older to you?" Danae pivoted in her mirror, admiring the way the folds of slate gray cloth spilled down her body. For her fourteenth birthday, she let Biton talk her into wearing a full dress instead of a dress tunic and leggings since they were going to a symphony. The effect was becoming, making her long limbs seem graceful and stately.

Her hair felt right now that her father had shown her what to do, but Danae was disappointed to see that she still looked young. So young. Yesterday, fourteen had seemed a good age; now, she only wished to be older. Sixteen, like Biton would be soon, or maybe even twenty.

"I don't," Danae sighed, slumping in front of the mirror and turning away. Biton was lying on her bed and tossing her brush, catching it repeatedly. He looked dazzling in black satin and silver bangles. "Let's face it, the best clothes in the world won't make me look like a girl."

Biton caught the brush and sat up, tossing it onto her vanity. "I've got an idea. Put on something else and call Yuka in really quick. I need a needle, thread, and a penknife."

"What? A knife? What are you planning?" Even as she argued, Danae reached for the silver clasps at the shoulders. "Yuka?" The slave waited on the other side, as she always did, and bowed as Danae summoned her. "Master Biton needs a needle, thread, and a penknife."

If the request confused Yuka, she didn't show it as she bowed again and hurried off to find the supplies. She had been with the Othonos her whole life, so Yuka was well trained in keeping her expression polite, something Danae had always admired.

Danae waited in her shift while Biton lifted the dress and turned it inside out, looking for something that she couldn't discern. "Grab your least favorite silk scarf or tunic." He had his cheek between his teeth, his kohl-darkened lashes casting shadows across his skin. "Yes, I think this will do...."

Yuka arrived as Biton started to fold up the spare scarves, Danae watching from the bed. "Would Master Biton like for me to sew something up?" Yuka asked, gaze kept respectfully on the floor.

"No, thank you, Yuka. I appreciate you getting that for me." He held out his hand for the sewing case, and Danae waved her back into the hall. Maybe Yuka would go help her mother in the kitchens, or with the wash.

"What are you doing, Biton?"

His hands flew over the fabric, picking out seams that Danae had not even noticed were there. He ran his hand back through his hair, brushing it off his face. "I'm just adding a few... adjustments."

She didn't have much experience with sewing—the art of making clothing was less appealing than dancing—but Biton looked like he'd done this before. Danae sank back while he worked, her mind wandering. "I heard papa saying things were going well at the border. As much as such things can I suppose...."

"Yes, everyone at the city office is really optimistic. Some are even saying that Liria was foolish to ask for war. We've a larger population, more resources, and more talented craftsmen. That means better weapons, better armor. Really, they're outmatched."

She supposed all that was true, but the Lirians were more experienced with fighting. "Don't you think the larger army would win?"

He shrugged. "From what I understand, it all matters: numbers, training, gear, food. A starving soldier can't fight."

"Nor can a frightened novice," Danae murmured, nervous about speaking her opinion rather than parroting her parents' views. But it was Biton; he wouldn't laugh at her.

"That's a good point. Nobody at work has mentioned how little we've used our army in recent years. They wouldn't stand a chance against our navy, though."

Danae's mind flickered to the Lirian Imperator's Tupa Galan bride. Liria didn't have much of a navy, but Tupa Gali did. However, Biton turned his attention back to her dress, slipping the folded scarves into the pocket he had created. Understanding bloomed within Danae. "You're making curves!?"

Biton flicked his eyes up at her, a rakish grin tilting his lips. "Of course. What did you think I was doing?"

"How was I supposed to know? A hidden compartment for a pirate sword or stolen jewels?" Biton's gaze drifted towards the window, and Danae sighed in exasperation. "I wasn't making a suggestion!"

"Next time," Biton promised, sewing close the pocket with the scarves. He repeated the process and stood up, turning the dress right side out. "Put it on now."

Danae grabbed the gown, pulling it back over her narrow hips and reclasping the shoulder pieces. She turned to look in the mirror and gasped. It worked! "Biton, you mad genius!" She looked as if she had breasts. Not huge ones, but more than she had.

Now she looked older.

Danae turned left and right, admiring how the cloth spilled over the silk scarf lumps. "I could be a beauty, don't you think?"

Biton

Biton stretched, and came to stand behind her in the mirror. "You already are a beauty; you just haven't realized it." Danae scoffed but continued to toy with the padded dress, going so far as to cup the scarves as if they were real breasts. He snorted, and Danae spun, blushing.

"Biton! Don't make fun! I couldn't help it. I just wanted to...." She cupped them again, and he shook his head. "It really is fun."

"I would never!"

"You spend a lot of time *looking* at Erose's chest—"

"That was *one* time!"

Danae rolled her eyes, reaching up to unclasp the shoulders of her dress again. "Here! Wear it! You'll see what I mean; you just want to touch them!"

Biton sighed, though his lips still twitched upward. She could make him feel such a strange mix of happy and exasperated. Still, he had never seen Danae so excited about her own appearance, and that depression from earlier was still near the forefront of his memory. "Alright, fine."

He slipped out of his shirt and pulled the dress over his head. Danae came over to help him with the fastening at the shoulders and playfully patted the fake chest. "What do you think, my lady?"

"Oh, Councilor Biton, you look *so* splendid in your new gown!" she adopted a lofty tone, stepping aside so Biton could see his reflection in the mirror.

He froze, his eyes widening. Feeling welled in his belly, and if he couldn't see it himself, he might have thought his stomach was billowing out. "This is... different."

Biton placed his hands on his hips, then ran his fingertips along the side of his jaw.

A knock sounded at the door, and Danae turned to answer it. Voices murmured behind him, but Biton kept staring at himself in the mirror. He stepped forward and placed one palm against the glass. "There you are."

"Biton?" Danae appeared in the mirror behind him. "My parents are waiting for us. It's time to go. Can you give me my dress back now?"

Biton shook his head, trying to clear the fog. "Yes, of course." He glanced back at the mirror. Perhaps it wasn't exactly right. But it was close. He pulled the dress over his head and tossed it back to Danae. "Well, hurry up then. We don't want to be late for the symphony."

⇑ ⇑ ⇑

Sixth Moon, 1800, Diosion

"Happy birthday, Biton." Danae deposited her gift—imported silks—into his lap, where he sat in the throne-like chair in the center of the garden.

"Thank you, Danae." He had a way of smiling that made her feel like she was his favorite person at the party.

Flowers bloomed in an explosion of color around Biton, reflecting in his mirror-silver tunic so that he looked all the more colorful. The flute of bubbling liquor held in his left hand looked like one of his sparkly accessories.

At sixteen, Biton and the older council member's children were allowed to drink alcohol. Danae would stick to the punch provided for younger guests. "There are a lot of people here." There was Ion, glass in hand, with Adohnis and Callista. Neither brother nor sister were old enough for their own drinks, though Adohnis was not far from it. Erose, of course, was in attendance, laughing with Yolanta and Peta Leos.

Usually, Peta lived in the Leonis province, but with the war at the border, the Council met more frequently, and members of the other council families were in Diosion.

"Yes! Isn't it wonderful?" He sounded like his first taste of alcohol was starting to get to him, and she grinned.

"It's only sunset Biton. Better not lose your head too soon, right?"

He blushed and set the liquor down. "Always the voice of wisdom. I'm tired of sitting in this chair. Let's go talk to some of the others."

Danae nodded, letting Biton lead the way over to Ion and Adohnis, where they stood beside the fountain. Soon the others joined. The group felt a little oppressive to Danae, but Biton was laughing and clearly enjoying being the center of attention.

Erose slid in beside Biton, and Danae repressed the urge to roll her eyes. "Biton, shall we dance? I saw the musicians when I came in earlier."

"Who will lead, though?" Adohnis's voice was sharp, the insult unspoken and clearly understood.

Biton wore a low-cut tunic with a string of black stones dripping down the center of his chest. His black-satin hair swept back from his face in artful braids at his temples, and his eyes were painted with smokey grays and blacks. He looked like a fairy tale made flesh.

He didn't seem to be able to answer, and in that silent moment, Adohnis spoke again— out of pettiness or embarrassment, Danae didn't know. "I mean, Erose is showing as much cleavage as Biton and less makeup!"

"You sound like a *Lirian*, Adohnis," Erose snapped, her cheeks red with indignation.

"What? Like I'm the only one who has noticed?"

Danae looked to Biton, ready for his witty remark or laughing retort, but he had gone strangely pale. And the fact that Biton was rendered speechless made Danae's temper flare as it never had before. Without considering the consequences, Danae stepped forward and planted her hands on Adohnis's chest. With one solid shove, he toppled back into the fountain, flailing. When he finally got back to his feet, water dripping from his hair and clothes, cheeks red with rage, Danae realized what she had done.

"Oh, Adohnis, you're *so* clumsy. I can't believe you fell into the fountain like that." Erose's voice was dry and drawling. For once, not even Ion came to Adohnis's defense.

Peta started to giggle, then a couple of the others joined in. Adohnis hauled himself out of the fountain shivering and rushed off, servants moving out of his way as they brought forth trays of little treats.

"So, dancing?" Erose asked, snuggling up to Biton. This time it didn't bother Danae.

"Yeah, alright." Biton's previously joyous mood was much subdued, but he turned to the dance floor with the others.

Biton

Biton wasn't typically tired after social events. If anything, he felt revitalized by them, infused with an energy he could get from no other source: not sleep, rest, or time outdoors. He *needed* people, their interactions and intricacies, the way others might need time alone. Today, though, when the door to his room closed behind him, he heaved a sigh of relief.

Adohnis's remarks felt like a weight across his shoulders. It had been moons since Biton began to portray himself more honestly through his clothing. Had Adohnis thought that all along? Had he been the only one? The others had been quick to stand up for Biton, but they could have done that for any number of reasons. To keep their social status in the group or because they wanted something from him.

All except for Danae. She really cared.

"Master Biton." Keme's voice tugged him from his thoughts. "I had not expected you back so early. Are you well?"

Keme had his hands full of Biton's dirty sheets, the bed behind him recently made, fresh winter cotton turned down in preparation for sleep.

"Thank you, Keme." Biton stumbled over and hugged the Emaian like he had not in years, putting his arms around the older man's waist beneath the sheets.

Awkwardly, since his hands were full, Keme laid his cheek on the top of Biton's head. "What is it, bright one?"

"Today, at the party, someone I thought was my friend said something cruel about how I look." He pulled away and sat on the bed, chewing on his cheek.

"Has this friend ever said anything before?"

"No. None of them have. I mean, sometimes, Adohnis can be an ass, but he's never come at me like that."

"Was he the only one?"

"Yes."

Keme nodded and sat down next to him on the bed. This was not, strictly speaking, acceptable behavior for a slave. They were not to sit in the presence of one of their masters, much less talk to or touch them without being directed, but in the privacy of Biton's room, they had long since passed such restrictions. Sometimes, it felt that Keme was more his parent than his parents were.

"People are like old snow. They have layers: ice crusts and soft powder beneath. We can't see what is below the surface. Perhaps Adohnis listens to the whispers his fears make and spoke out of a reaction to them rather than you."

"So, he might not really think those things?"

"I think it might be best to talk to him and find out. After you've both had time to thaw."

"Thank you, Keme."

He hummed. "You remind me so much of my child. I hope she also has found someone to tell her the ways of ice and sea and people."

A knock came from the door, followed by Danae's voice. "Biton?"

Keme stood and moved away, gathering his load of bedclothes. "Good night, Master Biton. I'll be nearby should you need me."

"Thank you, Keme." Biton touched three fingers to his lips. "Danae! You can come in!"

The girl entered, stepping aside so Keme and his burden could get past, and then paused by the door. She looked uncertain, fiddling with the front of her tunic. "Your mother said I could have the room next door."

"Why? You usually stay with me if you stay the night."

"I thought, maybe you asked her to... Perhaps you were angry with me?"

Biton gave her a tired smile. "Danae, you're my hero! Adohnis is older and bigger than you, and you stood up to him for me. You're like —like Avel. The bravest person in Phecea."

"He's not that much bigger than me." Shaking her head, Danae hurried over to where Biton sat, settling beside him and taking his hands. "I'm sorry he said those things. I think he might be jealous of you."

Biton's brows creased, and he scratched the back of his head. "I don't know why. Keme says it'd be a good idea to talk to him and see how things lie. I will after some time passes."

Danae shook her head, unable to say why Adohnis had been so

cruel, but she snuggled closer to Biton, wrapping her long arm across his shoulders and holding him tighter. "So you don't want me to sleep in another room?"

"No, of course not! I'm glad you're staying over tonight." Biton laid his head on Danae's shoulder, her well-formed curls tickling his cheek. He would overthink it if he was alone, turning Adohnis's words over in his mind. "Do you think any of the others feel the same things as Adohnis? About how I look?"

Danae pulled away from their hug to look Biton over, giving him the benefit of thinking about the question before she answered. It was one of the things Biton liked best about Danae. She considered his painted face, his low neckline, his jewels. "I don't know, Biton. I was jealous of how beautiful you are. Is that the same thing?"

"Mama says that jealousy is a sort of compliment. And you never treated my appearance as a bad thing."

"No, but that jealousy made me mean." Danae stood from the bed, pulling her tunic off and letting it crumple to the floor. Her leggings followed suit, and she hurried to Biton's vanity, where she'd left one of her satin sleeping bonnets. She tucked her curls inside to protect them, tying it about her head and climbed between the sheets in her shift.

Biton stood up and traded his tunic for a soft sleep shirt and trousers, stepping momentarily behind a screen to change pants. He spoke to Danae through it. "But did you think I was strange or wrong?"

"No. I was jealous because I wanted to be like you; why would I want to be strange or wrong?" Danae's eyes followed Biton as he came out from behind the screen, round and owlish. He crossed over to his vanity to wash his face in the basin of water there.

"Why do I have to act and dress a certain way just because I was born male? What does it matter to anyone else what I do? I think I look more like myself in nice things."

"Well... I..." Danae hesitated, watching Biton. It was a big conversation for a fourteen-year-old. But then again, Biton was just sixteen. "I guess people like clear answers? Like when you asked me if it was smart to go to war with Liria or not. And Erose said my answer wasn't an answer?"

"Why do I owe them an answer about whether or not I'm enough of a boy?" Biton could feel his face flushing with heat. He was starting to feel angry. Not at Danae, but at Adohnis and at anyone else who needed straight answers about someone else's identity. "This is just who I am. It's not their business. I just— I just want to be me and not worry about what anyone else thinks."

"I don't see how you could be anyone else, Biton. You're the pirate captain and the Dasan and the fastest rider. Pirates get funny looks sometimes, but that doesn't stop them, does it?"

"You know, Keme said something similar to me one time. I guess we can't all be wrong. Especially since you're probably the smartest person I know."

"You drank too much of the bubbly stuff!" Danae grinned at his compliment, pushing his shoulder lightly. "I'm not the smartest person you know. You work with the treasury and papa's office."

"You're just selling yourself short." Biton pushed her back, grinning now. The distress of earlier was feeling more and more distant. He yawned and propped his head on his arm. "Do you think we'll ever meet a real pirate?"

"I heard Dido say she was giving up painting and would seek out a ship shortly." Danae snuggled closer, resting with her cheek against Biton's chest.

"There's a real terror. The seas will never be the same again. Perhaps I'll convince her to take me along as her first mate, and we'll bring you back jewels and treasure."

"Be more ambitious, Biton. I'm certain you could be captain if you show her how to pull that coin from her ear. She's been trying for a while now," Danae's voice was muffled against his chest, but the laughter was still unmistakable. His sisters were getting older, soon too old for simple magic tricks, but Dido held onto her sense of wonder with both hands.

"Maybe. I wouldn't be so sure. She'd be Queen of all Pirates if given half a chance, and they'd never meet a fiercer leader."

A large yawn erupted from Danae. "You could be her pet parrot."

"At the very least, I could play lookout."

"Well, you're sixteen now. I can't stop you; you're pretty much a grown-up. But I'll miss you while you're off being the lookout, and I have to keep attending etiquette classes for another year."

"It'd be worth finding a band of pirates just to escape Mistress Afin."

CHAPTER 47: RHOSAN

FIRST MOON, 1800, CYM OR

Five Years before the Proclamation

Wynn left the menders' room half an hour after his first official Contender match. He was sore and bruised, the flesh over one of his eyes split like an overripe melon, and his recently dislocated left shoulder was still aching even though it had been shoved back into place. Still, Wynn felt amazing. His heart pumped a near-frenzied rhythm through his veins, his thoughts buzzing pleasantly in the back of his mind. He was twenty-nine, in the best shape of his life, and he had just won the title of Contender, best of the middleweights.

He stepped from the cells and into the warmer air of the sun-dappled arena, dodging Defeated around its edge until he came to a place where he could see inside.

Dyfan stood in the center of the arena. The stands were packed with Victors spilling out into the ranks of townspeople crowding the sides. This was the biggest match of the year. The Champion Class, the heaviest, most skilled fighters. Everyone in Cym Or wanted to witness Dyfan taking his fourth Contender title.

Or fail.

The thought eroded Wynn's post-fight euphoria like sugar left out in a thunderstorm. They didn't care if Dyfan lived or died, was injured, or injured another man. They couldn't see his gentleness, couldn't care. To them, the Defeated were not even human.

Across from Dyfan stood Cadel, flexing his back and chest muscles, and turning so the onlookers could admire him. Dyfan, in comparison, was a statue, nothing moving but his eyes as he scanned the pits. When his gaze fell on Wynn, the corners of his lips moved. Was that a smile?

Wynn's heart warmed despite his anger, and he reached out to press his clenched fists against the waist-high wall separating them. He looked pointedly from Dyfan to Cadel. *Keep your eyes on your opponent.*

Victor Eurig and Victor Kane came forward, handing over the weapons randomly selected for the match. Wynn supposed the Victors didn't want to declare which weapons would be used in case someone had a mind to tamper with them. By selecting minutes before the match started, they ensured a fair fight.

Fair. Nothing in Wynn's life was fair any more.

Victor Eurig handed Dyfan a long oval shield and short spear, but Cadel got a short spear and sword instead of a shield. Dyfan said a shield was the difference between winning or getting cut up, but Wynn had also seen his lover win a fight with two knives or just fists. This was a Contender bout. Not even the Victors would try to fix this match, right? It would likely go against their bloody religion.

Dyfan hefted his shield, spun his short spear experimentally, and turned to face his opponent. The Victors shook one another's hands as if they were the ones fighting and then fled the arena. Dyfan bowed. Cadel bowed. All this mock civility made Wynn's jaw clench; it was like dressing up a murder.

The call came, and the fight started. Cadel exploded forward, attacking with a swipe of his short spear, followed by a downward cut of his sword. Dyfan deflected both with his shield, standing his ground as Cadel advanced, not yielding. Wynn could hear bets being made nearby. Someone was talking about Cadel's ferocity. He wanted this win. Some said more than Dyfan did.

Dyfan twisted his shield to the side and cut forward, forcing Cadel to leap back or be sliced. Without a shield, Cadel would have nothing to protect him from Dyfan's spear. It didn't seem to matter. He was so fast. While Dyfan pressed his advantage, Cadel side-stepped and launched into another series of attacks. He got three hits in, giving Dyfan no time to return the attack before he was darting off again. If Dyfan could only land a blow, he'd slow Cadel down, but that was only if he could catch the other fighter.

"Dyfan is looking sluggish," said a fighter to Wynn's left. He couldn't look away to see which pit fighter said it.

"He's lost some of his passion," Osian agreed.

Wynn felt himself leaning forward, his knuckles digging into the wall's unyielding surface. All the Gods, let Dyfan get through this fight unscathed. Enyo, lend him the strength of the wilds. Let Maoz gift him with unworldly skill with the spear. Please, Esha, keep his body well, and Aryus stay their—

"This doesn't look like much of a celebration, Wynn." The voice cut off Wynn's fevered prayer, and he turned to find that Ifanna had slid up beside him. She wore a scandalously low-cut dress in a rich, emerald green. Black stones glittered in her hair and around her throat like she was hostessing one of Gruffyd's parties rather than roughing it at the arena.

Wynn bowed to her, resisting the urge to turn back to Dyfan struggling in the ring. "It helps to know the other fighters' weaknesses, Victor."

A shout went up, and Wynn turned to see Cadel scrambling back, a deep cut across his chest. Dyfan had landed a blow at last.

"You think you'll be fighting in Dyfan or Cadel's weight class?" Ifanna's incredulous tone made it clear what she thought of that idea. "Well, I didn't realize you were so ambitious, Wynn."

All right, so that had not been the best excuse. Wynn needed to continue watching, to assure himself that Dyfan would not be injured, but he also knew just how important it was to keep their closeness a secret. If the Victors found out, there was no doubt they'd use it against them. He forced himself to shrug. "Perhaps. Perhaps not. Even if I never fight them, I can learn from how they fight."

Cadel brought both of his weapons up and around in a crescent moon swipe, and it was Dyfan's turn to jump back, twisting as he did so. Cadel's sword and spear tip shrieked as they sliced across the metal of Dyfan's shield. Right at throat height. Sweat glistened on their bodies, and the sand coated their legs like ash. Dyfan didn't wait for Cadel to attack again, instead continuing his pivot until he was positioned to thrust with his short spear.

Cadel whipped to the side, bringing the spear shaft and sword up, creating a wall of wood and metal. He spun, too fast for proper comprehension, and dipped low, slashing at Dyfan's unprotected ankles. The big fighter jumped, lithe as a fawn. For all the talk, Dyfan wasn't doing badly. He just needed to find a tactic for attacking Cadel. He could dodge the blows easily enough.

"It looks to me like it's better to be quick than brawny. I knew Dyfan wasn't the brightest, but it looks like Cadel is just a better tactician." Ifanna said, and Wynn gritted his teeth, trying not to show that she'd needled him. He took a breath, then another, but when he looked away from his lover, he found his Victor's wife staring at him. Her brows were arched, her red-painted lips parted sensually. Wynn wanted nothing more than to take a step back, his shoulders tensing around his ears.

"I wouldn't count either of them out yet."

Wynn looked back and saw Dyfan and Cadel exchanging a series of blows, Dyfan taking all that Cadel doled out on his shield and Cadel having to concede ground. Doggedly, Dyfan stepped forward, attacked, stepped forward, attacked, pressuring Cadel.

Cadel's eyes were wide, and he shook his head as if to rid himself of sweat. Dyfan didn't waste time or energy on pointless movements. Wynn knew he'd rather let his eyes burn than take his gaze off his opponent.

"What is the style of fighting you favor, Wynn?" He glanced through his lashes to see Ifanna had taken another half-step closer as if she wanted a better view of Dyfan's fight, though her gaze was on him. He shuddered. "I think you're clever too. You know what's good for you."

A crash yanked Wynn back to the fight. He couldn't help it. Dyfan had Cadel on one knee, pressing down with his shield, which Cadel held back with both his spear and sword. Dyfan and Cadel were of the same class, but Dyfan was taller. He used that advantage now. Wynn could see Cadel's shoulders shake as he held Dyfan off himself, his teeth gritted, his eyes narrowed. Dyfan shifted, heaving into his shield arm. He was a boulder, and he would just crush Cadel.

"I'm just trying to stay alive," he said finally, hoping it would get her off him. "It's all too easy to die in the pits.

"But you're not just staying alive. You're a Contender. You're the absolute best of your class," Ifanna whispered, close enough that Wynn could hear her despite the shouting of the Victors and the clash of Cadel's sword against Dyfan's shield as he tried to beat him away.

Wynn felt the brush of long-nailed fingers at the underside of his arm, hidden from view to the rest of the world, and in that touch, he found the excuse he was looking for. "Pardon me, Victor," he said politely and took a step away as if to give the higher-ranked woman the appropriate amount of space. If she moved closer now, it would be clear to any watching what she was doing.

A bellow broke through his thoughts, and he turned in time to see Dyfan plummet, grasping at the back of his knee. Blood bubbled up from the wound, spilling too fast. Somehow Cadel had sliced Dyfan, bringing the better fighter down with a single cut.

"Widow maker's cut," Osian muttered, and the crowd screamed.

Victor Eurig and the white-robed healer appeared out of thin air, like Aryus could, pressing white bandages to the crimson leg. Dyfan screamed and thrashed at their touch. Wynn had never seen his lover cry out like that. Not during a whipping or when he was beaten bloody by fists.

It made his blood run cold and thick, so difficult to pump that his chest ached. Though he had never been a religious man, Wynn began to pray again, exhorting the Gods to protect Dyfan.

"Well, I guess Gruffyd will be angry tonight. He thought Dyfan was a sure thing." Ifanna sighed and swept a hand through her dark shiny hair. "But if I could have a gold piece for every time Gruffyd was wrong, I'd be richer than all the Victors put together. Goodbye, Wynn. Congratulations on becoming a Contender."

Wynn could hardly do more than glance at her as Dyfan was carried off the field.

⇑ ⇑ ⇑

Eleventh Moon, 1800, Cym Or

Shouting from the Defeated quarters grew louder. Even the most obedient Defeated were trying to sneak by to see what it was about, though Linn huffed, unimpressed, and commanded Wynn to continue chopping the wood while she built up the fire pit. One of the hunters had brought in an elk, and they would roast it outside, as the beast was too large for the kitchens.

One of the younger boys ran over, red-faced and panting.

"Well?" Linn asked.

"It's Victor Gruffyd hollering at that fighter, Dyfan. He came over to breed, but I guess he doesn't like Eira much because he won't do it. They already took the hammer to his hand, but he didn't seem bothered."

"Stupid man. Eira isn't that pretty, but that shouldn't matter. Victor Gruffyd got a bargain price on that stud since he lost his Contender Match this year. He'll not be happy to lose a deal." Linn huffed. "Are they getting his Victor then?"

"Ayup," the boy agreed. "Set him over by the henhouse, tied him up good, and left him to think on it while someone finds his Victor. Eira is crying, though."

"I'm going to go tend to the girl. You better finish splitting the logs before you go off to your own business." Her keen eyes were bright. Somehow, Linn always seemed to know everything. Somehow she must have sensed Wynn's closeness to Dyfan.

Wynn nodded stiffly, his shoulders tensing up around his neck. He didn't like that she saw so much, understood so much. Not when his relationship with Dyfan was so dangerous to them both. Still, she had been quiet about it. Whatever she suspected.

The ax handle had gone slick in Wynn's hands when he hefted it again, and he had to stop and dry his palms before continuing his work. He knew better than to ask himself why Dyfan had refused the order to breed with one of Gruffyd's Defeated. Wynn was afraid he already knew the answer.

Anxiety made him sloppy, but Wynn finished chopping firewood in record time. He left the ax buried in the stump he'd used for splitting and wound his way down the familiar track to the henhouse. He could see Dyfan's huddled form before he got there. He crouched down near the other warrior, just out of reach. He still hadn't worked out what to say.

"Hey."

Dyfan shifted slightly, keeping the hand that had been smashed with the hammer cradled in his lap. Only two fingers were swollen and discolored. He had undoubtedly sustained worse injuries, but it looked painful.

"Hello."

"It's been a while now, but do you remember when you gave me that advice about not getting angry?" Wynn snapped off a twig, using the sharper end to trace nonsense patterns in the earth.

"I am not angry."

"Then what's going on?'

"I won't," Dyfan's voice was a whisper, flexing his injured hand with a grimace. As if the pain was welcome.

"Won't tell me?" Wynn's eyes fixed on those bruises, on the way they blurred purple and yellow against Dyfan's brown hands. *I put those there.* The thought sprang unbidden, mocking.

"I won't breed."

Wynn couldn't hold his gaze for more than a few seconds. If they switched places, if Dyfan had been the Battle Defeated with a wife, what choices would he have made? What would Dyfan say if he knew Wynn had been married?

"They're going to hurt you if you don't." He broke the twig again, the two halves biting into his palm. "I'm not going anywhere. I won't stop this—us— if they make you do it."

"They can't hurt me." His bloody hand seemed to argue against that, but Dyfan didn't consider pain the way the other fighters did. He never complained as he was sliced open and sewn back together. Wynn had only seen him break down after losing that fixed fight.

His body did not matter as much as his soul.

There was a clamor from the front of the compound, and Dyfan grunted again. "You better go, Wynn. Victor Eurig is here."

"They can take you away. Send you to the mines. What then, Dyfan? Will that not hurt you?" He was breathing hard, his chest tightening. There would be men coming up the path any moment, coming to beat Dyfan, to hurt him.

And it was Wynn's fault.

Dyfan held out his uninjured hand. "Come here."

Wynn flinched back. His hands were starting to shake. "They'll take you. They'll take you too."

"No. Wynn —" Dyfan's tone was steady, but his words came out quickly. "They would never take me. I am a fighter, remember? Where would they put me? I will never earn them as much money as when I am in the pits— Come here." He strained against his ropes, skin turning red and then white as they cut off circulation. Reaching for Wynn.

"No. No, you're wrong. They take so much—" He shook his head, back and forth like a dog with ear mites. "They just take and take—" Boots crunched against the gravel, too close and heading nearer. Wynn froze. Tensed. Trembled harder.

"Run, Wynn. Go back to your quarters. Run!" He hissed, still twisting and straining against his ropes as if to get free. As soon as the Victors were within sight, Dyfan howled curses, thrashing like some insane, trapped animal.

They paused, baffled by his behavior. "He was calm earlier, Eurig, I swear. I broke a few fingers, nothing more." Eurig nodded thoughtfully as he watched Dyfan, spittle flying from his lips.

Something of Dyfan's urgency pierced the fog of Wynn's thoughts. "Run," he had said. Just like Wynn had told Nia and Owynn. *Run.*

He turned to go, but he was shaking, his weak knees hardly keeping him upright. He had to run, had to escape the Victors, had to hide. Behind him, Dyfan yelled, and the hair along Wynn's spine stood up beneath his clothes. He had to go. He couldn't leave.

The henhouse stood between Wynn and the Victors, but they were coming closer. They wouldn't miss him. They would see him and understand, and then they would be able to hurt Dyfan. They'd be able to hurt them both.

Unless he hid.

The entrance to the henhouse was small, but Wynn was not a broad man. He shimmied in and curled tight within the dark, trembling as the Victors came.

Dyfan

Dyfan made a show to keep Wynn from their scrutiny as he disappeared into the henhouse. By the time Victor Eurig and Victor Gruffyd ordered him to quiet down, Dyfan was panting. His throat felt raw.

"Dyfan, what is this all about?" Victor Eurig asked, his tone reasonable. Dyfan felt a slight pang of guilt. His Victor had always been a reasonable man. He paid for Dyfan to train and eat extra, only setting him in the best fights. But it didn't change the feeling Dyfan had in his gut; he could not bed another. Not a woman, not a man.

He just wouldn't do it.

"He broke my hand," Dyfan said, though it hardly bothered him. As a fighter, broken fingers would hamper his training and his bouts.

"Yes, because you refused to breed."

Dyfan could hear the hens clucking in the house behind him. Wynn was surely in there, panicking and trying to keep quiet. Dyfan couldn't let them see him in such a state. "I do not wish to breed with her."

Victor Eurig's brows rose. "I didn't ask if you *wished* to."

"See?! He won't! What are you going to do? I paid for that seed!" Dyfan could smell the drink on Victor Gruffyd even feet away. The stench of wine and ale always followed him these days. Wynn's earnings kept him in coin.

"What do you want me to do, Gruffyd? It's not like I can force his cock to stand up." Victor Eurig barely tolerated the man, brother-by-law or not. He thought Gruffyd a lush and a dolt and really only valued his coin. "Dyfan, is the woman too ugly? Perhaps we can find another, more suitable—"

"No. I do not wish to breed with anyone."

The silence stretched on as Victor Eurig stared at him. Dyfan wanted to take up a defensive position, but being tied as he was, all he could do was wait. Finally, Victor Eurig nodded. "Very well. If you will not breed, we will find other ways for you to earn additional coin. Perhaps in the lesser pits?"

The lesser pits were seedy, disreputable places that would have fighters use crude weapons, broken glass, or attack wild animals. They were nearly as much a death sentence as the mines, but Dyfan knew his Victor wouldn't risk his life. He was trying to scare Dyfan into relenting. It wouldn't work.

"Yes."

Victor Eurig stared at him for a long time, but Dyfan didn't flinch. He was not bluffing. He would readily enter the lesser pits if it meant no longer breeding. He'd fight a bout a day if that was what it took.

His Victor must have read his resolution because finally, he gestured for Dyfan to be untied. It was an exercise in fortitude to not glance over his shoulder. To walk away without looking back, without knowing if Wynn had recovered from the fear. But he did it. Even if it felt like daggers pierced his gut.

CHAPTER 48: THE WESTERN SEA

THIRD MOON, 1800, VILLAGE OF TAQQIQ

Five Years before the Proclamation

*I*n these southern, untouched reaches of the Emaian Tundra, the Emai still put up their illus in circles around a place to gather, their villages rich with the bounty of the sea and all that it provided, be it whale, fish, seaweed, or urchin. They did not carry the thin, half-starved wariness of the Emai on the northern border, but still, these people wore fear like clothes, like it was this and not the generations of belief that bound them together as a people. All the Emai feared the slavers, so even in the farthest sea-side reaches of the Tundra, they would trade their poison for weapons, armor, and protection.

Iniabi stood in one such Emaian town, warm in the safety of an illu and surrounded by the smells of her childhood. Guilt was a living thing in her belly as she listened to the medicine woman claim that this was not the only ship to sail this far in search of poison. Iniabi did not quite want to believe her.

"And they had someone who could speak Emaian too? Who could barter for poison and whale-goods?"

"Yes, but they were not like you. They didn't know our ways." The medicine woman lingered on Iniabi's light hair and snow-kissed skin.

It seemed to Iniabi that the woman implied something with those words. Something about an Emaian selling poison was worse than a foreigner, and she didn't know how bad Iniabi's position really was. Before she could reply, the medicine woman pressed on, "How long have you lived with these... *people?*"

"It doesn't matter." Iniabi tried to hide her guilt at this rude treatment of a medicine woman. "I am here to work out a trade. Do you wish for weapons or not?"

The woman's gaze pierced Iniabi's chest, into her heart and her past and all the long hours spent doling out poison for an addicted northerner. But no. She must not have seen because she gestured to several large earthenware jugs behind her. "Do you have enough to trade for this?"

Iniabi swallowed. It was more poison than she had ever seen in one place, and she turned to confer with the captain in Phecean. "She's willing to trade all that, Captain. Do you want to make an offer?"

Iniabi knew the *Flying Night* did not carry enough goods to afford so much poison. The only sensible thing to do would be to trade for part of it, but Captain Ira's face was gaunt and dark with hunger. She would kill herself with it if left alone. Just... upturn one of those jars and die in twisting, screaming nightmares.

"What does she want, exactly?" The captain's eyes weren't fixed on Iniabi or the medicine woman but on the jugs filled with sacred poison. "Food? Money?"

Iniabi kept her voice level. "Money is pointless this far south. There is no one to take it. They want grain to ease their winters and weapons to protect themselves from slavers. They'll take kava if we have it—the tea is something of a delicacy."

The captain stood. "We'll give her everything she wants, but we'll have to return to the ship to get the supplies."

There weren't enough supplies on the ship. Iniabi knew that. Taaliah, standing next to them, knew that. Neither one of them said anything. Iniabi turned back to the medicine woman and spoke in her native tongue. "The captain wishes to return to her ship to take stock of what we have to offer."

"Alright. Go with your captain." The woman's voice was steady, but her gaze fixed on the captain as if she knew she was untrustworthy.

The captain strode out after nodding to the medicine woman, Taaliah behind her. Iniabi followed a few steps behind, hearing pieces of what they said but not the entire thing.

"If we—"

"But we need enough rations—"

"You know how much—"

Iniabi watched the snow-drenched paths between the illus for pale, white-haired faces. She only saw a few, and those the countenances of warriors, stern-eyed and careful. No children darted from whalebone structures, their sloping sides clear of snow. She half-wanted to run, half-wanted to see herself among them.

They passed quickly through the town, Captain Ira's boots tracking black ash from the central fire into the snow. Iniabi stepped around it, light-footed, and between the last few rows of illus. Jaya waited for them, arms crossed over her chest and her expression stony. Jaya had been promoted since Leon's death, and she wore the title of Navigator like a new kiati. Iniabi looked away.

The captain gestured for Jaya to fall in line with them, doggedly continuing her way to the shore and the *Flying Night*. It wasn't until they were well outside the Emaian village that Ira turned, looking between the three of them.

Jaya spoke first, "Captain, Liria passed an ultimatum. I saw the posters in the town."

"What now?" the captain sounded irritated.

Jaya glanced Iniabi's way before responding, her tone harsh. "Anyone carrying Emaians or Emaian goods will be considered Emaian and subject to the laws governing them."

The captain stared at Jaya for a long moment, her gaze disbelieving. "The laws...."

Iniabi went cold, understanding dawning like the sun over the harsh winter landscape. "You mean any found carrying Emaians or Emaian goods will be taken as slaves." She was a liability, but the captain would never leave her, not when it would mean losing access to poison. She would keep a death grip on Iniabi even as she lost her sanity until they both died in mutiny. "The Lirians have been unable to capture the *Flying Night* for years. Is this new declaration really so different as the threat of beheading all pirates face if caught?"

"A beheading is an instant; slavery is the rest of your life. I won't pay for your—"

The captain cut Jaya off. "Enough talking. We have a trade to complete."

For a moment, Iniabi stood as though stunned. She could remember a time when Iago, Cai, Nil, Neus, and Jaya had been like family. She remembered loud meals with all of them, Jaya throwing an arm over Iniabi after practice, Iago sitting with her on deck as the sun went down. When had it all gone so wrong? Would she have survived if she hadn't handed the captain that first string of poison shells?

They reached the ship, and the captain called all crew to the deck rather than heading belowdecks to tally their supplies. Iniabi shifted from foot to foot, uncertain of just what this meant.

"Tomorrow, we raid the Emaians."

The pirates nearest Iniabi shifted, frowning. One murmured, "What is she talking about?"

Another shushed the speaker, and the captain pressed on. "These Emaians think they can insult us by overcharging for their goods. Well, I'm happy to teach these heathens a thing or two about commerce. Once we get what we want, we leave these waters for a while."

"And go where?!"

"Ingola, Zolela, or Tupa Gali. Anywhere with less horseshit than these fucking Lirians and Pheceans. We're not part of their petty wars, but we have already been dragged into them. I'm tired of it, aren't you?"

"That's right!"

"True!"

Raising her hands for quiet once more, the captain looked around the crowd. Whatever she saw in her crew made a grim smile twist her lips. "Then we will take what we need!"

Iniabi looked not at the captain but Jaya, who stood off to one side. The Ararian's thick brows were pulled into heavy lines, and her many earrings glittered in the dying sunlight. She must have felt Iniabi's gaze because Jaya glanced her way, and for a moment, their eyes met.

Iniabi felt as though she had swallowed the Tundra, and all the snow and ice lay frozen at her center—empty and desolate.

With that, the captain turned away, heading into her cabin with her best fighters, presumably to plan the attack on the Emaian village in greater detail. Jaya didn't follow the Pirate Captain, instead turning to head below deck.

Iniabi stood on the deck for a long moment, irresolute. She felt like a ship without sails, set adrift in the middle of a dark sea she did not understand. The world around her had lost all meaning, and she didn't know how to chart a new course.

The crew on deck began to disperse, people turning to their jobs or other small tasks to keep themselves occupied. The few that passed Iniabi shot her dark looks. The rumors were spreading: that she was responsible, in part, for the captain's insanity or that she had gotten Leon killed. She was alone here— reaping the consequences of a choice she had made as a much younger girl, for just trying to survive. It was so clear how her future aboard this ship would play out that she did not need poison to see it.

She would become a slaver, attack her people like one of the men that had burned her home, stolen and raped the people that had flourished there. She would kill them, those people of her blood, and earn herself a few more wretched moons parceling out poison to the captain until either a fit of rage, the captain's death, or a terrified crew member killed her. There was no point, no good ending,

But they were at port now, and there was somewhere better than the ocean depths to escape to.

CHAPTER 49: THE WESTERN SEA

THIRD MOON, 1800, THE FLYING NIGHT

Five Years before the Proclamation

*I*niabi rose with the shift change, slipping onto the deck when there were the least amount of sailors to spot her. She padded to the leeward rail, where dinghies nudged the ship's side, instead of hanging from their places above the deck. Why bother? They would be in use again soon. Iniabi's lips twisted in a wry smile, and with the ease of long practice, she slipped overboard, shimmying down a single rope.

Four of the *Flying Night's* six longboats bobbed softly against the ship's side like pups bumping up against a bitch's belly. Quietly as she might, Iniabi left holes in three so they would sink, still tied to the *Flying Night.* They would have to be hauled up or cut away before the ship could sail again.

The fourth boat Iniabi began to row. She dipped dripping paddles into a wine-dark sea and watched as her home of six years grew small with distance. She didn't think she would miss it. One day, she might think fondly of the time she'd spent growing up with Iago, Cai, and Jaya. When Vlassis was teaching them to fight, and the captain was nothing more than a figurehead somewhere on the periphery of their lives. That all ended when Iago died in a desperate battle to avoid capture by the Lirian military. Jaya would never be the friend or companion Iniabi wanted, and the captain could only need and despise her false Emaian medicine woman.

It was still dark when the longboat reached the shore. Iniabi tugged it high away from the tide, careful not to puncture the hull. It might be of use again. When she was finished, three guards stood waiting on the rocks above her, spears in hand and expressions carefully blank. When Iniabi had imagined coming here, she had expected to slip over snow and ice like the silent Emaian hunters of her childhood. No matter. She would go even if it had to be at spear point.

It wasn't, though. When Iniabi held up her hands and went quietly to the guards, they led her through the village to the illu of their chief, their spears held loosely upright as they went so that Iniabi felt less like a prisoner than a guest. In the uncanny way of medicine women, the elder arrived before Iniabi, so the chief and his spiritual advisor sat in the center of his home. His wife heated kava tea, bustling through the tent like a soft-faced wren.

"Thank you for meeting me," Iniabi said when a cup of the stuff had been put in her hands. It smelled like Manaba. "But I'm afraid that I bring bad news.

⇈   ⇈   ⇈

Morning found Iniabi with a sling in her hand and her thin, wicked sword belted to her waist. She stood among other Emaian warriors, the sounds of their spears and their stone pouches rattling like bones. They stood before the village at dawn, the streets behind them filled with hidden traps—pits, flaming oil, poison. Anything that might stop an enemy invader. They would retreat in that direction when the time came, but they didn't need to worry about the very young, old, or infirm. They hid in the Tundra, away from the fighting.

Chief Toklo and the village's medicine woman, Uki, daughter of Massak, stood before the rows of able-bodied warriors. Iniabi had high hopes, standing shoulder to shoulder with strong, young Emaians. The pirates could only fill two long boats at a time— no more than forty of them could land before they would have to return to the ships to get more.

This had to work. The only other option was death or a desperate existence alone on the Tundra.

"You smell interesting," a voice murmured at her elbow, and Iniabi turned to see who was talking. It was probably the strangest conversation opener Iniabi had received, and the novelty of it made her curious. A girl around Iniabi's age stood clutching a spear, her almond eyes bright with amusement, her cheeks a wind-rubbed red only a lifetime of living on the Tundra could produce. Her light hair was braided in two ropes that fell over her shoulders, and her cheeks were well rounded. Where Iniabi was all sharp angles, this girl had been sculpted in smooth curves.

"What do I smell like?"

To her bafflement, the girl leaned closer, sniffing Iniabi's shoulder. "You smell like steel and the ocean, but underneath that, you smell... spicy. You smell like danger, but I like it. It's not the bad kind of danger, like a broken ice flow. More like the good type of danger, like learning to hunt in deep winter."

Iniabi was so surprised her cheeks warmed, and she had to look away from this pale-eyed girl who was so interested in a black-eyed pirate. To cover her confusion, Iniabi leaned over and sniffed the other girl's shoulder. They were almost of a height. "You smell like fresh snow, smoke, and whalebone." Like the Tundra. Like home.

"I'm Qimmiq. My father is Toklo."

"I am Iniabi, daughter of Manaba." She glanced sideways at Qimmiq. "Are you ready for the battle?"

"I've hunted, but I don't think I want to hurt people, even if they are trying to steal from us...."

"Me neither," Iniabi admitted, thinking of Iago and what she should have told him the night he died. "I lived among those people for years. But we do what we must to protect each other. This village needs those goods to survive. I'll bet you're a good fighter, and I'll have your back."

"Iniabi, daughter of Manaba, come here."

Iniabi flashed Qimmiq a reassuring smile and strode forward to stand beside Toklo. "Yes, Chief?" On the horizon, she could see the *Flying Night* sailing slowly towards them, her great, majestic bulk silhouetted against the dawning sky. Iniabi shifted uneasily. She had not expected them to get the ship in so close.

"You will fight by my side, but first, I want to try reason. If they know we plan to fight back, perhaps they will reconsider this madness. Will you translate as you did before?"

Toklo was a tall man with a trim beard lining his jaw and the same almond eyes as his daughter. He must have had Qimmiq very young because he didn't look all that old, yet he was still chief. Leader of the Taqqiq. Iniabi could not shake her feeling of unease—there was no reasoning with Captain Ira. The woman was mad, driven insane by the poison she should have never taken. Still, Iniabi nodded. She desperately needed these people to accept her. "Yes, Chief, but let us not talk long. They could use that time to fill this beach with fighters."

He pressed three fingers to his lips and strode forward, a handful of his warriors following suit. They would meet the raiding pirates on the beach.

Time stretched inexorably. The *Flying Night* sailed closer, Iniabi trying to parse the distance. Was this in range of the ballistae? Would they turn their ship-hunting weapons on people? It seemed two ages passed before five long boats were let down the side.

Something cold and dark and familiar sank through Iniabi's veins, though it took her a moment to figure out what it was. She was afraid, afraid for these people and herself. Somehow, the crew of the *Flying Night* had managed to haul up the boats and patch the three Iniabi damaged. How quickly had they found them after Iniabi left? She should have cut the ropes.

Heavy minutes passed while the long boats rowed to shore, and the pirates finally landed, dragging them up the beach and out of the tide. Nearly a hundred lined up behind Captain Ira Mirelli, flanked by Jaya and Taaliah. The three women made a fearsome picture standing together like that: the captain with her curls and scarred lip, her too-thin face and hard eyes; Jaya with the shaved sides of her head and the tattoos that covered most of her dark-skinned body; and Taaliah with her long, swinging braids and missing eye. They were all armed, but something about seeing the captain in the forefront eased Iniabi's fear just a little. She had never seen the captain put herself in danger, not for any prize. Perhaps they did want to talk after all, and the pirates behind them were simply a show of force.

"Very good, Iniabi!" the captain called, a strange smile twisting her lips. Iniabi was careful to look only at her and not at Jaya. "You brought us the leader of the heathens so we can end this quickly; that was smart. Perhaps I ought to promote you."

Iniabi did not translate this, nor did she reply to her once-leader. Instead, she looked to Toklo and spoke in her native tongue. "How would you like to begin?"

He held out a hand, a gesture for the pirates to stop in their approach. His expression was solemn, his voice steady as he spoke, "We do not wish to fight you, but we will not sit by and allow you to rob us. Offer us fair trade, and you can have what you want. If you will not deal with us fairly, then leave. No one has to die today."

Iniabi straightened and translated this as though she had never met the sailors of the *Flying Night*, as though they were foreigners she had to speak to for the sake of her people. She added nothing, embellished nothing, simply gave them the chief's words with her face as straight and solemn as his.

The captain's face pulled into a snarl. "I *need* this Iniabi. You know that. Tell him he doesn't have to get his people killed for a bit of medicine. Give us what we want, and we'll go." Iniabi wasn't sure if that was true, but she told Toklo what the pirate said.

He never looked away from the pirates on the snowy beach, his breathing and movements easy, as if he were a battle-hardened warrior, not the chief of a remote village. "We will not give away our sacred poison. We will not slice away piece after piece of ourselves to accommodate greedy foreigners. They have come onto our land, our territory, and we will treat them as guests or invaders. The choice is hers."

If it were Iniabi's choice and not the chief's, she would give up the poison. There would always be more urchins in the sea, and Liria's recent declaration meant that pirates coming to trade or steal would eventually be a thing of the past. She would not have pitched this village against one hundred seasoned pirates if they would leave with nothing but poison. When she whispered this to him over the shushing sound of the waves and all the breathing, fidgeting soldiers on the beach, he shook his head.

"No, Iniabi. We have little left but our pride and tradition."

Iniabi did not say that he had these people, too, instead giving the captain his reply.

"He would let his own people die for a little medicine?"

Iniabi did not translate this. "Says the woman who will slaughter for it."

"I have my own worries, Iniabi. You've benefited from our butchery for years now and this is the first I've heard you complain of it." The captain held up her fist, and somewhere distant, Iniabi heard the snap of the ballista firing.

The first bolt struck the ground between the two groups, shattering into a thousand wood splinters. The second's aim was true. Iniabi flung herself bodily at the chief, knocking him down, and the spear pierced the chest of the warrior standing directly behind him. The warriors of the Emai screamed their fury in battle cries, and the two groups plunged towards each other, weapons raised. It was chaos, but a chaos Iniabi knew well.

She stood, pulling the chief up with her while his remaining guards fought to keep the pirates away from him. The Emai were already getting pushed back between their illus. The ballistae fired again, bolts piercing whale-skin tents. It was more demoralizing than anything else. No one hunched in the illus of Taqqiq Village.

Iniabi shoved her sling in her belt and drew her sword, pushing into the fray, fighting to get forward where the captain and her officers had last been standing. Killing them would end this sooner. The Emaians fell back in droves, retreating to the safety of their traps, and Iniabi was forced to go with them or risk being surrounded by foes.

The pirates followed and were punished for their eagerness when pits lined with sharp stakes opened beneath their feet. Iniabi ignored their screams. She slid her sword through the neck of one of Taaliah's cronies, a man Iniabi had known since first boarding the *Flying Night*. She sliced through the belly of a night shift sailor and opened the cooper's thigh. Iniabi didn't see Cook, and for that, she was grateful. The big Ingolan man had always been kind to her.

Something burned against her shoulder, and Iniabi pivoted to deflect the glancing blow of a blade. As she whipped her sword up to slash it across her attacker's belly, she saw Jaya's dark-eyed glare. Taller, stronger, and seething with anger, Jaya didn't hesitate in her attack, thwarting Iniabi's initial cut and diving in with a brutal kick to her thigh. The muscles in Iniabi's leg spasmed, and she thought she might fall, but years of fighting on the rocking decks of ships kept her upright, if just barely.

"Thought you'd come after me yourself, did you, slaver girl?" Iniabi snarled, darting around Jaya. She scored a shallow cut across her upper arm before jumping back again. Someone swung for Iniabi's head from behind, a whisper of wind that just missed the back of her throat. The sailor screamed even as Iniabi glanced behind her, and Qimmiq bounded away, her spear bloody.

Jaya spat at Iniabi's feet and raised her blade, her dark skin already wetted with blood. "At least I'm not a liar. Come on! Let's fight!"

"I never told the captain to take urchin spine. I told her to sell it, that she could make a fortune." Iniabi kept her distance. She was more patient than Jaya. Faster than her too. She'd not lose her calm.

Jaya took long strides to close the distance between them, trying to catch quick Iniabi. "Oh? Poor Iniabi, she didn't mean to kill Cai and drive our Captain into madness. Poor Iniabi. She didn't mean to whisper lies into the captain's ear and get Leon murdered. You're a snake, a viper. You can't be trusted because you corrupt everything you touch." She swung her blade, chopping across Iniabi's torso in a blow that would cleave her in two if it had made contact.

Iniabi was already coming in at a different angle, the tip of her sword puncturing Jaya's thigh before she was gone again. "I'm the only reason your precious captain is still alive! She signed her own death the moment she drank the urchin spine. She should have just lined her fucking pockets! Cai was an idiot who should have taken care of himself, and Leon was a mutineer."

"You believe these falsehoods, don't you? Are you just stupid or as crazy as Ira?"

"I'm a fucking runaway slave, Jaya. A kid who watched her village murdered and raped and put into chains, and you know what? I fucking *survived*. And I'll be damned if *you* will take that away from me."

Jaya hesitated, her parry slower than it should be. Behind her, Iniabi could see the captain of the *Flying Night*, ax in hand and blood spattered across her face. She swung and buried her weapon into the meat of a retreating Emaian's back. Iniabi didn't slow, taking advantage of Jaya's confusion, and drove the tip of her thin blade into the Ararian's foot, pinning her to the ground. Jaya screamed, seeming to forget all her training, and fell back, grabbing at the hilt of Iniabi's sword even as the Emaian yanked it from the other girl's flesh.

Blood spilled over the snow, and Jaya couldn't do more than clutch at her injured limb and shout in a language Iniabi didn't know. She spared the girl she'd pined for a glance and flew toward the captain. She would end this fight. She would end it now.

Iniabi stepped between burning illus and tried not to breathe in the stench of whale-skin smoke, her mind full of images from a past she did not want to remember. It had smelled like this the day she sat beside her best friend and watched Piav die. The men who put her in chains and whipped her until she was close to death looked like this too. All around her were the sights and people of her childhood, and for the second time in Iniabi's life, they burned.

This time, though, Iniabi was not a too-often beaten little girl. She was twenty-two and strong from weapons training and hauling ropes. She had her sword in one hand and a pouch of stones bumping against her thigh, clothed in Emaian furs. Iniabi would not be helpless again.

The captain did not see Iniabi until she was upon her. Iniabi whipped up her thin blade, air whistling, and carved a cut into the captain's sunken cheek to match the scar on her lip. The captain roared in pain, backhanding Iniabi hard enough to send her reeling into the snow—impossibly strong. There must be urchin spine in her veins even now. Iniabi rolled to dodge the fall of the captain's ax, and lost her sword in the chaos. No matter. There had been a time when a rock swung between cords was all the weapon Iniabi needed.

She danced back and loaded her pouch, swinging the stone inside to the left and right, weaving it across her body the way Piav had taught her. She had never told Mika's father how much it meant that he stepped in and treated her like another daughter, but she hoped his spirit could see her now, defending their people from these foreigners. Let Piav and Manaba and Yura and Tonraq all lend her their strength and pride.

"Would you rather be a slave, girl?" the captain snarled, just like Manaba had.

"*Never.*"

The captain lunged forward, and Iniabi released her missile. It hit the captain squarely between the eyes, and she dropped to the icy mud beneath her. All around Iniabi, the sounds of battle still raged. Whaleskin smoke mingled with the smell of blood and urine. Weapons and voices clashed. Pirates ran past, dragging seal skins and whale oil. And still, despite all of this, Iniabi could not ignore the spark of triumph in her gut. The captain who despised and used her was dead. Taqqiq would survive this onslaught. Iniabi was finally free.

CHAPTER 50: LIRIA

FOURTH MOON, 1800, EGARA

Five Years before the Proclamation

"What's he doing, papa?" Cassia held onto Luce's arm as they passed messengers and soldiers in royal livery. Even in the capital, the stench of war was inescapable. A young boy nailed posters into the granary's wall depicting a heap of half-naked people strewn across each other, their faces contorted in drunken ecstasy. Two children, dressed modestly in Lirian garb, stood to the side, staring at the orgy with horror and fear. The little girl wept, and the older boy beside her, a brother Luce thought, wrapped a protective arm around her shoulders. At the bottom of the poster, it read, "PROTECT LIRIA FROM THE DEBAUCHERY OF PHECEA! PRESERVE OUR WAY OF LIFE!"

Luce grimaced, turning Cassia away before she could get a good look at the poster and all that it exposed. Of course, it was *right*. Pheceans were immoral, flesh-obsessed lechers, the embodiment of greed and lust, but he didn't want his little girl to know that. Not yet. She was too young and innocent to understand the realities of Phecean degeneracy. "He's putting up posters to explain why we must fight our neighbor, Phecea."

"Why do we need posters for that? The Imperator said we must.

He knows what the Almighty wants." He appreciated her loyalty, how she believed that since the Imperator set Liria to war, then it was right, but not everyone had Cassia's keen understanding. Even if she was correct about the Imperator's connection to the one God. Of course, if the war went badly for the Imperator, some might claim he didn't have the Almighty's favor, and the nobility could plot against him.

"Some Lirians need to know more. It's hard to fight and to have sons going off to battle. It is scary, so they must be reminded that if it were not for their sons and fathers, Liria would fall to Phecea, and our righteous way of life would be lost."

Cassia frowned, but after a moment, nodded in some comprehension. "And posters will do that?"

"They will help."

CHAPTER 51: PHECEA

ELEVENTH MOON, 1800, SESSIS

Five Years before the Proclamation

While most Council families concerned themselves with the entire province and left their cities to separate leadership, that did not seem to be the case in Sessis. Settled in the fertile farm country of the Aetirieum province, the Aetos family seemed to have infected the entire city. Danae asked her father why so much Sessis was marked by their colors, and he smiled without it reaching his eyes.

"The Aetos lineage is vast. Councilor Myron Aetos has three brothers and two sisters. Each of those siblings has several children of their own, some of whom are old enough to have babies too. Myron's next oldest brother, Councilor Baccus, has nine children. With so many family members looking for responsibilities, the Aetos have taken many positions of authority in Sessis. The city honors them by reflecting their colors."

Danae thought it sounded more like the city had been overrun, but she understood what her father didn't say aloud. He found it tacky but wasn't rude enough to disparage a Council family in their province. The Aetos handled much of the crafted good production in Phecea and a significant portion of the crops, though they couldn't compete with the larger Zodrafi province for the sheer amount of vegetable and grain exports.

This year's Council meeting in Sessis would not be conducted in the Aetos estate, which must be too crowded, but instead, in a large state building that hosted many official and commerce-related events. Of course, no one would sleep in the black stone building. Danae thought it was rather ugly.

The Councilors owned townhouses in every province seat, and any accompanying administrators that did not would either stay with friends or find lodging in the city. That was why the Mavros carriage traveled behind them. Biton and his father would be dropped off at the state building with Danae's family, and servants would take the carriages to the Othonos townhouse to unpack.

She hadn't been to Sessis before; if she had, it had been as a small child, and Danae didn't recall much of it. So far, it was like every city she had visited but less pleasant. The garish black and red were overwhelming, and the gridlike pattern unnatural. Diosion, an older city, had streets winding around the bluff, a path people had trodden for hundreds of generations.

White-skinned Emaians with gray hair and eyes milled about in an overabundance. Diosion was the bigger city, yet it was clear that Sessis hosted a much larger slave population. Danae looked away from the window as the carriage crested the hill. She felt small.

They pulled to a stop, jarring Danae out of her musing, and the slave who rode at the back opened the door. Danae waited for her parents to descend before climbing out and looking around.

"Ah, the great *monolith*," Danae's mother murmured, her tone precise, though the words were humorous. So her parents thought the black building was poorly designed too. It looked like a black box. No decorations, no craftsmanship on the exterior. The grounds were green with late spring grass, but no other plants softened the terrain, and the black walls surrounding the building felt more like a trap than security.

"It's practical," her father said, his voice a soft warning.

"I suspect constructing it here, at the hill's apex, provides a nice breeze and excellent views," Danae said. Arsenio smiled at his daughter and then took his wife's arm. Biton and his father approached, and Danae looped her hand through her friend's elbow, speaking in a whisper. "Breeze or no breeze, it *is* ugly."

Biton tried to hide his smile in imitation of his father's calm expression, but Danae could see it leaking from the corners of his eyes. "It looks to me like someone built it to withstand an army. All sense and no beauty. Who do you think they were trying to protect themselves from?"

"Have you forgotten all your history lessons? Before Liria and Phecea, dozens of states existed north of the Emaian Tundra, and they were *always* fighting. Perhaps, when this keep was built, the Aetos were at war."

Biton shrugged, his black eyes on the dark-stone building. "Still, it *is* horrid. No wonder the Aetos family moved into a more comfortable manor."

"Papa was saying there are many of them, but I don't remember any during etiquette. I suppose they have their own masters here...." Danae had met a few Aetos during the annual Council meetings, but she only remembered them as a pack of wild boys, prone to wrestling, racing, and making a lot of noise. She hadn't spent much time with them. "Do you think there will be anything good in the market?" Her mother had said that if Danae and Biton wished, during the week of meetings, they could go shopping. After all, Biton was old enough to supervise.

"Oh, isn't Sessis known for its exceptional clockwork and inventions? Perhaps we could find a flying machine or a trebuchet!" Biton's cheeks made hills of his darkened eyes, and his gaze shifted to the distance. "Would you get in a flying machine if you could? I would! I wonder how high I could go?"

"I don't know. I suppose it depends on who designed the machine...." The state building's palm-thick doors opened with a creak. It almost made her feel nervous as if entering a derelict ruin.

The halls inside were uncommonly low and dark for lack of windows. Every four steps, a whale oil sconce offered up a feeble, yellowed light that just illuminated the path and the portraits between them. It was a lovely collection: expertly rendered scenes from each of the five provinces, and yet, the art did not take away the old, cramped feel of the place.

Biton didn't seem to notice. "I don't know if they've built any yet. I just heard it from Ion and Adohnis a few moons ago. Evidently, someone submitted a design for one that made it all the way to the Diosion patent office—Ion's dad works there, remember? Anyway, Ion and Adohnis were arguing about whether or not it would fly. Wouldn't it be amazing if it could?"

His energetic speech was cut off as they arrived in the main hall. A Phecean steward flanked by two Emaian slaves stood waiting for them. "Greetings, Councilors Othonos and Administrator Mavros. Would you like to be shown directly to the assembly hall?"

Danae stood straight as her parents conferred with Administrator Mavros and then her mother turned. "We'll get dinner tonight." She kissed her daughter's cheek and nodded to Biton before all the adults headed into the assembly hall. Which left Danae and Biton to find their way to the room where the Council members' children would be gathered.

They made their way through dim halls to a ballroom-like chamber filled with more children than Danae had ever seen during Council meetings. They were predominantly smaller, ten or eleven years old, but plenty of teens attended as well. Most wore the black and red of the Aetos house, so Danae didn't have to guess where they came from, though she spotted the Leos twins and the little Adamos girl among them.

Danae understood *now* why the Aetos family didn't bother bringing their children to Diosion. There were too many!

Five boys chased one another, shouting joyfully despite being indoors, and across the room, Danae recognized Ion, Adohnis, and Callista, though they were mostly obscured by the sea of Aetos. "Oh."

Biton squeezed her hand where it lay on his arm and gave her one of his most charming smiles. "Come on! Let's start with Ion and the others."

He tugged her across the room, deftly avoiding two toddlers squabbling over the same toy ball, to reach the others. Adohnis spoke first, a tentative smile on his lips. "Hi, Biton. Hi, Danae." He had been over-friendly since he and Biton had made up their quarrel.

"Hi!" Biton said. "Have any of you managed to speak to this crowd?"

"A few," Ion shrugged. As one of the oldest of the group, nearing seventeen, he had developed an effortless air of confidence, though his dry humor hadn't become softer. "You know how the Aetos are... prolific."

A stampede of them hurried past, chatting amongst themselves, seemingly uninterested in the newcomers, and Biton grinned. "Is there any entertainment?"

"I heard someone talking about a poet tomorrow, but it appears that for today, we're to keep ourselves busy."

Danae turned to look around the room again, daunted. Off to her left, a group of five boys chatted. They looked close to her age, and two were even vaguely familiar. As an Othonos, Danae thought it might be her role to play diplomat. Sweaty hands released Biton, and she crossed the space between the two groups, bowing politely to the Aetos boys.

With red or black tunics and brown or black hair, there was not much difference in appearance. She suspected they were cousins, if not brothers. The tallest boy noticed her bow and stopped talking, bowing in return. His cohorts remembered their manners and joined in.

"I'm Danae Othonos."

"I know who you are. I've seen you at other Council meetings," the tall boy said, a wry smile across his full lips.

Danae struggled to remember the names of the Aetos children she had met. There was Bas and Pello... Pello was the younger one who hadn't attended Council meetings in a few years. She supposed the tall boy could be Pello, though he had changed drastically.

"Pello?" Her tone was incredulous.

"Indeed. I've grown a bit, eh? You look like you have too, Danae." Pello certainly had grown—exclusively up. He had been a fat little boy, and now he was tall and broad-shouldered. His light brown eyes swept over her slender form, pausing ever so slightly on the padding at her chest, courtesy of Biton, before moving over her hair, oiled and curled. His smile widened, and Danae felt as if she had eaten a bowl of live fish, and they flopped around in her belly.

She had no idea what to say to that, though she liked how it felt when he looked at her that way. Silence stretched between them. *I should say something. Say what?! Thanks so much for noticing I'm the second tallest person in the room besides you, and oh, by the way, my chest isn't real?*

No!

What would Erose say in a situation like this?

"You're not so fat."

Death. Danae wanted to die. Why had she said that?!

Pello laughed, a deep, raucous sound. Her skin burned with embarrassment, even as Biton approached their group, concern written across his face. "Danae. Is everything alright over here?"

Danae shook her head, then nodded, then shook her head again, mouth clamped shut. The Aetos boy chuckled and bowed to Biton, his cousins or brothers or whoever they were following suit.

"Biton! Little Danae here just told me I'm not so fat anymore, do you agree?"

Biton blinked, glanced at Danae, and then took a breath. "Well, I'd have to agree with her! Good to see you, Pello!"

"And you, Biton, though I must say you don't look like you've gotten any skinnier," his tone was teasing, as Biton had always been a slender person. "And Danae! I'd almost say you gained weight, though it suits you."

"It's Biton's," Danae sputtered, glancing down at her chest.

"She means the dress!" Biton blurted, speaking too fast. "I designed it especially for her, and the shape suits her. Don't you think, Pello?"

Danae flushed and resisted the urge to wipe her sweaty palms on her tunic. She was their resident diplomat and cleverest speaker, and she had utterly lost her wits. Subtly, Biton touched her arm, and she leaned into him. He must have thought she'd lost her mind. Apparently, she had.

"Sure, it's a nice dress." Pello shrugged, the movement graceful and lazy. His slow grin slipped over to Biton, and he pushed his hands into his pocket trousers. "So, Biton, you didn't bring any of your horses, did you? Cause I'd love another go at winning my honor back."

Danae giggled because it was silly to think that honor was something that could be won or lost, but as Pello cast her a glance, she realized he wasn't kidding. He was more interested in racing than the strangeness taking hold of her.

"No. My father and I traveled in company with the Othonos family. Even if I hadn't, you might not want to challenge me so quickly. Crane is still the fastest horse in Diosion, and his foal, Dasan, will be even faster."

"Yes, but as Danae pointed out, I'm not so fat now and a far better rider. Perhaps I could convince you to ride one of my mounts?"

"You're on!" Perhaps a bit of air would do Danae some good too.

⇑ ⇑ ⇑

With the final Council meeting of the year completed, Danae's father claimed a celebration was in order. The war, with its complication of supply chains and distribution, made this Council meeting particularly arduous. More than once, when Danae was near the Council chambers, she heard raised voices and heated debate. An unusual occurrence, as the Councilors normally found amenable ways to reach an agreement, and if that didn't work, a vote would settle it before anyone had to shout.

Tempers were hot with Phecean soldiers losing their lives. Danae hadn't considered that people were dying on the front lines since the papers only proclaimed that things were going well on the border. When Danae asked, her mother said there was the truth, and then there was the ugly truth. The people of Phecea didn't want to know the uncomely, emotional side. Just the facts. And the facts were, both sides were evenly matched: equal victories and losses.

These thoughts swirled around Danae's head as she watched the nobility milling about. The ballroom was festive with floral arrangements and musicians but still had the underlying feeling of utilitarian starkness. The Leos family had made the trip from Leonis for the celebration, as well as the other ruling families: Adamos from the Adamithi province, Othonos from Othonisis, and Zodrafos from Zodrafi, where the war was being fought on the border. The garish Aetos red and black were somewhat muted with the additional colors, and Pello looked particularly handsome in all black. Tall and commanding. It didn't matter that he was a few moons younger than Danae; he seemed so mature.

Biton shone across the room, his formal tunic made of a material like liquid copper. As if a bucket of the stuff had just been poured over him in lovely drapes and swashes. He'd initially been so upset about the boycott of Tupa Galan silk, as Tupa Gali was supporting Liria in the war. Still it seemed to her that the limitation had only pushed him to further inspiration. She had no idea how he managed it, but he was a drop of sunlight.

She was supposed to be moonlight, but Danae thought the cream-colored tunic was more like milk. It certainly didn't have the effect she'd daydreamed about: Entering the ballroom with her curls dotted with pearls and her meager figure on display, Danae would turn heads. Pello Aetos would notice her and smirk the way he did and bow deeply, not because of her status but because of her beauty. And he'd say so, in front of everyone.

And Danae had practiced what she'd say back. She'd smile, demure and coy, like Erose or one of the other older girls, and nod. *This? Oh, it was nothing!* Her beauty effortless. In reality, she had spent far too long in the mirror, and even Biton said a good artist knew when to stop painting.

Pello would stay by her side all night, and they'd discuss cultured things like music and poetry, and he'd become shy, pulling her aside to tell her a poem he had written just for her.

And then...

Well. She wasn't sure what would happen after that.

But it didn't matter anyway because she walked in with Biton at her side, and Pello only said they both looked fit. Fit!? Like she fit into her outfit or she ran a lot? Fit. Like a puzzle piece. She, at least, tried the little lines she had given herself, determined not to be inarticulate as she was most of the week, but with her *Oh this? It was nothing!* Pello grinned and turned to Biton, the more interesting of the two Diosionites, and talked about *horses*.

So Danae stood there, smiling and nodding whenever Biton graciously included her until Callista came over and asked Danae about music. Grateful for a topic she actually had something to say about, Danae replied, but she supposed talking near the boys was annoying, because they moved off into their own group, which grew to include the other horse enthusiasts.

Eventually, the dancing started, and Danae would not partake in that, even if Pello did ask her, though it seemed like he would not, as he was busy eating. So she stood feeling a little forlorn. Of course, she knew he wasn't interested in her as a flirt or anything. He smiled at her and looked her over, but he smiled and looked the other girls over too. He was just a friendly fellow.

It was growing hot within the ballroom, so many bodies mingled, and thin windows cracked open to allow a measly breeze. It wasn't enough. She needed more air. Danae moved along the wall, going unnoticed until she found a balcony. The door was unlocked, so while no one was out there, she didn't think it was off-limits. A swift wind snapped through her clothes, cooling her. Danae sighed, grateful for the relief, and strode forward to wrap her hands about the railing.

Below, she could see the perfect grid pattern of Sessis laid out in the flickering lights of candles and fires. The door to the balcony swooshed open behind her, and Danae smiled. Biton would always find her. "Tired of dancing already?"

"Dancing? I hate dancing." The voice was not Biton's cheerful tenor but a wry drawl.

Her heart hardened into lead, and Danae pivoted to see Pello, two glasses in hand and a smile on his face. "I guess you were expecting someone else?" He let the door shut behind him, cutting off the noise of the party.

"I thought you were Biton."

"Ah, no, he's the center of the dance floor. It's a shame he's nobility, even from a meager family. He should have been a performer."

"He *is* talented," Danae agreed, wondering what she had eaten to make her feel like a worm on the end of a hook.

"Here." Pello handed her one of the glasses, and Danae brought it up for a sip. The taste was sickly-sweet with a bitter edge. Liquor. But she wasn't even fifteen yet, nor was he! He must have seen her surprised look despite the poor lighting because he laughed again. "I have like a hundred brothers and cousins; my family can't keep track of who is old enough or not. Don't you like it?"

Not wanting to seem childish, Danae tried another sip. Still terrible. But she smiled and nodded.

"So, what are you doing out here, all alone?"

"I was just looking at the lights below and thinking about the war."

Pello came to stand beside her, glancing once at the candlelight map before focusing on her face. "Those are strange thoughts, Danae Othonos." She shivered at the way he said her name. Oth-on-os. Drawing out the middle to sound like a whisper. "Don't most young nobility think about perfecting their arts?"

"I think about that too, sometimes."

"Hmmm, Biton said you play the harp well."

"Well enough." Danae tried another sip of her drink and decided it was too sour to enjoy.

"How modest." Pello leaned closer, smiling. Danae felt as if her feet were molded to the balcony floor. She couldn't move as he inspected her. "What are you good at, then?" Danae shook her head, unable to think of a single thing. His smile grew even wider. It would consume her soon; Danae knew it. The idea wasn't entirely unpleasant. "Not dancing, or speaking, or the harp… Perhaps your passions lay deeper?"

"I don't know," Danae admitted, her voice soft.

"Let's find out, hmmm?" Pello leaned closer, his hand gripping her shoulder, pulling her into him. His lips, hot and firm, pressed into hers. He smelled of spices and liquor and something earthy. Perhaps his sweat. Danae didn't dislike the smell.

Pello pulled away and looked into her face. Whatever he saw there made him laugh again, and Danae blushed. "Well?"

"Not terrible. Here, let's try again."

CHAPTER 52: THE EMAI

NINTH MOON, 1800, VILLAGE OF TAQQIQ

Five Years before the Proclamation

Iniabi sat in the cleared space for a new illu, lashing two long, curving rib bones together and trying to imagine the immensity of the whale that grew them. They were charred on the edges but stronger than the timber on the *Flying Night*. More resistant to fire, too, as they had survived the burning of the illu they were salvaged from. Much of the village had been put back together that way by using the surviving pieces. This, though, was the first illu that Taqqiq was constructing in a new location. It would be Iniabi's when they were done.

Iniabi looked up from the work she did with clumsy fingers and tried to imagine what it would be like to live in an illu of her own. She could make furniture to fill it, build her own fires, and drink her own kava. She could take a wife and choose a place for herself among these people. They felt less like strangers every day.

The idea was... new. It left Iniabi's belly roiling either because it was different from what she had expected or because there was another path for her still. Perhaps she would feel differently when it was more than a circle of dirt and bare whalebone.

One of the women, Sona, started up a working song, a cheerful tune that Iniabi knew, though she could not remember the words. She hummed along with the others, tying animal gut string until her fingers ached. A few village hunters stopped by, their arms full of skins. There was no whale, as none had been spotted in some time, but elk, wolverine, and goat. Qimmiq was among them, and Iniabi smiled and raised a hand when she saw the chief's daughter. "You've been busy!"

The plump girl nodded and paused to inspect Iniabi's work. It was not as neat as the others. Iniabi had never done this in the village of Nec as it was not typically a duty of the medicine woman or medicine woman in training. "This will be your home?" Qimmiq shifted her hold on the pelts, glancing around the clearing. Iniabi had chosen a spot in the middle of the village's illus. Not too far from the gathering place at the center or the sea. "It's not such a far walk from my illu. You have good taste."

Qimmiq smiled, and tentatively, Iniabi smiled back. Six moons had passed and the start of a new year since the pirates' attack on the village, and yet she still couldn't quite believe how easily the other Emaians had accepted her into their ranks. It wasn't instantaneous, but the growing trust was real, unlike anything she had experienced on the *Flying Night*. Her value wasn't measured in the lives she took in or the poison she spilled but in her sweat and daily contributions. The Emaians asked much of her, but when Iniabi filled their requests, they didn't ask more.

One day, if she grew old or got hurt, they would still value her. They cared for no foreign power and turned away none that wanted to live their way of life. There would never come a day that they did not need and want her, so long as she did not betray that trust. So long as she never told them she'd been a little poison girl who had traded dreams to live.

"When will you be done here?" Qimmiq asked, readjusting her armful once more.

"Well, it won't be the fastest illu ever built," Iniabi said with a wry smile, standing and stretching her hands up over her head. "I'm afraid that I'm awfully slow at this work. I'm strong enough, though. Would you like help?" Iniabi blushed a little, suddenly reminded of a much younger version of herself, making Mika laugh by puffing out her chest and claiming she'd be as strong as any Emaian man one day.

Qimmiq nodded and pressed her burden into Iniabi's outstretched arms. "I meant when would you be done *today*, silly. I was going to ask if you wanted to have supper with me." The chief's daughter started to walk again, though her pace was slow and a bit meandering. Iniabi fell in step easily.

She felt a little awkward and uncertain of what to say. Iniabi had never courted anyone, not really. Jaya had turned against her before she'd even had the chance to try. She didn't know what to say to a pretty girl that could hunt and fight and had never sold poison. Especially when that girl seemed to want to be around her. "What are we having for dinner?"

"Is that a yes, then?" Qimmiq's light eyes flickered to Iniabi's face, her heart-shaped mouth pressing into a bit of a pout. "Or are you a picky eater after all the fancy spices on the ship?"

Iniabi laughed, her cheeks making crescent moons of her eyes. "I think you overestimate the fare available to pirates. I've lived off everything from raw mussels and boiled snow to bilge rats." It was true, but the thought of Cook's stews still brought a shot of homesickness that Iniabi hadn't been expecting. She took a deep breath and let it fade before turning to Qimmiq with a crooked grin. "I guess that means it's a yes then."

"Well, it's only elk, not exotic rats, but I think you'll like it. Everyone says my cooking is good." She gestured for Iniabi to put down her load, the illus in this part of the village ready for lashing the hides to their exteriors.

The bundle of furs made a soft whump as Iniabi dropped it into the earth, and she straightened, though she was careful not to wrinkle her nose. Not all the smells from her childhood were pleasant, but she didn't want Qimmiq to think she was finicky. "I'd rather have elk than rat any day," she said with a tentative smile. "Though, of course, the company is the real draw."

Her words earned a smile, and Qimmiq pushed one of her two braids over her shoulder with a sly look. "Of course, my father will be there as well...."

That didn't surprise Iniabi. Emaian children did not leave their family's illus upon coming of age. They often didn't leave upon choosing husbands or wives, so multiple generations might live together until they spilled out for lack of space. Iniabi's childhood, alone with Manaba, had been a strange one among her people, but she was accustomed to the press of bodies—life in the crew quarters of the *Flying Night* had seen to that.

"Good! Maybe it will give me a chance to make a good impression."

"Tonight, then?"

Iniabi nodded, a smile clinging to her lips like kelp to a swimmer's legs. "Tonight."

⇑ ⇑ ⇑

Iniabi arrived at Qimmiq's illu sore, tired, and nervous. She had taken the time to wash and braid her thick, white hair. It was getting too long to wear loose all the time, but Iniabi liked it too much to cut it shorter. She didn't have many sets of clothes, but she'd pulled on a clean kiati; one didn't often get the opportunity to sup with the lovely chief's daughter and her family.

Outside, Iniabi paused, hesitating, and then chided herself. She had leaped into battle with fewer qualms than she felt stepping into the illu of a girl who seemed to like her. Iniabi wasn't sure why this was so frustratingly hard. She had never worried this much about speaking to Jaya, though, to be fair, that relationship had never been more than a dream. Iniabi took a deep breath and rapped her knuckles against the spar of whalebone next to the entrance, and when a voice called out, she stepped inside.

Qimmiq's family illu was a warm place filled with the warm smells of roasted meat and smoked kelp cakes. It was nowhere near as neat as Manaba's had been. Sleeping pallets lay strewn with furs where their occupants had left them that morning, and belongings lay haphazardly mingled. Iniabi loved it. She wanted someone to share her space that way, to mix their things with her things until there was only 'ours.'

Qimmiq sat at the fire, carefully turning over thin slices of sizzling elk heart and liver, her father sitting nearby while he mended a tunic. Her mother, Akna, fussed at them both for whatever crude joke had them laughing. Iniabi took it all in, and a sudden love for her people and their ways of life filled her throat until it was difficult to breathe. This was *her* place, this town, this Tundra. The first place she had chosen for herself.

Chief Toklo waved Iniabi over, and she sat by the fire near Qimmiq, taking the opportunity to lightly brush Qimmiq's shoulder as she passed. Akna, Qimmiq's mother, put a warm kelp cake in her hand and joined them. The salty, fruity smell made Iniabi's mouth water, and she bit into it eagerly, the smoked cake bursting in her mouth. "Thank you!"

"So," Akna started, and Qimmiq inhaled audibly beside Iniabi. "Tell me, Iniabi, were your parents fighters as well?"

"Aada!" Qimmiq hissed, her already pink cheeks turning all the brighter. "Iniabi doesn't want to talk about that sort of thing!"

Chief Toklo settled beside his wife, his smirk hidden behind his kelp cake. "What?" Akna asked, her brows raising over her high forehead. "I just want to know a bit more about her!"

Iniabi took a bite of elk liver to cover her hesitation. "My Aada was a medicine woman," she said, hoping they would not press her about the father she knew nothing about, that her mother had never chosen. "I was going to be one too, but I did not get to finish training."

"Is that what you would like to do? Perhaps Uki would allow you to resume your training?" Chief Toklo said.

"Ataat! Iniabi is a *warrior*; you saw it yourself," Qimmiq chided, and when she looked over at Iniabi, her eyes were wide and filled with admiration. Iniabi's stomach flipped, and her mind skidded to a stop like an elk trying to change directions running full-tilt on an ice field.

"I— Yes. That's who I am now." When she dragged her eyes away from Qimmiq, Iniabi's belly shivered. She did not want to paint herself in blood and gypsum, to wail spirits to the shore and split open her tongue to better take the poison.

"She's a good warrior, better than many of ours. I saw her, like smoke dancing through the air, leaving enemies fallen behind without a trace of her path." Qimmiq sighed and bit into her kelp cake.

"Alright, alright." Chief Toklo held up his hands in defeat.

Akna seemed more likely to press the issue, but Qimmiq chimed in before the older woman could speak. "Iniabi, how do you like your new illu?" Though it wasn't finished, Iniabi had slept in it the last few nights, looking at the stars through bare spars. It wasn't quite cold enough to keep her from reveling in the idea of owning her own place.

"I love it," Iniabi said, with real feeling. "Thank you for giving me the materials. I know things in the village are still difficult after the attack, and it means a lot to me. I feel like I belong here."

"You're more than welcome," Chief Toklo said, his voice sincere. "Even before the pirates' attack, we were small, but with so many dead, we need every pair of hands. Whether they are building, healing, hunting, or protecting."

"Yes," Akna agreed. "It's also good to add to our young people... It has been years since the Taqqiq last faced an attack from foreigners."

That caught Iniabi's attention. "You've been attacked before? By slavers? And the Taqqiq survived?"

Akna and Toklo's faces became solemn, and Qimmiq's mirrored theirs, though with less sincerity. "Before Qimmiq was born. It was a hot summer for us, so the Tundra was more welcoming to Lirians than usual. Perhaps they had picked through all the northern villages and were fishing for dregs. Whatever the reason, they came."

"Did the village fight them off? How long did it take to rebuild?" Suddenly, the illu seemed far away, and Iniabi's mind buzzed. If one village could fight them off, why not more?

"It took us too long to rebuild, but yes. We fought. I wouldn't say we won, as many were lost to the Lirian's chains or blades, but they left with only half of our people and many of their own dead."

Akna closed her eyes. "My sister and brother were lost that day, both to the blade. The snow froze red that winter, and everywhere you walked were the puddles of your loved ones. It took years for the ice to fully cover the scars."

"Uki says the Lirians were overtired and underfed when they

arrived. They didn't come by sea but by land. They must have marched across the Tundra for weeks to find us."

Disappointment was bitter on Iniabi's tongue, and she took another bite of elk to disguise the taste. "I'm sorry for bringing up such a dark time. Perhaps I could teach the village's strongest to fight like the northerners do. We recovered enough weapons from fallen pirates. Though not, of course, if it took hands away from more important tasks."

Akna opened her eyes again, and the shadows lingering there darkened the pale silver to storm gray. Toklo gripped the back of her neck, massaging, and the tension in her body seemed to fade. "Thank you, Iniabi, for that offer. Once we have rebuilt, I think it is a good idea."

CHAPTER 53: THE EMAI

ELEVENTH MOON, 1800, VILLAGE OF TAQQIQ

Five Years before the Proclamation

Iniabi woke to wind howling past her illu and struggled out from beneath her furs into a frigid night. She didn't feel as though she had been asleep long. Her body was too aware, too unrested. She had likely only just begun to drift off. It was dark outside, but the sun sank below the horizon early in the Tundra, especially so far south.

Iniabi shivered even as the wind shook her home once more. It had seemed so strong last moon when they finally completed the work, the whalebones tough and sturdy in their gut lashings. Now, though, Iniabi was uncomfortably aware that there was nothing but skin and bone between her and the incoming storm. Perhaps she ought to double-check the ties.

Torn between staying inside where it was warm and dry and out into the wet howling wind, Iniabi jumped when the bone frame that served her for a door opened and someone appeared in the portal. Iniabi's first reaction was to lunge for her sword, lying in its scabbard beside her sleeping pallet. She took two quick steps in its direction, her eyes on the figure entering her home. They didn't look like they'd been trying to be subtle.

The bundled figure moved, pulling the wrappings away from her face, revealing plump pink cheeks and bright eyes. Qimmiq's brows rose up her forehead as she took Iniabi in, and then she smiled. "I came to see if you were alright. Ataat says this is a big storm, and new illus sometimes don't do so well." Though Qimmiq said she was coming to ensure Iniabi's home was safe from the weather, she didn't look around at the neat piles of belongings, instead focusing on Iniabi.

Iniabi's heart rate, already elevated from waking abruptly to an unexpected visitor, wouldn't slow down. Qimmiq's pale eyes were a prison that Iniabi couldn't seem to escape. She wasn't sure she wanted to.

Qimmiq stepped closer, her smile staying in place.

"You were worried about me?" Iniabi said, attempting a light, teasing tone. She stepped towards Qimmiq too, though she didn't completely close the distance.

"Of course, you're new to the village; this is a new illu... I didn't want the wind and ice to blow you away or leave you frozen."

"Why, chief's daughter? Would you miss me if it did?" She felt taut, strung tight as a hare who'd spotted a wolf, and to break some of the tension, she chuckled. "It has been a long time since I've lived in the Tundra. Perhaps you think I'll be helpless in one if its storms."

With two handbreadths between them, Qimmiq stopped smiling, her attention unwavering. "I never think you're helpless, but I would miss you if you blew off into the wind. Sometimes I don't think you're real. You came out of the ocean like driftwood, washed and beautiful and new."

There was a hard lump in Iniabi's throat. Would Qimmiq still think so if she knew everything that she had done? That she had dealt in sacred secrets and spurned the peaceful ways of the Emai? Iniabi reached out and took the other woman's hand, too nervous and entranced to hear the storm or even to see anything but the flash of pale eyes in the dim light of a whale oil lantern. She tugged Qimmiq closer. "I can't leave with the wind. I would miss you too."

Qimmiq came easily, docile in her grip. She moved closer than Iniabi had initially intended, pressing against her body. Even with their clothes between them, Iniabi thought she could feel Qimmiq's heat radiating off her in waves. "Are you going to kiss me?"

A little, nervous laugh passed unbidden from Iniabi's lips. "Do you want me to?" Her body felt as trembling as a loose flap of sail in high winds—she could not quite let go of the fear that, at any moment, Qimmiq might push her away in disgust.

"I've been waiting since you saved us from the pirates." Qimmiq's voice sounded sincere, and her expression was rapt, not snide or sickened. She leaned closer, her lips slightly parted. Slowly Qimmiq's gaze moved from Iniabi's eyes to her mouth.

The tension was too much—Iniabi couldn't wait any longer. She closed her eyes and brushed her lips to Qimmiq's, the storm-chilled skin of her cheeks a balm to Iniabi's fevered ones.

Qimmiq hummed a sound of approval and wrapped her hands into the front of Iniabi's kiati. Pulling them closer, the other woman deepened the kiss until all the breath left Iniabi's body, and she had to break away to gasp. The chief's daughter grinned fiercely and arched her brows in a silent question, though Iniabi had no idea what it was. "Are you alright?"

"Yes," the word left Iniabi in a rush. "I mean, I've never kissed anyone before, but yes. I'd like to kiss you again if you would like to. It's—um— warm and very nice, and I like you s— Sorry."

She winced inwardly. Iniabi was so much more vulnerable here. These people knew she'd been a pirate. They knew she'd done horrible things, even if they did not realize just how bad. There was no Captain Ira or brothel mistress or even Manaba to keep her on her guard. She felt soft and loose and bare. Perhaps she should have been more careful. She would make a fool out of herself if she didn't keep control. Maybe she shouldn't have let Qimmiq get close enough to disarm her.

The other woman laughed without any barbs. "You've never kissed anyone? How can that be? You're a dashing warrior! You fight like you're dancing, and you smell like fire and steel."

Iniabi's belly was a knot too tangled to loosen. A half-smile hovered uncertainly about the corner of her lips. She was old to have never kissed anyone—she knew that, and it made her feel defensive.

She tried to shrug it off. "There weren't many options with the pirates, and some foreigners have strange customs against the idea of two women as—as lovers."

"Oh, I don't know much of the world. I didn't realize that would be an issue...." Qimmiq's hands roamed along Iniabi's neckline, thick-gloved mittens brushing against bare skin. "I might have kissed and been with other people before, but you know so much more about... well. Everything."

Qimmiq's tone dissolved some of the fear clenching Iniabi's muscles. Her gentleness was a balm, a safe place from the world of cruelty she had known before, and for a moment at least, she let herself trust it. Iniabi relaxed against Qimmiq, tucking her face in the other woman's neck to press a kiss there. "It doesn't bother you, then? That this is new for me?"

Though they were nestled together, Iniabi could hear the smile in Qimmiq's voice as she pulled herself tighter to the ex-pirate, "Why would it bother me? I suppose I *am* greedy because I wanted to bed you as soon as I could, and perhaps we'll wait longer now if you even want to bed me, but that's not a problem. Your kisses are enough."

"I—" Iniabi's face was ablaze, and she was suddenly grateful that Qimmiq could not see her face as they were. She'd dreamed of the different ways her body might fit with another's, one hand beneath the blanket in her hammock, but now, presented with the opportunity, she felt a little overwhelmed. "Soon, I think. I just need a little time."

Qimmiq nuzzled against Iniabi's throat but then pulled away. The wind seemed to be redoubling its efforts, its howls turning into screams. "Take all the time, Iniabi. I think you should know I only kiss one person at a time. And only those who have the hearts of women. It's not the way for everyone, but it is with me."

Iniabi breathed past the squirming of her belly and nodded. "I don't want to kiss anyone else while I'm— while I'm with you. And I am the same as you. I've never wanted men. Really, that's why I've never— with anyone.

I—" The walls of Iniabi's illu shuddered in a particularly nasty gust of wind, and Qimmiq cut herself off, looking around. Her lips tightened into a nervous line. "Perhaps you should stay in my parents' illu tonight with me? I promise I'll keep you warm."

Iniabi reached out and touched the nearest wall without moving away from Qimmiq. She loved this place, this home of her own. Even if she did not have much to put in it. "Are you sure you don't mind?" It was strange to have someone else worry about her or offer kindness for no other reason than they cared.

Qimmiq laughed. "Why would I mind? I'll sleep better knowing you're safe and warmer with you by my side."

Blushing, Iniabi nuzzled close again to save herself from having to put together a coherent answer. She gathered her parka, her sword, and a few extra furs before letting Qimmiq lead her out into the snow and then into the warmth of her bed.

⇑ ⇑ ⇑

Iniabi woke in a daze of happiness and gently extricated herself from Qimmiq's arms, careful to keep the beautiful woman snug beneath her furs. It was early yet, but the wind outside had died away and the first timid rays of sun lightened what sky she could glimpse out of the hole above the firepit. Quiet as a hare, Iniabi slipped her feet into soft boots and pulled on her coat, buckling the thin, wicked sword about her waist. Then, she stepped outside. She wanted to check on her illu, to make sure it had made it through the night.

When she turned from the door to Qimmiq's home, however, Iniabi stilled in horror. The illus nearest the chief's were intact but past that, many of them were in shambles. They lay toppled over on their sides, some of them torn open, their contents strewn across the snow. Everything they had rebuilt was destroyed, with more besides, the buildings of Taqqiq fallen like bodies on a battlefield. Iniabi took a slow step and another, then she was running, dashing towards the collapsed homes. She found people huddled together under their furs, their faces stricken with the dread of yet another tragedy. Iniabi helped them up and sent them to the chief. It was much the same with each home she passed, though a few had lost even more. A new mother wailed beneath her destroyed home, holding the blue-lipped corpse of an infant, and further out, two elders lay unbreathing in the snow, their pale skin nearly the same color and their arms still clasped around each other.

For a moment, Iniabi wondered why they hadn't fled for shelter when their homes were destroyed, but she remembered her experiences with blizzards. They were just as likely to wander further into the Tundra as reach shelter, and their best hope was to wait out the storm and pray they made it through the night.

The farther she went, the more extensive she realized the damage was. While she had been safely wrapped in Qimmiq's arms, much of the village had suffered, and the knowledge of it left her guilty and grief-stricken. They had all worked so hard to rebuild after the pirate attack, and for what? A single act of natural fury had destroyed all but the oldest and sturdiest of illus.

Iniabi found Uki, the medicine woman, in her home—shaken but unharmed. She had the far-off expression of one who had recently taken poison, her wrinkled skin dark beneath her eyes. Iniabi went to her and helped her up from her sleeping pallet, supporting much of the older woman's weight. "What did you see, Uki, daughter of Massak?"

Her voice was hoarse as if she had been shouting for hours, "Bones sprout from a sea of blood."

The older woman's eyes were on Iniabi, and she had difficulty keeping her expression neutral. A shiver was traveling up her spine, a feeling of weight, of destiny. "And then? What happened next?"

"You," Uki croaked, and her nails dug into Iniabi's arm. "Where you go, the blood washes clean. All that is left is snow."

Iniabi stilled. It was so close to what Iniabi saw the first time she took the poison. The future she'd glimpsed was near now, a slow tide coming in to wash clean the beach. She laid a hand on the medicine woman's arm. "There has been a disaster, elder. Your poison dreams must have carried you through it. We need to go, to speak with the chief. There will be people that need healing."

Uki, daughter of Massak, stared up at Iniabi for a breath. For two. Then she blinked, and the tension broke. "Yes...yes. Take me to the chief."

It was slow work to guide Uki through the snow. The elder was weakened by the use of poison, her frail limbs trembling with fatigue. It would be days before she felt herself again—Iniabi well remembered the feeling.

When they arrived at the chief's illu, Toklo was standing in the open door of his home, ushering in the sick and injured. Uki's competent apprentice, Tatik, was just visible through the portal. The middle-aged woman was tending to the sick with a skill that suggested she had long ago been prepared to take over as medicine woman when Uki was no longer able to attend her duties. Qimmiq and her mother worked together to pass out bowls of stew rich with elk meat, mussels, and seaweed.

Iniabi helped Uki to the chief, and by some unspoken agreement, the three of them stepped away from the crowd. Toklo looked tired, his face wan. Though Iniabi did not have the right to this type of meeting, neither of the two village leaders waved her away.

"More than half the village has lost their illus. We only grow closer to the peak of the storm season, and our supplies are greatly diminished." Toklo reached up as if to rub his hand over his face in exhaustion but stopped himself. He glanced around the gathered Emai and straightened his shoulders. "We should send hunting parties out at once to start rebuilding our food and pelts."

"The older children can search for herbs, and I will make reserves for medicine and poultices," Uki added.

"Good. Yes. We can have the elderly and those with children share the remaining illus. It doesn't look like it will storm tonight, so those strong enough could sleep outdoors if we make a big enough bonfire."

Iniabi looked between them, her brows creased. They spoke as if they planned to stay, to begin again with even fewer hands to help along the work. She would be without a home, and though the prospect of slipping into Qimmiq's furs each night was not unwelcome, she did not think that the village would be able to come back from this. There simply weren't enough resources.

She took a deep breath. "Chief, elder, I believe trying to start over now would be foolhardy. We're out of resources and have only just finished rebuilding from the pirate attack. To do so again would leave us vulnerable for moons to come, especially without the raw materials we had last time."

Uki frowned as she turned to look at Iniabi and the ex-pirate prepared to be shot down. Instead, the medicine woman only examined her face, leaning into Iniabi's strength to keep her upright. "What would you suggest then, Iniabi?"

She looked, wide-eyed, between the chief and the medicine woman and then swallowed. "We should go north, find a village close enough to reach on foot, and then add our strength to theirs. We will always be stronger in greater numbers."

Chief Toklo and the medicine woman looked at one another, their faces shifting slightly as they seemed to exchange some silent conversation. Finally, the chief nodded, and Uki let out a deep breath as if she were already wary of the trek, though it had not yet started. "Sinqiniq is our closest neighbor, nearly a hundred miles northwest."

A hundred miles. It seemed impossibly far away with so many young and elderly, but if they had to, they could make sleds to pull them in. Iniabi nodded sharply, trying to look confident. "We can make it if we're careful, if we help each other and hunt along the way. A week of traveling, if not a little more, and then we will be safe.

Uki tightened her grip on Iniabi's arm. "We follow the Snow Bringer."

CHAPTER 54: RHOSAN

FIRST MOON, 1801, CWM OR

Four Years before the Proclamation

Wynn ran his chisel down a wood plank, taking off a long, smooth strip. It joined the curling pile at his feet, and he tested the feel of the groove his last pass left behind. It was getting there. With the ease of long repetition, he lifted the chisel and pressed its tip against the wood, filling his cluttered workshop with the rasps of tool on timber.

He almost didn't notice the knock on the door when it came, but it must not have been the first. Wynn opened the door to the impatient form of a wealthy farmer that lived nearby. His clothes were well made, embroidered with vines along the trim, but his face was weathered and his hands perpetually dirt-stained.

"Penvro," Wynn said with an easy smile. "I'm glad you came by today. I finished your wife's new rocking chair just this morning. Would you like help getting it out to the cart?"

The farmer's face creased all along his crow's feet and smile lines, and his teeth flashed, surprisingly white. "Why, Wynn, you're nearly a week early! I wish your old dad could see what an excellent job you've done running this shop."

"Me too." Wynn led the way farther in, dusting off his hands on a rag he picked up. When they reached one of the far corners of the small room, he lifted a thick canvas cover from the chair, revealing warm, oiled wood and the graceful curves of carved vines and flowers.

Penvro whistled. "That is truly beautiful work. Do you mind keeping it here a few more days? I don't want to ruin the surprise by bringing it home before the wife's birthday—that is, if it doesn't make Nia pink with jealousy!"

Wynn laughed along with him, then gestured towards the still-unformed project he had begun that afternoon. "I'm working on something for her now. It'll be a cradle when I'm done with it."

"Aw, really?" Penvro buffeted Wynn across the shoulder like a small boulder. "You and Nia are gonna have a baby? 'Bout time, lad! You'll make a great father."

Wynn waved him off, unable to hide his grin. Even as light footsteps came down the stairs leading to the home above the shop.

"I swear, Wynn, you'll have told the entire town by nightfall." Nia laid a hand on her still-flat belly, neatly dodging the beginnings of a graceful wardrobe for the village chief. "We've only known for sure since yesterday."

Wynn didn't bother looking sheepish, even with Penvro guffawing beside him. He just smiled at his soft, brown-eyed wife. "I'd crow it from the rooftops if I didn't think it'd disturb folks' sleep."

She shook her head, but he could see where the corners of her lips edged upwards. "Why don't you see Penvro out and pick us up a bit of bread to go with supper before the bakery closes for the evening?"

He kissed her on the cheek and did as he was bid, stepping into the chill of a late-winter dusk. All along the dirt road, little shops and homes stood huddled together as though to fend off the cold, their bright faces pretty even in the fading light. Wynn patted Penvro's team of cart horses as he clucked them forward, then hurried off toward the bakery, his hands in his pockets and his chin lifted to hum a happy tune.

THERE's a hearth for me
    and a fire for me,
    kettle hangin' from its hook.
    There's a hearth for me
    and a heart for me,
    babe nestled in his nook.

. . .

WYNN WOKE ALONE, his mouth dry and his toes stiff in the biting cold of a North Rhosan spring. No fire lit his stone cell—there was no place for one, and his coverings could not keep out the chill.

It had been a long time since he had dreamt of the days before his capture. A long time since he had even thought of them. How many years had it been now? Six? In the beginning, Wynn often wondered where Nia and their son were, if they had gotten away, survived the raids, and made it to one of the temples below the mountains.

He certainly hoped so.

Wynn stood and stretched, searching for the worn boots he'd been assigned that winter so that he might bully his freezing feet inside. Waking up in the pit cell was still strange, but it meant that he could slip down the hall to see Dyfan before morning training. Another benefit of winning matches.

Today, however, he paused before the entrance, uneasy after his dream. It was hard to place the feeling, hard to understand what was knotting in his chest. He stood there, breathing slowly until he thought he had it.

Guilt. He felt guilty.

Did seeing Dyfan mean betraying Nia?

They had been happy, him and his wife. He loved her. He loved their son. In the days before his capture, Wynn would have never considered needing anyone else. He would have spent the rest of his life just on those two people and never felt he was missing anything.

But Wynn sent them away when his village was raided. And he had not promised to find them. They would have been empty words—Nia understood. He stayed to be killed or captured so that they might get away. There was not even any guarantee that they made it to safety.

Still, Wynn had taken vows. He had stood beneath an ancient oak and bound his hand to hers. He had promised to care for her, to seek solace in no other person's arms. Did he owe it to Nia to follow that vow even now, even in the clutch of the Victors?

No easy answer came to him, and yet Wynn did not want to abandon Dyfan. The warrior did not speak much, but it wasn't hard to imagine how lonely his life had been. Wynn shook his head, still uneasy, still guilty, and stepped into the hall.

⇑   ⇑   ⇑

The lesser pits weren't worthy of their name. It was an ill-cut arena in the frozen ground half a day's walk from Cwm Or surrounded by rows of roughly hewn seats to give Victors and townspeople a good view. There was nothing noteworthy about the grounds. No training areas or housing for fighters. Nothing official or time-honored. They were thrown together so haphazardly that they radiated an air of impermanence.

The matches reflected this sense of fleeting urgency with weapons made out of whatever spectators brought and bouts arranged with little care for the participants' skill. Fistfuls of money were won and lost, by far less than anything Dyfan's Victor would win in the real arena, but then, Victor Eurig wasn't here to win coin. He wanted to win Dyfan's compliance.

He would not.

Scratching the shaved sides of his head, Dyfan ignored Victor Eurig's looming presence, instead watching a contestant kick at a snarling dog. The dog jumped away from the blow and whipped around to snap at the human's leg. The man, a craftsman or a farmer, screamed in pain and punched the dog's skull. The dog let go of his leg but launched at his raised arm.

"You'll go next, Dyfan. Since you're a well-known Contender, I had to agree to a few concessions to even the odds," Eurig's voice was bored, and Dyfan didn't look his way.

Someone pried the man and dog apart, and it seemed the crowd thought the dog had won the fight. Dyfan was prone to agree, as the man cursed and bled, and the dog was only limping slightly.

"Victor Eurig, here is the rope."

Dyfan turned to see a blond volunteer handing over a heavy coil of rope. They glanced at Dyfan once and then quickly looked away. Afraid of the crazy Defeated. Good. Let that reputation carry him safely through these matches.

Victor Eurig turned with the rope, gesturing for Dyfan to come closer. "One of those concessions. You'll wear this tied around your waist, the end trailing off. To slow you down."

Since there was no point in speaking, Dyfan only nodded. Of course, they wanted to slow him down. Of course, they wanted to make it fairer to whatever Defeated or townsperson had the ill luck to fight him. It didn't matter if it was fair or not to Dyfan to be trailing a rope that would trip and tangle him. Tied or not, he'd win. He had to.

Wynn was waiting.

The arena was emptying, people haggling over their bets, and the debris from the last few bouts cleared away to leave the raw earth waiting. "No weapons?"

Victor Eurig finished securing the knot at Dyfan's back and then came to stand at his side. "There will be a club and a shield waiting in the middle."

As he spoke, three men stepped into the arena. They were smaller, younger men, boys likely trying to make some coin or prove themselves. It didn't matter why. They chose to fight Dyfan, perhaps thinking they would be safer in a group.

They weren't wrong. "Rules?"

"Don't kill them."

That seemed to leave the question of whether they were allowed to kill him unanswered, but Dyfan wasn't going to spend all day chatting with his Victor. The sooner he ended this charade, the sooner he could get back to Wynn.

No crier proclaimed the fighters' names, the weapons they would use, or the rules of conduct. Only a man off to one side shouted that the bout was about to start, and with that, the three younger men rushed him at once. The swiftest, a young man with black hair and a pinched face, stooped to pick up the club in the center of the arena. He brandished the weapon like a sword, pointing it at Dyfan's face.

Dyfan ducked the first blow, but in the moment his eyes were cast downward, the second boy, stocky like the mountain people, launched into his belly and knocked Dyfan onto his back. A fist collided with his jaw, a dull pain. The boy was fat but not particularly strong.

As the boy raised his hand, Black Hair brought the club back to land a blow. Dyfan bucked and rolled with the fat boy atop of him, letting his opponent's shoulder take the smack of the falling club.

Dyfan shoved Mountain Boy aside and lunged to his feet and rammed his shoulder into the distracted Black Hair. They both flew backward, and now Dyfan straddled Black Hair, wrestling the club out of his grip. He managed to get one resounding knock against the boy's ribs when something yanked Dyfan off his opponent.

A moment too late, he realized the remaining opponent had joined the fight, gripping the trailing rope tied around Dyfan's waist and using it to heave the bigger fighter off of his friend. It was a valiant attempt, the slight boy's pale face crimson with exertion. Dyfan used the club like an ax, slicing it down onto the taut rope. The force jerked the boy forward, making him trip and stumble into Dyfan's grip, where he tossed him aside as easily as a bag of grain. These young men were nothing but bones and skin, no weight to them. The small boy collided with Mountain Boy, still recovering from the club to the shoulder, and they fell into a pile of limbs.

There was no time to breathe or think as Black Hair took the opportunity to attack, kicking Dyfan hard in the stomach. His breath wooshed out of him, and Dyfan didn't have any thoughts other than the wave of nausea churning his gut before he felt hands wrap around the club, twisting. Trying to pry it out of Dyfan's grip. He spat and threw a punch, landing it on the boy's jaw, but he didn't release the club. They struggled for a moment when the boy lashed out with another kick, this time to Dyfan's balls.

He dropped the club and fell to his knees. In the real pits, blows to the genitals were considered unsporting. No one did it. Of course, it would be different here. It'd been stupid to leave himself open to that sort of attack.

Some sense of self-preservation raised Dyfan's tear-filled gaze, and he threw himself backward in time to avoid a blow from the club. Mud spattered where it hit the earth, Black Hair holding the club two-handed to get more power. He reacted quickly, raising the club to strike another blow. Again, Dyfan kicked back, sending himself a few hand lengths away from his attacker. His fingers brushed against something hard. Somehow, he had crawled right into the shield, left forgotten in the center of the arena.

He swung it up just in time to block the next attack. The clang echoed through the arena, and Black Hair careened back, the force sending him off balance. Dyfan didn't wait, lurching to his feet and using the edge of his shield to smack the underside of the boy's jaw. It was the boy's turn to spin backward, landing hard on his front, the club flying out of his grip and off to the side. He shook his head as if disoriented, and Dyfan caught movement in the corner of his eye. The others were on their feet, and Pink Face ran for the weapon. Dyfan grabbed the length of the rope around his waist and pulled it taut, tangling his feet.

Pink Face fell, and Dyfan broke into a sprint, the club filling his vision. The air was full of shouts and figures, dim and ill-shaped, jostled one another for a better view. The Contender, the Fighter Dyfan, scrabbling around in the mud with three boys like an untrained southerner. Victor Eurig would make more gold today with this single demeaning match than everyone else in the lesser pits for a moon.

Just as his fingers wrapped around the club's handle, something rammed into him again. Stumbling forward, he swung around to smash the butt of the club into his attacker's shoulder and back, hammering his ribs with a volley of small but painful blows. Mountain Boy clung to him, the weight nearly enough to drag Dyfan down when Pink Face joined him.

Enough was enough. Dyfan lifted up his foot and brought it down atop Mountain Boy's. Toes gave beneath his boot, and the boy screamed. The rope was a mud-caked mess, all the more heavy from the moisture it picked up from the ground, and as Dyfan turned, it tangled the boys clinging to him. Mountain Boy whimpered and writhed away, his foot mangled. Tangled but no longer an opponent. Pink Face, clinging to his club arm, dripped slick tears, his face wan with fear. Dyfan knew the look. He'd seen it in plenty of inexperienced fighters before.

He didn't need the club to hurt the boy, and he raised his fist, letting it collide with Pink Face. It didn't take more than one sound punch to make the kid fall, limp and unresponsive. *Don't kill them,* Victor Eurig had said.

Well, Dyfan wasn't sure he would adhere to that edict.

Black Hair reappeared then and, lacking enough sense to know when the fight was lost, ran at Dyfan. The fighter raised his club, ready to finish it when the boy dropped to the ground. Before Dyfan could realize what was happening or what insane battle tactic the child was trying, dirt, sand, and snow flew up at his eyes. The boy had taken a fistful of the arena floor and thrown it into Dyfan's face.

Unbidden, Dyfan's eyes shut to protect him, and the boy collided with him, knocking them both off kilter. Even with his eyes closed, Dyfan felt the rush of air that was an oncoming attack and yanked his head to the left, feeling a fist barrel past him. He didn't need his eyes to win this cursed fight. He brought his foot around, hooking it against the boy's knee, and yanked him off his feet.

It hurt to pry his eyes open, but Dyfan did, resettling his grip on the club before bringing it down on top of the boy's leg. A resounding crack split the arena, and Black Hair's scream cut off as he turned his head and vomited. When Dyfan brought the club away, he could see a clear indent in the boy's leg, the rough cloth of his trousers sinking in as if his limbs were made of clay, not bone.

The crowd bellowed, some in horror, some in excitement. These onlookers probably hadn't seen anything so brutal in a long time. Ordinary people didn't fight like this. They weren't Defeated. They weren't pit fighters.

Animals. That's what Wynn compared the pit fighters to. Wild animals.

Dyfan hadn't ever felt like one before.

He chunked the club away from the mewling boy and walked to his side of the arena, where Victor Eurig waited with a small smile on his lips.

His fingers dripped countless pieces of gold.

CHAPTER 55: RHOSAN

FIFTH MOON, 1801, CWM OR

Four Years before the Proclamation

For the first time in two weeks, Wynn stepped into the pits. It was evening, his escort of free men already moving away to discuss the next day's fights with peers. Despite the new-spring color on the trees, it was cold, each flick of wind leaving chill bumps patterned across Wynn's skin.

Last time he stood here, Wynn had not seen Dyfan. He hadn't been in his cell, hadn't been scheduled for any fights. Of course, the other Defeated were all-too-eager to spread the reason why, their faces bewildered by the sudden refusal of one of their own to breed. It was just part of the pit fighter's existence. Some of them even enjoyed it. To refuse the Victors, to take the punishment of the lesser pits over a few nights' breeding... it was unheard of.

And the injuries he sustained...

Wynn closed his eyes, his lips tightening against the pain in his belly. He had to get to Dyfan, and convince him to give in to Victor Eurig's demands. He was only going to get hurt more by refusing.

He shoved his way into the hall, shouldering aside other Defeated carelessly in his rush. They moved, sliding out of his way as though he were as dangerous as the animals Dyfan fought these days—a side-benefit of winning in the pits. Wynn had never wanted to be feared, yet his growing reputation for calculated savagery had its upsides.

The farther he walked from the arena, the quieter the halls became. Most fighters would be retiring to the barracks soon—it was foolish to enter the ring exhausted. Wynn couldn't bring himself to care. He would rather fight tired and lose than see Dyfan carried back from the lesser pits again.

It was ghost-silent by the time Wynn reached Dyfan's quarters, and he slipped in without bothering to give a warning, crossing the floor to Dyfan in a few short steps.

For all that Wynn gave Dyfan no warning, the larger fighter didn't startle. He was lounging on his cot, admiring the scrapes and bruises crossing his knuckles and forearms, looking up only long enough to see the intensity of Wynn's face before resuming his inspection. Dyfan wouldn't speak about what happened in the lesser pits. Sometimes other fighters saw or heard of it, and then Wynn would know. Bears, wild cats, three untrained boys against Dyfan. Barefisted fights that didn't keep track of points but only blood. The more brutal the bout, the longer it would take for Dyfan to recover enough to return to the main pits. To the horrifyingly honorable version of pit fighting.

The healing cuts along his arms looked like claw marks.

Dyfan shifted, making a spot for Wynn beside him on the cot. As if Wynn had come to lay alongside Dyfan. To chat about bouts and tactics.

Wynn didn't take the offered place, his feet rooted to icy stone. "You can't go on like this." His shoulders were tight as his expression, and his fists clenched at his sides. The shiny pink of the skin ringing those claw marks made his stomach writhe. It was his fault Dyfan was being hurt like this. It would not have happened if he'd just turned the other fighter away from his room that first night a year and a half ago.

Dyfan sighed, likely tired of this discussion. They had some version of it every time they spoke, and the larger man rarely had much to say on the matter. He'd sit quietly, listen, and respond flatly that he would not breed anymore. That he didn't mind the lesser pits —they didn't frighten him. He could and would survive.

Even if it was slowly tearing him apart, piece by piece.

"Wynn...." Dyfan's voice was low, almost soothing as if he could placate Wynn on the matter.

Wynn jerked back as though struck, tightening his fists until his nails pressed half-moon gouges into the center of his palms. "It's tearing me apart, seeing— You can't do this any longer. What will happen to us if someone finds out why you're doing this?"

"Sit?" He straightened up on his cot, no longer in a relaxed recline. His keen features sharpened, turning serious. As soon as Wynn settled beside him, Dyfan took his hand, crushing it within his own. "I don't want to harm you, Wynn. But I will not breed anymore. Don't be angry."

Wynn tugged his hand away. "I'm not angry. I'm—" Guilty? Afraid? He shook his head to clear his thoughts. "Why, Dyfan?"

The question seemed to stump him, and Dyfan opened and closed his mouth several times before finding no answer. He only shrugged. As he always did.

Wynn stood up and paced away, his movements jerky and rigid. What else could he say? The one person he still had, the one person he had allowed himself to care for in this cursed place, was going to destroy himself, and he would not even tell Wynn why. "Is it because of me?"

Dyfan

Dyfan shook his head. "It's me. I've changed." He watched Wynn prowl, growing more still as Wynn became more agitated. In many ways, they were opposites. Dyfan was calm and focused when Wynn became frustrated or tense. He had no words when Wynn could speak for hours. But mostly, they understood one another.

Mostly.

"I can't anymore." Perhaps another Defeated would have been ashamed to admit it. A male's prowess was often equated to that of his cock and his stamina. But it wasn't that. Before, he had bedded females like he trained. He could lift heavy rocks or practice drills, but it wasn't a *real* fight.

Now... Now, it felt as if they were asking him to enter the arena for a match he had no business partaking in. And he simply couldn't do it.

Dyfan stood, covering the distance between them swiftly. He took Wynn's hand again, but this time, placed it over his steadily beating heart. "I can't." Did he understand what Dyfan meant? Could Wynn create the words Dyfan simply did not have? Dyfan hoped so, pressing his desire to be understood into his gaze.

He needed Wynn to fill the silence Dyfan created. He needed Wynn to realize this was not his fault and stop worrying about the lesser pits. Never in his life had Dyfan felt so free. So right. He was happier this way. Except for how much it worried Wynn. He couldn't have that.

Leaning forward, trusting that no other fighter would be nearby, he risked a kiss.

Wynn didn't pull away, but neither did he seem to understand. The other man just looked at him, the same mixture of worry and frustration written across his features. "If our situations were reversed and it was me in the lesser pits, how would you feel? Would you be able to let it go?"

"I would understand. If you said you couldn't do it anymore, Wynn. I would understand." Dyfan rarely cursed his quiet nature. He often found that those who spoke too much let their tongues get the better of them, sounded like fools, and started fights. But now, with words failing him, Dyfan felt a pang of frustration. Perhaps even desperation.

He needed Wynn to understand him. What was it that he felt? Why couldn't he bed the female Defeated anymore?

When he thought of entering those rooms, of disrobing and mounting those women… He felt sick to his stomach. He thought of Wynn, and his heart stuttered. His mind wheeled, and his pulse hammered so loudly in his ears that Dyfan could not think of anything else.

But when he laid with his head on Wynn's chest, or his fingers roved through Wynn's unruly hair, every piece of Dyfan felt at peace. And laying with another would shatter that.

What were the words to explain all this? What was the feeling?

Grunting in exasperation, Dyfan turned away, looking out at the darkened sky beyond his cell window. Victor Eurig had not stopped paying for him to have the best view despite his disobedience. The cool breeze licked over his face and neck, calming him some.

Wynn rocked forward until his forehead pressed into the center of Dyfan's neck. For a long time, neither of them spoke. They stood there together.

"I'm just tired of seeing you hurt." Wynn's hands slipped up his sides, wrapping tight around Dyfan's waist until they were pressed together, Wynn hugging him from behind. "You can't leave me here alone. I can't— I can't lose you."

"I would never leave you." He promised, knowing it was a falsehood. How could he promise that when he could die at the hands of Victor Eurig? Or a random spear in the pits? Or a wild animal in the lesser pits?

Still, he would promise Wynn anything to keep him happy.

Dyfan turned in Wynn's grip, wrapping his arms about Wynn's neck, tugging him closer. Many of their couplings were rough and fast, stealing moments where they could. As satisfying as those could be, Dyfan cherished the secret seconds where they could be tender together. To hold one another, to whisper against each other's skin. To kiss, to protect, to share breath. The intimacy of those moments was more profound than anything Dyfan had ever experienced.

Those quiet, soft moments with Wynn were worth a hundred lesser pit fights.

"Never." He promised again, wishing it was true.

CHAPTER 56: THE EMAI

ELEVENTH MOON, 1800, THE EMAIAN TUNDRA

Five Years before the Proclamation

While they walked, Uki told stories.

"The third Emaian to bear the title Dasan," she started, "was a humble fisherman. His name was Tongortok, and one day, while reeling in his net, he found a pearl."

Iniabi walked in front of a mass of Emaians. There were nearly a hundred of them, each carrying their most essential belongings over as many layers of clothing as they could wear. Beside her walked the old trapper, Deniigi. His white skin was scoured by so many years of wear by the sun and wind that he looked craggy, half melted. He was sharp as a well-honed blade, though, his small pale eyes constantly searching the snow.

Behind them, Uki continued. "Tongortok, eager to gather more treasures for the one he hoped to impress, dove into the frigid waters of the Taruiq Bay in hopes of finding more. Instead, he pierced his palm on the spine of a black urchin."

When Deniigi slipped away from the group, Iniabi almost didn't notice. Her eyes were on the horizon, her mind on the story. He was always doing that— disappearing into the snow only to return later with an elk, a clutch of rabbits, or a hem full of berries. The man had an uncanny understanding of the Tundra.

"Tongortok only just made it back into his small boat before the hallucinations set in. He dreamed that the sun sank to set fire to the sea, that the waves became the tongues of a sea serpent that reared up and swallowed him. He dreamed he floated atop the night sky, not quite dead and not quite living until finally, dawn came, and sense returned to him. Weakened, it took Tongortok two more days to return to his village."

Iniabi turned, searching for Qimmiq amid the crowd. She relaxed when she saw her, laughing about something with one of the village's other hunters. Qimmiq was fine. Most of the Emai were, and they took turns dragging those who struggled in sleds.

"Many in Tongortok's village had believed him lost, so they rejoiced when he returned, but before he gave into the celebration, he took the experiences he had gained to his medicine woman. Life for Tongortok's village returned to normal for a time, but the medicine woman was busy perfecting a tincture from the spines of the black urchin.

"She came to them after taking this concoction, this poison, to tell them of an attack coming from a neighboring clan that wanted more land and wealth. The chief hesitated, but Tongotok spoke of the effects of urchin, and eventually, they prepared for battle."

A lone hawk rode the wind high above Iniabi's head, its gray and red wings catching the sun's light. It would find no food here unless Deniigi had dressed his kills nearby. There was nothing to Iniabi's eye but the unending white of the Tundra.

"When Tongortok strode into that battle, his village called him Dasan, for he had brought them the gift of reaching into the future."

"Who is your favorite Dasan?" Qimmiq's voice was low, almost conspiratorial, as she fell in step with Iniabi. She was nearly as silent on the snow as Deniigi. "Uki, Daughter of Massak, likes Tongortok the most. She tells his tale often. I prefer Hey more."

"It seems odd to pick a favorite one of the Emai's protectors. They all watch out for us." The answer sounded too much like Manaba, and

Iniabi hurried to add, "I think I like Inneq's story the best, though. When I was little, I wanted to ride a hawk to the sun."

"And be up so high?" Qimmiq shuddered, her wind-kissed cheeks paling at the thought. "No, thank you. We were made with arms and legs, not wings or flippers. We're supposed to live on land; didn't anyone tell you that, Iniabi?"

Iniabi gave her a crooked grin. "Wasn't Hey stranded at sea when his boat was caught in a storm? My Aada said he rode home on the back of a whale and then shared its meat and bones with his village."

"What? He wasn't in a storm. He sang to the whales, and they came from the sea to listen to his sweet voice." Qimmiq gave Iniabi an odd look.

"I suppose some of the stories we tell are different in the north," Iniabi said, shrugging. "I like your version, though. I'll bet if you stood on the beach and sang to the sea, the whales would come to listen."

"Yes," Qimmiq agreed, pulling her furs tighter across her wonderfully plump body. "I'd sing, and they'd come up to see who was butchering an elk so close to the shore."

Sona overheard this comment and laughed, calling, "That's true! Iniabi, don't ask her to sing!"

Qimmiq shot a dirty look over her shoulder and straightened her furs while Sona and her partner laughed. "These people have *no* respect for the chief's daughter."

"Well, I suppose if you got the whales to come in out of curiosity, that would still be something. Then, they would have to respect your singing no matter how bad it is." Sona's partner, Miki, groaned, but it only made Iniabi's smile wider.

"Is that really the type of Dasan I would want to be? The death singer?" Qimmiq shook her head. "I'd rather be a regular villager and not known for my terrible voice."

"The death singer has a ring to it. I understand, though." She didn't, really—Iniabi didn't want to be a regular anything— but Qimmiq could be if she wanted.

When they reached the village of Sinqiniq, Iniabi followed at the rear of the line, one hand on the end of the makeshift sled she pulled alongside a young boy. Cheerful lines of smoke coiled over the tops of illus tucked against the curve of a half-frozen river. Iniabi could not hear or smell the sea—hadn't been able to in days—so they must be decently inland. Perhaps these people would have never heard of a ship called the *Flying Night*.

A greeting party awaited them at the village outskirts, and when the remnants of the Taqqiq stopped, Iniabi wound her way to the front to listen to what was said.

"Who are you?" one of the young hunters asked. "And why have you brought so many people to our home?" His hands were white-knuckled around his spear as though he feared attack from their motley group.

Chief Toklo slowly spread out his hands, which were empty of weapons. "I am Chief Toklo. We are the Taqqiq, but after an attack by pirates and a sea storm, our village is no more. We seek to treat with the Chief of the Sinqiniq."

"Treat away." The dry voice came from a short, muscled woman with white hair braided back from her face. Like Iniabi, she had dark eyes. "I am Chief Sakari of the Sinqiniq." Something about her tone brooked no nonsense and made Iniabi want to stand straighter. The Sinqiniq had accepted a chief with slaver blood. She wasn't sure whether to be ecstatic or in awe.

If Chief Toklo noticed or cared that the Sinqiniq leader wasn't pure Emaian, he didn't show it, instead pulling off one of his mittens to expose his hand. He kissed three fingers respectfully and dipped his head in a nod. "Chief, I have brought my people across the Tundra in hope of finding refuge and community."

"The last I heard of the Taqqiq, there were many more of you than this." Her eyes turned from the gathered Emai and back to their chief. "You wish to combine our peoples, then? You have no plans of returning home?"

Only now did Iniabi see an issue with this plan. If Sakari did not allow Toklo to continue to govern his people or give him a prominent place in her council, he would have to turn over the welfare of his villagers to a stranger. He must have known before, and that knowledge made Iniabi respect him even more. He was willing to risk his position as chief for the safety of his village.

"My people are my home. Wherever they are safest is where we rest." Akna came up to stand beside Toklo as he spoke, and Qimmiq behind her parents. The gathered Emaians fell silent, listening and waiting to see what the chief of the Sinqiniq would do.

Chief Sakari stood motionless and impassive for a long moment, and then she gave a sharp nod. "Come. We will not leave neighbors to the cold. You will all be given homes to stay in for the time being. We have much to discuss about how this will work for both our villages, but you are welcome."

All the tension went out of Iniabi, and she stepped with her people into their new home.

⇑　　⇑　　⇑

"Chief Toklo," a young, clever-eyed woman said, "There is room for three with Elders Tikaani and Naunja." Iniabi thought this must be the Sinqiniq's medicine woman because, despite her youth, the others of her village deferred to her.

Iniabi stood next to Qimmiq, close enough that their shoulders touched. The contact was like a thin line of comfort, an anchor in a new sea. Akna put her hand on her husband's arm, and they both glanced toward Iniabi and Qimmiq. Iniabi shifted uneasily. She could sleep somewhere surrounded by strangers if she needed to. She'd done it for years on the pirate ship and would be safe here among her people. She opened her mouth to say as much but Akna spoke first.

"These two stay up all night whispering. You know how girls in love are. Let us go with Uki and Tatik, and they can stay with people who don't want to go to bed so early."

Iniabi knew she was blushing. Was she in love? Was this what love felt like, this twisty, exciting feeling in her belly?

"You two are together, then?" The medicine woman only looked vaguely curious.

"Yes," Iniabi blurted, then glanced at Qimmiq. She only relaxed when she saw that her round cheeks were pink as well. Qimmiq was smiling.

Iniabi sighed in relief.

"Well, then we'll put you with Elders Tikanni and Naunja — those two sleep like the frozen, except for the snoring. They won't be bothered. What are your names?"

"Qimmiq."

"Iniabi, Daughter of Manaba." That name had seemed a burden once. Now, it proved Iniabi belonged.

The medicine woman nodded sharply. "Chief Toklo, Akna, you and your medicine women are welcome in my illu. There is space enough for five."

So the assignments went on. After a time, Iniabi began to yawn in boredom. There was not much to see from the center of this village. She glanced at Qimmiq and then to the chief, whose focus was still on the work of dividing his people into small enough groups to assimilate. They wouldn't need Iniabi or Qimmiq any time soon, so Iniabi took the beautiful hunter's hand, and they slipped away from the commotion.

"Have you heard much about this village before?" Iniabi asked when they were far enough away to speak without anyone noticing. They walked through the middle of three rings around the center of the village, the packed gathering area occasionally visible through the illus. There was something strange about how this village was set up, but Iniabi couldn't figure out why.

"We've traded with them before, but only if we couldn't get trade from the sea. I never got to come—I was too young—but father and the old chief knew each other. What do you think of them?"

"This is a new chief then? I think her mind has a lot more to say than her mouth does."

"New enough. Trade was good off the port for as long as I can remember, so I don't think we had any reason to trek all this way. So she could have been chief for ten or so years."

Perhaps the strangeness lay in the three rings of illus. Iniabi had never been in a village with more than two; even then, the second one was not often complete. It was easily the biggest village that she'd heard of. But still, something seemed odd. She knew what when they'd gone nearly in a full circle. "Where is their medicine woman's illu? Does she not live a little away from everyone else to better hear the spirits?"

"I don't know… Uki's was off a bit… But she was getting older, and we had been talking about moving her closer…."

"What are you looking for?" A voice sounded behind them, and Iniabi held onto Qimmiq's hand tighter when the other woman jumped. They both turned to see a round-faced child, their eyes narrowed in suspicion, a strange expression on such a young person.

Iniabi glanced at Qimmiq. "We were just talking, not looking for anything. But we are curious. Where is the medicine woman's tent?"

"In the center of the illus, *of course*. The chief and the medicine woman have illus next to each other. That way, they always know what the other one is doing." They rolled their eyes and shuffled closer, their thick layers of pelts making them waddle. "My Aada says you are ocean people. Sedna, Daughter of Meriwa, says some seafaring Emai can turn into seals. Do you turn into a seal?"

"Not I." Iniabi crouched to bring her eyes level with the child's and spoke conspiratorially. "Only the most beautiful women among the ocean people can wear seal skins and slip beneath the waves. I've yet to see her do it, but I'm pretty sure that Qimmiq here can."

The child turned to look at Qimmiq with something close to accusation. "Do it."

Qimmiq shook her head. "Without the ocean, I cannot change."

This seemed to stump them, and they let out a forlorn sigh. "Only women can turn into seals?"

Qimmiq glanced at Iniabi and shook her head. Iniabi gave her a shrug and a small smile. "That's what pirates believe, but we Emaians know it has more to do with love for the ocean than gender. I think Tongortok could, too."

She straightened again, dusting snow off her leggings. The sun was setting in the distance, casting the sky in pinks and reds reflecting in Qimmiq's hair. Iniabi's belly flipped a little at the sight.

Her words seemed to soothe the child because their frown dissipated and was replaced with curiosity. "You're sleeping in old Naunja's illu. She smells funny."

"How romantic," Qimmiq murmured.

"Hanta, what are you doing?" The voice was stark, and the three Emaians turned to see Chief Sakari. The child didn't seem all that impressed by their chief's stern look.

"Talking."

"I see that," the chief said. "Why are you bothering these women?"

"I wanted to see if they could turn into seals, but they won't."

"Seals? I see." The corners of her chiseled lips turned slightly upward. "This is true, Iniabi, Daughter of Manaba? You will not turn into a seal for my kin?"

"I'm afraid I lost the ability because I stayed too long out of the water. Now I can only walk on two legs like the rest of the Emai."

"There, see, Hanta? It's not kind to point out someone else's difficulties. Go home now; dinner will be ready soon." The child opened their mouth, perhaps to protest, but a look from their mother made them rethink it.

"Where are *they* eating dinner?"

Chief Sakari's cheek twitched as if she were suppressing a smile. "With their new hosts, who are not smelly."

Hanta, apparently embarrassed to have been caught bad-mouthing the elders, scuttled away in their too-thick clothing. The chief waited until her child was out of earshot and then turned to Iniabi and Qimmiq, her expression serious.

"Chief Toklo says you're a fighter, Iniabi, Daughter of Manaba."

Before Iniabi could reply, Qimmiq spoke, "Yes, she is. She's marvelous. The best fighter you've ever seen."

The chief arched a brow. "Bold words, Qimmiq, since you do not know the skill of my fighters."

Something about this chief unnerved Iniabi. She reminded her of Manaba and Captain Ira, but more controlled, harder to predict. It left Iniabi feeling wary and uncertain. "I can hold my own," she said, her skin too taut. She would not lay beneath the thumb of another. Never again. Iniabi was going to make her own path.

"Good. I came to invite you to join my warriors tomorrow. As the tribes are combining, Chief Toklo and I have been trying to ensure everyone has a place and a task. Qimmiq, you'll be joining the hunters."

Iniabi nodded. "I'll be there. Hopefully, to live up to my friend's words."

"We'll see."

CHAPTER 57: PHECEA

SECOND MOON, 1801, DIOSION

Four Years before the Proclamation

*D*anae opened the door to the Mavros music room, surprised to find it quiet. With Melba, Zina, and Voleta all determined to become excellent musicians, the room hardly ever seemed empty of scales and sonatas. Today, though, the girls must be with tutors or out with friends because when Danae stepped through the door, canvas and paints clamped awkwardly beneath one arm, only Biton stood within. His side was turned to her, his eyes focused out the window, and he didn't immediately look around when Danae entered. Danae felt loath to disturb him. He was biting his cheek in thought or worry, and his dark brows were drawn together over subtle gold eyelids. His black hair had gotten long. It hung down his back with no adornment but the braids looping back from his temples. He wore a long-sleeved linen tunic in blush pink.

She was staring. It was just that he made a nice picture, framed in the window's light.

"It's so quiet in here." Danae smiled, turning to set down her canvas and paints. She was supposed to work on a portrait, and this room seemed the best place.

"Oh, hello, Danae. Dido and Dara are with their riding instructor, and the others have gone into town to walk through the market."

He looked... not sad precisely, but not happy either. Preoccupied perhaps?

"Well, we don't get much time, just you and me, so I suppose I don't mind them being gone. Especially with my apprenticeship tour coming up soon." She pulled the canvas up, showing Biton the rough sketch of him. She was no master painter, but it wasn't the ugly thing it would have been when she first started. "What do you think?"

He touched his face and smiled. "I think that's a fair likeness. Who is your drawing instructor? Maybe mother could hire them to help Dido."

Danae snorted and looked around for the best light. Really, where Biton stood beside the window was perfect. "Here." She grabbed one of the tall stools and placed it beside him, gesturing for him to sit. Turning to set up her supplies, Danae glanced back at Biton. He squirmed on the seat, plucking at his tunic until it lay just so. "Are you alright? You seem... quiet."

"I'm fine!" Biton's voice was a little too high and cracked on the second word. He cleared his throat. "Am I just supposed to sit here?"

"Well, yes, Biton. That's how modeling works. You sit, and you're supposed to inspire me or something. You know... be a *muse*. A-muse me." It was a poor joke, but she didn't like how solemn Biton seemed.

Biton laughed, but it wasn't quite the cure she was looking for. The hills between his brows were still there. "Clever, Danae. Is having me try to be still amusing? What are you going to do with this portrait, anyway?"

He shifted again, and Danae squinted her eyes at him. Did he look... nervous? Around her? When had they ever been nervous around each other?

"Maybe I'll make it your birthday gift. Seventeen this year." She needed a few more things. "Keme?" she called, and the door opened to the music room.

He bowed his head. "Mistress?"

"I need several glasses of water and rags to wipe my brushes on."

"Yes, mistress." He bowed again, but as Danae turned back to her jars of paint, she saw Biton's gaze latch onto Keme. He seemed to take strength from the Emaian.

"Thank you, Keme." Biton took what looked to be a deep, steadying breath. "Well, make sure to make me pretty."

"Ha, as if I have to try. You do all that on your own. I'm just going to ensure you have a nose this time...." Danae set a dollop of inky blue paint on her pallet, then white, red, and pink. All the colors in her jars. Biton would need all the colors. She started to fill in the shadows, the dark places: the spot at his temple where his hair pulled away, the line of his black lashes, the shadow beneath his folded hands. For a time, the only sound was the dabbing of her brush against the cloth canvas and the creak of the stool as Biton moved. After the third time he shifted, changing the angle of his chin, Danae sighed and put her brush down. "Biton, I told you to go riding this morning before I came over. You keep moving!"

"Well, there's nothing to do," he said. "I *did* go riding this morning. I went for a trot with Crane and then came back to the stables to see Dasan."

"Alright... If you're certain...." Danae lifted her paintbrush. He hadn't been so fidgety last time he sat for her, but that was well over a year ago. Perhaps he just had more energy.

The room was silent again, filled with nothing but late-morning sunlight and the strokes of Danae's soft brushes against her canvas. Biton even managed to sit still for a few moments, though she looked up after adding the middle pigments to find him gripping the edges of the stool on either side of his thighs, his face pale.

"Um, Danae? Do you remember my last birthday? The things Adohnis said?"

"You mean when I pushed him in the fountain?" She squinted, trying to get the color mixture for his pink tunic just right. It was less pink and more... dusty. "Of course, I remember, and I know you've made up, but I don't feel like apologizing." Perhaps a dot of black would do the trick?

"Oh, that's alright. But do you remember what he said?"

Now it was too dark. Danae sighed and looked up from her pallet. Biton was staring at her. "Ummm." What had Adohnis said? That

Biton wore girls' clothing? That Biton should pick a side? Something like that. "I do...."

"And afterward, how we talked about me being who I wanted to be?"

"Yes, about how you're the pirate captain?"

Biton took a shaky breath. "Or the pirate queen... Danae, will you call me Basia? From now on?"

Queen.

She looked over Biton's gilded eyes and long inky hair. His beautiful clothes and the uncomfortable way he sat on the stool, as if ready to dart up any moment. To flee. From her.

She thought about how perfectly he danced and included her whenever she was left out. Biton was kind to everyone, even when they were rude, annoying, or downright mean, like Adohnis had been.

Basia was a girl's name.

Pirate *Queen.*

"Oh," Danae put her brush down. "Alright." She swallowed, wondering how best to react. His expression was painfully intent. No. Basia. Her. *Her* expression. And that made Danae pick up her brush. "You moved again."

Basia

All of the tension in Basia's shoulders relaxed, and she slumped forward slightly in her seat. Should she laugh or smile or cry? The relief was almost as overwhelming as the fear had been, and some uncertainty still swirled in her belly. Danae had said alright, but she might treat her differently.

"Basia, can you sit back up? You're leaning out of the light."

Basia did smile then, wide and full-toothed so that she felt it in her eyes. A tear rolled down her cheek, dusted gold by her face paint, and she wiped it away before Danae could see.

Keme had been right—he usually was. He had stood beside her at the city's edge, on a cliff overlooking the Great Eastern Sea, and told her that she did not owe anyone the truth of herself. But, if she let them know, she might be surprised by how accepting they were. She just had to give them a chance.

Danae was naturally the first person she'd given the chance, but now, armed with Danae's acceptance, she could tell others too. One day people would come to the city office and she would be introduced as Basia Mavros, administrator to the great Confederacy of Phecea.

She would be who she had been all along, and everyone else would see it too.

Basia, daughter of Cyril and Iris Mavros and protector of the Confederacy. Dashing, bright, brave, smiling Basia.

"Don't forget the gold!" she told Danae. "I want to look like I could ride all the way to the sun on the back of a flaming eagle."

CHAPTER 58: PHECEA

FOURTH MOON, 1801, ADAMITHI

Four Years before the Proclamation

Basia splashed cold spring water over her face one-handed, the other clasped around Crane's reins while the stallion drank his fill. Around them, the land rose in gentle, sloping hills: grass-furred and dotted with yellow shrubs. The sky was an unending blue field above, and though it was only fall back in Diosion, the air in the Adamithi province was winter-cold. They were not so far from the Emaian homeland here.

Crane shook his head, jangling his bridle and sending water droplets pattering back into the stream, his soft, red nose dark from the wet. He enjoyed this as much as Basia did: long days of riding with all of Phecea spread out around them. So far, Adamithi looked like no place she had ever seen. Most of the Confederacy was flat plains, ending in cliffs that jutted above the Eastern Sea. Not so in this hilly province in the shadow of the Psilos Mountains. There were no walls here, no buildings, nothing to hem her in. Just endless tree-broken green.

"Let's get back to the others, shall we?" Basia mounted and clucked her horse toward the main road—if the narrow dirt track deserved such a name. The carriage carrying Danae, her tutors, and all of their things had passed her only a quarter of an hour prior, and the thing moved at a damnably slow pace. "Alright, Crane, do you want to see how quickly we can overtake them?"

Basia squeezed her calves, and the stallion obligingly sped up to a trot. She didn't push him to go any faster, and still, they reached the others in a few minutes. The Psilos Mountains were in full view at the crest of the hill Danae's carriage was climbing: snow-capped giants, peering down on all the world. Keme called them the Nonnocan Peaks.

Basia handed Crane's reins off to one of the guards Councilor Arsenio Othonos had sent to protect his daughter and then leaped easily onto the carriage's step, swinging open the door to slide inside.

"Danae! Have you seen the mountains? We must be nearing Iretetra!"

"How many times have I asked you not to leap into the carriage while it is moving, Mavros?"

Basia gave Danae's tutor, Master Annas, her most charming smile. "I do believe you've mentioned it."

"Basi!" Danae's voice was full of reprimand, but she was smiling. The Othonos heir sat in a coat and warm breeches, sheaves of paper balanced on her knees where she had spent the day taking notes. Basia thought she looked like she could use a ride.

"Adamithi is beautiful riding! You really have to see it!"

"I still have my lessons," Danae murmured, though she sounded less than enthusiastic. As the heir to her parent's responsibilities, including their seats on the Council, Danae had to be educated in the aspects of Phecean life, like philosophy and the arts, and the specific skills needed to run Phecea. She had a lot more studying to do than Basia. With Danae's fifteenth birthday only a moon away, she would soon start her apprenticeships, which would eat into study time.

Basia sighed, which only seemed to further raise Master Annas's ire. He straightened his already impeccable posture to look down his narrow nose at the uncouth teenager. "I believe I shall take it upon myself to speak with Master Ida about your curriculum. It seems to me that you are not getting enough stimulation from your studies, Mavros."

Basia winced. That just sounded like more lessons. "Apologies, Master Annas."

The master sniffed, straightened his delicate spectacles, and returned his gaze to his book. With a ruffling of pages, he began to read aloud.

"Before the formation of Liria or the Phecean Confederacy, the lands north of the Emaian Tundra were ruled by several powerful city-states. Unclear borders and competition over natural resources lead to centuries of war between these factions. By 1632, the lands currently known as the Phecean Confederacy were under the control of the five families we know well today. These five families— Adamos, Aetos, Leos, Othonos, and Zodrafos— had established an uneasy alliance that allowed them to consume smaller city-states. West of the Psilos Mountains, however, one power managed to overrun all competition. This family, once known as the Loratos, restyled their nation as Liria and set out to conquer the rest of this continent. It was this threat that led to the formation of the Phecean Confederacy. The five heads of the city-states not under Lirian control met to discuss terms for their new nation. Each family was to have two seats on a Council, one for each of the heads of the state. These Councilors are sometimes married couples, but this is not always the case. For example, from 1714 to 1743, the Aetirium was ruled by two Aetos sisters, Sappho and Daphne, and our current Zodrafi and Aetos seats are held by siblings."

Basia yawned and turned her face to the window. That was nothing any well-educated Phecean would not know, and she found that her mind drifted as Master Annas paused in his reading to direct a question at Danae.

"What significance does this piece of our history hold for you, Danae Othonos?"

She looked away from the window to see Danae blush slightly. "It means whoever I marry will get the second seat on the Council since I have no siblings." Master Annas raised his brows.

"Good. Or?"

"Or...." Danae glanced Basia's way as if she had the answer. "Or another noble can be voted into the Council seat, but they will have to drop their family name and adopt Othonos instead."

"Very good. It is a big responsibility since your spouse will not just be your partner in life but also in politics. Only nine other people in our nation will experience such demands. The process of the Council voting in a new member is a rare one. In our history it has only happened three times and those were all in our nation's infancy. Mavros." Master Anna's unwavering gaze latched on to Basia. "Who was the last person to be voted into the Council, and from which family?"

Basia blinked. How had this become a quizzing session for her?! "Umm...." she stole a look at Danae, hoping that her friend would have the answer. Danae mouthed a name, but for the life of her, Basia could not read her lips. "Ummmmmmm...." Danae mouthed the word again, more emphatically, Kaa—os. What did that mean? There were several lesser noble families with names that started with Ka, and practically all noble families ended with -os. "Kaaa...donnn...nos?"

"You give me hope for the future of the Confederacy, Mavros. Pray tell, what family name changed from Kadonos? I've never heard of it."

"I believe, Master Annas, that it was the Killos family, specifically Calliope Killos, who was voted into the Leos seat when Jannas Leos refused to marry."

Master Annas gave her a dry look. "Thank you, Othonos." He straightened his papers and turned one over, reviewing his notes. "Next, we will discuss Lirian exports and the Phecea's long-standing reliance on their Emaian breeding programs."

Basia tried to listen—she really did—but as the pitched roofs and coiling stonework of Iretetra rose around the carriage, her mind wandered to the city and the things she would see there.

⇑   ⇑   ⇑

Danae had never seen so much strange food. Diosion was a coastal city, though perched high on the cliffs above the Eastern Sea; Aphodes sat right on the bay, the city's edge melding into the salt water. There were familiar dishes, such as scallops and clams, but also something bug-like, red, and tough-shelled. The creature was served whole, its little black eyes staring at her from across its plate. Beside it rested a bowl of something that still moved.

Councilor Minos Leos assured Danae and Basia that it was a delicacy, a creature pulled straight from the bay and onto their plates. It was supposed to be dead, despite the wiggling. Danae hadn't brought herself to taste it yet, though etiquette dictated she must sample each dish.

"*You* try it," she whispered to Basia as Councillor Minos conferred with Master Annas and Mistress Ida on the itinerary for their stay in Aphodes.

"You *first*." Basia wrinkled her nose and, copying one of the administrators to her left, reached out to pick up one of the red prawns. She pinched off its tail and found the white meat within. "Oh! It's spicy!"

The administrator gave her a wink and raised the head of his prawn to his lips with a contented slurp, but not even Basi was brave enough to try that.

These people were insane. Slurping sea bug brains and butts. Danae's lips wobbled as she brought one piece of wiggling tentacle up to her mouth. She tried to convince herself to open, to put the "food" on her tongue, but her mouth would not comply. "Basia," she hissed, "I am your *best* friend *and* an Othonos. I order you to eat this for me."

"Over my cold body. I've never been more glad I'm *not* an Othonos."

"*Hussy!*"

Basia snorted and had to pretend it was a cough when Councilor Agni turned. That was at least a little satisfying, but now Danae had paused too long with the squirming morsel at her lips.

"Othonos, don't play with your food. You're supposed to eat it," Master Annas said, and all eyes turned her way. Expectant. Was there a polite way to shudder in revulsion?

"Of course," she said, and without letting herself think too much about it, popped the thing into her mouth. It moved against her tongue, and Danae chewed aggressively, determined to make it stop.

The table was very quiet.

"Well? What do you think?" Councilor Minos Leos asked, lips

parted in a small smile as he took a sip from his cup. Danae couldn't respond right away because she was still chewing. And chewing. And chewing.

Finally, when the bite went down, she nodded. "It's very... *fresh.*"

Both Councilors laughed good-naturedly. "A diplomat indeed. It's alright, Danae. You don't have to eat more."

Basia gave her an impressed glance from behind her fifth or sixth sea bug. "May they sing epics of your bravery for centuries."

"It's not so bad once you get used to the texture," Peta said from across the table. A few years older than Danae and Basia, the Leos daughter wore the traditional loose tunic of a floaty material that danced in ocean breezes. Her twin Aesop shook his head.

"Are you two going to the maiden voyage celebration of the Helen? Most of the nobility in this region will be there."

It sounded like something Danae would enjoy, but she didn't know if Master Annas would permit such a thing. His schedule was *very* tight.

"Oh, you must," Councilor Agni Leos chimed in. "What's the point of being young if you don't experience all that Phecea has to offer? Don't you agree, Master Annas?"

Put on the spot by a Council Member, Master Annas purpled but nodded. "Of course, within reason." His stern gaze turned to Basia, who was eyeing the near-empty bowl of sea prawns with something akin to longing. "I suppose Mavros could act as... *chaperone* for Danae."

Basia looked up, giving Master Annas a sheepish smile. "Uh...Of course! I'd be happy to."

⇑ ⇑ ⇑

The *Helen* was a three-masted galleon, a behemoth of a ship, but constructed in smooth lines. A military vessel, she was dark and stern, especially compared to the bright backdrop of Aphodes's cheery merchant flotilla. The deck was littered with small, round tables, their coverings held down with ship lanterns and miniature rope coils. Emaian slaves in crisp white linens held silver platters laden with wine and delicacies. To the south, the city lay like a handful of jewels, a scattering of brilliantly painted buildings above the harbor.

Basia thought it looked like the perfect scene for a pirate attack, but so far, the most exciting thing was the *Helen's* three great ballistae firing as her officers paraded onto the deck in full dress uniform.

"How can we lose the war with ships like these? Liria will fall in a matter of moons." Basia threaded her arm through Danae's. "Do you want to get a closer look at the ballista?"

"Alright, but you have to promise you're not going to try to fire it." She pulled Basia closer, smile indulgent. They had both donned the Aphodian style of tunic, composed of four gossamer layers of lightly dyed fabric. Cut short at the tops of their knees and belted at their hips rather than their waists, the hem seemed to make Danae uncomfortable. She kept tugging it down over her long legs.

Her curls frayed in the wind, but her cheeks were bright. Most of the nobility in attendance were from lesser families who resided within Aphodes or nearby, but Basia had spotted a few of the Aetos clan.

"*Fine*. I won't fire it."

She pulled Danae over to the massive crossbow-like weapon, trying to determine just how large the spear it launched was. Would it punch a hole in a ship? Or harpoon a whale? She turned to see what Danae thought when she caught sight of Pello Aetos. He stood well behind Danae, bent to whisper something into the ear of a girl hanging off his arm.

"That fish-fucking whore!"

"Basi!" Danae's voice was sharp with surprise, her brows arching in alarm. "What's gotten into you?"

Well, there just weren't any better words to describe Pello.

Basia looked at Danae. Should she show her? It would hurt her feelings, yet it didn't seem right to let Danae continue to think Pello was her beau.

"Are you alright?" Across the ship, Pello looped his arm around the girl's waist, pulling her to him. His hand traveled dangerously close to her rump. This was the boy Danae had been pining after for the last six moons. They exchanged painfully saccharin letters that Basia had the *pleasure* of hearing Danae repeat because she thought the stars lit themselves on Pello Aetos's smile.

Basia groaned. "*I'm* alright. But you're not going to be."

"What do you mean?" Danae looked down at her short tunic and patted her hair, awkward and nervous. "Do I look stupid?"

"You look like a vision. He's the one that looks like an artless fool." Basia took Danae's arm and gently turned her around.

Danae's reaction was like a physical blow, and she fell back against Basia's chest. "I… But, I thought…." Pello bent to kiss the unknown girl's fingertips, a flirtatious smile on his slimy face. "I need to go. Right now. Basia."

Danae turned away from the scene, but her movement seemed to catch Pello's attention because he looked up. His face contorted with surprise and then blanched. Pello yanked his hand away from the strange girl's rear and stepped forward as if to speak to them.

"Go on," Basia told Danae. "Head off the boat, but don't go far. I'll catch up, and we can ride back to the Leos estate together."

She turned back to Pello, straightening the gossamer tunic beneath its belt. Really, boots were the thing for unpleasant confrontations, but she'd make do with sandals. He made as if to go around her, to get to Danae. Idiot. Basia blocked his path again. "I don't know where you think you're going."

"Look, Bit—"

"It's Basia. Like Danae told you in her last rather heartfelt letter." Basia crossed her arms over her chest and glared up at him. "You're not going to follow her."

"Basia, then. It's not what it looks like. I really do care for Danae, but she lives in Diosion, and I live in Sessis. You're a bo— You're sixteen, you know what it's like. We have desires!" Pello craned his neck to watch Danae's fleeing form, shifting on his feet as if he were thinking about running after her.

Basia stepped in front of him again, her lips twisting in distaste. "You're barking like a bitch in heat. Danae's too good for dogs that can't control themselves. Go find some other female to sniff."

"Don't be such a brute, Basia. I do care about her. But we're young! It's not as if we talked about getting married or anything. You're being heartless. I know she doesn't have other beaus. She'll be lonely." Pello looked away from Danae's retreating form and straight into Basia's face.

"You hurt her, you ass! Stand down, or I'll call her guards. You do not get to insult the Othonos heir and then harass her about it."

"Alright, alright. But tell her I'll write."

"She'd be better off listening to snakes," Basia growled, but she took a step back. "Go back to your date, Aetos."

When Pello turned around, Basia sprinted down the ship's ramp and found Danae waiting on the pier. She was red-eyed, but she wasn't crying. She looked as if she wanted to.

"Hey, Danae. I got rid of him. Do you want me to call a carriage?"

"Yes. I don't want to be here anymore." She tucked her hands against her sides, determinedly looking anywhere but at the *Helen*.

There were a few Emai in the white uniform of those serving the guests stationed at the bottom of the ramp. Basia spoke briefly to one of them, securing a carriage for herself and Danae before returning to her friend. "They're on the way. We just need to walk back to the end of the pier."

"Alright," she murmured, sounding distracted as she turned to stride away from the ship and Pello. Danae made it through the carriage ride and the Leos estate before they finally reached her bedroom. Then she flopped onto the mattress like a sack of wet wool and dissolved into tears.

CHAPTER 59: THE EMAI

FOURTH MOON, 1801, ADAMITHI

Four Years before the Proclamation

Iniabi reached out a hand to Pakuk, the other loosely wrapped around a simple, wooden staff. She heaved him up, though the man was a foot and a half taller than her, and dusted the dirt off his shoulder. "Do you see what I mean now? If you stand still, you're going to take the hit. You've got to *move*. Get out of the way of my swings or block them, and then attack while I'm off balance. Don't get so preoccupied with trying to win that you forget to watch yourself and lose your shins to a Lirian blade."

"But I like winning," he complained.

"Trust me, you'll like staying alive more." Around them, the sounds of grunts and clacking wood were balm to Iniabi's ears. Many of Sinqiniq's fighters *were* good, but they had never trained like Iniabi had aboard the *Flying Night* with Lirian weapons and a Phecean fighting instructor. They'd not first wet their spears on Lirian military, mercenaries, and sailors. Now, they were beginning to shape into something deadly. The first well-outfitted Emaian fighting force with the weapons the Taqqiq village had salvaged from the pirate attack. Iniabi straightened her spine and fixed her grip on her staff. "Again. Let's see if you can stay on your feet this time."

Iniabi fell into the familiar mind space of sparring, pointing out places where Pakuk could improve. Most of her days were like this—working with the warriors of the Sinqiniq and Taqqiq peoples when they weren't needed to help smoke elk or build illus. It left her body sore and her mind full of teaching exercises, but all her charges had improved, and Iniabi was as fast as she'd ever been.

The peace Iniabi had found in Taqqiq hadn't left her, but it felt good to spar, to fight. This is what she was really good at—not tanning hides or helping to hunt. She stepped back after she dropped Pakuk again, happy that it had taken longer this time. He was learning. "Alright, get up and—"`

Shouts rang out from the edge of the village, and Iniabi froze mid-sentence. She touched the sword at her hip with one hand and then turned to the people around her. She was not their leader. She was not their chief. She wasn't even the most experienced one among them, just a half-Emaian bastard that had taken to the sea with pirates for six years. And yet, this was her home now, and Iniabi needed help defending it.

"Grab any weapon you have and follow me!" Her voice rang out clear and loud across the clearing. All those years at sea had taught her to project over the sounds of storm and battle. Pale faces turned to look at her. "Our people need us!"

There wasn't any more time to wait. Iniabi turned and ran from the rough patch of earth where they trained, the staff still clutched in her fist and her sword slapping regularly against her thigh. Whatever attacked them, this would not be a repeat of Nec. She would not allow it to happen.

Qimmiq would be alright. She and the other hunters had gone out early that morning, slipping out from their furs and leaving Iniabi to sleep the last gray hour alone. They would be out on the Tundra stalking elk, safe fro—

Iniabi turned between two illu to see a Lirian soldier, his fist wrapped around one of Qimmiq's braids as if it were a lead rope. Her face was bruised and gore-streaked, her eyes wide with fear, but when Qimmiq saw Iniabi, something akin to relief broke over her features.

She believed that Iniabi would save her so completely that even as she stood there, still in her captor's grip, she calmed. Iniabi had never held so much trust.

She wasn't going to lose it.

"Iniabi!" Qimmiq squeaked just as the Lirian turned to see her standing there.

The soldier wasn't ready for Iniabi's attack. She was on him before he could get up his sword, before he could breathe, slamming the butt of her staff into his gut. When the staff proved too dangerous with Qimmiq so near, she dropped it and drew her knife. Iniabi broke her only rule and took a shallow cut to her hip so she could kill him faster, thrusting the entire length of her dagger up through his chin and into his skull. He fell when she yanked it out, her body shaking and her vision tinged with red. "Qimmiq," she whispered. "Qimmiq."

Qimmiq had fallen with the Lirian as he died, his hand still buried in her hair, but with a wince, she pulled herself free. For a moment, the two women stood staring at each other in shock, and then Qimmiq threw her arms around Iniabi, shaking. "They found us out hunting! They chased us here! I was so afraid." She buried her face against Iniabi's shoulder, her voice muffled, "I knew you'd save me."

"Yes. You're safe." Iniabi pulled back and put her free, unbloodied hand against Qimmiq's cheek. "There are more of them, though. I need you to help me. Can you help me, love?"

"Yes. Yes."

"I need you to get anyone who can't fight to the center of the village. Put bows or slings in the hands of anyone who can use them." More of the fighters ran up behind Iniabi, some with bloodied weapons. "We're going to stop them from getting to you, but just in case, I need you to help me stop anyone from getting taken today."

Qimmiq clutched Iniabi's hands but then released her. "Be safe."

Iniabi pressed her forehead to Qimmiq's, stealing precious seconds with her lover. "I'll see you after this is over, Qimmiq. I promise."

They shared one last breath, and then Qimmiq stifled a sob and turned away.

Iniabi stepped back and pointed to the outer ring of illus with her blood-soaked knife. The warriors were still behind her, their eyes reflecting red. Few of them had ever killed anyone before, and all those were probably from the pirate raid on Taqqiq. "Spread out! When you find them, shout! Don't attempt to kill them alone!"

They scattered like snow, tearing through the illus, Iniabi first among them. She stalked the gray and brown structures like a wolf amid trees, hooded-eyed and hungry. She wanted to spill blood, to slake her anger with the slavers' destruction. She would lose no one. No one.

A scream pierced the air, and Iniabi swung towards it, shifting her knife to her right hand so she could draw her sword with her left. The sound came from outside the ring of illus, and she loped towards it on impatient feet.

Three Lirians kept watch over several of the hunters that had gone out that morning—they must have come across the hunting party on their way home. The Sinqiniq warriors fanned out behind her.

They attacked as one, charging over the snow to rescue their bound neighbors. These Lirians were quicker to react— they were prepared for an attack. One raised his crossbow, and a bolt buried itself into the woman closest to Iniabi, killing her before she could scream. There was no time to look. Pakuk's staff batted the crossbow out of his hands, and then Iniabi could do nothing but block the blows of the Lirian in the center. He was tall and broad-shouldered, his uniform different enough from the others to denote a higher rank. The leader fought like a dancer, quick and silent.

Iniabi was faster.

She ducked his blows, always just out of reach and never attempting to swing back. "Fucking coward," he cursed in his own tongue. "Animals—"

The man's frustration created the opening Iniabi needed. He swung out hard and missed, leaving his torso completely exposed for just long enough. Iniabi's sword opened him from his waist to his chin in a single deep stroke. He fell back, gurgling.

The crossbow soldier had managed to knock Pakuk's staff from his hands and was advancing, his sword held up menacingly. Iniabi grabbed him from behind and shoved her sword through his ribs.

Behind her, another warrior felled the last Lirian and untied their captives.

"Get to the center of the village," Iniabi told the hunters. "Protect those who can't protect themselves."

She and the warriors turned back to the village, but most of the attackers had been slain. Iniabi killed a fleeing soldier with a thrown dagger, then another with a flick of her sword. Pakuk took one out with a brute-force blow to the skull. Qimmiq had done her work well. There were no Emaian bodies or captives on the outskirts, and the warriors made quick work of the last knots of fighters.

A little farther in, Iniabi found the prone form of their youngest fighter, a girl named Sila. She'd been quick and smart, but she lay now with a bolt in her heart, the second Emaian fatality of the battle. Iniabi keened when Pakuk leaned down to pick her up, a single, low call that the other fighters around her took up until it rose, haunting as snow spirits, above the village.

They were still calling when they reached the village center, every one of the Lirians lying dead in the snow behind them. Pakuk laid Sila before the medicine women Sedna, Uki, and Tatik, alongside the body of the other woman who had fallen.

They would mourn together later. Now— Now, they needed hope.

Iniabi let the call die from her throat. "The Lirians are dead! May their spirits wander the Tundra alone for an age. They will not be taking Emaians today!"

For a long moment, there was silence in the gathering space, the faces of the people around them tight in fear and grief. It was like they could not quite believe that they had escaped that unavoidable fate, that death sentence that was a Lirian slave raid. They could not live through their neighbor's destruction and believe they might turn away the same fate when it reached their doors.

And then, Pakuk threw back his head and howled. The warriors around him took up the noise, screaming war cries into the white sky with enough fervor to boil the blood in Iniabi's veins. She felt feverish with excitement, as powerful as the Dasan who'd flown to the sun. She was Iniabi, Daughter of Manaba, warrior of the Sinqiniq, and she had led these people in battle against the Lirians. They had *won*.

Iniabi stretched her neck to the sun and added her war call to the clamor.

Cries still filled the air when a hand linked with hers, and she turned to look at Qimmiq. Her cheeks were no longer blood-stained, and her face was tight with something bright.

Toklo and Sakari stood at the center of the clearing. "We need to get any wounded to Uki and Sedna," Qimmiq's Ataat started. "Assess the damage to our homes."

Sakari nodded. "For the warriors who slew our foes and the hunters who protected us even after their ordeal, some rest. Everyone else, let us prepare a feast! We will drink tonight and mourn our fallen in the morning."

"Come with me," Qimmiq whispered into Iniabi's ear, tugging her away from the collected Emai.

Something in Qimmiq's eyes felt like the same rush she'd gotten from the battle cries, something hot and alluring. Iniabi took a deep breath, trembling as the adrenaline began to leave her body. It was just now noon.

Quickly they wove through illus and cooking fires and skinning frames until they came upon the half-constructed illu Qimmiq and Iniabi had started to build. Qimmiq ducked through the open archway and pulled Iniabi along with her, spinning faster than Iniabi had ever seen her move.

Qimmiq pressed against Iniabi, their lips forming a single line as she wrapped her arms around Iniabi's hips. When Qimmiq pulled away from the fevered kiss, her face was smeared with blood. The ex-pirate wondered for a moment where it had come from, but then she realized she was speckled with the red stuff, her hands coated like a second pair of macabre gloves.

"You fought them off, Iniabi." Qimmiq's voice was breathless, her eyes wide and round. "I've never met anyone like you."

"I'm just so glad you're alright." Iniabi trembled, fighting to hold herself still. She felt almost like she was coming down from urchin dreams, the poison leaving her limbs in shakes and starts. "I saw you, held by that soldier, and I— I—" It was getting harder to talk. Iniabi reached out to touch Qimmiq's arm and left a streak of blood there, bright red against the pale fur of her coat.

"Shhh...." Qimmiq leaned closer, brushing her lips against Iniabi's. "Shh, you saved me. You saved us *all.*" The other woman's lips moved across Iniabi's jaw and then nuzzled against her neck. After a moment, she eased away, hands coming to pull Iniabi's gloves off, one finger at a time. Qimmiq started to push aside the neckline of Iniabi's furs, warm lips leaving shivering touches everywhere they landed.

"Qimmiq...." Iniabi shoved off her outermost furs, the worst of the blood spatter falling with them. Free of the stuff, she shivered, leaning into Qimmiq's touches. She felt hot despite the cold and her skin flushed beneath Qimmiq's mouth. With clean hands, she tugged off the other woman's mittens. She wanted those fingers free. She wanted so much.

It didn't seem to matter to Qimmiq that the roof of the illu was open to the sky or the wind whipped through the uncovered door because she pulled her furs off quickly, tossing them aside as she had Iniabi's gloves. She didn't stop undressing until she stood in nothing but her boots and a thin undershirt, long enough to brush the tops of her thighs and hide the V of her legs. Iniabi was dizzy from the soft curve of her lover's body through the fabric, and Qimmiq smiled when she saw Iniabi's gaze on her. Qimmiq brushed her fingers down the length of her legs before peeling back the hem of her shirt. "Do you...?"

Iniabi tore her gaze from the pale sliver of Qimmiq's thigh beneath the rising hem of her shirt. She was already halfway out of her boots, her fingers working in a clumsy rush to rid herself of her tunic. "Yes, Qimmiq. Yes, I want—"

"Good. Me too." She slipped her fingers under the hem of Iniabi's trousers, using the ties to pull Iniabi in for another kiss. Iniabi winced in pain, her body suddenly reminding her of the cut she took to the hip.

"My brave warrior," Qimmiq said, kneeling before Iniabi to better inspect the wound. It wasn't deep, though it hurt. Qimmiq brushed cool fingertips against the cut, and which stung more, but Iniabi couldn't bring herself to care much, not with Qimmiq nuzzling against her thighs like that. "Should I kiss you and make it better?"

Qimmiq looked up, grinning a challenge, and Iniabi had to reach out and take hold of one of the illu's spars to keep herself upright. There was a bonfire blazing to life in her belly, and somehow, she knew it would spread. "I— Yes. Yes." Below her, Qimmiq's back was a gentle slope, widening to hips just covered by the thin shirt, the pale rounds of her toes tucked beneath the curve of her ass, and her breasts soft silhouettes. Iniabi had never seen anything so beautiful.

She all but lost her mind when Qimmiq brushed a dainty kiss over her leggings, between her legs instead of on her hip where the cut was. The hunter raised one eyebrow, her lips quirked in a half-smile, and when she peeled off the leggings, Iniabi felt no pain at all. It was like her mind couldn't hold it, not at the same time as Qimmiq's teeth lightly nibbling the inside of her thigh. Little breaths of air escaped Iniabi's mouth each time the other woman moved her mouth closer, a tiny "hah" punctuating each kiss or bite. Iniabi ran her hands through pale, feather-soft hair, brushing it back from Qimmiq's face until her mouth met Iniabi's center, and all the world fell away.

She stayed upright only because of her grip on the whalebone, one hand still in Qimmiq's hair. She stayed that way one minute, two and then sank slowly to the floor on the illu, her legs trembling. She'd been shaky before. Now, she couldn't stand.

"Sorry, Qimmiq. I can't. Not while you're doing that."

"Don't apologize for that."

Qimmiq licked Iniabi, one long, fast swipe, and giggled when Iniabi yelped at the intensity of it. "Qimmiq!"

The smile in Qimmiq's voice was somehow dangerous. "What? Do you want me to stop?"

Enough teasing. Iniabi put a hand on the top of Qimmiq's head and guided her mouth back down. The other girl went eagerly, groaning into Iniabi so that her whole body vibrated until she was rising through the depths of warm salt water into blinding, shocking light. Suddenly, the press of Qimmiq's tongue was as bright and uncomfortable as the kiss of flame.

Iniabi scooted back and lay panting, her legs still trembling occasionally. Qimmiq laid her head on Iniabi's belly, her hair a spill of silver across Iniabi's breasts, and Iniabi had the sudden, absurd fear that Qimmiq could not possibly be comfortable there so near Iniabi's sharp hip bones. Iniabi's body had known near-starvation for too many years before finding Taqqiq, and training as a warrior kept her whipcord sharp. She'd never be as soft as her lover.

"I'd like to do that to you," Iniabi said, as their breaths took on the same rhythm. The sun had passed out of view, and wind cooled Iniabi's hot cheeks.

She could just see the curve of Qimmiq's smile as she nuzzled against Iniabi's side, one hand coming to cup Iniabi's breast. Slowly her thumb drew circles around Iniabi's nipple, making it stand. "It's my secret, I can't tell you how, or you'll be too good for me."

Iniabi squeezed her eyes shut, running one hand down the other woman's neck and shoulder. Her mind rushed to show her how she would never be as good as Qimmiq— her past as a pirate, a poison dealer, her thirst for blood. The way her body refused, even now, to soften into the full shapes of maturity. Iniabi didn't repeat any of it. "There's nothing in the world that will ever be good enough for you, Qimmiq of the Taqqiq."

Her words seemed to startle Qimmiq out of her relaxed stupor, for she sat up suddenly, staring down at Iniabi through curtains of silver hair. When had her braids come undone? "You are good enough, Iniabi, Daughter of Manaba. You saved me, my village, and the village of Sinqiniq. You fought back when everyone else lost hope." She bent closer and pressed her brow to Iniabi's, sharing her breath. "I think I'm in love with you, Iniabi. You're the most exciting, brave person I know."

Iniabi framed Qimmiq's face with her hands, cupping her cheeks between her palms so that her thumbs rested on the other woman's cheekbones. For a moment, she said nothing, just stared up into blizzard eyes and tried to memorize the feeling of Qimmiq's hair just brushing her too-taut skin. "I'm in love with you, Qimmiq."

A breath wooshed out of Qimmiq, and she leaned in to press a kiss against Iniabi's mouth. When she pulled away, she looked up to the sky above them. "Then let's go dance and celebrate."

"I don't know if my legs will work enough for dancing," Iniabi groaned, but she let Qimmiq pull her to her feet, and after a few starts, they managed to get dressed and slip out of the illu. The celebration lasted long into the night, and they lost themselves to drinking and dancing until it came time to find the secret world of their illu once more.

CHAPTER 60: THE EMAI

SEVENTH MOON, 1801, VILLAGE OF SINQINIQ

Four Years before the Proclamation

"The hunters have seen signs of slavers again," Toklo said. He sat in the center of Sakari's illu next to Uki. The other two medicine women, Sedna and Tatik, were present, along with Chief Sakari and two elders from each village. Iniabi sat on one side of this esteemed council and fidgeted with impatience.

"The Pheceans and Lirians were at war. I suppose it was too much to hope for them to kill each other off. Now, they want slaves again," Iniabi said, speaking up before any others could voice their opinion. It was not strictly polite, but she did not have time to listen to them repeat the same quibbles. "More slavers means that we will face more attacks. Our village is too large, too prosperous to escape notice."

"We are far south and far inland. For years, we have lived without issue. Our hunters know not to leave tracks. Our people know not to make fires that will leave smoke. We are bigger now, but that means we have more resources to dedicate to hiding and securing ourselves." Sinqiniq's medicine woman's voice was steady and reasonably toned as she spoke, her gaze not coming to rest on Iniabi but Chief Sakari instead.

"Just this moon, we lost *two* lives to slavers. All around us, Emaians will be torn from their homes, raped, murdered, or shoved into the cramped bowels of disease-laden ships and then sold to work until they die miles from home. How drenched are Phecea and Liria with the spirits of Emaians who had no medicine women to show them the way home?" Iniabi took a deep breath, calming herself. Her voice was rising, which would not help her case in this circle. When she spoke again, it was decidedly softer. "My home was protected, and they took it all the same. We have proven that we can turn them away. We can end this suffering."

"By seeking out our destruction?" Toklo frowned as he spoke, looking at Iniabi as if she had grown a second head. "If we hunt down the Lirians, they will become aware of us. They will hunt us too. They aren't rabbits; they're wolves, Iniabi."

"They are not wolves. Wolves understand the Tundra. They know not to stray too far from their territory. The Lirians lose men every time they step foot into our lands because they do not know how to survive here. We would only need to attack at night, to burn their supplies or set their horses free. They would not survive long enough to make it home, much less to raid us. And they would have no one to fight, no one to follow back to a village."

Uki spoke up then, raising a surprised grunt from Toklo. "Iniabi speaks true. Violence is not the Emaian way, but it is certainly the Lirian one. Perhaps we should show them what it is to be alone and afraid, cold and defenseless on the Tundra."

"Uki, Daughter of Massak, you surprise me. Would you so willingly send our warriors off to die?" Akna said, her voice tense. Her eyes turned to Iniabi. "Would you leave your lover to mourn you so soon?"

"You ask them to die every day you keep them here where they cannot stop an attack until it is upon them!" Iniabi hit her leg with her fist. "Sila and Yun died because we did not know the attack was coming. Qimmiq might have been among them if I hadn't reached her in time. Waiting here, not knowing when to expect an attack wears down our warriors, and we are just as vulnerable to a surprise as the Lirians are. But if we decide instead of letting them decide for us, we won't lose warriors like Sila and Yun. I won't have to find my lover in the hands of a slaver."

The illu was silent, some faces thoughtful, others defiant. Finally, Chief Sakari spoke, her crisp manners breaking the tension. "Nothing will be decided today. War is a serious business, something we won't jump into impulsively, but neither will we sit by and do nothing. I think we can all agree to that."

Uki nodded to Iniabi. It was clear she was expected to leave now while the elders discussed other matters of the tribe. Iniabi gritted her teeth and stood, so angry that she could feel the heat in her cheeks. "I pray that you do not wait too long, Chief Sakari, for the lives that will be lost in the interim."

Iniabi swept from the illu, hurtling blindly away and into the village. Why must the elders be such cowards?! They stood between Iniabi and the end of Emaian safety. Her warriors were eager to fight. They kept their weapons sharp, trained daily, and whispered about tactics over their cook fires. They were ready for war, ready to follow Iniabi.

She crashed into the nearly-finished illu she shared with Qimmiq and pressed her hands over her eyes. The elders just did not understand what it was like. They had never been ripped from their homes, never felt the cold clamp of steel about their throats. Next meeting—no. Tomorrow, she would go to them again. She would tell them her story and show them the scars on her back that not even Qimmiq could stand to look at. She would show them and then—

"Iniabi?" Qimmiq's voice broke her chain of thought, and Iniabi looked up, surprised to see the dark sky behind her lover. How long had she been pacing in their illu? Qimmiq's face was contorted into something wary, and she let the flap of furs fall shut behind her as she came all the way into their home. "Aada said you left the council meeting angry… Are you still mad?"

The wariness in Qimmiq's expression reminded Iniabi of a much younger version of herself, standing half-cloaked in the folds of her home so that Manaba would not notice her. Guilt fell like wet snow over the fires of Iniabi's rage, and she shivered. Iniabi opened her arms to her lover and softened her posture. "I am still angry. The chiefs and elders would not hear my arguments. They think I'm foolhardy, but their timidness puts us all in danger. I'm so afraid of finding you in a slaver's arms again. I'm so afraid that if there is a next time, I'll be too late."

Qimmiq closed the distance between them, some of the tension she carried melting out of her face, making it soft and sweet again. Wrapping her arms around Iniabi's waist, the other woman hugged her tightly and then released her. "I understand. Another attack would be terrible, but you would protect us like before. I don't want you to go out there and get hurt when you could be safe here with me." Qimmiq's gloved hand slipped down Iniabi's arm, and their fingers entwined.

"I didn't protect everyone, though. We lost two warriors, one no more than sixteen. If next time they attack at night or in the evening while we're around our cooking fires instead of practicing with our weapons in hand, there's no telling how many more we could lose. The only way to be safe—the *only* way—is to attack them first, to keep them from reaching us." Iniabi rested her head in the crook of Qimmiq's neck. "I love this village, these people. I can't lose any more of them, not when I can stop it. Don't you understand?"

"I know you're a protector and a warrior. You don't like not doing something, but I think you may have forgotten how Emaians are. We talk everything out. Over and over again. We want all voices to be heard, even if that takes a little longer." Qimmiq laid a kiss on the crown of Iniabi's head, but she stiffened despite the affection.

"I wasn't stuck aboard that pirate ship long enough to forget who I am, Qimmiq. I know what it means to be Emaian." She stepped back and turned so that Qimmiq couldn't see her black slaver's eyes. "I just hope they don't talk so long that it puts the village in danger."

Iniabi felt Qimmiq withdraw, her voice pinched, "I didn't say... I didn't mean... Iniabi! I was just saying it's the Emaian way to take time with these things. Aada and Ataat are just being careful; surely you should understand that?"

Iniabi took a deep breath and forced her shoulders to relax. "I can try," she said, though as she and Qimmiq curled up to sleep that night, she could think of nothing but the fact that they had been careful too long. It hadn't helped them before.

⇑   ⇑   ⇑

One week later, Iniabi lay next to Qimmiq in their furs and waited for her to fall asleep. They were both loose-limbed and bare, Iniabi's hand resting comfortably on her lover's side. She listened while Qimmiq's breath deepened, evened out, while her limbs twitched with the coming of sleep. Overhead, an owl called out its hunting song, and Iniabi let the low coo permeate her skin. She, too, would be hunting soon. Like the owl disappearing into the night and home safe before morning.

Qimmiq sighed, slipping deeper into dream rhythms. She was fully asleep now, but Iniabi lay still and waited another hour before rising and slipping into her clothes. Iniabi tucked the furs around her lover's body and regretted, for a heartbeat, the necessity of leaving such a warm scene. But there was nothing for it, and she would be back before dawn. Someone had to protect the people even if the chiefs would not condone it. Iniabi belted on her sword and slipped into the night.

She found ten warriors waiting for her, crouched at the edge of the village along with Deniigi, the old trapper that had helped her and the Taqqiq reach Sinqiniq. When Iniabi joined them, they all rose silently and headed west until they could speak without being heard in the village.

"Deniigi has found signs of Lirians camped dangerously close by," she said, keeping her voice low. "We're going to ensure they don't leave the Tundra alive. It will be a quick raid; destroy their supplies and return home without a trace."

In the moonlight, Iniabi could see the wolfish grins of her warriors. They were a pack, flying out over the night on fleet feet, hunting in their territory. This was Emaian land, and they would keep the Emaian people safe from these intruders.

No one spoke, instead turning as one to follow Deniigi as he stepped forward. Despite the silver and black painting the landscape, he walked easily, making no noise. He seemed to know the location of every snow drift or shrub that might creak beneath his boot. The others of her party were stealthy, to be certain, but none moved with such eerie grace across the Tundra.

Too soon, Deniigi stopped, pointing down a small slope. The Lirians had found a natural depression in the earth and made their camp in the sparse shelter it gave. Even this late at night, she could hear a few voices. Sentries.

Coming to stand beside her, Deniigi whispered, "We can go around the front, where the hill ends, or down the slope. It's slick but not impossible."

Iniabi nodded shortly, her hand on her dagger. They would need to kill the sentries quickly to be able to sneak in and set fire to the supplies. "Which way is quietest?"

"Around the side. If someone slips on the crest of the hill...." Deniigi didn't wait for her response, instead turning to lead the group of warriors out and around until they finally could see the front of the camp.

The Lirians had made their camp in straight, unnatural lines, a box sitting in the wilderness. The front two tents would be commanders or leaders of some sort, and the back two were supplies and a healer. If they built in a circle, there would be no corners or edges for Iniabi and her wolves to hide behind, but the Lirians couldn't learn.

The first sentry showed himself while they kept silent and waiting. Iniabi's leggings were soaked with snow where she lay against the stuff in the shadow of a heavy drift. One of her wolves blew a dart laden with untreated urchin spine, and he dropped like so much senseless meat. Iniabi crawled closer, crouching behind the corner of a tent until the next sentry approached. Her knife seemed to leap from her hand, burying itself in his throat. A soft thump her told her that her wolves had taken a third sentry as well.

Together, they moved like shadows to the tents in the back, which must hold the supplies. A fourth sentry—one they had not expected caught sight of them then. His mouth rounded in surprise, his pimpled face oddly childlike in its wide-eyed expression. The soldier managed a half-strangled shout before Pakuk wrapped heavy hands around him from behind, and a sharp-faced woman named Capun put a knife in his heart.

Iniabi permitted herself a predatory smile as they slipped around to the entrance of the supply tents. This was all going so well. They were in without alerting the sleeping Lirians. All that was left now was to set fire to the—

The clink of a chain behind her halted Iniabi's thoughts. She knew that sound. She would know that sound every day that she lived, and it would haunt her alongside the crack of a whip and the keening of Emaian voices.

She turned, her heart thudding, to find the huddled forms of a dozen Emai in chains. They were pressed together as she remembered being, their bodies drawing warmth from each other beneath shared furs. They were out in the open, of course. Not permitted shelter. Just huddled between the camps so the sleeping Lirians would hear any escape attempts.

Iniabi's plan could not go forward. Destroying the supplies now would condemn these captives to death just as surely as their captors. They would have to fight, to kill every one of the Lirians if they wanted to free the Emai. And there would be no pretending this hadn't happened when they arrived back home with escaped slaves in tow. Iniabi closed her eyes. She would be punished for this. Qimmiq would be so angry.

And yet, she could not leave these Emai to die.

Iniabi turned to look at her wolves. They had fallen still, waiting for her to give them the word. "Leave the supplies," she hissed. "Freeing the Emai is more important. Kill as many of the slavers as you can before they wake to fight us."

Again her wolves grinned wide and fanned out to do as she bid. The small group of Emaians chained together was likely a hunting party or ice fishers, though that seemed unlikely this far from the coast. Whatever the reason, they were caught now and fell silent as Iniabi and her wolves crept into the Lirian camp. Wide eyes and pale faces stilled into masks of alarm and confusion, the youngest gasping in disbelief. Someone shushed the boy, and the only sounds filling the Lirian camp were the fires crackling and the muffled clank of chains as they dropped away from hands and feet. She didn't wonder where Deniigi had gotten the keys; the blood on his gloves was answer enough.

Only five more Emaians remained chained together when a shout rose, cut off in a strangled gurgle. Iniabi spun to see Capun's knife sliding across the throat of a Lirian soldier, half-dressed and black hair mussed with sleep. He must have come out of his tent to piss and found them instead.

His shout was enough, and voices clamored from all sides.

Iniabi didn't wait to let her enemies come to her, instead leaping over the fallen body of Capun's kill and ducking into the tent he had been exiting. Two more soldiers were inside, struggling to escape their bedrolls and grab their weapons. Perhaps someone would have said it was dishonorable to slay men half-dressed and trapped in their beds, but Iniabi thought stealing children from their homes to force them into slavery was worse. Her blade slashed across one Lirian's belly, and he screamed as his guts spilled out over his blankets. The other started babbling in his language, holding his hands out to stop her. The front of his pants darkened as he pissed himself.

For just a moment, the man looked human— afraid of death, of dying so far from home. Then, Iniabi remembered the bodies chained together outside. She flicked her blade across his throat, giving him a faster death than his companion.

Outside the tent, the camp was chaos. A few of the captured Emaians had taken up the weapons dropped by dead soldiers, but without understanding how to use them, they mostly got in the way, tripping up her wolves and making their task harder. The other freed slaves clustered against the hill, hiding the faces of their youngest to save them from the slaughter. Iniabi's fighters howled, filling the night with eerie cries as they hunted down their prey. The Sinqiniq fighters did not escape unscathed. Even as Iniabi watched, Pakuk took a deep cut along his bicep, and Aniki lay back against a tent, clutching a wound in her thigh.

Iniabi leaped back into the fray, fighting alongside her wolves to kill the last handful of remaining Lirians. It did not take them long. Soon, the Tundra was silent again, the sky above them lightening slightly with the first hints of dawn. They had won, and no Emaian lives had been taken, but still, Iniabi could not breathe easily. The day's trials were only just beginning.

She wiped sweat and blood spatter from her forehead. "Capun, bandage Aniki's thigh. Yotimo, take a look at Pakuk's arm. I don't need anyone dropping from blood loss on the way back. Everyone else, take what weapons and supplies you can carry. It's time to go home."

⇑ ⇑ ⇑

The sun was up by the time Iniabi made it back into camp. She did not try to hide what she had done—there was no point. By now, the village would know that she and a party of warriors had slipped away in the night. Many would have even guessed why. She stepped through the first ring of illus with her head held high and the youngest of the rescued Emai, a child of perhaps three or four, balanced on one hip. Let them look at her now, unbloodied and victorious. Let them see the people that followed her tucked carefully in the middle of her warriors and tell her she had done the wrong thing.

Let them. It would not stop Iniabi. Nothing would.

As they strode deeper into the village, the people of Sinqiniq and Taqqiq looked up from their skinning, their weaving, their mending. Many stood. Some even raised their voices in the howls of wolves preparing to hunt. Almost all of them showed some respect. Good. Iniabi would use that one day if she must.

When the party reached the center of the village, they stopped. It was empty, as it often was in the middle of the morning, but many of the villagers who had seen them come in now stood behind them, in between illus or crouched in the snow. Iniabi hadn't anticipated that she'd be facing the consequences of her actions with an audience, but so be it.

"Yotimo, please fetch the medicine women. Pakuk and Aniki need care, as well as some of our newly freed friends." Iniabi set the child down to stand on their own two feet.

As Yotimo disappeared between the illus, the voices of the

onlookers rose in a whispering hum. Everywhere Iniabi looked, pale faces eyed her, some craning their necks to better see the freed Emaians she had brought with her.

The clamoring stopped, and Iniabi turned in time to see why. Chief Sakari stood, finely chiseled face perfectly controlled, her expression giving nothing away.

"What is this, Iniabi, Daughter of Manaba?"

The rest of the crowd hushed, and she could hear the wind whistle through the village. A lone dog barked in the distance.

Part of Iniabi wanted to quake, to bend and ask for forgiveness. The same little girl who'd been so afraid of Manaba's wrath, so desperate to placate the captain, still lived somewhere within her. But to do that now, to take their victory and turn it into something to be ashamed of, would only dishonor the warriors that had fought alongside Iniabi, who had gone into the danger of the Tundra and brought back lost souls.

"Chief Sakari," Iniabi said by way of greeting. Yotimo returned with the medicine women behind them, and Chief Toklo stepped from his illu. "We've returned with neighbors that need our help. They were taken by slavers and might have spent the rest of their lives in Lirian hands had we not freed them."

Chief Toklo stared at the Emaians behind Iniabi and then walked to stand beside the Chief of the Sinqiniq. His back was straight, and his mouth a thin line. "You led some warriors to attack the Lirians in the middle of the night?"

Out of the corner of her eye, Iniabi caught movement. She shifted just enough to see Qimmiq pushing through the gathered crowd, her face red with exertion. She must have run back to the village when she heard Iniabi had returned.

What had Qimmiq thought when she awoke alone?

Iniabi swallowed guilt like bile and straightened her spine. "Yes," she said, pitching her voice to carry. "We attacked when we learned our enemy was close enough to put the village in danger and saved a dozen captives in the process."

Akna and two elders joined the chiefs, and Uki was aided there by Tatik. Sakari and Toklo murmured to one another, and the shorter woman stepped forward to speak. Her pale eyes never left Iniabi's face, and though her tone was stern, Iniabi had the strangest sensation of approval, as if Sakari's words were not her true meaning. "You went directly against the council's decision. We specifically told you to wait while we came up with a resolution for the nearby Lirians. Instead of respecting your chiefs, medicine women, and elders, you went out on your own whim and put the tribe at risk. Do you think yourself above the ways of your people, Iniabi?"

"I seek only to serve my people." Iniabi did not look away, not even to check on Qimmiq. "Whatever the cost, I will fight for them."

Again, Iniabi felt as if Saraki was on her side, despite the frown crossing her lips. "Those are pretty words that do not answer my question. We have all agreed to live by our ways, respecting the elders, council, and chiefs. You have gone against our wishes, no matter how noble the reason. Should I treat you as if you are above our laws, Iniabi, Daughter of Manaba?"

The crowd around them shifted, starting to whisper again. Tension grew. As Iniabi looked at Chief Saraki, the short woman shook her head slightly. "No, Chief Saraki, Chief Toklo. I am not better than our traditions. I will accept whatever punishment I receive, though I will not regret my actions."

One of the rescued Emaians, a large man who helped carry the children, stepped up. "Chiefs, Elders, please… Iniabi saved us from the Lirians. I know I do not belong to this tribe, and my voice is not one of yours, but I beseech you, be fair in your justice."

His words were like a stone thrown into a still pool, ripples of disgruntled remarks and looks spreading across the villagers. They didn't seem to want Iniabi to be punished at all. Chief Toklo and Saraki exchanged a look, and Qimmiq's Ataat stepped forward.

"Two days of isolation, Iniabi. I hope you use the time to think about your place in this tribe and what it means to be one of us. You cannot just do whatever you please and still live in harmony amongst your neighbors."

"Yes, Chief." If this was the price of her successful raid, then so be it. Iniabi had faced far worse trials than two days alone on the Tundra.

She had the feeling that she would face worse again. Her path would not be an easy one.

Chief Toklo stepped aside, and villagers made a path out of the illu. "Go now."

Iniabi turned and left back through the ranks of her warriors and the escaped slaves, past the woman she loved. Iniabi searched Qimmiq's face as she went, but Qimmiq only turned away as Iniabi fell through the cracks of the village and out into the snow.

CHAPTER 61: RHOSAN

FIRST MOON, 1802, CWM OR

Three Years before the Proclamation

The pits were cacophonous, a swell of sound rising in steady crescendo, pounding on the stone like a gale. The sun was high overhead, painting the blood on the pit floor too bright, even as a boy came to dust it liberally with sand.

Wynn was up next. He could hear slurred voices yelling his name along with wagers: Five gold pieces for Gruffyd's Defeated. Seven for Eurig's new man, the fighter that had beaten Dyfan in the Contender matches.

All Wynn could think about was that Dyfan's cell had been empty last night, just as it had during the previous moon's fight and the moon before. There had been six bouts since Wynn had laid eyes on Dyfan. Half a year without the one person in this place he cared about.

"Next Contender Match," the announcer bellowed, "Wynn, property of Victor Gruffyd, and Cadel, property of Victor Eurig! All wagers must be in before the start of the match! Today's weapon: the morning star!"

Dyfan had been pitted against two mountain lions, rumors said.

Others said three. They thought he was lucky to be alive. That he asked for it by refusing to breed.

Someone shoved Wynn towards the ring. The announcer must have called his name, but he'd been too lost in thought to hear it. He stepped down into the shallow dirt bowl. Where they fought for the enjoyment of people who controlled what they ate and when they shat and who they fucked.

"Defeated, lift your weapons!" The morning star felt good in Wynn's hands. Heavy. "May the best fighter take the match!"

It wasn't Cadel's fault that Eurig had ordered Dyfan to the lesser pits. He certainly hadn't chosen this life, hadn't asked to be bought by Eurig after beating Dyfan.

But he did represent an opportunity.

Wynn stood frozen in the center of the ring, his hands wrapped around the hilt of the morning star, his eyes glued to his opponent. Cadel was experienced in the ring. Wary. He would not make impulsive mistakes, and he was bigger than Wynn. He had just dropped into the weight class Wynn recently rose to. Wynn stretched, yawned, and waited. Cadel began to pace, his gait slightly awkward. He seemed to be favoring his right knee. Wynn smiled.

The crowd roared for blood. They didn't like it when fights started too slowly. It was boring, having to wait for their Defeated to bloody each other. Wynn looked up, searching the stands where the Victors lounged, his eyes passing over dozens of them until he spotted the cool mask of Dyfan's Victor. Eurig had taken Dyfan from him for moons.

And now, there was someone of Eurig's in the ring.

Only the whistle of a heavy object moving through the air alerted Wynn of Cadel's first attack. He leaped backward, avoiding the spiked head of his opponent's morning star. It had been a test, a cautious blow to see whether or not Wynn's apparent distraction was a ruse.

What a waste. If he had acted faster, swung harder... Wynn might have lost the match then.

Instead, Wynn turned and spat into the earth before raising his weapon. Cadel closed the distance between them, and a few glancing blows filled the ring with the sound of screeching metal before he danced away again. Still cautious, still testing.

Wynn played Cadel's game, letting his blows come just a little too slow, just a little too weak. Gruffyd's voice rang out over the crowd, "Wynn, take him out already!"

The Defeated almost smiled. He wasn't going to take Cadel out.

He was going to ruin him.

The next time Cadel came in, Wynn was ready for him. He feinted, starting a blow like he had half a dozen times before, only to change target, slamming the spiked ball into Cadel's unprotected midriff. The other Defeated crumpled inwards. When Wynn moved in to knock him off balance, he fell with little resistance, his face purpling as he gasped for air.

All Wynn had to do was keep him from getting back up. A blow to the kidney, maybe. A foot on the other man's chest. Instead, Wynn reared up and brought the full weight of his weapon down on Cadel's right knee.

It shattered. Like eggshell, like cheese. Crumpling in on itself with a gush of blood. Cadel screamed, and the sound wasn't human. Was hardly even animal.

Had Dyfan made a sound like that when the cats injured him?

Wynn dropped his weapon and stepped away, panting. Sweat dripped in lazy lines down his back. The Victors were roaring again. They always did.

"And the match goes to Wynn, property of Gruffyd!" The announcer hauled Wynn's fist into the air. Victor Eurig hadn't moved. He stood as still as Wynn, unaffected by the noise.

Gruffyd gripped Wynn's shoulders. Somehow, he had made it down to the ring. "Next, Wynn will be coming to you. Keep an eye out for the Victory tour!"

Finally, Wynn tore his eyes from Eurig. Tour? What if he didn't see Dyfan before he was taken away? What if Dyfan was killed in the lesser pits while he was gone? Wynn shivered despite the heat of battle, and once it began, the shaking would not stop.

Irritated, Gruffyd shoved him toward the arena's edge. "Quickly now! Someone get him to a cell."

What did it matter if these people saw him shake? He would be taken from this place to maul other captured men, and for what? So they could destroy Dyfan? Wynn clenched his fists, half fighting the Defeated who came to escort him back to his cell. Let him return to the pit. Let him die in it.

They got him back, though, eventually. Into the little stone room, away from the noise and the blood. In the quiet, Wynn sank to the ground, his heart thudding against his rib cage as though trying to escape it. The other Defeated left him there, habituated to his attacks.

They were taking him away.

Would he ever see Dyfan again?

CHAPTER 62: PHECEA

FIFTH MOON, 1801, DIOSION

Four Years before the Proclamation

The hardest part of getting out of the Mavros estate was escaping her rooms. There was no reason for a rough-clad girl to be leaving the bedroom of the eldest Mavros daughter. If anyone saw her, they would raise the alarm, and Basia's chances for excursions alone in the city would be over.

It was a good thing she had Keme.

He could exit her room or stand in the hallway without raising suspicion, so, when he gave her the all-clear, Basia could slip from her room in a servant's homespun garb and into the narrow stairway just a couple doors down.

From there, it was easy. She only had to remember to hunch her shoulders and keep her eyes down, and then Basia was just one of the servants constantly moving through the bowels of a Phecean noble household. To get back in, she would need only a basket or a parcel, and she would look as though she was returning from some errand. Really, it was a weakness, she supposed. But one no other noble thought to take advantage of.

At the door to the kitchens, she was stopped. A fearsome woman with a nose like a clothes iron and a stained white smock gripped her by the upper arm. Basia's heart held its breath. Had she been too cocky, thinking she could slip out without question?

The woman shoved a pail into Basia's arms. "Fill this with water from the well and be quick about it."

Basia relaxed and ducked her head. "Yes'm." It was better to do the chore than have the kitchen staff ask questions later.

She filled the bucket, surprised by its weight, and sloshed the water when she set it in the kitchen. Amid all the chaos, she only earned a sharp glare. After that, it was easy enough to slip away. In the noble quarter, the Mavros estate was closest to the market, with the grand Othonos home the farthest, seated at the highest point on the cliff above the Eastern Sea. The other houses lay in that manor's wake, draping the cliffside until they met the town, which curled on down to the harbor and the sea. Diosion was shaped like twisted letter C, so the Othonos estate looked down on the harbor at the bottom of the crescent.

The market was excellent entertainment if you were a noble with coin to spend, but it was full of the upper crust of Phecean society: brightly colored merchants held out wares for men and women from aristocratic families, and guards in crisp uniforms watched for signs of theft. In her current garb, Basia would stick out unless she looked like she was on a specific errand, which didn't fit her current mission at all.

Basia wanted to see more of Phecea's people than just the nobility she had known all her life. Living on the cliff above them was like living in a beautiful, protective cage. One couldn't see much peering through the bars.

So, Basia would have to go where the people were.

The market faded behind Basia in a cloud of noise and smells, replaced by quieter streets lined with homes and shops that primarily served the middle city. Couples and families strolled past, enjoying the warm fall evening after the surprising heat of the day. They spoke in small groups or drooled over window displays of carpentry or sweets. None of them glanced twice at Basia. Many of these families likely had members who served in the noble quarters; it was nothing strange to see a servant girl returning home in the evening.

As Basia went on, the cheerful facades of stone homes and storefronts draped in brightly colored awnings faded into dimly-lit buildings with soot-stained windows and too-watchful residents. Ahead, the city's great warehouses rose above the harbor, blocking the sea from view, though Basia could trace the curve of the noble quarter, arching up and to the north. The one exception to this downtrodden scene was a bar, too close to the warehouses to be particularly high-class, too far from the harbor to be a brothel or a gambling den. It was plain stone on the outside with a dark cherry door and a sign advertising a storyteller named Madame Rhea Gabris. The windows were clean. There was a waft of fiddle music and a low hum of voices coming from inside, and several groups of people stood around the front, talking or smoking from long, narrow-bored pipes.

Basia knew from previous excursions into Diosion that the Cormorant's Rest had the best dark ale on this side of the Bathi and that it drew a uniquely varied list of patrons. She had never been inside before, but she didn't hesitate in front of the door. Basia gripped the handle and stepped into a world of noise and smells. There were only a few empty tables and none of these were near the central fire where someone had set a stool for Madame Rhea. The fiddle player balanced his case upon it and placed his instrument inside. There were so many voices, all trying to be heard, that Basia had no idea how she could learn anything useful, but she pushed her way to an empty table regardless. She wouldn't let one of her precious nights away from the Mavros estate go to waste.

"May I get you anything?" Basia tore her eyes from the room to focus on the Emaian woman standing at her table. She was better dressed than most slaves, and while she kept her eyes downturned, her lips were pursed in something like annoyance.

"Yes, please. I would like a tankard of the house ale and a bowl of whatever is over the fire. It smells great." She tried a smile, but the woman just held out her hand.

"That will be two coppers." Her Phecean was heavily accented, and she pronounced every syllable as though they lay uncomfortably in her mouth. Not like Keme. He spoke the language as well as any Phecean, though he was a captured slave rather than a bred one. This server must have been captured, too, despite the rarity of captured slaves in Phecea.

Basia felt around in her pocket for the smallest coins, careful not to draw out any gold or silver, and placed them in the woman's palm. "Thank you."

This last courtesy seemed to surprise her. The woman glanced over her shoulder, where the room's attention had turned to the storyteller settling herself before the fire. She looked at Basia again, hesitated, and then brought three fingers to her lips.

It was the Emaian gesture of respect. Keme had explained it to Basia years ago, but it seemed to symbolize more than he let on. Like a word that had taken on a new meaning between a group of friends.

Basia touched three fingers to her lips. It was like saying, "should you wish to speak, I will hear you," or close to it. Keme said it didn't translate well to any spoken language, much less Phecean.

The woman's eyes widened again, and she turned to disappear into a door behind the bar. Basia had the sinking feeling that she had drawn attention to herself when she ought to have just been here to listen.

"There once was a man who lived in Diosion by the name of Azarios. He had a good life. He ran a business selling the work of great artists and devoted his life to the gift of beauty. He made it possible for the people of Diosion to find the art that most moved them. He had a caring family and a well-kept home but never married. Azarios was misfortunate in one respect: he fell in love with one of his artists, a woman named Niky who had already married another.

Azarios knew that this was folly. He had not set out to love someone he could not be with. Still, it seemed as though his love for Niky was both inevitable and inescapable. She understood him, and no craft was as graceful as her sculptures.

Because he was a man of understanding, Azarios turned to the philosophers of Diosion for guidance. He went to the halls of the nobility to attend their lectures and so first heard the advice of a young noble: "It is of utmost importance to be honest before anything else. No matter what you say, so long as it is the truth, the outcome will always be the best possible result, even if you fear what will come about due to your words."

Azarios left the noble quarter feeling like a great weight had been taken from his shoulders. He would tell Niky how he felt, and if she never spoke to him again, he would at least have done the right thing. However, on his way through the market, Azarios was stopped by the sight of another philosopher.

This man wore plain linens over his warm skin. He was in his prime and beautiful. 'Of all the things we say to each other, our vows are the most important. Those who would break a vow or come between the promises of others are the worst of us.'

Azarios was stricken. If he told Niky the truth, was he attempting to come between her and her husband? Even if he expected nothing of her, wouldn't telling her be the wrong thing to do?

Azarios turned from the square and found a small public garden where an older woman scattered stale bread for pigeons. Her eyes were creased, but she had a gentle smile. He sat beside her, and after a time, she spoke, though he was unsure if it was to him or the birds. 'All that we have, we will lose in time. So appreciate what you have while you have it. Do not lose it for want of something more.'

The art seller sighed. If he were to take her advice, he should just appreciate Niky for her art and understanding and not lose them out of a desire to tell her how much he cared. This was perhaps the most selfless option: Niky would keep his friendship and be untroubled by his confession.

He stood and wandered back to the street to find his way home, but halfway there, he encountered a crone crouched along the path. A cloth was tied around her blind eyes, and her outstretched hand was thin with extreme age, her knuckles bulging along her fingers. 'There is nothing greater in this life than love,' she told him as he placed a coin in her palm. 'Be wary of losing it. For without it, you will never truly be happy.'

Azarios made it to his home, but he was more unsettled than ever. Should he be honest and selfish, silent and giving? Should he cherish what he had or gamble for the love he would otherwise never have?

He could make no decision, find no course. And so Azarios did nothing.

He did not tell Niky the truth or lie for her happiness. He did not cherish her or give her the chance to love him. He spent his life without solving his dilemma, so they were fated to find each other again in the next life and face the same problem."

Basia blinked. She hadn't expected the story to end so dismally, and evidently many of the audience shared her dismay. There were low murmurings among the guests, but they seemed to have lost some of their revelry.

A tall, slender person with short, brown curls stopped at Basia's booth and rested their arm on the back of her chair. "So, what did you think of the story?"

Basia was taken aback. They were beautiful in red and black silk, with a long, pointed nose and high cheekbones above lovely pouting lips. For once, she didn't have an answer right away.

"I thought it was a horrible choice." A tall woman with skin darker than Arsenio Othonos and hair shaved nearly to her scalp slid into the seat opposite Basia. "People don't want bad endings at the beginning of the night. She should have saved that one until everyone was deep in their cups." She flashed a startlingly white smile to a thin, pale scholar who walked with a cane, his opposite arm clutched around a book. He lowered himself into the seat next to her.

"I think the entire thing is based on a faulty premise. How would this Azarios even fall in love with Niky if he knew she was already taken? It's just silly."

The slender person sat beside Basia, pushing her over with a bony hip. "I heard a rendition down on the docks where Azarios gets over himself, tells her, and then has a fantastic time with Niky *and* her husband."

"You did not, Lex!" The dark-skinned woman rolled her eyes at them. She was as muscled as a soldier, her hands bound in leather gloves with studded knuckles. "That's just what *you* wanted to happen."

They shrugged and looked back at Basia. "You didn't answer my question."

She blinked at them. She didn't know any of these people. Did they just want her table, or had they singled her out because she was alone? "Who are you?"

Instead of answering, the one called Lex gave her a sharp, appraising look. "You said 'thank you' to your Emaian server."

"So?"

"We'd like to buy you a drink, is all." They smiled, and the dark-skinned woman flagged down another server.

"That level of courtesy is decidedly uncommon around here," she said.

"I'd go so far as to say that most Pheceans are rude." Lex had an easy way of talking. Slow and drawn out. They couldn't be much older than Basia.

She was having a hard time keeping up. All three of them were a bit larger than life. "You're not Pheceans?"

"Of course we are!" The scholar looked rather put out. "Well, except for Zol. Are you really that dull? Ilia said you knew the gesture and everything."

"Don't be so hard on her, Eros!" The woman, evidently Zol, said. She pounded the scholar on the shoulder good-naturedly, and he hardly kept his seat. "I'm Zolelan, though I've been here so long I don't see how it really matters."

The Emaian woman that had taken Basia's order arrived at the table then, carrying a tray laden with tankards and bowls. She handed them out to choruses of "Thank you, Ilia" and winked at Basia when handing over hers. None of the others failed to treat her courteously, and Basia couldn't help but wonder what Keme would have thought of this bunch. They were as vibrant as any pirate crew she had dreamed up.

"I'm Lex, that's Eros, and the big scary one is Zol if you hadn't figured that out by now. You could call us the Society of the Preservation of Not-Being-Assholes—"

"Society for the Preservation of Courtesy!" Eros cut in.

"Yeah, sure. Didn't you hear the story? You shouldn't spend so much time listening to philosophers."

Basia leaned forward. "I thought it was about getting over yourself so that you could bed married women and their husbands?"

Lex guffawed at that, and Zol spewed half of the ale she was in the middle of swallowing. Eros just sighed. "Yet again, I am surrounded by heathens...."

They didn't speak of slaves again that night, but the banter continued until Basia could hardly hold herself upright. It felt as though the liquor in her belly kept sloshing around, pulling her off balance in one direction or another. It was a miracle that she made it back to the Mavros estate and into her rooms, but when she did, she fell into a drunken slumber.

⇑ ⇑ ⇑

The note Basia received in the morning only said two words: *come quick!* In Danae's familiar looping script. It was almost too early to count as morning, the sky tinted with the barest blush of pink. Basia dragged herself out of bed, squinting at the uncomfortable brightness, and dressed herself to go. She rode with the messenger back to the Othonos estate.

The mixture of last night's liberties, the uncomfortable sway of the carriage, and worry turned Basia's belly into a knot of squirming grubs. She thought she might throw them up, spill slimy maggot bodies all over the seats of the Othonos's carriage. Danae had never sent such a short message before or so early in the morning. If she was at home, she had to be safe, right? Nothing bad would happen at the Othonos estate. Was it her parents? Something else?

Despite the note's urgency, the servants and slaves in the Othonos house didn't seem worried or in a rush. One bowed to Basia, as always, and showed her to the sitting room as usual. No one hurried her up the stairs to Danae's room. An Emaian slave came with the customary tray of treats and bowed to Basia before asking if she needed anything else. The house was quiet.

Councilor Arsenio came in to greet Basia, as he often did when she visited, though this was the first time she had seen him in many moons. The Council was busy these days, with the war building momentum. Danae was often alone in the house as her parents traveled between the provinces attending Council business.

Despite the earliness, Danae's father looked well groomed, as if he had already been awake for some hours. He nodded in greeting to Basia and turned toward the tray ladened with tea and sweetened rice cakes. "Good morning, Basia—correct?" He glanced over his shoulder as he spoke, smiling more as Basia nodded. "Do you take honey in your kava?"

Something in Basia relaxed at the Councilor's greeting. Her friends and family had not had much trouble calling her by the name she had chosen for herself, but even their support had not quite been able to quell her fears of what Danae's father would think. He was the leader of their province, one of the ten most influential people in the Confederacy, and he thought she was Basia. Like she knew she was.

Basia cleared her throat. "Yes, sir."

Councilor Arsenio nodded as he settled into one of the gracefully carved chairs across from Basia and sipped his cup of kava tea. "I'm glad you're here, Basia, though I can't imagine what it is my daughter needs you for so early. I was thinking about you the other day. A spot has opened up in the office that handles shipping and trade. As you surely know, with this war, Phecea stands to lose access to many goods our citizens rely on." Councilor Arsenio leveled brown gold eyes onto Basia, the same eyes his daughter shared. "I've seen your creative thinking in action, though admittedly more to do with social situations than forging trade alliances… I think you would be an asset to Phecea."

Basia forced herself to swallow the kava in her mouth rather than spitting it onto the floor. A position in Phecea's trade office was second only to being an ambassador and often was an essential step to becoming one. The Office of Trade answered only to the Council rather than to the leaders of individual provinces, and positions could only be attained through appointment by a council member. It was the sort of opportunity that would entirely change Basia's life, not to mention that with her training to be a Trade Official, her spot in the city office would become available. Maybe her sister Melba would be able to take it after her birthday at the beginning of the year, securing them both prominent positions in the government.

No more would people say the name Mavros was failing.

"I—" Basia realized then that she had been quiet too long. "Thank you, Councilor. I cannot begin to say how grateful I am for the opportunity."

"Excuse me, Mistress Basia?" That was Yuka, waiting by the door to the sitting room, ready to show Basia up to Danae's room.

Councilor Arsenio nodded in dismissal. "We'll talk more, yes?"

"Yes, sir!" Basia bowed, the low formal bow for a respected leader, trying not to stumble or vomit. Her knees felt weak and shaky all the way out of the room.

Yuka strolled up the stairs and towards Danae's room at the end of the hall, and her pace further implied that nothing terrible had happened to her mistress. Yuka bowed as Basia went through the doors and shut them behind her.

"Basia! Good, you're here. Look!" Danae towed Basia over to the standing mirror in the corner and then stood in front of it. "Watch." Danae waited until Basia's gaze was on the mirror, and then bounced on her toes.

Basia cocked her head, more than a little confused. The gauzy curtains hanging from Danae's windows had been thrown open, and the light was making her head pound. She couldn't keep up with everything this morning, which perhaps was a good thing. If she tried, she thought it might test her stomach too much.

"Did you see it? *Look*!" Danae jumped more forcefully this time. She wore a light summer tunic and leggings, curls tousled as if she had spent the morning toying with them.

"Um, your curls *do* look particularly bouncy this morning." Basia hooked her ankle around the stool at Danae's vanity and pulled it over so she could sink into it. Humors, it felt good to sit down. The Othonos estate stairs were brutal.

"My curls? What are you talking about?! You must be blind. Look!" Danae's enthusiasm, usually welcomed, was grating this early in the morning. She turned, pulling her tunic tight down her front. She pivoted left and right. Eyes bright, smile eager.

And there, barely more than a pinprick stood out the smallest of curves from her chest. The starting of breasts.

"Congrats, Danae! Welcome to puberty." Basia gave her a winning smile, only slightly less charming than usual. For her, puberty was a nightmare, a betrayal of her body that she did her best to hide or change. It would seem a miracle for Danae, who had long beaten herself up over her lack of curves. "See? I told you it would happen!"

Danae glowed as she turned to inspect herself in the mirror again, admiring how the tunic fell over her chest. "I've got a few hairs under my arm, too."

"Nice! You're practically an adult now. We should throw a party and not tell anyone we're celebrating your arm hairs, but secretly that'll be what it's for."

Danae blushed, turning away from her mesmerizing reflection. "Are you well? You look... pale."

"I'm fine! I made a few friends in the city last night and might have drunk a bit too much." Basia winced, suddenly remembering a blurry scene somewhere along her fourth tankard. She'd been gawping at Lex.

"What do I call you?"

"I told you my name! Did you forget already? It's Lex. L. E. X. Maybe we ought to cut you off."

"No, I mean, do you prefer him or her?"

"What does it matter, kitten? We both know you're attracted to me."

Basia groaned and hid her too-pink face in her hands. "I think I made a fool of myself."

"How? You always know what to say. Did you call anyone fat?"

"Well, no...."

"Well then! You're likely over thinking it. Now." Danae's smile widened, standing to return to her reflection. "Could we make new tunics that are sleeveless, or... I don't know... lower cut?"

Basia smiled. That was something she could do without putting her foot in her mouth. "Call Yuka and ask her to bring us sewing supplies. Oh, and plenty of tea."

CHAPTER 63: PHECEA

ELEVENTH MOON, 1801, LEFKARA

Four Years before the Proclamation

Danae stared out of the window in her room in the Zodrafos estate. It was quiet, the paper in her hand half-forgotten. Outside, the streets were clean, swept red clay that glowed in the last hours of sunlight. A few well-dressed citizens walked past, but most traveled in carriages when leaving the noble quarter. Probably because the rest of the city was so much worse—dirty, dark, strewn with starving poor and wounded soldiers. Danae again wondered about the difference in patrols between the markets and the wealthier areas of Lefkara.

She had asked Master Annas, and his answer had only confused her more.

"Let us exercise our minds. What, Othonos, is the *most* important part of Lefkara? Consider its placement on the Ligo Bathi River, and its proximity to the border."

Danae recalled the image of Lefkara on a map. The smaller branch of the Bathi River was north of the city, and to the west was Liria's border. Which location was more vulnerable? More valuable? Before she could answer, Master Annas spoke again.

"Now, consider what Lefkara's importance is to Phecea. The

nation and soldiers need food, so the farmlands *must* be protected. But, if the border goes unguarded, then Lirian forces will come through and attack the city and our ports along the Bathi. How do you choose which to focus on?"

Danae frowned. She didn't know. "But what about the people?"

"Another essential consideration. Lefkara has a strong population of artists, thinkers, craftsmen, and soldiers. Do you protect the regular citizens, the valuable farmers and artists? The soldiers who protect us? The nobility who run the government? If you need to feed and arm more soldiers, where will the gold come from? Who will pay for their food and gear?"

Danae shook her head. "I do not know."

"It is a great responsibility. One you are learning to shoulder. Your time shadowing Councilor Janus Zodrafos will hopefully shed some light on the matter for you."

Having retired to her room early, Danae still grappled with the question. The city wasn't desolate by any stretch of the imagination, but it was tense. Poised for trouble. The constant vigilance left everyone, nobleman and merchant alike, holding their respective breaths. She wondered how long they could go on like this. Lefkara had been under regular attacks since the start of the war in 1800.

With a sigh, she looked away from the window and turned to settle at the writing desk. She had promised Basia she would write as often as possible while touring Phecea. Of course, she had known it would happen when she turned fifteen, yet when her parents explained it was time, Danae felt blindsided. All fifteen-year-olds in Phecea started their apprenticeships— even Council members' heirs, who traveled to learn from the Confederacy's leaders.

It was a year touring the provinces and learning to be one of the ten rulers of her country. A year away from her home and her family and her friends. It might as well have been a lifetime.

Danae looked down at her paper. She would not tell Basia how often she cried without reason or that her breasts, small as they were, were tender and swollen. Nor would she tell her friend how fearful things felt here. How it seemed to Danae that Phecea sat on the edge of a sword, waiting to fall off one way or the other. Victory or defeat, strength or starvation.

She picked up her pen.

Dear Basia,

I already miss the bright streets of Diosion, and I've only been gone three weeks. The ride to Lefkara was tedious, the roads often muddy from late spring rains. I told my guards that I could ride to keep the carriage from getting stuck, but they assured me I must not. Apparently, my status as Othonos heir makes me too precious to ride out in the open. Even in the empty countryside where there is no one to see.

Instead, I spent the entire trip with Master Annas droning about the duties and administrative responsibilities of being a Council Member. As if I don't know from first-hand experience. Have I not spent countless moons alone in the Othonos estate because mother and father were away seeing to that work?

You know I am not prone to rude remarks, but I had to bite my tongue during those days locked in the carriage. Now that I've arrived in Lefkara, I wish to be back in that cursed carriage. This city is not the Phecea I know. People rush through the streets, and soldiers on and off duty are everywhere. Their rigid uniforms and tendency to carouse at night are disconcerting.

The streets are dirty, and many buildings are in ill repair. I know Diosion is not a utopia, but we do not let our poor get so... wretched. I have even seen lines forming for the bakeries and market stalls, and Master Annas says that supplies are less abundant here, so there are fewer food stalls. People have to wait. They don't have the choice to shop as you and I are used to.

I find myself both disturbed by this truth and wishing I didn't have to know it. Am I a coward for not wanting to look upon their discontented faces? Is it foolish to miss the bright, beautiful streets of Diosion when people are struggling here?

Who knows.

I hope you are doing well and that your new position in the Trade Administration is proving as interesting as we hoped it would be.

I cannot believe we won't see each other for a full year. I'm not ashamed to admit I miss you, though not as drastically as when I first left. The loneliness is not so bad, not because I have gained new companions, but because I am growing accustomed to my own company.

Yours,
    Danae Onthonos.

⇑   ⇑   ⇑

First Moon, 1802, Phecean Confederacy, Diosion

Dear Danae,

The news of Lefkara is troubling. Here in Diosion, we only hear good tidings of the war: that the Lirians are unable to gain a foothold or that we have turned them aside at sea. If Lefkara is as you describe it, then this cannot all be true. The Confederacy is under more strain than the Council would have us believe. I understand they don't want us to panic, but even in the Office of Trade, hopes for a quick end to the war are high. I don't think we are prepared for any other outcome...

Diosion has changed in your absence. The streets are still beautiful, and the sea still sparkles below our cliff-hang overlook, but we have started to see shortages as well. They aren't called that here. They say, we are sending as much as we can to feed the brave soldiers on the front. They say, "How can you grieve the loss of wine and fine cloth while the vineyards grow provisions and the ships keep your coast safe?" And so, no one seems to mind. It is frightening to think that we might not have these things because the farms are being trampled by booted feet and the ships lie beneath the sea.

Ion has left to join the war front. He is the youngest son of his family, and they were proud to send him, but Adohnis has not been the same since he left. I think that they had some sort of disagreement just before, but I haven't had a chance to ask. All of our friends seem wrapped in new jobs and responsibilities.

I'm still so grateful—

"Still so grateful that you met me?"

Basia jumped, bumping into Lex, where they peered down over her shoulder. The loft above the Cormorant's Rest was otherwise empty besides the old table where Basia sat and the barrels and boxes of backstock needed to run a popular pub. Two floors down, the tables were likely filling with patrons, but it was inaudible from where she worked on her response to Danae.

"No. Don't you have anything better to do than read over other people's shoulders?"

Lex sighed dramatically and dropped into the chair at Basia's right. "Of course. You're more than just grateful you met me. You're probably ecstatic. Unbearably joyful. Downright flooded with inescapable, overflowing happiness." It would have just been silly, perhaps, if it wasn't for the too-knowing smirk they flashed in Basia's direction.

Basia could feel the tips of her ears reddening, but she resolutely turned back to her letter.

I'm still so grateful to your father for offering me the job in the Trade Office, but it certainly keeps me busy. There's so much to learn! Evidently, that Ingolan magic woman left because of the war—they're really finicky about their mages being used in battle— and our sanctions didn't work against Liria at the beginning of the war because they had already wrested total trade rights from Tupa Gali. Not to worry though! We just managed to form an alliance with Zolela that should make a big difference against Liria.

I've been seeing a lot more of those friends—

"Oh! Is this the part where you talk about me instead of boring things like war and trade agreements?"

Basia groaned and pulled her letter closer to her chest. "Can't you go bother someone else, Lex? It's not yet time for the meeting."

They sighed and stood, trailing their fingers across Basia's back, so she had to hide her shiver. "Alright, but hurry up. The others will be here soon. Do you want anything from the bar?"

"Just a cup of tea, thank you." It was hard enough to keep her head straight with Lex around, much less with alcohol in her belly.

—those friends I told you about before you left. They're an interesting

bunch, and they keep me on my toes. I'll have to introduce them to you when you get home.

Be careful, Danae! Do what your guards ask—they're there to keep you safe. Maybe you can ride when you're not so close to the war front? It still seems so long before you get home, and I can't wait to see you again. I miss you so much! Learn lots and travel well.

WITH LOVE,

BASIA MAVROS

EROS WALKED IN, one spindly arm over-filled with books, leaning heavily on his cane. Once, Basia would have rushed to aid him, to take the books out of his arms or pull out a chair for him to sit in. Now, she understood that it would only frustrate him. Lex said Eros was born with one half-useless leg and had spent a good amount of his time since then proving that he was just fine without it. Basia wasn't about to disagree.

"Hey, Eros," she said as the scholar sat down. "What'd you bring for us?"

He hooked his cane on the table and sat back with a remarkably self-satisfied smile. "You'll just have to wait until the others get here. I don't want to ruin the surprise."

Basia eyed the dusty tomes. What could possibly be hidden in such an uninspiring package? Certainly nothing worth being so smug about? She didn't have time to press further, though, because both Lex and Zol came barreling up the stairs. Lex slid around the table and threw themselves into one of the seats opposite the door. They propped one elbow on the table, hand open towards Zol, who sat down only a little more sedately. She repeated the motion, gripping Lex's slender hand.

"Alright, so the rules are the first person's hand to touch the table loses. For five gold pieces."

Eros groaned. "Not this again...."

"You got it. I'm warning you, though, you might want to back down. I got an old sailor to teach me a trick that will win every time." Lex's eyes were bright, and their lips cracked in a savage smile.

Zol just rolled her eyes. "On three: One, two... three!"

Lex's hand smashed into the table so hard their eyes watered, and they shook their fingers to stop them from stinging. "Zol, you brute! Why'd you have to do it so hard?"

"My turn!" Basia leaped up from the table. "I bet one gold piece I can last twice as long as Lex."

Zol cracked one eyebrow. "Who're you betting? Me or them?"

"I'll take the bet." Lex moved over one seat so Basia could take the chair across from Zol. "It's a simple game. You just have to prove that you're stronger than our brave Guardswoman."

"Stronger than *you*, you mean." Basia put her elbow on the table and flexed her hand, cocking her eyebrow at the Zolelan woman. "What do you think?"

She reached out and took Basia's grip in her own strong, callused fingers. The studded gloves she wore were surprisingly smooth. Zol smiled so that her cheeks made mounds of her honey eyes. "I think a passing breath of stale summer wind is stronger than that ridiculous creature."

"Well then, my bet seems secure."

"I wouldn't count your gold before you've got it, noble girl."

Basia rolled her eyes at Lex and then turned back to the table. "On my count: One, two—"

The door banged open, and both Zol and Basia flinched. Ilia stood, one hand on her hip and her pointed features drawn together in a sneer. She flipped her alabaster hair back over her shoulder. "Well, if it isn't the Society for the Preservation of Absolutely Nothing Useful. I don't know why Vel lets you use this space. We could have more storage."

She dropped the tray full of drinks on the table, and Lex smiled charmingly at her. "Thank you, Ilia! I forgot I'd left that downstairs."

"I believe Velia thinks we could accomplish much for your people within Phecea," Eros said. He glared hard enough at Basia and Lex that Basia had to check to ensure they weren't freezing over. "If only we could stop playing and begin the meeting."

Zol sighed and leaned back. "Yes, thank you for the reminder, Ilia."

The Emaian woman huffed and rolled her eyes, turning to go back downstairs. She and Vel would be busy for hours.

"I have proof that slavery in the confederacy began in response to the formation of Liria," Eros started, folding his warm, pale fingers into steeples above his stack of books. "Loratos began the practice, and slave labor was one of the tools they used to conquer so many of the original city-states. The early Phecean Confederacy, eager to adopt any advantage in the war to turn away Liria, took up the practice. Over time, slavery became so integrated into both cultures, they began to consider it the norm. Emaian slaves became chattel, to be traded between Phecea and Liria like grain or timber."

The gravity of what they faced struck Basia then. Hundreds of years of habit, tradition, and convenience. Beside her, Lex shook their head, curls falling artfully over their well-structured face. "It's such a big, pervasive thing to try to stand against."

"Where do we even start?" It was the first time Basia had ever seen Zol anything less than confident.

She thought of Keme, of his stoic advice, his steady support. Of the family and home he once had. She thought of Ilia and Vel and how Ilia had to pretend to be a slave just to exist within the Confederacy. This couldn't be allowed to continue, but neither would it crumble in a day.

Basia took a deep breath. "I think I have an idea...."

CHAPTER 64: THE EMAI

FIRST MOON, 1802, VILLAGE OF SINQINIQ

Three Years before the Proclamation

Iniabi lay belly-down in the snow, ignoring the spread of cold through her torso, the slight dampening of her tunic as her body heat melted the powder beneath her. The white wolf pelt draped over her head and body kept her warm enough even as it blended her form into her surroundings. Below her stretched the Tundra, cloaked in white but for the stubborn protrusions of rock or sparse plant life. Something moved, a flash of sun reflecting off steel. And then again. Iniabi smiled.

The Emaian woman slipped backward off her raised hill and around to the plain below, moving slowly, carefully. The closer she got, the easier it was to see the still, fur-cloaked form. The armor that gave him away, a glint of light against the white and gray. When Iniabi was close enough to touch him, she rose from the snow like one of the wraiths that stalked these plains and looped a thin cord around his neck, planting her knee in his back and letting her weight bear down upon him. It took a few moments, his weakened fingers scrabbling at the snow, at Iniabi, at the weapons sheathed at his waist. He died ignobly, yet it was still a fairer death than what he would have given Iniabi.

She stepped back, raised a hand in signal, and began to loosen the dead man's belt, removing his sword, quiver, and long knife. She took the armor strapped to his chest, legs, and arms, dumping out his bag to sort through what was inside. Useful items went to one pile and cast-offs to another. These were all for the Wolves, Iniabi's small but growing group of fighters. Emaian weapons had their place—they fed the village, kept predators at bay, turned away small raids— but they could not match Lirian steel for close-quarters fighting.

There was no way to get weapons in the Tundra without taking them off the bodies of those you killed, so that was what they did. And if her warriors were squeamish, Iniabi reminded them that wolves were scavengers, and these people did not deserve their thoughts.

Iniabi's hands were in the sentry's pockets when the two new wolves instructed to tail her arrived. "Yutu, why do we only attack their scouts?"

"Because they are alone," Yutu murmured, wincing as the movement of his lips caused the dry, cracked skin to split. He wiped at the blood. He'd been out too long without protection from the wind and the cold. He needed fat to smear across his skin.

"That makes them easier targets." Iniabi added flint to her useful pile and then began to refill the man's satchel with the things they needed. "We can't attack the main body of their force with our current numbers. There are just too many of them. Why else?"

Yutu didn't respond, but Maniitok did, a smile tugging at his lips. "If more and more scouts don't come back, they'll be afraid to go out. Scout duty will feel like a death sentence. Their chiefs—"

"Commanders," Yutu corrected, using the Lirian military term for leaders.

Maniitok rolled his eyes. "Their *Commanders* will have to choose who goes and who stays. And every time the scouts don't come back, their Commanders don't get reports on what's out here."

"They don't know where we are," Yutu said. "They're blind."

Iniabi smiled and gestured to the remaining pile as she tossed the sack over her shoulder. The two warriors began to pick up the weapons and armor. "Right on all counts. The only thing you missed was what you're holding now. Every scout we take means more weapons and armor we can use against them. Now, let's head home. No trace, like Deniigi showed you."

⇑   ⇑   ⇑

With a handful of new warriors in tow, Iniabi slipped into the little camp growing off the side of Sinqiniq. She stepped through the circle of rough tents and cooking fires, touching a shoulder here or making a joke there. At the center, she straightened and looked at the pale faces around her. "It's time to sharpen your claws! Deniigi has slipped out into the Tundra to find us a target. We move again at dawn."

A few voices rose in approval, yipping like excited foxes. Capun approached and slung her arm over Iniabi's shoulder with easy familiarity. "About time. I was getting skinny without a proper hunt. Look at my arms. They're *tiny!*" She tightened her grip on Iniabi, effectively putting her in a headlock.

Iniabi gripped Capun's arm, braced the other woman's weight against her hip, and tossed her overhead. "You know, I think you're right! That was easier than the last time you tried." Cackles rose across the camp as Aniki made an over-exaggerated show of pulling Capun to her feet and dusting off her shoulders. Iniabi let them laugh.

Capun smirked as she shoved Aniki playfully and then straightened up. "Are you eating with us tonight?" Some nights, if things were too quiet in her and Qimmiq's illu, Iniabi would share a fire with her wolves instead.

"Not tonight," Iniabi said. "I'll come for you before dawn."

She turned away then, winding through the rings of illus until she found her way to the home she shared with her lover. "Qimmiq?" she called, stepping through. "I'm home."

The smell of grilling elk greeted her, and Qimmiq turned around with a handful of dandelion greens, dropping them into the already simmering pot. Her long braids dangled precariously close to the fire, and her eyes were bright as she smiled at Iniabi. "I'm nearly done with supper."

Iniabi relaxed, the tension she'd been holding sluicing away like cold-tight muscles in warm sunlight. She stepped farther inside, kissing her lover and warming herself by the fire. "What did you make? Do you need me to do anything?"

"It's just meat and greens," Qimmiq murmured, her lips curving into a shy smile. "Did you want something sweet? I have a bit of goat milk and some cloudberries... We could make some akutuq?"

The cold, creamy dessert might have been pleasant if she hadn't spent the day crawling through snow, but Qimmiq wouldn't want to know about that. "You're sweet enough for me."

The other woman blushed and gave Iniabi a gentle push away. "Am I? That's good to know. Now I won't have to go to the trouble of making desserts!"

"I can make them then." Iniabi turned to strip out of her wet layers, laying them across the drying line hung between two spars of their illu. The feeling of taking off half-frozen clothes in a warm illu was near blissful. "I can make cloudberry and kelp pudding, sugarpine mushrooms, or even nagoonberry fishskins."

Warm arms wrapped around Iniabi's waist, pulling her close against Qimmiq's chest. "Stop talking, you silly creature. We both know you're a terrible cook."

Iniabi shivered at the contact of Qimmiq's hands on her bare skin, and she paused with a dry tunic still in her hands. "You never know; I just might surprise you."

"Surprise me into throwing up, maybe. Iniabi, you're half-frozen." Qimmiq's hands moved up and down Iniabi's sides. "I wish you wouldn't push yourself like that; it's not good for you to go out and freeze half the day away. Besides, you know the elders don't agree with you seeking out trouble."

Iniabi tried to keep her body from tensing. Qimmiq would be able to feel it the moment she did. She could repeat, *again*, why she did this and who she did it for, but it did not seem to matter how many times Iniabi said she fought Lirians for the love of her people. Qimmiq would not understand. She wanted only to be safe, warm, and happy, even if that meant that somewhere, other Emaians were being taken. The elders were just as closed-minded. Someone had to fight for the people.

Iniabi took a deep breath. It was so nice to be held like this, so warm. She did not want to invite another silent night. "Push myself? All I did today was play training games with new warriors."

"Games?" Qimmiq didn't release Iniabi, and hope bubbled in her gut. This didn't have to be a silent argument.

"Yes, just teaching them to move or hide in the Tundra. You should think about showing the hunters to catch more game."

"I suppose it could help," Qimmiq agreed after a long pause.

Iniabi relaxed into her lover's arms and let her worries melt away.

CHAPTER 65: PHECEA

NINTH MOON, 1802, APHODES

Three Years before the Proclamation

Danae could barely hear the clanging of the harbor bells over the shouts of the people flocking past her carriage. Screams and yells broke through the night, and the crowds flooding Aphodes's streets scattered. Master Annas grabbed Danae by the back of her neck and hauled her down into the center of the carriage as an iron arrow the length of a grown man and heavier than two sacks of grain whistled through the air. Something thundered to the left of the carriage, and the panicked horses whinnied, the box heaving like a ship.

If the ballista attack on Aphodes didn't kill her, Danae thought the horses would lose their minds and take off with her locked inside with Master Annas.

"We have to get out of the carriage!" Danae yanked herself away from her Master, but he was stronger than he looked. She could see the whites of his eyes and the thin lines around his mouth compressed into deep furrows as he shook his head. She suspected he was trying not to lose his mind to fear. Like the horses.

"You will be crushed in the crowd."

"Not if we go with the flow."

"We cannot–" Master Annas never got to finish his sentence as the carriage swung to one side. Danae screamed and realized too late that the box was tipping over. Something had hit them and knocked the carriage off its wheels.

They teetered on two wheels, and Danae's belly rose into her throat, choking off her voice. Then they were falling. She slammed into the carriage door and felt the glass of the window splinter against her hands, which she had thrown out to pointlessly catch herself.

Something heavy hit her from behind, and Danae's arms buckled. She fell onto the broken door, but just as the weight crushed her, it was gone. She looked over her shoulder and saw Master Annas, forehead bleeding, pulling himself to his feet. He planted one foot on the cushioned seat and slammed his palm into the opposite door. It flew open, and Danae saw the night sky, the clouds overhead painted red and orange, reflecting light from the harbor.

It hadn't been cloudy when she went to bed, a brisk ocean breeze keeping the sky clear. Why was it cloudy now?

"Get up, Danae," Master Annas ordered. Danae shifted and remembered her pain.

"M-my hands," she mumbled, looking down at her palms. They were red too. Blood.

"It doesn't matter. Get up right now, Othonos, before this carriage is crushed."

Danae blinked stupidly at her bleeding hands, wondering if it would hurt more to keep the glass shards in or to yank them out.

Something lifted her up, and Danae felt hands at her elbows and then about her waist. The driver set her on the cobbled street and then clambered back atop the carriage to help Master Annas.

The horses were gone, the remains of their harnesses dangling from the hitch of the carriage. The driver must have cut them free. Danae looked for the supply wagon she and Master Annas had traveled with all these moons, then remembered that Yuka and the others hadn't come with her. She was too precious, too important to keep in Aphodes while the Lirians attacked. Should Phecea win, Councilor Minos and Angi, the heads of the Leos family, would send her things once the fighting had settled.

Danae took a shuddering breath and regretted it. Her lungs burned, and she coughed until her belly ached. She covered her nose and mouth and squinted up at the sky. It was a haze of smoke, not clouds, reflecting bright light from the harbor.

The Aphodes harbor burned.

Gasping, Danae turned to watch the people of Aphodes pushing past, babies held on hips, bags thrown over their backs. They looked like a school of fish, swimming desperately upstream to avoid the net. How had the Lirians slipped past their naval patrols? How had they gotten a fleet so far along the Phecean coastline?

Someone knocked into Danae, and she lurched forward, colliding with another shoulder. She turned, trying to avoid a burly man carrying a child, and instead bumped into a cluster of young women. They didn't push her, but neither did they step aside. Bodies pressed in, and Danae blinked, trying to orient herself. Where was Master Annas? Where was the carriage?

Something brushed against her hand, and Danae yelped, pain lancing up her wrist and making her palm throb. "Stop." No one reacted, and the crowds pressed her uphill, away from the harbor. "No. I have to get to Master Annas."

Danae looked over her shoulder, trying to spot her party, but despite her height, it was too difficult to make out details over the sea of bobbing heads. She looked forward, up the crest of the hill leading into the city proper, and saw a troop of soldiers running in sync. They cut a swath through the fleeing citizens, and Danae stepped aside just as they hurtled past, feeling the touch of cool metal as their shields acted as a knife, cleaving through nobility, merchants, and slaves.

She took the opportunity their passing made and slipped away, finding an empty doorway to huddle beneath. Danae clutched her bleeding hands to her chest, hot tears tracking down her cheeks. When had she started crying?

It felt like an hour, but it couldn't have been that long when she finally saw Master Annas again. He and the Leos driver hurried up the hill, the crowds thinning now that most of the harbor was evacuated. She could see Master Annas opening his mouth, his lips forming words her ears couldn't hear over the roar of the attack.

He was shouting her name.

The distance between them seemed to stretch and grow, getting wider than the Bathi River. She blinked, shaking her head, trying to keep her mind from playing tricks on her. She was so tired, her body pummeled from human rapids.

"Master Annas!" she called, but he didn't turn. She would have to go to him.

Danae straightened her shoulders, trying to give herself an imposing air, but it didn't work. Shoulders and elbows still shoved her. Danae took a deep breath, rallied herself, and pushed forward. An age passed before she half-grabbed, half-fell into Master Annas.

He jerked, turning with a frown before his too-wide eyes focused on her. Her tutor tucked one arm about her shoulders, and Danae couldn't tell if he was trembling or if she was as they fled the burning city.

⇑ ⇑ ⇑

Ninth Moon, 1802, Diosion

Basia stood in the Trade Office entrance and pulled on a long coat over her clothes and satchel. It was already dark outside, despite the lengthening days of early spring, the setting sun shrouded by weather. It had been a rainy season, and today was no different; outside, droplets pattered the pavement in an uneven tattoo.

"Humors, I will be glad when this rain lets up." It was Ines, the woman who sat nearest Basia in the office, her Ingolan descent written on her pale skin and dark hair. It looked like she was hesitating, gearing herself up before her walk through the damp evening.

Basia gave her a sympathetic glance. "You and me both. I—"

"Basia Mavros?" A man in a battered cloak stepped through the door, bringing rain and wind along with him. He wore a bulging satchel at his side, a newspaper in his grip. He handed it to her with little decorum, and she tucked it under one arm. "Your paper."

"Thank you."

Ines seemed to have found what fortitude she needed to face the rain because she had already slipped away. Basia pulled her cloak tight about herself and stepped, at last, into the night. There were not many people on the streets. The rain was cold, the cobblestone roads of Diosion slick. It would be easy to fall, easy to be robbed. No one that didn't have to be out in it would be. Poor Zol. She was on duty tonight in the harbor—she and all the other guards would have an uncomfortable night of it.

Basia pulled her collar tighter around her neck, shivering at the trail of a frigid raindrop rolling down her spine. There was the bakery that carried that delicious spanakopita Lex liked to bring for lunch, its windows still brightly lit, and beyond that, a couple doors down was a clothier. Basia glanced over her shoulder as she passed the display of winter furs and ducked into the alleyway beside it. No one paid attention. All those on the street were too busy trying to stay dry.

There was a doorway leading into a dark building on the opposite side of the alley as the little clothing shop, so Basia tucked herself inside to wait out of the downpour. It was eerie to stand in so dark and unfamiliar a place, surrounded by the smells of rain on stone and the refuse thrown into the alleyway. The torrent of water made a translucent curtain, blurring the world around her into indistinct shapes. She might have been anywhere in the world.

"Hey." Basia relaxed slightly at the sound of Lex's warm voice. They stepped close to share her shelter, droplets beading on their collarbone just a few inches from Basia's nose. Their usual sandalwood scent was muted, mixing with the smells of water on skin. "You look like you've had a scare. Did you have to wait long?"

She shook her head. "No. I left work late. What took you so long to get here?"

"I had trouble getting away too. We got in a shipment at the end of the day—Are you sure you're alright, Basia?" They placed a hand on her cheek, and Basia had to fight to keep herself from leaning in. She loved the way Lex said her name. "You're too cold."

She closed her eyes, willing herself to focus. She was here to bring Lex the trade documents they needed—their ships couldn't sail without them. "I brought the papers. You should have everything you need to get our first friends to freedom."

"Come here. You're going to catch a cold, and then where would we be?" Lex pulled her close against their chest, and Basia did lose her breath then, sighing into the embrace as though it was the one thing she had always been missing.

"I—"

"I'll take the papers in a moment. When's the last time you let yourself just enjoy something nice? You spend so much time working for the Confederacy, for the E— for our friends."

Basia took a deep breath, filling up her lungs with the smell of them, the feel of their arms wrapped around her. It shook as she let it back out again. "I think I would like something nice with you."

Lex chuckled, and she could feel it vibrate in their chest. "Of course, you would."

They kissed her, and all the world with all its worries fell away like rain from a lightened cloud.

When Lex left with the papers they needed to take to the harbor, Basia waited a moment in the doorway where they had met, the smell of Lex's sandalwood scent still lingering in their wake. Her cheeks were so flushed that when she pressed cold fingers to them, she could feel the heat radiating into her hands, and her heart was a raging patter in her chest, much faster than the trickling rain. She took long, slow breaths, trying to calm herself, but joy and desire kept slipping around her control.

Lex had kissed her. By every philosopher in Diosion, she had been hoping they would for weeks. *Finally.* And it had been so worth waiting for.

Basia eventually left the dark sanctuary, reveling in the raindrops that hit her skin. Did they leave behind steam as they trailed off? She thought they must. She was glowing.

It wasn't until Basia had made it home to her family's estate that she remembered the paper. She shucked off her wet clothes, leaving them strewn haphazardly around her room, and then fell into bed humming to herself, the paper held up in front of her.

APHODES KEPT FROM LIRIAN CONTROL

THIS MOON, TUPA *Galan warships filled with Lirian soldiers managed to slip by the Phecean Fleet guarding the mouth of the Bathi River and attack the important port city of Aphodes, one of the biggest trade hubs in the Confederacy.*

Sources say that Phecea prevailed against this attack, successfully keeping our northern shore free of any Lirian invaders, but reports of the damage wrought to the city are unclear. Plumes of smoke were seen as far as the town of Bais following the attack, and many of the seaside port's bright, painted plaster buildings have been reduced to rubble.

We here at the Diosion Crier are still awaiting more reports, but it is safe to assume that no ships will be docking in Aphodes for some time. As much of a blow this is, we can be grateful that Liria has not gained a foothold in Phecean territory during this long war...

BASIA DROPPED THE PAPER, her chest suddenly growing cold. Danae was supposed to have arrived in Aphodes earlier this moon. Had she been caught in the attack? Had she escaped? Surely Danae would have been protected—as the Othonos heir, she was too important not to be, and yet—

Leaping to her feet, Basia threw on her damp cloak and boots, racing down the stairs to the stable. The Councilors kept late hours these days, working through the night to combat the war. If she took Crane, she'd make it to the Othonos estate before they retired for the evening, and maybe Danae's parents would know more about where their daughter had gone.

CHAPTER 66: RHOSAN

FIRST MOON, 1803, GWAETH

Two Years before the Proclamation

The landscape of northern Rhosan hadn't changed in the years Wynn spent locked in Cwm Or. The great, evergreen forests still stood, broken only by spars of rock and snowfall. Trees still trembled with snow over winding paths. Wagon ruts mixed brown and white. The winter sun was a pale eye watching over it all.

Wynn sat on the back of a wagon, his spine pressed into the rough curve of a grain sack. The wood beneath him bit into his thighs with every jolt, but he didn't bother to shift—he'd been waiting here long enough now that he knew it would do little to alleviate his discomfort. Somewhere ahead of him, two horses rode alongside the wagon. Gruffyd and Ifanna, if she hadn't given up the saddle for the wagon's padded seat.

"Go now," he told himself for the thousandth time. It would take so little effort to push off the back of the wagon and into the underbrush. He knew they were headed into Gwaeth and that it was a port city. He only had to hide until Gruffyd and Ifanna had left to search and then slip onto a ship. Fewer vessels left northern ports at this time of year, but surely, there would be *something* to take him away from this place.

If he could make himself leave.

Wynn gripped the planks on either side of his legs until his palms began to take on their shape. Early in the trip, Gruffyd had chained him here; now, nothing held him back. The Victors had grown too used to his docility, too lazy after moons of rough travel. He could just... drop. Walk away.

He would be *free*. Free to let the cold air of a Rhosan winter fill his lungs, free to go where he wanted when he wanted... Free as a hawk or one of the dragonkin.

And yet...

A great wall grew between his mind and limbs, a stone artifice that pushed back whenever he tried to come near it. At the thought of climbing that resistance, of tearing down the wall, Wynn's limbs protested, quivering dully against his tendons. He could not bring himself to do it. He could not leave Dyfan.

Not after all these years. Not after the feeling of him pressed close. Precious moments stolen in the dark.

After a time, the view around him began to change. The forest fell away to cleared land, the crisp smells of pine replaced with woodsmoke. They were nearing Gwaeth, and still, Wynn had not dropped from the wagon. He gave up the pretense of trying and curled himself tight against the grain sacks behind him.

They arrived, as they always seemed to, right before a fight.

The village of Gwaeth was smaller and meaner than any others they'd yet traveled through. Its muddy streets were mostly empty, the facades of its few buildings grimy with damp and earth. A miasma seemed to hang over the space: part fog, part salt, and stinking of fish.

Gruffyd stopped only briefly to ask for directions to their pits, and when he pulled up next to them, Wynn thought the place was laughable. Men stood in clusters around a simple rope barrier. The ground inside was churned and blood-spattered but level. No one had made the pretense of digging it out. Wynn supposed it was too cold to bother this far north. In the center of the ring, two men grappled—shirtless despite the frigid weather.

Gruffyd stepped over to mingle with those watching the fight, to line up bouts and a place to stay, Wynn assumed. He had never asked. Didn't bother speaking to his captors at all. His life had narrowed to endless waiting, only occasionally broken by fights or new places to sleep.

"Don't look so grim." Ifanna held out a thick woolen blanket for Wynn. He hadn't seen her step behind the wagon. As he reached forward to take it, she stepped closer. For a moment, their fingertips touched. "You'll win against these Defeated. You always do."

Wynn took the blanket warily, breaking contact as quickly as possible without provoking her. Ifanna's attention had only grown since he had accompanied her to Kirit's temple, but she never seemed to notice his distrust of it.

She opened her mouth to say something else but then seemed to notice her husband's returning figure. Instead, she shrugged, turning to arrange her braided locks in a fit of vanity. "Good luck, Wynn." She straightened her tunic and brushed past him as she made her way back around the wagon.

"Big day tomorrow, eh," Gruffyd said a couple moments later. And maybe it would be, for him.

⇑　⇑　⇑

Wynn didn't see the pits again until late afternoon the following day; by then, the crowd had multiplied. The rope barrier was packed with onlookers shouting and jostling each other for a better view. Wynn could see little of the fight inside, but it looked bloody.

The fight ended before he could get close, and then the mass of people swallowed him whole, swelling up around him only to drop him back inside the pit with a dozen other Defeated. What was this? A melee? Wynn turned, casting around for a weapon, a stone—anything. He had never fought so many others at once. He needed some sort of advantage—*there*. In the pit's center, a few rusty weapons clustered in a pile: a whip, a mace, and a couple of knives. Wynn gathered himself to charge, only to find the hands of countless onlookers swarming up from the other side of the barrier to hold him back, wrapping around his arms, tangling in his clothes and hair. They smelled of earth, sweat, and sour breath.

"No cheating now, boy."

A whistle sounded close by, and the hands let go. Wynn didn't hesitate. He charged forward, stumbling in his hurry, and cleared the yards to the center faster than any of his opponents. His fingers closed over the mace handle, nails cracking against the earth below. The others were on him then.

Wynn swung wildly, spinning to take out anyone close, and caught another Defeated in the face, crushing his jaw at the joint. Dirt sprayed into his eyes as another man fell to his right. The flash of a knife was all the warning he had to leap away. A red-haired man darted forward, and Wynn brought the mace down on his shoulder before scrambling back again.

There was no art to this fight, no clever tactics. It was moving too fast for any of that. He just acted, reacted—an animal devoid of human reason. The only thought in his mind was survival.

All these years, and it still boiled down to live or give up.

The melee lasted a moon, and then it was over. The Defeated before Wynn took out another with a knife throw to the throat. Wynn bashed in his skull. The sheer volume of all the throats and hands around him built up like a wave, crashing into the already blood-dampened shore.

The hands were on him again, drawing him out and away from the ring into some shelter. Gruffyd's rooms? In the wake of all that noise, the silence was bewildering. Did they mean to leave him here while they celebrated? He supposed it was better than being shown off.

Hours passed. A healer came in and left again, leaving neat rows of stitches behind. Wynn didn't remember getting wounded. The sky outside darkened to night. The fire, built high before a wide, fur-strewn bed, began to ebb. Waiting broken only by fights.

How many men had he killed this time?

The door's rusted hinges pulled Wynn from his thoughts, though he did little more than blink. If someone wanted to kill him now, he'd probably just let them. He was too tired to fight anymore. He didn't feel at all. The fear that once controlled him, stole his reason and humanity, no longer had a hold. Nothing did.

If he felt anything anymore, it probably would have been resignation when he saw who entered. Not Gruffyd, who surely was still off drinking, but Ifanna. She held a fine fur coat about her body, belted in place with something gaudy and thick, and leaned against the inn's thin door after she shut it, studying him.

Her dark, wavy hair was loose, and he could see she'd freshly applied color to her lips. Red. Like poisonous baneberry.

"Do you pray before your fights, Wynn?"

It was a loaded question. A test. The Victors cared only for one God, not the coalition he had worshiped his whole life. He could lie, but he didn't think pleasing her was the way to go. She wanted something from him, and he didn't want to give it to her. "No."

Her brows quirked, and then her lips parted in a cunning smile. "No? Given up on your Gods, have you?" She stepped away from the door, and Wynn realized it was locked. For the first time since leaving Cwm Or, he felt the twinge of fear.

"Just on yours." He turned away from her, focusing on the fire instead. On anything else instead.

"Defying a God? Kirit would approve of the spirit, if not the stupidity. Besides, he accepts your tribute whether you pray or not."

Ifanna walked to the small table pushed into the sparse room's corner and reached for a pitcher he hadn't noticed sitting there. She took two wooden cups and filled them from the pitcher. Wynn could smell the spiced wine from where he sat beside the hearth.

"If your God loves spirit, I doubt he considers the pit fights tribute at all. We fight not for courage but because we are forced to."

Ifanna collected the full cups and turned to smile at Wynn again. He didn't meet her eyes. "You win, you mean. You don't fight. You win. Other men would fail where you have only conquered. A Contender already. If Gruffyd were in your position, I doubt he'd do so well. He's going soft with age."

Wynn spat into the fire. Her regard left him with a sour taste in his mouth, and he hunched his shoulders against the inescapability of this room. He wanted out. He wanted Dyfan with his warm hands and calming presence. Fuck freedom. Wynn just wanted to be safe again. "Perhaps you should start a match for Victors, then, and let me be."

"Hush. You don't really feel that way." Ifanna settled beside him, the white of her fur coat collecting dust and dirt from the floor. She set the spare cup of wine next to Wynn's knee and took a sip out of her cup. "Think of how much better your life could be if we were friends."

What would it really matter? This place was worse than any Cursed Realm from which the Gods might have freed themselves. It chipped away pieces of him, crumbled his sanity, left scars on his body, took years of his youth and strength. One day there would be nothing left.

And yet, he knew he was kidding himself. He had seen Dyfan come back from the lesser pits half in pieces. She could do that to him. She could see him killed, or ensure that he never laid eyes on Dyfan again, the gentle, blue-eyed giant he could not bring himself to leave. This existence was impossibly crushing, but it could still be worse.

Ifanna seemed to take his silence as compliance as she set her cup aside and turned to look at him fully. She traced one long-nailed hand up his leg, stopping just short of his sex. When Wynn looked up, he could see something calculating in her gaze. She tilted her head to the side, exposing her long neck. "Come here."

Wynn's heart was breaking, but he could see no way out.

CHAPTER 67: PHECEA

ELEVENTH MOON, 1802, KYDONIA

Three Years before the Proclamation

Danae fumbled with her reins, the bandages around her palms making it difficult to shorten or lengthen the leather with any dexterity. Her mount, a borrowed gelding, slowed his pace at her slack grip. Master Annas, jostling on a feisty mare, hauled back on his reins too sharply, and she came to an abrupt halt. He muttered darkly, though Danae couldn't make out the words, and pressed his heels against her side. She picked up a forward trot.

It would have been funny, Danae supposed, if it wasn't for their situation. Master Annas, unable to keep his mount at the pace he wanted, Danae fumbling around with her docile gelding— like some sort of comedy play, written deliberately to point out their foibles. Now, it was just another piece of unfortunate truth in Danae Othonos's life. She held back a tired sigh and clucked her gelding forward despite her too-loose rein, trying to collect them. Ahead, Master Annas had gotten his mare to halt again, and it seemed he was giving up as he dismounted and waited for Danae to reach him. When she did, he just walked beside her, leading his mount by the bridle.

Around them, four thousand Aphodian troops and refugees stumbled forward. Few others had the luxury of a mount, their backs laden with children and the few objects they'd managed to save from their burning homes. Somewhere, a high voice sang a song of mourning, their pretty voice broken by a dog's frantic barks. They had brought the taint of smoke with them into the marshes and fields north of Kydonia.

Master Annas's once navy robes now looked more gray, covered in dust from the road, and the hems were permanently blackened from mud and blood and soot. Several places were torn, and Master Annas's usually trimmed beard was scraggly. His cheeks were sunburnt, and the lines around his mouth, nose, and eyes were deeper than when he and Danae had started this trip.

By the way her tutor peered at her, Danae knew she didn't look any better. Aside from her bandaged hands, her wild curling hair was squashed under a straw farmer's hat, and her travel tunic was stained with sweat, horse snot, and mud. Danae looked away from Master Annas's appraising gaze.

Three weeks, they traveled with the other refugees from Aphodes. Three weeks, they slept on the ground, surrounded by hundreds of others. No one had carriages or feather mattresses. No one had baths or chefs or anything but the clothes on their backs and the few possessions they had managed to escape with.

"Tell me, Othonos," Master Annas said, his voice taking on the droning quality of a lecture. Apparently, fleeing across a war-torn country wasn't reason enough to skip her lessons. "What tactical advantages does Kydonia hold?"

"With the Bathi at its western side and the great walls surrounding the city, it is a fortress." It was a poor answer, undetailed, but Danae didn't care. Her backside ached from riding endlessly, and she couldn't concentrate on anything aside from the unpleasant present. Tactics be forgotten.

"True. But you fail to mention the city's access to the Ligo Bathi. Just half a day's ride south, the smaller river provides yet more shelter. Its currents aren't as swift as the main branch, but with Lefkara perched near the mouth, it provides quick transport for troops and supplies."

"I understand, Master Annas. I just... I'm *tired*." Danae felt her reins slipping through her bandaged hands again and gave up on riding too. Maybe walking would ease her rump. Pulling her gelding to a halt, Danae dismounted with a wince. Her knees ached, and her legs felt heavy.

"I know you are, Othonos. We *all* are." His tone, kind and yet steadfast, only made Danae feel worse. Once she got to Kydonia, she'd be the Leos's guest, though she doubted they had gotten out of Aphodes faster than she had. She'd live in their fine estate for a moon or so, resuming her apprenticeship tour when the Leos returned, while all these refugees would still sleep wherever Kydonia could fit them. She could go home at the end of all this. Diosion stood proud and safe.

The Aphodians couldn't say the same.

She was behaving like a spoiled child. Danae swallowed her fatigue and tried to smile. "Kydonia has other advantages, Master Annas."

"Oh?"

"Yes, I believe the garrison from Aphodes has been reassigned to Kydonia as well."

"How do you know that?"

In truth, she'd been waiting in line for the latrine and overheard a few soldiers talking about it. Or rather, complaining. But it wasn't as if she could tell Master Annas what she overheard waiting to relieve herself. Danae shook her head demurely. "It's hard not to hear things when you're in a... a *caravan* of this size."

He gave her a pointed look but then smiled. It was good to see her tutor do that again. Even for a moment.

"Well, more fortifications for the military is certainly an added bonus. Ah, here we are. Once we crest this hill, if memory serves me, we'll have an attractive view of Kydonia."

Danae looked up the long winding road and bit back a moan. It looked like it would take most of the afternoon to reach the top. *Don't be a baby,* she chided herself. *Everyone else is doing it, and once we're at the top, we can go down into the river valley and finally reach safety. Maybe you can even have a bath.* The idea gave her strength, and Danae strode purposefully alongside Master Annas.

By the time they reached the hill's crest, the sun was dipping low in the sky. She'd probably have to sleep one more night out in the open. Already other refugees were setting up camp on either side of the road. Grim faces and low voices. Shouldn't they be relieved to see salvation?

Master Annas stopped, his mare obediently following him. Danae glanced down the hill and across the valley to the walled city of Kydonia. Banners flew from towers and turrets, and to her left, Danae could see the distant glimmers of the river.

And there, sitting like great sea snakes in the middle of the Bathi River, were Lirian warships.

⇑   ⇑   ⇑

Eleventh Moon, 1802, Diosion

Lex's home was a surprisingly simple affair. It was stone, blocks rising into a plain V above a single room tucked into their family's warehouse. They had stark furniture: a wooden armoire and a couple chairs, a simple wooden table. Their only luxuries were a long, clear mirror propped on one wall and a thick-mattressed bed.

Basia loved it.

"What's the point of having a place for your clothes if you're just going to drape them over the bed and chairs?" she teased, propping her head on their bare chest.

Lex was slow to respond, somnolent from sex. "How else am I to look elegantly ruffled all the time?"

"Elegantly ruffled? You mean you look like a ruffian of the highest order."

"Yes, exactly."

They lay quietly for a time, Lex's breathing beginning to lull Basia into a warm, comfortable sleep, drenched in the red smells of spice and skin. Perhaps they could have sex again in the morning, or else just lay like this in the moments before the day began.

"Do you think we're doing all we can? For the cause? It never feels like enough. For every captured Emaian we help back home, thousands are still enslaved in Diosion, and that's not even touching the bred Emaians."

Basia stirred herself back to wakefulness, propping herself up on one elbow and examining Lex's face. Their expression was uncharacteristically uncertain, something she'd never seen them show before. "Yes, but if we send bred Emaians to the Tundra, what would they do? They wouldn't have family there, wouldn't know how to survive the climate. Yes, they would be free, but at what cost?"

"It's just— I don't think we're making a difference."

"We can only afford to buy so many, Lex. We do what we can with what we have."

"Mmmm." She could tell they didn't agree with her.

"Our first group of Emaians should make it back across the border soon. Do you think they made it? Do you trust those people Eros knows in Pangnir? What if they sell our friends back into slavery, or worse, to Liria?"

Lex reached up to pull Basia back down to them. "Eros swears they're trustworthy."

"Maybe we should make the trip with the next group. Just to make sure."

"And leave behind the Trade Office and my parent's merchant company? It's not like Zol can exactly walk away from her position on the guard either, and I don't think Eros would be up for the journey."

"What about Ilia? She could pretend to be one of them."

"Vel would kill us if anything happened to her."

Basia took a deep breath and chewed on the inside of her cheek. "It just feels like so much to trust someone with."

"You know, you're going to gnaw your mouth bloody if you keep doing that."

Basia stopped and shot them a look.

"Yes, I suppose. But we're doing the right thing, Basia. You know how they live here. Can you imagine being torn from your home?"

"I— Yes, of course, but—"

"It'll all work out, I promise." They pulled her in closer and pressed their lips to hers. "Don't borrow trouble, love. I just wish we could do more."

Basia sighed into the embrace and relented. She would find a way to ensure those they saved made it safely to their homeland, but for now, it would have to wait until morning. "You're right, I suppose."

Her ungracious tone earned her a snort and a lopsided smile from Lex. They raised a hand to trace the curve of her jaw. "Have you heard anything about your missing friend?"

"No." The word came out as a whisper, Basia closing her eyes from the sudden fear and worry. She had gone an hour or two without thinking of the danger Danae must be in, lulled into the warmth and desire of Lex's bed, but now it returned in full force. "She was in Aphodes when the Lirians attacked, but no one knows where she is now. Her parents are in pieces— *I'm* in pieces. Lex, I don't want to lose her. She's like family to me."

"There's word from people in Leonis province that the burning of Aphodes was on purpose. The Leos Councilors burned their own harbor to keep the Lirians from landing." They ran a hand down Basia's side. "There's no way they would have put the Othonos heir in danger, right? It'd be madness."

"Then why hasn't anyone heard from her? It's been almost two moons."

"Maybe she just hasn't gotten to someone who can send her post. She'll be alright, Basia. Her keepers won't let anything befall her."

Reluctantly, Basia allowed herself to be comforted. Let Lex be right. Let Danae be safe.

⇑   ⇑   ⇑

Eleventh Moon, 1802, Kydonia

Booted steps echoed through the streets of Kydonia and into the stone walls of Danae's borrowed room. She looked away from the open window and back at the mirror. She didn't look like herself anymore. Her cheeks were hollowed and red from days in the sun and wind, and her hair was bleached, closer to copper or gold than the tawny brown it had always been. Her eyes— Well. They were still light brown, but the circles beneath looked like purpled bruises.

Danae shook her head at her reflection and straightened her borrowed yellow tunic. There was nothing for it; there was no Basia here to save the day with face paints and a fantastic adventure story. Danae was alone.

Her lower lip quivered in the mirror, and she turned away before she could fall to pieces. Now was not the time to cry.

She hurried out of the room provided by Commander Dimos and down the stairs into the main hall of the garrison. The Commander decided that the Othonos heir would stay with the military's might rather than somewhere more tactically precarious. The Leos home in Kydonia was perched above the main walls for the breathtaking views. Views, Commander Dimos had said, weren't worth taking a bolt for.

Danae agreed. Besides, the Leos hadn't made it to Kydonia. Presumably, they were still in Aphodes, dealing with the aftermath of the Lirian attack. With no other Council members in attendance, that gave Commander Dimos the responsibility of protecting Kydonia, so she yielded to his direction.

Soldiers hustled past, some remembering to bow, others too busy to be bothered with the girl lurking about the garrison. Danae didn't mind and instead wove her way to the conference chamber. Murmured voices told her plenty of people were in attendance. Slipping through the half-closed door, Danae pressed herself alongside the edge of the wall, peering at the table ladened with maps and figurines.

"It's no good," Commander Dimos said, pushing a carved figurine of a Phecean warship away from Kydonia. "The few ships that survived in Aphodes cannot come down the Bathi in time. Besides, they're needed in Aphodes."

"Commander Faidon in Lefkara has sent word; he can spare two thousand soldiers, or one thousand sailors, but not both."

"What are our latest estimates of Liria's numbers?" Commander Dimos held out his hand, and a competent, steel-haired apprentice deposited a sheaf of papers there. The room was quiet as Commander Dimos glanced over the reports, the lines on his forehead growing deeper. "The reports indicate that Liria has some ten thousand men headed this way: one more warship coming downstream, plus those men already camped on the far bank of the Bathi. Our ballistae can't reach them. If we send our troops across the river, they will be cut off from us."

"The Lirians are probably hoping we try to send our fighters across now."

"If we don't attack the five thousand now, we'll have to fight ten thousand in a few days," Danae didn't know the name of the woman who spoke, but the ribbons on her shoulders indicated she was a decorated officer.

Silence hung in the air, and Commander Dimos sighed, rubbing his jaw with his free hand. "This city was built to last a siege, but if we just lock up the gates and hunker down, Liria will sweep past and raze Phecea from here to Lefkara and probably all the way up to Aphodes. Not to mention what they'll do to all the refugees along the northern road."

"We don't have the numbers to face them in open combat. Kydonia has four thousand troops as well as the two thousand from Aphodes."

Danae swallowed and pressed against the wall. This seemed hopeless. What would they do? Lirians surrounded them on all sides; their numbers put them at a disadvantage, *and* they had the Aphodian refugees to protect.

Commander Dimos stared at the map, with the little ships painted in Lirian colors and the fighter figurines painted in Phecean. He leaned forward and picked up one of the Lirian ships, studying the craftsmanship of it for a moment. Then he nodded. "Someone get me a messenger bird for Lefkara. We will not lose Kydonia to those Lirian pigs, not while there is breath in my body."

⇑ ⇑ ⇑

Eleventh Moon, 1802, Kydonia

Battle was worse than the screaming of refugees fleeing Aphodes while it was ablaze. People screamed here, too, their voices mingling with the clang of steel and the thudding impact of ballistae bolts. Danae huddled by the westernmost battlement on the thick stone wall surrounding Kydonia and watched as Phecean people flung themselves against Lirian men. This high up, it was difficult to tell who was who or what, *precisely*, was happening. All she understood was the thrashing, pulsing mass below her were thousands of people slicing each other up.

When the battle first started at the break of dawn, she could tell the Lirians from their red uniforms, but no longer. Blood and dirt and gore spattered everything. The four thousand Kydonian troops kept their line, unable to push the Lirians back but also refusing to give up a single inch of the earth below the wall. Lirians spilled onto the banks every hour or so, shepherded across the dangerous mountain river by their horrid warships.

Each time a fresh wave of Lirians arrived, Danae thought her heart would stop from fear. How could Pheceans hold them back any longer? How could they hope to win this?

A hand landed on her shoulder, and Danae flinched involuntarily. Master Annas had found her at last. He'd tow her back to her room, to 'safety' and perhaps lecture her on the roles of an heir. She had to stay alive, first and foremost, and being up on the battlements was putting that at risk. She turned, ready to argue with him, only to see it wasn't Master Annas who had her but Commander Elena.

She frowned at Danae, but when Danae didn't look away, she nodded. "You're the Othonos heir, aren't you? What's your name? Dana?"

"Danae," she whispered, and of course, the Commander couldn't hear her. The other woman didn't seem to care anyway, as she glanced down at the battle.

"Looks bad, doesn't it?"

The patriot in Danae wanted to protest, to say Phecea would always prevail, but the girl who had fled Aphodes and listened to her parents' hushed conversations late at night knew better. So she nodded. The Commander removed her hand from Danae's shoulder and rested it on the pommel of her sword.

"You ever seen fighting before, Dana?"

"I was in Aphodes when it burned."

"Were you? That was an interesting tactical move. Sort of like biting your nose off to spite your face. But it worked. Phecea holds Aphodes, not the Lirians."

"Maybe Aphodes was a distraction." Danae wanted to shrink away when Commander Elena looked her way, the older woman's eyes narrowing.

But she smiled. "You're a clever girl. Or a cynic."

"Or both."

Commander Elena nodded again. "Or both," she agreed just as a horn sounded. Danae looked over the wall and saw yet another shipload of Lirians disembarking. She'd lost count, but she thought that meant there were seven thousand Lirians on this side of the Bathi now. Seven against four. That didn't seem possible. It looked as if the banks of the Bathi had swollen with fall floods, only instead of water, it was filled with blood and bodies and Lirian steel.

"Where are the soldiers from Aphodes? What about the Lefkarans?" Danae asked.

"They're where they're supposed to be," the Commander explained in an irritatingly calm tone. She glanced at the sun, covered with sparse clouds, and shook her head. "It's a waiting game. Battle always is."

"And if we wait too long?" "You won't know if you were too late until it's over."

"So, you're saying it's actually all a gamble?"

The Commander could probably see the dislike in Danae's face because she smiled sadly. "Life is a gamble, Dana Othonos. You were born to Councilors. You're noble and educated. I was born to a merchant family, one of eleven children. The only way I'd be able to pursue anything was by becoming a sword for Phecea. We take what we're given, and we make the most of it."

"And you think sending our soldiers down there to buy time is making the most of what you were given?" Danae wasn't sure why she spoke so boldly to this woman, but she couldn't justify the lives ending down there.

"Like I said, I won't know till the end of the day. When Phecea's flag still flies over Kydonia, or a Lirian one rises instead."

The Commander glanced at the sun and at the battle below. As if her looking signaled it, another set of horns blared. Danae winced, readying herself to see more Lirians ferried across the Bathi. Instead, when she hardened herself enough to look, it was to see a Phecean warship coming around the bend in the river. It headed straight for the Lirian ones, hurrying to turn to face their opponent rather than acting as a ferry. Three Lirian ships against one Phecean one, but at least no more Lirians would join the battle on the Kydonia side of the river.

A second set of horns sounded, answered by a roar like an avalanche echoing off the stone walls of Kydonia. Danae looked around and gasped. There, to the left, a thousand Pheceans thundered toward the battle, their horses covered in armor which glinted in the sunlight.

Danae could hardly breathe but didn't dare take her eyes off the second force of Aphodian soldiers, also mounted, crashing into the flanks of the Lirian army. The signal seemed to bolster the soldiers at the front as the fighting redoubled.

With the Lirian warships occupied by the arrival of Lefkaran sailors, the Lirian army had its back against the mighty Bathi. Pheceans pressed into the army from all sides, pinching the Lirians until they had nowhere to go. Some soldiers did jump into the Bathi. Danae wasn't sure if they thought drowning would be a better death than a Phecean blade or if they were foolish enough to try and swim the freezing channel, but it didn't matter. Most stayed and fought.

And died.

At the end of the day, Phecea's flag still flew above Kydonia.

CHAPTER 68: LIRIA

ELEVENTH MOON, 1802, EGARA

Three Years before the Proclamation

Never in his life had Luce seen General Gais look so stricken. His knuckles were white where he held a stack of reports. There was a greenish tinge around his lips, and he kept licking them as if his mouth were too dry. The highly polished table within the war room in the Imperator's palace reflected General Gais's strained features back up at him, making him appear doubly worried. The dark paint around his eyes was even smudged a bit.

"How many dead in Kydonia?" The Imperator's voice growled from his place at the head of the table, and Luce resisted the urge to flinch. The battle for the eastern shore of the Bathi River had been brutal. That they lost ten thousand Lirian soldiers would have made it unacceptable, but worse, Phecea still held its side. Ten thousand dead, and Liria hadn't gained any more ground.

"Ten thousand, Imperator." General Gais at least kept a quaver from his voice. He was a strong, proud man who would not shame Liria now by appearing weak. Luce felt the smallest spark of pride for the general, leader of the entire Lirian army, after the Imperator, of course.

"Do you find this result acceptable, General?"

"No, Imperator, I do not."

"What do you have to say for yourself, then?"

General Gais glanced at Luce once and then bowed to the Imperator. "I advised against this decision, Imperator."

Of course, it was true. Both Luce and Gais had argued against the attack, stating too little preparation and intel, but the Imperator had insisted they press forward after their success with Aphodes. Phecea seemed to be crumbling. Why wouldn't they push their advantage? But one did not point out the Imperator's part in this failure! Not as Gais did. Luce felt the other commanders shifting. No one murmured, but the air in the room was tense. They were more frightened of the Imperator's silence than of his shouts.

"What did you say?"

"Imperator, I—"

The Imperator unsheathed his sword. Luce knew it had been crafted by the finest smiths of its age and was carried by each Imperator, dating back to the first from the Loratos family. Now, it flashed through the air, and with a muffled thump, General Gais's head fell to the floor. Gais hadn't even straightened from his bow.

Something warm dotted Luce's face, and he resisted the urge to wipe at it. Blood. Luce blinked and stared down at his polished boots. They, too, were speckled red.

"Vice General Nonus." The Imperator set his blade on the table, and it dripped more of General Gais's lifeforce onto the ancient wooden surface.

Years of training kept Luce in place, bowing to the Imperator. Was he about to be punished as well? He had argued against the attack initially. What would Camilla and the children do if he were gone?

He swallowed the bile in his throat. "Imperator, I am yours to command."

"You are now the General of all my armies. Do not fail me."

Luce bowed again and saw a droplet of blood join the others on his boots. His face was dripping with the stuff. "No, Imperator. I will not fail you."

CHAPTER 69: THE EMAI

THIRD MOON, 1803, VILLAGE OF SINQINIQ

Two Years before the Proclamation

*I*niabi stood on the deck of the Flying Night. Jaya and the navigator, Leon, were at the tiller. They made a strange pair, with his pink, Ingolan coloring next to her ebony skin. For a moment, they glared at her, Iniabi standing alone against their onslaught. She found herself entranced by the darker line around the edges of Jaya's pink-brown lips.

"Be careful not to anger her, Leon," Jaya taunted, her lips curling into a snarl. "You don't want to end up like Cai, do you? Pushed from the top of the mast to your death. The storm was probably only to cover the deed, don't you think? Why else would she have insisted he climb without a rope?"

Leon laughed, the sound dark and macabre. "Iniabi's a slinking murderer. A poisoner here to doom us all."

"Poison? Where is the poison?"

Iniabi whirled to see the captain's corpse struggling up the stairs, half-crawling, pulling herself up with grasping, skeletal fingers. One of her eye sockets was an empty, crow-pecked hole, and her face had split open along the scar cutting through her lip. Maggots oozed from the gash, from her mouth. She coughed on them, spewing writhing white bodies onto the deck.

"Poison!" she screamed. "Give it to me, Iniabi! I need it."

Iniabi turned to flee, to jump the ship, to get back to the Emai at any cost, but the captain screamed again, and Jaya and Leon took hold of her arms. They shoved one of the great earthenware jars of poison from Taqqiq into her hands, and desperately, the captain fell to her knees before Iniabi. She felt her arms lift, raising the jug of black urchin spine to the captain's decaying lips and began to pour.

The thick, dark liquid filled the captain's mouth, mixing with the maggots, the blood, the flaps of skin sloughing from her face. "No!" Iniabi sobbed. "No! It's too much!" But when she tried to pull away, the captain gripped her wrists with unbreakable fingers, greedily gulping down the poison.

Until it wasn't the captain but Qimmiq kneeling before her, her dark eyes wide and loving, black staining the beautiful, pale skin of her cheeks. She looked like she had the first time she'd kneeled in front of Iniabi like this, coy and stunning, her mouth working eagerly at the lip of the jug. But slowly, that began to change.

Qimmiq's cheeks grew sunken, purple bags forming under her eyes. She began to choke, shoving Iniabi's hands back even as more poison filled her mouth, spilling down the front of her elkskin hunting tunic. She gasped for air, struggling against Iniabi's hold, and still, Iniabi forced her to drink more of the poison. Cuts opened in Qimmiq's skin, oozing as thick, black tears began to run from her too-dark eyes.

Iniabi looked up to see her wolves, their eyes silent and expectant. "I have to do this! I have—"

Iniabi sat up in her sleeping mat and struggled outside, heaving into the snow until bile rose in her throat and spilled in a thin, steaming stream. It tasted vile, burning, and her body convulsed well after anything stopped coming up. She sank to her bare knees, cold sinking into her limbs even as sweat froze against her skin.

It was a gray predawn. Qimmiq had already left to hunt, and Iniabi had never been more glad to wake alone. She did not want Qimmiq to see her like this.

She shoved mouthfuls of snow onto her tongue until she'd scrubbed away the taste of vomit, and her teeth ached with the cold. Iniabi stepped inside, dressed, and armed herself for a long trek.

⇑ ⇑ ⇑

Iniabi found what she was looking for five or six miles from Sinqiniq. It was midmorning, steam rising from her furs as she hunkered in the shadow of a copse of fir trees. The force of raiders spread out before her was roughly the same size as hers, a group of about fifty or sixty meant to take hunting parties or smaller villages. It looked as though there were a few captured Emaians among them already, souls unlucky enough to be taken from their homes or work. They huddled in the center of the camp even as the northerners sent out a couple of scouts—likely looking to increase their haul before they turned north once more. She killed the scouts to give herself time and then sprinted back to Sinqiniq.

A force of fifty was too many for Iniabi's fighters, even with the element of surprise. Though these were not soldiers, northern cutthroats had more steel and armor than her fighters. Not to mention an average education in using them that Iniabi's piece-meal group of hunters and warriors could not hope to defeat. And yet, Iniabi would not sit idle while a horde of raiders camped so close to her home. Qimmiq was out on the Tundra hunting— it could have just as easily been her curled in the snow, chains clamped around her neck.

Somehow, Iniabi didn't think Qimmiq would see it that way. For a moment, an image of her kneeling as she was forced to guzzle seer's poison flashed before Iniabi's eyes, and she had to work to keep her stomach from disgorging its contents again. She shook herself.

It was just a dream.

The faithful warriors that followed Iniabi's cause had made a camp for themselves on the edge of Sinqiniq. They weren't unwelcome, not exactly. After Iniabi's punishment following her first attack on nearby Lirians, the chiefs and medicine women had begrudgingly given up trying to stop her. Uki even seemed to support Iniabi, lending her further credence. It only made sense. Most of the warriors from both villages now threw in their lot with hers— trying to keep them from this work, this calling would only create an unnecessary power struggle. Iniabi was all too eager to let the chiefs handle Sinqiniq's day-to-day needs, but should they get in her way again, they would not like the outcome.

Her people, through no prompting, had made the distinction between themselves and the rest of the village visible with this camp, but Iniabi couldn't say that she minded. It made it obvious to any with eyes just how many liked her ideas. The Emai were tired of living under the fear of raids and slavery. They were ready to rise up.

There were no illus among this smaller camp, only rough, elk-skin tents propped up with bone and wood. Blackened circles showed the places where they built fires for warmth and food, and there were a couple bare patches where even now, warriors practiced. As a whole, they looked restless, uncertain without her there to lead them.

No matter. She had a task for them today.

Iniabi swept into the camp, calling orders. "Capun! Pakuk! Deniigi! Gather into two groups. I will lead one and Deniigi the other. Pakuk, you're with me. Capun, make sure everyone has the best weapons we can give them and food and water for the rest of the day. Tonight, we fight."

⇑   ⇑   ⇑

Yutu huffed as he spoke, his eyes bright and his cheeks red. "The raiders— have split— twenty-five north—twenty-five west."

Pakuk grunted in approval and looked at Iniabi expectantly.

She turned away from them, peering out from the trees they crouched between to where she could just make out the fires of the western camp several miles off. A slow, wolf-like grin spread across her lips, and she readjusted the white wolf pelt slung over her shoulders. It was working! Of course, it was. The idiot foreigners would not suspect such a ruse from slaves.

"Yutu, find Maniitok and get him to take word to the few left at the west camp to get out of there. We don't want them fighting anyone. From there, they'll need to head to the camp where the captured Emai are being kept."

She moved back away from the treeline, the northern 'camp' laid out below them, a collection of old cloth and campfires meant to look like a hunting party from afar. Between these makeshift dwellings were tripwires and thinly disguised pits—anything to put the field of battle further to Iniabi's advantage. "Is everyone ready?"

"Hungry," Pakuk murmured, and Iniabi knew he didn't mean for food.

Time stretched on in silence as the foreigners drifted towards them. They were not Lirian or Phecean soldiers—they were too roughly geared for that— but Banished men looking to make a little gold. Inland pirates come for the most valuable asset of the Tundra: the Emaian people.

They moved stealthily, in groups of two or three that Iniabi could only just make out against the snow. She might not have seen them if she had not been looking. Perhaps they learned their craft from Emaians in villages where they lived among the natives of the Tundra. Like Nec in Iniabi's early years. There was something particularly unpleasant about men who would turn that knowledge against those who gave it to them, and Iniabi relished the chance to kill them.

When the raiders arrived, they charged in with swords bared and torches raised, shouting at the top of their lungs. It was a clever tactic that left half their number surrounding the tents to grab any who might flee. Iniabi was willing to bet they had caught many a slave using similar methods, but not tonight. When they hit the camp, the first few slavers fell to traps as snow-and-cloth covers collapsed over spear-filled pits. Confusion spread among them. They had been expecting to find screaming people at their mercy—instead, they got howls.

Iniabi started it off—a long, eerie call—and at the sound, the first wave of her people stepped from the trees. Some of them held javelins, others whirled slings in tight patterns around their bodies, and when they let them fly, death fell like snow onto the Tundra. Iniabi held her breath while a second volley flew, but these men were not untrained. Though a dozen fell, the others began to form up, and drew their swords. Iniabi gave a sharp call, and her people melted back into the wood.

Even now, with their numbers halved again, Iniabi refused to face the enemy openly. It was too uncertain a thing with their weapons and armor. She would lose fighters, and unlike the seemingly neverending stream of their enemies, she did not have any to spare.

She would not have to meet them on the field, though. The raiders, assured of their prowess despite the trap they had unwittingly fallen into, charged into the woods where her force hid. It was a poor decision. As well-trained as these men were on even ground, they stumbled through the forest like newborn elk, tripping over roots and falling into the knives of her people.

Battle, perhaps, was not the right word. This was slaughter, and Iniabi did not even get a chance to wet her blade.

After, when they'd hauled the bodies into the open to liberate them of their supplies, the other, smaller force of Emaian warriors met up with them again, headed by Capun and trailing two dozen freed slaves. Iniabi scanned them, taking note of a bandage around Aniki's temple and a sluggish scrape on Maniitok's bicep. At the very least, all twelve people she had sent were there, their arms full of gathered supplies. One of them even led a similarly-burdened horse of the sturdy, shaggy kind foreigners brought into the Tundra. "Capun! Tell me how your attack went."

The woman smiled, nodding toward the freed slaves. "We did as we were told, Kaneq Amaroq. We're loyal wolves." Kaneq Amaroq. Ice Wolf. Iniabi smiled, thinking back to the Ice Hearted warriors that had guarded the edges of Nec. It was certainly a moniker she could get used to. "Got the prisoners free from the few slavers left behind to guard them. It was easy enough."

Capun looked around the little clearing, her gaze lingering on the bodies of the raiders. Not one had survived. Iniabi pressed three fingers to her lips in respect and gratitude. "You did well."

Deniigi approached, his hunter's furs splattered with blood, though his face was clean. "We need to go before the other force realizes the fire was a ruse to lure them away."

"They're too stupid to notice until they're already there and find the empty tents," Capun said.

"Don't underestimate your prey," Deniigi's voice was rough.

Iniabi nodded sharply. "He's right. They've probably already found out, and I think we've had enough fighting for the day. We'll head home before they come looking for their missing slaves. Capun, Pakuk, assign everyone into small groups. We'll make fewer signs of passage that way. We don't want to lead them back to Sinqiniq."

Pakuk and Capun turned away to follow her orders, but Deniigi remained at her side. He waited until the others were out of hearing range and reached into his furs. He pulled out a folded-up piece of paper. Iniabi tensed inwardly. She didn't want to give away that she wouldn't be able to read it.

"I found this on one of the raiders," he murmured, unfolding it to reveal a painting. The woman portrayed there looked like plenty of Emaians, with white hair and skin, though her eyes were dark like Iniabi's. The shape of her face was nondescript, and Iniabi shrugged. It didn't look like anyone she knew. Deniigi frowned and pointed to the letters above the painting. "It says they're looking for *you*, Iniabi. They're offering money to anyone who will give information about you."

She laughed, taking it from him and holding the picture next to her face. "Doesn't look much like me, does it? Let them look. What does gold matter to the Emai? All we have ever wanted was our freedom."

Somehow, though, she didn't think Qimmiq would have found it so amusing.

Deniigi shook his head, though he at least stopped frowning. "You're costing them gold, Iniabi. They make money off our people, and you've been slowing them down. The Emai don't care about gold, that's true, but the Lirians certainly do. Be careful, Kaneq Amaroq. They're coming for you."

Iniabi took a deep breath and looked out at the parties of her fighters—her *wolves*— disappearing into the Tundra. "Let them come."

She would be waiting.

CHAPTER 70: RHOSAN

THIRD MOON, 1803, CWM OR

Two Years before the Proclamation

It was meant to insult Dyfan, having to walk alongside his Victor's wagon. Prized pit fighters did not shamble next to wagons, holding doors and fetching barrels of mead or wine. They did not go anywhere, really, besides the arena for training, their quarters for rest, and compounds for breeding. They were fighters. Not to be towed about like pets, but stabled, fed, and exercised precisely.

Dyfan didn't care if he hauled sacks of barley from the market. He didn't care if he had to clean out muck piles or wash soiled clothes. He didn't care if he had to fight three men armed with rusty blades while all he had were his fists.

He was freer than ever before, and it was worth it all.

He didn't let it show. He limped next to Victor Eurig's carriage and hung his head slightly. He let his breaths fall uneven, like the slice in his leg hurt him terribly. Let Victor Eurig think he was suffering. Let him try to embarrass Dyfan. It didn't matter anymore. It never would again, as far as Dyfan could reckon.

The freedom of choosing who touched his body, and who Dyfan cared for was more important than pain, or pride. It was more important than life itself.

Though his right eye was swollen from a match two days ago, Dyfan could see well enough. The village was like a disturbed beehive. People buzzed around, gossiping about Victor Gruffyd's victory tour and subsequent feast. Excited to eat and get drunk on Gruffyd's coin and to see what a talented fighter his Defeated had become. Dyfan was excited as well, though he had to school himself to appear bored.

Wynn was home. And Dyfan's belly flipped at the thought.

They passed an old structure that had once been a temple for a lesser God, and Victor Eurig beckoned for Dyfan to come closer. His steady gaze was chilly, and Dyfan made sure not to let his expression change. Victor Eurig could not know how impatient Dyfan was to arrive at Victor Gruffyd's compound. He could not know how unaffected Dyfan was by the torments he had been put through.

"You should be embarrassed. Gruffyd's Defeated is half the fighter you are, yet he is a rising star while you sink into the muck."

Dyfan doubted his Victor wanted an answer, so he only nodded. Perhaps, a lifetime ago, he would have been irritated. But now, he felt Wynn's success as his own. Watching Wynn lose had never given Dyfan pleasure. Now the idea made him physically sick.

"You should have had a tour and your fourth Contender title. You should be whelping fighters, not opening wagon doors."

He agreed with Victor Eurig. Dyfan had all the makings of a Contender last season, yet he couldn't participate in enough bouts to qualify, mostly due to his injuries in the lesser pits.

Dyfan nodded again, watching a group of young men jostling each other as they passed. They were dressed in bright, clean tunics, and as the young men spotted Dyfan, they slowed, elbowing each other and murmuring. Likely, they had grown up watching him fight. Dyfan's pride bucked against the limp and the slumped shoulders he wore for Victor Eurig. He didn't want others to think him slow or weak.

"Are you listening?" Victor Eurig's voice, normally so controlled, was sharp. Irritated.

"Yes, Victor."

"Well? What do you have to say for yourself?"

Dyfan shuffled a bit more. He'd not tell his Victor that he could win if he weren't always injured. And he wouldn't concede on the breeding matter. So there was nothing to say.

Victor Eurig tsked and waved his hand in dismissal. Dyfan slowed his steps so he no longer walked beside the wagon seats.

Dyfan had been learning more about Cwm Or through all these errands. As a pit fighter, he hadn't much reason to see the settlement or its people, but now he enjoyed his little walks to the market or the miller. The people of Cwm Or were strong, fighting types. Men and women boasted broad shoulders, well-muscled arms, and dense cores. They favored plain colors, furs, and cloaks.

Mothers scolded children with smiles hidden in the corners of their mouths, and men debated heatedly about crops, prices, fights, horses, dogs, and the weather. Many knew him on sight and, despite his status as a Defeated, were engaging. Often, he would be asked to lift heavy things or arm wrestle a random passerby.

Dyfan never did, quietly ignoring them all, but he liked how interested they were in him. It made him feel less… empty.

It seemed to Dyfan that the market was the heart of Cwm Or, and the blacksmith was the arm. Everyone, even children, was armed, and they got their weapons from the blacksmith. Daggers, belt knives, swords, spears, clubs. To Dyfan, the smithy was much like the kitchens he had hoped to belong to as a child. Bright, warm, and filled with life. People bustled in and out, and the smith herself was constantly hammering or shaping.

The marketplace was in the center of the settlement and smelled heavily of spices, sweaty bodies, and food. There were stalls for everything a person could ever need. Fresh produce, dried goods, cloth, leather, metal. Even now, on the eve of Victor Gruffyd's massive feast, the smithy was sparking as they walked the center of the city proper.

Each compound was placed along a circular arc around the settlement with the Pits at the center of it all. Victor Gruffyd's compound happened to be directly across from Victor Eurig's, so the walk led them through the thick of Cwm Or rather than around.

Usually, this wouldn't bother Dyfan, but the closer they came to Victor Gruffyd's compound, the slower the carriage had to move. People were in the streets, or on horses, or in their own wagons, all thronging towards the feast. Clogging things up. Bogging them down.

Dyfan wished he could simply shoulder past them all and finally see Wynn.

⇑   ⇑   ⇑

The entrance to Gruffyd's main hall was among the largest in Cwm Or. Grand double doors led into the room from the outside, flanked by polished bronze candle sconces and glinting urns. The stone floor was layered with an enormous bearskin that Gruffyd claimed to have slain in his youth, its wide mouth bared to the door. On the opposite wall, two archways led into the main hall, and a tapestry depicting a victorious Contender hung directly between them. Gruffyd placed Wynn in front of this before the first guests were welcomed inside.

Dozens of people walked past him— Victors and their families, prominent Defeated trailing behind; merchants, craftsmen, warriors. Anyone that Gruffyd had deemed important enough to come. Some of them stopped to look at Wynn. A few even tried to speak. But, Wynn had become stone. His feet had grown into the floor, his face immobile. He could look nowhere but the doors before him.

Dyfan might step through them.

Would he smile or frown? Would he even meet Wynn's gaze? Did Wynn want him to? He had given Ifanna what she wanted while Dyfan languished in the lesser pits for refusing to breed. He might not want anything to do with Wynn. He might not come at all.

People streamed into the hall, more people than Wynn thought could possibly fit, and still, Wynn didn't see him. He began to lose hope. It was not as though he could miss the broad-shouldered giant in a crowd. The barrage started to thin, people trickling through the doors in twos and threes. He would be called in soon so the Victors could ogle him during the feast.

Then, Victor Eurig stepped through the door. His retinue was one of the largest, and in the back, black-eyed and stooped, stood Dyfan. He was a shell of his former self, much reduced in size and power, and still, Wynn could not have imagined being so happy, so relieved to see him.

Despite a swollen eye and a defeated air, Dyfan's gaze blazed across the space, pining Wynn to the spot. As ratted and worn down as he seemed, the larger man still held Wynn's attention as he had the first time they met. Steady. Assessing.

Many of the other pit fighters said Dyfan was crazed, dangerous. They dropped his stare, or avoided looking at him at all. Wynn didn't think they could be more wrong.

It wasn't madness; it was intensity. Passion.

And it told him everything he needed to know. Dyfan was still his. Nothing had changed in his absence except for him.

The rest of the visitors passed without Wynn's notice, disappearing into the room beyond like so many ants. The Defeated sent to fetch him had to say his name three times before he looked up at her. When he did, he stepped into the other room eagerly, finding Dyfan with his eyes for a moment before he was positioned alongside the other Defeated fighters. They lined the western wall of the hall, and from where he stood, closest to the head of the table, Wynn couldn't see his lover, though he had an excellent view of the feasting. The Victors tore great bites from fowl until grease ran from their chins and left long, dark stains in their beards. They drank, and laughed. Their wives made easy conversation—even Ifanna, though she glanced towards Wynn a few times while he steadily avoided her. Through it all, Gruffyd boasted, exaggerating Wynn's feats and the difficulty of their travels in equal amounts.

It was much as the Victor's feasts usually were, and Wynn ached to see it over.

He glanced down the line of Defeated, struggling to catch some glimpse of Dyfan. Would he be sent to sleep with Gruffyd's Defeated again? Would they be able to see each other? Perhaps Wynn was wrong for wanting to after what he'd done.

As the feast dragged on, it seemed that Victor Eurig was not drinking as much as the rest. In fact, he barely sipped from his cup. Occasionally, he cast Gruffyd a look that could almost be categorized as disgust.

Would he stay sober enough to return home at the end? It seemed likely. Wynn's hopes only plummeted further until Victor Eurig gestured with his cup. Dyfan stepped into view, stooping to hear whatever his Victor murmured into his ear. With a deferential nod, Dyfan turned to leave the hall.

Wynn refocused his gaze on the opposite wall, fighting to keep his expression blank. Most of the Victors had devolved into drunken stupor, a few slurring over improbable anecdotes, and some even asleep in their chairs. Few aside from Victor Eurig seemed to have retained their faculties, and he was having a quiet but intense discussion with an older man, his gray-tinged beard falling below the table. Wynn took a deep breath, counting heartbeats. Fifty… One hundred… Three hundred since Dyfan had left.

When he reached five hundred, he turned and slipped into a side door leading to the hallway, muttering, "Outhouse," to the Defeated girl that waited just beyond. He made for the nearest exit onto the grounds and then paused, sheltered by a thick swath of shadow.

Where would Eurig have sent Dyfan? He had no business in the rest of Gruffyd's holdings—he wasn't picking up any trade. He certainly wasn't here to breed. The only other thing on the compound that belonged to Eurig was his wagon. Wynn blinked. Of course.

The stable was quiet as he neared it, dark but for a lone lantern swinging just inside the entrance. Doubt checked his pace. Had he been wrong after all?

But, no. Wynn entered the wide doors to find Dyfan slipping out of one of the stalls, his eyes on the floor. There was hay in his hair and clothes, clinging to him like fur. His black eye looked even darker in the dim light, a hollow in his strong face.

"Dyfan," Wynn whispered, stepping closer, one hand half-outstretched.

The larger man stopped and looked up, momentarily tensing before he saw Wynn. Dyfan scanned the stable once, then crossed the distance between them with a few limping strides. He wrapped his arms about Wynn's shoulders and pulled him close. Wynn closed his eyes, melting into the embrace despite the guilt in his chest. "Wynn," Dyfan mumbled into Wynn's neck and redoubled his grip. The bigger man took a deep, shuddering breath, and Wynn realized Dyfan was trembling. "We didn't get to say goodbye."

Wynn tucked his face against his lover's chest, shaking with the force of silent, body-wracking sobs. They'd not been able to say anything. Dyfan had been in the lesser pits, fighting impossible battles, when Wynn found out he was to be taken on tour. They'd been apart all the long moons since. He wanted to tell Dyfan everything: about Ifanna, about the attempts to leave, about all the lives he'd taken in bloody, melee fights.

He couldn't do it. Not now. If Wynn lost Dyfan, it would break him. He was already only pieces of a man. Dyfan held him tighter until Wynn thought he might not be able to breathe in his crushing grip, but it felt too good to be shielded this way to complain.

They stood that way, bodies pressed together until they were one thin line, but Dyfan finally pulled back. He brushed his fingers across Wynn's neck, pushing his red hair away with a frown. He winced as he stepped back, and Wynn wondered what sorts of injuries his lover had sustained in the lesser pits. "I thought... I thought maybe you would escape."

"I couldn't do it. Freedom was there, and I just couldn't leave. Not — not with you here."

Dyfan's blue-green gaze was black in the darkness of the stable, and he watched Wynn unblinking for a long moment. Then he nodded. "I understand. There are some things I cannot do either."

"The lesser pits. You're hurt again, and— I—" Wynn took a deep breath. The words were caught in his throat, so thick and heavy he couldn't make himself spit them out.

"It's alright," Dyfan whispered, holding out his hand. "We don't have to talk about it. We're together now, and that's really... That's all I want."

"Me too." Wynn took Dyfan's hand and guided him close once more.

CHAPTER 71: RHOSAN

FIFTH MOON, 1803, CWM OR

Two Years before the Proclamation

Clear nights were the coldest, even in spring. Without its blanket of damp-cotton clouds, the land north of the mountain bled its warmth into the heavens in exchange for moon rays and constellations. Most nights, Wynn didn't think the trade was worth it. For all their furs, the cells given to the best Defeated were stone and did not hold their warmth. Stars couldn't keep you from freezing.

Tonight, though, he would take the cold for the light to see Dyfan's muscle bunch and writhe beneath his skin. To watch as the strong man's goose-pimpled arms trembled, their contours cast in alternating silver and shadow by the bars on the cell window. Wynn leaned back, slowing their coupling, just to see the scars on his lover's back painted in colors other than blood and dirt. Then pressed in again so that his shadow would hide the Victors' marks from view.

Dyfan groaned again, and Wynn had to still, had to take great gulps of the frigid air to keep from losing himself in the sound, artless as a boy. His thighs tensed, and he placed warning hands against Dyfan's back. "Oh. Be still, a moment." The other fighter just gave a quiet laugh and pushed back, pressing into Wynn's thighs, the bones of his hips. It was a deliciously cruel move. A little, insistent give-me-more that had Wynn folding in on himself, pressing his forehead to the small of Dyfan's back. He had to think of breathing, just of breathing and the tightening of his legs.

Only then Dyfan was chuckling again, his body quivering with the out-of-breath rhythm of it, bouncing against Wynn's body. Dyfan loved this, curse him. Loved that he could make Wynn shake with the effort of holding his own release in check. Wynn growled and bit him, but it only made Dyfan chuckle more, and then there was no helping it. His choices were to stay still, to let Dyfan pull his orgasm from him in little gasping breaths and wiggling pushes, or to take it for himself, running up to the cliff so that he might dive further from it.

Wynn took the dive, and in the space of a few pulses, he was falling, a near-unbearable warmth starting at his waist and tingling outwards until he slumped against Dyfan, boneless and spent.

He didn't feel the cold any longer.

Dyfan stretched out flat on the cot, and Wynn went down with him, only managing to lift himself from his lover after long moments of warm stupor, his senses full of the smells of Dyfan's skin. When he did move, they arranged themselves much as they always did: Dyfan lying on his back, Wynn half-draped against him.

"Do you think this will last forever?" As in the length of their lives. Forever was really a child's word for a child's grasp of life. Wynn had lost that surety in his existence late, well after adulthood. How long had Dyfan held onto his?

"Forever?" Dyfan's voice had the drowsy, complacent tone of one too content to muster much energy. His blunt fingers idly traced the line of Wynn's spine, the deep tenor of his voice gravely with suppressed laughter. "I don't suppose you can last forever...."

Wynn snorted. "No thanks to you."

Dyfan's fingers trailed up Wynn's back and buried into the hair at the nape of his neck, tugging on the shaggy locks. "I want it to last forever."

"Me too." Wynn pressed his hand against Dyfan's belly and slid it up the length of the other fighter's chest. How was it possible to want another person this much? So much that it felt as though even the possibility of losing him was something to guard against. So much that he would never get enough time with Dyfan, not if he lived for centuries. For forever. Wynn was heavy with the necessity of Dyfan, stone-chested with it. How had he ever thought he could run away alone?

Dyfan inhaled sharply and tightened his grip in Wynn's hair. Blue-green eyes cracked open to cast Wynn a steady look. Appraising, challenging, amused. As Wynn's fingertips brushed against his collarbones, Dyfan's calloused hand came to cover his. Stopping him from moving his touch elsewhere. "What is this, Wynn?"

"What do you mean?" Wynn asked, his chest growing heavier.

Swallowing, Dyfan turned Wynn's hand over where it rested above his heart. He rubbed his thumb gently across Wynn's palm but shook his head. "I don't... I'm just warm and...." He shrugged, clearly trying to find the words. So often, they eluded Dyfan. With a touch more urgency, he pressed Wynn's fingers against his heart. "Here."

Wynn turned to press his lips into the soft skin between Dyfan's shoulder and chest, his throat tightening with emotion. For all that the other fighter could not quite express himself in words, Wynn had no trouble grasping his meaning. "I love you too, Dyfan."

His lover let out a shaky breath and leaned forward, pressing his lips to Wynn's.

Dyfan

Relief made Dyfan giddy. His heart bounced around his chest as the words settled into his soul. Love. The purring warmth in his chest whenever he thought of Wynn, the ache in his belly when the other man was gone. Fizzling nerves in Dyfan's heart when he and Wynn lay together, arms looped about one another. It was *love*.

He didn't think anyone had ever loved him before. Perhaps his mother, all those years ago, but she hadn't been given a choice, had she? Mothers and fathers didn't choose who they loved. But Wynn, he was at choice. And with that freedom, he had chosen *Dyfan*.

Dyfan let his lips drag across Wynn's jaw and down his throat, urgency painting his thoughts. The other man tasted of salt and earth, the firm line of the muscles in his abdomen luring Dyfan further down.

Wynn's chest ballooned with a sigh that pressed his body against Dyfan's mouth, but as the fighter neared the v at Wynn's hips, he pushed Dyfan's face away. Still sated from their earlier bout. "Here," he murmured and rolled over, so his chest pressed into the furs.

Dyfan leaned forward, running his hands over the breadth of Wynn's shoulders, down his ribs, over his hips, across his ass. His skin felt like the fabrics some of the Victors' wives wore, unbelievably smooth against Dyfan's rough hands. Dipping down, Dyfan let his lips trace the bold lines of muscle across the shoulder blades of the man he loved. Who loved him.

A sigh eased over his tongue, and Dyfan tried the words. A whisper only. Just to see how they felt coming out. "I love you."

Wynn sighed out his reply, the words barely audible. "I love you."

How words could make shocks of starlight flood through Dyfan's veins, he didn't know, but they did. His throat tightened, and the fighter moved across Wynn, kissing his neck and shoulder. There couldn't be a single breath separating them. He couldn't wait any longer. Every thought narrowed down to the feel of Wynn beneath him and the perfect sound of his breaths.

Fights felt like this at times, where the world faded to nothing but a spear in his hand and a shield on his arm. Just Dyfan and his opponent. Only, now he didn't feel the pinpoint focus of battle, but instead the peace of something more. As if he belonged in this moment with Wynn.

Dyfan buried his face against Wynn to muffle the moans he couldn't keep from escaping. Below him, Wynn cried out as well, a single, crystalline note choked off as he turned his face into the furs. It hung in the air for a moment as though frozen by the chill.

And then an answering jingle came from the hallway beyond.

Dyfan stilled, the world shattering around him, but Wynn hadn't noticed. He laughed and pressed back against the bigger warrior. "Now who can't last forever?"

There wasn't even time enough to warn him.

An unfamiliar face in the familiar garb of an arena guard stood at the door. His eyes were wide, his mouth open in a soft gasp of surprise. Even as Dyfan watched, his lips twisted. Wynn noticed there was something wrong, then. He turned towards the door, stiffening like a cornered animal.

The guard slammed the bars to Dyfan's cell and locked them inside before disappearing into the dark.

For a moment, Dyfan wondered if it was real. Had a guard seen them? Caught them? But as the seconds passed and Wynn moved to dress, Dyfan realized what happened. Numb with confusion, the Defeated didn't hear the first few things Wynn said, an odd buzzing filling his ears as he finally bent to pick up his discarded clothing.

He knew what would happen next. What happened anytime a Victor gained something over a Defeated. Blinking slowly, Dyfan turned to Wynn, who was still talking. It was just sound.

Wynn froze then, his mouth still open, molded around the words that he no longer seemed to have the ability to speak. Neither moved for long moments, and then Wynn stepped close and reached up to wrap one hand around the back of Dyfan's neck. He tugged the taller man down until they stood with their foreheads pressed together, fists buried in each other's clothes.

"We can get through this," Wynn said, and then more guards arrived to take him away.

⇑ ⇑ ⇑

None of Victor Eurig's men touched him as they moved through the halls. It was as though they thought his particular affliction contagious. *This was the creature responsible for Dyfan's time in the lesser pits?* their eyes asked, and Wynn didn't know how to answer them, so he kept his eyes on the floor instead, counting the stones between his cell and Dyfan's.

Wynn was bleeding. He could feel the warm drip of it sliding down from a cut on his brow opened by the force of a clenched fist. His face would be purpling already, the marks of Eurig's men chosen for their visibility. Eurig wanted Dyfan to see that Wynn was hurt. Gruffyd had left when they began to do it, like a parent unable to watch their child's punishment.

"He's the reason I'm still here, fighting for you!" Wynn had wanted to scream at him. In the end, the Defeated remained silent.

Wynn looked up when they reached Dyfan's cell. His lover was stock still, unblinking in the manner he often had before a bout. Hyper-focused, he watched every move the guards made, and his expressionless face somehow bespoke great violence. Dyfan looked as dangerous as they had always made him out to be. His gaze drifted over Wynn's bloodied brow and bruised cheek before whipping to the cell door as another entered.

Victor Eurig's voice was honey smooth, coming to stand beside Wynn, hands meticulously clear as he bared them before Dyfan. "I was annoyed to be called from my bed so early this morning, even more so when it was your training master who bade me come. What more irritation could you possibly afford me, Dyfan? I feed you, I train you, I keep you in clothes and under a roof, and yet these past years, you have been little more than a burden. And, I thought to myself, 'Now that rutting Defeated will take my sleep too!?'"

Dyfan didn't look at Victor Eurig as he spoke, instead keeping green-blue eyes leveled on Wynn's as if willing the smaller man to know his meaning purely through that stare.

"And then I find out they have caught you lying with this... Defeated." Victor Eurig's tone dripped with distaste. To him, Wynn was only a Battle Defeated. Unworthy, ill-suited to the glory of the pits. "And I realized what an opportunity you have presented me with, Dyfan. Your sloppiness has shown me how to direct you."

That caught Dyfan's attention, and finally, he blinked, gaze wavering. Was it fear or suppressed rage that made him shudder? Did he understand yet what Eurig was doing? Wynn did, and he'd pray to Kirit the rest of his life if only it didn't break Dyfan.

"Yes, I can see you understand. You're a simple fighter, but you've always employed strategy. How to take your opponents down the most efficient way possible." The Victor gestured, and a guard brought a whip forward. The leather pommel creaked in Victor

Eurig's grip as he uncoiled the line. Tendons in Dyfan's neck stood taut, visible in the first blushing rays of morning.

Eurig stepped out of Wynn's line of sight, but Wynn didn't turn to watch him. *I won't flinch*, Wynn told himself. *I won't do it.* He'd lived with pain for nearly a decade now. What was another cut, another lash? He would be stone so that Dyfan would not see that he hurt.

The first strike was a line of fire across his back, but Wynn didn't so much as twitch. He kept his jaw locked down, his eyes on Dyfan's.

The whip struck again and again, and still, Wynn was silent, swallowing the pain like it was poison he could keep from Dyfan. Until the weapon tore open his shirt, splattering blood across the stone. He gasped then. Hardly a sound, but his facade had cracked.

It was all Dyfan needed. He stepped forward, breaking his stance, the lids of his eyes fluttering in some inexpressible emotion. "Stop." His voice was hoarse as if he, too, had been holding back screams of pain. Victor Eurig immediately let his whip arm fall to his side.

"Yes? What is it you wanted to say, Dyfan?"

The younger man's hands shook as he offered them, palm up. Placating. Pleading. "I-I'll do what you want."

"You'll resume your breeding rounds?"

Dyfan's gaze never left Wynn's face. "Yes."

Victor Eurig started to roll up the whip, no sadist looking to hurt Wynn. Why would he? The Victor had gotten what he wanted after all. "To be clear, Dyfan, Victor Gyffud is willing to let me pay to inflict... ah... *motivation* on Wynn whenever necessary. In case you forget your place again."

"I won't." It was a promise; Wynn knew it by the way Dyfan lowered his gaze. Differential to his Victor. He would never put Wynn in danger.

And so, Wynn would be the tool they controlled him with.

Nothing could change that. Dyfan had gone into the lower pits when he only thought he was betraying Wynn. For his lover's physical safety, there was nothing Dyfan would not do. Wynn sagged against the knowledge, and when Eurig's men directed him back toward his cell, he made no move to stop them.

CHAPTER 72: PHECEA

TWELFTH MOON, 1802, DIOSION

Three Years before the Proclamation

"Basia, wake up."

Basia groaned, struggling to pull apart gummy eyelids. She had been up too late, pouring over documents for the Society, and it didn't seem possible that it was already morning. Humors, she had to stop doing this. It was exhausting. She just didn't know how else she was supposed to get everything done.

Finally, she looked up, taking in the shape of Keme's pale face, lit strangely as it was by a lantern.

"Keme, what is it?"

"A messenger arrived from the Othonos estate. They want you to come right away."

Basia sat up, flinging her covers off. "Did they say why?" Could it be about Danae? She had been missing for so long now—three moons without so much as a word. Perhaps they had finally gotten a clue about her whereabouts, or maybe they'd even received a letter. For once, Basia didn't bother with her appearance but threw on the first pants and blouse that she found.

Keme shook his head, his lips pulled into a grim line. "No, they just said to come. They sent their carriage."

"Forget the carriage. I'll take Crane. He's faster."

THE COBBLESTONE PAVERS lining the Othonos drive clattered against Crane's shoes, announcing her arrival. She saw a sleek black carriage sitting in the middle of the path, and her heart dropped. It looked like the formal sort of coach nobility used to transport their dead.

Danae was alive. She *had* to be because Basia just couldn't handle any other possibility. Never mind that she was caught in Aphodes during the attack or that so many other brigands and soldiers had been nearby. Danae couldn't be dead. Basia couldn't— She—

Basia barely had the wherewithal to throw herself out of the saddle and toss Crane's reins to Yuka's mother, a woman she had known her entire life, who came to show her in.

She hurried past, forgetting formalities or niceties, and let her feet lead the way to the waiting room. The door was half open, and Basia didn't bother to knock, stepping inside only to feel her heart drop.

Danae's mother sat in one of the beautifully carved armchairs, her face in her hands. Her shoulders shook with silent sobs. Andromyda Othonos, Councilor to Phecea and one of the most proper women Basia knew, wept openly. Basia looked around and saw Master Annas slumped in a chair by the window, his eyes half shut. She had never seen the tutor look so worn down. His clothes were dirty, his Master's robe gone, his chin dark with stubble.

Basia took a half-step back. "No. No no nonono." Her heart was breaking, spilling out of her chest like so much refuse in the streets of lower Diosion. This couldn't be happening. It couldn't—

A large hand came to rest on Basia's shoulder, and she turned to look up into Councilor Arsenio's face. His honeyed brown eyes were red-rimmed, too, as if he had been crying, but he smiled. "Basia." He stunned her by pulling her in for a hug. He was such a tall man that Basia's nose barely reached his collarbone and he smelled nutty, warm, and sweet. Argan and myrrh. Just like the oil Danae used in her curls.

Basia felt tears well up in her eyes, and in the safety of Arsenio

Othonos's embrace, she let them come, her shoulders shaking with the force of her loss. "D—Danae...."

He held her a moment longer and then coughed, straightening up. "She's up in her room. Go. You should see her."

Basia pulled herself away, her wet cheeks cold from the sudden current of air against them. She didn't want to see Danae, not laid out on some sheet like a felled sapling, but as herself—long, shy, smart, and kind. She'd been waiting all this time for Danae to come home. She couldn't come home like this. She couldn't do this to Basia, to her family!

The stairway up to Danae's room ended too quickly, its often interminable length suddenly too short. Basia wanted to turn, run back into the night, and throw her arms around her horse's warm, sweet-smelling neck. She didn't, though. She stepped unstoppably onwards until she reached Danae's door.

She raised her hand to knock and then realized how pointless that was. Steeling herself, she pressed the door open. There stood Danae, half-dressed and barefoot in the middle of her room. She shrieked when she saw Basia and threw the brush she had been holding, though it missed Basia's head by a few inches.

"Basi!" Danae turned away, grabbing a cotton robe and pulling it over her shoulders. "What is wrong with you?! You scared me half to death!"

"You?!" Basia rushed into the room and threw her arms around her best friend. "You went missing for three moons, and then I get a message from your parents in the middle of the night, and there's a black carriage outside, and everyone looked like they had been crying, and your mom had her face in her hands, and your father *hugged* me! Danae! I thought you were dead!"

Basia felt Danae's thin arms wrap about her shoulders and had another shock. Danae was almost as tall as her father now. "Basi, they thought I was dead too. I guess they're crying because I'm *not* dead. Emotion is a funny thing." Danae pulled away from their hug and smiled into Basia's eyes. "I'm sorry I couldn't come home in a more fashionable carriage; the black ones were the only ones available to hire in Kydonia."

"Who cares if it was fashionable! I'm just so glad you're home!" Basia left tear-damp kisses on both of Danae's cheeks and stumbled back enough to see her face. "Why were you in Kydonia? Don't you know that's where all the fighting was?! You look like you're older than me now."

Danae shook her head, and Basia realized it wasn't just the sun-soaked color of Danae's skin or the lightening of her curls that made her look older. Her rounded cheeks were sharper now, her jaw more pronounced. Danae didn't look like a little girl anymore. Experience had stolen the remains of her childhood. That thought saddened her, but Basia pushed it away as she watched Danae rub her palms. "I left Aphodes rather abruptly, and Kydonia is a stronghold... It proved to be, but only through clever maneuvering. Basi... This war..." Danae swallowed and let her hands drop to her sides. "We're not winning."

CHAPTER 73: PHECEA

THIRD MOON, 1803, DIOSION

Two Years before the Proclamation

Danae suppressed a shudder as she stepped over a puddle of unknown origin and hurried to catch up to Basia, who strode through the lower streets of Diosion with a level of confidence Danae thought unwise. It wasn't that Diosion, even the poorer districts, was a cesspit of crime and poverty. But there were refugees here. The occasional thief. As they passed open doorways, Danae saw families crammed into tight rooms and people with dark eyes that lingered on her fine linens and gold bracelets.

Where Danae was slim due to heredity, people here were skinny with hunger. Hunger could make a reasonable person do unreasonable things. "Basia!" she hissed as she caught up, tucking her hand nervously into the crook of her friend's elbow. "Where are we going down here? How did you even find a tavern in this district?" She knew what desperation looked like thanks to her time with the refugees from Aphodes—even the kindest person could turn with enough stress.

"What? Oh— I just listened. Most everyone in the city says that this is the best place to get a drink, and for good reason. Just wait! I'm sure you'll like it."

They stepped over another puddle, and Danae wished she hadn't worn her wrap-up sandals. Boots would have been better, though ridiculous, with her short tunic dress in the Aphodian style. The drainage down here was terrible, and Danae wondered how many people fell ill because of that oversight. She would speak with her parents as soon as she got home and tell them how the lower city needed its sewage system completely re-evaluated.

Something splashed against her toes. Alright. She'd take a bath, *then* speak to her parents.

Basia insisted they didn't need guards, and at the time, Danae had agreed. They often traveled into the city together—shopping and visiting the eating houses. Never before had she felt so exposed. The gaze of a man with a deep scar across his face, still red and puffy, followed them around a corner. Had he been a soldier, mutilated in war, and sent home? Had he been in Kydonia? One of those wading through bodies and blood? Danae swallowed, and her mouth tasted like the sea. Why would a soldier be down in the squalor? Shouldn't Phecea provide ample housing for its wounded soldiers and sailors?

These thoughts unsettled her. Her mother and father often discussed ways to create opportunities and livelihoods for the refugees, but it seemed like so many filled these streets.

What was the saying? A worker without a job is a thief who hasn't stolen yet.

Her grip tightened on Basia's arm. "Are you certain about this? We've never been down this way before…."

Basia laid her hand on her friend's arm. "Danae, relax. They're just people. I don't know how many times I've been here. Dozens definitely. Maybe more."

Just people? The crowds in Aphodes had *just* been people. People trampling one another to get out.

Basia's office was well behind them, but still, she led them onwards so that the warehouses of the lower city blocked their view of the sea. A quarter of an hour passed. Then more.

Master Annas had warned her in Lefkara, where crime had started to rise, that Danae would be a target for attacks or muggings because she had, and they did not. She'd seen the proof on the road from Aphodes, though many didn't see her as nobility, not when she was as ragged as the other refugees. She rubbed the scars on her hands where the broken carriage window had dug into her flesh. "Basi...."

"We're here." Basia gestured to a simple stone building with windows bright from the flicker of lantern light within. It had a swinging sign hung just above the entrance that read, "The Cormorant's Rest," in beautiful white calligraphy with little, black-winged birds poised as if to dive. People stood talking outside, but they seemed more absorbed in each other than a pair of newcomers.

"Well? What do you think?"

Slowly, Danae inspected the sign, the door, and the street around the pub. It had been swept recently, and she didn't see any puddles. "Well... I suppose if you say it's the best ale in Diosion...." If Basia loved The Cormorant's Rest, Danae would at least try it.

Basia grinned at her and swung the door open, spilling noise, music, and laughter into the street in waves. It was only louder inside. A musician on the stage, hammered a twangy dulcimer with two small, curving tools. Slurring patrons sang a folk tune about fish and hooks while the musician grinned at them. Basia took her arm and led her deeper into the chaos.

Considering the walk down, Danae was blatantly surprised at the atmosphere inside. No one looked as if they were ruffians or thieves. People smiled, and while they were mostly merchants and workers, she spotted fine linens and jewels too. Lesser nobility, perhaps. People mingled and sang and drank. Nothing smelled of piss or blood.

She felt herself letting out the smallest breath of relief. This was more like the Phecea she had grown up in, though admittedly a bit rowdier.

"This is where we usually sit." Basia led her to a quieter table along the wall, away from the thick of noise and people. "The others should be here soon. I invited all of them, but I'm not sure who will make it."

With her back protected by a wall, Danae let her gaze travel over the patrons and the Emaian slave coming to take their order. "I would like to meet Lex, at least."

Basia blushed a lovely peach shade that complimented her pale blue blouse. "You will. They won't miss it. They promised. And we are a little early."

"Well, if we're early, then I suppose we should try this best ale." Danae looked around and waved at the Emaian. She stood out, so pale against the warm tones of Phecea. "I'll pay. What do you want, Basi?"

Basia

Basia looked from Danae to Ilia in mild dismay. The Emaian woman gave nothing away but waited patiently with her eyes downcast—the perfect picture of a slave. Danae hadn't thought twice about beckoning her over to serve them, hadn't stopped to consider how unlikely a small pub owning a slave was, or what Ilia might mean to Basia and her friends.

"Um... I'll have the house ale." Basia cleared her throat and met Ilia's gaze as it briefly flicked to her face. How would Danae react if she knew about the Society? If she knew about Basia's great work to free the Emai enslaved in Phecea? She shifted beneath the table.

She had never kept anything from Danae, and certainly never so long, but what else was she to do? There was no giving up the Society. It was too important.

Danae slipped a few coins from her purse and laid them on the table rather than placing them in Ilia's hand. She nodded, indicating that she would take one as well. "I had never thought of you as an ale-drinker, Basi. More champagne or spiced wines. I do like the atmosphere. Everyone seems to be in a good mood, which is a little harder to find these days."

Basia nodded her thanks to Ilia as she left, trying to swallow her guilt. She had never treated the woman like a slave before. "Yes. I think it has to do with the entertainment, though the first time I came, the storyteller seemed to favor morose tales."

"Well, I'm glad it's a happy song today."

"Me too."

Basia turned to look through the sea of patrons and caught a glimpse of someone who looked remarkably like Lex. They had the same height, the same rich, warm skin, and the same soft curls. And yet, they wore a clean, linen tunic with a perfectly conservative neckline above fitted leggings and sandals. Basia had never seen them look so... *proper*.

"Hello," Lex said when they reached the table and flashed Basia and Danae their most charming smile.

"Lex! You look positively—"

They held up their hands. "Don't say it. Dashing, right? Lovely? Absolutely devastating?"

"I was going to say 'respectable.'" Basia slid over so that Lex could take the seat next to her. "But all those other descriptions are fitting as well."

Lex snorted and kissed her cheek before turning to Danae. "Hello! Danae, I presume? It's nice to finally meet you."

"A correct presumption. Is Lex short for a more formal name you'd prefer I call you by?" Danae smiled, unblinking as Ilia slipped up, depositing their drinks on the table.

"Thank you, Ilia," both Basia and Lex murmured, more out of habit than anything, but when Danae said nothing, Basia could feel Lex stiffen slightly beside her. "My family name is Tasseas, but I don't go by anything but Lex. What about you, Danae Othonos? Would you prefer to be called something aside from your first name?"

Basia knew the way Danae tilted her chin, the way her gold-brown eyes widened slightly. She was deciding if Lex's words were a challenge, an insult, or a genuine question. Danae had asked if Lex had a more formal name out of politeness. Basia wouldn't have just anyone call her Basi; that was reserved for Danae.

"No. People usually just call me Danae or nothing at all. So," to anyone else, Danae's tone would sound polite and friendly, but Basia detected a hint of nerves, a wobbling in her friend's voice. "Basia says your family operates traveling caravans. Does that mean you get to travel yourself?"

Lex leaned back in the seat, their arm brushing Basia's. Perhaps it had been a challenge. Perhaps Lex had just been playing. Either way, they seemed happy enough to let it go. "The Tasseas name is big in merchant circles. We operate vessels and deal primarily in the textile trade, though recently, we've branched more into raw materials for the war effort. I haven't gotten to travel much. My family is more interested in me learning the trade from their books and ledgers."

"Humors, did I come at the wrong time, or what? Books and ledgers? Is that really what people talk about when they meet new friends?" Zol leaned over the back of Danae's booth, looking down at the top of the smaller woman's head. "Hi there. Danae right? Mind if I sit with you?"

Danae jumped slightly as Zol spoke, turning to see Zol looming over her. Basia had forgotten, or perhaps never really realized, how overwhelming her friends could be. Danae's eyes flickered to Zol's exposed biceps and up to her keen golden eyes. She shook her head, stopped mid-shake, and nodded. "Y-yes. Please do sit."

Zol bit her lip and looked at Basia, then sighed and sat down. "I'm sorry for coming up behind you like that. I didn't scare you, did I?"

Danae

It suddenly occurred to Danae that she wasn't being the diplomat she was raised to be. She blushed and found an embarrassed smile to accompany it. "I apologize. My behavior is unacceptable. I was so focused on Lex I didn't hear you come up, and I won't lie and say I'm completely comfortable here. Basia may have mentioned to you two that I was recently traveling?"

Lex looked at Zol. "Yes, she mentioned it."

"More than once." The guardswoman chuckled good-naturedly.

"Well... I had some experiences in Lefkara, Aphodes, and Kydonia that made me realize I had previously lived in a golden bubble. Actually, a golden and cream bubble. I was startled, but I should not have reacted so childishly to you, Guardswoman." Danae didn't want Zol to think she was frightened of her just because she was strong. Zol looked like the granite statues Danae and Basia had studied as children. Perfectly formed and intimidating with muscle.

"Well, Councilor, that's a fine apology," Zol said, obviously searching for the same kind of gravitas that Danae spoke with. When it evaded her, she shrugged and fell back into more comfortable patterns. "You can leave your bubble behind while you're here. The Cormorant's Rest welcomes all types. Even that lout there."

"Me? A lout? Why you cad! You fiend!" Basia shoved Lex, and they sniffed haughtily. "What I mean is, yeah. Just be yourself. Have a drink and kick back."

Casting Basia another look, Danae nodded, picking up her cup. Be herself? It seemed like an odd thing to say. She was polite, a person who sought out diplomatic words and the middle ground where everyone could, hopefully, be happy. Yet it seemed at The Cormorant's Rest that her manners were considered falsehoods.

It made sense that Basia had slipped into this crowd as smoothly as she navigated noble circles. Basia had the natural gift of sociability and an easy nature. Whispers of her childhood swirled around Danae. The sense of not belonging, of being the odd one. The ugly one.

Though she had never liked ale, she brought the cup and its dark contents up for a sip. Heavy and rich in flavor, she knew enough to agree it was a good batch, if still too thick for her taste. Not that she would insult them by saying so. Despite the racket of the stage and singers and patrons, their table was growing quiet.

Basia glanced around them, her discomfort clear as a well-ground telescope lens for anyone who knew how to look. She faltered for a moment and raised her glass. "How about a toast? To new friends?"

"I'll toast to that. And to new ventures." Lex raised their glass as well.

Zol copied them. "And to good ale and fine music."

Danae raised her glass alongside the others and swallowed when they did. It was a struggle to find something to say. What if Lex accused her of being disingenuine again? Or tried to bait her into a fight or something? Danae didn't know what she had done to offend Basia's lover, but it appeared that Lex didn't like her from the start.

The guardswoman seemed like a safer conversationalist, so Danae turned to her, noticing again how strong she was. "Why did you join the city guards? Was it an ambition you had since childhood, or perhaps some early inspiration due to… something else?"

"Well, Councilor," Zol started. "That's an interesting story, though not all of it is legal. My commanders know the whole of it, and as I have proved myself to them and my crimes were not committed against any Phecean, they have seen fit to allow me to keep my position. It all started when a small Zolelan orphan stole a loaf of bread...."

And so the conversation limped on, smoothed over in part by the interest Zol's story provoked. Danae could not imagine stowing away on a ship bound to a foreign land to escape the prison sentence that was the Zolelan price for theft.

Danae nursed what little she could of the ale and made sure to leave good silver on the table for the bar's staff as she waited for Basia to return from wherever she had gone with Lex. Probably to say goodbye.

"I'm sorry again, Zol. For my initial reaction. I know you might think I'm unnatural and stiff, but I do mean it." She looked up at the muscular woman, trying to force sincerity into her face. Danae wasn't a fool. Lex didn't like her. Or was rather unimpressed. She knew when someone was unimpressed with her, as Danae Othonos normally was found wanting. But it seemed like Zol might forgive her.

Zol shifted in her seat, but she nodded. "I don't see why you wouldn't mean it. You seem nice enough to me."

Nice enough, to me. Danae understood the unsaid thing there. *She thought Danae was alright, but not everyone here would.* "Thank you, Zol. For believing me."

The guardswoman nodded uncomfortably, and then Basia was back, her face flushed becomingly. "Danae! Are you ready to trudge back up the hill? I'm sure Zol will want some rest before tomorrow's shift, eh?"

Zol nodded. "The sun comes too early after nights with friends." She made her farewells and slipped out, surprisingly quiet and lithe for so impressive a figure.

"I thought you said I wasn't supposed to trudge anymore?" Danae murmured, slipping off her seat and trying her best not to glance around at the patrons. Would any try to follow them? Now that it was dark out, what little comfort Danae had gained slipped away.

Lex was there, watching her with dark eyes. Assessing. Finding her to be false or a coward. So Danae didn't ask if they could pay for a carriage. "Thank you for showing me The Cormorant's Rest."

They smiled their mouth wide beneath almond eyes. "Of course! The Rest will always welcome you."

"Yes! We'll have to come back sometime, Danae!" Basia grinned at both of them, her eyes bright with ale and cheer. She kissed Lex's cheek and stepped towards the door. "See you tomorrow for lunch, love?"

"Always!"

"Alright, let's get home."

CHAPTER 74: LIRIA

TWELFTH MOON, 1802, EGARA

Three Years before the Proclamation

The painting hung in a gilded wood frame. The artist, a Lirian, had gone to the painstaking trouble of painting each leaf on the tree branches, each puddle of sunlight on the forest floor. It depicted an idyllic scene of the cypress forest in the coastal lands just south of the Green Sea, an area Luce had visited during the first year of his marriage to Camilla. The place held fond memories for him, and the painting had been commissioned by Camilla on their tenth wedding anniversary. So, she said, he would always remember those sweet days.

He studied the painting now, hoping to feel happier or at least calmer. If he squinted, Luce was certain he could just make out the distant coastline, the waters aqua green, the beaches rising mounds like the underside of clouds. If he closed his eyes, could he hear the wind blowing through the cypress, a breeze scented by loam and salt?

Almighty, all he could hear was his heart hammering and the unevenness of his breaths. Ever since General Gais had been so permanently demoted, Luce felt as if a heavy stone had been planted on his chest, its weight pressing down on his ribs so that it was impossible to fully expand them.

He recognized the sensation from his raiding days when he would fight the barbarians with his own steel. Panic. Simmering and ever-present, it dictated every moment of his waking hours, and seeped into his dreams, so he woke to the swish of the Imperator's sword and the thud of his head hitting the floor.

How would he accomplish what no one else in the entire Lirian military had? How could he address both the Pheceans and the Emaians? Liria was stretched thin, near the point of breaking. If he redirected troops from one area to shore up a weakness, he would create another vulnerability. And how was he to address the Emai? When had they learned to change camps and drill their people in warfare? When had they learned to leave traps and dart off into the tundra, leaving no trace? When had they learned anything without Lirians there to lead the way?!

His head pulsed, and Luce opened his eyes, his vision filling with cypress trees. So much for calming himself. He frowned and rubbed at his amputated wrist, feeling how tense the muscles were there. If his hand were intact, it would be fisted.

A knock made him jump, and he gritted his teeth at his foolish nature. The Imperator wouldn't expect results so soon. Would he?

Camilla smiled as she entered his study, a tray of mint tea and a dish of wheat noodles served with fire-roasted tomatoes in hand. Of late, she'd been delivering all his meals. He hadn't the time to spare for supper at the table. Not with four children and two grandchildren to keep safe. Not with an entire army to organize.

She set the tray down and peered into his eyes, hers narrowing in dissatisfaction. He knew what she would say. He was too tired, working too hard, or he needed a break.

"When are you going to ask me for my opinion?" she asked.

"What?"

"You heard me." She crossed her arms, lips pressing into a thin, severe line. If she gave one of his children that look, Luce would feel sorry for them. As it was leveled on him instead, he felt embarrassed, as if he had been caught doing wrong.

"I... Camilla, you are a brilliant woman, but I doubt even you can solve this problem. It's more than just tactics and numbers. It's... It's facing the unknown. How can I plan for something I don't understand and don't have the means to learn? How can I think like a barbarian or a whore?" Luce shook his head. "It's impossible."

"You mean it's uncomfortable."

"Uncomfortable?"

"Yes, you don't want to delve into the mind of a Phecean or a slave, so you won't. You're an honorable man, so you don't want to practice thinking dishonorably. But, Luce, answer this. Which is more dishonorable? Failing your family and country, or entertaining barbaric, disgusting thoughts?"

When she put it like that, Luce had to admit being a failure to his family was much worse. "I wouldn't even know where to start!"

"Start with the simplest problem, of course." Camilla's expression softened then, and she placed her hands on his shoulders, using her thumbs to dig into the tight muscles. He groaned in appreciation. "That's how I run this house. If I thought about everything that had to happen on a given day, week, or moon, I'd drive myself mad. Instead, I just focus on the morning."

"Right...." Luce wasn't sure he understood, and it seemed Camilla could sense that from his tone.

"I don't wake, get the children ready, make the menu for the week — and you know how hard that has been with the food shortages of late— practice my paintings, visit Valeria and the grandchildren, and make you tea all at once. No. I wake, pray to the Almighty for a righteous day, and wash. Then I ensure the children are awake and bathed. While the slaves prepare breakfast, I remind the children which tutors will be arriving and when they are expected."

"Mhmm...." Luce nodded, understanding a bit better now. "You just focus on breakfast or the tutors, then the menu."

"Yes, and if I can't make the menu because I don't know what is at the market, I arrange for the wash to be dealt with. Something easier that I can handle now."

Well, he *could* handle the supply chain issue caused by Phecean ships. "Can you make sure a letter is delivered to the Vice Admiral as soon as I am done writing it?"

Camilla stopped massaging his shoulders and came around, her smile almost smug. On anyone else, it would have been, but on her, it was just right. "Of course, my love. Is there anything else?"

Luce stopped searching for a clean sheet of paper long enough to clasp his hand over his heart. "Thank you, my brilliant wife."

"Anything for you, my dear."

CHAPTER 75: LIRIA

FIRST MOON, 1803, EGARA

Two Years before the Proclamation

"Camilla!" Luce called as he waved for one of the servants to open the crate he'd brought home from the market. "Camilla!"

She appeared at the top of the stairs, her dark hair lightly mussed as if she had been lying down. "Yes?"

"Look what's in this crate." He gestured with his wrist, smiling when her eyes shot to the crate, her brows arched. She must recognize the insignia of the Imperial Navy.

"Are you bringing us naval rations now? Has it gotten to that?" Though her words were casual, Luce saw the tension in her jaw belaying her worry. Certainly, things had been tight for all of Liria.

He smiled more. "No."

That seemed to pique her interest because Camilla glided down the stairs, gesturing for one of the servants to pass over the crowbar in his hand. Pride swelled in Luce's belly. Camilla was stronger than she looked, and her will was iron. With the screech of nails on wood, the lid came off, and she peered inside.

"Oh!" She tossed the crowbar onto the table with little ceremony and reached into the crate to pull out a bundle of bright yellow fruit. "It's Tupa Galan, isn't it?"

"Yes, a starchy fruit that can be eaten baked, fried, or boiled."

"But we haven't had shipments from Tupa Gali in—"

"Moons," Luce agreed. "I've concocted a plan with the Navy, a joint effort to keep the Pheceans too busy to access our western shipping routes. This crate is off the first ship in port, but dozens more are making berths."

Camilla raised the yellow fruit to her nose, sniffing it. She swallowed hard, and Luce realized that her cheeks were sharper than he remembered. How many meals had she eaten less than her fill to ensure their children and staff were well fed?

Too many.

This was just the start, he promised himself. He would keep making progress and winning small victories. Not for Liria, or the Imperator, or pride. But for Camilla and their children.

CHAPTER 76: THE EMAI

SIXTH MOON, 1803, SINQINIQ

Two Years before the Proclamation

Pakuk grappled with another man, close in height if not weight. They tore at each other's furs, each scrabbling to get to the other's throat or eyes so that slivers of flesh showed along their chests where their trappings had come loose. Iniabi came to a stop nearby, but neither man slowed or glanced her way. She didn't even know the new fighter's name. There were just too many recruits. Every day, it seemed there were people to add to the roster, yet Lirian raids had all but dried up.

Iniabi sighed, stepped to the nearest tent, and took a pail of melting snow—still mostly frozen—from the side of their fire. She looked at it, judging its volume, and then upended the entire thing over the two fighters. They came up gasping.

"Pakuk, go help dig latrines. And you, get a fresh pail of snow and set it to melt by that fire."

Both men grumbled, but as Pakuk turned to comply with her orders, the new man sighed and did the same. At least they would listen to her, even if they were fighting like dogs.

As Iniabi turned to leave the wolf camp, Deniigi slipped up beside her, silent as a hare in the spring snow. "That's the third fight this week. Things are getting tense here, Iniabi."

"I can't make the slavers appear." It was a poor excuse, and Iniabi knew it. Her wolves could not stay here—they would soon rival the village's numbers. They would over-hunt and over-forage the land, forcing the hunters to range farther or the village to change locations. She wouldn't ask that of the people here.

"Wolves with nothing to hunt will fight amongst themselves. If there aren't any elk in your territory, then expand your reach." The trapper had never been afraid to speak his mind, and she had always appreciated that trait, but now it was unneeded. She *knew* her warriors needed a task. She even knew what to do next. There was just one person keeping her here.

Iniabi sighed. She shouldn't give up hope before she tried, but she did not think the coming conversation would be pleasant. "Start preparing to go. Get me a list of things we need to leave, and I'll see if the chiefs will help us."

Rather than replying, Deniigi simply slipped off, his fur-lined boots leaving minute impressions in the snow. The man was of substantial size, and yet he never left tracks. It was baffling. Maybe he was actually a spirit, sent to aid and guide her?

She shook her head. Not even Manaba had managed to haunt her—she doubted any other spirits would have bothered to try. Iniabi ambled through the wolves' camp, watching for more signs of unrest. She found them everywhere, but still, her thoughts were on the illu she was avoiding.

Hanta, Chief Sakari's child, ran up to her while she wandered. They held a cup of something steaming in one hand and a clutch of rocks in the other. They had never seemed to warm to Iniabi, though Qimmiq and the child had eventually forged an understanding.

Now Hanta squinted up at Iniabi. "Sedna's baby is fat, and Qimmiq likes to pinch her little legs. Qimmiq likes fat babies, did you know?"

"I didn't," Iniabi said dryly. There were ways for two wives to raise a child among the Emai, but Iniabi did not have the time for any of them. Not when she had over a hundred warriors to keep from killing each other. She sighed. She would never be exactly what Qimmiq wanted, no matter how much the other woman loved her. "What are your rocks for?"

"For throwing." Hanta's tone bordered on incredulous as if Iniabi were foolish to not know that already. They lifted their clutch of palm-sized stones and then, with impressive accuracy, pelted Iniabi's belly with one.

It stung, and Iniabi rubbed the spot a little ruefully. "I'll leave you to it then." There was really no sense in waiting any longer. If she was going to do this, Iniabi needed to do it now. Otherwise, she might never. She sighed again and turned her steps towards home.

Qimmiq wasn't there when she arrived, as was to be expected. The hunting parties would be wrapping up their day's work, cleaning and skinning the carcasses that would feed the village for the next few days. Without the bright, cheerful chief's daughter, the illu felt dark and empty. Their sleeping furs were still mussed from the previous night, a few cooking utensils scattered around the firepit. With a wait ahead of her and nothing else to occupy her hands, Iniabi began to tidy the home she had built with Qimmiq.

It was nearing evening when Qimmiq returned home. She stepped through the door just as Iniabi finished mending one of her shirts, Qimmiq's hair coming loose from her braids and her clothes stained with dirt and blood. Iniabi's heart exploded in her chest, her gut writhing with nerves. "Hello."

"Oh, you're back early." Qimmiq smiled distractedly as she pulled off her parka and dropped it beside the door. "I didn't think I'd see you before supper. We tracked this big caribou today, and he led us to a herd. We were able to take a few of the older males, so Sinqiniq will do well for the next few weeks."

"That's a relief." Iniabi struggled to sound normal. "I know that things have been tense with the wolves here. The village is having to find more and more food."

"Well, we'll find a way." As Qimmiq spoke, she went about her usual routine of coming home from a long day of hunting. She filled a pot with snowmelt and set it atop the low fire Iniabi had built, then untangled her braids, letting her hair fall free over her shoulders. It was a scene Iniabi was intimately familiar with, comfortable knowing the domestic routine of her lover. Next, Qimmiq would change all her clothes and wash her hands and face before starting preparations for dinner.

"The wolves can't stay here, Qimmiq. Not the way they're growing."

The whalebone comb in Qimmiq's hand stalled halfway through her hair. Pale eyes met Iniabi's, and her usually pleasant smile was replaced with a tense line. "Where will they go then?"

"Where they're needed." Iniabi stood, too fidgety to be still any longer. "We've made tremendous strides here. The Lirians haven't dared to send soldiers this far south in weeks. If we could do the same north of here, pushing farther and farther, we could eventually chase them out of our Tundra. We could be free."

"We are free here in Sinqiniq. We have an illu, friends, and a village. We have each other." Qimmiq set down her comb with deliberate carefulness as if she were trying to control herself, but Iniabi saw the tremble in the other woman's hand. "I like our life here."

"I love our life here too," Iniabi said, the familiarity of this argument draining some of her nervous energy. In its wake, she was tired. "I just can't rest while there's still work to be done, Emaians to reach. I— I was lost for so many years. I finally found the thing I need to do."

"But what am I supposed to do? You're going off with the wolves to fight the Lirians, and I'm... what? Staying behind in the illu, hoping you'll remember me?"

"You could come with me. I would want you there."

For a few seconds, Iniabi let herself hope. She saw her and Qimmiq both leaving, leading the wolves towards the salvation of their people, working together on strategy and the unceasing trials of feeding and caring for a hundred people moving through the Tundra. They could do it. They could stay together.

"You want me to become a warrior?" Qimmiq's voice was softer, her eyes widening in surprise and hurt.

"No, I just want the person you are with the talents you have." She felt stripped bare, all her vulnerable insides spilling like blood on snow. "Come with me. Please, Qimmiq. I don't want to lose you."

She could see Qimmiq's throat bob up and down as she swallowed, and she stood face to face with Iniabi. "I don't want to lose you either." She reached slowly to brush a thumb along Iniabi's cheek, and Iniabi closed her eyes at the sudden tenderness of it. "But... I want a life. A home. A family. How can I have those things if we're moving around, always in danger, never building something permanent?"

"I didn't say never," Iniabi said, part of her still trying though she understood. She tucked loose strands of white hair behind Qimmiq's ear. "Just not now."

"Iniabi, Daughter of Manaba, warrior and pirate and visionary." Qimmiq cupped her cheeks and pulled Iniabi close enough to lay a kiss across her brow. "You are the most extraordinary person I've ever met, but... I think I want ... an ordinary life. And I don't think you'll ever be happy with that."

Iniabi let some of the weight of her head rest in Qimmiq's cupped palm. "No," she said, "No, I couldn't," and with those words came a surprising amount of relief, like they'd both been wearing masks, pretending to be people they weren't and were finally allowed to shed the farce. She smiled sadly. "It took us an awfully long time to figure that out."

"Two years isn't that long. After all, it took you ages to even kiss me." Qimmiq shared the sad smile Iniabi gave her and gestured to the pelts beside the fire. They both settled onto them, and Qimmiq tucked her hand into Iniabi's. The chief's daughter still shook, but she seemed calmer as if she felt the relief too. "Besides, when I was younger, the excitement was what I wanted. I just... I'm sorry, Iniabi. I changed."

Iniabi squeezed her hand and laid her head on her lover's shoulder. "So did I. When I first came here, desperate and purposeless, all I wanted was a home. I don't think I was ever made to be still, though." Life hadn't let her be.

Qimmiq nodded. "Well... That's that then, isn't it? You'll go off with the wolves, and I'll stay here and try to... make a life." She shook her head as if the idea was impossible. Iniabi knew it wasn't. Qimmiq was beautiful, kind, and a strong hunter, and when Iniabi left, she'd even have her own illu. Once her heart mended, Qimmiq would have plenty of potential romantic partners. "Oh, Iniabi, I wish we could want the same things."

"Me too," Iniabi said, but it wasn't entirely true. She would never want anything as much as she wanted to chase the slavers out of her home.

CHAPTER 77: THE EMAI

SEVENTH MOON, 1803, BIKKISI

Two Years before the Proclamation

Iniabi leaned back against the pale, flawed bark of a red alder trunk, the slender length pressing against her spine. Her back ached from a moon of carrying all the food and water she would need, and she relished the chance to stand straight and stretch. Around her stood the entirety of Iniabi's small war council— Tatik, Uki's apprentice and medicine woman to the wolves; Deniigi; and Poallu, an escaped slave who could read both Lirian and Phecean. She had a clever mind and knew much about the northern cultures from the time she'd spent serving them. The Amaruit camped a little ways away in the foothills of the Nonnoccan Peaks, several miles north of Bikkisi.

"We're running low on supplies," Tatik said, careful to keep her voice low lest someone overhear. Certainly, they were away from the pack, but Iniabi appreciated the medicine woman's cautious nature. "With every batch of captured slaves we free, our ranks increase but so do our hungry mouths. We need to feed them. We need to clothe them."

Deniigi nodded in agreement. "I think these little raiding parties aren't enough now."

"But Bikkisi is a stronghold. The Pheceans rely on the shipping from there, especially now with their conflict with Liria affecting their northern ports. They won't let it go easily." Poallu crossed her arms, her expression tense. The Lirians might have been her original captors, but the Pheceans had held her leash for many years.

Iniabi hummed and crossed her arms as well. Her ranks had swollen since she'd left the Sinqiniq, but still, one hundred and fifty Emaian warriors against a city of a few thousand were horrible odds. Iniabi wasn't about to lose her force to a pitched battle, not with so many lives depending on them. She much preferred to even the field before getting embroiled. "Is there any way we can get in, get what we need, and get out again? Perhaps causing a decent amount of chaos along the way? We can always come back after our ranks have filled out more."

"The harbor is well guarded, as their trade ships are their most valuable things," Poallu spoke first, her mouth pulled into a mulish line. She hated the Pheceans and wanted to fight them, but she still carried the fear of her old captors. The conflict roiled off the woman in palatable waves, and Iniabi didn't envy Poallu her situation.

"They seem organized from our reports. Regular patrols, some sort of curfew where the citizens are all in their boxes by moonrise." Deniigi shifted, taking his hunting dagger out and shining it with the hem of his coat.

"Perhaps we can reach their supplies and even the odds that way? Surely they keep their drinks and food in some dry, warm storehouse?" Tatik offered.

"And what, we take it?" Deniigi asked.

"No, we spoil it. If half their fighting force is stuck in the latrines, and the other half hasn't had any food for two days for fear of gut cramps, then they won't be very good fighters."

Deniigi stared at Tatik as if she were brilliant or even a little frightening. Slowly, he smiled.

Tatik smiled back at the tracker, and Iniabi shifted, uncertain. If they went with this plan, they'd be a fox fighting a bear, and a bear with stomach cramps was still more likely to win.

"How can we know which food will go to their soldiers and which will go to the normal people?" Poallu asked.

"Do you mean the slave takers or the slave users?" Iniabi snorted. There were no *normal people* in Bikkisi. "We *will* spoil the food after our raid, not before. We'll strike silently in the dead of night, steal as much food as we can carry, and ruin the rest. Let them sicken and starve. When we come back, it will make taking the city easier. For now, though, I won't destroy the Amaruit for the sake of a single port."

Tatik and Deniigi nodded, but Poallu frowned, and even before she started to speak, Iniabi knew what she was going to say. "Some of the Pheceans don't like slavery. I was helped by some. Should we hurt those who want to do good along with those who do harm?"

"Do you know of any allies to our cause within Bikkisi?"

Poallu shook her head. "Just because I do not know them doesn't mean they do not exist." Iniabi appreciated Poallu's candor and ability to think beyond what was in front of her, but her insistence that some Pheceans were good could be taxing at times. For a moment, Iniabi's mind flickered back to Uki coming to meet Iniabi before they left Sinqiniq. The old woman had whispered a warning even as she'd blessed this journey. *You might be Ice Hearted, Snow Bringer, but do not underestimate warmth.* Iniabi shook her head.

"Unless we have proof of allies, we will move forward. Weakening the port will make it easier to take once we have greater numbers." Iniabi rolled her head between her shoulders, stamping her feet against the ever-pervasive cold. "How many half-northern warriors do we have? We'll need spies to get in and find out where their stores are."

Deniigi met her eyes and shrugged. "Enough."

↑ ↑ ↑

By the time the spies returned, Iniabi was pacing like a caged wolverine, walking through the organized camp with no real purpose other than to *move*, to feel as though she were doing *something*. She twitched with impatience, and when she saw Capun and Yutu slip into camp, Iniabi had to restrain herself from running to them.

Instead, she went and found her council and waited for the spies to come to her.

It took longer than she would have liked, but eventually, they gathered in the same forest clearing as before. Capun was bright-eyed, and her silver-white hair was hidden beneath a cloth headwrap. Yutu bounced on the balls of his feet as Deniigi settled against a tree.

"Well?" he asked.

"Their storehouses are near the ports. I guess for convenience," Yutu explained, stuffing his hands into his pockets. He looked excited to be part of the council meeting.

"We could easily kill the six guards and sneak in. They have patrols that come around on a schedule. I watched them walk this square design through their streets, looping around every twenty minutes. We'd need to get in and out between patrols 'cause if they come by and see the guards are down, they'll raise the alarm." Capun seemed to remember her headscarf and pulled it off, folding it up and stuffing it under her arm.

"Is twenty minutes enough time?" Poallu asked, looking at Tatik.

The medicine woman nodded. "Ruining food is not a time-consuming art. Really it will be transporting the goods we want for ourselves that will eat up the most time."

"Could we buy more if we distracted the nearest patrols? Delay them from coming past the warehouse," Deniigi suggested, looking to Iniabi.

"Good idea. We'll have a second, smaller party for the distraction. Thank you, Capun and Yutu. You'll get orders shortly." Iniabi nodded, dismissing them, but Capun hesitated.

"You should know, we overheard some talk in the city. Lirians captured the *Flying Night*."

Iniabi went still, an unnamed feeling surging in her chest. "Thank you, Capun. That information may be of use."

ᛏ   ᛏ   ᛏ

Iniabi stood in the shadows between two buildings, breathing in the nostalgic stench of a refuse-steeped alleyway. She felt like she was back in the streets of Angillik, except that this time she did not have to scurry back to a tiny cliff for safety. She wasn't alone.

Behind her stood three wolves—Capun, Pakuk, and a new fighter named Anjij. None of them made any sound. To do so might have given them away. The streets of Bikkisi were as still and silent as the Tundra after thick snow, all the citizens tucked away in their homes. Perhaps that was a product of the war because Iniabi didn't remember a similar rule in Angillik. Of course, Bikkisi was also under Phecean control, so they might do things differently.

She shifted, her shoulder brushing rough brick—the whole city was made of the stuff, the jagged edges creating claw-like shadows where the moon struck them. Ahead was the tall, guarded building holding most of the city's food stores, rising blunt and square into a clear sky. Somewhere not too far, a strange, owl-like cry pierced the night, one short coo followed by a longer one. Iniabi smiled. The distraction party was in place.

On silent, hide-wrapped feet, Emaians slipped from hiding and into the streets, careful to keep out of sight of the slit-like windows above. Iniabi was one of the first to the doors. She moved like fluid, like poison, her body strong with the thrill of it all. She killed the first guard just as one of her wolves suffocated his partner. From there, it was easy. The wolves made quick work of the remaining guards, and Iniabi settled into the corner of a window to keep an eye out, watching as her people slipped in and out of the building with broad sacks.

"It's hard to believe this city was once Emaian," Capun's voice was kept low as she came to stand beside Iniabi, looking around the brick walls with open distaste. "It's so… wrong. Nothing makes sense here. They've fought every natural curve and turn of the earth."

"Nothing about this city was ever Emaian," Iniabi said, turning to look at the fox-faced woman. Her tone was dull, but she smiled a little, so it didn't sting. "Except the land beneath it. I wish we could take it back now."

"What would we even do with it? Tear it to the ground?" Capun thumped her hand against the brick corner of the storehouse. "These people don't understand anything."

"That would be better than letting them keep it."

Capun grinned. "We could do it. Rip it down, brick by brick. Let the Tundra reclaim what was taken."

"We will, one day. We'll come back and take this place apart until it all lies in the sea. We'll—"

Shouts rose, and Iniabi whipped back around, her heart pounding. In the streets below, the last few laden wolves were being rushed by soldiers. Iniabi turned from the window, cursing under her breath.

Behind her, Capun hissed like an angry fox. "What are they doing here so soon? We should have had another ten minutes, at least!"

There was no time to worry about that now. "Get down there!" Iniabi hissed, even as she took the stairs two at a time. She could feel Capun just behind her, a shadow to her shadow as they rushed past two wolves still determinedly tearing open the remaining food. "Leave it!" At this point, Iniabi just wanted them safely away. They could always attack again later; they just had to be alive to wield the blade.

She and Capun hit the streets together, Iniabi's wicked little sword ringing as she pulled it from its sheath. The chaos had not quite broken out into a full battle—many, if not most, of Iniabi's fighters had already made it away, and the last few were putting up a brave fight. It seemed that the Phecean soldiers had not realized just how many Emaians had infiltrated their city when they followed those responsible for Iniabi's distraction back to the warehouses, so there were not many of them to kill. Not all of her people had made it, though. Yutu lay dead in the streets, his arms tangled beneath his limp body and the spear he had just earned buried in his back.

Iniabi wheeled away, anger making her incautious. She flung herself at the nearest soldier, battering aside his sword and ducking within his guard to plant a dagger in his belly. His face went pale with agony, and when she dodged his counterstrike, he fell to the damp, dirty stone. Iniabi wanted to scream, wanted to retch or kill. She had led her people here. She had sent Yutu to die.

The soldier gurgled, pulling the knife out in a gush of blood as though he wanted to die faster. Iniabi let him. Let these slave takers bleed out in their own refuse-choked streets. Let them suffer. Not far, but easily out of reach, she caught sight of a soldier taking aim with a crossbow. Iniabi flinched, searching for somewhere to hide, anything to stop the bolt. Should she wait and try to dodge or—

The crossbow fired with a dull twang, and suddenly, Capun was there, falling against Iniabi, her mouth open in pain or horror. Iniabi caught the slim, sharp woman, keeping her upright even as she shuddered and twitched. Blood fell in streams down the curve of her back, and her hands clutched, claw-like, at Iniabi's sleeves. Horns sounded across the city, alarms threatening to bring more soldiers, and Iniabi's breaths were coming in fast gasps. "Run!" she told her people. "Get out of here!"

They dashed into the snow and trees of the Tundra, and beneath that black-broken sky, Capun died in Iniabi's arms.

CHAPTER 78: RHOSAN

SIXTH MOON, 1803, CWM OR

Two Years before the Proclamation

*P*ain blossomed through Wynn's gut, radiating up until his stomach spasmed, and he choked on bile before rough hands hauled him upright. The remains of his supper dribbled over his chin and down the front of his chest, bare as he slept in little more than woolen pants and shawl. The warmth of his vomit contrasted against his chilled skin, and Wynn flinched away as he was hauled out of his cot. Gods, let the beatings be over. Dyfan had said he would breed! They didn't need to hurt Wynn any longer.

The two Defeated at his side were field workers, strong from years of labor and emboldened by taking him in the middle of the night. Wynn yanked out of their grips, lunging to his feet only to find a third Defeated waiting with a club in hand.

He knew these men. They were part of Gruffyd's compound. Why were they attacking him?

The man with the club swung at Wynn, who pivoted to take the blow on his shoulder. The contact of the wood against his flesh ached, and Wynn grunted, facing his enemy. Maybe they were turning on him because of the Contender Matches or Dyfan. Whatever the reason, he wouldn't take this without a fight.

Wynn pushed past the pain in his back and kicked, his barefoot landing in the meat of the club wielder's thigh. He gasped, and the two who had initially accosted Wynn grabbed him by the arms.

"Stop it!" one ordered, but Wynn kept fighting, twisting so he could grab his captors as they grabbed him. They grappled, and he slammed the two Defeateds' heads together before something knocked against his raw back.

Pain blazed up his spine, and Wynn fell to his knees. He blinked away tears as another entered the room, her form resolving into cream skin and feminine lines. Ifanna pushed back the hood of her cloak, her dark hair billowing out around her face, her lips pulled into a sneer.

Wynn struggled to brace himself, to look up at the woman who— He'd—He closed his eyes. "What do you want from me? Haven't you already had everything?"

Was it because of Dyfan? Did she think because she'd fucked him on the tour, she owned his heart? Or was this just a point of pride, a way of breaking him for chasing the one beautiful thing this foul place had? It wouldn't work. Wynn would never regret loving Dyfan, not even if he'd betrayed him in the end by giving in to Ifanna.

"I want nothing from you, Defeated. Nothing but the truth." Ifanna gestured to the men, and they hauled Wynn back to his feet. "Leave us." The Defeated did as she ordered, and Wynn thought briefly of charging. He could kill Ifanna—break her skull against the stone walls of his tiny room. He could get past her and steal a horse. He'd go through town this time to lose the hounds before slipping into the wilderness.

But that would mean leaving Dyfan, and there was still no way to know if he would make it.

He took a deep breath and spat blood. "What truth?"

Her gaze narrowed as she took him in, and her frown deepened. "The truth about you."

"About me? I'm sure you know about Dyfan and me. Did you think I loved you? Is that the truth you're after?" Wynn laughed, curse the consequences. "If I had thought I had a way out, that night on the tour would have never happened. But what can I do against a Victor? I love Dyfan. There's your bloody truth."

"Love?" A sickening laugh escaped Ifanna, cold and full of anger. "You think I'm after love? What kind of idiot do you think I am?" She pushed aside her cloak, revealing she wore nothing more than a thin underdress. She was here to take him again, to manipulate him into doing what she wanted. Wynn flinched back. He wouldn't. He wouldn't do it. Not again. She couldn't force him. She knew he loved Dyfan, but she couldn't hurt Eurig's Defeated for no good reason, and she couldn't hurt him too much without Gruffyd noticing. He would not let her touch him.

But no, her scant clothing revealed the easy swell of her belly, the heaviness of her breasts. These shapes had been Nia's once when she bore Owynn.

Ifanna was pregnant.

"No." The word escaped Wynn in an involuntary whisper even as he began to count backward. It had been four moons, maybe five. "No, no, no...."

Ifanna pulled her cloak closed, hiding the pregnancy from view. She glared at Wynn a moment longer and then turned. It appeared that his answer had been truth enough for her. Wynn's mind reeled. He remembered, after the first fight he won, Gruffyd claimed he would get rich off of Wynn by making him stud like Dyfan.

Wynn had told Gruffyd he was barren. He'd even faked breeding with a few females to prove the point. Gruffyd must have believed it and told Ifanna he was sterile.

That had been why she chose him.

Had he done this to himself? Was it his fault that he had been used this way? Punishment like how Dyfan had been put in the pits when he refused to breed?

What was he thinking? No sane person would force another to choose between being used as an animal or fulfilling the sexual whims of their captor in exchange for safety. Anger surged within him, so hot and sharp that it brought tears beading to the backs of his eyes above his iron-clamped jaw.

"You do not get to blame me for what you coerced me to do,

Victor. If I lied to keep myself from being used like an animal, so godsdamned what? *You* pulled me from my home, from my wife and son, and put me in this godsforsaken cage so that you could make me fight and make me fuck and use me to satisfy your own debased cravings. If you didn't want to be pregnant, you've only your own sick nature to blame."

He laid back down on his pallet, curling in on himself, careful with new and old injuries. He supposed she'd chosen to have him attacked tonight because no one would look twice at the bruises right after Eurig had him beaten.

Ifanna's back stiffened, and she turned in his doorway. Her eyes flashed in the dim lighting, her cheeks reddening with anger. There was no way she felt shame. "You better watch how you speak to me, Defeated. If I told Gruffyd how you took me against my will, what do you think he'd do to you? To your little lover? Hmm?"

Wynn snorted. "By now, I'm willing to bet you've already told him it's his. You better have. You're showing. If you'd waited after you first found out, it would have been clear to everyone that you were trying to hide it. Do you really think he'd believe you had kept an assault from someone so inferior in power from him for moons? No. You've already taken care of your own safety."

She stood for a moment longer, her hands balling into fists. Ifanna was as trapped in this as he was. She gave him one last withering glare and left his room with a swish of her cloak.

The night was quiet all around, the Defeated quarters almost peaceful in the dark. As he lay alone and his anger cooled, Wynn began to shiver in fear and fever.

What could he possibly tell Dyfan that wouldn't push the other man away from him?

⇑ ⇑ ⇑

A week after his beating, Wynn was beginning to feel a little more human. He no longer ached with every movement or retched with sudden nausea during physical exertion. As he poured cold water from Gruffyd's pond over his sweat-slick limbs, he could see where the dark purple of his bruises was fading to a sickly yellow-green.

Scooping handfuls of wet sand from the bottom of the pool, he scrubbed off days of dirt and bloodstains, letting them wash away and wishing he could clean the memories from his mind just as quickly.

Ifanna was pregnant with Wynn's second child, a product of her mistreatment of him, and his betrayal. Dyfan didn't know, but their Victors knew enough about Wynn and Dyfan's relationship to force Dyfan to breed.

And there was nothing Wynn could do about any of it.

He was trapped, the only decision still in his power that of whether or not to tell Dyfan about the baby, about the night in Gwaeth when he had chosen to betray his lover for a few moons' peace instead of earning Ifanna's ire—something he'd reaped eventually regardless.

If he told Dyfan about the baby now, while the other man was already afraid for Wynn and struggling with being forced to breed, it would only make Dyfan's situation worse. If Wynn knew him at all, then Dyfan would not be able to let Wynn be beaten for his own freedom. He would just be betrayed, alone, and still completely within the Victors' grasp.

And yet, how much of that was an excuse? Wynn *wanted* to protect Dyfan, to keep him safe and healthy, but he was *so* afraid of losing him. What if Dyfan no longer wanted anything to do with him?

Wynn dumped another bucket of water over his head and shivered violently. The water was only up to his waist, and above it, his flesh pimpled in the cold, the weak light of a gray morning not even enough to paint the shadows of the evergreens standing around the pool's western edge. He still didn't know what to do, but not deciding was as much a decision as choosing a path.

He left the pond and dressed slowly, moving with the rheumy speed of a much older man, until a young runner interrupted him halfway through. Wynn glanced at the boy, standing a little ways off and staring wide-eyed at Wynn's large, scarred body. He was a Defeated kid. Hopefully not destined to be a fighter.

"What is it?"

The boy swallowed. "Ifanna wants you."

"Of course she does."

Wynn pulled his shirt on, hiding the remains of his injuries from view and turned to leave, wending his way through the compound and towards the Victors' home.

Linn waited for him in the great hall, her too-bright eyes narrowed as she gestured for him to hurry up. He'd kept Ifanna waiting too long. "What have you done now?" she hissed, straightening his plain tunic impersonally. "She wants you in her private rooms."

"I don't know," he lied. "There's no telling what any of them have in mind."

On the opposite side of the great house as Victor Gruffyd's, Ifanna's rooms were lavishly appointed. Obscenely so. Thick, woven carpets covered the wooden floors, and the walls were draped in tapestries depicting battle scenes featuring a molten figure. Kirit. The Defeated quarters were made of mud and thin wooden slats, and here she was, protected by stone, thatching, and warmth.

The hearth crackled merrily, contrasting with Wynn's guilt. Ifanna sat at a little table, the surface cluttered with jewelry, combs, perfumes, and face paints. She ignored Wynn as he bowed and busied herself with painting her lashes. She made him stand there waiting a long time before she finally turned, brush in hand, to give him an overly sweet smile.

"I wanted to congratulate you, Wynn. Gruffyd just told me the good news."

He watched her warily like one might study a snake laying languidly in their path. No matter how docile she looked at a given moment, she was always ready to bite. "What news?"

Her eyes widened in surprise, though he suspected it was feigned, and her smile deepened, making lines about her mouth and eyes. Ifanna was younger than Gruffyd, but he wasn't sure how much. Was she past thirty winters? "Why, your elevation in weight classes! Your training master says you qualify to be in the second largest class, and of course, you're a sure thing for the Contender Matches."

It seemed unlikely that Ifanna had invited Wynn here just to talk about pit fighting—she had never been particularly interested in the sport unless you counted the bodies of those who participated in it. They had already dismissed with the bluff that she could have him blamed for her pregnancy, so this was likely just some method or another to get back at him. The question was, how? Well, if she could play her part, he would play his. Wynn bowed. "Thank you, Victor."

"Of course," Ifanna went on, ignoring his false humility. "Victor Eurig's big stud just went down in weight class. I guess all those lesser pit fights really did him in. So... I suppose you're in the same division now."

And there it was.

Wynn stilled ice in his veins. They were going to make him fight Dyfan, or, he supposed, they would *try*. He wouldn't do it. Consequences be cursed. He'd let them kill him if it meant not hurting his lover.

So long as they didn't hurt Dyfan to force his hand.

Ifanna nodded as if she had read his mind and set aside her brush. She stood, running one hand possessively down her belly, drawing attention to it. "That's why I talked Gruffyd into buying another set of breeding rights from Eurig. I said, 'why not hedge our bets? If Wynn is the Contender this year, well, we already own him, but if Dyfan is, then we'll get one more whelp out of him before Eurig increases his rates.' You know Gruffyd, he's always liked a bargain." Before Wynn could react, she reached for the stupid little bell on her desk. She shook it, and Linn appeared in the doorway. "Has Victor Eurig arrived yet?"

Linn bowed her head. "Yes, Victor, he's in the courtyard."

"And Nimue is ready?"

"Yes, Victor," Linn murmured, her gaze flickering to Wynn once before darting back to the floor.

"Perfect. Linn, show Eurig inside. Wynn, show his stud to the breeding quarters."

CHAPTER 79: PHECEA

FOURTH MOON, 1803, DIOSION

Two Years before the Proclamation

Basia walked up from Lex's loft without seeing the streets around her. Lex's voice was still as loud in her ears as though she had never left, their pointed face, tight with anger, still swimming before her eyes.

"I just don't understand, Basia. How can you spend so much time with a slaver? She doesn't believe the same things you do."

"She's a good person. It's just how she was raised. I only know better because of Keme!"

"Doesn't she have a personal slave too?"

"Well, yes, but—"

Lex hadn't let Basia finish, blazing on through with their point. "She had all the same opportunities as you, and yet you ended up with us, and she's going to be one of the next propagators of slavery in Phecea."

"Lex, you don't know her."

"Did you tell her about us?"

"No, of course not, I—"

"See! Even *you* don't trust her."

Basia bit her lip and just avoided walking into a messenger with an armful of packages. She waved in apology and continued on, her eyes turned to the cobblestone of the streets beneath her feet.

It wasn't that she didn't trust Danae—she did! Danae just hadn't ever been told stories of the Dasans or the Long Pilgrimage. She didn't know that the Emai were just people. People who had been taken from their homes and forced into servitude under the guise of 'education' or 'betterment.' She would understand if Basia explained it to her.

Wouldn't she?

Basia forced herself to stop chewing on the inside of her cheek. Danae would know she was worrying if the other girl caught her doing it, and she had finally made it to the hall where they would meet. Now, she just had to find her friend.

The sound of a pen scratching against paper caught Basia's attention, and she turned a corner to find Danae. She stood scribbling with unblinking intensity on a makeshift table held up by an Emaian who braced the board with her back to provide a surface for writing. By the looks of her uniform, the Emaian was from one of the messenger groups around Diosion. For a few coins, one could have a message sent to anyone in the city, even if it took all day to track them down.

Danae's writing sped up, and dots of ink splattered her hand, but she signed the document and waved off the Emaian, turning to face Basia with open arms. "I apologize for keeping you waiting."

Basia looked between the Emaian woman rushing out into the city and her friend standing with her arms outstretched and thought she might cry. In the end, though, she hugged Danae quickly and stepped back. "What was all that about? It looked urgent."

Danae's assessing look changed to one of mild discomfort. Her eyes shifted to follow the slave, and she shook her head. "Things in Lefkara are growing... *tense*. Liria continues to press forward, eating up territory lines. My father sent me a message to say that I will attend the Council meeting on our limited supplies this evening."

Three years ago, a Council meeting at night would have been an odd event. Unheard of. But since the start of the war, and especially since the beginning of the new year, the Councilors and their heirs were meeting in a never-ending flurry of debates and tactical planning committees.

It was a wonder Basia got to see Danae at all.

"Your father knows this already, but I'm afraid that the trade alliance we brokered with Zolela is in danger of falling apart. Nearly a third of the ships they have sent laden with goods have been raided or sunk. It could just as easily be Lirians or pirates, and we can't take more vessels from the front lines to provide them with an escort. We offered to pay for escorts, but Papa says the treasury is already straining under the weight of the war."

"The lines on the Bathi are so thin. I saw the list of stipends we're sending families of the deceased... Basia, it's *terrible*." Danae slipped her hand down Basia's wrist, weaving their fingers together.

Basia turned her eyes to their intertwined fingers, her mind half on the cost of this bloody war and half on the argument with Lex that morning. "It *is* terrible," she said, and overhead, the great clock tower of Diosion tolled eleven. Basia tugged Danae back towards the front of the hall, using the excuse of moving to drop her hand. "Come on. Do you still want to see the play? It'll be starting any moment."

Danae

"Of course." Danae watched as Basia moved away and ahead of her. She knew her friend well enough to recognize that something was amiss. Basia normally took her by the hand and led her around. Now she kept looking away, leaving distance between them. Maybe Danae was imagining it. After all, they *were* in a bit of a hurry. "Do you want a drink? I could find some while you catch Adohnis and Callista?"

"Yes! That sounds good. They're probably already seated. Will you get me something light?" Basia smiled at her, but it was distracted, and she left abruptly, her head tilted to search for their friends.

The theater was nearly empty, the patrons spaced out and huddled into smaller groups, their voices high and faces tight. Danae didn't have to overhear their conversations to know what they spoke of. What else would they have to talk about? Certainly, musicians still created new songs and compositions, artists painted and carved, and dancers danced. But the muses had abandoned Phecea, and it seemed the only inspiration left came from the military, the war, or the bravery of common people.

Danae approached the bartop, crowded despite the smaller audience. Drinking would never lose inspiration, she supposed and had to wait to order.

She watched the soldiers in front of her, a group of three women, likely home on leave or newly conscripted and due at the border soon. Their uniforms were clean, their boots polished. There was a simplicity to the lines that Danae had found unappealing when she first saw it but now felt familiar.

"My mother said she went to the slave pens to buy a new kitchen girl, but the prices were ridiculous. Forty gold for an unskilled girl?"

"That's nothing. We got a letter saying the Council would buy our able-bodied Emaians from age sixteen to forty. Apparently, they need workers for the new farms they're establishing along the coast."

Danae kept her gaze away from the soldiers as she continued to eavesdrop. She didn't want them catching her listening in.

"Did your parents sell?"

"Of course! They're patriots. But now it's more expensive to buy replacements."

"The man said that inventory is low…."

She supposed it was better to complain about the price of slaves than the lack of food. With Liria pressing forward, Phecea had lost many acres of farmland. She attended the Council meeting discussing what was to be done, and at the time, thought asking loyal Pheceans to sell their working slaves to become farmhands was a reasonable solution.

These women seemed to think otherwise. But her father had said it was impossible to keep everyone happy anyway. The soldiers got their drinks, and Danae was finally able to order.

Ten minutes had passed before Danae found Basia, Adohnis, and Callista, so she hurried to sit next to Basia as performers appeared on stage. "Here, Basi." Danae handed her friend a drink. White liquor from root vegetables and pomegranate juice. It looked pretty, though

Danae had forgone it for kava tea instead. Basia was a better drinker than she was.

"Mmmm...." Basia took a sip of the pink concoction and smiled. "That's really nice. Thanks, Danae! Adohnis says he just got a letter from Ion. He's been promoted! Can you imagine our Ion in charge of a phalanx of soldiers?"

Adohnis leaned around Basia, grinning broadly. "In his letter, he said he'll work his way up to commander. Then he could attend war councils with you one day!"

"That's a big promotion," Danae agreed, wondering if it reflected Ion's skill and knowledge or a vacancy that needed filling. But that seemed like a terrible thing to say aloud, especially in front of Adohnis, so she smiled instead. "I doubt he'd enjoy sitting on the Council after such an active career. I swear my rear is getting flatter. Basia, wouldn't you say my backside is looking plank-ish?"

Callista rolled her eyes, shaking her head. "Basia would never say that about you, Danae!"

"Of course not!" Basia was quick to agree.

"Unless, of course, a flat rear was a sign of prestige. Come patriots, let us see who has spent the most time sitting for our nation!" Adohnis made a show of standing and looking at his own butt, and Callista yanked him back down into his seat while Basia tried to hold in her giggles.

Danae managed not to laugh aloud, and the rippling of a flute proclaimed the show's start. People hushed and settled in. Danae leaned against Basia's shoulder, ready to enjoy the show. "I must be very patriotic. I swear I spend all my time sitting or walking to the next Council meeting. It's been too long since we got to have any fun."

Basia nodded, though she shifted a little uncomfortably. "Yes. It's been—what?— a moon since we went to the Cormorant's Rest together?"

The woman on stage asked soldiers in the audience to stand and be applauded for their service, something Danae had never seen in a public gathering before. Beside her, Basia raised her hands to clap, while Adohnis did so enthusiastically on Basia's other side.

Clapping, she glanced at Basia through her lashes. They hadn't spoken much about The Comorant's Rest, Lex, or Zol. Mostly because they were both so busy, but also because neither seemed to know what to say. Danae had liked the place well enough, though not the location. And Zol was interesting and friendly…

But she wasn't sure what to say about Lex. They were good-looking, and clearly, Basia cared for them, but Danae only felt she had made a fool of herself with Basia's lover. She didn't want to lie to Basia and say she thought Lex was nice because, in truth, she wasn't convinced of their niceness. So she said nothing, and Basia kept her silence too.

"Maybe we could have a sleepover like we used to? It's been an age. I could come over after the Council meeting tonight."

Basia glanced at her and turned back to the stage. "Oh, sorry, Danae. I already promised I'd spend time with Lex tonight. Maybe later this week?"

"Of course," she agreed, though her heart paused. It sounded like one of those half promises nobility made to one another. *Oh, I'm sorry, I already have an event that day. Perhaps another time?* How many times had she heard her mother say such things to the various lesser nobility who invited the Othonos Councilors to every party they hosted?

But why would Basia give Danae a half-truth? A dismissal?

"Is something wrong?" Danae whispered, knowing it was rude to speak during a performance but still unable to hold her tongue. Basia was her dearest, closest, oldest friend. They shared everything and knew every secret. Had Danae upset her somehow?

"A lot's wrong. The war, people dying, the shortages, the issues with the trade alliance… Everyone's a bit worried."

Adohnis looked around Basia. "The show's starting!"

Danae flushed and pressed her lips together, giving Adohnis an apologetic smile. She had meant to ask if something was wrong with Basia. But instead of getting an answer, she got a list of the world's woes.

Danae sighed and focused on the play, ignoring her gut churning.

Sixth Moon, 1803, Diosion

Basia walked down the stairs to her parent's great hall and saw the life she had lived anew through Lex's eyes. Compared to the rest of the city—the middle-quarter homes, the warehouses, the Cormorant's Rest—this place was the height of opulence. Mavros was only a minor noble name, yet they were always surrounded by slaves who waited on their every need. The feast thrown for her today would have fed a hundred. The coin that went into their stable could have housed three families.

She could see how Lex might find this indulgence grotesque even without considering the lives taken to create it. And yet, this system had been in place long before any of its current members lived. Did that make them immoral for taking part in it? Or were they simply blind, in need of someone to explain so they might change?

"Basia?"

She looked up from her feet to see Melba standing at the bottom of the stairwell, her deep blue tunic a lovely contrast against the pale stone walls of their home. Basia stopped chewing on her cheek long enough to smile at her oldest sister. "Hi, Mel."

The younger girl put her arm through Basia's to walk with her. "It's your birthday, Basi," she said, adopting Danae's nickname for Basia just as the other Mavros children had. "You're not supposed to look so worried on your birthday."

Dido ran out to meet them, her black hair cut short above a brilliant black eye. "Basia always looks worried."

"I do not!"

"Do too!" Melba chimed again, but she squeezed Basia's arm. "Did you tell Basia what happened to your face?"

Dido covered the purple bruise with one palm and sighed. "The stable boy tried to tell me I don't have five sisters. So I walloped him, and he landed a lucky blow."

"Dido! Who taught you to fight?"

"I did. So there. But, anyway, Mama says I can't go to any parties until I look like a noble again." She rushed forward and hugged Basia around the waist. "Dara's present is from me too. Don't believe her if she says it isn't."

Dido darted around them and hit the stairs running. By the time Basia and her sister reached the great hall, the twin had already disappeared from sight.

Inside, the cavernous room was decorated in winter colors: gauzy navy window drapes and white flowers. The tables were set with cream, and several guests held delicate wine flutes in a frosty blue.

"I'll bet Danae's here!" Mel said, her voice pitched a little too high as though she were trying to cheer Basia up. "Do you want to go find her?"

"Lead the way."

It was easy to spot Danae as she stood a half-hand taller than all her companions. When Melba called out, Danae looked up over the heads of the lesser nobility surrounding her and smiled. She met Basia's eyes but dropped the stare quickly as they approached. It was clear she had noticed Basia's change in behavior recently, for all Basia's attempts to appear normal. It was just that Lex's words about trust had risen around her, a miasma that Basia could find no safe way to pierce.

Her cousin, Acantha, and Erose turned to greet Basia, crooning about her birthday and the party. Danae waited to be one of the last to approach, bowing respectfully. "Happy Birthday, Basia."

Basia tried for a smile. "Hi, Danae! Thanks for coming."

Thankfully, Melba was all too eager to fill in the gaps. "Are you still playing? I'm so busy with my apprenticeship at the Treasurer's Office that I've hardly had time to practice!"

Danae's focus lingered on Basia before shifting to Melba. "It's hard to find time, but a life devoted to the arts means sacrificing other things to find your true self. I play every night before bed. I know you'll find your rhythm soon, Melba."

"Oh, no wonder you're so good." Melba huffed, evidently not as interested in the work it would take to practice every night as she was the result. "I don't know if I can do that. I get home so tired...."

"You're capable of more than you think!" Basia's face ached from the strain of keeping up a smile. Humors, she hated this. Hated lying to her friend, squirming every time they were together, but what else could she do? Endanger the Society and all their work? If Danae thought shutting them down was the right thing to do, then there would be no stopping her.

She's going to be one of the next propagators of slavery in Phecea. Lex's words were so stuck in Basia's head that she couldn't see around them.

"That's true. Hard work pays off in the end, though at the time it might not feel like it." Danae smiled at Melba, but the conversation was interrupted by Callista coming forward. She bowed to Basia, and while she was smiling, something shadowed her eyes.

"Happy Birthday, Basia," she held out a gift wrapped in painted paper.

It was strange to see Callista without her older brother, and as Basia looked around the ballroom, she realized that Adohnis wasn't just missing from his sister's side but from the festivities altogether.

Danae must have noticed, too, because she said, "Is Adohnis ill?"

Callista shook her head, her throat bobbing visibly as she swallowed. What was going on? "He was not well enough to come. He sends his apologies, Basia."

Always the diplomat, Danae changed the conversation, likely because Callista seemed so tense. "We wish him a fast recovery. Basia, are you going to open Callista and Adohnis's gift?"

Basia took the long, cylindrical package and peeled back the paper to reveal a hard leather tube. Her brow creased slightly in bemusement. There was a fastening at one end that she unclasped to find thick paper coiled inside. Basia had to hold the case under one arm and get Melba's help to unroll it; so stiff was the paper that it wanted to coil immediately back on itself. When she could finally see it, Basia gasped.

"It's by the artist, Atreo Drakos," Callista said. "Adohnis and I both hope you like it."

The gift was a map of the world, beautifully rendered in gorgeous color from the farthest coast of the wild country north of Ingola to the tip of the Emaian tundra at the base of the globe.

"Callista, it's amazing!" Carefully, Basia put the precious thing back into its protective case. "Thank you! And tell Adohnis I said thank you to him as well."

Callista's smile was too quick, her nod overly enthusiastic. "I will, and happy birthday again. Basia."

Danae

Danae turned towards Callista. It wasn't as if Basia wanted to spend much time with her, and Callista seemed so tense. "Would you like something to eat? I saw a tray of honeyed dates floating around somewhere."

She nodded and they linked arms, strolling through the partygoers in search of the gooey treats. Danae was careful to keep her conversation light, watching through the corner of her eye as Callista's shoulders slowly dropped away from her ears, and the odd angle of her fake smile changed into a more natural one.

Dates in hand, Danae settled on one of the hall's many cushioned seats and let her attention flicker around the room. Lesser noble families made up most of the crowd, and several of their peers were entirely missing.

She knew of three who had joined the army or navy and others whose apprenticeships were keeping them away. She doubted the Leos twins would attend any social gatherings as long as the war continued. After the loss of Aphodes and their home, the Leos were overseeing the construction of ships in the Bay of Kosorus. The war with Liria was more real for them. Personal.

Danae nibbled on a honeyed date while Callista popped a whole one into her mouth. "I hope you're not feeling poorly too, Callista."

"I'm not sick." Callista looked around. They were secluded. Basia was across the room talking with Erose and a few others, and most of the nobility was focused there. Callista took in a deep breath and turned to face Danae. "Adohnis is not sick either."

Danae nodded slowly. She had guessed as much. "He and Basia made their peace years ago...."

"No. No, it's nothing like that. We got word from Ion's family today. They will tell everyone else soon, but I didn't want to ruin Basia's birthday...."

Danae's mind jumped to Ion, promoted and on the front lines. If the news was bad enough to keep Adohnis from the party and everyone else, then... Dread made Danae silent, unable to ask for more details. She didn't think she truly wanted to know, but it appeared that once Callista started speaking, she could not stop.

"Ion's dead. He died three weeks ago, but we're just now learning of it. Adohnis has been writing him letters all these weeks. Writing a dead man. I don't know what's wrong with me, but that's all I can think about. All those things that they won't say to each other. Letters unread." A single tear slipped down the younger girl's cheek, and Danae reached to brush it away.

"Callista, you don't have to be here. You gave Basia her gift. I'll make your excuses. You should be home with your brother." Poor Adohnis. Ion was his best friend—more really. Danae couldn't imagine the pain and grief he was suffering. If Basia died...

She pushed back her panic. Now was not the time to selfishly think of herself and Basia. Callista was trying to stop her tears, and people were starting to glance their way. Danae stood, fanning out her formal tunic to block Callista from view.

"I-I can stop. It'll be alright... It's Basia's birthday."

"No." Danae surprised herself with how firm her voice sounded. "You must go home. Grieve. I'll tell Basia what has happened once the party is over."

Callista looked up at her, eyes wide. In a sudden movement, she embraced Danae, hugging her tight. Almost painfully. Danae wrapped her arms around Callista and then stepped away.

"Goodbye, Callista."

"Goodbye, Danae."

Danae watched her leave and then turned to survey the room. Basia didn't seem to have spotted Callista's emotional departure. Good. Rolling her shoulders, Danae banished the thoughts of Ion, dead on some battlefield, and smoothed her expression into one of mild engagement. She joined the group talking near Basia, and while she had no interest in the topic, she nodded and smiled and even added something here or there.

She hated to think it, but she was eager for the entire affair to be done. Basia kept glancing at her with a smile like a pinch in the side. Fake. Bright in theory but with no real joy. It made Danae long for the *real* Basia. Wherever she had gone. It felt like moons since Danae had seen her best friend. Her best friend, who hugged her back and to whom she could talk for hours into the night.

What if things didn't get better, and something happened, like Ion and Adohnis? It had been strained for such a while now. She thought they had been themselves when she first returned from her disastrous tour, but perhaps that wasn't true. Had the year apart damaged their friendship? Or was it Lex? Danae knew Lex didn't like her, but she didn't understand how that could trump years of friendship.

She didn't love anyone romantically. No one loved her that way. Perhaps this was normal? She couldn't bring it to her parents, not with Basia keeping the relationship quiet.

"Danae?"

Blinking, Danae looked up from her cup, realizing she had been staring into it for several long moments. "Yes?"

"Don't you agree the prices for slaves are astronomical?" Erose asked, her saccharine smile, once an annoyance, was now a welcome distraction.

"I think the prices now reflect the responsibility one should consider before buying a slave. That includes education, clean clothes, quarters, and training if you need a skilled laborer. It's not something to be taken lightly."

"I suppose that is one way to look at it, but haven't we always taken care of our slaves? We're not Lirians. Besides, the slaves on the market now are *captured*, not bred. They're untamed."

The topic moved on and Danae found her eyes drifting back around the room, only this time, she didn't find Basia looking back at her. In fact, the other girl seemed to have vanished altogether.

Basia

Basia lay in the bed she had slept in all her life and stared at the ceiling. It showcased a mural of a flaming hawk climbing towards the sun—a gift from her parents for her thirteenth birthday. Basia used to imagine that she rode on the back of that great creature, climbing upwards to steal fire from the sun, but tonight she did not feel so brave.

Keme's stories were all very clear on the subject of bravery. It always came as part of doing the right thing: the heroes stood up for their people or their families, and they did not have to lie to do it.

There were several things clear within Basia's mind: The Society's work was critical. They were freeing people, changing lives. They were the only bastion of change against an oppressive system that had lasted hundreds of years. Without her and the papers she could create, they would not be able to perform the service they did for as many slaves as they could afford to save. On the other hand, it was most definitely not moral to lie to one's friends. Basia felt like the man in the story she had heard the first time she had gone to The Cormorant's Rest. No option she took could be entirely right.

So then, what was the least wrong? Lying to her friend or putting the Emai they could save at stake for a moment's honesty? Basia groaned and rolled over, hiding her head beneath her pillow. She knew which path she would take but loathed having to take it.

Muffled from beneath the layers of linen and down, a knock sounded on the door, and Basia's chest tightened. By all order, let it not be Danae. "Come in!"

"Basi?" Danae's voice clanged through the room. Basia could hear her door open and then whisk shut. Just the two of them, in her private quarters. When she looked around, Danae was still standing against the door as if uncertain if she could come in all the way, if she would be welcome. "You left your party...."

Basia sighed and sat up, tossing aside her pillow. "I just needed a moment. Are there a lot of guests still here? I can go back down."

"I asked the servants to bring in instruments. Your sisters are currently playing."

"Thank you, Danae," Basia said and rubbed her hands against her face. She knew she must be smearing her paints, but she couldn't bring herself to care.

Silence echoed between them for a moment, and Danae finally moved away from the door. She walked around the scattered gifts and selected one wrapped in cream and gold paper. Her friend handled it with trepidation but came to sit on the bed beside Basia.

"Do you want good or bad first?"

"Well, the bad, I suppose— Or no. Tell me the good news so it won't be colored by the bad."

Danae handed over the gift. "Here."

Basia's fingers trembled slightly, but she peeled back the layers of paper to find what first appeared to be black cloth. "Is this silk? But how? We haven't traded with Tupa Gali in three years."

"Ingolan."

Basia's eyes widened. The stuff was nearly impossible to get, between the cost and distance of shipping from the northern continent and the sheer amount of time it took to produce. She turned back to the package and slowly lifted out a stunning gown. It was lightest at the shoulders, a mauve that deepened into purple and black in a seamless fade down the length of the dress. It was long and slender with bare arms and a hint of opals at the clasp over the right shoulder. Basia sighed in wonder. It was simply the most perfect piece of clothing she had ever seen, and it fit her to the letter. "Danae," she said, her voice hushed. "It's— It's *wonderful*."

"I had it made just for you. I thought... I thought it looked like you. When I drew it for the seamstress, I was thinking of everything Basia Mavros means to me. About when we were children, and you were the Pirate Queen. About when we were in Mistress Afin's etiquette classes together, and you were the epitome of grace and all things beautiful." The other girl swallowed and blinked, looking away. "I just know the woman you are is the most glorious thing I've ever seen. I thought, when this stupid war is over, you might want to wear it out or something. I don't know. Take Lex somewhere glamorous."

Basia reached out and, for the first time in moons, wrapped her arms around her best friend. She didn't know what to say. She had been horrible, really. And whatever she had to do for the Society didn't mean that she had to punish Danae for the crime of being born into this way of life.

When she pulled away, Basia realized she had shed a few tears as well. "Thank you, Danae. For seeing *me*."

"Always." She wiped away Basia's tears. "Now, the bad...."

Danae told her of the news she had learned from Callista, and they held each other as they grieved.

CHAPTER 80: PHECEA

SECOND MOON, 1804, DIOSION

Eleven Moons before the Proclamation

Basia stepped from the Trade Office into the cool wash of evening. The skies were still pink from the path of the sun, recently set, and despite every appearance of warmth, Basia shivered. The worst of summer was past, the days slowly beginning to cool, yet they had not quite come to fall.

There was a crier on the corner of the street where the Trade Office met the wider thoroughfare. Her face was pink with passion, and she spoke too loud, too fast. "Our brave soldiers have been turning aside the Lirians at every front, and you can do your part too!"

If every crier who spoke on the bravery of Phecean soldiers were to be believed, the war ought to have ended years ago. Still, Basia stopped a moment to listen. She was curious about what the Council thought its people could do to help the war effort.

"The young people of Phecea have put down their crafts, music, plows and books. They have marched to the front so that you will be safe here. And yet, the country still needs its crops. Those soldiers need good weapons. Who then can fill that place if not our slaves?

Lend your Emai to the government, and make a *real* difference in the war today!"

Basia chewed her cheek and turned away from the crowd. They appeared concerned, some of them. Others bright-eyed. Her pockets contained the papers for four different slaves, all being shipped to the southernmost port in Phecea to be smuggled across the border and into the Emaian Tundra. To freedom. How many of these people would call her a traitor? How many would turn on her for returning these people to their homes?

For a moment, Basia swayed. How could she and her friends stand against something so big? Something so pervasive? Was there even any point? Or were they like minnows, worrying the sides of a whale?

She swallowed and took a deep breath, but it was the thought of Keme that steadied her the most. Their efforts mattered to the people they helped, at the very least. To their families, their people. That would have to be enough for now.

Basia's feet turned eastward, following the curving thoroughfare that connected all of Diosion. She passed the homes of the upper city and the warehouses below and finally came to the harbor as evening was settling into night. Zol would be on duty by now, standing at the docks and checking the papers of those shipping controlled goods within the country. Basia had only to find her and give her the bundle in her pocket. Lex would take care of the rest.

So close to the water, the wind was a grasping hand, tugging at Basia's hair and clothes like her sisters had when they were smaller. The sea was gray and moody, the last traces of warm colors completely gone from the sky. Everything stank of fish and damp, and the boards beneath her feet were stained black.

A line of people stood before a plain wooden kiosk where a guard sat. Basia could not make out Zol's features, but this was where she had been told to find the Zolelan woman. A handful of guards blocked traffic headed further into the docks, sending all those that didn't have clear authorization to the line behind Basia. No one around her spoke or gossiped, but a couple of the guards laughed over something Basia could not quite hear.

Basia shifted. Her heart was beating too fast for the calm scene. She felt too exposed. Anxious. There was no reason for it. It would be Zol at the kiosk taking her papers. And besides, they were entirely legal. Lex had bought the slaves at auction just like Basia had the moon before and Eros the moon before that. Basia forced herself to take another deep breath as the line moved up. It would all be fine, and then she could leave this cold place and return to the warmth of the upper city.

The line moved up again, and suddenly, Basia could see within the kiosk if she leaned out slightly. It was not Zol at all but a stranger. A pale woman with tight, tired eyes.

Basia's stomach knotted like the great cables that held Phecea's ships in the harbor. Where was Zol? She had said this would be her post for the foreseeable future. She had not sent word that she would be stationed somewhere else. Zol should have at least let The Society know. Basia pressed her hands to her face, but when she removed them, she caught one of the guards eyeing her too closely. It took effort to give the appearance of normalcy.

It shouldn't matter, *right?* The papers were legal. It was only that she had overheard the crier on the way that made her so uneasy. They had kept all of their operations above board for a reason. Besides, it would look too suspicious to leave now. The guards had noticed her, and she was near the front of the line.

"Next!"

Basia stepped forward and laid her paperwork on the counter. She tried for a smile. "Good evening." It came out too nervous, and the guardswoman frowned.

"Alright, what do we have here?" She pulled the papers towards her, and even though the question was certainly rhetorical, Basia opened her mouth to fill the silence.

"Just papers for the transport of a few slaves." She tried to smile again, but the woman wasn't looking. Her frown deepened, and her dark brows pushed together to form one severe line. The guardswoman looked up at Basia quickly.

"Wait here."

None of the others had required the guardswoman to leave her post, and the change in routine made Basia more nervous than anything else. She couldn't see where the woman had gone, but she knew she could not flee now. Her name was on those papers. If something was the matter, they would simply find her at the Mavros estate. She glanced over her shoulder. The people behind her were paying too much attention.

"Where did you get these slaves?"

Basia swung back to see that the woman had reappeared in the kiosk. Her face gave nothing away. "They were purchased at auction by a colleague of mine. Are the papers in order?" Of course, they were. She had drawn them up herself.

"Not quite."

A rough hand gripped Basia around her arm, tugging her out of line. She jerked away out of fear or instinct, but the guardsman holding her had no trouble keeping his grip.

"What is this?! Unhand me. You have no right to treat me this way."

The man was unmoved by Basia's outburst. He hardly looked at her as he drew her further away. "You are under arrest for the transport of stolen goods and the falsification of trade documents."

CHAPTER 81: LIRIA

SECOND MOON, 1804, EGARA

Eleven Moons before the Proclamation

Tiny, crystal mosaic tiles covered the stairs leading into the Imperator's thermal baths, the patterns of precise geometric diamonds in a dozen colors. Luce knew because he scrutinized them as the leader of all of Liria padded across the mosaic floor in nothing more than a sarong. He wasn't sure if being summoned to the Imperator's private bathing pools was an honor or a bad sign.

He supposed there must be some trust as the Imperator was unarmed if one didn't count his numerous personal guards standing along the columned walls. But still, Luce couldn't shake the knot in his stomach as he waited for permission to be granted to speak.

The Imperator stepped into the first pool, traditionally lukewarm, and settled onto one of the seats carved into its side. Luce glanced his way and then around the airy room. Along with the mosaic floors and columned walls, the domed ceiling was painted blue to trick the mind into believing it was the sky rather than marble. Sculptures lined alcoves and corners, great works of beauty as old as the pools.

One, in particular, reminded him of Camilla: a beautiful woman with a gauzy dress clinging to her plump thighs and waist, loose around her chest. How did the artist make the stone look light? The woman's gaze didn't linger on the pool or the floor below as many of the more demure statues, but straightforward, her air somehow challenging.

"You're smiling, General Nonus," the Imperator said. His words brought Luce back to the moment, and he clasped his fisted hand over his heart, bowing to the ruler of all.

"Yes, Imperator."

"This surprises me, as I've brought you here so that you might explain your proposal. Why would Liria allow a ceasefire with Phecea? We're *winning*." The Imperator's tone was annoyed but not seething angry. Perhaps the thermal baths were helping.

"We are gaining ground against Phecea, Imperator. That is true." He resisted the urge to point out that it was thanks to *his* tactics and pressed on, "But our stock of slaves is dwindling. With our forces split, we cannot commit as many raiders to the Emaians as we need, and we've sold most of our breeding inventory. Since we *are* winning, I suspect the Pheceans will be all too happy for a ceasefire."

The Imperator cupped handfuls of the murky mineral water and spilled it over his chest and neck. "Are you saying that Emaian dogs are besting you in battle, General?"

"No, it's not battle, what they are doing. It's less militaristic and more like the swarming of a bee hive. I believe we simply require a less straightforward approach to capturing the Emaians. If they want to act like animals, we'll herd them up like cattle or sheep."

"Herd?" The Imperator's expression was thoughtful, and the knot in Luce's belly lessened an inch.

"Yes, but to herd, we need many soldiers, so we can ensure not one slave escapes the flock."

The Imperator nodded slowly and stood, the water in the bathing pool gurgling. The Imperator left wet footprints on the tile as he headed for the next pool. Steam rose from its surface, the edges bordered by a geometric design of squares and triangles. The Imperator sloshed into the hot water, going so far as to dunk his head under as well. When he emerged, his cheeks were pink, and his eyes were glassy.

"How long would you need, General, to capture more Emai?"

That was a delicate question. The truth of the matter was, the tundra-lovers were becoming more hostile, more evasive. Slippery as the fish they so loved. But if he admitted any weakness, the Imperator would be displeased. More time to train his troops, create strategy, and sail south would ensure a higher chance of success. But, he understood his Imperator would find leaving the war too long... *distasteful.*

Luce could still hear the thud of General Gais's head as it hit the floor and feel the splatter of hot blood against his cheek. The blood of his friend and leader. Luce could not afford for that to happen to him. Camilla and Ignatious and all his children and grandchildren relied on him. He would *not* leave them.

His spit tasted of salt, and Luce recognized the sensation. He might throw up soon. He swallowed and pressed forward, trying for a thoughtful and reasonable tone, "Timing is not ideal, Imperator. As you know, now is the best season for raiding. The sailing is the least dangerous from twelfth moon to third moon. I hate losing ships to simple storms; it's too wasteful. There is no way we could train and resupply our armies soon enough to set out now, as I believe we aren't even expecting our next shipment from Tupa Gali for another moon. We have a few troops south already, so it is not as if we have completely stopped raiding. They will continue while we prepare the rest."

The Imperator draped his arms across the back of the bathing pool, letting his head lull to one side. He was listening but slowly sinking further into the hot water. "Mhm."

"With that reality a factor in our raiding plans, I would suggest a year or so... We could retrain the northern troops and give them all a few weeks' reprieve to increase morale. If the Almighty is willing, some soldiers will find out soon after returning to duty that their wives are pregnant. Providing for a family is a great responsibility, and so they will be additionally motivated to do well for Liria. After all, when Liria thrives, so too do they."

Luce paused in his speech as the Imperator climbed out of the hot pool and headed to the scaldingly hot pool. His skin was already carnation pink, yet he didn't flinch as he stepped into the water. The General followed his leader over, waiting by the side of the pool until the Imperator had resettled himself. Luce wasn't certain how long the Imperator could stand staying in the near-boiling water, so he spoke quickly once the Imperator gestured for him to resume.

"If we suggest the ceasefire, Phecea will see it as a sign that we want peace." The Imperator frowned at that, and Luce pressed on. "We know there will be no peace until Liria and Phecea are united and whole once more, but give the Pheceans a taste of it, and they'll be loathe to resume fighting when the ceasefire is over. They aren't warriors like us. They are weak and lazy. If their troops return home, the Pheceans might find it impossible to get them to come back to the battlefield. A little rest might make them easier to defeat."

"It could make them stronger, as you suggest it will make our men."

"It's a possibility. A small risk, I agree, but I do not believe in my heart that the Pheceans have the fortitude that Lirians do. Let them return to their orgies and debauchery. Let them get fat on feasts and soft-handed playing with clay or paint. Our men, after no more than three weeks' rest, will resume training. They will come back stronger, faster, and more determined."

The Imperator drummed his fingers along the edge of the hottest thermal pool, creating a slow beat like a horse's canter. Luce tried not to move, despite the moist, hot air and the sweat slipping down his back. "Very well, General Nonus. Draw up your plans, and we'll meet with the Pheceans for a ceasefire. I have an audience with Ingolan bankers next moon, so make it prompt."

Luce let out a small breath, bowing deeply to the Imperator. "Yes, Imperator."

The ruler of Liria stepped from the hottest pool, steam billowing off of him in great plumes. He looked like a man emerging from a volcano, and Luce almost envied the Imperator when he plunged into the ice pool. Steam rolled off the water, and the Imperator was under for so long Luce was starting to feel worried when he came to the surface, gasping. He slicked back his dark hair from his face and lifted one hand to wave Luce away. A dismissal.

After an additional bow, the General turned on his heel and marched from the Imperial bathing pools. It wasn't until he reached the top set of stairs that he allowed himself to relax and really accept that he had done it. He had convinced the Imperator to call a ceasefire on Phecea and focus on Emaian raids. Luce touched his throat, where his head would have been severed from his body had the Imperator thought his plan cowardly. Oddly, it ached as if his muscles could imagine what that pain would feel like.

CHAPTER 82: RHOSAN

SIXTH MOON, 1803, CWM OR

Two Years before the Proclamation

Never in his life had Dyfan been so conflicted about returning to the arena. He had always considered the pits where he belonged. The routines, the structure of training and meals: it all was familiar and comforting. His cell was all his, and he knew every detail of the arena. But now, as he escaped the gaze of Eurig's guards, Dyfan wished he had been taken anywhere but here.

If Wynn hadn't been in attendance, maybe it would have been tolerable to return to training, to behave as if nothing had happened, but as it was, his love stood shirtless and ready to spar. Dyfan couldn't bear it. He turned to flee to his cell and the privacy it could afford him, but the head training master caught him by the eye.

"Where are you going? You missed morning training and are supposed to prepare for the Contender Matches."

Dyfan flinched, looking toward the arena where the men were starting to gather. He didn't want to go there. He didn't want to be seen at all.

His hesitation caught the training master's attention, and the man came closer, one hand balled into a fist. "Don't give me trouble, Dyfan. I've had enough because of you."

Dyfan heaved a breath and finally nodded. His training master was a fair man. He didn't deserve the ire of Victor Eurig, which he had certainly been getting due to Dyfan's recent difficulties.

Fine. He would train. Dyfan went to stand in line with the other Defeated.

Like the very sun itself, Dyfan was acutely aware of Wynn. He always had been. Now it was painful not to look at his lover and, at the same time, the only thing the fighter could do. If he looked at Wynn, he was sure the older man would see his shame. Smell the woman Dyfan had bred with not even an hour ago. He would know Dyfan had done his duty, risen to the occasion despite not wanting to, and broken the one vow he had made himself.

Shame knotted with self-loathing. Dyfan had thought himself better than an animal. He thought since he loved Wynn, that when the time came, he would not be able to perform with the female Defeated. But she rubbed soft hands over the length of him and used her mouth until he was ready. And, curse him, he reacted. His body betrayed his heart. Just another Defeated, doing as he was commanded. Obedient to his Victor and no one else. Not to Wynn and not to himself.

The Defeated across from him hefted his club and small, round shield, and automatically Dyfan did the same. A call came out; left line attack, right line defend. Dyfan leveled his shield to take the blows. Thump. Thump. Thump.

The sound reminded him of the cot they had lain on, clacking against the wall as he—

Without warning, Dyfan turned from the line, vomit spewing from his lips, unbidden. His sparring partner stopped and called for a training master. One came over, bucket and ladle in hand.

"Are you sick?" The master asked, and Dyfan shook his head, spitting out the last vestiges of bile. "If you're sick, you need to see a healer. You know how quick illness spreads in the arena."

Again, Dyfan shook his head, taking the offered ladle and swishing his mouth. Spitting that out too, he swallowed a few clean mouthfuls of water, hefted his shield once more, and waved the master off.

His line attacked now, and Dyfan resettled his grip on the club before stepping forward. The urge to be sick faded as he bashed his club into the shield. Over and over again. The other Defeated flinched and pulled his shield higher, eyes rounding with something akin to fear. "We're just sparring."

Just sparring. It was never *just* sparring. They were practicing to kill one another. They were following the orders of the Victors. They were obedient dogs, doing as they were told, no better than beasts.

The call went out to switch again, but Dyfan ignored it. He swung harder, savoring the burn in his arm as the club cracked across the shield, ringing out as wood smacked metal.

"Hey!"

Sweat ran down Dyfan's brow and into his eyes, making them burn. He shook his head, a dog with fleas, and pressed onward. His club fell again and again. He grunted with the effort of it, wanting the wood to break off in his hand, the metal to concave, or the swirling of his thoughts to stop.

They didn't.

"Dyfan!" Someone shouted his name, but Dyfan didn't look around. Didn't stop in his pursuit. His hand stung as the club started to splitter and break. Pieces flew off as he hammered the metal shield, obscuring his vision. "DYFAN!" The rough wood under his fingers bit into his palm, chafing as he followed the retreating shield, his target fleeing.

Dyfan charged, tossing his shield towards an approaching training master, whip in hand. It was dead weight anyway.

The Defeated he pursued threw the shield aside and Dyfan turned, following its arc until it landed in a cloud of red arena dust. Dyfan wrapped both hands around his mutilated club and raised it over his head, bringing it down with a resounding crack. He repeated the gesture, making the same thud of fucking that female. His blood roared in his ears, and Dyfan beat the shield until it finally bowed, and his club fell to pieces. Useless. Panting, Dyfan yelled, grabbing the shield with blood-slick hands and bashing it into the earth over and over and over again.

Reality washed over him with a cold dousing of water. A training master stood with an empty bucket at his side as Dyfan rounded on him, glaring. His hands became fists, ready to fight a new foe. Anything not to think. Not to feel.

The training master stumbled back a few steps, and Dyfan paused. They never shied away from him. He looked around slowly, feeling eyes all around. The Defeated and training masters watched him. Mouths agape, eyes wide. No one spoke. His shoulders rose and fell in a silent pant and Dyfan turned to leave.

He glanced towards Wynn and nearly vomited again at what he saw. Wynn's skin was ashen, lips compressed into a tight line. He looked afraid.

Well, he should be. Dyfan was as disloyal as a buck during rut. Not a man.

No one stopped him as he stalked out of the arena and back to his private cell. No one called after him or told him to get back in line. Not today.

⇑ ⇑ ⇑

That night, Wynn picked his way through the hallways to Dyfan's cell with more care. It had been a week since he'd tried this. Two moons since he and Dyfan had been caught together in the other fighter's prison. Still, he could not rest leaving things as they were. Not after Dyfan's display of anger during practice.

Wynn did not see guards on his way, though that did not give him any sense of ease. They would be nearby, and they would be listening. He did not understand the sudden increase in their attention, but it worried him. Not least for future chances to spend time with Dyfan.

When Wynn arrived at his cell, Dyfan gave every appearance of being asleep. He lay on his side, facing away from the door, his broad back sloping down into the cover of an animal hide. His shoulders, though, were tense—too high about his neck for sleep— and his breaths were shallow and quick.

"Dyfan. Annwyl," Wynn whispered, trying out the taste of the endearment on his tongue. He liked the two-syllable shape of it in his mouth, the softness of the consonants and how they lay together.

The larger man stiffened and wound his arms about himself,

holding tight. Turning into a stone ball. Dyfan made no move to acknowledge Wynn in any manner. Wynn glanced at the door. Still no sound of guards. "Dyfan?" He stepped closer until he could lay a hand on the other man's back. He leaned down to place a kiss on his shoulder. "Can we talk?"

For a moment, it seemed as if Dyfan would not respond at all, aside from tightening his grip on his belly, but with a sigh, he sat up. Bringing his feet up to brace against the edge of his cot, Dyfan's knees created mountain peaks that hid half of his expressionless face. "What?"

Wynn drew his hand back, shocked by the coolness in Dyfan's tone. He took a deep breath and tried again, fear climbing through him like a tide. He reached out and tried to take Dyfan's hand.

The fighter pulled it away, and Wynn stepped back. He deserved this. He deserved to have Dyfan turn away from him, to be alone. He had betrayed Dyfan for safety, for the good grace of a woman who only wanted to use him. It was his fault that the Victors had anything over Dyfan at all.

Tears pricked the backs of his eyes. "Dyfan, I— I'm so, so sorry."

Green-blue eyes leveled on Wynn's face for one breath. Two. Five. Eight. Finally, Dyfan blinked and looked away. "Don't say that," he muttered. "Don't say sorry to me."

"I am sorry. I feel like this is all my fault." Wynn wrapped his arms around himself and looked down. He should tell Dyfan about Ifanna now; just open his mouth and say it. But fear rose hot and sticky as tar to glue closed his teeth. "I got us caught last time I came up here."

Dyfan shifted and then stood, walking away from his cot. He turned to stare at Wynn, one hand coming to clutch at his gut. "You didn't. And you... You're not the disgusting one. You shouldn't touch me."

"You don't disgust me. You never could. I love you. Please, I—I won't touch you if you don't want me to."

"You shouldn't love me, Wynn."

"Well, I do," Wynn growled. "I don't know why you don't want this now that the Victors know. Unless it has something to do with me...

and then— and then I guess I can't change that. Maybe I deserve it. I do deserve it."

"Stop it, Wynn. You know it's not you." Dyfan's shoulders tensed up his neck, threatening to touch his ears. "I just... I can't."

Those were familiar words. It was what Dyfan had said before when he'd rather fight in the lesser pits than breed when Eurig told him to. He just couldn't. He just wouldn't. "Alright." Wynn took the few steps to the door, Dyfan turning as he passed so that he never had to look Wynn's way. "If you can't, I won't make you."

"Good."

Wynn stepped out into the night alone.

CHAPTER 83: PHECEA

SECOND MOON, 1804, DIOSION

Eleven Moons before the Proclamation

Danae felt a mixture of disbelief and glee as she watched Peta and Sion before the altar, hand in hand, agreeing to tie their lives together forever. She hadn't thought Peta was much older than herself, yet here she was, getting married to a noble from Zolela. It wasn't a love match but a political one, as Danae's marriage would be, yet the two seemed close enough. They stole glances and smiled, and when the official told them to kiss, Peta and her new groom complied eagerly.

Danae looked away, worried that the seat beside her was *still* empty. Basia rarely missed important gatherings, and a formal wedding was a big affair. She couldn't recall the last time there had been a genuine celebration in Diosion, outside private homes. Rations had gone up again, produce in the markets was limited, and there were reports of concerning movements from the Emai. As if Phecea needed any more trouble.

So a formal wedding, a binding of two families, was something to celebrate. Yet Basia wasn't here. Her sisters, parents and friends were. Was she ill?

Danae clapped and stood as the other onlookers did, trying to focus on the moment as Peta and Sion walked past, hand in hand. They smiled as if they had accomplished some great task, which, Danae supposed, they had. Was it not one of the many responsibilities of a Council member's child to make alliances through marriage? Her mother and father had said as much.

"It'll be your turn soon, won't it, Danae?" She turned to see Master Annas, watching Peta and her groom as they embraced each other's parents as custom dictated. They were all family now.

"Not so soon. I'm only seventeen." Most children wouldn't get married until they were closer to twenty. She felt incredibly young watching Peta and her new husband grinning at one another. Never had she felt close enough to anyone to share her entire existence with them. Besides Basia.

"A few years, they'll fly by fast enough. Especially with this war," Master Annas murmured, sipping a bubbling Zolelan delicacy from his flute. It was strange to see Master Annas drinking and dressed so lavishly. Danae only thought of him as her strict teacher. Perhaps he noticed her attention and so straightened his tunic. "I was married once, you know."

Danae shook her head.

"Yes, a beautiful woman from Liria." The location startled her, and Danae schooled her features into a polite mask to avoid offending her Master. "A love match. I didn't care that her family looked down on me or had no grasp of the arts."

"I suppose love conquers all."

"Hardly. Love can't keep you civil in disagreements or make you see eye to eye on how to raise children. I thought love was all that mattered, but in the end, it was the only thing that held us together for so long. Our lives, children, and passions should have kept us knitted together, but instead those differences only became frayed threads."

She wondered how much Master Annas had been drinking. He seemed awfully melancholy, though she agreed with his logic. Her parents often warned of the weaknesses of love marriages. Harmony and sweet kisses wouldn't keep you happy. It wouldn't make the marriage strong. Compromise and understanding did.

Master Annas's voice pulled her from her thoughts. "Where is your shadow?"

"I haven't seen Basia today."

"Hmmph… Well, I must go congratulate the bride and groom." Master Annas nodded to her and strode off, leaving Danae alone by the table of bubbling drinks. Off to her left, a few people spoke about the price of slaves. It seemed that it was all anyone wanted to gossip over. Well, that and the war.

"Recently, I've heard an explanation for the price change that differs quite a bit from what the Councilors have been telling us."

That pricked Danae's interest enough for her to step closer under the guise of tasting one of the little honeyed phyllo cakes further down the table. The other two men standing with the speaker were eager to encourage him, thankfully. What could he know that the Councilors didn't?

"Evidently, the Emai are arming themselves and killing any civilized parties that enter the tundra. Savages. Can you imagine it? Who in their right mind would choose violence and death over a chance to learn and serve one's betters?"

"Hey. Danae?"

Danae jumped and spun to find one of the least likely faces she might have imagined. Lex stood behind her, clothed in attire that would have been more fitting on a noble, their usually warm skin wan with worry or apprehension. They looked as though they had been crying, their eyes puffy and red-rimmed.

"Hello, Lex. You're looking sharp." Danae didn't want to say well because really Lex looked… Off. If Lex was here, then perhaps Basia had simply been sitting with them instead of her for the ceremony. The thought hurt, as Danae believed she at least warranted a greeting, but perhaps they had arrived late and then couldn't find a seat and… "What's wrong?" The tension in Lex's shoulders, and the way their eyes kept shifting around the crowd caught Danae's attention.

Something was the matter.

"It's— Can we talk somewhere private? Also, thank you. You look nice as well. It's just that it's rather urgent that I speak with you."

"Of course, ah…." Danae looked around the crowd of gathered

nobility. It didn't seem like anyone would notice if they disappeared for a minute or two. She could afford to be a bit rude if it was about Basia, which she suspected it was. What else would Lex speak to her about?

She watched a servant disappear behind a strategically placed statue and nodded. That was likely a private hallway for servants only.

"Here, this way." Danae gestured for Lex to follow her and eased around the edge of the ballroom. She smiled, nodded, and said a few greetings but evaded getting sucked into any conversations before reaching the exit. "After you."

Lex ducked into the passageway and took a few long-legged steps further in, supposedly to check for listeners. When they came back, their hands were shaking as if they were so full of energy they might at any moment begin to vibrate.

"Alright. Yes, I think this should be good…." They turned back to Danae and then looked away again unable to meet her eyes. "It's about Basia. She needs you."

"What does she need me for? Where is she?"

"It's my fault," Lex said, which Danae thought was likely true, though unhelpful at the moment. Lex rubbed their face with their hands. "Basia's been— She's in prison, and I can't get to her. You have to help me get her out!"

The words rang in the air between them, incomprehensible. What could that even mean? Basia, in prison? How could Basia be in prison? It didn't make sense. Danae felt her polite mask falter and morph into a glare.

Lex was making fun of her, proving how gullible or desperate for approval Danae was by getting her to leave her friend's wedding. And she had fallen for it. She had thought Lex had something important to say.

"I don't understand your jokes, Lex. And I don't appreciate you making me think something was truly wrong." Her voice came out clipped. Basia, in prison? Lex should have thought up a more believable lie.

"Humors, Danae. I'm not joking. You'll see for yourself if you just come with me. Basia was caught with papers for the transport of slaves that she didn't know were illegal. I should have just told her! Then she might have been more careful. She'll lose everything if we don't *do* something."

"You've had your fun at my expense, Lex. Let it go."

"Damn it, Danae! Open your eyes! Would Basia really miss this sort of thing? There have got to be dozens of foreign diplomats here, and she cares more about ending the war than almost anything else. Fuck it. You know what? I knew you couldn't be trusted. Maybe Zol will be able to vouch for her." Lex started to turn away, hot, angry tears filling their eyes.

"Why would Basia have transport papers for any slaves, illegal or otherwise?" Basia's position in the trade administration had nothing to do with slaves. She worked directly with agriculture and shippable goods. This wasn't making sense, but Danae had the terrible feeling that... that Lex wasn't lying or joking. They were crying, and the desperation tinting their voice seemed *real*.

"What so you can get her in even more trouble? Coming here was such a huge mistake. I'll just go turn myself in. I'll tell them she didn't know the papers were illegal, that she thought she was just doing her job."

"Except, the transport of slaves *isn't* her job, Lex. If you knew anything about her position in the administration, you'd know that. So, whatever trouble you've gotten her into, your confession won't free her." Danae's heart started to pound in her chest, making her breaths come quick. This was real. "What did you do? Why is she handling slaves at all?"

"Fuck, *fuck*. We were freeing them, alright? Are you happy now? You can end all of our lives and go on living in your perfect little bubble, riding around on the backs of the people you steal and rape and pillage and force into labor! Just help me get Basia free before you destroy us and condemn an entire race of people."

Lex's words felt like stones against Danae's flesh. Basia was freeing slaves? She knew there was a shortage, so why would she do such a thing? Danae looked away from Lex, unable to stand another second seeing their indignant face. They thought she was some monster, a

Councilor's child, proud and proper and fake. Danae had only ever wanted to be real, and yet she had never fit in as herself. The only person who liked Danae the way she was was Basia.

So even if Basia had been sneaking around behind Danae's back, getting mixed up with the rough lot at The Cormorant's Rest, and breaking laws... Danae would not abandon her.

"Which jail has her?"

Basia

The middle city jail stood several blocks south of the main curving road that connected the various quarters of Diosion. It was a stone building constructed from great blocks of the same limestone that made up the cliffs the city perched on. It sported no decorations, no carvings, or window hangings. It was just metal bars and bare stone sluiced clean with sea water every morning.

It wasn't as dirty as Basia had imagined a jail cell might be. They had put her in a room by herself, roughly the size of a small closet. It had a simple cot bare of anything but a straw mattress that looked as though it had not been restuffed since the cell's inception and a clay pot with stains that belied its intended use.

Basia had not yet stooped to using the pot. Just across from the entrance of her cell, two guards sat at a table playing a game involving dice and glancing up at her at regular intervals. They had a bet over whether Basia's sex was the same as her presented gender, and she did not particularly want to give them the chance to discuss it further. She would just have to hold onto the contents of her bladder until their shift ended, which hopefully would be soon. Until then, all Basia could do was tug her coat tighter about her and huddle against the far wall of the cell.

In the time since the arrest, Basia had put together some of what must have happened. The slaves they were freeing were Lex's. The Society had agreed to keep their operation as above-board as much as possible. They would buy the slaves they were assisting rather than *take* them. Of course, that meant that they could only help so many... Had Lex gotten impatient with so slow a process? It would be like them to laugh at the consequences and take the higher risk for a theoretically higher gain. How many times had they sent Basia down to the docks over the last two and a half years with documents that could get her imprisoned? A handful? A dozen? All while trusting that Zol's commander would always place her in a position to approve the illegal papers. Basia supposed that Zol was in on Lex's plan, or she had also been in danger without knowing it.

This imprisonment would be the end of Basia's career, at the very least. Slave stealers did not become Trade Ministers. And there was no telling what her parents would think. It meant irreparable damage to their standing. More if they did not disown or distance themselves from her. Danae wouldn't understand. How could she? Basia had never found a way to explain it to her.

One of the guards stood up, a lean man with skin too small for his body so that it sunk in around all of his wiry muscles. He rattled the bars to Basia's cage. "Go on, let's see it. Is there something dangling between your legs?"

"Maybe it's telling the truth, and it's just the flattest-chested woman you've ever met." The other guard hardly looked up from the dice. He would know about Basia's chest since he'd spent most of the 'search' groping it.

Basia let her head drop to her knees. Had it all been worth it? Her life as she had expected to live it was over. There would be no more future in the Trade Office, no more freeing slaves. She would be stuck here with idiots who wanted nothing but to prod and examine her body to determine if it lived up to their expectations.

The guard's keyring rattled, and Basia looked up just in time to see him thrust it into the lock. She shrank back involuntarily, tightening her arms about herself. She wouldn't let him touch her. She would fight first if it came to that. Basia knew she wasn't very strong—she had never studied the arts of war— but she was boney. She could bite, thrash, or shove the sharp points of her knees and elbows into the soft parts of his flesh.

He watched Basia shrink, and her fear only seemed to spur him on, a smirk covering his face. "Come on, don't be shy. It's a long shift and not a lot to do."

"I don't see what that has to do with me." Basia tried to imagine herself stone, her arms fused together over her curled knees. She should not budge. Unless, perhaps, there was an opportunity to maim him. Frustratingly, horrifyingly, tears began to rise behind her eyes.

The clanging of the exterior door was perhaps the most beautiful sound she had ever heard. The prison's commander stepped in, his uniform unblemished with wrinkles or stains, unlike the guards who watched her. Behind him, Basia thought she recognized a familiar halo of curls. His expression, stern already, morphed into something akin to rage. "Captain Mihail, why are you in this prisoner's cell?"

The captain stepped back, saluting his commander respectfully. If he was sorry to be caught in bad behavior, he didn't look it. He only glanced her way and then stepped aside. "Assisting the prisoner with its supper."

"*Her.*" The voice echoed through the cells, crisp and polite and still stern. Danae stepped past the commander, who nodded respectfully to her. Danae might not have a military rank or a weapon, but she had the Othonos name and likely their gold too. And that seemed to have been enough to grant her entry to Basia's cell.

The captain didn't successfully hide his smirk, though he at least had the good sense to cast his gaze downward as Danae glanced his way. She looked aloof, as if the captain was so beneath her she couldn't even bother to deign him with her full attention.

Basia swallowed, searching her face for some sign of what her friend thought. It was strange to see Danae in the jail, with her beautiful blush-colored dress and diamonds at her lobes. She looked like a Queen or Empress, her hair fanning out in the semblance of a crown.

"Basia," Danae urged, stepping closer. "You are extremely late for Peta's wedding. We have to go now if you're going to see her off."

Basia dashed a few tears escaping down her cheeks, looking from Danae to the commander. She could leave? She didn't have to stay here with the groping, hateful guards? She unpeeled her fingers from their place clutching her knees and stood, wobbling slightly. It took a moment for her to be able to speak. "Yes, of course, Danae."

"Well, come along then." She turned on her heel, and Basia saw a flash of gold as she shook the commander's hand. "Thank you for your assistance, Commander."

"Of course, Mistress Othonos." He slipped his hands into his pockets and bowed a touch too low. How much had Danae paid him to get Basia out?

Basia stumbled after Danae through the prison and onto the street. Lex was waiting there, their face stained with tears and pale with stress and guilt. She knew at once that she was right. It had been them. Lex had attained the slaves illegally and then set Basia up to take the risk whether they had meant to or not.

"Basia!" Lex breathed, relief turning their face into something beautiful. Soft looks from sharp eyes. "You're alright! Thank the Humors. I don't know what I would have done—"

"Without me." Danae's voice broke in, sharper than Basia had ever heard it before. "Basia would have stayed in that terrible place *without me*. Thanks to *you*. She's not alright, Lex. She was sitting in a prison cell, being accosted by foul men. Do you know what dim men like to do to beautiful people? Did you think of that?"

Lex reached out to touch Basia's shoulder, and she flinched away. "It's not like I meant for that to happen, Basia. It was for— we are *saving* people."

Basia couldn't look up. "I just want to go home."

Danae stared at them for a long moment, the color slowly fading from her cheeks. "Both of you. Both of you are reckless and thoughtless. You think you're saving people? You're being *selfish*. Basia's family would be in a terrible position if this little incident were made public, as it would have been tomorrow morning when the arrest reports went out. Never mind that Basia would have spent years in prison for theft. I'm certain the other prisoners would be incredibly understanding of your position, *Biton*."

Danae spat the name out as if it tasted foul on her lips, and Basia flinched away. It might as well have been a physical blow. She had never thought of what might happen before, never understood the consequences because she had never realized she was breaking the law. Basia *would* have gone to a male prison. Never mind that she was Basia and not Biton.

"We're selfish? Only an Othonos could possibly make this about family position. Your family is only where they are through the destruction of other lives. And that's a dead name! Hasn't she been through enough?"

Basia wished they'd both just stop fighting. She wanted to curl up quiet, to be hugged. Now, Danae would never forgive her, and Lex had betrayed her.

"Explain that to the magistrate." Danae's voice was frigid. "Explain to the guards and the courts and everyone in the prison that Biton is dead and Basia is all that matters. And you're right, *Lex*. I do care about family. Basia *is* my family. If you hadn't been able to find me, she would have been stuck in that cell with those guards, and everyone would have been alerted to her thievery, and then even my *name* wouldn't be able to save her from *your* folly!" With that final fact thrown into their faces, Danae turned on her heel and strode off, the train of her beautiful gown dragging through the muck of the city streets.

CHAPTER 84: LIRIA

FOURTH MOON, 1804, ABOLO

Nine Moons before the Proclamation

Most Lirians considered Abolo one of the most beautiful places in all of Liria, but Luce was decidedly not of that opinion. Certainly brightly-colored buildings clinging to the cliff were a marvel of art and engineering, and the waters were clear enough to put the coral reefs on display. Abolo did host a myriad of rocky beaches and tidepools, providing a never-ending stream of delights from the ocean, but Luce didn't care for fish, and he hated climbing up and down the endless stairs.

Tactically speaking, Abolo's harbor allowed Liria a secure port for supplies and military shipping, but whoever had thought to build directly into a sheer cliff face had been either a genius or a madman. On days like today, where Luce's legs trembled as he marched up the stony path, he suspected the city's architect had been nothing more than a sadist.

Three moons, he had been posted in Abolo. Three moons, he had eaten nothing but kelp and stinking fish and slept with the ceaseless buzz of the tides outside his window. And for what? The army was returning from the tundra with empty ships, and the longer the barbarians put up this tedious tantrum, the longer he was away from his home and family. Without Camilla to temper his moods and aid him with her clear mind, Luce's grasp on the situation was painfully tight. If he didn't produce results for the Imperator, then being stuck in Abolo was the least of Luce's worries.

Luce ignored the respectful salutes and bows as he strode across the training yard. He had a pile of reports to muddle through and a headache pounding behind his eyes. The Imperator expected results on the Emaian front, and the truth was, they simply were not providing them. His gut clenched at the thought, and Luce nodded curtly to a soldier as he jumped to open the door to the command building, bowing as the General strode past.

"Who has the newest reports from the southern troops?" Luce demanded. He hated the communal command building, with its low ceilings and vinegar smell. Abolo was so damp that mildew grew rapidly, and the soldiers constantly washed the walls to eliminate the rot. And with Commander Vais still back in Vindium, Luce was saddled with nervous newcomers and lazy soldiers. What he wouldn't give for one competent, driven man. He needed things to go right. He didn't want to leave Camilla and his family alone. If he was killed by the Imperator, then what would happen to them?

A few soldiers sat at low desks around the front room. One too-skinny young man raised a hand in a shaky salute, his warm skin sallow with fear and a thin beading of sweat dampening a patch of hair above his upper lip too sparse to be granted the title of mustache. "I do, sir," he said, somehow managing to get through the words without stuttering. "We've lost another four raiding parties, and six others have come back empty-handed since the last report."

Luce held back a growl of frustration building in his throat. He didn't want these men afraid of him; a good leader *inspired* his men, not terrified them. Luce nodded in understanding and tucked his truncated wrist against his side lest he tap it on his leg in irritation. *It's not their fault,* he reminded himself. *These men aren't the ones failing Liria. They're just the messengers.*

"Very well... ah...." He couldn't remember the skinny boy's name and arched his brow, waiting for the boy to spit it out. Perhaps if he took the time and patience, he could train one of them to be a proficient aid.

"Kaeso," the boy said, wiping a nervous hand across his mouth. Swiping the little hairs to the right did nothing for the appearance of his facial hair. "Kaeso Bellator, sir."

Luce nodded again and fought past the pounding in his head. There had to be something he was missing. Some small piece he could focus on and fix. "Very well, Bellator. Find me the captain of the next ship heading south. If our men cannot produce results on their own, then they must be provided with more detailed instructions."

"I—uh— that is, if you want to hear it, sir, I have another piece of information." Kaeso squirmed as though he wished he were anywhere else but in that meeting.

Luce suppressed a sigh. "Yes?"

"There is a slave working on one of Abolo's old double-masted trawlers catching fish. She isn't Emaian. She's Ararian—taken from a pirate vessel carrying Emaian goods— and she claims she knows something about the she-demon plaguing the tundra."

"A slave?" Luce didn't trust slaves, but information on the elusive Emaian leader could be highly valuable. "And you know of this slave because...?"

"She's making something of a nuisance of herself, sir. She harassed her handlers into sending the information upward."

Perfect. Luce wanted nothing more than to be harangued by an Emaian collaborator. "Bring her in, Bellator. I'll take mint tea in my office while I wait."

It was some time before the boy returned with the slave in tow. The girl had the dark skin and hair of an Ararian, close-cropped to her skull so that he could see the black strokes of a vicious tattoo beneath it. The unwomanly musculature of her arms and the ink that fouled them turned a perfectly acceptable face unappealing. Her jaw jutted out mulishly, and Luce looked away from her unpleasant expression as Bellator plunked a cup of mint tea on his desk. Luce would have preferred that sooner, but at least the boy had remembered at all.

"Do you speak Lirian?" he asked the slave, not bothering to look her way as he lifted the steaming cup to his nose. Breathing in the familiar scents, he allowed himself a moment of relaxation, willing himself home. Camilla was just on the other side of the door, they would have stewed leeks over farro for supper, and then he would fall asleep to the sound of his children attending their chores and assignments. As he exhaled, Luce found himself in a better mood.

"Lirian? Some. Phecean is better," the slave said in a clumsy accent. The moment of relaxation evaporated as reality crashed back in. He didn't know many Ararians, but they were known to be an unrelenting people with strict rules and ethos. It was likely this brute hadn't gotten along with the sensibilities of her nation and so fled into piracy.

"Then we can speak in Phecean. I am told you wished to see me."

"You're the one in command? The Captain?" She looked around his unadorned office, but her expression didn't give away her emotions.

Luce set his cup down. "I'm not with the Navy, so my rank is not that of Captain but General. But yes, I am in charge."

"You're the one who put posters up about Iniabi."

"I did order posters to be put up," he agreed, reaching to take up his cup again. He would not give away the importance of accurate information regarding the rabble. If the girl was right, he now had a name. Iniabi.

"You want to know more about her. Your posters said you'd pay for information."

"I don't pay slaves."

"I don't require payment, only freedom."

Luce set his cup down and gestured for the woman to sit. "You're a known smuggler and obviously in bed with the Emaians. Why would I free you?"

"I am not in bed with them!" she snarled, her hands curling into fists. Behind her, Bellator shifted, as if nervous. She glanced over her shoulder at him, and after a heated moment, loosened her fists. "I want my freedom, and I have plenty of information about Iniabi. Give me what I want, and you can have what you want."

Luce wondered if he could simply torture the information out of the woman. She looked rough enough, but few could withstand dry drowning for more than a few days. Torture could take too long, though, and it wasn't a given that the information provided in desperation would be accurate.

What was one Ararian slave set loose? At least she wasn't Emaian.

"Fine, what's your name?"

"Jaya."

"Alright, sit down Jaya, and tell me what you know of this… Iniabi."

Her shoulders relaxed, and Jaya the soon-to-be ex-slave settled into the chair across the desk from Luce. "She lived as a pirate for six years—that's how I know her. We taught her to fight and sail, and speak as many languages as we could. And then she killed our captain."

Luce made no move to encourage the woman to speak. It seemed she had been preparing her little diatribe for some time. He did glance up at Bellator, and with a subtle nod, the boy hurried to collect ink and paper.

"We found her selling her people's poison. It's supposed to be sacred, but when it suited her, she exploited them. Iniabi is without conscience. If she thinks it will benefit her, she will do it."

He knew of the drug, having received too many reports from those stationed in Ifratem detailing its casualties. He forbade it within his unit when he had been a commander still going on raids, but not all commanders felt they could dictate their soldiers' personal time. It didn't surprise him that this Emaian bitch sold the stuff. "What are her weaknesses? How old is she? Does she have a family?"

"No, Lirians killed her family. Well, her Emaian family." Jaya gave him a long look.

"She's half Lirian?" he clarified.

"Yes. Her father was Lirian. I don't know if he's still alive. I'm sure no one knows who he is."

"Distasteful and unhelpful. What else?"

"She doesn't have many weaknesses aside from selfishness and a willingness to bite the hand that feeds her. I mean, she's disgusting, but I don't see—"

"What do you mean, *disgusting?*"

The slave rolled her eyes, and Luce resisted the urge to slap her. "She likes women."

"Women?"

"To fuck."

Luce lifted his cup of tea to hide the smile crossing his lips. "Go on." Perhaps this irritating woman would be worth his time after all.

CHAPTER 85: THE EMAI

THIRD MOON, 1804, AMARUIT WAR CAMP

Ten Moons before the Proclamation

The Amaruit lived in a sea of tents, moving like the tide and adding more to their ranks every time they neared the shore. There was a steady stream of recruits from the south —young, able-bodied Emaians adding their strength to Iniabi's wolves. Their number neared five hundred, even after the losses they'd suffered here and there at Bikkisi and occasionally in smaller raids.

Iniabi stepped between waist-high tents, their occupants spilling out of them in various stages of wakefulness while more of her warriors returned from their night watches to find their furs. A little ways away from her tent, a group of them clustered around Poallu in a tight ring.

The language they spoke was slippery and lilting, nearly as familiar to Iniabi as her mother tongue, but when one of the escaped slaves caught Iniabi watching, they stopped speaking Phecean. One after another, they pressed three fingers to their lips in respect, and Poallu glanced over her shoulder to see who stood there. She smiled when she saw Iniabi and beckoned for her leader to join the circle of chatting Emai. "We're just catching up on the way of things in Phecea. They're doing worse than Liria, it would seem."

"Worse how?" Iniabi asked, her interest piqued. Perhaps there was a weakness there that she might exploit.

"Well," a young woman Iniabi didn't know said. She must have recently returned to the Tundra because she wore a parka thrown over foreign clothes. "The Pheceans don't have the special trade agreements that the Lirians do. My ... the family I was with, they would talk about it often. The Lirians have special arrangements with another country to the north. And that is the nearest place to ship goods from, so Phecea has to ship from further countries. Their farmlands have regularly been overrun by Lirians, so their natural resources are dwindling. That is why the family sold me. They could not afford to feed me."

Iniabi wondered how long the girl had lived in Phecea. It seemed to Iniabi's ear that the newcomer had a Phecean accent even when speaking her native tongue. She must have been taken incredibly young. "How did you come to return to the Tundra?"

The girl shook her head in open confusion. "These Pheceans bought me at the slave market and gave me papers to ship here. They said I shouldn't be a slave anymore."

Iniabi looked at Poallu, her eyebrows raised. "Did you put her up to that? I know you're convinced that Pheceans are somehow better than Lirians, but I'll not treat their raiders any differently."

Poallu shook her head. "No, I didn't tell her to say that. You should ask around the camp, Kaneq Amaroq. There are a few others who have similar stories."

The girl was nodding, and Iniabi hummed thoughtfully. "Do you know the names of those who sent you?"

She shook her head. "There was a group of them. Young people who spoke with passion and treated me kindly. One was a beautiful girl who knew a bit of our language. But they didn't give names. I suppose it was to be careful in case I told someone that would get them in trouble."

"Makes sense," Poallu agreed. "The northerners are probably strapped for free labor."

The new woman looked at Iniabi with a thoughtful tilt to her chin. "I... I still have friends in Phecea. I can write, and they can too. If... if I can get a message to them, perhaps they could find the answers you seek, Kaneq Amaroq?"

Iniabi looked at her for a long moment, her thoughts far away. The newcomer said that there was a beautiful girl who spoke their language, and unbidden, Iniabi's mind conjured images from her first foray into the world of urchin spine and dreams. There had been a beautiful girl in that poison sleep, soft, warm-skinned, and curly-haired. Was this the foreign girl Iniabi was meant to find? "Yes," she said finally. "Find them if they exist, but be careful. If we have allies in Phecea it won't help us to get them in trouble."

"Yes, Kaneq Amaroq. I will be." The girl kissed three fingers and turned to leave as if to set to her new task at once. It seemed with Iniabi nearby, the other newcomers didn't wish to continue their conversation, and the group broke apart, filtering off to other tasks. Poallu gestured for Iniabi to join her at the little fire they had gathered around, and Iniabi squatted.

"I would offer you some soup, but my pot is mostly water and herbs," Poallu murmured, her gray eyes flashing with unspoken meaning.

Iniabi understood. Her own soup had been just as thin, and her clothes sat looser and looser upon her body. Food was a constant struggle with a force this large. "How difficult would it be to get goods from nearby villages?"

"Not that difficult," Poallu said, but she paused, chewing on her bottom lip. "It might be easier to send some of the wolves home. There is talk of it already; with smaller numbers it would be easier to keep the rest of the pack fed."

"We would be making ourselves weaker for it." Iniabi looked away over the endless peaks of tents interspersed with the pale trunks of birches and sugar pines or warriors going about their work. She would not disband. Not while there was still so much to do. "For now, send scouts to whatever villages they can reach to ask for aid, and I'll organize a few of our war bands into hunting parties. It's not yet time to lay down our swords."

When Iniabi returned her attention to Poallu, it was to find the other woman staring at her for a long breath. She held Iniabi's gaze but, finally, nodded. "Yes, Kaneq." Though she complied, Iniabi felt the hesitation and knew what it meant. Poallu, too, wanted to return to her village. To a home. To an illu and familiar routines and comfort. She wasn't alone.

The Emaians were winning, for now. But Iniabi feared their progress would be destroyed the moment they stepped away from the battle.

⇑   ⇑   ⇑

That evening, Iniabi was drawn away from her makeshift maps by a commotion on the edge of the camp. She rose smoothly, motioning to Tatik and Deniigi to accompany her. They all stood quickly and made their way through the maze of tents that provided her wolves shelter from the late summer winds. It was almost warm this far north, the mild weather setting Iniabi's skin sweating below her tunic.

"What do you think it is?" she asked the others. "More recruits?"

"Maybe the hunters brought back something big. Caribou?" Tatik murmured. Deniigi shook his head in doubt. For an old tracker like him, Iniabi's large collection of fighters was a nightmare. They scared off game for miles.

Three figures stood at the edge of their camp, Iniabi's wolves waiting on the other side. Three was a small number, and they had approached from the west. The only thing to the west was a Phecean port town called Pangnir.

Iniabi caught a young man's arm and smiled when he gaped at her, half-stunned. "Go get Poallu and bring her to me." He nodded sharply and raced off, stumbling over himself in his haste.

If these were more freed people from Phecea, then perhaps Poallu would be the best person to see them settled in.

The newcomers clustered at the edge of camp, speaking to the guards but not attempting to enter. There were two men—strong and with the look of hard laborers—and a woman roughly Iniabi's age with classically pale hair and skin. Her features were a devastatingly familiar delicate porcelain, and she was taller than most other women Iniabi knew. It made sense. She had been tall as a girl too.

"Yeah. Just looks like new recruits," Iniabi murmured. Fear spiked her heart rate, and she had to work to keep her breathing even. "I'm sure you all can take care of this?"

Tatik shrugged affably, but Deniigi's eyes followed her as she fled. He could probably tell something was amiss, but she couldn't stand there and pretend any longer. She'd give herself away, or someone else would.

That was Mika at the edge of camp. Iniabi's childhood best friend come back to haunt her after the slavers took her away. It was Mika's fault that Iniabi had never become a slave—it was her fault Iniabi had been flayed and left to die in the snow by the slavers who had raided Nec.

She could tell the Amaruit about Iniabi, about, about— About what? Iniabi shook herself forcibly even as she stalked towards the opposite side of camp. Mika didn't know that Iniabi had sold poison in Angillik or prepared it for the Captain to keep herself alive. She would have been a slave then, far away from port towns and pirate ships.

Iniabi forced herself to take a deep breath, resisting the urge to press handfuls of snow into her face. Snow wouldn't take off the tint, the warm undertones of slaver's blood beneath her skin. It would not take her black eyes and give her pale ones. Instead, Iniabi slipped into her tent, digging through the furs, knives, and small implements necessary to live in the camp until she found a small goat stomach pouch. She opened it with shaking fingers, breathing in the chalky smell.

Gypsum.

The scent took her back to her childhood, to mixing powder into paste for Manaba. She still remembered how to do it, the cold water from her pail slick and clumping against her fingers. Manaba had always said it must be perfectly smooth.

When it was ready, Iniabi smeared the white paint over her face, her neck, her hands. It dried against her in a stiff second skin, and when she leaned over her pail to peer at her reflection, she saw Manaba looking back at her, her face bisected by a branching red river.

Iniabi shrieked and fell back, waving away a worried wolf when he stuck his head in to check on her. A second glance showed her features reflecting back at her, black eyes on purest white, her mother banished to the Tundra's endless expanse.

After a few more moments to herself, Iniabi spoke to the guards on watch and the patrols coming in, making her rounds through the encampment. Mika was probably settled in by now. She wouldn't even have to talk to her. She'd just return to her tent after arranging the next day's scouting and foraging parties.

She had nearly made it when a slim figure stepped out between two tents, blocking her path. Iniabi instinctively reached for her sword but stopped when the moonlight shone off silver hair. "Iniabi?" the figure whispered, and though Mika's voice had deepened as she aged, she still sounded like the girl from Nec all those years ago.

Iniabi didn't know what to feel. Here stood a living relic, someone from the ruin of her raided village, alive and whole and *real*. Here stood the girl who had let her be beaten until she lay at death's door, freezing in the snow. She was someone from Iniabi's dangerous past.

Mika came closer, her gray eyes wide with disbelief. She scanned Iniabi, who resisted the urge to hide or squirm in discomfort, and reached out one hand. Palm up.

Uncertain, Iniabi offered her hand as well, and Mika took it, her grip hard. Iniabi suppressed the urge to flinch but couldn't hold back her gasp of surprise when Mika yanked on their connected hands, pulling Iniabi in for a crushing hug. "It *is* you."

Iniabi reacted slowly, but after a few tense seconds, she allowed herself to relax into Mika's embrace, wrapping her arms around the pretty woman's waist. "Yes. It's been so long, I know. But it is me, Mika."

"I thought you were dead. I thought you died that day...." Mika hugged her tighter. "I'm sorry, Iniabi. It's my fault that happened. I was young and afraid and I wanted my mother, but I shouldn't have let you... shouldn't have blamed you."

Iniabi took a deep breath, letting her rib cage expand against Mika's arms and using that pressure to ground herself. If this was her instead of Mika, apologizing to the Emai for selling, bastardizing their deepest secrets, for turning on them in favor of what safety she could find on a pirate ship crewed by an addict she helped create…

Iniabi was sorry too. For so much.

"I forgive you, Mika. Welcome home."

It seemed those were the words Mika needed to hear because she gasped, shoulders shaking in suppressed wails. They stood that way, Iniabi half holding up the taller woman until finally, Mika broke away. She pressed her hands to her face and then, as if she couldn't help herself, took Iniabi's hand again. "I can't believe you're here. That you're leading these warriors to protect the Emai. How did this come to pass? Were you taken by other Lirians?"

Iniabi shook her head mutely. "No. But it's a long story. If you'd like, you could sit by my fire tonight and tell me all that has happened to you."

"That is a long story too, but I will sit by your fire." Iniabi gestured toward her tent farther up the row. It didn't seem as if Mika could keep herself quiet because as they started to walk, she spoke again, not waiting for a fire or a meal to spill her truth. "After the Lirians left you in the snow, we were loaded onto a boat and taken north. It was bad sailing and… well. Not all of us made it to Liria."

The fire was just a collection of charcoal when they reached it, but Iniabi had a bit of wood and kindling. She set about coaxing it to life while she listened, putting water for stew over the flames.

Mika accepted the broth without pausing in her tale. "Lirians keep captured Emai for themselves most of the time. Aada and I were bought and used as kitchen slaves. After what happened to you and the others, I was afraid. I didn't want to get in trouble, so I was quiet. I was good. I did what they asked me to."

Hadn't she done the same on the *Flying Night*?

"I lived like that for a long time. Being a slave is no good, but it wasn't all bad. I had food and shelter and Aada. It wasn't a life I wanted, but it was a life." Mika looked down at her cup, seeming to realize it was still full. She took a gulp and then pulled a face. It must have been a long time since she had any food caught and cooked in the Tundra. "But Aada got sick. Coughing all the time. Soon the Lirians didn't want her working in the kitchens 'cause they said it was unclean. So she started working making wool and weaving. She did that for a year or so, and then...."

The grief was still plain on Mika's features, and for a moment, Iniabi felt guilty, remembering how she had challenged Manaba's spirit on a rooftop in Angillik. If anything, she had been relieved to be free of her Aada. "Then what happened?"

Mika blinked and set her cup aside, coming to life again. "Well... like I said. I didn't want to be killed or whipped, so I was good. I think that's why they chose me. Do you know about the... About how the Lirians get more Emaians?"

Iniabi's gut went cold. "They come here and take more of us."

"No. Most of the ones they sell aren't from the Tundra." Mika picked up her cup of broth, holding it between her hands as if to sap its warmth. "They're... It's... I can't remember the word for it in Emaian. They *make* more slaves."

"They— they made you—" There was a roaring in her ears, a wild avalanche-fall pressure building up behind her breastbone. Mika had wanted children once, but great seas, not like that. "Did they— Did you—"

"They took me to the place where the others live. They aren't Emaians. They don't know our language or about snow or illus or anything, but they look like us. I suppose that's all that matters." Mika's tone was distant, her face carefully blank. "I can't have children, so I didn't stay there very long. That's when I was sold to the Pheceans."

Iniabi stood and crossed around the fire to put a steadying hand on Mika's shoulder. "I will stop them, Mika. I will kill them in droves, burn down these... these *breeding* places and free those descendants who don't even know how to live like us. Will you tell the others? They need to know just what we are fighting against."

Mika looked up into her face, eyes still unblinking, but something changed, and her expression softened. "I will tell the truth. I won't lie ever again. I promise, Kaneq Amaroq."

CHAPTER 86: THE EMAI

SIXTH MOON, 1804, AMARUIT WAR CAMP

Seven Moons before the Proclamation

One year after leaving the Sinqiniq, the Amaruit found a place to camp in the center of a valley between two snow-slick hills northeast of the Nonoccan peaks. They put up their tents the same way they might construct a village—concentric rings upon rings around an open circle at the center. To Iniabi's eye, there were fewer of them now, though, in all reality, the few warriors that had left so far shouldn't have been enough to make a visible difference.

They were not deep enough into Emaian lands for the bonfire lit at the center of their camp, the flames seeming to leap higher as the night wore on. Hopefully, the hills around them would hide them from slavers' searching eyes. Iniabi's wolves danced around the blaze, their voices lifted in echoing song and their feet pounding the rhythms traditionally played by caribou-skin drums. Tatik stood near the center of this, her exposed skin caked in white gypsum and her arms raised above the two warriors standing to either side of her.

The revelry bloomed and shuttered around Iniabi, waves of sound against a lee shore. She couldn't seem to make herself smile, much less relax the stiffness in her shoulders. This wedding had been Tatik's idea—a way for the wolves to let off steam as the slave raids seemed more easily turned away each day. Many of them felt the war was already won, and they should go home and celebrate their newfound freedom with their families.

Iniabi was sure they were wrong.

The slavers would not give up so easily—not when they thought the Emai belonged to them, that it was their right to tear strangers from their homes. No. Retribution was coming, and her wolves needed to be ready for it. No matter how many Emaians the Lirians bred in their despicable barns, they would always be hungry for more flesh if only her wolves would see it.

"You're frowning, Kaneq Amaroq." Poallu appeared at her side, but Iniabi didn't jump. The ex-Phecean slave had come a long way in a short time, turning into one of the swiftest, quietest wolves. That, and her ability to read and write, made her an invaluable counselor to Iniabi, though they had a tendency to disagree. "Most people smile at weddings."

"Most weddings don't take place this close to enemy lands," Iniabi said, raising a brow. "Do you think it's too late to ask them to sing more quietly?"

"Do you mean whisper? It wouldn't be much of a celebration if the spirits couldn't hear us. Besides, the Lirians are afraid of us, you know that." Poallu lifted her cup of fermented root liquor, eyes roaming over Iniabi's empty hands.

"I know that I'm surrounded by a bunch of Emaians who celebrate when the fish finds their nets instead of when it is cooking on the fire. There's still work to do yet."

Poallu clasped Iniabi on the shoulder, a little too familiar. "If you're hungry, there's fish by the bonfire. Relax! You've earned it. Your plan to get support from nearby villages means our bellies are full."

Iniabi shook her off and turned away. "I will be the first to dance when this war is finally over."

"What war? Look around you! This is victory!"

Iniabi turned and surveyed her war camp again. To one side of Tatik, Pakuk laid a spear and net at the feet of the girl he was going to marry, taking the first few steps in the dance that would bind them to each other. Around them, warriors drank and laughed, slapping each other's backs and congratulating themselves on their feats of strength or bravery. Somewhere nearby, a young woman boasted about the lover waiting for her at home. Very few of them kept alert or had their weapons close to hand.

"All I see are fools," she said finally, the word leaving her throat in a harsh growl.

"Those are cold words, Kaneq Amaroq."

Iniabi met Poallu's eyes then, if only briefly. "I am the coldest wolf."

Amaruit's leader turned her back to the celebration and strode for the edge of camp until the darkness of the Tundra beyond swallowed her small form.

The night was deep, powder-soft flurries visible in the distant light from the Emaian camp. Iniabi shivered as she stepped between the trees growing from the northernmost hill guarding their little encampment. There had been no forests near the village where she'd grown up, and still, the closeness of looming trees made her skin itch.

No tracks led from the camp and into the surrounding land. Perhaps this was because the scouts Iniabi had sent out had covered their footprints remarkably well, but she doubted it. How many were dancing in the center of the camp instead of protecting their fellow warriors? Soft. The last few moons had made them all soft and insubordinate as well.

Iniabi stepped deeper into shadow, following the curves and dips of the land so that she would be invisible to searching eyes. There was something strange in the air, a smell that did not fit with the spice of crushed nettles or the cleanness of snow. Iniabi supposed it might have been the lingering wisps of smoke that must still cling to her clothes and hair, but she doubted it— there was something *wrong* beyond the valley where the Amaruit reveled.

She turned her feet towards the feeling, ignoring the tiny signs of small animals that had made their homes in the cold. Trees passed by her, dark watchers, and the stars spun slowly like nets cast over the sky. After a time, the smells of people grew thick—horse and sweat and refuse, but it was not until Iniabi reached the edge of the wood that she saw them. A party of what must have been a few thousand camped in a depression on the other side of the same hills that sheltered the Emai.

Iniabi stilled. She felt no surprise, no horror, only a budding chill that seemed to bloom like hoarfrost at her center. There was no telling from this distance whether the soldiers below were Lirian or Phecean. In truth, it did not matter. Iniabi could pick out their supply tents like ticks in a dog's fur—bulbous, fat, and ready to be plucked free.

Her first instinct was to return to her warriors, to raise them from their drunken bliss and set them on the enemy that had finally begun to amass in response to their efforts. But what good would liquor-addled wolves do besides stumble into the enemy camp and get themselves killed? It was better to let the invaders do the work for her.

The leader of the Amaruit slipped back down the hill and into camp, where she made a point of sitting by the fire, drinking, and congratulating Pakuk and his new wife. The new day would bring enough blame. Iniabi had no desire to be included in that frenzy.

⇑   ⇑   ⇑

Iniabi woke the next morning well-rested. There was a new resolve in her limbs, and she took a moment to revel in it, stretching beneath her furs as much as she could in the cramped confines of her small, worn tent. She searched herself for any signs of doubt but found none—she needed to move forward, needed to continue the fight, and to do that, she needed this army.

Outside, the camp was already stirring. Soldiers on breakfast duty sent knives slicing through the skinned bodies of hares, splitting bone with sharp cracks. Still others drained the blood from the hanging carcass of a caribou, fat droplets spilling slowly into a waiting bowl. Iniabi slipped through this massacre to find one of her pack leaders.

Manirak was a thin man, his hair so close-cropped that she could see the curve of his skull beneath it. He had big, sad eyes and two fingers missing on his right hand. He sat, mopping up the last of his stew with a slice of iffiaq, a fried bread they made from stolen grain whenever they could get their hands on it. Manirak ate with the mechanical efficiency of one who cared nothing for what they were consuming but needed sustenance anyway. Iniabi put a hand on his shoulder. "Finish your meal and gather enough warriors for a couple of scouting parties."

He didn't even bother to ask why—just stood, dropped off his bowl, and went about the work. Iniabi liked that about him. The man had lost more to the slavers than most. After Banished slave-sellers took his wife and child, he survived and found another village where he began to start again with a new lover, only to lose her to Lirians as well. He certainly wasn't about to ask for the war to end before it was finished.

While she waited for Manirak to return, Iniabi took a bowl and slice of bread for herself, trying to eat the savory mixture quickly to avoid losing its warmth. The fat and gristle of the unidentified game stuck to her teeth, slimy against her throat, yet she ate it without complaint. She'd known true hunger too often to do otherwise.

When Manirak returned, Iniabi was finished with her food, her belly warm and full. She looked over them with a satisfied air. Twenty well-equipped warriors stood before her, all clothed in a strange mixture of Emaian furs and stolen Lirian steel. Manirak leaned on an enormous two-handed ax, its metal head half buried in the snow-melt muck in front of him, and he leaned towards Iniabi to confer with her.

"How would you like to split them?"

"Most of them will be in a large group heading southeast to Bikkissi. A dozen will be scouting north of here. I've heard of stirring around the port—the Pheceans might be landing ships there for raids while our focus is northward." Iniabi did have some reservations about Bikkissi, but it was not the port that made her lips tighten and guilt prick painfully at her chest.

Manirak, ever the capable leader, relayed the instructions without raising his voice, his movements brisk and competent. Iniabi liked that about him, and she made a mental note to give him more authority in the future, should she have the need. She watched the proceedings without taking part—there was no need to step on Manirak's toes— until she saw that Mika had been put in the smaller group. Those headed to the north.

For a moment, Iniabi could see nothing but memories—she and Mika sitting shoulder-to-shoulder while Manaba led their village in prayer, helping each other with chores, talking beside the fire when an arrow took Piav through the throat. Mika telling the slavers that Iniabi had stolen from them when they were taken.

She shook her head sharply. "Manirak, have the new girl, Mika, stay behind. Her grasp of languages is more useful here."

He only nodded once and made it so.

⇑ ⇑ ⇑

It was after noon the next day before word of Iniabi's dawn scouts returned. She sat on a stump, one hand cushioning her chin, and let no emotion spill onto her features. Several of her wolves were arguing about why they should return to their families.

"We've been out in the Tundra for a year now! We've cleared our land of Lirians, and it's time to return home. Our people need us."

Tatik, the medicine woman, sat nearby, her expression pulled into tense lines. "Uki is getting older, but Sinqiniq has Sedna, and she specifically said she wanted me to follow Iniabi."

Many pairs of eyes drifted to her then, some hopeful, some worried. She was, after all, the leader.

The Kaneq Amaroq stood, her shoulders square and her white hair falling long over her shoulders. She took deep breaths of cold air, and when the others were silent, she opened her mouth to speak. "I wish we did not have to leave our homes, my wolves. I wish we could have stayed in the easy warmth of our illus and the company of our villages. I dream of a day when no Emaian will march to war or lift a spear to die defending their homes from slavers. I want to go home too, to curl up in the arms of my loved ones and sleep away from the wilds."

Iniabi paused for a moment, allowing others to join their circle. She had not idly chosen the previous night's bonfire for her meeting place. The smell of smoke coated everything, and ash went up in delicate puffs as Iniabi stepped across the fire's discarded bones.

"You have done good work, my wolves. The Lirians and

Pheceans who step on our land now fear our spears. They cannot send raiding parties like they once did to take away our people, and they hesitate now before entering the Tundra at all. For this, I congratulate you."

Iniabi raised her right hand and pressed three fingers to her lips, offering all those who gathered before her a sign of respect.

"But you are fools if you truly believe that we will stay safe if we lay down our weapons and return home. The slavers still come. In a moon or two, they will tell their people that the Amaruit no longer protect the Tundra. They will come back with their steel weapons and armor. They will sail their ships back to our harbors. They will ask us to pay in blood and poison for their enjoyment. Some of your sons and daughters will be taken. Some of your spouses will be used, and some of you will live untouched but forever with the knowledge that you failed to save your people."

Silence stretched out between her and the wolves. Some nodded or stared at her with fevered intensity, but many—too many—frowned.

"So we are to stay here forever? Roaming the Tundra in the hopes that an enemy will appear? Even the Lirians get to go home."

It surprised her that Pakuk spoke, his arm looped over his new bride's shoulders. He had been one of her first fighters. One night of marriage, and he wanted to return to an illu and a cooking pot? Iniabi had to suppress a scoff.

"No, not forever. Just until the war is won."

Shouts broke out at the edge of camp, panic blowing through the tents like blizzard winds. Several of the wolves gathered around Iniabi broke away, running to assist, to find out what had caused the disturbance. Iniabi yelled orders over the din, demanding that her wolves stay calm, stay organized. The last thing they needed was to devolve into chaos. More of the Emai joined the gathering at their camp's center if only to hear the news. Tatik looked ready to bolt to someone's aid but unsure what direction to choose.

After a few moments, three blood-drenched fighters made their slow, agonizing way to Iniabi's circle, the woman in the lead bleeding profusely from a gash across her forehead. Arrows still protruded from her shoulder. "Kaneq—" she started, the words catching in her mouth. "They're... they're dead."

Iniabi stepped forward, reaching out to steady the woman. Her skin was damp and clammy, her cheeks lacking any color. "What? Who is dead? Speak, warrior. I've got you."

"Dead... dead...." The woman's eyes unfocused, and she slumped limply in Iniabi's arms, her weight half-dragging the Kaneq Amaroq into the ash of the bonfire. Behind her, one of the other wolves, a man, coughed blood into pure snow.

"The scouts," he said, drawing in rattling breaths past red-speckled lips. "They're all dead. Four thousand Lirians are coming."

Guilt poisoned Iniabi's blood. She had ordered this. She had commanded twenty of her wolves to go unknowingly into the arms of their enemies. She had sent them all to die, and now the Amaruit would have no choice but to face four thousand Lirian soldiers in battle.

And yet, this time, when Iniabi asked her wolves to ready themselves for war, they all came. There would be no talk of going home again.

CHAPTER 87: PHECEA

FOURTH MOON, 1804, DIOSION

Nine Moons before the Proclamation

"Mistress?" Danae looked up from her harp, resting her hands against the strings to quiet their singing. Yuka stood on the threshold of the music room, eyes downcast deferentially. Normally the Emaian woman would never interrupt Danae's practice time, so the interruption was likely from the only higher authority than herself in the Othonos house—her parents.

"Yes?"

"Your mother and father would like to see you in their study." Yuka bowed her head a bit more and stepped aside, clearing the path. Danae held back a sigh and nodded. It wasn't Yuka's fault that her parents' only free moment these days was late in the evening when Danae practiced.

Standing, Danae straightened the nightgown she had already donned and touched her hair. It was a mess, but then she hadn't left the Othonos estate in three days. She'd been neglecting social events whenever possible. "Thank you, Yuka. I'll go to them now."

The sound of her bare feet padding against the polished wooden floors echoed in the silent halls, most servants and slaves already abed. Danae had started to notice how empty the estate could be since

Basia didn't come over and Danae was left home often. She had hoped that the ceasefire would mean that Arsenio and Andromyda Othonos would have more time to spend at home, but it seemed that their efforts were now focused on repairing damages to Lefkara and Aphodes, accruing trade alliances, and refilling the Phecean treasury.

Her parents were even busier than they had been before the ceasefire. Or maybe she just noticed it because she was alone where she had not been before.

After Basia's release from prison, Danae didn't have the stomach to spend much time with her friend. She just couldn't understand why the other woman would risk so much— her family's name, her status in the trade administration, her freedom. Basia had tried several times to explain or talk to her, but it didn't feel right. Danae wasn't a ruffian who broke laws. She loved Phecea and respected her country, and patriots didn't go around thwarting the systems meant to protect Phecea.

As she approached her parents' shared study, Danae could hear her father's voice, raised and harsh. He wasn't the sort of man to shout, so this was enough to shock her. Though she knew it was rude, Danae eased closer.

"—Emaians in our lands! Twenty dead in the raid! Supplies *stolen*. As if Phecea can afford to lose even a single outpost!"

"We're sending reinforcements. It'll be handled." Andromyda's voice was softer, more reasonable.

"By the time the reinforcements get there, the rabble will be long gone. Bikkisi is too far, too isolated. It's vulnerable."

"We've never had these types of problems before. It's a valuable port—"

"That's why they attacked it. Lirians on our doorsteps and Emaians at our back gate—"

"Shush, Arsenio. Danae will be here any minute."

Her father huffed a sigh, and Danae waited to the count of twenty before she resumed walking, pointedly making noise.

When she knocked, her father's voice was under control again. "Come in, Danae."

Her parents were seated on ornate sofas placed around a low table, though Danae suspected her father had been pacing before. The table before them was tidy, but the desks facing the large windows were strewn with papers. Shelves lining the walls, filled with charts and maps and books, and stately windows provided an attractive view of the garden beyond, an ever-changing painting. It was the focal point of their office, bringing the outside in. Of course, as it was now night, nothing was visible but the distant harbor's lights.

"Danae, please, come sit with us. Have some kava." Her mother gestured to a steaming pot and a tray of small treats. Despite the late hour, it looked as if her parents were ready for a long conversation. Settling across from them, Danae watched as her father poured her a cup of kava tea. Their expressions were bland, and Danae reminded herself to do the same, schooling her features into stillness.

A small part of her wondered if they had somehow found out about Basia, the slaves, and the prison or if they knew that Danae had used the Othonos name and gold to get Basia out. Phecea didn't condone bribery after all.

She forced herself to take even breaths, refusing to let the nervous impulse to swallow win out. This could be about anything. Moons had passed, and they hadn't heard about Basia. There was no need to give herself away.

Her father spoke first, leaning forward and clasping his hands together between his knees. His tunic matched the hand-knotted rug below, patterned gold and white and red in brilliant hues. "Danae, next moon, you will be turning eighteen. Though it is a bit young, your mother and I believe it is time to discuss suitable matches with the right families."

"Matches?" Her mind was drawing a blank. What did he mean? Danae glanced at her mother, who tilted her chin in a subtle nod.

"Yes, for marriage. Alliances."

Marriage? Most nobility didn't marry until they were at least twenty! Danae's heart plummeted. She had thought she would have a few more years to work herself out. To learn precisely what it was to be Danae Othonos, Councilor to the Phecean Confederacy. "Oh."

"We won't broach a marriage just yet, but we want the right families to know it's coming. Just the *temptation* will help us forge the right alliances." Did that mean they were looking outside of Phecea for a match? Would she be tied to a foreigner who didn't know or respect the humors and the arts? Her stomach squirmed, but Danae only nodded.

"Don't worry. Your mother and I won't let you be committed to someone undesirable. You're the Othonos heir." Danae usually found her father's smile reassuring, but it didn't help her now.

"I understand."

"Is there anything you'd like to know, Danae? Or say? We're not demanding this of you. We believe you're ready, but if you don't...." Andromyda's words made Danae flinch.

"No. No. If you think it's time, I agree," she said hastily, pulling her lips into a smile even if she knew it was a poor one.

She was spared from thinking about the subject of her early marriage by Yuka's second arrival. The slave bowed deeply as she entered, and Arsenio gestured for her to speak.

"Mistress Basia has come." Danae's heart flopped in her chest. How much more of this could she take?

"Very well, we're done here, Danae. You may go." Arsenio smiled at Danae, already standing to approach his desk. Danae felt herself automatically standing, nodding to her parents, and following Yuka down the stairs into the formal sitting room where Basia always waited.

Normally, Danae would *want* to talk to Basia about this—Emaian raids, a tentative ceasefire with Liria, and her parents deciding to have her marry so early. Basia would hold and talk with her through the night.

Well, the old Basia would, the Basia who was her friend, who didn't hide things from her and sneak around breaking laws. The Basia who hadn't chosen ruffians over the life she and Danae had been promised since birth.

The new Basia... Danae didn't know who she was or if she was even a real friend.

Without thinking, Danae bowed to Basia as she entered the sitting room. The servants had left her the little tray of her favorite treats; they knew her preferences as well as they knew Danae's. After all, Basia had been in the Othonos estate almost every day since they met some eight years ago. She was her best friend and family and everything else.

Or she *had* been.

Danae stiffened and looked away. "Hello."

Basia

"Danae!" Basia stood up, knocking into the untouched platter in her haste to rise. She just managed to catch it by the edge before she sent the whole affair tumbling onto the carpet. "I— thank you for seeing me. I know this is your practice time, but I really need to speak with you."

Perhaps her short stint in prison had irreparably destroyed Basia's relationship with Danae, but even so, she couldn't just let things lie. Danae had meant too much to her for too long.

"I wasn't practicing. I was speaking with my parents." She swallowed and moved to sit in the chair opposite Basia.

Basia relaxed slightly. Danae was speaking to her, not just offering excuses to leave. That had to count for something, didn't it? "What were you talking to them about?"

"My future."

"Your future? As in ruling the province?"

Her friend folded her hands on her knees, one of the signs of Danae trying to find something diplomatic to say. Basia chewed the inside of her cheek, her brows creasing. Since when had Danae needed to choose her words so carefully around her best friend? "As in my marriage and my place on the Council."

Basia flinched back. "Already? You're not even eighteen yet! You should have years before you have to marry."

Danae looked away. It was difficult to tell what she thought about the matter, but Basia knew Danae often felt outcast or awkward around their peers. Marrying so young wouldn't make things easier.

"It doesn't matter. Things are bad with the war and the Emai. It's my *duty* to stabilize them."

"So you think what I'm doing is betraying my country?" Basia's face tightened, and her teeth tore a bloody rent into the side of her cheek. She swallowed iron and tried to slow the sudden surge of anger that rose within her chest. "I'm sorry. I didn't come here to fight. I came to try and make things right between us."

"I think you're betraying your family and me. You're behaving recklessly. You lied to me, your supposed best friend, for years."

"I made a choice between telling you and saving lives, Danae. If you had to lie to me to save someone, would you do it? Phecean, Emaian, what does it matter? These are people we're talking about. Human beings. You know the words of the great philosophers better than I do. Law is not the same as morality. We have to hold ourselves to higher standards than the letters of past magistrates."

"The morality of it won't save you, your friends, or your family. I love you, Basia. And it's that love that makes it so hard for me to see you do this."

"But it's so much bigger than just me and my friends. This is a problem going back half the span of Phecea's existence. Can you imagine how many people have been torn from their families to serve us over the last two hundred years? How many have died? If we could change it, we would be saving generations of life on this continent." Basia ran her hands back through her hair, so frustrated with the whole situation that the room blurred around her. This was right. It had to be. So why was Danae having such a hard time understanding?

"Basia, I just... I can't worry about anyone else. Or anything else. Our country is at war; this ceasefire won't last forever. And Phecea isn't going to be how it was before. I'm going to change too. Don't you realize that? And I'll be married and making alliances, and I can't worry about you getting—" She looked around as if suddenly afraid someone would overhear them. Danae didn't bother to finish her sentence. "I think it's better if you go home, Basia."

Basia stood up, her hands shaking. She had to actively work not to ball them into fists. "I have stood by you your entire life, and now you're going to cast me aside because I've become too much effort? Humors, Danae, I'm not asking you to join me. I'm asking you not to abandon me for doing something I know has to be done!"

"You're not asking me to join you? So what was that with Lex and

Peta's wedding? I'm not abandoning you, Basia; I'm trying to protect you!"

"Yes, by pushing me away!"

"Do you want me to ask you to stop? Do you want me to beg you to stop, Basi? Should I fall on my knees?" She sunk to her knees in demonstration. "I will. If I thought it would make you safer, to keep you from this dangerous world? I would beg. I would weep and plead. I would do anything if I thought you would stop. But it won't help, will it?"

Basia scowled and turned her back on Danae's prone form. "So that's it then? I either have to stop making a difference in my country, or you'll have nothing to do with me? Fine. At least I can acknowledge that a problem exists. You're stuck so high up in this estate that you can't even see what's going on in your own city. If I have to work to solve it without you as a friend, I *will*."

She didn't turn to look at Danae again but sailed through the door and down the Othonos estate's thousand steps.

CHAPTER 88: PHECEA

SEVENTH MOON, 1804, DIOSION

Six Moons before the Proclamation

The heat of flickering coals seeped into the Council meeting, so Danae's thick cotton tunic stuck to her thighs with sweat. Despite her best efforts, Danae found it difficult to listen attentively to the Councilors gathered and administrators of the various divisions. Trade, treasury, law. All the heads Phecea forced together, trying to find a solution to Liria's increasingly worrisome movements.

And though Danae knew it was an important meeting, her mind wandered to the heat and how her eyelids drooped in slow blinks. All she wanted was to sleep. Every evening there was a social event or art installation or performance to attend, and every morning she and her parents rose before the sun. Meetings and contracts and discussions. She rarely had time to practice her harp anymore, let alone rest.

So she couldn't listen to what Commander Faidon said about Liria and their acquisition of Emaians in border villages. Her mind was too tired to take it in.

Perhaps if she just closed her eyes for a moment...

"My reports claim their last deployment south was four thousand strong." Danae forced her eyes back open, fighting against the weight of leaden lids. It was the spymaster speaking, a small, dark-eyed woman with one of the most unremarkable faces Danae had ever seen. She might have been anyone, Lirian, Phecean. She could have passed for Tupa Galan, too, with some effort. "With a force of that size, they should greatly increase their intake."

"You mean you haven't confirmed their yield?" The Commander sat back in his seat, spider-leg fingers steepled before his eyes.

The spy just shrugged. "My sources haven't gotten word to me yet. I suspect being on the Tundra is affecting their ability to communicate."

Councilor Arsenio raised an eyebrow at that. "Well then, all we can do is wait. What of our plans to fortify Lefkara and Kydonia?"

Danae reached for her glass of water. Maybe if she drank enough, she would wake up more? "Kydonia is making good progress, but Lefkara—"

A slave came up behind Danae, passing her a folded note. She jumped as they murmured her name, pulling her attention away from the discussion. She took the note and read it.

Come quickly.

It was Basia's lazy scrawl, for all that she hadn't bothered to sign it. Danae looked up to see her mother's brow creased with worry. "Yes. It's just too close to the front. Humors, how did we lose so much land?"

She and Basia hadn't communicated directly in moons. Not since that terrible scene in her parents' sitting room when Danae begged Basia not to get herself in so much trouble, and Basia said she'd rather end their friendship than stop her recklessness.

Conflict roiled in her gut. If Basia said to come... Was she in trouble again? Perhaps Lex had been arrested or something equally bad?

"—right, Danae?" She looked up, startled to see her father's eyes on her. "It's been a rough few weeks. A rough few years, if I'm to be honest. We'll all think more clearly after a break. Shall we reconvene this evening?"

Others murmured around her, and Danae nodded in agreement. She needed to think. She needed to sleep, really. But with Basia's note folded into a tiny square in the palm of her hand, Danae didn't return to the Othonos estate, instead walking to the Trade Administration building, hoping to find Basia there.

She didn't even make it to the street. Basia stood just outside the main building of the administrative compound located just south of the market and on the western side of the city so that its eastern windows faced the sea. She must have found a messenger slave and sent the note from there. Basia was dressed in her usual, effortless way, her dark hair cut short and fashionably styled about her face. Nothing else about her appeared normal. Danae didn't think she had ever seen Basia so... unreadable.

"Good, you're here. Come with me." Basia turned on her heel and strode purposefully into the square.

"Basia— Wait!" Danae strode after her friend, her voice pitched low so no one would overhear. They hadn't had any substantive conversations in moons, barely looking at each other during social events. Now Basia was rushing off, demanding Danae follow? "Is this about Lex?"

"No, it isn't." Basia didn't turn around, didn't even look back at her. She headed out of the administrative compound, and instead of turning left towards the bar, the prison, and the warehouses, she turned right towards Diosion's sprawling marketplace.

It felt strange to trail after Basia rather than walk alongside her. They continued further down, the shade cast by the taller government buildings fading into shorter market stalls. Danae tried to think of something to say or ask, but each time she opened her mouth, no words came out. The breach between her and Basia seemed too great to bridge with simple words.

Even apologies didn't seem like enough.

What would she even apologize for? Saving Basia from that terrible prison? Being afraid for her dearest friend? Abiding the laws of Phecea?

So she didn't say anything as they wended through the busy streets of Diosion's center. Where were they going?! This was a part of the market Danae had not been to before. The farther they went from its center, loud and lush even in the midst of war, the dingier the stalls and wagons became until, on the very western edge, merchants sold their wares from nothing more than colorful cloths spread over the ground. The cobblestone ended here, and just past its border was a crowd of dirty-sandaled people in luxurious clothing standing around a simple wooden stage. Behind it, a sea of carriages stretched— some covered and some caged, but all seemingly burdened with pale people. Basia turned then, though only briefly. "Have you been here before?"

Danae scanned the empty stage and the people milling around as if waiting for something. She had not been here before, though she could guess what might be coming. Danae shook her head.

Basia nodded and pressed forward. She was narrow-shouldered and slender, but she had enough height and presence that most of those in front of them veered away. All her life, Basia had been kind, polite, and affable, but today she spared not a word for the wealthy merchants and nobles around them.

As they got closer to the stage, Danae saw a simple wooden podium. A thick-limbed man stood half-turned away and spoke to an aid, though one of his wide arms still rested on the stand before him. Behind the man stood a line of Emaians, chained together by great links of iron wrapped around their throats. They seemed to go on forever.

"That male looks strong enough. Do you like him for farm work?"

"I'm more interested in the little female. They're so much easier to train when you buy them young."

Similar strains of conversation floated past them as they moved, but Basia said nothing until they were nearly at the base of the stage. "Do you know why they chain them like that? By the throat?"

It felt as if a chain were around *her* throat, constricting her words. "No," Danae choked out, trying to breathe through her parted lips. It stank down here. She hadn't known humans could smell like that—a mixture of dung and something sour, like bad milk. All the Othonos slaves were bred. They'd been in her family for generations. Had any of them been captured initially? Had they been bought here?

A man stood off to one side, holding a set of keys. He must be the leader of the raiders who had captured these Emai, ready to reap his rewards for braving the Tundra. She was a little surprised they had allowed one of the Banished into Diosion, but then this was the edge of the city.

"Often, when they are first taken, they are so frightened and desperate to escape this torture they will break a hand or foot to escape. They'll tear it bloody from the manacle, sometimes so badly that they never regain use of it. But then, what is a hand to your whole life?"

On the stage, the man behind the podium seemed to agree with his assistant. He nodded and turned to face the audience, pressing his forearms to the podium and leaning on them so that his head jutted out like a carnival mask. A twitching vein in the center of his forehead darkened as he opened his mouth to yell. "All right, citizens, the first captured specimen is a male, seventeen or eighteen, with good teeth and no health issues whatsoever. Just look at that muscle development! Sticks right out against his snow skin. He'll make a fine hard laborer, just you bet. So who will start the bidding today? Do I hear five hundred gold pieces, five hundred gold pieces? How about six? Do I hear a six? Oh! Seven, in the back there!"

Around her, the crowd erupted into chaos, the leading citizens of Phecea screaming out numbers, shoving each other to better view the merchandise. Spit flew, and bodies clustered around her. Basia made no move.

Despite herself, Danae huddled closer to her friend. Or... Whatever Basia was now. Cowed by the aggressive crowd. The Emaian standing on the stage looked scruffy and underfed despite the auctioneer's assertion that he was strong. Had he been that way when he left the Emai or had the journey to Phecea made him so unkempt and malnourished? She wanted to look away rather than stare, but Basia watched unblinkingly.

Danae stepped closer again, letting Basia's back shield her as she watched the auction continue. The boy sold for an astounding nine hundred gold pieces and was shuffled off the stage to be replaced by a little girl. There was quite the commotion as the little girl cried and clung to the legs of a young woman, perhaps her sister or mother, screaming, "Aada, Aada!" The woman wailed as the guards pried the girl's arms from about the older slave's limbs.

Danae's stomach clenched.

The auctioneer began yelling while the little girl's cries still rang in the brisk, wet air of a Phecean winter. He leaned even farther forward, his face reddening. The vein splitting his head swelled to a deep purple with the effort of making himself heard over the din. "Just listen to that healthy set of lungs! This young female will be easier to train than any other slave you see here, and she'll be worth more years of labor! Imagine not having to replace your scullery maid or laundress for the next fifty years!"

The crowd's roar, which had only decreased slightly for this latest pitch, swelled forward again. Their screams mingled with that of the child and her mother, whose spirit seemed to have broken past the point of silence. She could not bear to watch while these strangers haggled over her daughter's life.

"Do I hear a five hundred? Five hundred? How about a six? Six hundred for fifty years of work?"

Basia did step forward then, her clear voice ringing through the crowd like the peel of a bell through a thunderstorm. "I'll take the child and the mother for two thousand gold pieces!"

Danae blanched. Where would Basia get so much gold?! It wasn't as if her family was sitting at the top of the noble quarter, with gold to squander in such ridiculous quantities. She supposed Basia's cohorts might contribute funds, but Basia was, by far, the wealthiest of the lot. Were they stealing the money to buy these slaves? It didn't seem as if Lex was above thievery, though Danae struggled to remember the laws of Phecea, with the mother screaming, the child crying, and the people bidding.

It was too loud, too crowded. She couldn't think.

"Sold!" The auctioneer screamed again, and Basia nodded.

The woman Danae once would have considered her closest friend in all the world looked down at her so coldly they might have been strangers. "Go home, Danae. You'll want to distance yourself from this next part. Sending them home isn't illegal, but I doubt any of these *loyal* Phecean patriots would agree with it."

She stepped away, shoving through the sea of bodies to the area behind the stage where the two slaves were being led. And with that, Danae was alone amidst the stampede.

CHAPTER 89: LIRIA

SIXTH MOON, 1804, VINDIUM

Seven Moons before the Proclamation

"General?" Lucilius looked up from his mint tea to acknowledge Commander Vais's presence. Setting his cup down, he pushed back from his desk and stood.

"Are they ready?"

"Yes, General. I was able to find seven for sale."

Luce nodded and gestured for Vais to lead the way. They strode in sync past the well-appointed offices of various high-ranking military leaders and down into the lower levels of the military compound outside Vindium. This close to the Psilos Mountains, it was cold most of the year, and Luce wore a fur coat over his winter uniform. The extra layers made the climb down into the dungeons less biting, and his severed wrist was secretly wrapped in an extra layer of wool. Camilla had made the cuff, sewing one into the sleeve of all his winter uniform shirts so that no one but she and Luce would know of the unsanctioned addition.

Despite the excellent craftsmanship of Lirian builders, the dungeons were perpetually damp and smelled faintly of mold. Luce shivered as Commander Vais unlocked a cell. Inside, seven captured Emaians huddled in proper Lirian dress. All female, all young enough to be of good breeding age. Each was shackled to the wall to ensure they could not interfere with one another. He nodded.

"Very good, Commander. Tell me their details."

Commander Vais straightened his papers and gestured to the first woman. She kept her head lowered, her shoulders caved forward. "Higalik, found in 1799, estimated at 24 years of age. It looks like she's been trained in kitchen, laundry, and general household tasks."

"Look at me, Higalik," Luce commanded. The girl flinched but turned her face to him. Her cheeks were rounded and her nose short and flat. Her eyes were the same as all Emaians: gray and too wide. Her silvered hair lay in a thick braid down her back. He couldn't tell if she was attractive or not, as such things never appealed to him. Who would be interested in vermin? "Do you speak Lirian?"

She nodded. "Yes, General."

"Where did you reside before you were put to sale?"

"Abolo, General."

That explained why she was so fat. Even with food shortages, people in Abolo could always fish. Luce looked to the next girl. Where Higalik was fat, she was rail thin.

"Iqaluk," Vais read off. "Found in 1800, estimated at 18 years of age, trained—"

"Would you bed her, Commander?" Luce interrupted. Commander Vais choked on his words and turned to look at Luce as if he had lost his mind.

Luce smiled, knowing it was a disgusting question. Vais was of good breeding and a fine officer. He would never bed a slave, and it was an insult to say as much. But, according to Jaya, he needed an attractive woman for this.

"General?" Vais managed to keep his tone polite.

"If she wasn't a slave or an Emaian? If she had beautiful dark hair and skin and didn't stink of fish and snow. Would you think her lovely?"

Commander Vais looked at Iqaluk again, who hung unmoving. After some consideration, the Commander shook his head. "No, I would not."

"Why?" Luce asked.

"Because she is too young, too skinny, and too meek."

Luce nodded and gestured to the next girl. Her hair was chopped at her chin, thick and uneven in places. Her gray eyes seemed closer to green than the others, and she had a scar slashing across one lid and onto her cheek. A fighter, then. "What is her information?"

"Soyala. Found in 1802, along with two children. They've been kept together to train the children in more useful trades. Estimated at 27 years, so a bit old but—"

Luce raised a hand, and Vais stopped speaking. Soyala had watched him the entire time, her expression guarded. She wasn't cowering, she wasn't sniveling, and while she was scarred, a most unbecoming trait in a woman, there was something of Camilla in the way she held his gaze.

"Do you speak Lirian?"

"Yes," she replied, her accent thick.

"Have you been taught to read and write since you were liberated from destitution?"

She nodded again. "Yes."

"What are your children's names?" Luce stepped closer, eyeing her body. She was slim but still looked like a woman, not a girl. She had full lips and a small pointed nose.

Soyala frowned then, and Luce arched a brow. Her children's names would be a matter of public record; there was no point in hiding it, though he understood the urge to protect one's offspring. Everything Luce did was to keep his family safe. Finally, she spoke, proving she was smart enough not to be obstinate for the sake of it. "Kaya and Sesi."

"And they are?"

"Two girls, seven and five."

That was good. Not so young as to need her attention every day, but young enough to still be little children. Sweet and innocent, even for heathens. He could see the gleam in Soyala's eye. She loved them just as much as Camilla loved their children.

"She will do, Commander. Take the others and return them to the slave market."

"Yes, General, right away."

Luce gestured for Vais to unlock Soyala's manacles, and once she was loose, he nodded for her to follow him. He doubted she'd attack him here, in the military compound. Besides, she had her children to think of. He was counting on that fact.

They hadn't made it one story above the dungeons before she spoke. She was quick to talk and certainly didn't understand her place, but that would make her more believable for what he needed. "What do you want with me?"

Luce glanced over his shoulder to see Soyala staring up at him. She was surprisingly short, her head barely reaching the top of his shoulder. "It is not what I want, but what you want."

"What *I* want?"

"Yes, what you want, Soyala. I won't pretend to understand a barbarian's mind, but I do understand mothers. No matter where they are in Illygad, all mothers want the same thing."

"What's that?"

"For their children to be safe and happy."

"They are slaves. How can they be safe and happy?"

Luce tightened his jaw. She was newly captured, new to Liria. She hadn't experienced its bounty and generosity. She'd only lived here during the war. He stopped before his office door and turned to face the Emaian. "They can be educated and trained for good trades. They can remain together, and when this war is over, you can rejoin them." Luce opened the door to his office, even allowing the slave to go first, a courtesy she likely hadn't experienced before.

Soyala hesitated but then entered the room. Minimal in decoration, it mostly boasted shelves of books, a map of the Sunetic States, and his desk. "Or?"

Good, her mind was sharp. She understood that nothing was free. He settled into the chair behind his desk, gesturing for her to take one of the others. Another attempt at appeasing her. Soyala sat and watched him with her too-pale eyes. "Or, they can be sold into hard labor. Say… a mine or quarry. They could be sold separately, and you could never see them again."

She didn't blink, and Luce felt a small smile tugging at his lips. He had chosen the right woman. "How do I ensure this doesn't happen?

"It's simple, really. You just have to report to me all you see and hear."

"Where? Where will I see and hear?"

"In the camp of the slave revolt, of course."

"You mean their leader? You want me to spy on her?"

Luce nodded and picked up his cup of mint tea. It was still warm. He sipped it with satisfaction. "Yes. Do you think you can do that, Soyala?"

Her lips twisted as if she tasted something sour, but Luce could tell the moment her thoughts returned to her daughters. Their fate depended on her obedience. "And if I get caught?"

"Should you prove yourself useful before such an event, I will honor our bargain and ensure your daughters are given the best opportunities for someone in their station. Should you get caught before that time, I will assume you deliberately blundered so that the Fish Queen known as Iniabi would stop you, and I will treat your children as the bastards of a traitor."

"Then I will not get caught," Soyala whispered, her pale eyes so bright it looked as if they held the sun. She was determined.

Luce smiled. "Good. Then we have an accord."

CHAPTER 90: RHOSAN

ELEVENTH MOON, 1803, CWM OR

Two Years before the Proclamation

"It's too cold. It was foolish of Tegan to flee now."

"She had an opportunity and took it. You're saying you wouldn't, in her place?"

"In the middle of winter? No."

Dyfan pulled his woolen shawl tighter about himself, imagining the biting cold Tegan must feel now, lost in some snowbank. He shivered despite himself and resisted the urge to look at Wynn. They sat only a hand's breadth apart, yet Dyfan felt the chasm between them widening every moon.

His gut clenched in an angry promise that his meal would not stay with him long, and he resisted the urge to rub his swollen belly. He didn't want the other fighters to know of his weakness, and he didn't need Wynn asking if he was alright.

It wasn't wise for Tegan to flee the pits now, in the dead of winter, but he was starting to understand the desperation that would compel her to try. Perhaps she had a lover too and couldn't stand to face them for the shame of her crude betrayal? Perhaps she couldn't say no but didn't wish to say yes, so all she had left was a knotted ball of bile that woke her every morning and settled like a stone in her gut every night.

Most Defeated knew trying to flee was futile, especially in winter. The Victors had hounds to hunt down runners, food, warm clothes, and money. Most Defeated were only dressed well enough not to die but could never survive in the open without additional supplies.

Cursed Realms, Dyfan didn't even know how to start a fire or hunt. He couldn't tell his place in the world by the stars, as some said they could. Even if he knew how to use the stars as a guide, he didn't know where to go. Illygad was a blank canvas for him. The shape of Rhosan was a mystery. Of course, he knew Cwm Or, but that had only happened after Victor Eurig had demoted him. Before, Dyfan wouldn't have been able to tell anyone where to find the smith or the butcher. His world was small. Deliberately so, to keep him reliant on the Victors. It was the way for all born Defeated. "What did you do on cold nights before?"

"You mean before I was taken?" Wynn moved, and it was the restless fidgeting of the caged bird. "It's just eleventh moon, not the height of winter. I bet Tegan could have made it."

"How? She was born Defeated. She could no more hunt or find shelter than I could."

"No one has to teach the fox to find a hole. So long as she has the sense to follow the river, it wouldn't be that hard. You can go a lot longer without food than water."

Dyfan shifted to peer down his nose at Wynn. The other man's gaze was fixed on the gossiping Defeated some yards away. "Maybe *you* could. You're getting fat, old man." It wasn't true. But Wynn *had* gained weight of late. Gruffyd paid for him to have larger portions, and the training masters insisted he did extra sets of all the exercises. As a result, Wynn was getting bulky with muscle.

Wynn looked up at him in shock, his warm eyes wide. With a familiar twinge of guilt, Dyfan realized that they hadn't joked together in moons—not since they were caught together, and he was forced back into the breeding rounds. "We could do it. If we only got the chance."

"What?"

"You and me. We could escape." Wynn twisted so that Dyfan could see his face. His worried brows were pinched, and his eyes were sad. "We could get away from this place and its rules and its Victors, and you could love me again. We'd just have to find an opening."

"Wynn, there aren't openings. Not for fighters who win. Not for Defeated like me...." Victor Eurig was not so sloppy as Victor Gruffyd. He always made sure Dyfan was properly monitored. He'd never escape. "And I didn't stop loving you."

"I— I just feel so alone these days." Wynn rubbed his eyes with his thumbs. "You hardly want me around you."

The urge to comfort Wynn, to drape an arm about his shoulders and pull him in close, collided with the fear that someone would see and use that act of kindness to hurt Wynn, leaving Dyfan frozen. He wanted Wynn around. Stupidly, selfishly he wanted nothing more than to sit next to Wynn near the gates and eat their meals, talking about their days. He longed for the familiarity and ease of the past but didn't know how to get back there.

"Are there any Old Gods who can turn back time?"

"None that dwell in this cursed place." The words came out choked. He sounded hollow, wrung-out, depressed. "I just don't understand. What can I do to prove we can still have this? Why do you have to let the Victors get between you and me?"

"They didn't," Dyfan felt the words ooze out of his mouth like that morning's vomit. Unbidden, they pushed past his tongue and teeth until they fell to the earth between them. "I did."

"They did! You can't believe that! You *proved* you weren't unfaithful in moons and moons of horrible treatment and lesser pit fights to not breed. You're only doing it now to keep me safe, and still, you insist on punishing us both!"

Wynn's intensity only made Dyfan withdraw. "You don't understand. I... I thought..."

"Only because you won't *talk* to me!" Wynn was crying, tears streaming down his face in a snow-melt river, and his limbs beginning to shake like they did in one of his attacks.

Other pit fighters were starting to peer their way. Dyfan gave them a cold look, and most glanced away, still afraid of him despite his diminishing form, but he was certain they were trying to listen. He watched as a tear ran down Wynn's pointed nose and dripped off the tip. His poor man, trembling and miserable because Dyfan couldn't control himself. It was all so unfair.

"Wynn," Dyfan placed his hand on the earth between them. Tentatively, Wynn took it. "I don't know how to explain the things I feel. I've always needed you for that."

"I can't read your mind. Sometimes, you're going to have to tell me."

"I will try. After we got caught, I thought they would force me back into the breeding rooms but... that I wouldn't be *able* to do it." Dyfan closed his eyes. He took a shuddering breath, determined to keep his eyes shut so he couldn't see the disgust in Wynn's when he finally explained his deplorable nature. "I... I thought I... My manhood *wouldn't*. But... It *did*."

Wynn

Wynn looked away. *That* was what had caused all these moons of pain? What would Dyfan think, Wynn wondered, if he knew what he had done when Ifanna pushed herself on him on the Victory Tour? He had given in to her wishes with far less fight than Dyfan and for less reason. Wynn had *performed*. The other man would probably shrink away, repulsed. If he knew, Dyfan would rid himself completely of something already dying.

There was a chance that if Dyfan knew what Wynn had done, he wouldn't blame himself so much. He'd realize they were both broken and fallible, two men struggling to live and love each other in a place determined to grind them into dust. They could accept it and move on, go back to how things used to be— teasing and tenderness in whatever spare moments this life allowed.

There was the chance, though, that telling the truth wouldn't have that effect at all. Dyfan might renounce Wynn or withdraw, retreating deeper into himself until the thing that sat beside Wynn was only a shell of his friend, the man he loved impossibly out of reach. He may never forgive Wynn.

This moment, painful though it might be, was the closest Wynn had felt to Dyfan in moons. They were talking! Working things out! Was he willing to risk losing that now?

He looked at Dyfan again, at the sag in his shoulders and the pain in his eyes. He'd waited too long. "Anwyl, I don't blame you for that. Your heart does not directly control the rest of you."

Dyfan shook his head slowly, the woad tattoos on the sides of his shaved head like wind or rain. "I wanted it to. I love you; I don't want any part of me to…to *want*… anyone else."

"I just miss you. I know breeding is not your choice, and I don't blame you for anything that happens in those rooms."

Silence stretched between them, and Dyfan finally let out a breath. At first, Wynn thought it was a sigh, but then Dyfan sucked in another one and another until Wynn realized that his lover was sobbing. Silently, without tears, but it was clear that the deep, shuddering inhales and exhales were disguised weeping. Dyfan, by all the Gods, tugged on Wynn's hand, pulling him closer. Not pushing him away. "I'm sorry. I'm sorry, Wynn. I wanted to be a better man for you."

"You're the best man I have ever known." Wynn closed his eyes and tucked his face against his lover's neck until the world seemed to fade around them. "I love you."

Dyfan's calloused fingers gripped the back of Wynn's neck, holding him closer. "I love you."

For several long minutes, they sat curled together while Wynn's heartbeat slowed and Dyfan's trembling gradually ceased. Guilt and relief warred in Wynn's breast. He had his lover back, yes, but he hadn't come clean about what he'd done.

The night deepened as the Defeated finished their dinners, bowls and spoons clinking as they were set aside. Wynn sighed. Guards approached with torches, and the Defeated that had been at the arena that day were leaving in ones and twos. "Have you seen the list for the Contender Matches?"

"No. No one has said what they were…." Dyfan said, and Wynn tensed. "Have you?"

"Not the whole list." Wynn looked at the scuffed ground between his feet. "They moved me up to heavyweight."

"I told you you were getting fat."

"That means they'll pit us against each other. Sooner or later."

Wynn felt Dyfan freeze. They both knew what that would mean. These fights didn't end with first blood. No. A Contender had to defeat his opponent unquestionably. That meant serious injury. Sometimes cripplings. The man he had beaten last year still walked with a limp.

Dyfan's arms tightened about Wynn. "Then you'll win."

"No. Don't you get it? You don't get to decide that for me."

The guards would be arriving soon to escort Wynn back to Victor Gruffyd's holdings. They didn't have much time to discuss this. Not now. And the fights weren't until after the first moon of the year.

Dyfan shifted, letting Wynn go. They stood. "I love you, Wynn. I will not fight you. If I see you in the arena, I will lay down my sword. Happily so."

"I wonder what they'll do to us then. Two dogs who won't fight." Wynn shook his head, but his face softened, the mountains between his eyes becoming hills. "I love you too, Dyfan."

CHAPTER 91: THE EMAI

SIXTH MOON, 1804, AMARUIT WAR CAMP

Seven Moons before the Proclamation

Sun glinted off armor as the Lirian horde crested the hill that bordered the Amaruit's valley to the north. Around Iniabi, the camp was a chaos of torn-down tents and bodies struggling to collect everything they needed, pulling on packs and weapons and coats. They hadn't broken into full panic yet.

But Iniabi felt hysteria rise in her chest.

She had done this, had called this flood of Lirians down on her own people like a plague. There was no plan, nowhere to go. Only four thousand armed and armored soldiers against a rag-tag group of half-trained Emai in fur and stolen steel. Even had the Emai been as well trained and well-equipped as their foes, they'd not have stood a chance. She needed a trick, an advantage, *anything*.

"Iniabi?" Mika's voice broke through her reverie, and she turned to see the girl of her childhood infatuation watching her, a spear in one hand and her pack gripped in the other. "What are you doing?"

"I—" Iniabi faltered. She was packed, her tent and sparse belongings folded into the sack on her back, her thin, wicked little sword on her hip, and a glaive taken from a fallen Lirian in one hand. What was she doing? She hardly knew. "Waiting for the wolves to ready themselves."

Mika nodded, her pale eyes sweeping over Iniabi, assessing. An old memory flickered before Iniabi's eyes, a smaller Mika transposed over the one that stood before her today. *You have slavers' eyes.* "You look like you did when we were younger, watching your Aada."

Iniabi had thought she'd destroyed that part of herself, destroyed it as she killed the captain who had taken Manaba's place. She clenched her fist around the glaive. "Go get my pack leaders."

Mika didn't reply but instead turned to do as Iniabi commanded. It took less than five minutes for her to return with Deniigi, Manirak, and Amka in tow. All had a similar look of wariness. Controlled and yet ready to flee.

"Kaneq Amarok," Deniigi murmured by way of greeting. "Silla is on her way."

Iniabi nodded, her neck and shoulders tight. *What are you doing?* Mika's question went round and round in Iniabi's head. *What are you doing? What are you doing? What are you doing?* All of these people—nearly five hundred warriors and escaped slaves— relied on Iniabi's decisions to keep them safe, and instead, she had decided to bring the might of their enemies down upon them.

"I've got the wolves prepared for a long run, Kaneq Amarok," Deniigi said, his weathered face pulled into stern lines. He knew as well as she did that running wouldn't be enough to escape the avalanche of Lirians coming their way.

"If we head north, we could try to lose them among the foothills of the Nonnocan Peaks?" Amka suggested, but Manirak was already shaking his head.

"We've grown too large to hide."

"We have to try *something*," Amka shot back.

What are you doing? What are you doing? What are you doing?

Warmth spread across her hand, and Iniabi looked down as ungloved fingers interlaced with hers. She followed its wrist and arm up to find Mika standing there. When their eyes met, Mika nodded slowly. She squeezed Iniabi's fingers, and Iniabi remembered her poison dreams. This was not how she would die.

Iniabi let go.

"Gather your people. You are each responsible for the warriors under your command should we be separated. I will take one-fifth of the group—the wounded still well enough to run, the new recruits yet unassigned, and my hand-picked fighters. Mika, go get Tatik and have her perform rites for anyone too wounded to come. They are each to be left a dagger. Leave as your groups are ready and head due west. We'll meet on the banks of the Nattiq. Don't forget that we are faster than these trespassers."

Mika didn't hesitate, nor did Deniigi, but Amka paused, frowning. "Leave them behind?"

"We cannot lose the Amaruit for the sake of a few. All those who can move must come. The ones we leave behind... They will have more choice than the slaves before them, and their souls will be cared for."

Amka's frown didn't lessen, but she dipped her head in agreement and turned to do as she was bid. Silla ran up then, pounding up to them with her pale cheeks pink-touched and her breath coming quick. "They're coming! They've started the descent into the valley!"

"It'll take the trespassers time to navigate it. Go, gather your groups!"

Within the hour, Iniabi's pack of wolves circled around her, hard-faced and frightened. There were more wounded and untrained than she had hoped, but she dispersed her best people among them, and they set out together, flying across the Tundra as only the Emai could, the ashes from Pakuk's wedding fire still clinging to their boots.

They ran for hours. The Lirians were a dark line receding into the horizon, a mass big and black enough to blot out the snow. They sent their shaggy mountain horses ahead, the riders carrying big flags to relay Emaian positions back to the main force. Emaian slings took the first of these down, but they had since been smart enough to keep out of bow range. It was a clever tactic, but it was ruining Iniabi's plans. The river was before them in all its black, frozen beauty, and she had hoped they'd have lost the Lirians by then.

The first few groups—Amka and Manirak's—had already reached the bank, and the Lirians were still after them. They were running out of places to go! If the wolves made a stand here, they'd be crushed against the ice— five hundred new slaves for northern homes and breeding grounds, if so many survived.

When Iniabi's group reached the river, she turned, the shine of sun on metal helmets dazzling her eyes. They were getting closer.

"We're going to have to cross!" She shoved her way through the terrified Emai, shouting directions as she went. "Drop your packs! Take nothing but your weapons!"

Even her older wolves, ones whose faces she recognized from years of fighting, paused at her instructions. It was winter, but this far north, the river might not be frozen solid. To cross might doom them all, but to stay here was certain death. Iniabi grabbed a woman by the pack, yanking it off her shoulders. She blinked and started to comply, and those around her hurried to do the same.

Iniabi approached the bank, staring across the misshapen ice. It wasn't smooth as a lake or pond would have been, carved in dips and ridges where the flow of the water below had pressed the upper crust of ice up and overlapping. Some areas were like sea glass, blue-green in color, others white as fresh snow. Deniigi appeared at her side, stepping out onto the ice with deliberate care. It groaned but held.

He knelt and pulled his hood off to press an ear to the surface, closing his eyes as he listened. Iniabi had no idea how he could possibly hear anything above the racket of the wolves tossing aside their belongings.

"Can you hear the river below?" Mika asked, and Deniigi straightened up.

"Are you certain about this, Kaneq Amarok?" he asked.

"I don't think we have any other choice. Start your people over first, Deniigi. You'll be the best at finding a path. I'll take the last group because mine is the smallest."

Deniigi nodded and took another step onto the ice, his gaze downward, his movements precise. A few of his wolves followed suit, stepping where he stepped, but a younger man, new enough that Iniabi didn't know his name, balked. He stood at the edge of the frozen river, hands balled into fists at his sides.

"I can't. We can't! We'll drown!" He shoved into those around him, and people started to push back. If he kept this up, she'd have a fight on her hands. The Emai would turn on each other and die in droves when the Lirians found them. Iniabi tossed her pack aside and strode up to the young man.

"Go," she ordered, but when he turned to face her, the whites of his eyes showed, and she saw not a man but a frightened animal.

"I'll drown!"

"Great seas!" Iniabi reached for her sword to use the hilt to knock the stupid boy unconscious, but he chose that moment to throw a wild punch. She ducked and launched forward, crashing into his belly and propelling him off his feet. The boy squawked like a gull trapped in a net, but it was enough to stop him.

"Tie him up!" Mika helped Iniabi rise, watching as nearby wolves jumped to comply. The boy screamed until they stuffed a gag in his mouth and bound his hands and feet.

Iniabi looked back at the dark tide of Lirians, a faceless sea of monsters. Closer and closer. How many miles separated them now? Four? Five? Not enough.

"Carry him across. Go! Go now!" she shouted.

It was agony to watch the wolves start their way across the Nattiq, ten or so at a time. As each group reached the halfway point, the next wave would start the precarious process of picking their way across. Fifty wolves were safely on the other side. Seventy. Two hundred. Three hundred.

The Lirians' rhythmic, drumming footfalls chorused with the creak of their armor and saddles. When Iniabi turned to look at her enemy, she could make out their faces. Distinct and clear. Their first lines brandished spears, a wall of jagged steel points.

"Go! Go now! All of you," she ordered the last two hundred wolves, turning not toward the river but back to her enemy.

"What about you, Kaneq Amarok?"

"I'm coming. Just go now."

Iniabi waited until the last of her people stepped onto the ice and then began to follow them, using the butt of her glaive like a staff as she picked her way across the surface. The ice creaked and groaned, but then any Tundra-walker could tell you that ice was not silent. Especially not the ice formed above a fast-flowing river.

She was halfway across when the first Lirians reached the ice. Their shouts carried over the frozen water, their light, lilting language garbled by distance and distress. They no more wanted to cross than the wolves had, and all the better. Iniabi didn't want them coming after her.

Over her shoulder, in quick, stolen glances, she watched as the first of them came. Iniabi closed her eyes and prayed to the Tundra, prayed that the ice would break and the river would swell with the bodies of drowned trespassers. The ice held. The Lirians began to advance. Slowly at first, but with growing confidence until whole squadrons of them shared the river with the retreating stragglers of Iniabi's army.

She gritted her teeth. The Lirians were going to overtake them. Her wolves had lost too much time at the water's edge, and now their enemy marched fearlessly across in an endless stream, not pausing between each phalanx they sent over. Iniabi's decision to force the Amaruit into continuing this war would only kill them all. Pain pricked behind her eyes, and for a moment, Iniabi thought that her slavers' blood would send a hot rush of tears down her face, but no. The Emai could not cry.

With a howl, Iniabi lifted her glaive and flung herself at the nearest crack, a long, spidering thing, tracing its way through the ice. She shoved the blade inside as far as it would reach and then heaved it to the side, clenching her teeth at the sound of ice cracking as the split widened and spread. On the nearby bank, the last of Iniabi's followers had reached safety, and they turned to shout for her. Idiots. Didn't they know they ought to be running? She didn't have time to tell them, instead keeping her eyes on her work.

"To steal from Liria is to ask for pain." Iniabi lifted her glaive like a slaver's whip and plunged it into the flesh of her home. "To steal from Liria is to ask for pain."

At first, the Lirians did not seem to understand what was happening. They continued to march across the rough expanse of wave-like ice, their boots crunching against the surface. As the cracks widened, though, the blasts of ice blocks coming apart soon had their attention. They broke out in a run, some heading for Iniabi and others for the shores, but none of them made it. In the end, it was the Lirians, all their hundreds spread out across the river charging in thoughtless panic that shattered the surface.

There was no time to feel triumphant. Iniabi ran, dodging surging ice that mountained into the air as it collided together, leaping over yawning openings filled with black, churning water that soaked Iniabi's boots and made her skin ache with cold. She felt like she was atop the *Flying Night* in a storm, only the ship was breaking beneath her, so many shards of jagged timber. A vast, wet chunk of river ice descended on Iniabi, and she threw herself to the next, landing hard enough to leave her gasping, her fingernails tearing open as she scrabbled for a hold on the ice. It collapsed beneath her, dropping her halfway into the water, so numbingly cold that it left her panting, her body seizing. She pulled herself up inch by agonizing inch, jumped to the next slab from all fours, and tumbled off the far edge.

The world, split by the piercing thunder above, dropped into sudden silence, the churning current of the water spinning Iniabi out of control. She grabbed for rocks, for fallen trees, for anything. If the current caught her, she was dead, and the Amaruit would just have to learn how to go on without her. Iniabi had saved them. They would not be lost today.

CHAPTER 92: PHECEA

TENTH MOON, 1804, DIOSION

Three Moons before the Proclamation

"It's been two years now—"

"Closer to three, really." Eros interrupted Zol from his place at one end of the table in the Cormorant's Rest. She nodded to him graciously, but Basia had to hide her yawn. It was late, their meeting pushed back into the hours surrounding midnight since Zol's shift changed from day to evening.

Lex seemed to echo Basia's impatience. "Alright, then. Three years. But how many have we saved?"

Eros sniffed and shuffled his papers. "According to the reports Zol has given me, we have saved one hundred and thirty-three captured individuals over the last thirty-four moons."

Basia went cold. That wasn't right—it couldn't be. They were only freeing two or three slaves a moon, spreading the cost between them as much as possible. "But—"

This time it was Lex who interrupted her. "How many are still enslaved?"

"The population of Othonisis Province is roughly two and a half million; of course, slaves aren't counted in the five-year census, but current estimations are at one Emaian for every five or six Pheceans. There is no way to know the numbers of bred versus captured."

That silenced all of them. So many... Were they really having any effect at all?

"That's—that's almost half a million Emai in this province alone." Zol didn't seem to be able to quite grasp the sheer magnitude of the problem they were facing.

Eros gripped her shoulder, but he didn't have much consolation to give. "Othonisis *is* the most population-dense province in Phecea."

"Still...." Basia swallowed hard. They had put so much work into making a difference.

"We've got to help more each moon!" Lex slammed a palm down on the table. "It's the only way we'll be able to make an impact."

Basia rounded on them, anger building behind her eyes like a tidal wave. She could hardly see around it. "More each moon?! Lex, we knew from the beginning that all we could afford was two or three a moon. After thirty-four moons, we should have saved seventy, maybe eighty people. So where did the other fifty come from, Lex?"

"I don't think your math's quite right, Basia. And there were moons, especially in the beginning, when we were able to do more...."

"My math is excellent, is it not, Eros?" Basia swung to glare at the other two, but Zol wouldn't meet her eyes. "Well?"

Eros cleared his throat. "Yes, that is correct."

Basia shoved her chair back up from the table and stood. "So, *Lex*, where did they come from? You swore not to resort to thievery after I wound up in prison, didn't you? Where did you get the Emaians?"

"Basia, I—"

"You *lied* to me!" She swung around to Zol. "And you helped them!"

The Ararian woman's dark face flushed crimson. "Give me a break, Basia. I can't contribute money the way the rest of you do. It's the least I can do to get whatever poor souls you bring me onto ships!"

"We're not going to change the system through thievery!"

"And why not? I saved *fifty* people. That's dozens of more families reunited. Dozens who are no longer enslaved. Basia, you're being unreasonable. This works! I've proven it does!" Lex stood up as well, their chair crashing into the oaken floor of the Rest's attic.

"Yes, by getting me imprisoned!"

Lex rolled their eyes. "*Briefly*. We knew there were going to be risks!"

"Here's a risk for you: you either operate above board, or I'm out! No more money, no more trade papers, no more anything. Get it? And you know what? You are not about to lie *with* me one night and lie *to* my face the next! You and me, we're done."

The door to the room crashed open to reveal a red-faced Ilia. "What are you doing up here? You're disturbing the guests! Isn't this supposed to be a *secret* society?"

Basia swallowed down her next barrage, for all that her anger was still a living, pulsing thing living just beneath her skin.

"Fine. I'm done with all of you. *I* won't be the reason no difference is made." Lex shouldered past Ilia and thundered down the stairs, leaving Basia in stunned silence. She hadn't expected them to give up on the Society rather than on thievery as a tactic.

Eros sighed. "Might I suggest that we adjourn the rest of this meeting? Things have gotten a little too heated."

"I'll say," Ilia agreed, and Basia felt a rush of guilt. How was this her fault? Lex was the one lying and not following the plan.

Zol just stood and left the room without ever looking Basia in the eyes.

⇑ ⇑ ⇑

Danae's hand shook as she took notes for the Council meeting. She was glad for the distraction of note-taking because the topic made her queasy.

"We have to press more people into service. Provide incentives besides patriotism."

"We can't pay them more." Cyril Mavros cut in, frown making his ordinarily pleasant face tight and angry. "The treasury is stretched as it is. We simply can't increase sailors' and soldiers' stipends."

"Perhaps we could give the public a heroic image of our soldiers? I know several playwrights and poets who would be happy to create loyal, brave Phecean material. Posters in the streets for the play, public readings—"

"If the enlistment rates are any reflection of your propaganda tactics, they don't work with any significant influx. We need staggering numbers to keep Liria off our borders."

"Then what do you suggest, General?" Arsenio Othonos cut in smoothly, keeping the military commander and the Public Relations Administrator from jumping down each others' throats.

General Catia sighed and shrugged, his shoulders looking all the broader in his stark uniform. Danae watched his expression, pulling distastefully at the corners of his mouth. He knew whatever he was about to suggest would not go over well. She kept her pen close to her paper, ready to record his words as soon as he said them.

"Conscription."

Danae wrote the word and looked to her mother and father. Phecea had never forced its citizens into military service. Not once. Of course, Phecea had existed with minimal conflict for centuries, so the need for that many soldiers hadn't arisen. Now, they needed soldiers and sailors. And fast. The Council had tried to press the importance of enlisting on its citizens. Patriotic posters and newspaper articles had initially spiked enlistment, but as Liria started to overrun Phecea's borders and battles were lost, the public's opinion shifted. They didn't want to die in some horrible muddy ditch or drown at sea in water painted red with the blood of their friends. She couldn't blame them.

But now... Now they needed to train new soldiers for the inevitable end of the ceasefire. Liria would not let this go. They were rabid dogs, Phecea the bone they drooled after.

Arsenio Othonos sighed heavily. Danae realized there were lines around his mouth she hadn't seen before. When had her father gotten wrinkles? "Very well, the Council will discuss it. But if we conscript, more of our craftsmen and farmers will be gone. Our workforce will diminish, and we already have a supply issue."

The Agricultural Administrator squawked. "We already have too few hands in the fields!"

"Then we need to get more," Andromyda said, placing a

comforting hand on her husband's knee beneath the table. "We need more slaves."

"Our supply of slaves was eighty-seven percent Lirian-sourced. Obviously, we've not been able to buy from Liria in almost five years."

"Then we procure them ourselves. In higher numbers," Despite Andromyda's reasonable tone, Danae's heart faltered. She thought of the slave auction Basia had forced her to attend. She remembered the little girl screaming for her mother. Not bred to purpose, as most Phecean slaves had been, but stolen from the Emaian Tundra.

"Ehm...." Danae cleared her throat, and her parents glanced her way as others around the table continued to debate a trip into Emaian lands. "Perhaps it would be easier to train the youth to work in the fields?"

Her father smiled, indulgent. "Creative thinking is always welcome, but Emaians are strong workers."

"This is the best course of action for Phecea," Andromyda said, smiling at Danae and turning her attention back to the debate.

"But—" Danae kept from wincing when her parents' eyes widened slightly, their only sign of surprise. She normally wouldn't argue with them, especially not in a Council meeting. She lowered her voice so that no one else would overhear her words. "They are people too... Taking them from their homes—"

"Huts," Andromyda cut in, correcting Danae smoothly. "Taking them from their *huts*. And the frozen wasteland. We educate them, feed them, give them proper clothes."

"But they didn't ask—"

"Darling, this is how things have always been," Arsenio brushed a curl away from Danae's face. She knew the tone. The conversation was over.

It was difficult to take notes the rest of the meeting, her mind slipping back to the expression on Basia's face when she bought that mother and child. The way she glared at Danae, so certain that she was right and Danae was the villain. When the law was on her side, Danae had to be right.

And yet.

She couldn't look as they counted the votes because she knew the result without looking.

"Unanimous vote. We will procure a minimum of four thousand Emaian slaves to cover the fields and fill our workforce." Her father's voice echoed in her mind even as the meeting disbursed. Four thousand Emaians yanked from their homes. How many would be ones that Basia had bought and shipped back?

CHAPTER 93: PHECEA

ELEVENTH MOON, 1804, DIOSION

Two Moons before the Proclamation

Spring in Phecea was usually stunning. The trees painted Diosion's stone streets in rich yellows and lime greens, and the warmer temperatures were a welcome relief after winter's frigid chill. This spring, however, was beginning in fits and starts. It was already the eleventh moon, and still, the new growth had yet to take hold, hampered by unseasonable frosts.

Basia tugged her coat closer about her shoulders and tried not to think about how cold her toes were, even protected by a thick pair of leather boots. The market seemed reduced, though it was unclear whether that was due to the weather or the war. There were fewer craftsmen now and less money to buy their goods. There were even fewer soldiers within the city—all who could be spared had been sent to the front.

She was on the western edge of the market that evening, somewhere along her walk from the Trade Office to the Marvos estate. It wasn't on her way, not really, and Basia wasn't sure exactly what had brought her so close to the slave auctions. She couldn't save anyone just now. Not with Lex gone and the Society struggling to find a new way to ship their refugees home.

And yet, here she was. Perhaps it was habit or intuition because just as Basia convinced her feet it was time to turn towards the cliffs and the fine landscaping of the noble quarter, she caught a glimpse of wild curls.

Danae stood at the back of the slave auctioneer's crowd, not quite close enough to be part of the throng but too near to have come for anything but the auction. Basia stiffened, reading the lines of uncertainty and discomfort in the tense curve of the other girl's shoulders. Why had she come here? What could she possibly need? The Othonos family was far too wealthy to stand in the dirt and barter for their slaves. All of them were bred in-house.

Basia couldn't decide whether to stay, to go find out why Danae had come here, or to turn and run away home. It would be easier to hide, she thought, than peel open the wounds between her and Danae again.

In the end, the choice was taken from her. Danae turned. Black eyes met gold, and Basia knew she had been seen.

Danae's face was already twisted into subtle lines of displeasure, likely from watching the auction. As she looked at Basia, those lines disappeared, only to be replaced with caution. She stared at Basia for a long breath and then nodded respectfully. "Basia." Despite the racket, she could hear Danae's voice well enough. Carefully polite.

"Did you enjoy it so much you had to come back for a second time?" The words were out of Basia's mouth before she had time to stop them, as though her tongue was a sleeping adder that had chosen that moment to strike. She was angry. Angry and tired, and she had been more alone in the last moon without Danae or Lex than she ever had before.

Her friend twitched, the only sign that Basia's angry words had landed. The Othonos heir glanced toward the auction and then back to Basia, shaking her head. "No, I didn't enjoy last time. I didn't enjoy this time either." She stepped closer to Basia despite the tension between them. Looking down, Danae revealed her hand, which had been hidden in the pocket of her tunic. She opened her fist, exposing a piece of paper folded into the smallest square possible. She considered it and then handed it to Basia.

Basia thought about slapping it to the ground, about turning and walking away and leaving Danae standing like that, her hand outstretched. Alone. Instead, Basia unfolded the note. It was a line of credit affirmation from a bank. It said Danae Othonos was approved for up to seven thousand gold. A ridiculous sum for an eighteen-year-old noble girl to carry around in her pocket.

"I was going to try and ...bid, but...."

"Why?"

"Well, I thought I'd just walk over to The Cormorant's Rest and sign them over to you." Danae's gaze wavered on Basia's face, perhaps surprised by what she saw there. "Are you alright, Basia?"

"The Cormorant's Rest?" Basia blinked, unable to quite comprehend. The world seemed to be shifting faster than she could grasp the changes. Her anger was fleeing, and in its absence, she felt only exhaustion.

Danae's hand came to rest against Basia's elbow, warm and gentle. "I'm sorry, Basi. I was afraid. I still am. But I am sorry for my words and my... Shortsightedness. Come, let's get something to eat."

Basia looked down at Danae's hand on her arm and then reached for her. "I left Lex," she said, and a few hot tears escaped with the words. Basia dashed them hurriedly away.

"I'm sorry, Basia, that must have been difficult. I won't pretend to know what it's like to be in a relationship... But I know I felt terrible these moons that we weren't together, so I can only imagine what it would be like with someone so important." As she spoke, Danae led them through the market, back into the cleaner, tame streets nearing the noble quarter.

"They were lying to me. Stealing slaves and saying that they were obtained legally. Risking everything." Basia leaned into Danae, taking comfort in honesty and simple physical closeness. What did Danae mean, someone so important? There had never been any relationship as important to Basia as this one. "Now, they've gone and taken their ships with them, and we have no way to save anyone."

Danae

That seemed unfair. Would Lex really leave something they truly believed in just because Basia wanted to do things legally? Danae knew there was probably more to the story than that, but ultimately it seemed childish to shut down the entire operation. And with Lex no longer part of the little slave-freeing gang, it seemed unlikely to continue.

Relief battled shame. Danae had started to look at the Emaians in her family's estate and around Diosion, thinking about where they had come from and what it would have been like. It was harder to not notice them, as she had done before. Her entire life, not seeing the white ghosts wandering around Phecea. She should want to help.

"Well," Danae nodded to an eating house that she and Basia frequented when they were younger. The crowds were thin; so many patrons were now soldiers, sailors, or workers. She hoped the eating house would make it despite hard times. The Ingolan style food was a rare delicacy. "It might be for the best. The Council approved a large acquisition order for more Emaians. That's where so many of the troops disappeared to. South."

Basia winced. "That really doesn't make me feel any better about not being able to help. That just means more people are torn from their homes."

Danae glanced at Basia, but before she could speak, the eating house proprietor came forward, wide grin in place. He was a pale man with curling blond hair and watery blue eyes. "Mistress Mavros! Mistress Othonos! It's been too long!" He bowed politely, and Danae bowed as well.

"Master Quentin."

"Here, here, come have your spot by the windows. A good view for my old customers. Will it be the usual?"

Long habits of politeness had not left Basia in all her nights in rougher establishments. She made a familiar bow to the proprietor and nodded. "Yes, please." When they were seated, her eyes wandered to the window, one cheek hollow and her lips twisted as she masticated the inside of her mouth. "I'm not giving up, you know."

"I'm not saying you should, Basi. I'm just saying soon things will be very precarious." Danae looked around; the eating house was not very full despite it being dinner time. No one would overhear them. "The Council voted, and there will be mandatory conscriptions soon. Farmers and workers won't be doing their jobs anymore. They'll be going to war."

It still baffled her that Phecea could be so desperate as to force her citizens into military service. The first time in their proud history. People would be angry and confused. Pheceans weren't used to being told what to do.

"So the Council wants to put slaves in their places." It wasn't a question. Basia rubbed her face with her hands and breathed into the spaces between her fingers. "There's got to be another way. Hasn't there?"

It seemed like too big a question to have a simple answer. Yes. No. Perhaps. Danae wasn't certain that Phecea could exist without their free workforce. Who would have time to pursue their passions, the arts, and reach a higher understanding if they were always working? But still, she could not deny that the Emaians weren't benefiting from the arrangement as she had been told her entire life. Her enlightened existence seemed selfish if it was due to someone else doing the work for her.

But there simply wasn't enough gold to pay everyone for these jobs. Agriculture alone would fall flat. It took many hands to plant and tend fields. She knew this from experience; her time during her tour through Phecea was spent observing Councilors dictating how many tons of wheat or rye would be harvested. The sheer numbers…

"It is possible…." Danae paused as Master Quentin hurried over, placing the tasting plate before them with a flourish. Ingolan savory tarts. Little pastries filled with cheese and meat. As soon as she smiled and nodded, he moved away, and Danae dropped her voice. "It is possible the Emaians will address this issue on their own. There is a…." rabble raiser didn't seem like the right word now. "A *revolutionary* who seems to be organizing the Emaians. They are fighting back."

"I've heard whispers… It's true, then? I expect this revolutionary won't much care for the soldiers heading their way."

Danae picked up one of the tarts. "No, I don't think they will." She was a little proud of how dry her voice sounded. Like her father, making bland understatements. His humor wasn't always obvious, but Danae found herself emulating it. "She's a woman, from the reports I've heard."

"A real-life Pirate Queen— or Ice Queen, I suppose." Something of the Basia Danae had grown up with sparkled in that smile, and there was a familiar tilt to her jaunty brow. "But what will the Council do if the troops come back empty-handed?"

"Liria was our predominant source of Emaians before the war— there's no way Banished traders will be able to keep up with their numbers, especially not if they face organized resistance. I suspect the Council will have to either allocate more resources to acquiring Emaians or, if that is deemed unprofitable, address the workforce. If we cannot get Emaians, how will our fields be tended? Our mines and quarries?"

That thought tickled at the back of her mind, but the more Danae tried to grasp the idea, it slipped away.

"Are you not hungry?" She had eaten two tarts already, and Basia still sat with an empty plate before herself.

"It's hard to eat when your belly's so full of worry."

With the rationing in Diosion, Danae suspected things would only get worse. She'd never gone hungry before, aside from a few days after she had fled Aphodes with the other refugees, and she doubted her family would go hungry in the coming moons. Still, her father had already said many Pheceans would have to go without.

War was a hungry beast, consuming all in its path.

Danae straightened up in her seat. "Basi... Do you know how much the treasury spends quarterly on this conflict?"

Basia looked up from chasing a piece of wine-stewed beef around her plate. "An astronomical amount. Pardon me, Danae, but curse these blasted Lirians. It is damnably hard to make any worthwhile changes in the middle of a war."

"Well, I suppose with that dark mood it is." Danae tried for a lofty tone, one that Erose would probably use at one of her little tea parties. She even went so far as to pick up her glass and sip, looking away from Basia with a coy air.

"What do you mean?"

"Basi, you simply have to think creatively. If we're losing money hand over fist, which we are, and our raiding parties become unprofitable, then perhaps Pheceans would be willing to consider another way."

She was paying attention now, her food forgotten. "What other way?"

Danae glanced around the half-empty restaurant and then leaned closer. "If the Emaians prove that they aren't worth the effort, money, and focus to capture, then they might resolve this slavery issue, in part, for us. You know they have that revolutionary."

"What is the revolutionary going to do for us? Besides hopefully keep Phecea from getting more slaves."

"She can do a lot, Basi. If properly funded, an Emaian revolution could be quite compelling, I would imagine." Danae set her cup down, watching Basia's expression. If the Ice Queen's revolution was costly enough, the Council would have to reconsider the current slave structure in Phecea. But revolutions were tricky things to handle. How many histories around the world were peppered with unsuccessful ones? "What if *we* help her, Basi? Help *her* help *us*?"

"Humors, Danae, I could kiss you. That's brilliant!"

Danae felt her cheeks heating in a blush, and she looked away from Basia's bright, smiling face. She didn't know if it was brilliant, but it was certainly a bold idea.

Even if it was treason.

CHAPTER 94: RHOSAN

TWELFTH MOON, 1803, CWM OR

One Year before the Proclamation

Wynn wiped sweat off his brow and straightened up, stretching up to ease his cramping back. On either side, there lay piles of firewood, split into uneven, rounded triangles. It was a crisp day: chilly, but the sun was high overhead and shining hot enough that the long hours of work had left Wynn dripping. He piled a stack of spoils into his arms and trekked off to the kitchens.

In Gruffyd's estate, the kitchens were at the back, tucked in on the bottom floor so that the Victors and their guests could prance above them, the Defeated out of sight and largely out of mind. They opened into a courtyard where the Victors kept a chicken coup and a few hogs. Wynn's chopping block was only a little farther, at the wood's edge, and the Defeated lived off to the south of the big, west-facing keep. Wynn picked his way through the yard, stepping over animals and dirty children, their parents yelling for them. Defeated were everywhere. Beating rugs, shining silver, collecting eggs, and mending sheets and drapes.

Wynn found Linn in the kitchen, standing over something delicious simmering on a fire. Sage and butter left rich trails of scent through the air, and for all that it was a much smaller space, there seemed to be just as many Defeated within, bodies thumping into each other as they scurried to finish their tasks. Linn stood like a queen, her cheeks dusted with flour and a wooden-spoon scepter held in the clenched fist pressed to her hip.

"Linn!" Wynn called as he approached, touching her shoulder to get her attention over the clang of knives and pans. "What has this place so stirred up? It's like an overturned ant hill."

She snorted. "Gruffyd's had all sorts of things delivered for this party he's throwing a moon from now. Half of them are trying to find places to store it all, and the other half are trying to keep Ifanna happy. Kirit knows why she's in such a high temper now that she's safely delivered the babe, but whatever it is, it seems like she's forgotten to be mad at you. Now, go put that firewood down and pick up some boxes."

"Lovely as always, Linn."

The shipments Gruffyd had bought were in carts on one edge of the courtyard, and the other Defeated unloading it were eager to fill his arms with goods.

"Don't drop it," Morwen said, handing him his third box. She had a face like a cliff—all edges—and a knack for making alcohol out of anything.

"What is it?"

"Booze. The good stuff. Shipped up all the way from Aberdwyr and the folks who sold it to him claimed it came from Ingola." She pronounced the name like a drunk walked: lopsided and heavy on the front end, grinning like a red wolf.

"Like the Victors need anything fancy to knock themselves senseless. I wonder if the vintage will make it go quicker or slower than their usual horse piss."

Morwen's eyes sparkled, but she had the sense not to respond. There were those among the Defeated who would trade tales for privileges.

"Who all is Gruffyd trying to douse? All of Cwm Or?"

"Every Victor of the region, I heard. Or all of them with Contenders." Morwen shot him a side-long glance. "All of which'll be on display, I imagine."

Wynn grimaced as he turned away, his shoulders dragging with the reminder of the coming matches.

⇑   ⇑   ⇑

Dyfan had probably wiped down the sword forty times already, but he continued smoothing the oiled cloth across the tempered steel despite the metal's high shine. This wasn't because Dyfan believed the sword needed extra attention but because he was using the task as an excuse to watch the guards. The day was one of ice and biting winds. Anyone who had a choice was still within their homes. A storm blew in the night before, rain that turned to ice the moment it hit the earth, and crackling thunderheads kept the Defeated awake in their cells.

Once or twice Dyfan had worried about Wynn, alone at Victor Gruffyd's, but since his lover hadn't suffered from many fear attacks in the past few moons, Dyfan told himself Wynn was fine.

The storm left bitter cold and precarious surfaces. Training was effectively pointless, as half the Defeated who didn't live at the arena still hadn't arrived. Wynn included. The frozen world inspired the guards stuck on duty, so they gathered little sticks and hay, and a few larger logs stored in the stables. Dyfan kept his hands moving even as guards set the hay in one small pile, twigs in another, and logs in a third. They were going to start a fire.

Dyfan wanted to know how.

The branches of ice-coated trees creaked and groaned, threatening to break atop their heads. The noise was eerie, echoing off the sleet-carpeted ground and reverberating through the empty arena. All the other Defeated had retreated to their cells, some with hot meals, others having to wait until supper.

Dyfan would eat later. Now, he watched the guards at their work. One dug at the earth, clearing away the ice and snow until the usual red sand appeared. In this small wallow, he placed a generous handful of the hay while his fellow pulled out his dagger. The fighter didn't flinch as the man brought the tip of his blade to his thumb, pressing until it pierced his skin and a red drop welled up.

The guard drew his thumb over one of the larger sticks. It was difficult to tell from where Dyfan watched, but it looked to him as if the guard had made an arrowhead with his blood. The guard furrowed his brow in what Dyfan could only assume was concentration. Everyone seemed to hold their breaths until smoke started to rise from the stick.

The guard smiled and blew gently on it, and the smoke started to wither, but in its stead, red and yellow flames bloomed. He blew again, and they grew, then he set the burning stick down on the pile of hay, his fellow guards feeding it the smaller sticks they had set aside.

With their fire made, the guards seemed to remember him, and Dyfan set the practice blade back on its rack before they could question why he was there. Dyfan stored that piece of knowledge away, tucking his cold-blushed hands into his armpits. Just for someday. If he ever needed it.

Climbing the stairs to his cell, Dyfan paused on the landing, staring at the frozen world through a barred window. He could see over the pit walls, and into the forested world beyond this high up. Little stacks of smoke rose up here and there, presumably from people's hearths. Dyfan watched the smoke dance in the sky, buffeted by the harsh, combative winds. With a sigh, he resumed climbing to the second level, mind turning back to the fire magic he had witnessed in the arena.

If there were runes for fire and protection, as he had seen in the past, there were probably runes for other things. Maybe to tell directions or to hide someone in plain sight. No Defeated would ever be taught these things, but then, when did a Defeated only learn what his Victors wanted him to? Hadn't Dyfan learned more of tactics and hand-to-hand than Victor Eurig had ever expected? How many times had Dyfan studied another man's face and learned what nature lay beneath his mask? No one had told him to trust Wynn; many had openly scoffed at the soft-handed Battle Defeated. They wouldn't have bet, nine years ago, that Wynn would be a Contender. And yet, Dyfan had seen something there.

He strolled towards his cell, mind buzzing with too many thoughts.

"Hey." The sound of another voice made Dyfan jump, but it was just Wynn, the long-faced fighter sitting casually on Dyfan's cot. He should have noticed his lover's presence upon entering his cell, but Dyfan's mind was wrapped up in the concepts of fires and runes. "I got here late and headed inside when I saw the other Defeated leaving the arena," Wynn said. "I'd have found you if I thought you were still out there. Were you training?"

"No." Dyfan shook his head, freeing his hands from his armpits to rub them together. He glanced over his shoulder once, wondering if anyone bothered to listen in. Not immediately spotting training masters, guards, or other Defeated, Dyfan sat beside Wynn. "I was watching the guards build a fire."

Tugging one of the pelts over their thighs, Dyfan let his leg rest against Wynn's. He could feel the other man's warmth through his breeches and realized that Wynn must have been waiting a good while.

"Really? Did you learn how to do it? I wish I could teach you."

Dyfan's eyes narrowed, and he responded in a bland tone. "Defeated don't need to know how to start fires. You know that."

Wynn blinked in surprise, then seemed to catch on. "Yeah, of course. It was a silly thing to say." He stood up and walked around the cot so that he might lay down on the side furthest from the door and spoke in a bare whisper. "I might have gotten fat, but I still think you're big enough to hide me if you lay on your side."

With a grunt, Dyfan swung his feet onto the cot, rolling onto his side, so his back faced the cell door. He lifted the pelt so that Wynn could scoot beneath it, looping his arm lazily over his lover. It would be good to share warmth.

"Now, can you tell me?" Wynn's lips moved, feather-quiet. He wiggled close to his lover though Dyfan knew he must be cold compared to Wynn's warm skin.

He huffed a sigh, dipping his head down to rest his chin atop Wynn's head. "They pricked one guard's finger and drew an arrowhead on the wood. I wasn't close enough to see it in detail... You didn't learn magic before?"

Wynn's heavy brows drew together as though huddling for warmth. "The old ways... My grandmother taught me some, though not many people used magic even when I was free. Why prick a thumb when flint is plentiful or ward a home when you have a heavy, oak door? Perhaps, if we had shielded ourselves better, the village would not have been lost to the Victors."

"I don't know," Dyfan murmured, turning to kiss the top of Wynn's head. He didn't want to bring up dark memories for his lover. "Are you cold?"

"No, annwyl. I could still make a fire rune or ward. I could teach you. All you need is an offering of blood and intent."

He could never learn those skills—not in front of the Victors or the guards. Defeated weren't supposed to know such things. He smoothed his hand down Wynn's back. It was strange that even nine years later, Wynn could forget that. "It's pointless. Don't waste your time on that, Wynn."

"I know. It's just nicer to think about magic than the Contender matches. They're getting so close. A couple weeks away."

His gut clenched at the thought. Two weeks and then he'd step into the arena. He'd fight a handful of heavyweights, and then it would just be him and Wynn. There was no doubt in his mind that Wynn would defeat the others; he was too good now.

If only Dyfan hadn't lost so much weight to his bouts of shitting and vomiting. If only he hadn't gotten injured so many times and convalesced for so long, then perhaps he'd still be in the champion weight class and Wynn only a heavyweight, and they'd never be faced with this impossible task.

He knew he'd never hurt Wynn, never fight him, but a shameful part of Dyfan wondered what was worse. If he fought Wynn and won, at least he'd be swift. If they both refused... What would Victors Eurig and Gruffyd do to them? It wouldn't be swift.

Victors weren't meant to be disobeyed.

"Wynn, I... I think maybe you should win."

"No." Wynn's voice came as a growl, hard and angry. "We've already talked about this, Dyfan! I won't do it!"

Dyfan tightened his grip on Wynn, holding him closer. "Listen to me. We can't go on defying them. We have to give them a winner. If you win, then maybe Victor Eurig won't breed me as much."

Wynn fell silent, shoving Dyfan's arms away, though he didn't answer at once. Dyfan could *feel* how angry he was in his short, sharp breaths and the height of his shoulders around his ears. "You know I can't—*won't* do anything that might make them breed you more. But — *Gods,* Dyfan! Can you imagine having to hurt me? I don't know if I even can."

"I know." Dyfan reached for Wynn again, half-afraid he'd pull away. "But I can't be responsible for them hurting you either. If we don't fight, they'll hurt us both. At least, if you win, it's on our terms. That's something. Isn't it?"

"It's not fair!" Something seemed to break within Wynn, and he began to shake, sucking air for great, wracking sobs.

Wynn didn't fight Dyfan as he pulled him closer, one arm tucked across Wynn's back, the other hand planted firmly on Wynn's chest. "It's fair if I get to keep you, Wynn. That's all that matters to me." Dyfan tried to breathe slow and deep. Maybe Wynn would copy him and find calmness. "We can practice in secret. We can fix the fight the way the Victors do."

"Alright. For you, annwyl, I'll do this. We'll fix the fight."

CHAPTER 95: THE EMAI

ELEVENTH MOON, 1804, AMARUIT WAR CAMP

Two Moons before the Proclamation

Soyala breathed in the crisp scents of snow and ice and regretted that her daughters weren't here now, joining her in exploring the Tundra. She had been a hunter when she was free and roamed for miles across the sloping land. The freedom of coming and going whenever she pleased was intoxicating now, and Soyala wondered how she had ever taken it for granted before raiders captured her. How had she not known what a privilege it was to kneel in the snow, reveling in its cold kiss even as the warm blood of a kill soaked her hands? Was she blind, back then, to the beauty of open space that stretched on forever? No walls, no streets, no noisy, smelly, pushing people.

Just the sun, the snow, and Soyala.

She breathed deeply as she turned away from the empty Tundra and back toward the camp of Emaian warriors, crouching in a valley like a fox ready to spring upon a vole. The Lirian had told her of the reported size of the Fish Queen's 'rabble army,' but Soyala hadn't understood what those numbers meant in reality. He was wrong, too, if she had any head for numbers. There were far more people here than the mere five hundred he had led her to expect.

Never in her life had she seen such a thing. The largest village she knew of could fit within the camp four times, and even as she watched, more warriors approached, melting out of the surroundings.

Was there another camp nearby? A sister or twin, just as large? Just as formidable?

It was easy enough to slip through the spirals of tents, her elk-skin clothes and silver hair making her one of many. Even if it was a lie.

People, Emaians, were everywhere, filling every space, every open tent flap, every clearing with a cooking fire in the center. None looked to be older than fifty, and none younger than fifteen, and while some were short, and others tall, some slim and a few bordering on fat, they were all straight-backed, bright-eyed, and strong.

These were not the Emai she knew. No one kept their chins tucked to their chests to stay unnoticed. They did not flinch or hunch their shoulders. She could not hear the clank of chains.

Soyala checked herself, straightening her shoulders as the others did and remembering her purpose. She could not be intimidated by these warriors. She could not fail.

Raised voices drew her attention to the center of the war camp, and she eased through the crowds to find herself two rows back from a spectacle in the middle. A woman, as short as Soyala and whipcord-skinny, stood on a tree stump. She wore a razor-thin sword, and gypsum caked her face. The chalky mixture made her dark eyes stand out, and Soyala resisted the urge to recoil. Slaver eyes. Black, without souls.

"They understand nothing but violence! Nothing but taking! Stealing! Raping!" The woman had to raise her voice as she spoke, as the Emaians watching echoed her words, the truth of their lives. The truth of any Emaian. They were all slaves in the eyes of Liria and Phecea, whether or not they wore collars. "So we will speak to them in the language they understand! We will take the fight to them! We will force them to acknowledge the strength of our people! No longer will any nation look upon the Tundra as something to be exploited!"

The large woman beside Soyala nodded fervently, letting out an excited yip, much like a wolf or fox. Others joined her in the eerie cry, and Soyala bit the inside of her cheek. All the fine hairs on the back of her neck lifted. These warriors were loyal to their chief. It would be difficult to spy on her effectively, let alone get information back to the Lirian.

But if she didn't, her daughters would pay. And Soyala could not allow that. Would never allow that.

"For generations upon generations, we have been a peaceful people, but our ways have not protected us. Our enemies have no place in their hearts for peace and bounty. If they will not learn any other way, we'll give them what they can comprehend! We will come like a white tide to their lands and ensure no Emaian is ever taken again!"

Soyala's heart jumped. The idea of fighting off the Lirians and keeping the Emai safe was intoxicating. But like a bucket of snowmelt tossed across her face, she knew it would never happen. This army was impressive by Emaian standards, but she had lived in the belly of the beast. The Lirians were better armed, better trained, and ruthless as only the soulless could be.

Black eyes seared her face, and it was all Soyala could do not to flinch as the Fish Queen stared at her. Maybe this woman knew the heartlessness of Liria, but she didn't have the hunger of a Slaver. She had not sheltered her daughters from the hands of their enemies in Lirian lands. She had not sat with their leader and taken his bargain. Soyala held Iniabi's gaze and was glad it was the other woman who looked away first.

CHAPTER 96: LIRIA

FIRST MOON, 1805, EGARA

The Proclamation

Luce dipped his bread into the wine at his left and selected a small piece of cheese to accompany the bite. The sour-sweet of the wine would go nicely with the salty fat of the cheese. Sweat rolled down the back of his neck, dampening the collar of his dress uniform. He waited for the Imperator to take a bite before placing the morsel in his mouth. After the staggering loss at the Emaian river, Luce knew every meeting with the Imperator could be his last. He had to keep proving he was a loyal General. There was nothing else he could do.

"When will your next report come in from the rabble, General?" the Imperator asked. He plucked a plump fig for his plate with two long, thick-knuckled fingers and examined it, his lips pursed. It was a deep bruise purple, shiny as a black eye, and when he dipped it into the carafe before him, honey oozed down his fingers like blood.

Soyala's first report had come in ill-formed letters twelve days after she had arrived in the Emaian war camp. She informed him of Iniabi's influential power and hatred for the Lirians. Her note had other details about the number of warriors present and their preparedness to fight. "She is joining them as a hunter, so she should be able to wander off regularly without raising suspicion. I have a series of men stationed at various outposts who know exactly who she is and her importance to our cause. All she must do is give a message to one of them, and they will send it by bird."

All of that was to say, there was no guarantee when the next message from his spy would arrive, but there was no reason to expect long periods of silence. The Imperator nodded and dipped a piece of bread into herbed oil. "And you are certain she will not betray Liria?"

"Most definitely. Your wife is a mother now," he smiled and saluted the Imperator with his wine. He wanted the Imperator to think they were friends or... companionable at least. If Luce was likable, the Imperator might think twice about beheading him. "Think of what she would do for her children."

"Anything. She would eat my heart if it meant keeping our child safe."

Luce suppressed a shudder. Tupa Galans were a little wild, still uncivilized. "All mothers are the same. She will be loyal to us."

"Very good. Then, it seems the Emaian situation is under control for the time being. Tell me your plan for Phecea now that—"

A knock interrupted them. "Yes?" the Imperator snapped, and the door opened to reveal a sweaty runner.

"Imperator, a message from the south."

"The south? What is this? Give me the message." The Imperator held out his hand, but the messenger didn't deposit a letter.

"It's a verbal message, Imperator."

"Who has the authority to send a verbal message to the Imperator himself?" Luce asked, wiping his fingertips on the napkin in his lap. Another bead of sweat trickled down his spine, and he resisted the urge to squirm.

"It is not just to the Imperator, General. Copies of this message have been sent to all high-ranking Lirians."

"Enough. Give the message."

The boy nodded and straightened his shoulders, taking on an air of importance. When he spoke, it was in the fashion of someone long practiced in reciting to an audience. He didn't stutter or stumble on the words.

"The following proclamation is in the voice of Iniabi, Daughter of Manaba, Free Warrior of the Emaian Tundra, and Kaneq Amaroq of the Amaruit, the protectors of the Emai.

Greetings, rulers of the slave nations Liria and Phecea. Today I offer you a choice. You may immediately cease the conquest of my people, free those you have enslaved within your borders, and remove your people from the Emaian land you currently occupy south of the Nonaccan Mountains. Doing so will earn you the right to your peoples' lives in the sanctity of your new borders. You will have peace, if not an alliance, with the Emai.

Should you not take this choice, then the only option I have left for you is war. I will raze your cities, slaughter your people, steal your children. I will come out of the dark and put an end to the two hundred years of atrocities you have heaped upon the Emai, and I will take revenge in your blood and land until the black sea rises and none alive remember the names of your so-called civilizations.—"

CHAPTER 97: PHECEA

FIRST MOON, 1805, DIOSION

The Proclamation

"—Your future is in your hands. I await your responses, though not eagerly. If you do not reply within a moon, I will consider your choice the second. It matters not. My people thirst for blood, and I yearn to give it to them."

Danae tried not to look Basia's way, not to react at all as silence filled the ballroom. The messenger had arrived in the middle of a small gathering of Phecean nobility and said he had a message that must be read aloud. The music stopped, and the crowd turned to hear the news, curious and excited. Sometimes new plays were announced this way or great works of art. Creatives enjoyed a bit of drama.

Instead, it was a declaration of war. Not from Liria, but the Emai.

No one moved. No one spoke.

Finally, her father came forward, taking the messenger aside. Danae dared to look at Basia, who held her face in a carefully concerned expression. They had only sent one shipment of goods to the Emaian revolutionary leader, and yet it seemed as if it were the push to start the entire system tumbling.

Fear coated Danae's throat. She had wanted to help end slavery.

She had watched those auctions and looked at the white-skinned Emai as people, not heathens, and Danae had known in her heart it was wrong. But she hadn't thought it would all happen so quickly. She hadn't thought her involvement would escalate to full war.

Now Phecea would face two enemies or be forced to drop slavery to keep the Daughter of Manaba from attacking.

Had she betrayed her country?

CHAPTER 98: RHOSAN

FIRST MOON, 1804, CWM OR

One Year before the Proclamation

Wynn had never seen so many people in Gruffyd's hall. They stood in clumps of five or six or sat at small tables, all dressed in winter finery: embroidered jackets and long-sleeved dresses. An entire room had been set aside for their fur coats. Wynn and the other Contenders were on display, standing around the room in no particular pattern. Unlike the warmly-dressed Victors, many of them, himself included, were bare-chested despite the cold. Wynn was glad to see that Dyfan was decently clothed for the weather.

Dyfan wasn't looking his way. The other Defeated hadn't all evening, and it was for the better that way. They needed to stay apart, to keep any of the Victors from becoming suspicious until they were too drunk for it to matter. It would be a while yet for that. Party-goers were still arriving and seemed more interested in discussing the upcoming battle or showing off their Defeated than consuming refreshments. If they stayed sober, it would be difficult to get time alone with Dyfan to go over their bout before the fight tomorrow.

For a moment, Wynn wondered if the other Defeated on display would be a problem. They would not consume any alcohol. They would be clear-minded all evening, and some might notice if he and Dyfan went missing. If one of them saw them slip out, they could alert the Victors. Maybe even catch him and Dyfan practicing their fixed bout. Wynn couldn't imagine the favors that would win; the choicest food, better quarters, maybe even an easy retirement, mind still intact. He caught himself eyeing the others and stopped. It would not help him to set any of them on edge now.

"Wynn." Ifanna's voice was like the screech of vultures to a dying man. She stood arm in arm with Victor Eurig's wife, and in their winter-dark colors, their resemblance was uncanny. Both women were almost beautiful. Their necks were pommels, and their faces were full of blade angles. "Fetch Blodwyn and I the tray of meats from that table."

"Are you sure he's perfectly docile?" Blodwyn asked, her voice the mirror of Ifanna's. "Eurig believes he destroyed Cadel out of pure spite. He didn't have to shatter his knee."

"Oh, they're *all* animals in the pit." Ifanna waved an airy hand. "*Now*, Wynn."

Wynn took a deep breath. "Yes, Victor Ifanna."

"See?" Ifanna purred, but the rest of her sentence faded as Wynn hurried to carry out her demands.

Dyfan was standing at the back of the hall, one of the furthest points from the wide entryway. He was framed in brilliant red by the tapestry hanging behind him. It was a beautiful color, though it reminded Wynn too much of blood, and his stomach turned. He forced himself to take a deep breath. It would all work out. He would get to practice with Dyfan tonight, and tomorrow they would put on a show for Cwm Or that would keep them safe and together.

Wynn took another deep breath. There were no longer any Victors entering the hall. It seemed full to bursting. Every space not taken by a Contender or a Defeated servant was filled by laughing, drinking Victors. The sheer mass of them made Wynn's chest clench, but he focused on the feeling of air moving through his nose. He could not afford to have a fit of terror now. It would bring too much attention.

Forcing himself to move, Wynn returned to Ifanna, tray in hand. She took a single piece of the delicately sliced salmon and laid it on her tongue. "Would you like any, Blodwyn?" The other woman shook her head, and Ifanna waved. "Take it back, Wynn, and bring us the platter of dates."

A handful of like errands later, irritation warred with doubt in Wynn's belly. Ifanna wasn't drinking, not like the others. He supposed she might not want to drink due to the baby. He'd need his mother soon enough. All around them, the Victors downed Gruffyd's too fine liquor, yet she still played her petty little games. She was too aware of Wynn for him to slip away.

Wynn wiped sweat off his brow with the back of a hand. The kitchens were as loud as the hall, and there seemed to be as many bodies, though less finely dressed. At least they were warmer. The skin of Wynn's bare chest was shriveling with the cold.

"What is it this time?" Nimue hardly spared him a glance. "Seth, go out and fetch wood; we need to make more bread."

"Ifanna's goblet was *dirty*," Wynn drawled.

Nimue took the offending goblet, inspecting it quickly to see it was not dirty in the least. Still, she swapped it for a new one, adding the used one to the already prodigious stack waiting to be washed. "You watch yourself, Wynn. The Victor's are not to be trifled with."

"Yes, Nimue." Wynn swiped a bottle of fine wine from the rack near the hearth and held it to the Defeated woman. "For the lady Victor."

She waved him off. "Yes, yes. Now out of the kitchen. You're just getting in the way."

He hardly made it out before stopping for Seth, whose arms were overloaded with wood. Wynn hesitated, suddenly indecisive, and reached out to ruffle the boy's hair. "Stay out of trouble."

Seth smiled despite his burden. "Are you taking that wine for yourself? Mama says drinking makes a man foolish." His eyes were the same green-blue as Dyfan's.

"Your mama is right," Wynn said, laughing. "You listen to what she says."

"Alright, if you carve me another lion?"

Wynn just snorted. "We'll see." He left feeling strangely saddened. In another life, he would have loved the chance to raise Dyfan's son.

Wynn thundered up the steps and back to Ifanna's table, dodging Defeated and Victors on his way. During his time in the kitchens, the sound here had only crescendoed, spilling into the night like so much muddy snow melt. At Ifanna's table, Wynn placed the fresh goblet and wine before her and Blodwyn. "Compliments of your husband, Victor Ifanna." He need not have worried. Her hands were already full with a tankard of mulled cider, and Blodwyn reached forward to uncork the wine.

"Yes, good. Now, Wynn, go find us my dice. They're in my personal chambers." Ifanna's gaze lingered too long on his lips and chest, and Wynn backed away uncomfortably.

"Yes, Victor Ifanna."

She was drinking, finally, but still, Ifanna was too aware of him. If anything, she seemed only to notice him more the more she drank. He set off in search of Dyfan.

Dyfan

Dyfan waited with the shadows, tucked into the alcove beneath the main stairwell. His gut gurgled, nervous because he was planning to break the rules, but he ignored it. He wasn't supposed to throw the Contender matches either, and he still was going to. What was a little secret training compared to that?

Laughter echoed through the great hall and bounced down the hallway, distorting until it sounded like a pack of baying hounds. Dyfan scanned the crowds for Wynn. He'd last seen him bringing Victor Ifanna a goblet.

Wynn would be sneaking off any minute now.

Or he should have been. Wynn's face was turned away as he slipped into the alcove, one hand resting on the wall. He looked like he was searching for something, but even as Dyfan watched, he turned and smiled. "Hey. How're you holding up?"

The words stuck in Dyfan's throat, so he only nodded, his chin jerking in an abrupt affirmation that he was "holding up" well enough. He wasn't shitting his guts out and wasn't crawling out of his skin. If he could just hold it together, they would be alright. Like outlasting an opponent in the pits, stamina would win this fight. Or so he told himself.

"Ready," he said.

Wynn reached out and gripped Dyfan's arm. "I love you."

And that was why Dyfan would do this, fix this fight in the hopes that the Victors would let them be. "Now?"

Wynn's brow furrowed, and he glanced back out into the crowd. "I can't get away from Ifanna. She keeps sending me on errand after errand. She's drinking now, so hopefully it won't be much longer."

Dyfan glanced where Victor Ifanna and Victor Eurig's wife, Blodwyn, sat, laughing and drinking. Wynn was right. Already Ifanna was starting to look around. Probably for Wynn. She seemed to enjoy tormenting him particularly. "Why is she so focused on you?"

Wynn closed his eyes, an expression like pain contorting his features. "I— I'll tell you after. Not here."

"Alright. Later."

"I'll see you in just a few minutes," Wynn said and looked around again, back to the ant-hill swarm of people. "Be careful."

Dyfan watched Wynn bring a tray of tarts over to Victor Ifanna, who took one bite and then sent Wynn away with the tray again. When he returned, Dyfan saw he had, of all things, a handkerchief. Victor Ifanna wiped her red-painted lips and sent him off again. Time dragged on, and the rest of the Victors drank and ate and enjoyed themselves, but Victor Ifanna seemed fixated on Wynn. What had he meant, he would tell Dyfan later? What was there between the dark-haired woman and Dyfan's lover that would make her so petty?

Finally, she waved Wynn off, and he passed by Dyfan as he climbed the stairs to the Victor's private quarters. Cold skies, Dyfan didn't want to practice up there, where they could get caught so easily! But as Dyfan waited, Wynn didn't come down again.

Fine.

If this was their last opportunity to practice their mock battle, then so be it. Wynn must win the Contender matches tomorrow. There was no other option.

Minutes passed before Dyfan dared to move from the alcove, heading directly for the doors that would lead him outside. Let people think he needed to relieve himself. As soon as he was out of sight, Dyfan changed his course, ducking around the side of the compound and towards the kitchen's welcoming light. Defeated bustled here and there, not noticing Dyfan was out of place. He found the servant's stairs and took them two at a time. Now that he was moving, his body jittery with anticipation, Dyfan felt certain they would be successful. He would find Wynn, and they could practice while the Victors were busy with their food, wine, and music.

The upper level was empty as Dyfan mounted the top step, all Defeated busy with the party downstairs. There were sets and sets of doors, and all he knew to do was check each. He stopped before a tall pair of filigree double doors, and knowing it would do no good to look around, Dyfan only opened them. As if he had every right to be there, as if he belonged.

He had barely shut the doors when he realized his mistake. There was someone in this room, but it wasn't Wynn. Victor Gruffyd sat slumped at his desk, one hand wrapped around a long-necked bottle, the other fiddling with a knife atop a stack of papers. Dyfan bowed automatically, and when he straightened, he saw that Victor Gruffyd's eyes were red-rimmed and glassy. Had he been weeping?

"Yes?" Victor Gruffyd asked, his voice fuzzy with drink.

Dyfan tried to think of a lie, for a reason why he was up here and couldn't. He hadn't ever been good at those sorts of things. He looked instead to the basket set in the chair beside Victor Gruffyd and realized with surprise it wasn't filled with blankets as he first thought. It wasn't a basket at all but a bassinet.

Victor Ifanna's baby lay within, face smooth with sleep.

"What do you want?" Victor Gruffyd's voice was sharper this time, and Dyfan wondered if he could just leave. Just turn around and walk out. Would the Victor even remember his strange behavior tomorrow?

"Uh... Victor Eurig sent me," Dyfan lied finally.

"For what?"

"What?" Victor Gruffyd's face, already red, darkened. He was irritated. If Wynn showed up now, Victor Gruffyd would know they were planning something. Perhaps even tell the other Victors. Then his and

Wynn's plans would be for nothing. "Um. Victor Eurig wants to place a bet with you, Victor. About tomorrow's matches."

"Oh. Fine. Sure. A bet." Victor Gruffyd's gaze left Dyfan, much to his relief, and settled on the sleeping baby. Slowly he lifted his bottle to his lips and took a long pull. Dyfan watched the Victor's throat bob as he swallowed three mouthfuls.

This was strange behavior for a Victor, especially Gruffyd, who seemed to enjoy being the center of attention. He was always the loudest, brightest, most annoying Victor at any event. Now, at his own feast, he was locked away with his son in his office?

"How much do you wish to bet on the outcome of the Contender Matches, Victor?" Dyfan asked, glancing around the office. There was a map of what he suspected was Thloegr on one wall, the continent of his birth reminding Dyfan of an ill-formed thumb.

The desk was untidy with papers, empty inkwells, and spilled wax. It appeared chaotic, though, for all he knew, the stacks of documents were related. Squiggling lines divulged nothing of their meaning.

Laughter echoed below, and Dyfan shook his head, trying to focus. Wynn might come looking for him soon.

"It doesn't matter— Doesn't matter how much I bet. That fucking Defeated—" Victor Gruffyd's voice trailed off, and Dyfan looked once more at the man. His gaze was still on the sleeping baby. He drained the last of his bottle and then tossed it aside. The shattering of glass added to the commotion echoing through the halls. "My fucking bitch wife and that bastard Defeated have made a fool out of me for the last time."

How had Wynn made Victor Gruffyd a fool? Dread knotted in Dyfan's jaw, clenching until his teeth creaked in protest. Did Victor Gruffyd know about their plan to throw the fight? How could he? "Wynn is loyal to you, Victor—"

The older man laughed, cutting Dyfan off. "Loyal? That stinking— Defeated— bedded my wife!"

Shock left Dyfan speechless. Why would Wynn bed Ifanna? She wasn't a Defeated who he could be ordered to breed with to produce other Defeated.

Slowly, Dyfan looked at the baby in the basket as Victor Gruffyd did. He couldn't remember when she'd had it. Him. It was a son. Maybe four moons ago? Wynn had been on tour when she'd conceived.

She'd gone with Victor Gruffyd on the Victory Tour.

Despite himself, Dyfan stepped forward, peering at the baby more closely. He wasn't much to look at. Just pink skin and fat little hands, but he did have the start of hair. Little whisps at the crown of his head.

Red whisps.

Victor Gruffyd laughed again, and he sounded unhinged, the crackling of his voice edged with desperation. "See it, don't you? See his fucking features?"

Numbly, Dyfan nodded. Yes. He could see Wynn in the boy, even this young. And Wynn had said he'd explain why Ifanna hated him so much. So there was something to explain. "Why?" his voice was a croak, his throat constricted with betrayal.

"Why?!" Victor Gruffyd guffawed. "Because women are sluts and Defeated are dogs. Don't you fuck whatever Victor Eurig tells you to?"

Yes, he did. But no one would tell Wynn to breed with Ifanna... Not unless... Dyfan frowned. Wynn had been married to a woman. He'd said as much. Maybe, after all these years, Ifanna had wanted him, and he wanted her. Maybe he wasn't like Dyfan. Maybe Dyfan wasn't the only answer for Wynn.

His stomach clenched, and Dyfan took a step back.

"Disgusting, isn't it?" Victor Gruffyd was looking at the baby again, and Dyfan realized he didn't mean Wynn and Ifanna.

"It's just a babe," Dyfan said, surprised by how steady his voice was.

Gruffyd looked up then. Dyfan could see the whites of his eyes. "It's an affront to Kirit and to our way."

"It's just a little boy."

"See? That's why you're Defeated, and I am not. You just take someone shitting on you. I won't stand for it." Victor Gruffyd gripped the knife and leveled it at Wynn's child.

Ice ran through Dyfan's veins. Not fear, not the worry that had hung off him like a cloak for so long. But the calm, cool sensation he always had before a fight.

He might be a Defeated, but it seemed Gruffyd had forgotten one crucial thing: Dyfan was a pit fighter and had been one all his life. He was not some meek Defeated. He was a Contender.

Dyfan lunged forward as Gruffyd plunged the dagger's tip toward the bassinet. The blade pierced Dyfan's forearm instead of the baby, and Gruffyd barely had time to blink before Dyfan used the hand of his injured arm to wrap around the man's wrist, forcing it up and away. He didn't stop when he knew the knife was well away from the baby, nor when he felt Gruffyd's fingers release the hilt. Dyfan twisted until the small bones of Gruffyd's wrist ground and snapped beneath his fingers.

Gruffyd bellowed in pain, and Wynn's baby finally woke up. He squalled his protests, but Dyfan didn't stop. With his free hand, he punched Gruffyd's face, and when the drunkard reeled back, Dyfan wrapped both hands around the back of the man's skull. He thrashed out at Dyfan with his good arm, but his feeble hits against Dyfan's ribs felt like snowfall against his skin.

Dyfan tangled his fingers into the too-long hair at the back of Gruffyd's head and slammed his forehead forward onto the desk. A loud crack emanated from the impact, and the man stopped moving, though Wynn's baby redoubled his screaming. Dyfan spared the child a glance and saw that he had little droplets of red on his cheek. Dyfan's blood must have dripped on him when he stopped Gruffyd's dagger. Dyfan slammed Gruffyd's head into the desk three more times to ensure he was dead. Then he tossed the body aside and turned to pick up the wailing baby.

The little boy was smaller than a loaf of bread, though twice as heavy. He stared at Dyfan with familiar brown eyes and screamed all the more. Dyfan was sure he was a horrible sight to behold.

"It's alright," Dyfan told the baby, who kept crying, flailing his little arms around in protest. "I've got you."

Dyfan turned, wondering if someone would come upstairs because of the crying, and found he had an audience.

Wynn stood in the doorway, his mouth open with shock and fear.

He was panting, his chest rising and falling in the rapid breaths of someone who knew danger was upon them. He met Dyfan's eyes and, after a long moment, seemed to master himself.

"You killed him." It wasn't a question.

"Eventually."

"To protect my son?" Wynn stepped slowly into the room, reaching out to cup Dyfan's arms around the baby. He ran a long, calloused hand along the baby's arm and a fat little hand wrapped around it.

Dyfan swallowed, looking down at the baby, who was finally quieting. Did he know Wynn was his true father? Was that why he stopped crying? How could he? "Yes."

Wynn nodded and stepped away to search Gruffyd's body, removing his coin pouch with quick, deft movements. "We can't take him with us, annwyl. He's too small, and he'll be safe here now that Gruffyd is dead."

"With us?" Dyfan didn't understand. Where were they going? Did Wynn still want to practice for tomorrow's Contender Matches? He looked at the baby and realized his blood was soaking into the baby's swaddling blankets. Slowly, Dyfan put him back into his bassinet, looking for something to wrap his wrist with.

"Aryus curse Gruffyd's soul. I'm going to need clothes. At least Eurig put you in something sensible. We'll go through the town, lighting fires as we pass—that ought to keep them busy for a time."

"Fires?" Dyfan didn't see any bandages, so he just wrapped his good hand around the wound. Wynn's eyes followed the movement, and he ripped off a strip of Gruffyd's cloak to stem the flow of blood.

"Or perhaps just the stables. Speed matters most now."

"What do you mean?"

"I mean, if we don't run now, they're going to kill you for this." Wynn finished tying the makeshift bandage and looked up at his lover. "Let's go. Through the servant's stairs before someone comes looking. I'll grab something from the laundry or the Victors' coat closet on the way."

Go? Wynn meant to flee. To run away from Cwm Or and the

Victors in the dead of winter. Away from the pits and matches and everything Dyfan had ever known.

He looked at his bandaged arm. It wasn't as if he could just sneak back downstairs, and no one would be the wiser about who smashed Gruffyd's head in. There was proof in his wound that he'd had an altercation. But if they went into the wilderness, how would they survive?

Dyfan shook his head slowly. He hadn't thought when he protected Wynn's son. He'd just acted. Stupid, foolish impulsive. All the things he had told Wynn not to be. And now. Now they were trapped.

Running was as much a death sentence as staying, but at least if they stayed, Wynn would survive.

"I can't, Wynn. I don't know how to be free."

"You were born free, Dyfan. They had to teach you not to be."

Was that true? He'd been born Defeated. His mother had been chosen because she was big and strong, and his father was a Contender. His life had been plotted before he'd even been born. Wynn spoke as if freedom and life beyond Kirit's territory were something everyone could take to. That everyone would belong to.

But Dyfan wasn't sure that was a fact.

Still, hadn't he defied the Victors by loving Wynn at all? And again, when he refused to breed? Wasn't he willing to go against their wishes, despite being a Defeated, by fixing the Contender matches for Wynn?

What of his decision to end Gruffyd's life and save Wynn's baby?

Was that not the choice of someone free? Free of will, if not of body?

Dyfan looked out the window past Gruffyd's sprawled form. The moon was rising high. Morning was six hours off. The Victors would be tired and hung over, but they would rouse in time for the Contender fights.

Dyfan looked back at Wynn, his brown eyes steady and patient, and felt his heart warm. "Alright. Let's go."

DRAMATIS PESONAE

Rhosan

    Afan (Af-ahn): Dyfan's first son
    Blodwyn (Blood-win): Victor Eurig's wife
    Cadel (Cah-del): Fighter in the pits
    Dyfan (Dif-ahn): Fighter in the pits
    Ein (Ine): Fighter in the pits
    Eurig (Yur- ig): Victor, owner of Dyfan
    Gar: Defeated
    Gruffyd (Gruff-id): Victor, owner of Wynn
    Gwilm (Gwillmm): Defeated
    Ifanna (If-ah-na): Victor Gruffyd's wife
    Igor (Ee-gor): Fighter in the pits
    Iorath (Ee-or-rath): Defeated Healer
    Jeston (Jess-ton): Aryus follower, Defeated
    Kane (Cane): Victor, owns Cadel
    Kerwyn (Kur-win): Victor
    Liliwen (Lil-ee-win): Defeated
    Linn: Defeated
    Mona (Moh-nah): Defeated
    Nia (Nee-ah): Wynn's wife
    Nimue (Nim-way): Defeated

Osian (Oh-see-an): Pit fighter
Owynn (Oh-wen): Wynn's son
Trevyn (Treh-vin): Contender
Wynn (Win): Recently captured Defeated

Liria

Balbina Nonus (Bal-bee-nah No-nus): Luce's first granddaughter
Caius Nonus (Cai-us): Luce's father
Camilla Pontius (Cah-mil-ah Pon-tee-us): Luce's wife
Cassia Nonus (Cass-ee-ah): Luce's second daughter
Gaius (Guy-us): General
Ignatious Nonus (Ig-nay-shus): Luce's first born son
Kaeso Bellator (Kay-so Bell-ah-tor): soldier
Lucilius Nonus (Loos-il-ee-ous): Soldier
Sabina Nonus (Sah-bee-na): Luce's first daughter
Vais (Vai-is): Commander
Valaria (Vah-lair-ee-uh): Ignatious's Tupa Galan wife

Phecea

Adonhis (A-dahn-is): Callista's brother, noble child
Aesop Leos (Ay-sop Lay-os): Twin to Peta, Leos heir
Afin (Ah-fin): Mistress of etiquette
Agni Leos (Ag-nee): Mother to Aesop and Peta, Councilor
Annas (An-as): Danae's tutor
Andara Mavros (An-dar-ah Mav-ros): Twin to Dido, youngest Mavros child, goes by Dara
Andromyda Othonos (An-drom-mih-da O-thone-os): Danae's mother, Councilor
Arsenio Othonos (Ar-sin-ee-o): Danae's father, Councilor
Atreo Drakos (Ah-tray-oh Drac-os): Artist
Azarios Aetos (Ah-zar-ri-os Ae-tos): Noble child, cousin to Pello
Baccus Aetos (Bac-us) : Brother to Myron, council member
Bas Aetos (Bas): Brother to Pello
Basia/Biton Mavros (Bahs-ee-ah/Bih-ton): Mavros eldest child, noble.
Calliope (Cah-lai-oh-pee): Noble child

Callista (Cah-lis-tah): Adohnis's sister, younger than Danae and Basia, noble child

Cyril Mavros (Sih-ril): Basia's father

Danae Othonos (Dan-ay): Heir to the Othonos council seats

Dido Mavros (Die-doh): Andara's twin sister, youngest Mavros

Dimos (Deem-os): Commander in Kydonia

Eleni Adamos (Eh-lane-ee Ad-ahm-os): Coucilor's daughter, noble

Eros (Air-ros): Member of Basia's society

Erose Cirillo (Air-ros Seer-il-oh) (feminine version of the name): Noble child

Faidon (Fade-on): Commander in Lefkara

Gelene Adamos (Geh-lane): Council member

Ida (Ai-duh): Basia's tutor of economics and trade

Ion (Ee-on): Noble child

Iris Mavros (Ai-ris): Basia's mom

Janus Zodrafos (Jan-us Zo-drah-fos): Council member

Karan (Cah-ran): Master of music

Keme (Kim-eh): Emaian slave

Lex: Society member

Melba Mavros (Mel-bah): Second Mavros child

Minos Leos (Mine-os): Councilor, father to Peta and Aesop

Myron Aetos (My-ron): Councilor

Niky (Naik-ee): person in story

Pello Aetos (Pay-loh): noble child

Peta Leos (Pee-tah): Aesop's twin, Leos heir

Rhea Gabris (Ray-ah Gah-bris): Storyteller

Sousanna Adamos (Su-sahn-ah): Council member

Voleta Mavros (Voh-lay-tah): Fourth Mavros child, goes by Leta

Yolanta (Yo-lahn-ta): noble child

Yuka (Yoo-kah): Danae's personal Emaian slave

Zina Mavros (Zeen-nah): Third Mavros child

Zol: Society member

Village of Nec

Iniabi, Daughter of Manaba (In-ee-ah-bee): Emaian girl

Kallik (Cah-leek): Villager, married to Tapeesa and Yura

Manaba, Daughter of Ooyu (Ma-na-ba, Oo-yew): Medicine woman for Nec, Iniabi's mother
Meriwa (Meh-ree-wah): Tundra walker, Ice Hearted
Mika (Mee-ka): Villager, daughter of Sani and Piav
Piav (Pee-ahv): Sani's husband, Mika's father
Sani (Sahn-ee): Mika's mother
Tapeesa (Tap-ee-sah): Wife to Yura and Kallik, villager
Tonraq (Ton-rak): Tundra walker

The Flying Night
Avignon (Av-in-yon): pirate
Cai: Pirate boy
Cook: The cook/Surgeon
Gita (Ghee-tah): Pirate
Iago (Ee-ah-go): Pirate boy, friend to Iniabi
Ira Minelli (Ai-rah Mih-nel-ee): Captain
Jaya (Jai-ah): Pirate girl
Leon (Lee-ahn): Navigator
Morys (Mor-iss): Pirate
Neus (Noos): Twin to Nil, pirate child
Nico (Nee-koh): Pirate
Nil: Twin to Neus, pirate child
Taaliah (Tahl-ee-ah): Bosun
Tegan (Tee-gan): Pirate
Vlassis (Vlass-iss): Quartermaster

Village of Taqqiq
Akna (Ak-nah): Toklo's wife, Qimmiq's mom
Deniigi (Din-ee-ghee): Old trapper/warrior
Sona (So-nah): Villager
Tatik (Ta-teek): Uki, the medicine woman's, apprentice
Toklo (Tok-loh): Chief, Qimmiq's father
Uki, Daughter of Massak (Oo-kee, Mah-sak): Medicine woman
Qimmiq (Kim-eek): Daughter of Toklo and Akna

Village of Sinqiniq

Aniki (Ah-nee-kee): Warrior
Capun (Cah-poon): Warrior
Hanta (Han-tah): Chief Sakari's child
Naunja (Na'aun-jah): Married to Tikaani, village elder
Pakuk (Pah-kook): Warrior
Sakari (Sak-ar-ree): Chief
Sedna (Sed-nah): Medicine woman
Sila (See-lah): Village girl, tries to be warrior
Tikaani (Tih-kahn-ee): Village elder

The Amaruit
Anjij (Ahn-jeej): Warrior
Maniitok (Man-ih-tok): Warrior, stoic and dependable
Poallu (Poh-ahl-loo): Warrior, escaped slave from Phecea
Yotimo (Yoh-tee-moh): Warrior
Yutu (Yoo-too): Warrior

FOLLOW L&S FABLES

Join the Illygad family and keep abreast with the latest updates and releases from L&S Fables!

You can join our newsletter at lsfables.com for exclusive sneak peaks of upcoming releases, short stories, and deals. Listen to the L&S Fables Podcast everywhere you find podcasts and email us your fan art at LivSterlingFables@gmail.com.

Your reviews mean the world to us!!!

ALSO BY THESE AUTHORS

Call of Calamity

Vassal

Goddess

Shepherd of Souls

Shepherd of Souls

Death Seeker

Song of the Lost

The Last Contender

Kindle Vella

The Thistle Queen's Thorns

Made in the USA
Monee, IL
11 March 2025